THE WORLD'S CLASSICS

## AYALA'S ANGEL

ANTHONY TROLLOPE (1815–82), the son of a failing London barrister, was brought up an awkward and unhappy youth amidst debt and privation. His mother maintained the family by writing, but Anthony's own first novel did not appear until 1847, when he had at length established a successful Civil Service career in the Post Office, from which he retired in 1867. After a slow start, he achieved fame, with 47 novels and some 16 other books, and sales sometimes topping 100,000. He was acclaimed an unsurpassed portraitist of the lives of the professional and landed classes, especially in his perennially popular *Chronicles of Barsetshire* (1855–67), and his six brilliant Palliser novels (1864–80). His fascinating *Autobiography* (1883) recounts his successes with an enthusiasm which stems from memories of a miserable youth. Throughout the 1870s he developed new styles of fiction, but was losing critical favour by the time of his death.

JULIAN THOMPSON has been Lecturer in English at Hertford College, Oxford since 1984.

THE WORLD'S CLASSICS

ANTHONY TROLLOPE

# *Ayala's Angel*

*Edited with an Introduction by*
JULIAN THOMPSON

Oxford  New York
OXFORD UNIVERSITY PRESS

Oxford University Press, Walton Street, Oxford OX2 6DP

Oxford New York
Athens Auckland Bangkok Bombay
Calcutta Cape Town Dar es Salaam Delhi
Florence Hong Kong Istanbul Karachi
Kuala Lumpur Madras Madrid Melbourne
Mexico City Nairobi Paris Singapore
Taipei Tokyo Toronto

and associated companies in
Berlin Ibadan

Oxford is a trade mark of Oxford University Press

Introduction, Note on the Text, Select Bibliography,
and Explanatory Notes © Julian Thompson 1986
Chronology © N. J. Hall, 1991

First published 1881
First published by Oxford University Press 1929
First issued as a World's Classics paperback 1986

British Library Cataloguing in Publication Data
Data available

Library of Congress Cataloging in Publication Data
Trollope, Anthony, 1815-1882.
Ayala's angel.
(The World's classics)
Bibliography: p.
I. Thompson-Furnival, Julian.  II. Title.
PR5684.A9  1986  823'.8  86 2572
ISBN 0-19-281747-7 (pbk.)

5 7 9 10 8 6 4

Printed in Great Britain by
BPC Paperbacks Ltd
Aylesbury, Bucks

# CONTENTS

## ACKNOWLEDGEMENTS

I should like to thank Stephen Wall and A. O. J. Cockshut for help and advice given during the preparation of this edition.

# INTRODUCTION

*Ayala's Angel* provides one of the more extra-ordinary statistics in Trollope's extraordinarily pro-ductive career. At 243,000 words it is longer than the conventional Victorian three-volume novel, yet it was composed in only seventy-one of Trollope's three-hour working-days, mostly on an Alpine holi-day, and allowing for an intermission for a first trip to Iceland, itself written up in magazine and book-form. And Trollope, who was sixty-three and had spent the winter touring South Africa, had intended 1878 to be one of his quieter years! He was probably tired, as well as justifiably proud, when he cele-brated, in a letter to his Australian friend G. W. Rusden, the completion of his '80th tale' (under-lined three times).

Yet the finished novel bears few signs of hasty composition, and none at all of weariness of spirit. It is, moreover, the brightest book Trollope had writ-ten since the completion of the Barchester Chronicles in the mid-sixties. The previous novel, *John Caldi-gate*, had been overhung with Puritan gloom, and the next, *Cousin Henry*, was to be a concentrated study of guilt, cowardice, and procrastination. But *Ayala's Angel* is uniquely zestful, quite free from sombreness, stodginess, or even, given its author's age and indifferent health, from nostalgia. It has become critically orthodox to stress the pessimism of Trollope's art in his last decade, but the general reader who comes to *Ayala's Angel* without presup-positions, will find exuberant romantic comedy,

underpinned by a calm and serious view of life, and
a pervasive humour which may be done broader, but
which is surely never done better elsewhere in
Trollope.

Despite its sustained richness and quality and its
distinctive freshness of tone, *Ayala's Angel* has
tended to be classed with Trollope's less frequently
read novels. Early reviews were favourable, and the
novel has been mildly popular with the general
reader, but the critical attention attracted has been
slight. One of the more sensitive accounts is that of
R. C. Terry (*Anthony Trollope: The Artist in
Hiding* (1977)), who compares it with Shakespearean
Romance. This is a valuable comparison, but the
novel is more ebullient than late Shakespeare.
Serene resolution, for the old men in *The Winter's
Tale* or *The Tempest*, often means that every third
thought shall be their grave. In *Ayala's Angel* the
old lady and gentleman who share a railway-com-
partment with the hero and heroine in Chapter
XLVI are very much alive. They do not look to the
young generation as a hope for the future, but flirt
outrageously with them. Discussion may range over
such topics as whether or not young ladies should be
ornamental, and whether or not the window should
be open; but by the end of the scene it is clear that
the old lady and gentleman seem to suspect what
Ayala does not herself know yet, that she is in love
with Stubbs. Other middle-aged characters like Sir
Thomas Tringle and Reginald Dosett, Lady Albury
and the Marchesa Baldoni are far from 'Time's
doting chronicles'. And Trollope's world is far more
the world of all of us than the magical world of late
Shakespeare. There are ironic place-names (Stubbs
finally wins Ayala in 'Gobblegoose Wood'), and
whimsical, almost private jokes (such as the moment

when Augusta, a sow's ear if ever woman was, is employed in making a 'silk purse'). But where Shakespeare makes the setting of *The Tempest* fantastic, the fantasy in *Ayala's Angel* arises largely from the imaginations of the characters themselves. All the characters remember their fairy-tales and ballads. Colonel Stubbs sees Ayala as a 'princess'; Ayala's 'Angel of Light' becomes a knight dwelling in a castle; Stubbs is seen as a friendly talking bear; Ayala is always 'Beauty', her various suitors, as often as not, 'Beasts'. Frank Houston dons shining metaphorical armour to win Imogene Docimer, and even the blundering Tom Tringle, drunk in Soho. is seen as 'that very bellicose young City knight'. A world of chivalric romance and bewildering transformations is always on hand to lend richness and wonder to the behaviour of the characters, who are, after all, mainly concerned in the conventional novelistic quest for husbands and wives. One of the strengths of living life like a fairy tale is that the wise saws and sententious allusions common in Trollope are strangely redundant in *Ayala's Angel*. Ayala does not know that 'beautiful description of a "sallow, sublime, sort of Werther-faced man"' with which Trollope introduces Stubbs. Trollope is fond of quoting Horace—but he tells us that Lucy gets at the poet's meaning without having read him. As the novelist heaps up the literary and sub-literary commonplaces which middle-aged worldly wisdom likes to reach down from its mental shelves (*Ayala's Angel* is as allusive as any of his novels), he is perhaps suggesting that we are as often as not dulled by them as edified. Ayala may be ignorant and naïve, but she is also delightfully engaging, because she lives in a fresh world, like the world of fairy-tales, beyond the range of literary allusions, and without

immediate recourse to the distilled wisdom of somebody else's lifetime.

*Ayala's Angel*, then, is a novel in which fantasy is
continuously accessible, yet at the same time a fully
realistic novel. The theme of the main plot (Ayala's
search for an ideal husband, or 'Angel of Light') is
the way that fantasy is immersed in, and functions
as a part of everyday life. At first Ayala seems a
rather silly self-styled Shelleyan highborn maiden,
setting herself up in her mind with her ideal Angel
in 'the tower of the castle from which she could look
down upon the inferior world below'. She is not keen
on eating, or at least on monotonous meals at Kingsbury Crescent with her poor relations, and wonders
whether Nature might have managed the business
of nutrition more nobly had we 'sucked it in from
the atmosphere through our fingers and hairs, as the
trees do by their leaves'. And when she refuses
Colonel Stubbs simply because he has a red beard
and an ugly name, we are inclined to agree with the
Marchesa Baldoni that Ayala 'is one of those human
beings who seem to have been removed out of this
world and brought up in another'. The Marchesa is
partly right of course. Ayala is impractical because
she is immature, but there is nothing otherworldly
about her. Bohemian South Kensington, when she
was a little thing among the blue china cups of her
artist father, liked to think of her as 'Ayala the
romantic; Ayala the poetic!' In fact she is an ordinary, healthy young girl with ordinary, if strongly
concentrated dreams. Trollope's point is that many
adolescents have ideal fantasies corresponding to
Ayala's 'Angel of Light', and that like Ayala, they
bend their fantasies to suit the accidents of the real
world with an unconscious mental sleight-of-hand.
At Stalham aspects of the Angel are glimpsed in an

energetic pony, a glittering river, and a fine day's hunting, and we realize that Ayala is twisting her dream to suit the excitement of her entry into fashionable life. It is not surprising that in the course of the novel the Angel metamorphoses into the aspect of Colonel Stubbs, red hair, gargoyle face, and all, and that on the last page of the novel Ayala believes that she has indeed been handed over to her 'Angel of Light'. Ayala is not the less true to her Angel because, at a given point in the novel, she is not sure what the Angel represents. Trollope might easily have written a conventional novel of disillusionment, stripped Ayala of her dreams, and reformed her into a model housewife. Indeed, it seems at one moment when an explicit 'separation takes place between herself and the spirit that had haunted her', that he is going to do this. But in Trollope as in life few conversions are complete. The dream recovers, and a good thing too, perhaps, because Stubbs has his own Romantic side. He has a 'picturesque but inconvenient' cottage in the Scottish Highlands, likes half-jokingly to see himself as King Solomon, and, as Trollope notes, 'the Ayala whom her lover had loved would not have been an Ayala to be loved by him, but for her dreams'. Ayala is at least constant to her pragmatic fantasy. She may be unable to account for the vagaries of her behaviour or for the mysteries of the Angel, but she is aware, without any hint of self-regard, that she is a very lucky girl: 'I wonder', she concludes, 'whether there is anybody in all the world who has got so completely everything that she ever dreamed of wanting as I have.'

*Ayala's Angel*, like so many of Trollope's later novels, is a work of considerable human range. Ayala—'our pet heroine'—may be the novel's psy-

chological triumph; but in the subsidiary characters
too, Trollope explores the dignity and the potency
of the dream-worlds so many of us carry around with
us. Foremost among these studies is the unrequited
lover, Tom Tringle. Ayala obviously finds him physically repulsive, and compares his attempted
embraces, which she has to suffer throughout the
book, with those of a 'Newfoundland dog . . . unpleasant because dripping with muddy water'. But
Trollope makes it clear that Tom's vision of im-
mortal love is as sincere and heartfelt as Ayala's
own—perhaps more so, as it is focused on a human
being and not a spirit, and has the added merit of
undiminished constancy. Tom's problem is that
along with his perfect devotion as a courtly lover, he
also happens to be a sentimentally vulgar oaf. Trollope's argument is that sentimentally vulgar oafs
have every right to be in love, and it is particularly
praiseworthy in one when he pursues his dream to
the point where a self-respecting Romeo, never
mind a self-respecting man-of-the-world, would
have given it up.

Tom Tringle is in fact a 'hobble-de-hoy', a type
with whom Trollope had had notable success before
(see Charley Tudor in *The Three Clerks* and
Johnny Eames in *The Small House at Allington*),
and one might suspect from the opening description
of Tom, who is 'stout and awkward, but without
that settled air which age gives to heavy men', that
Trollope, as he certainly does with both Tudor and
Eames, is going to draw on his own amatory experiences as an overweight and somewhat callow Post
Office clerk back in the eighteen-thirties. Yet neither
Tudor nor Eames could quite touch Trollope's
heart as Tom Tringle evidently does. Both of them,
like Trollope himself, became successful public men,

Tudor a facile journalist, and Eames a redoubtable
Civil Servant. Neither has Tom Tringle's disadvan-
tages of enormous wealth, and the disabling freedom
from responsibility which goes with it. Tom is a
wastrel who quickly acquires a police record and is
eventually sent off in disgrace (like the egregious Sir
Felix Carbury in *The Way We Live Now*) on a
global tour to get him out of the way. His only aptitude—apart from a tendency to earn laughs at his
own expense—is to love hopelessly, constant in a
losing cause that has never had a glimpse of victory:
'and yet he fought out his battle to the last gasp'. It
is this that earns him the respect of his creator. Both
Tudor and Eames have their respective dreams of
love. But Tudor, despite inadvertent episodes with
a young barmaid and her basilisk guardian, wins his
Katey Woodward easily enough. Johnny Eames's
passion for Lily Dale is, on the contrary, one of the
types of Trollopian unrewarded love. But if Lily refuses Johnny she remains his friend and confidante,
and he gets close enough to her to understand, un-
spokenly, the complex psychological predicament
which causes her to refuse him, and which he may
even find attractive. Tom succeeds only in tempor-
arily 'taming' Ayala, and in reducing her first
impression of him as a 'beast' and 'devil' into an
extraordinary and rather interesting fact of life. As
Trollope concludes, Tom Tringle's truth to his
dreams has much to recommend it: 'The merit is to
despair and yet to be constant.'

Trollope's portrait of him is often masterly. His
seedy dissipations in Faddle's company and in
favour of Signor Bolivia's bank-account are simply
absurd, of course, as are his Aguecheek-like mach-
inations to bring a horsewhip or a rapier to bear on
Colonel Stubbs. But there is no hint of Aguecheek's

meanness of spirit, or his cowardice. Tom Tringle has the firm-footed recklessness that marks so much real bravery: 'He had no disinclination to be hit over the head himself, if he could be sure of hitting the Colonel over the head.' He may have an instinct for making the worst of himself—witness the cheap jewellery he wears to woo Ayala, and the novelettish syntax which would make the most heartfelt intention sound insincere ('Rain—what matters the rain?', 'Ayala;—stay yet a moment!') Yet he has his father's business-sense too. When he buys the necklace that is to bribe Ayala into submission, he is quick to point out both to his father and to Colonel Stubbs that he has got 20 per cent off cost price by paying cash, and when, Ayala having proved suitably unimpressed, he is forced to sell it back to Ricolay's, we hear he only lost thirty pounds on the whole transaction. These impractical practicalities are, in their own way, as effective as all the impossible idealism when it comes to making the character of Tom Tringle tell; and if the grounds for considering Tom the hero of the book (see Trollope's apology for him in Chapter LXI) are perhaps debatable, yet there is ample evidence for setting him somewhat above Ayala as a character extraordinarily constant to rather ordinary dreams.

Other characters in *Ayala's Angel* are also defined by their rich inner world. Paradoxically eminent among these is the grand financier, Sir Thomas Tringle, who is quite clearly most satisfied and most alive when in 'the little back parlour in Lombard Street' where he is something of an artist in the manipulation of his own and other people's millions, and an acknowledged authority on international finance in the age of the purchase of the Suez Canal shares. Lombard Street clearly means

more to Tringle than either the town house, the
country house, or the Scottish mansion his efforts
there have earned him, and this devotion, combined
with a freedom from crude acquisitiveness, make
the portrait of Sir Thomas Tringle (balance being
the principle of Trollope's art) a welcome antidote
to the adverse view of the city financier presented
in *The Way We Live Now* (1875) and *The Prime
Minister* (1876). Here Trollope had presented the
merchant-prince Melmotte and the stock-jobber
Ferdinand Lopez outwardly as tyrants in a world
of financial conquest and possibility, inwardly as
frightened men, trying to bluff and bully confidence
in fictitious companies and commodities. Both are
portrayed with considerable psychological acumen,
yet Trollope's view of the money-market is sharply
critical in these novels, and even satiric. In the
milder atmosphere of *Ayala's Angel* Tringle is
shown as a craftsman whose labours bring him satis-
cation and fulfilment. It is not a rose-tinted portrait.
Sir Thomas does boast, as a matter of course, about
his deer-forests and waterfalls; there is a bullying
roughness in his voice such as might bring a board-
room to book, and the spirit of the age has forced
him to lend his name to prospectuses for dubious
concerns. Yet he would never let the Melmottes,
Lopezes, Fiskers, and Grendalls of this world stand
with him behind his counter. And his repudiation of
the Faddle family has about it a touch of chivalry.
Here his son Tom has taken a junior Faddle on
excursions into Soho:

Do you know what Faddle and Company are,—stock
jobbers, who ten years ago hadn't a thousand pounds
in the way of capital among them! They've been connected with a dozen companies, none of which are
floating now, and have made money out of them all!

Do you think that Travers and Treason will accept a young man as a partner who associates with such people as that?

Sir Thomas, in his private life, is a bit of a softie. There are even moments in his relations with the younger generation where he resembles the Duke of Omnium in *The Duke's Children*, Trollope's finest study of a relationship between a father and his children, composed in 1876, but not published until 1880. Sir Thomas is more impulsive than the Duke in the earlier novel, and his critiques are less dry, but he is outmanoeuvred just as often, and when, in exasperation, he can find nothing more momentous to satirize, has a tilt at his offspring's preference for modish slang. 'Confounded', he tells Tom, 'is a stupid foolish word, and it means nothing.' We remember that the Duke was equally unimpressed by his son Silverbridge's preference for 'awful' and 'beastly'! Gertrude and Tom heap folly upon folly, Augusta's scrounging husband lays a heavier and heavier hand of obligation on his shoulder, but Tringle, like Palliser, grows in stature the more he gives way. When uninspiring Captain Batsby, who has somewhat unwillingly eloped with Gertrude to Ostend for the sake of the latter's Romantic preconceptions, goes on about the 'way in which we were separated at Ostend being very distressing' to his feelings, Sir Thomas intercepts him with: 'Not improbably. I have always observed that when people are interrupted in the performance of some egregious stupidity their feelings are hurt.'

Sir Thomas has some particularly wry dealings with perhaps the most entertaining character in the book, his parsimonious son-in-law, the Honourable Septimus Traffick. Traffick does not promise much at first in the way of rich inner life and personalized fantasy. When he first comes to Queen's Gate as a suitor for Augusta he is an unprepossessingly heavy and unhealthy young man of forty using his father Lord Boardotrade's 'mushroom peerage' and his own seat in Parliament to get himself a suitable wife. There is no look of luxury or audacity about him, and it comes as a rich surprise when, in the space of the novel's first volume, he flowers into perhaps the most efficient sponger in Victorian fiction. His technique is flawless. Not content with the income from the £120,000 Sir Thomas has settled on Augusta, he sets about treating the home and belongings of the 'London merchant-prince' as his oyster. Like his father, who wears his patrician's toga grandly in the only scene in which he appears, Traffick is always ready to flatter his father-in-law's munificence in public, and to pour a gallon of condescension upon it. Realizing that brazen guests are run after more readily than craven ones, he wonders if Sir Thomas ought to move his stables at Merle Park a little, suggests improvements that might be made in the standard of claret at dinner, and raises the tone of Queen's Gate society with the importation of miscellaneous Honourable Miss Trafficks. There is nothing else quite like him in Trollope. Lord Mongrober, who provides sour critiques of Dick Roby's wine in *The Prime Minister*, and who never gives a dinner in return, is a mere cameo in comparison; the 'irrepressible Crocker', the obscure Post Office clerk who inveigles acquaintance with the aristocrats of *Marion Fay*, looks thin and coarse beside Traffick. A consummate egoist, Traffick is a man who likes to take everything upon himself, whether or not he is capable of performing it, paying as little as possible for the privilege, and remaining unfailingly true to his own high estimation of himself. 'I know that at bottom [Sir Thomas] has a thorough respect for me,' he confides to his wife. As the book progresses, Traffick's zeal for self-advertisement, acquisition, and interference in the affairs of others, rumbles on in the background, until it reaches a climax as he attempts to choose a suitable husband for Gertrude. He has little to gain from this, and his moralizing is simply that of an inveterate busy-body, as when he declares with pleasing irony that Frank Houston will not suit Gertrude for when a man has nothing else to do he is sure to spend all that he can lay his hands upon. He then proceeds to interfere with Sir Thomas on Captain Batsby's behalf, setting Captain Batsby's marriage portion at half his own (with suitable deductions for Batsby's imprudent behaviour), and assuring the trusting Captain of his abilities as ambassador: '[Sir Thomas] is rough, as you say, but he is not hard-hearted, nor yet stubborn. I can do pretty nearly what I like with him.' Unfortunately Sir Thomas bridles up and Traffick gets his marching orders, which is a pity, because he has by this time convinced not only himself but the reader that he is essential to the conduct of the book. He may delude himself—but he makes plenty of capital out of his delusion. He has infinite powers of resilience. Like Ayala, he is a dreamer: and his dreams help him through life as conveniently as she is supported by hers. As Colonel Stubbs points out:

He has learnt the great secret than a man cannot be cut who will not be cut. As it is worth no man's while to protract an enmity with such a one as he, he suffers from no prolonged enmities. He walks unassailable by any darts, and is, I should say, the happiest man in London.

In a novel with so many dreamers, practical and impractical, it is perhaps as well that Trollope should offer a substantial inset commentary on artist-life, both through the opening reminiscence of Egbert Dormer, and through the portrait of the sculptor, Isadore Hamel, and his offstage father, who lives in voluntary exile, and in scorn of the conventional properties, at Rome. Trollope had not had a very happy time introducing the art-world into his novels before *Ayala's Angel*. He had tried his hand at guying fashionable portrait-painters in the chapters of *The Last Chronicle of Barset* which deal with Conway Dalrymple and Mrs Dobbs Broughton, but had succeeded only in producing cumbersome farce. In life, Trollope was an indefatigable art-tourist who believed in standing before pictures till he dropped, or lying on the floor where benches were not provided in galleries—'a hard-working amateur', N. John Hall concludes in *Trollope and His Illustrators*, 'possessed of both the enthusiasms and liabilities common to that status'. His account of 'The Art Tourist' in *Travelling Sketches* is a most amusing manual on the craft of coarse picture-appreciation. But in *Ayala's Angel* he is not concerned with appreciation, or even pretension to appreciation, but with men and women, and his view of the fringes of artistic society is a telling one. Take, for instance, the few glimpses of the porcelain Bohemianism at Egbert Dormer's 'bijou' house in South Kensington with its 'republican' constitution, and its propensity for doing 'tricksy' and dainty things at high speed: 'They were a family who ran up and down with the greatest alacrity.' Or take his sketch of the pompous combative young sculptor, Isadore Hamel. Trollope begs the question as to whether he will progress beyond pretentiously allegorical figures of 'Italia

United' or 'The Prostrate Roman Catholic Church'
to works of real imagination. He will probably try
his hand soon enough at 'a likeness of Mr. Jones,
when he comes to sit for his bust at the request of
his admiring friends'. The important thing is that
he dresses the part, convinces Lucy that he is as
'handsome as could ever have been any Apollo', and
gets through the novel without deterring Sir Thomas
from making a settlement on her. And Frank
Houston's schemes to paint society-portraits are at
least as dilettantish as those of Henry Gowan in
Dickens's *Little Dorrit*. It is possible to speculate
that Trollope constructed his arty hangers-on from
material gained during his friendship with Millais,
his favourite illustrator; or perhaps from expatriate
sculptors who were familiar with his mother, Fanny
Trollope, in the days of her Florentine circle; or
from friends of his brother, Tom Trollope, during
the latter's days in Rome. Whatever their origin, the
Dormers and Hamels are highly convincing, and it
is fitting that Trollope should deal with them only in
their human, and not in their professional relations.
The kind of serious discussion of art and artists that
appears in Henry James's *Roderick Hudson* would
be out of place in *Ayala's Angel*.

  The inset love-story of Frank Houston and
Imogene Docimer is perhaps the only point in the
novel where the inner lives of the characters are not
quite rich enough for the roles assigned them. Frank
has been disappointed in a legacy and now must
choose between a moderately futile existence of
limited luxury, and the constraint of marriage on a
limited income. He is a variation on the typical
Trollopian male lover who can adduce precepts but
not quite live up to them, and can be set in company
with Frank Greystock in *The Eustace Diamonds*,

Paul Montague in *The Way We Live Now*, or
Harry Clavering in *The Claverings*. Frank has a
quick intelligence, a ready wit, and a modicum of
culture, but has a damaging inability to be serious
about anything. Some of his early letters to Imogene
—racy commentaries on his attempts to carry off
Gertrude Tringle and some of the Lombard Street
millions—verge on the heartless, and are certainly
whimsically self-regarding. His chaffing of the
pseudo-romantic Gertrude Tringle when she wants
to get him to elope is only moderately funny, be-
acuse it is also his habitual tone with the genuinely
passionate Imogene. Even when he is considering
returning to Imogene (the passage dramatizing putting off decision-making is characteristically Trollopian) his deliberations get muddled up with all
the trivia of club gossip which are the normal background to his existence. Love on a crust and a garret
to Frank is by turns a cottage or a cottage-garden at
Pau, Brittany, or Castlebar, never a practical proposition, until he is pitchforked into marriage by
Aunt Rosina's sentimentalism and the pressure of
events. It is hard to criticize him much—he is the
moral casualty of idleness and lassitude. But Trollope's detailed exposition of his superficiality throws
into sharp relief the dearth of information we are
given about Imogene's devotion to him. She is very
fond of telling herself that as a woman she is in-
evitably dependent. Yet, modest as are her expecta-
tions in life, and disagreeable as is her plight as the
perpetual property of her brother Mudbury
Docimer's baggage-train, it is clear that much of the
time she thinks she is bemoaning her woman's lot
she is really bemoaning her inexplicable devotion to
Frank Houston. She knows she is attractive enough
to turn into an adventuress like Georgiana

Longestaffe (in *The Way We Live Now*) or Arabella
Trefoil (in *The American Senator*) and do better
than either in catching a rich husband. Yet she
remains constant to Frank. Trollope seems to be
attempting another investigation of the complexities
—even the perversities—of female devotion, as he
had with Emily Hotspur in *Sir Harry Hotspur of
Humblethwaite* or Emily Wharton in *The Prime
Minister*. Yet in this case as in those the portrait is
damaged by being too externalized. It is clear
enough that Imogene is strongly attracted to Frank
sexually. The emotional charge of the waterfall
love-scene in the Tyrolean Alps is much stronger on
her side than on his (it is interesting to note that
the setting is very similar to that of the crucial love-
scene between Emily and George, also cousins, in
*Sir Harry Hotspur*). Equally striking is the dramatic
detail in the chapter entitled 'A Cold Prospect' of
Imogene standing before Frank 'putting her two
hands up to her head, and brushing her hair away
from her forehead'. Moments like this are charac-
teristic of Trollope's art at its surest; but Imogene's
passion is dealt with elliptically on the whole, and it
is very difficult to tell whether she gives herself to
Frank at the end of the book in a spirit of self-
sacrifice, self-punishment, or unexamined female
constancy, vanquishing male dilatoriness 'by the
absolute sincerity of her love'. This is not a merely
perfunctory secondary love-plot, like, for example,
the vapid affair between Carstairs and Mary in *Dr
Wortle's School*; but it seems to lack the rounded
vitality and psychological specificity of the remainder of the novel.

*Ayala's Angel*, then, in so far as it can be said to
have any predominant theme, is about the richness
and ubiquitousness of fantasy, and the narrow and

uncertain border that separates ideal visions from real life. This is perhaps a strange subject for so apparently dry-souled and realistic a writer as Trollope to tackle. Yet he does not write in the spirit of the High Classicist, who is suspicious of dreams, nor of the High Romantic, who prefers them to real life. He perceives that the truth is richer and subtler than either would admit. In *Ayala's Angel* dreams rise out of reality, and are modified by reality.

JULIAN THOMPSON

# NOTE ON THE TEXT

THE manuscript of *Ayala's Angel* is preserved in the Yale University Library, and is listed in Appendix B to Gordon N. Ray's 'Trollope at Full Length' (*Huntingdon Library Quarterly*, 31 (1967–8)) as possessing 'minor corrections' in the author's hand. The 'Working Diary', publishers' agreements, and associated documents are in the Bodleian Library, Oxford, under the call-mark MSS. Don. c. 10. Trollope began the novel on 25 April 1878, worked intermittently at it until the end of July, and then continuously until completion on 24 September. The last fifty-four chapters of the novel were written in less than two months, Trollope taking only four days' rest in that time. In all, the composition of *Ayala's Angel* occupied only seventy-one working days.

The novel was offered to Alexander Ireland, to Blackwood, and to Macmillan in turn, but none were interested in the serial rights, and Trollope was eventually forced to sell these to the National Press Agency, who seem never to have made use of them. The novel was. however, serialized in the *Cincinnati Commercial*, running from 6 November 1880 to 23 July 1881. In book form, it was published in three volumes by Chapman and Hall in June 1881.

The present edition is a reproduction of the first Oxford World's Classics text of 1929 (reprinted 1951, 1960, 1968, and 1975). This has been checked against the text of the 1881 first edition, and the following emendations have been made: page 51, line 14 from foot, *out* for *our*; page 58, line 16, *unsubstantial* for *substantial*; page 214, line 5, *do it with* for *do with it*. A useful checklist of other possible corruptions was compiled by R. W. Chapman ('The Text of Trollope's *Ayala's Angel*', *Modern Philology*, 39 (February 1942), 287–94). I have adopted Chapman's suggestions on page 26, line 5 from foot, reading *at all* for *all*, on page 363, reading *namby-pamby* for *namby-mamby*, and on page 488, reading *dish* for *diet*.

## SELECT BIBLIOGRAPHY

THERE is no collected edition of the works. A facsimile edition of thirty-six titles (62 vols.), *Selected Works of Anthony Trollope*, has been published by the Arno Press (1981; General Editor, N. John Hall). Works by Trollope are also available in the Oxford World's Classics series; in Penguin, Dover, Alan Sutton, and Encore reprints; in the Harting Grange Library Series (mostly the shorter works), published by the Caledonia Press; and in *Anthony Trollope: The Complete Short Stories* (forty-two stories in 5 vols.), ed. Betty Jane Slemp Breyer (1979–83). The standard bibliography of the works is Michael Sadleir, *Trollope: A Bibliography* (1928; reprinted 1977). *The Letters of Anthony Trollope*, 2 vols., ed. N. John Hall (1983), is now the standard edition.

Recent years have seen an embarrassment of riches in biographical studies of Trollope. In 1988 appeared R. H. Super's *The Chronicler of Barsetshire*, in 1990 Richard Mullen's *Anthony Trollope: A Victorian in his World* and in 1991 N. John Hall's long-awaited *Anthony Trollope: A Biography*. All three have their merits, but perhaps Hall best blends insight with reliability. Victoria Glendinning is at present working on a fourth major biography. Of the earlier lives Michael Sadleir's *Trollope: A Commentary* still holds its own for eloquence and urbanity. The best primary sources of information about Trollope's life are T. H. S. Escott's memoir, *Anthony Trollope: His Public Services, Private Friends and Literary Originals* (1913; re-printed 1967), and the novelist's *Autobiography* (1883). Other useful tools are W. and J. Gerould, *A Guide to Trollope* (1948), and N. John Hall, *Trollope and His Illustrators* (1980).

The best bibliographies of criticism are Rafael Helling, *A Century of Trollope Criticism* (1956), and *The Reputation of Trollope: An Annotated Bibliography 1925–1975*, ed. John Charles Olmsted and Jeffrey Welch (1978); but see also Ruth apRoberts, 'Anthony Trollope' in George H. Ford, *Victorian Fiction; a Second Guide to Research* (1978), and the bibliographies published annually in *Victorian Studies*. A selection of contemporary criticism is reprinted in *Trollope: The Critical Heritage*, ed. Donald Smalley (1969), and contemporary responses are very fully discussed in David Skilton, *Anthony Trollope and his Contemporaries* (1972).

Of the many general studies of Trollope, the most useful are: Henry James, 'Anthony Trollope' in *Partial Portraits* (1888); A. O. J. Cockshut, *Anthony Trollope: A Critical Study* (1955); G. N. Ray, 'Trollope at Full Length', *Huntingdon Library Quarterly*, 31 (1967–8); Ruth apRoberts, *Trollope: Artist and Moralist* (1971; *The Moral Trollope* in USA); and James R. Kincaid, *The Novels of Anthony Trollope* (1977). Perhaps owing to its anomalous status in Trollope's *oeuvre*, extended critical studies of *Ayala's Angel* are few. The most sensitive seems to me to be that of James Kincaid, in his *The Novels of Anthony Trollope* (Clarendon Press, 1977); Robert Tracy's *Trollope's Later Novels* (Berkeley, 1978) includes a workmanlike, if rather heavy account of the book, and Andrew Wright, in *Trollope: Dream and Art* (Macmillan, 1983), indicates a parallel between the novel and *Pride and Prejudice*. J. Hillis Miller's influential *The Form of Victorian Fiction* (1968) uses *Ayala's Angel* as the basis of an important general account of Trollope.

# A CHRONOLOGY OF
# ANTHONY TROLLOPE

Virtually all Trollope's fiction after *Framley Parsonage* (1860–1) appeared first in serial form, with book publication usually coming just prior to the final instalment of the serial.

1815   (24 Apr.) Born at 16 Keppel Street, Bloomsbury, the fourth son of Thomas and Frances Trollope. (Summer ?) Family moves to Harrow-on-the-Hill.

1823   To Harrow School as a day-boy.

1825   To a private school at Sunbury.

1827   To school at Winchester College.

1830   Removed from Winchester and returned to Harrow.

1834   (Apr.) The family flees to Bruges to escape creditors.
       (Nov.) Accepts a junior clerkship in the General Post Office, London.

1841   (Sept.) Made Postal Surveyor's Clerk at Banagher, King's County, Ireland.

1843   (mid-Sept.) Begins work on his first novel, *The Macdermots of Ballycloran*.

1844   (11 June) Marries Rose Heseltine.
       (Aug.) Transferred to Clonmel, County Tipperary.

1846   (13 Mar.) Son, Henry Merivale Trollope, born.

1847   *The Macdermots of Ballycloran*, published in 3 vols. (Newby).
       (27 Sept.) Son, Frederic James Anthony Trollope, born.

1848    *The Kellys and the O'Kellys; or Landlords and Tenants*
        3 vols. (Colburn).
        (Autumn) Moves to Mallow, County Cork.

1850    *La Vendée; An Historical Romance* 3 vols. (Colburn).
        Writes *The Noble Jilt* (A play, published 1923).

1851    (1 Aug.) Sent to south-west of England on special
        postal mission.

1853    (29 July) Begins *The Warden* (the first of the
        Barsetshire novels).
        (29 Aug.) Moves to Belfast as Acting Surveyor.

1854    (9 Oct.) Appointed Surveyor of Northern District
        of Ireland.

1855    *The Warden* 1 vol. (Longman).
        Writes *The New Zealander*.
        (June) Moves to Donnybrook, Ireland.

1857    *Barchester Towers* 3 vols. (Longman).

1858    *The Three Clerks* 3 vols. (Bentley).
        *Doctor Thorne* 3 vols. (Chapman & Hall).
        (Jan.) Departs for Egypt on Post Office business.
        (Mar.) Visits Holy Land.
        (Apr.–May) Returns via Malta, Gibraltar and
        Spain.
        (May–Sept.) Visits Scotland and north of Eng-
        land on postal business.
        (16 Nov.) Leaves for the West Indies on postal
        mission.

1859    *The Bertrams* 3 vols. (Chapman & Hall).
        *The West Indies and the Spanish Main* 1 vol.
        (Chapman & Hall).
        (3 July) Arrives home.
        (Nov.) Leaves Ireland; settles at Waltham Cross,
        Hertfordshire, after being appointed Surveyor of
        the Eastern District of England.

1860    *Castle Richmond* 3 vols. (Chapman & Hall).
        First serialized fiction, *Framley Parsonage*, pub-
        lished in the *Cornhill Magazine*.

(Oct.) Visits, with his wife, his mother and brother in Florence; makes the acquaintance of Kate Field, a 22-year-old American for whom he forms a romantic attachment.

1861    *Framley Parsonage* 3 vols. (Smith, Elder).
*Tales of All Countries* 1 vol. (Chapman & Hall).
(24 Aug.) Leaves for America to write a travel book.

1862    *Orley Farm* 2 vols. (Chapman & Hall).
*North America* 2 vols. (Chapman & Hall).
*The Struggles of Brown, Jones and Robinson: By One of the Firm* 1 vol. (New York, Harper—an American piracy; first English edition 1870, Smith, Elder).
(25 Mar.) Arrives home from America.
(5 Apr.) Elected to the Garrick Club.

1863    *Tales of All Countries*, Second Series, 1 vol. (Chapman & Hall).
*Rachel Ray* 2 vols. (Chapman & Hall).
(6 Oct.) Death of his mother, Mrs Frances Trollope.

1864    *The Small House at Allington* 2 vols. (Smith, Elder).
(12 Apr.) Elected a member of the Athenaeum Club.

1865    *Can You Forgive Her?* 2 vols. (Chapman & Hall).
*Miss Mackenzie* 1 vol. (Chapman & Hall).
*Hunting Sketches* 1 vol. (Chapman & Hall).

1866    *The Belton Estate* 3 vols. (Chapman & Hall).
*Travelling Sketches* 1 vol. (Chapman & Hall).
*Clergymen of the Church of England* 1 vol. (Chapman & Hall).

1867    *Nina Balatka* 2 vols. (Blackwood).
*The Claverings* 2 vols. (Smith, Elder).
*The Last Chronicle of Barset* 2 vols. (Smith, Elder).
*Lotta Schmidt and Other Stories* 1 vol. (Strahan).
(1 Sept.) Resigns from the Post Office.
Assumes editorship of *Saint Pauls Magazine*.

1868   *Linda Tressel* 2 vols. (Blackwood).
       (11 Apr.) Leaves London for the United States on
       postal mission.
       (26 July) Returns from America.
       (Nov.) Stands unsuccessfully as Liberal candi-
       date for Beverley, Yorkshire.

1869   *Phineas Finn; the Irish Member* 2 vols. (Virtue &
       Co).
       *He Knew He Was Right* 2 vols. (Strahan).
       *Did He Steal It? A Comedy in Three Acts* (a version of
       *The Last Chronicle of Barset*, privately printed by
       Virtue & Co).

1870   *The Vicar of Bullhampton* 1 vol. (Bradbury, Evans).
       *An Editor's Tales* 1 vol. (Strahan).
       *The Commentaries of Caesar* 1 vol. (Blackwood).
       (Jan.–July) Eased out of *Saint Pauls Magazine*.

1871   *Sir Harry Hotspur of Humblethwaite* 1 vol. (Hurst &
       Blackett).
       *Ralph the Heir* 3 vols. (Hurst & Blackett).
       (Apr.) Gives up house at Waltham Cross.
       (24 May) Sails to Australia to visit his son.
       (27 July) Arrives at Melbourne.

1872   *The Golden Lion of Granpere* 1 vol. (Tinsley).
       (Jan.–Oct.) Travelling in Australia and New
       Zealand.
       (Dec.) Returns via the United states.

1873   *The Eustace Diamonds* 3 vols. (Chapman & Hall).
       *Australia and New Zealand* 2 vols. (Chapman &
       Hall).
       (Apr.) Settles in Montagu Square, London.

1874   *Phineas Redux* 2 vols. (Chapman & Hall).
       *Lady Anna* 2 vols. (Chapman & Hall).
       *Harry Heathcote of Gangoil. A Tale of Australian Bush
       Life* 1 vol. (Sampson Low).

1875   *The Way We Live Now* 2 vols. (Chapman & Hall).
       (1 Mar.) Leaves for Australia via Brindisi, the
       Suez Canal, and Ceylon.

(4 May) Arrives in Australia.
(Aug.–Oct.) Sailing homewards.
(Oct.) Begins *An Autobiography*.

1876   *The Prime Minister* 4 vols. (Chapman & Hall).

1877   *The American Senator* 3 vols. (Chapman & Hall).
(29 June) Leaves for South Africa.
(11 Dec.) Sails for home.

1878   *South Africa* 2 vols. (Chapman & Hall).
*Is He Popenjoy?* 3 vols. (Chapman & Hall).
(June–July) Travels to Iceland in the yacht 'Mastiff'.
*How the 'Mastiffs' Went to Ireland* 1 vol. (privately printed, Virtue & Co).

1879   *An Eye for an Eye* 2 vols. (Chapman & Hall).
*Thackeray* 1 vol. (Macmillan).
*John Candigate* 3 vols. (Chapman & Hall).
*Cousin Henry* 2 vols. (Chapman & Hall).

1880   *The Duke's Children* 3 vols. (Chapman & Hall).
*The Life of Cicero* 2 vols. (Chapman & Hall).
(July) Settles at South Harting, Sussex, near Petersfield.

1881   *Dr Wortle's School* 2 vols. (Chapman & Hall).
*Ayala's Angel* 3 vols. (Chapman & Hall).

1882   *Why Frau Frohmann Raised Her Prices; and Other Stories* 1 vol. (Isbister).
*The Fixed Period* 2 vols. (Blackwood).
*Marion Fay* 3 vols. (Chapman & Hall).
*Lord Palmerston* 1 vol. (Isbister).
*Kept in the Dark* 2 vols. (Chatto & Windus).
(May) Visits Ireland to collect material for a new Irish novel.
(Aug.) Returns to Ireland a second time.
(2 Oct.) Takes rooms for the winter at Garlant's Hotel, Suffolk St., London.
(3 Nov.) Suffers paralytic stroke.
(6 Dec.) Dies in nursing home, 34 Welbeck St., London.

Ayala's Angel

# CONTENTS

# CHAPTER I

## THE TWO SISTERS

WHEN Egbert Dormer died he left his two daughters utterly penniless upon the world, and it must be said of Egbert Dormer that nothing else could have been expected of him. The two girls were both pretty, but Lucy, who was twenty-one, was supposed to be simple and comparatively unattractive, whereas Ayala was credited,—as her somewhat romantic name might show,—with poetic charm and a taste for romance. Ayala when her father died was nineteen.

We must begin yet a little earlier and say that there had been,—and had died many years before the death of Egbert Dormer,—a clerk in the Admiralty, by name Reginald Dosett, who, and whose wife, had been conspicuous for personal beauty. Their charms were gone, but the records of them had been left in various grand-children. There had been a son born to Mr. Dosett, who was also a Reginald and a clerk in the Admiralty, and who also, in his turn, had been a handsome man. With him, in his decadence, the reader will become acquainted. There were also two daughters, whose reputation for perfect feminine beauty had never been contested. The elder had married a city man of wealth,—of wealth when he married her, but who had become enormously wealthy by the time of our story. He had when he married been simply Mister, but was now Sir Thomas Tringle, Baronet, and was senior partner in the great firm of Travers and Treason. Of Traverses and Treasons there were none left in these days, and Mr. Tringle was supposed to manipulate all the millions with which the great firm in Lombard

Street* was concerned. He had married old Mr.
Dosett's eldest daughter, Emmeline, who was now
Lady Tringle, with a house at the top of Queen's
Gate, rented at £1,500 a year, with a palatial moor
in Scotland, with a seat in Sussex, and as many
carriages and horses as would suit an archduchess.
Lady Tringle had everything in the world; a son,
two daughters, and an open-handed stout husband,
who was said to have told her that money was a
matter of no consideration.

The second Miss Dosett, Adelaide Dosett, who had
been considerably younger than her sister, had insisted upon giving herself to Egbert Dormer, the
artist, whose death we commemorated in our first
line. But she had died before her husband. They
who remembered the two Miss Dosetts as girls were
wont to declare that, though Lady Tringle might,
perhaps, have had the advantage in perfection of
feature and in unequalled symmetry, Adelaide had
been the more attractive from expression and bril-
liancy. To her Lord Sizes had offered his hand and
coronet, promising to abandon for her sake all the
haunts of his matured life. To her Mr. Tringle had
knelt before he had taken the elder sister. For her
Mr. Progrum, the popular preacher of the day, for
a time so totally lost himself that he was nearly
minded to go over to Rome. She was said to have
had offers from a widowed Lord Chancellor and from
a Russian prince. Her triumphs would have quite
obliterated that of her sister had she not insisted on
marrying Egbert Dormer.

Then there had been, and still was, Reginald
Dosett, the son of old Dosett, and the eldest of the
family. He too had married, and was now living with
his wife; but to them had no children been born,
luckily, as he was a poor man. Alas, to a beautiful
son it is not often that beauty can be a fortune as to
a daughter. Young Reginald Dosett,—he is anything now but young,—had done but little for himself with his beauty, having simply married the

estimable daughter of a brother clerk. Now, at the age of fifty, he had his £900 a year from his office, and might have lived in fair comfort had he not allowed a small millstone of debt to hang round his neck from his earlier years. But still he lived creditably in a small but very genteel house at Notting Hill, and would have undergone any want rather than have declared himself to be a poor man to his rich relations the Tringles.

Such were now the remaining two children of old Mr. Dosett,—Lady Tringle, namely, and Reginald Dosett, the clerk in the Admiralty. Adelaide, the beauty in chief of the family, was gone; and now also her husband, the improvident artist, had followed his wife. Dormer had been by no means a failing artist. He had achieved great honour,—had at an early age been accepted into the Royal Academy,— had sold pictures to illustrious princes and more illustrious dealers, had been engraved and had lived to see his own works resold at five times their original prices. Egbert Dormer might also have been a rich man. But he had a taste for other beautiful things besides a wife. The sweetest little phaeton that was to cost nothing, the most perfect bijou of a little house at South Kensington,—he had boasted that it might have been packed without trouble in his brother-in-law Tringle's dining-room,—the simplest little gem for his wife, just a blue set of china for his dinner table, just a painted cornice for his studio, just satin hangings for his drawing-room—and a few simple ornaments for his little girls; these with a few rings for himself, and velvet suits of clothing in which to do his painting; these, with a few little dinner parties to show off his blue china, were the first and last of his extravagances. But when he went, and when his pretty things were sold, there was not enough to cover his debts. There was, however, a sweet savour about his name. When he died it was said of him that his wife's death had killed him. He had dropped his pallette, refused to finish the ordered portrait of a princess, and had simply turned himself round and died.

Then there were the two daughters, Lucy and Ayala. It should be explained that though a proper family intercourse had always been maintained between the three families, the Tringles, the Dormers, and the Dosetts, there had never been cordiality between the first and the two latter. The wealth of the Tringles had seemed to convey with it a fetid odour. Egbert Dormer, with every luxury around him which money could purchase, had affected to despise the heavy magnificence of the Tringles. It may be that he affected a fashion higher than that which the Tringles really attained. Reginald Dosett, who was neither brilliant nor fashionable, was in truth independent, and, perhaps, a little thin-skinned. He would submit to no touch of arrogance from Sir Thomas; and Sir Thomas seemed to carry arrogance in his brow and in his paunch. It was there rather, perhaps, than in his heart; but there are men to whom a knack of fumbling their money in their pockets and of looking out from under penthouse brows over an expanse of waistcoat, gives an air of overweening pride which their true idiosyncracies may not justify. To Dosett had, perhaps, been spoken a word or two which on some occasion he had inwardly resented, and from thenceforward he had ever been ready to league with Dormer against the 'bullionaire', as they agreed to call Sir Thomas. Lady Tringle had even said a word to her sister, Mrs. Dormer, as to expenses, and that had never been forgiven by the artist. So things were when Mrs. Dormer died first; and so they remained when her husband followed her.

Then there arose a sudden necessity for action, which, for a while, brought Reginald Dosett into connexion with Sir Thomas and Lady Tringle. Something must be done for the poor girls. That the something should come out of the pocket of Sir Thomas would have seemed to be natural. Money with him

was no object,—not at all. Another girl or two would
be nothing to him,—as regarded simple expenditure.
But the care of a human being is an important
matter, and so Sir Thomas knew. Dosett had not a
child at all, and would be the better for such a wind-
fall. Dosett he supposed to be,—in his, Dosett's way,
—fairly well off. So he made this proposition. He
would take one girl and let Dosett take the other.
To this Lady Tringle added her proviso, that she
should have the choice. To her nerves affairs of taste
were of such paramount importance! To this Dosett
yielded. The matter was decided in Lady Tringle's
back drawing-room. Mrs. Dosett was not even consulted in that matter of choice, having already
acknowledged the duty of mothering a motherless
child. Dosett had thought that the bullionaire should
have said a word as to some future provision for the
penniless girl, for whom he would be able to do so
little. But Sir Thomas had said no such word, and
Dosett, himself, lacked both the courage and the
coarseness to allude to the matter. Then Lady Tringle
declared that she must have Ayala, and so the matter
was settled. Ayala the romantic; Ayala the poetic!
It was a matter of course that Ayala should be
chosen. Ayala had already been made intimate with
the magnificent saloons of the Tringles, and had been
felt by Lady Tringle to be an attraction. Her long
dark black locks, which had never hitherto been
tucked up, which were never curled, which were
never so long as to be awkward, were already known
as being the loveliest locks in London. She sang as
though Nature had intended her to be a singing-
bird,—requiring no education, no labour. She had
been once for three months in Paris, and French had
come naturally to her. Her father had taught her
something of his art, and flatterers had already begun
to say that she was born to be the one great female
artist of the world. Her hands, her feet, her figure
were perfect. Though she was as yet but nineteen,
London had already begun to talk about Ayala

Dormer. Of course Lady Tringle chose Ayala, not remembering at the moment that her own daughters might probably be superseded by their cousin.

And, therefore, as Lady Tringle said herself to Lucy with her sweetest smile—Mrs. Dosett had chosen Lucy. The two girls were old enough to know something of the meaning of such a choice. Ayala, the younger, was to be adopted into immense wealth, and Lucy was to be given up to comparative poverty. She knew nothing of her uncle Dosett's circumstances, but the genteel house at Notting Hill,—No. 3, Kingsbury Crescent,—was known to her, and was but a poor affair as compared even with the bijou in which she had hitherto lived. Her aunt Dosett never rose to any vehicle beyond a four-wheeler, and was careful even in thinking of that accommodation. Ayala would be whirled about the park by a wire-wig and a pair of brown horses which they had heard it said were not to be matched in London. Ayala would be carried with her aunt and her cousin to the show-room of Madame Tonsonville, the great French milliner of Bond Street,* whereas she, Lucy, might too probably be called on to make her own gowns. All the fashion of Queen's Gate, something, perhaps, of the fashion of Eaton Square,* would be open to Ayala. Lucy understood enough to know that Ayala's own charms might probably cause still more august gates to be opened to her, whereas Aunt Dosett entered no gates. It was quite natural that Ayala should be chosen. Lucy acknowledged as much to herself. But they were sisters, and had been so near! By what a chasm would they be dissevered, now so far asunder!

Lucy herself was a lovely girl, and knew her own loveliness. She was fairer than Ayala, somewhat taller, and much more quiet in her demeanour. She was also clever, but her cleverness did not show itself so quickly. She was a musician, whereas her sister could only sing. She could really draw, whereas her sister would rush away into effects in which the drawing was not always very excellent. Lucy was doing the best she could for herself, knowing something of French and German, though as yet not very fluent with her tongue. The two girls were, in truth, both greatly gifted; but Ayala had the gift of showing her talent without thought of showing it. Lucy saw it all, and knew that she was outshone; but how great had been the price of the outshining!

The artist's house had been badly ordered, and the two girls were of better disposition and better conduct than might have been expected from such fitful training. Ayala had been the father's pet, and Lucy the mother's. Parents do ill in making pets, and here they had done ill. Ayala had been taught to think herself the favourite, because the artist, himself, had been more prominent before the world than his wife. But the evil had not been lasting enough to have made bad feeling between the sisters. Lucy knew that her sister had been preferred to her, but she had been self-denying enough to be aware that some such preference was due to Ayala. She, too, admired Ayala, and loved her with her whole heart. And Ayala was always good to her,—had tried to divide everything,—had assumed no preference as a right. The two were true sisters. But when it was decided that Lucy was to go to Kingsbury Crescent the difference was very great. The two girls, on their father's death, had been taken to the great red brick house in Queen's Gate, and from thence, three or four days after the funeral, Lucy was to be transferred to her Aunt Dosett. Hitherto there had been little between them but weeping for their father. Now had come the hour of parting.

The tidings had been communicated to Lucy, and to Lucy alone, by Aunt Tringle,—'As you are the eldest, dear, we think that you will be best able to be a comfort to your aunt,' said Lady Tringle.

'I will do the best I can, Aunt Emmeline,' said Lucy, declaring to herself that, in giving such a reason, her aunt was lying basely.

'I am sure you will. Poor dear Ayala is younger than her cousins, and will be more subject to them.' So in truth was Lucy younger than her cousins, but of that she said nothing. 'I am sure you will agree with me that it is best that we should have the youngest.'

'Perhaps it is, Aunt Emmeline.'

'Sir Thomas would not have had it any other way,' said Lady Tringle, with a little severity, feeling that Lucy's accord had hardly been as generous as it should be. But she recovered herself quickly, remembering how much it was that Ayala was to get, how much that Lucy was to lose. 'But, my dear, we shall see you very often, you know. It is not so far across the park; and when we do have a few parties again——'

'Oh, aunt, I am not thinking of that.'

'Of course not. We can none of us think of it just now. But when the time does come of course we shall always have you, just as if you were one of us.' Then her aunt gave her a roll of bank-notes, a little present of twenty-five pounds, to begin the world with, and told her that the carriage should take her to Kingsbury Crescent on the following morning. On the whole Lucy behaved well and left a pleasant impression on her aunt's mind. The difference between Queen's Gate and Kingsbury Crescent,—between Queen's Gate and Kingsbury Crescent for life,—was indeed great!

'I wish it were you, with all my heart,' said Ayala, clinging to her sister.

'It could not have been me.'

'Why not!'

'Because you are so pretty and you are so clever'.

'No!'

'Yes! If we were to be separated of course it would be so. Do not suppose, dear, that I am disappointed.'

'I am.'

'If I can only like Aunt Margaret,'—Aunt Margaret was Mrs. Dosett, with whom neither of the girls had hitherto become intimate, and who was known to be quiet, domestic, and economical, but who had also been spoken of as having a will of her own,—'I shall do better with her than you would, Ayala.'

'I don't see why.'

'Because I can remain quiet longer than you. It will be very quiet. I wonder how we shall see each other! I cannot walk across the park alone.'

'Uncle Reg will bring you.'

'Not often, I fear. Uncle Reg has enough to do with his office.'

'You can come in a cab.'

'Cabs cost money, Ayey dear.'

'But Uncle Thomas——'

'We had better understand one or two things, Ayala. Uncle Thomas will pay everything for you, and as he is very rich things will come as they are wanted. There will be cabs, and if not cabs, carriages. Uncle Reg must pay for me, and he is very very kind to do so. But as he is not rich, there will be no carriages, and not a great many cabs. It is best to understand it all.'

'But they will send for you.'

'That's as they please. I don't think they will very often. I would not for the world put you against Uncle Thomas, but I have a feeling that I shall never get on with him. But you will never separate yourself from me, Ayala!'

'Separate myself!'

'You will not—not be my sister because you will be one of these rich ones?'

'Oh, I wish,—I wish that I were to be the poor one. I'm sure I should like it best. I never cared about being rich. Oh, Lucy, can't we make them change?'

'No, Ayey, my own, we can't make them change. And if we could, we wouldn't. It is altogether best that you should be a rich Tringle and that I should be a poor Dosett.'

'I will always be a Dormer,' said Ayala, proudly.

'And I will always be so too, my pet. But you should be a bright Dormer among the Tringles, and I will be a dull Dormer among the Dosetts. I shall begrudge nothing, if only we can see each other.'

So the two girls were parted, the elder being taken away to Kingsbury Crescent and the latter remaining with her rich relations at Queen's Gate. Ayala had not probably realized the great difference of their future positions. To her the attractions of wealth and the privations of comparative poverty had not made themselves as yet palpably plain. They do not become so manifest to those to whom the wealth falls,—at any rate, not in early life,—as to the opposite party. If the other lot had fallen to Ayala she might have felt it more keenly.

Lucy felt it keenly enough. Without any longing after the magnificence of the Tringle mansion she knew how great was the fall from her father's well-assorted luxuries and prettinesses down to the plain walls, tables, and chairs of her Uncle Dosett's house. Her aunt did not subscribe to Mudie's.* The old piano had not been tuned for the last ten years. The parlour-maid was a cross old woman. Her aunt always sat in the dining-room through the greater part of the day, and of all rooms the dining-room in Kingsbury Crescent was the dingiest. Lucy understood very well to what she was going. Her father and mother were gone. Her sister was divided from her. Her life offered for the future nothing to her. But with it all she carried a good courage. There was present to her an idea of great misfortune; but present to her at the same time an idea also that she would do her duty.

## CHAPTER II

### LUCY WITH HER AUNT DOSETT

FOR some days Lucy found herself to be absolutely crushed,—in the first place, by a strong resolution to do some disagreeable duty, and then by a feeling that there was no duty the doing of which was within her reach. It seemed to her that her whole life was a blank. Her father's house had been a small affair and considered to be poor when compared with the Tringle mansion, but she now became aware that everything there had in truth abounded. In one little room there had been two or three hundred beautifully bound books. That Mudie's unnumbered volumes should come into the house as they were wanted had almost been as much a provision of nature as water, gas, and hot rolls for breakfast. A piano of the best kind, and always in order, had been a first necessary of life, and, like other necessaries, of course, forthcoming. There had been the little room in which the girls painted, joining their father's studio and sharing its light, surrounded by every pretty female appliance. Then there had always been visitors. The artists from Kensington had been wont to gather there, and the artists' daughters, and perhaps the artists' sons. Every day had had its round of delights,—its round of occupations, as the girls would call them. There had been some reading, some painting, some music,—perhaps a little needlework and a great deal of talking.

How little do we know how other people live in the houses close to us! We see the houses looking like our own, and we see the people come out of them looking like ourselves. But a Chinaman is not more different from the English John Bull than is No. 10 from No. 11. Here there are books, paintings, music, wine, a little dilettanti getting-up of subjects of the day, a little dilettanti thinking on great affairs, per-

haps a little dilettanti religion; few domestic laws,
and those easily broken; few domestic duties, and
those easily evaded; breakfast when you will, with
dinner almost as little binding, with much company
and acknowledged aptitude for idle luxury. That is
life at No. 10. At No. 11 everything is cased in iron.
There shall be equal plenty, but at No. 11 even
plenty is a bondage. Duty rules everything, and it
has come to be acknowledged that duty is to be
hard.* So many hours of needlework, so many hours
of books, so many hours of prayer! That all the
household shall shiver before daylight, is a law, the
breach of which by any member either augurs sickness or requires condign punishment. To be comfortable is a sin; to laugh is almost equal to bad
language. Such and so various is life at No. 10 and
at No. 11.

From one extremity, as far removed, to another
poor Lucy had been conveyed; though all the laws
were not exactly carried out in Kingsbury Crescent
as they have been described at No. 11. The enforced
prayers were not there, nor the early hours. It was
simply necessary that Lucy should be down to breakfast at nine, and had she not appeared nothing
violent would have been said. But it was required
of her that she should endure a life which was altogether without adornment. Uncle Dosett himself, as
a clerk in the Admiralty, had a certain position in the
world which was sufficiently maintained by decent
apparel, a well-kept, slight, grey whisker, and an
umbrella which seemed never to have been violated
by use. Dosett was popular at his office, and was
regarded by his brother clerks as a friend. But no
one was acquainted with his house and home. They
did not dine with him, nor he with them. There are
such men in all public offices,—not the less respected
because of the quiescence of their lives. It was
known of him that he had burdens, though it was
not known what his burdens were. His friends,
therefore, were intimate with him as far as the

entrance into Somerset House,*—where his duties lay,—and not beyond it. Lucy was destined to know the other side of his affairs, the domestic side, which was as quiet as the official side. The link between them, which consisted of a journey by the Underground Railway to the Temple Station,* and a walk home along the Embankment and across the parks and Kensington Gardens, was the pleasantest part of Dosett's life.

Mr. Dosett's salary has been said to be £900 per annum. What a fund of comfort there is in the word! When the youth of nineteen enters an office* how far beyond want would he think himself should he ever reach the pecuniary paradise of £900 a-year! How he would see all his friends, and in return be seen of them! But when the income has been achieved its capabilities are found to be by no means endless. And Dosett in the earlier spheres of his married life had unfortunately anticipated something of such comforts. For a year or two he had spent a little money imprudently. Something which he had expected had not come to him; and, as a result, he had been forced to borrow, and to insure his life for the amount borrowed. Then, too, when that misfortune as to the money came,—came from the non-realization of certain claims which his wife had been supposed to possess,—provision had also to be made for her. In this way an assurance office eat up a large fraction of his income, and left him with means which in truth were very straitened. Dosett at once gave up all glories of social life, settled himself in Kingsbury Crescent, and resolved to satisfy himself with his walk across the park and his frugal dinner afterwards. He never complained to any one, nor did his wife. He was a man small enough to be contented with a thin existence, but far too great to ask any one to help him to widen it. Sir Thomas Tringle never heard of that £175 paid annually to the assurance office, nor had Lady Tringle, Dosett's sister, even heard of it. When it was suggested to him that he should take one of the Dormer girls, he consented to take her and said nothing of the assurance office.

Mrs. Dosett had had her great blow in life, and had suffered more perhaps than her husband. This money had been expected. There had been no doubt of the money,—at any rate on her part. It did not depend on an old gentleman with or without good intentions, but simply on his death. There was to be ever so much of it; four or five hundred a-year, which would last for ever. When the old gentleman died, which took place some ten years after Dosett's marriage, it was found that the money, tied tight as it had been by half-a-dozen lawyers, had in some fashion vanished. Whither it had gone is little to our purpose, but it had gone. Then there came a great crash upon the Dosetts, which she for a while had been hardly able to endure.

But when she had collected herself together after the crash, and had made up her mind, as had Dosett also, to the nature of the life which they must in future lead, she became more stringent in it even than he. He could bear and say nothing; but she, in bearing, found herself compelled to say much. It had been her fault,—the fault of people on her side,—and she would fain have fed her husband with the full flowery potato while she ate only the rind. She told him, unnecessarily, over and over again, that she had ruined him by her marriage. No such idea was ever in his head. The thing had come, and so it must be. There was food to eat, potatoes enough for both, and a genteel house in which to live. He could still be happy if she would not groan. A certain amount of groaning she did postpone while in his presence. The sewing of seams, and the darning of household linen, which in his eyes amounted to groaning, was done in his absence. After their genteel dinner he would sleep a little, and she would knit. He would have his glass of wine, but would make his bottle of port last almost for a week. This was the house to which Lucy Dor-

mer was brought when Mr. Dosett had consented to
share with Sir Thomas the burden left by the death
of the improvident artist.

When a month passed by Lucy began to think that
time itself would almost drive her mad. Her father
had died early in September. The Tringles had then,
of course, been out of town, but Sir Thomas and his
wife had found themselves compelled to come up on
such an occasion. Something they knew must be
done about the girls, and they had not chosen that
that something should be done in their absence. Mr.
Dosett was also enjoying his official leave of absence
for the year, but was enjoying it within the economical precincts of Kingsbury Crescent. There was
but seldom now an excursion for him or his wife to
the joys of the country. Once, some years ago, they
had paid a visit to the palatial luxuries of Glenbogie,
but the delights of the place had not paid for the
expense of the long journey. They, therefore, had
been at hand to undertake their duties. Dosett and
Tringle, with a score of artists, had followed poor
Dormer to his grave in Kensal Green, and then
Dosett and Tringle had parted again, probably not
to see each other for another term of years.

'My dear, what do you like to do with your time?'
Mrs. Dosett said to her niece, after the first week  At
this time Lucy's wardrobe was not yet of a nature to
need much work over its ravages. The Dormer girls
had hardly known where their frocks had come from
when they wanted frocks,—hardly with more precision than the Tringle girls. Frocks had come—dark,
gloomy frocks, lately, alas! And these, too, had now
come a second time. Let creditors be ever so unsatis-
fied, new raiment will always be found for mourning
families. Everything about Lucy was nearly new.
The need of repairing would come upon her by
degrees, but it had not come as yet. Therefore there
had seemed, to the anxious aunt, to be a necessity
for some such question as the above.

'I'll do anything you like, aunt,' said Lucy.

'It is not for me, my dear. I get through a deal of work, and am obliged to do so.' She was, at this time, sitting with a sheet in her lap, which she was turning. Lucy had, indeed, once offered to assist, but her assistance had been rejected. This had been two days since, and she had not renewed the proposal as she should have done. This had been mainly from bashfulness. Though the work would certainly be distasteful to her, she would do it. But she had not liked to seem to interfere, not having as yet fallen into the ways of intimacy with her aunt. 'I don't want to burden you with my task-work,' continued Mrs. Dosett, 'but I am afraid you seem to be listless.'

'I was reading till just before you spoke,' said Lucy, again turning her eyes to the little volume of poetry, which was one of the few treasures which she had brought away with her from her old home.

'Reading is very well, but I do not like it as an excuse, Lucy.' Lucy's anger boiled within her when she was told of an excuse, and she declared to herself that she could never like her aunt. 'I am quite sure that for young girls, as well as for old women, there must be a great deal of waste time unless there be needle and thread always about. And I know, too, unless ladies are well off, they cannot afford to waste time any more than gentlemen.'

In the whole course of her life nothing so much like scolding as this had ever been addressed to her. So at least thought Lucy at that moment. Mrs. Dosett had intended the remarks all in good part, thinking them to be simply fitting from an aunt to a niece. It was her duty to give advice, and for the giving of such advice some day must be taken as the beginning. She had purposely allowed a week to run by, and now she had spoken her word,—as she thought in good season.

To Lucy it was a new and most bitter experience. Though she was reading the *Idylls of the King*,* or pretending to read them, she was, in truth, thinking of all that had gone from her. Her mind had, at that

moment, been intent upon her mother, who, in all
respects, had been so different from this careful,
sheet-darning house-wife of a woman. And in thinking of her mother there had no doubt been regrets for
many things of which she would not have ventured
to speak as sharing her thoughts with the memory of
her mother, but which were nevertheless there to add
darkness to the retrospective. Everything behind
had been so bright, and everything behind had gone
away from her! Everything before was so gloomy,
and everything before must last for so long! After
her aunt's lecture about wasted time Lucy sat silent for
a few minutes, and then burst into uncontrolled tears.

'I did not mean to vex you,' said her aunt. '

'I was thinking of my—darling, darling mamma,'
sobbed Lucy.

'Of course, Lucy, you will think of her. How
should you not? And of your father. Those are
sorrows which must be borne. But sorrows such as
those are much lighter to the busy than to the idle.
I sometimes think that the labourers grieve less for
those they love than we do just because they have not
time to grieve.'

'I wish I were a labourer then,' said Lucy, through
her tears.

'You may be if you will. The sooner you begin to
be a labourer the better for yourself and for those
about you.'

That Aunt Dosett's voice was harsh was not her
fault,—nor that in the obduracy of her daily life she
had lost much of her original softness. She had
simply meant to be useful, and to do her duty; but
in telling Lucy that it would be better that the
labouring should be commenced at once for the sake
of 'those about you',—who could only be Aunt
Dosett herself,—she had seemed to the girl to be
harsh, selfish, and almost unnatural. The volume of
poetry fell from her hand, and she jumped up from
the chair quickly. 'Give it me at once,' she said, taking hold of the sheet,—which was not itself a plea-

sant object; Lucy had never seen such a thing at the bijou. 'Give it me at once,' she said, and clawed the long folds of linen nearly out of her aunt's lap.

'I did not mean anything of the kind,' said Aunt Dosett. 'You should not take me up in that way. I am speaking only for your good, because I know that you should not dawdle away your existence. Leave the sheet.'

Lucy did leave the sheet, and then, sobbing violently, ran out of the room up to her own chamber. Mrs. Dosett determined that she would not follow her. She partly forgave the girl because of her sorrows, partly reminded herself that she was not soft and facile as had been her sister-in-law, Lucy's mother; and then, as she continued her work, she assured herself that it would be best to let her niece have her cry out upstairs. Lucy's violence had astonished her for a moment, but she had taught herself to think it best to allow such little ebullitions to pass off by themselves.

Lucy, when she was alone, flung herself upon her bed in absolute agony. She thought that she had misbehaved, and yet how cruel,—how harsh had been her aunt's words! If she, the quiet one, had misbehaved, what would Ayala have done? And how was she to find strength with which to look forward to the future? She struggled hard with herself for a resolution. Should she determine that she would henceforward darn sheets morning, noon, and night till she worked her fingers to the bone? Perhaps there had been something of truth in that assertion of her aunt's that the labourers have no time to grieve. As everything else was shut out from her, it might be well for her to darn sheets. Should she rush down penitent and beg her aunt to allow her to commence at once?

She would have done it as far as the sheets were concerned, but she could not do it as regarded her aunt. She could put herself into unison with the crumpled soiled linen, but not with the hard woman.

Oh, how terrible was the change! Her father and her mother who had been so gentle to her! All the sweet prettinesses of her life! All her occupations, all her friends, all her delights! Even Ayala was gone from her! How was she to bear it? She begrudged Ayala nothing,—no, nothing. But yet it was hard! Ayala was to have everything. Aunt Emmeline,— though they had not hitherto been very fond of Aunt Emmeline,—was sweetness itself as compared with this woman. 'The sooner you begin to labour the better for yourself and those about you.' Would it not have been fitter that she should have been sent at once to some actual poor-house in which there would have been no mistake as to her position?

That it should all have been decided for her, for her and Ayala, not by any will of their own, not by any concert between themselves, but simply by the fantasy of another! Why should she thus be made a slave to the fantasy of any one! Let Ayala have her uncle's wealth and her aunt's palaces at her command, and she would walk out simply a pauper into the world,—into some workhouse, so that at least she need not be obedient to the harsh voice and the odious common sense of her Aunt Dosett! But how should she take herself to some workhouse? In what way could she prove her right to be admitted even then? It seemed to her that the same decree which had admitted Ayala into the golden halls of the fairies had doomed her not only to poverty, but to slavery. There was no escape for her from her aunt and her aunt's sermons. 'Oh, Ayala, my darling,— my own one; oh, Ayala, if you did but know!' she said to herself. What would Ayala think, how would Ayala bear it, could she but guess by what a gulf was her heaven divided from her sister's hell! 'I will never tell her,' she said to herself. 'I will die, and she shall never know.'

As she lay there sobbing all the gilded things of the world were beautiful in her eyes. Alas, yes, it was true. The magnificence of the mansion at Queen's

Gate, the glories of Glenbogie, the closely studied
comforts of Merle Park, as the place in Sussex was
called, all the carriages and horses, Madame Tonsonville and all the draperies, the seats at the Albert
Hall into which she had been accustomed to go with
as much ease as into her bed-room, the box at the
opera, the pretty furniture, the frequent gems, even
the raiment which would make her pleasing to the
eyes of men whom she would like to please—all these
things grew in her eyes and became beautiful. No. 3,
Kingsbury Crescent, was surely, of all places on the
earth's surface, the most ugly. And yet,—yet she
had endeavoured to do her duty. 'If it had been the
workhouse I could have borne it,' she said to herself;
'but not to be the slave of my Aunt Dosett!' Again
she appealed to her sister, 'Oh, Ayala, if you did but
know it!' Then she remembered herself, declaring
that it might have been worse to Ayala than even
to her. 'If one had to bear it, it was better for me,'
she said, as she struggled to prepare herself for her
uncle's dinner.

## CHAPTER III

### LUCY'S TROUBLES

THE evening after the affair with the sheet went
off quietly, as did many days and many evenings.
Mrs. Dosett was wise enough to forget the little
violence and to forget also the feeling which had been
displayed. When Lucy first asked for some household
needlework, which she did with a faltering voice and
shame-faced remembrance of her fault, her aunt took
it all in good part and gave her a task somewhat
lighter as a beginning than the handling of a sheet.
Lucy sat at it and suffered. She went on sitting and
suffering. She told herself that she was a martyr at
every stitch she made. As she occupied the seat
opposite to her aunt's accustomed chair she would
hardly speak at all, but would keep her mind always
intent on Ayala and the joys of Ayala's life. That

they who had been born together, sisters, with equal fortunes, who had so closely lived together, should be sundered so utterly one from the other; that the one should be so exalted and the other so debased! And why? What justice had there been? Could it be from heaven or even from earth that the law had gone forth for such a division of the things of the world between them?

'You have got very little to say to a person,' said Aunt Dosett, one morning. This, too, was a reproach. This, too, was scolding. And yet Aunt Dosett had intended to be as pleasant as she knew how.

'I have very little to say,' replied Lucy, with repressed anger.

'But why?'

'Because I am stupid,' said Lucy. 'Stupid people can't talk. You should have had Ayala.'

'I hope you do not envy Ayala her fortune, Lucy?' A woman with any tact would not have asked such a question at such a time. She should have felt that a touch of such irony might be natural, and that unless it were expressed loudly, or shown actively, it might be left to be suppressed by affection and time. But she, as she had grown old, had taught herself to bear disappointment, and thought it wise to teach Lucy to do the same.

'Envy!' said Lucy, not passionately, but after a little pause for thought. 'I sometimes think it is very hard to know what envy is.'

'Envy, hatred, and malice,'* said Mrs. Dosett, hardly knowing what she meant by the use of the well-worn words.

'I do know what hatred and malice are,' said Lucy. 'Do you think I hate Ayala?'

'I am sure you do not.'

'Or that I bear her malice?'

'Certainly not.'

'If I had the power to take anything from her, would I do it? I love Ayala with my whole heart. Whatever be my misery I would rather bear it than let Ayala have even a share of it. Whatever good things she may have I would not rob her even of a part of them. If there be joy and sorrow to be divided between us I would wish to have the sorrow so that she might have the joy. That is not hatred and malice.' Mrs. Dosett looked at her over her spectacles. This was the girl who had declared that she could not speak because she was too stupid! 'But, when you ask me whether I envy her, I hardly know,' continued Lucy. 'I think one does covet one's neighbour's house, in spite of the tenth commandment, even though one does not want to steal it.'

Mrs. Dosett repented herself that she had given rise to any conversation at all. Silence, absolute silence, the old silence which she had known for a dozen years before Lucy had come to her, would have been better than this. She was very angry, more angry than she had ever yet been with Lucy; and yet she was afraid to show her anger. Was this the girl's gratitude for all that her uncle was doing for her,—for shelter, food, comfort, for all that she had in the world? Mrs. Dosett knew, though Lucy did not, of the little increased pinchings which had been made necessary by the advent of another inmate in the house; so many pounds of the meat in the week, and so much bread, and so much tea and sugar! It had all been calculated. In genteel houses such calculation must often be made. And when by degrees, —degrees very quick,—the garments should become worn which Lucy had brought with her, there must be something taken from the tight-fitting income for that need. Arrangements had already been made of which Lucy knew nothing, and already the two glasses of port wine a day had been knocked off from poor Mr. Dosett's comforts. His wife had sobbed in despair when he had said that it should be so. He had declared gin and water*to be as supporting as port wine, and the thing had been done. Lucy inwardly had been disgusted by the gin and water, knowing nothing of its history. Her father, who had not always been punctual in paying his wine-merchant's bills, would not have touched gin and water, would not have allowed it to contaminate his table. Everything in Mr. Dosett's house was paid for weekly.

And now Lucy, who had been made welcome to all that the genteel house could afford, who had been taken in as a child, had spoken of her lot as one which was all sorrowful. Bad as it is,—this living in Kingsbury Crescent,—I would rather bear it myself than subject Ayala to such misery! It was thus that she had, in fact, spoken of her new home when she had found it necessary to defend her feelings towards her sister. It was impossible that her aunt should be altogether silent under such treatment. 'We have done the best for you that is in our power, Lucy,' she said, with a whole load of reproach in her tone.

'Have I complained, aunt?'

'I thought you did.'

'Oh, no! You asked me whether I envied Ayala. What was I to say? Perhaps I should have said nothing, but the idea of envying Ayala was painful to me. Of course she——'

'Well?'

'I had better say nothing more, aunt. If I were to pretend to be cheerful I should be false. It is as yet only a few weeks since papa died.' Then the work went on in silence between them for the next hour.

And the work went on in solemn silence between them through the winter. It came to pass that the sole excitement of Lucy's life came from Ayala's letters,—the sole excitement except a meeting which took place between the sisters one day. When Lucy was taken to Kingsbury Crescent Ayala was at once carried down to Glenbogie, and from thence there came letters twice a week for six weeks. Ayala's letters, too, were full of sorrow. She, too, had lost her mother, her father, and her sister. Moreover, in her foolish petulance she said things of her Aunt Emmeline, and of the girls, and of Sir Thomas, which

ought not to have been written of those who were
kind to her. Her cousin Tom, too, she ridiculed,—
Tom Tringle, the son-and-heir,—saying that he was
a lout who endeavoured to make eyes at her. Oh,
how distasteful, how vulgar they were after all that
she had known. Perhaps the eldest girl, Augusta,
was the worst. She did not think that she could put
up with the assumed authority of Augusta. Gertrude
was better, but a simpleton. Ayala declared herself
to be sad at heart. But then the sweet scenery of
Glenbogie, and the colour of the moors, and the
glorious heights of Ben Alchan, made some amends.
Even in her sorrow she would rave about the beauties
of Glenbogie. Lucy, as she read the letters, told herself that Ayala's grief was a grief to be borne, a grief
almost to be enjoyed. To sit and be sad with a
stream purling by you, how different from the sadness of that dining-room in the Crescent. To look
out upon the glories of a mountain, while a tear
would now and again force itself into the eye, how
much less bitter than the falling of salt drops over a
tattered towel.

Lucy, in her answers, endeavoured to repress the
groans of her spirit. In the first place she did acknowledge that it did not become her to speak ill of
those who were, in truth, her benefactors; and then
she was anxious not to declare to Ayala her feeling
of the injustice by which their two lots had been
defined to them. Though she had failed to control
herself once or twice in speaking to her aunt she did
control herself in writing her letters. She would
never, never, write a word which should make Ayala
unnecessarily unhappy. On that she was determined.
She would say nothing to explain to Ayala the un-
utterable tedium of that downstairs parlour in which
they passed their lives, lest Ayala should feel herself
to be wounded by the luxurious comforts around her.

It was thus she wrote. Then there came a time in
which they were to meet,—just at the beginning of
November. The Tringles were going to Rome. They

generally did go somewhere. Glenbogie, Merle Park, and the house in Queen's Gate, were not enough for the year. Sir Thomas was to take them to Rome, and then return to London for the manipulation of the millions in Lombard Street. He generally did remain nine months out of the twelve in town, because of the millions, making his visits at Merle Park very short; but Lady Tringle found that change of air was good for the girls. It was her intention now to remain at Rome for two or three months.

The party from Scotland reached Queen's Gate late one Saturday evening, and intended to start early on the Monday. To Ayala, who had made it quite a matter of course that she should see her sister, Lady Tringle had said that in that case a carriage must be sent across. It was awkward, because there were no carriages in London. She had thought that they had all intended to pass through London just as though they were not stopping. Sunday, she had thought, was not to be regarded as being a day at all. Then Ayala flashed up. She had flashed up some times before. Was it supposed that she was not going to see Lucy? Carriage! She would walk across Kensington Gardens, and find the house out all by herself. She would spend the whole day with Lucy, and come back alone in a cab. She was strong enough, at any rate, to have her way so far, that a carriage, wherever it came from, was sent for Lucy about three in the afternoon, and did take her back to Kingsbury Crescent after dinner.

Then at last the sisters were together in Ayala's bed-room. 'And now tell me about everything,' said Ayala.

But Lucy was resolved that she would not tell anything. 'I am so wretched!' That would have been all; but she would not tell her wretchedness. 'We are so quiet in Kingsbury Crescent,' she said; 'you have so much more to talk of.'

'Oh, Lucy, I do not like it.'

'Not your aunt?'

'She is not the worst, though she sometimes is hard to bear. I can't tell you what it is, but they all seem to think so much of themselves. In the first place they never will say a word about papa.'

'Perhaps that is from feeling, Ayey.'

'No, it is not. One would know that. But they look down upon papa, who had more in his little finger than they have with all their money.'

'Then I should hold my tongue.'

'So I do,—about him; but it is very hard. And then Augusta has a way with me, as though she had a right to order me. I certainly will not be ordered by Augusta. You never ordered me.'

'Dear Ayey!'

'Augusta is older than you,—of course, ever so much. They make her out twenty-three at her last birthday, but she is twenty-four. But that is not difference enough for ordering,—certainly between cousins. I do hate Augusta.'

'I would not hate her.'

'How is one to help one's-self? She has a way of whispering to Gertrude, and to her mother, when I am there, which almost kills me. "If you'll only give me notice I'll go out of the room at once," I said the other day, and they were all so angry.'

'I would not make them angry if I were you, Ayey.'

'Why not?'

'Not Sir Thomas, or Aunt Emmeline.'

'I don't care a bit for Sir Thomas. I am not sure but he is the most good-natured, though he is so podgy. Of course, when Aunt Emmeline tells me anything I do it.'

'It is so important that you should be on good terms with them.'

'I don't see it at all,' said Ayala, flashing round.

'Aunt Emmeline can do so much for you. We have nothing of our own,—you and I.'

'Am I to sell myself because they have got money! No, indeed! No one despises money so much as I do.

I will never be other to them than if I had the money,
and they were the poor relations.'

'That will not do, Ayey.'

'I will make it do. They may turn me out if they
like. Of course, I know that I should obey my aunt,
and so I will. If Sir Thomas told me anything I
should do it. But not Augusta.' Then, while Lucy
was thinking how she might best put into soft words
advice which was so clearly needed, Ayala declared
another trouble. 'But there is worse still.'

'What is that?'

'Tom!'

'What does Tom do?'

'You know Tom, Lucy?'

'I have seen him.'

'Of all the horrors he is the horridest.'

'Does he order you about?'

'No; but he——'

'What is it, Ayey?'

'Oh! Lucy, he is so dreadful. He——'

'You don't mean that he makes love to you?'

'He does. What am I to do, Lucy?'

'Do they know it?'

'Augusta does, I'm sure; and pretends to think
that it is my fault. I am sure that there will be a
terrible quarrel some day. I told him the day before
we left Glenbogie that I should tell his mother. I did
indeed. Then he grinned. He is such a fool. And
when I laughed he took it all as kindness. I couldn't
have helped laughing if I had died for it.'

'But he has been left behind.'

'Yes, for the present. But he is to come over to us
some time after Christmas, when Uncle Tringle has
gone back.'

'A girl need not be bothered by a lover unless she
chooses, Ayey.'

'But it will be such a bother to have to talk about
it. He looks at me, and is such an idiot. Then
Augusta frowns. When I see Augusta frowning I am
so angry that I feel like boxing her ears. Do you know,

Lucy, that I often think that it will not do, and that
I shall have to be sent away. I wish it had been you
that they had chosen.'

Such was the conversation between the girls. Of
what was said everything appertained to Ayala. Of
the very nature of Lucy's life not a word was spoken.
As Ayala was talking Lucy was constantly thinking
of all that might be lost by her sister's imprudence.
Even though Augusta might be disagreeable, even
though Tom might be a bore, it should all be borne,
—borne at any rate for a while,—seeing how terrible
would be the alternative. The alternative to Lucy
seemed to be Kingsbury Crescent and Aunt Dosett.
It did not occur to her to think whether in any
possible case Ayala would indeed be added to the
Crescent family, or what in that case would become
of herself, and whether they two might live with
Aunt Dosett, and whether in that case life would not
be infinitely improved. Ayala had all that money
could do for her, and would have such a look-out into
the world from a wealthy house as might be sure at
last to bring her some such husband as would be
desirable. Ayala, in fact, had everything before her,
and Lucy had nothing. Wherefore it became Lucy's
duty to warn Ayala, so that she should bear with
much, and throw away nothing. If Ayala could only
know what life might be, what life was at Kingsbury
Crescent, then she would be patient, then she would
softly make a confidence with her aunt as to Tom's
folly, then she would propitiate Augusta. Not care
for money! Ayala had not yet lived in an ugly room
and darned sheets all the morning. Ayala had never
sat for two hours between the slumbers of Uncle
Dosett and the knitting of Aunt Dosett. Ayala had
not been brought into contact with gin and water.

'Oh, Ayala!' she said, as they were going down to
dinner together, 'do struggle; do bear it. Tell Aunt
Emmeline. She will like you to tell her. If Augusta
wants you to go anywhere, do go. What does it
signify? Papa and mamma are gone, and we are

alone.' All this she said without a word of allusion to her own sufferings. Ayala made a half promise. She did not think she would go anywhere for Augusta's telling; but she would do her best to satisfy Aunt Emmeline. Then they went to dinner, and after dinner Lucy was taken home without further words between them.

Ayala wrote long letters on her journey, full of what she saw, and full of her companions. From Paris she wrote, and then from Turin, and then again on their immediate arrival at Rome. Her letters were most imprudent as written from the close vicinity of her aunt and cousin. It was such a comfort that that oaf Tom had been left behind. Uncle Tringle was angry because he did not get what he liked to eat. Aunt Emmeline gave that courier such a terrible life, sending for him every quarter of an hour. Augusta would talk first French and then Italian, of which no one could understand a word. Gertrude was so sick with travelling that she was as pale as a sheet. Nobody seemed to care for anything.* She could not get her aunt to look at the Campanile at Florence,* or her cousins to know one picture from another. 'As for pictures, I am quite sure that Mangle's angels would do as well as Raffael's.' Mangle was a brother academician whom their father had taught them to despise. There was contempt, most foolish contempt, for all the Tringles; but, luckily, there had been no quarrelling. Then it seemed that both in Paris and in Florence Ayala had bought pretty things, from which it was to be argued that her uncle had provided her liberally with money. One pretty thing had been sent from Paris to Lucy, which could not have been bought for less than many francs. It would not be fair that Ayala should take so much without giving something in return.

Lucy knew that she too should give something in return. Though Kingsbury Crescent was not attractive, though Aunt Dosett was not to her a pleasant companion, she had begun to realise the fact that it behoved her to be grateful, if only for the food she ate, and for the bed on which she slept. As she thought of all that Ayala owed she remembered also her own debts. As the winter went on she struggled to pay them. But Aunt Dosett was a lady not much given to vacillation. She had become aware at first that Lucy had been rough to her, and she did not easily open herself to Lucy's endearments. Lucy's life at Kingsbury Crescent had begun badly, and Lucy, though she understood much about it, found it hard to turn a bad beginning to a good result.

## CHAPTER IV

### ISADORE HAMEL

I T was suggested to Lucy before she had been long in Kingsbury Crescent that she should take some exercise. For the first week she had hardly been out of the house; but this was attributed to her sorrow. Then she had accompanied her aunt for a few days during the half-hour's marketing which took place every morning, but in this there had been no sympathy. Lucy would not interest herself in the shoulder of mutton which must be of just such a weight as to last conveniently for two days,—twelve pounds,—of which, it was explained to her, more than one-half was intended for the two servants, because there was always a more lavish consumption in the kitchen than in the parlour. Lucy would not appreciate the fact that eggs at a penny a piece, whatever they might be, must be used for puddings, as eggs with even a reputation of freshness cost twopence. Aunt Dosett, beyond this, never left the house on week-days except for a few calls which were made perhaps once a month, on which occasion the Sunday gloves and the Sunday silk dress were used. On Sunday they all went to church. But this was not enough for exercise, and as Lucy was becoming pale she was recommended to take to walking in Kensington Gardens.

It is generally understood that there are raging lions about the metropolis, who would certainly eat up young ladies whole if young ladies were to walk about the streets or even about the parks by themselves. There is, however, beginning to be some vacillation as to the received belief on this subject as regards London. In large continental towns, such as Paris and Vienna, young ladies would be devoured certainly. Such, at least, is the creed. In New York and Washington there are supposed to be no lions, so that young ladies go about free as air. In London there is a rising doubt, under which before long, probably, the lions will succumb altogether. Mrs. Dosett did believe somewhat in lions, but she believed also in exercise. And she was aware that the lions eat up chiefly rich people. Young ladies who must go about without mothers, brothers, uncles, carriages, or attendants of any sort, are not often eaten or even roared at. It is the dainty darlings for whom the roarings have to be feared. Mrs. Dosett, aware that daintiness was no longer within the reach of her and hers, did assent to these walkings in Kensington Gardens. At some hour in the afternoon Lucy would walk from the house by herself, and within a quarter of an hour would find herself on the broad gravel path which leads down to the Round Pond. From thence she would go by the back of the Albert Memorial, and then across by the Serpentine and return to the same gate, never leaving Kensington Gardens. Aunt Dosett had expressed some old-fashioned idea that lions were more likely to roar in Hyde Park than within the comparatively retired purlieus of Kensington.*

Now the reader must be taken back for a few moments to the bijou, as the bijou was before either the artist or his wife had died. In those days there had been a frequent concourse of people in the artist's house. Society there had not consisted chiefly

of eating and drinking. Men and women would come
in and out as though really for a purpose of talking.
There would be three or four constantly with Dormer
in his studio, helping him but little perhaps in the
real furtherance of his work, though discussing art
subjects in a manner calculated to keep alive art-
feeling among them. A novelist or two of a morning
might perhaps aid me in my general pursuit, but
would, I think, interfere with the actual tally of
pages. Egbert Dormer did not turn out from his
hand so much work as some men that I know, but
he was overflowing with art up to his ears;—and
with tobacco, so that, upon the whole, the bijou was
a pleasant rendezvous.

There had come there of late, quite of late, a young
sculptor, named Isadore Hamel. Hamel was an
Englishman, who, however, had been carried very
early to Rome and had been bred there. Of his
mother question never was made, but his father had
been well known as an English sculptor resident at
Rome. The elder Hamel had been a man of mark,
who had a fine suite of rooms in the city and a villa
on one of the lakes, but who never came to England.
English connections were, he said, to him abominable, by which he perhaps meant that the restrictions
of decent life were not to his taste. But his busts
came, and his groups in marble, and now and again
some great work for some public decoration: so that
money was plentiful with him, and he was a man of
note. It must be acknowledged of him that he spared
nothing in bringing up his son, giving him such
education as might best suit his future career as an
artist, and that money was always forthcoming for
the lad's wants and fantasies.

Then young Hamel also became a sculptor of much
promise; but early in life differed from his father on
certain subjects of importance. The father was
wedded to Rome and to Italy. Isadore gradually
expressed an opinion that the nearer a man was to
his market the better for him, that all that art could

do for a man in Rome was as nothing to the position which a great artist might make for himself in London,—that, in fact, an Englishman had better be an Englishman.* At twenty-six he succeeded in his attempt, and became known as a young sculptor with a workshop at Brompton. He became known to many both by his work and his acquirements; but it may not be surprising that after a year he was still unable to live, as he had been taught to live, without drawing upon his father. Then his father threw his failure in his teeth, not refusing him money indeed, but making the receipt of it unpleasant to him.

At no house had Isadore Hamel been made so welcome as at Dormer's. There was a sympathy between them both on that great question of art, whether to an artist his art should be a matter to him of more importance than all the world besides. So said Dormer,—who simply died because his wife died, who could not have touched his brush if one of his girls had been suffering, who, with all his genius, was but a faineant workman. His art more than all the world to him! No, not to him. Perhaps here and again to some enthusiast, and him hardly removed from madness! Where is the painter who shall paint a picture after his soul's longing though he shall get not a penny for it,—though he shall starve as he put his last touch to it, when he knows that by drawing some duchess of the day he shall in a fortnight earn a ducal price? Shall a wife and child be less dear to him than to a lawyer,—or to a shoemaker*; or the very craving of his hunger less obdurate? A man's self, and what he has within him and his belongings, with his outlook for this and other worlds,—let that be the first, and the work, noble or otherwise, be the second. To be honest is greater than to have painted the San Sisto, or to have chiselled the Apollo; to have assisted in making others honest,—infinitely greater. All of which were discussed at great length at the bijou, and the bijouites always sided with the master of the house. To an artist, said Dormer, let his art be everything,—above wife and children, above money, above health, above even character. Then he would put out his hand with his jewelled finger, and stretch forth his velvet-clad arm, and soon after lead his friend away to the little dinner at which no luxury had been spared. But young Hamel agreed with the sermons, and not the less because Lucy Dormer had sat by and listened to them with rapt attention.

Not a word of love had been spoken to her by the sculptor when her mother died, but there had been glances and little feelings of which each was half conscious. It is so hard for a young man to speak of love, if there be real love,—so impossible that a girl should do so! Not a word had been spoken, but each had thought that the other must have known. To Lucy a word had been spoken by her mother,—'Do not think too much of him till you know,' the mother had said,—not quite prudently. 'Oh, no! I will think of him not at all,' Lucy had replied. And she had thought of him day and night. 'I wonder why Mr. Hamel is so different with you?' Ayala had said to her sister. 'I am sure he is not different with me,' Lucy had replied. Then Ayala had shaken her full locks and smiled.

Things came quickly after that. Mrs. Dormer had sickened and died. There was no time then for thinking of that handsome brow, of that short jet black hair, of those eyes so full of fire and thoughtfulness, of that perfect mouth, and the deep but yet soft voice. Still even in her sorrow this new god of her idolatry was not altogether forgotten. It was told to her that he had been summoned off to Rome by his father, and she wondered whether he was to find his home at Rome for ever. Then her father was ill, and in his illness Hamel came to say one word of farewell before he started.

'You find me crushed to the ground,' the painter said. Something the young man whispered as to the consolation which time would bring. 'Not to me,' said Dormer. 'It is as though one had lost his eyes. One cannot see without his eyes.' It was true of him. His light had been put out.

Then, on the landing at the top of the stairs, there had been one word between Lucy and the sculptor. 'I ought not to have intruded on you perhaps,' he said; 'but after so much kindness I could hardly go without a word.'

'I am sure he will be glad that you have come.'

'And you?'

'I am glad too,—so that I may say good-bye.' Then she put out her hand, and he held it for a moment as he looked into her eyes. There was not a word more, but it seemed to Lucy as though there had been so many words.

Things went on quickly. Egbert Dormer died, and Lucy was taken away to Kingsbury Crescent. When once Ayala had spoken about Mr. Hamel, Lucy had silenced her. Any allusion to the idea of love wounded her, as though it was too impossible for dreams, too holy for words. How should there be words about a lover when father and mother were both dead? He had gone to his old and natural home. He had gone, and of course he would not return. To Ayala, when she came up to London early in November, to Ayala, who was going to Rome, where Isadore Hamel now was, Isadore Hamel's name was not mentioned. But through the long mornings of her life, through the long evenings, through the long nights, she still thought of him,— she could not keep herself from thinking. To a girl whose life is full of delights her lover need not be so very much,—need not, at least, be everything. Though he be a lover to be loved at all points, her friends will be something, her dancing, her horse, her theatre-going, her brothers and sisters, even her father and mother. But Lucy had nothing. The vision of Isadore Hamel had passed across her life, and had left with her the only possession that she had. It need hardly be said that she never alluded

to that possession at Kingsbury Crescent. It was not
a possession from which any enjoyment could come
except that of thinking of it. He had passed away
from her, and there was no point of life at which he
could come across her again. There was no longer
that half-joint studio. If it had been her lot to be
as was Ayala, she then would have been taken to
Rome. Then again he would have looked into her
eyes and taken her hand in his. Then perhaps——.
But now, even though he were to come back to
London, he would know nothing of her haunts. Even
in that case nothing would bring them together. As
the idea was crossing her mind,—as it did cross it so
frequently,—she saw him turning from the path on
which she was walking, making his way towards the
steps of the Memorial.

Though she saw no more than his back she was sure
that it was Isadore Hamel. For a moment there was
an impulse on her to run after him and to call his
name. It was then early in January, and she was
taking her daily walk through Kensington Gardens.
She had walked there daily now for the last two
months and had never spoken a word or been
addressed,—had never seen a face that she had
recognised. It had seemed to her that she had not
an acquaintance in the world except Uncle Reg and
Aunt Dosett. And now, almost within reach of her
hand, was the one being in all the world whom she
most longed to see. She did stand, and the word was
formed within her lips; but she could not speak it.
Then came the thought that she would run after
him, but the thought was expelled quickly. Though
she might lose him again and for ever she could not
do that. She stood almost gasping till he was out of
sight, and then she passed on upon her usual round.

She never omitted her walks after that, and always
paused a moment as the path turned away to the
Memorial. It was not that she thought that she
might meet him there,—there rather than elsewhere,
—but there is present to us often an idea that when

some object has passed from us that we have desired
then it may be seen again. Day after day, and week
after week, she did not see him. During this time
there came letters from Ayala, saying that their
return to England was postponed till the first week
in February,—that she would certainly see Lucy in
February,—that she was not going to be hurried
through London in half-an-hour because her aunt
wished it; and that she would do as she pleased as to
visiting her sister. Then there was a word or two
about Tom,—'Oh, Tom—that idiot Tom!' And
another word or two about Augusta. 'Augusta is
worse than ever. We have not spoken to each other
for the last day or two.' This came but a day or two
before the intended return of the Tringles.

No actual day had been fixed. But on the day
before that on which Lucy thought it probable that
the Tringles might return to town she was again
walking in the Gardens. Having put two and two
together, as people do, she felt sure that the travellers
could not be away more than a day or two longer.
Her mind was much intent upon Ayala, feeling that
the imprudent girl was subjecting herself to great
danger, knowing that it was wrong that she and
Augusta should be together in the house without
speaking,—thinking of her sister's perils,—when, of
a sudden, Hamel was close before her! There was no
question of calling to him now,—no question of an
attempt to see him face to face. She had been
wandering along the path with eyes fixed upon the
ground, when her name was sharply called, and they
two were close to each other. Hamel had a friend
with him, and it seemed to Lucy at once, that she
could only bow to him, only mutter something, and
then pass on. How can a girl stand and speak to a
gentleman in public, especially when that gentleman
has a friend with him? She tried to look pleasant,
bowed, smiled, muttered something, and was passing
on. But he was not minded to lose her thus immediately. 'Miss Dormer,' he said, 'I have seen

your sister at Rome. May I not say a word about
her?'

Why should he not say a word about Ayala? In a
minute he had left his friend, and was walking back
along the path with Lucy. There was not much that
he had to say about Ayala. He had seen Ayala and
the Tringles, and did manage to let it escape him that
Lady Tringle had not been very gracious to himself
when once, in public, he had claimed acquaintance
with Ayala. But at that he simply smiled. Then he
had asked of Lucy where she lived. 'With my uncle,
Mr. Dosett,' said Lucy, 'at Kingsbury Crescent.'
Then, when he asked whether he might call, Lucy,
with many blushes, had said that her aunt did not
receive many visitors,—that her uncle's house was
different from what her father's had been.

'Shall I not see you at all, then?' he asked.

She did not like to ask him after his own purposes
of life, whether he was now a resident in London, or
whether he intended to return to Rome. She was
covered with bashfulness, and dreaded to seem even
to be interested in his affairs. 'Oh, yes,' she said;
'perhaps we may meet some day.'

'Here?' he asked.

'Oh, no; not here! It was only an accident.' As
she said this she determined that she must walk no
more in Kensington Gardens. It would be dreadful,
indeed, were he to imagine that she would consent to
make an appointment with him. It immediately
occurred to her that the lions were about, and that
she must shut herself up.

'I have thought of you every day since I have been
back,' he said, 'and I did not know where to hear of
you. Now that we have met am I to lose you again'?
Lose her! What did he mean by losing her? She,
too, had found a friend,—she who had been so
friendless! Would it not be dreadful to her, also, to
lose him? 'Is there no place where I may ask of
you?'

'When Ayala is back, and they are in town, perhaps I shall sometimes be at Lady Tringle's,' said Lucy, resolved that she would not tell him of her immediate abode. This was, at any rate, a certain address from where he might commence further inquiries, should he wish to make inquiry; and as such he accepted it. 'I think I had better go now,' said Lucy, trembling at the apparent impropriety of her present conversation.

He knew that it was intended that he should leave her, and he went. 'I hope I have not offended you in coming so far.'

'Oh, no.' Then again she gave him her hand, and again there was the same look as he took his leave.

When she got home, which was before the dusk, having resolved that she must, at any rate, tell her aunt that she had met a friend, she found that her uncle had returned from his office. This was a most unusual occurrence. Her uncle, she knew, left Somerset House exactly at half-past four, and always took an hour and a quarter for his walk. She had never seen him in Kingsbury Crescent till a quarter before six. 'I have got letters from Rome,' he said, in a solemn voice.

'From Ayala?'

'One from Ayala, for you. It is here. And I have had one from my sister, also; and one, in the course of the day, from your uncle in Lombard Street. You had better read them!' There was something terribly tragic in Uncle Dosett's voice as he spoke.

And so must the reader read the letters; but they must be delayed for a few chapters.

## CHAPTER V

### AT GLENBOGIE

WE must go back to Ayala's life during the autumn and winter. She was rapidly whirled away to Glenbogie amidst the affectionate welcomings of her aunt and cousins. All manner of good things were done for her, as to presents and comforts.

Young as she was, she had money given to her,
which was not without attraction; and though she
was, of course, in the depth of her mourning, she was
made to understand that even mourning might be
made becoming if no expense were spared. No expense among the Tringles ever was spared, and at
first Ayala liked the bounty of profusion. But before
the end of the first fortnight there grew upon her a
feeling that even bank notes become tawdry if you
are taught to use them as curl-papers. It may be
said that nothing in the world is charming unless it
be achieved at some trouble. If it rained ' '64
Leoville ',—which I regard as the most divine of
nectars,—I feel sure that I should never raise it to
my lips? Ayala did not argue the matter out in her
mind, but in very early days she began to entertain
a dislike to Tringle magnificence. There had been a
good deal of luxury at the bijou, but always with a
feeling that it ought not to be there,—that more
money was being spent than prudence authorised,—
which had certainly added a savour to the luxuries.
A lovely bonnet, is it not more lovely because the
destined wearer knows that there is some wickedness
in achieving it? All the bonnets, all the claret, all
the horses, seemed to come at Queen's Gate and at
Glenbogie without any wickedness. There was no
more question about them than as to one's ordinary
bread and butter at breakfast. Sir Thomas had a
way,—a merit shall we call it or a fault?—of pouring
out his wealth upon the family as though it were
water running in perpetuity from a mountain tarn.
Ayala the romantic, Ayala the poetic, found very
soon that she did not like it.

Perhaps the only pleasure left to the very rich is
that of thinking of the deprivations of the poor. The
bonnets, and the claret, and the horses, have lost
their charm; but the Gladstone, and the old hats,
and the four-wheeled cabs of their neighbours, still
have a little flavour for them. From this source it
seemed to Ayala that the Tringles drew much of the

recreation of their lives. Sir Thomas had his way of enjoying this amusement, but it was a way that did not specially come beneath Ayala's notice. When she heard that Break-at-last, the Huddersfield manufacturer, had to sell his pictures, and that all Shoddy and Stuffgoods' grand doings for the last two years had only been a flash in the pan, she did not understand enough about it to feel wounded; but when she heard her aunt say that people like the Poodles had better not have a place in Scotland than have to let it, and when Augusta hinted that Lady Sophia Smallware had pawned her diamonds, then she felt that her nearest and dearest relatives smelt abominably of money.

Of all the family Sir Thomas was most persistently the kindest to her, though he was a man who did not look to be kind. She was pretty, and though he was ugly himself he liked to look at things pretty. He was, too, perhaps, a little tired of his own wife and daughters,—who were indeed what he had made them, but still were not quite to his taste. In a general way he gave instructions that Ayala should be treated exactly as a daughter, and he informed his wife that he intended to add a codicil to his will on her behalf. 'Is that necessary?' asked Lady Tringle, who began to feel something like natural jealousy. 'I suppose I ought to do something for a girl if I take her by the hand,' said Sir Thomas, roughly. 'If she gets a husband I will give her something, and that will do as well.' Nothing more was said about it, but when Sir Thomas went up to town the codicil was added to his will.

Ayala was foolish rather than ungrateful, not understanding the nature of the family to which she was relegated. Before she had been taken away she had promised Lucy that she would be 'obedient' to her aunt. There had hardly been such a word as obedience known at the bijou. If any were obedient, it was the mother and the father to the daughters. Lucy, and Ayala as well, had understood something

of this; and therefore Ayala had promised to be
obedient to her aunt. 'And to Uncle Thomas,' Lucy
had demanded, with an imploring embrace. 'Oh,
yes,' said Ayala, dreading her uncle at that time.
She soon learned that no obedience whatsoever was
exacted from Sir Thomas. She had to kiss him
morning and evening, and then to take whatever
presents he made her. An easy uncle he was to deal
with, and she almost learned to love him. Nor was
Aunt Emmeline very exigeant, though she was
fantastic and sometimes disagreeable. But Augusta
was the great difficulty. Lucy had not told her to
obey Augusta, and Augusta she would not obey.
Now Augusta demanded obedience.

'You never ordered me,' Ayala had said to Lucy
when they met in London as the Tringles were passing through. At the bijou there had been a republic,
in which all the inhabitants and all the visitors had
been free and equal. Such republicanism had been
the very mainspring of life at the bijou. Ayala loved
equality, and she specially felt that it should exist
among sisters. Do anything for Lucy? Oh, yes,
indeed, anything; abandon anything; but for Lucy
as a sister among sisters, not for an elder as from a
younger! And if she were not bound to serve Lucy
then certainly not Augusta. But Augusta liked to be
served. On one occasion she sent Ayala upstairs, and
on another she sent Ayala downstairs. Ayala went,
but determined to be equal with her cousin. On the
morning following, in the presence of Aunt Emmeline and of Gertrude, in the presence also of two other
ladies who were visiting at the house, she asked
Augusta if she would mind running upstairs and
fetching her scrap-book! She had been thinking
about it all the night and all the morning, plucking
up her courage. But she had been determined. She
found a great difficulty in saying the words, but she
said them. The thing was so preposterous that all
the ladies in the room looked aghast at the proposition. 'I really think that Augusta has got something

else to do,' said Aunt Emmeline. 'Oh, very well,' said Ayala, and then they were all silent. Augusta, who was employed on a silk purse, sat still and did not say a word.

Had a great secret, or rather a great piece of news which pervaded the family, been previously communicated to Ayala, she would not probably have made so insane a suggestion. Augusta was engaged to be married to the Honourable Septimus Traffic, the member for Port Glasgow. A young lady who is already half a bride is not supposed to run up and down stairs as readily as a mere girl. For running up and down stairs at the bijou Ayala had been proverbial. They were a family who ran up and down with the greatest alacrity. 'Oh, papa, my basket is out on the seat'—for there had been a seat in the two-foot garden behind the house. Papa would go down in two jumps and come up with three skips, and there was the basket, only because his girl liked him to do something for her. But for him Ayala would run about as though she were a tricksy Ariel* Had the important matrimonial news been conveyed to Ariel, with a true girl's spirit she would have felt that during the present period Augusta was entitled to special exemption from all ordering. Had she herself been engaged she would have run more and quicker than ever,—would have been excited thereto by the peculiar vitality of her new prospects; but to even Augusta she would be subservient, because of her appreciation of bridal importance. She, however, had not been told till that afternoon.

'You should not have asked Augusta to go upstairs,' said Aunt Emmeline, in a tone of mitigated reproach.

'Oh! I didn't know,' said Ayala.

'You had meant to say that because she had sent you you were to send her. There is a difference, you know.'

'I didn't know,' said Ayala, beginning to think that she would fight her battle if told of such differences as she believed to exist.

'I had meant to tell you before, but I may as well tell you now, Augusta is engaged to be married to the Honourable Mr. Septimus Traffick. He is second son of Lord Boardotrade, and is in the House.'*

'Dear me!' said Ayala, acknowledging at once within her heart that the difference alleged was one against which she need not rouse herself to the fight. Aunt Emmeline had, in truth, intended to insist on that difference—and another; but her courage had failed her.

'Yes, indeed. He is a man very much thought of just now in public life, and Augusta's mind is naturally much occupied. He writes all those letters in The Times about supply and demand.'

'Does he, aunt?' Ayala did feel that if Augusta's mind was entirely occupied with supply and demand she ought not to be made to go upstairs to fetch a scrap-book. But she had her doubts about Augusta's mind. Nevertheless, if the forthcoming husband were true, that might be a reason. 'If anybody had told me before I wouldn't have asked her,' she said.

Then Lady Tringle explained that it had been thought better not to say anything heretofore as to the coming matrimonial hilarities because of the sadness which had fallen upon the Dormer family. Ayala accepted this as an excuse, and nothing further was said as to the iniquity of her request to her cousin. But there was a general feeling among the women that Ayala, in lieu of gratitude, had exhibited an intention of rebelling.

On the next day Mr. Traffick arrived, whose coming had probably made it necessary that the news should be told. Ayala was never so surprised in her life as when she saw him. She had never yet had a lover of her own, had never dreamed of a lover, but she had her own idea as to what a lover ought to be. She had thought that Isadore Hamel would be a very nice lover—for her sister. Hamel was young, handsome, with a great deal to say on such a general subject as art, but too bashful to talk easily to the girl he admired. Ayala had thought that all that was just as it should be. She was altogether resolved that Hamel and her sister should be lovers, and was determined to be devoted to her future brother-in-law. But the Honourable Septimus Traffick! It was a question to her whether her Uncle Tringle would not have been better as a lover.

And yet there was nothing amiss about Mr. Traffick. He was very much like an ordinary hard-working member of the House of Commons, over perhaps rather than under forty years of age. He was somewhat bald, somewhat grey, somewhat fat, and had lost that look of rosy plumpness which is seldom, I fear, compatible with hard work and late hours. He was not particularly ugly, nor was he absurd in appearance. But he looked to be a disciple of business, not of pleasure, nor of art. 'To sit out on the bank of a stream and have him beside one would not be particularly nice,' thought Ayala to herself. Mr. Traffick no doubt would have enjoyed it very well if he could have spared the time; but to Ayala it seemed that such a man as that could have cared nothing for love. As soon as she saw him, and realised in her mind the fact that Augusta was to become his wife, she felt at once the absurdity of sending Augusta on a message.

Augusta that evening was somewhat more than ordinarily kind to her cousin. Now that the great secret was told, her cousin no doubt would recognise her importance. 'I suppose you had not heard of him before?' she said to Ayala.

'I never did.'

'That's because you have not attended to the debates.'

'I never have. What are debates?'

'Mr. Traffick is very much thought of in the House of Commons on all subjects affecting commerce.'

'Oh!'

'It is the most glorious study which the world affords.'

'The House of Commons. I don't think it can be equal to art.'

Then Augusta turned up her nose with a double turn,—first as against painters, Mr. Dormer having been no more, and then at Ayala's ignorance in supposing that the House of Commons could have been spoken of as a study. 'Mr. Traffick will probably be in the government some day,' she said.

'Has not he been yet?' asked Ayala.

'Not yet.'

'Then won't he be very old before he gets there?' This was a terrible question. Young ladies of five-and-twenty, when they marry gentlemen of four-and-fifty, make up their minds for well-understood and well-recognised old age. They see that they had best declare their purpose, and they do declare it. 'Of course, Mr. Walker is old enough to be my father, but I have made up my mind that I like that better than anything else.' Then the wall has been jumped, and the thing can go smoothly. But at forty-five there is supposed to be so much of youth left that the difference of age may possibly be tided over and not made to appear abnormal. Augusta Tringle had determined to tide it over in this way. The forty-five had been gradually reduced to 'less than forty',—though all the Peerages*were there to give the lie to the assertion. She talked of her lover as Septimus, and was quite prepared to sit with him beside a stream if only half-an-hour for the amusement could be found. When, therefore, Ayala suggested that if her lover wanted to get into office he had better do so quickly, lest he should be too old, Augusta was not well pleased.

'Lord Boardotrade was much older when he began,' said Augusta. 'His friends, indeed, tell Septimus that he should not push himself forward too quickly. But I don't think that I ever came across any one who was so ignorant of such things as you are, Ayala.'

'Perhaps he is not so old as he looks,' said Ayala.

After this it may be imagined that there was not
close friendship between the cousins. Augusta's
mind was filled with a strong conception as to Ayala's
ingratitude. The houseless, penniless orphan had
been taken in, and had done nothing but make herself disagreeable. Young! No doubt she was young.
But had she been as old as Methuselah she could not
have been more insolent. It did not, however, matter
to her, Augusta. She was going away; but it would
be terrible to her mamma and to Gertrude! Thus it
was that Augusta spoke of her cousin to her mother.

And then there came another trouble, which was
more troublesome to Ayala even than the other.
Tom Tringle, who was in the house in Lombard
Street, who was the only son, and heir to the title and
no doubt to much of the wealth, had chosen to take
Ayala's part and to enlist himself as her special
friend. Ayala had, at first, accepted him as a cousin,
and had consented to fraternise with him. Then, on
some unfortunate day, there had been some word or
look which she had failed not to understand, and
immediately she had become afraid of Tom. Tom
was not like Isadore Hamel,—was very far, indeed,
from that idea of a perfect lover which Ayala's mind
had conceived; but he was by no means a lout, or an
oaf, or an idiot, as Ayala in her letters to her sister
had described him. He had been first at Eton and
then at Oxford, and having spent a great deal of
money recklessly, and done but little towards his
education, had been withdrawn and put into the
office. His father declared of him now that he would
do fairly well in the world. He had a taste for dress,
and kept four or five hunters which he got but little
credit by riding. He made a fuss about his shooting,
but did not shoot much. He was stout and awkward
looking,—very like his father, but without that
settled air which age gives to heavy men. In appearance he was not the sort of lover to satisfy the preconceptions of such a girl as Ayala. But he was
good-natured and true. At last he became to her

terribly true. His love, such as it seemed at first, was absurd to her. 'If you make yourself such a fool, Tom, I'll never speak to you again,' she had said, once. Even after that she had not understood that it was more than a stupid joke. But the joke, while it was considered as such, was very distasteful to her; and afterwards, when a certain earnestness in it was driven in upon her, it became worse than distasteful.

She repudiated his love with such power as she had, but she could not silence him. She could not at all understand that a young man, who seemed to her to be an oaf, should really be in love,—honestly in love with her. But such was the case. Then she became afraid lest others should see it,—afraid, though she often told herself that she would appeal to her aunt for protection. 'I tell you I don't care a bit about you, and you oughtn't to go on,' she said. But he did go on, and though her aunt did not see it Augusta did.

Then Augusta spoke a word to her in scorn. 'Ayala,' she said, 'you should not encourage Tom.'

Encourage him! What a word from one girl to another! What a world of wrong there was in the idea which had created the word! What an absence of the sort of feeling which, according to Ayala's theory of life, there should be on such a matter between two sisters, two cousins, or two friends! Encourage him! When Augusta ought to have been the first to assist her in her trouble! 'Oh, Augusta,' she said, turning sharply round, 'what a spiteful creature you are.'

'I suppose you think so, because I do not choose to approve.'

'Approve of what! Tom is thoroughly disagreeable. Sometimes he makes my life such a burden to me that I think I shall have to go to my aunt. But you are worse. Oh!' exclaimed Ayala, shuddering as she thought of the unwomanly treachery of which her cousin was guilty towards her.

Nothing more came of it at Glenbogie. Tom was

required in Lombard Street, and the matter was not suspected by Aunt Emmeline,—as far, at least, as Ayala was aware. When he was gone it was to her as though there would be a world of time before she would see him again. They were to go to Rome, and he would not be at Rome till January. Before that he might have forgotten his folly. But Ayala was quite determined that she would never forget the ill offices of Augusta. She did hate Augusta, as she had told her sister. Then, in this frame of mind, the family was taken to Rome.

## CHAPTER VI

### AT ROME

DURING her journeying and during her sojourn at Rome Ayala did enjoy much; but even these joys did not come to her without causing some trouble of spirit. At Glenbogie everybody had known that she was a dependent niece, and that as such she was in truth nobody. On that morning when she had ordered Augusta to go upstairs the two visitors had stared with amazement,—who would not have stared at all had they heard Ayala ordered in the same way. But it came about that in Rome Ayala was almost of more importance than the Tringles. It was absolutely true that Lady Tringle and Augusta and Gertrude were asked here and there because of Ayala; and the worst of it was that the fact was at last suspected by the Tringles themselves. Sometimes they would not always be asked. One of the Tringle girls would only be named. But Ayala was never forgotten. Once or twice an effort was made by some grand lady, whose taste was perhaps more conspicuous than her good-nature, to get Ayala without burdening herself with any of the Tringles. When this became clear to the mind of Augusta,—of Augusta, engaged as she was to the Honourable Septimus Traffick, Member of Parliament,—Augusta's feelings were—such as may better be understood than described! 'Don't let her go, mamma,' she said to Lady Tringle one morning.

'But the Marchesa has made such a point of it.'

'Bother the Marchesa! Who is the Marchesa? I believe it is all Ayala's doing because she expects to meet that Mr. Hamel. It is dreadful to see the way she goes on.'

'Mr. Hamel was a very intimate friend of her father's.'

'I don't believe a bit of it.'

'He certainly used to be at his house. I remember seeing him.'

'I daresay; but that doesn't justify Ayala in running after him as she does. I believe that all this about the Marchesa is because of Mr. Hamel.' This was better than believing that Ayala was to be asked to sing, and that Ayala was to be fêted and admired and danced with, simply because Ayala was Ayala, and that they, the Tringles, in spite of Glenbogie, Merle Park, and Queen's Gate, were not wanted at all. But when Aunt Emmeline signified to Ayala that on that particular morning she had better not go to the Marchesa's picnic, Ayala simply said that she had promised;—and Ayala went.

At this time no gentleman of the family was with them. Sir Thomas had gone, and Tom Tringle had not come. Then, just at Christmas, the Honourable Septimus Traffick came for a short visit,—a very short visit, no more than four or five days, because Supply and Demand were requiring all his services in preparation for the coming Session of Parliament. But for five halcyon days he was prepared to devote himself to the glories of Rome under the guidance of Augusta. He did not of course sleep at the Palazzo Ruperti, where it delighted Lady Tringle to inform her friends in Rome that she had a suite of apartments 'au première'* but he ate there and drank there and almost lived there; so that it became absolutely necessary to inform the world of Rome

that it was Augusta's destiny to become in course of
time the Honourable Mrs. Traffick, otherwise the
close intimacy would hardly have been discreet,—
unless it had been thought, as the ill-natured Marchesa had hinted, that Mr. Traffick was Lady Tringle's
elder brother. Augusta, however, was by no means
ashamed of her lover. Perhaps she felt that when it
was known that she was about to be the bride of so
great a man then doors would be open for her at any
rate as wide as for her cousin. At this moment she
was very important to herself. She was about to
convey no less a sum than £120,000 to Mr. Traffick,
who, in truth, as younger son of Lord Boardotrade,
was himself not well endowed. Considering her own
position and her future husband's rank and standing,
she did not know how a young woman could well be
more important. She was very important at any
rate to Mr. Traffick. She was sure of that. When,
therefore, she learned that Ayala had been asked to
a grand ball at the Marchesa's, that Mr. Traffick was
also to be among the guests, and that none of the
Tringles had been invited,—then her anger became
hot.

She must have been very stupid when she took it
into her head to be jealous of Mr. Traffick's attention
to her cousin; stupid, at any rate, when she thought
that her cousin was laying out feminine lures for
Mr. Traffick. Poor Ayala! We shall see much of her
in these pages, and it may be well to declare of her
at once that her ideas at this moment about men,—
or rather about a possible man,—were confined
altogether to the abstract. She had floating in her
young mind some fancies as to the beauty of love.
That there should be a hero must of course be
necessary. But in her day-dreams this hero was
almost celestial,—or, at least, æthereal. It was a
concentration of poetic perfection to which there was
not as yet any appanage of apparel, of features, or of
wealth. It was a something out of heaven which
should think it well to spend his whole time in ador-

ing her and making her more blessed than had ever yet been a woman upon the earth. Then her first approach to a mundane feeling had been her acknowledgment to herself that Isadore Hamel would do as a lover for Lucy. Isadore Hamel was certainly very handsome,—was possessed of infinite good gifts; but even he would by no means have come up to her requirements for her own hero. That hero must have wings tinged with azure, whereas Hamel had a not much more ætherealised than ordinary coat and waistcoat. She knew that heroes with azure wings were not existent save in the imagination, and, as she desired a real lover for Lucy, Hamel would do. But for herself her imagination was too valuable then to allow her to put her foot upon earth. Such as she was, must not Augusta have been very stupid to have thought that Ayala should become fond of her Mr. Traffick!

Her cousin Tom had come to her, and had been to her as a Newfoundland dog is when he jumps all over you just when he has come out of a horsepond. She would have liked Tom had he kept his dog-like gambols at a proper distance. But when he would cover her with muddy water he was abominable. But this Augusta had not understood. With Mr. Traffick there would be no dog-like gambols; and, as he was not harsh to her, Ayala liked him. She had liked her uncle. Such men were, to her thinking, more like dogs than lovers. She sang when Mr. Traffick asked her, and made a picture for him, and went with him to the Coliseum, and laughed at him about Supply and Demand. She was very pretty, and perhaps Mr. Traffick did like to look at her.

'I really think you were too free with Mr. Traffick last night,' Augusta said to her one morning.

'Free! How free?'

'You were—laughing at him.'

'Oh, he likes that,' said Ayala. 'All that time we were up at the top of St. Peter's*I was quizzing him about his speeches. He lets me say just what I please.'

This was wormwood. In the first place there had
been a word or two between the lovers about that
going up of St. Peter's, and Augusta had refused to
join them. She had wished Septimus to remain down
with her,—which would have been tantamount to
preventing any of the party from going up; but
Septimus had persisted on ascending. Then Augusta
had been left for a long hour alone with her mother.
Gertrude had no doubt gone up, but Gertrude had
lagged during the ascent. Ayala had skipped up the
interminable stairs and Mr. Traffick had trotted after
her with admiring breathless industry. This itself,
with the thoughts of the good time which Septimus
might be having at the top, was very bad. But now
to be told that she, Ayala, should laugh at him; and
that he, Septimus, should like it! 'I suppose he takes
you to be a child,' said Augusta; 'but if you are a
child you ought to conduct yourself.'

'I suppose he does perceive the difference,' said
Ayala.

She had not in the least known what the words
might convey,—had probably meant nothing. But
to Augusta it was apparent that Ayala had declared
that her lover, her Septimus, had preferred her
extreme youth to the more mature charms of his
own true love,—or had, perhaps, preferred Ayala's
raillery to Augusta's serious demeanour. 'You are
the most impertinent person I ever knew in my life,'
said Augusta, rising from her chair and walking
slowly out of the room. Ayala stared after her, not
above half comprehending the cause of the anger.

Then came the very serious affair of the ball. The
Marchesa had asked that her dear little friend Ayala
Dormer might be allowed to come over to a little
dance which her own girls were going to have. Her
own girls were so fond of Ayala! There would be no
trouble. There was a carriage which would be going
somewhere else, and she would be fetched and taken
home. Ayala at once declared that she intended to
go, and her Aunt Emmeline did not refuse her sanc-

tion. Augusta was shocked, declaring that the little
dance was to be one of the great balls of the season,
and pronouncing the whole to be a falsehood; but
the affair was arranged before she could stop it.

But Mr. Traffick's affair in the matter came more
within her range. 'Septimus,' she said, 'I would rather
you would not go to that woman's party.' Septimus
had been asked only on the day before the party,—as
soon, indeed, as his arrival had become known to the
Marchesa.

'Why, my own one?'

'She has not treated mamma well,—nor yet me.'

'Ayala is going.' He had no right to call her Ayala.
So Augusta thought.

'My cousin is behaving badly in the matter, and
mamma ought not to allow her to go. Who knows
anything about the Marchesa Baldoni?'

'Both he and she are of the very best families in
Rome,' said Mr. Traffick, who knew everything
about it.

'At any rate they are behaving very badly to us,
and I will take it as a favour that you do not go.
Asking Ayala, and then asking you, as good as from
the same house, is too marked. You ought not
to go.'

Perhaps Mr. Traffick had on some former occasion
felt some little interference with his freedom of action.
Perhaps he liked the acquaintance of the Marchesa.
Perhaps he liked Ayala Dormer. Be that as it might,
he would not yield. 'Dear Augusta, it is right that
I should go there, if it be only for half-an-hour.'
This he said in a tone of voice with which Augusta
was already acquainted, which she did not love, and
which, when she heard it, would make her think of
her £120,000. When he had spoken he left her, and
she began to think of her £120,000.

They both went, Ayala and Mr. Traffick,—and Mr.
Traffick, instead of staying half-an-hour, brought
Ayala back at three o'clock in the morning. Though
Mr. Traffick was nearly as old as Uncle Tringle, yet

he could dance. Ayala had been astonished to find
how well he could dance, and thought that she might
please her cousin Augusta by praising the juvenility
of her lover at luncheon the next day. She had not
appeared at breakfast, but had been full of the ball
at lunch. 'Oh, dear, yes, I dare say there were two
hundred people there.'

'That is what she calls a little dance,' said Augusta,
with scorn.

'I suppose that is the Italian way of talking about
it,' said Ayala.

'Italian way! I hate Italian ways.'

'Mr. Traffick liked it very much. I'm sure he'll tell
you so. I had no idea he would care to dance.'

Augusta only shook herself and turned up her
nose. Lady Tringle thought it necessary to say
something in defence of her daughter's choice. 'Why
should not Mr. Traffick dance like any other gentleman?'

'Oh, I don't know. I thought that a man who
makes so many speeches in Parliament would think
of something else. I was very glad he did, for he
danced three times with me. He can waltz as lightly
as——' As though he were young, she was going to
say, but then she stopped herself.

'He is the best dancer I ever danced with,' said
Augusta.

'But you almost never do dance,' said Ayala.

'I suppose I may know about it as well as another,'
said Augusta, angrily.

The next day was the last of Mr. Traffick's sojourn
in Rome, and on that day he and Augusta so quarrelled that, for a certain number of hours, it was
almost supposed in the family that the match would
be broken off. On the afternoon of the day after the
dance, Mr. Traffick was walking with Ayala on the
Pincian,* while Augusta was absolutely remaining
behind with her mother. For a quarter-of-an-hour,—
the whole day, as it seemed to Augusta,—there was
a full two hundred yards between them. It was not

that the engaged girl could not bear the severance,
but that she could not endure the attention paid to
Ayala. On the next morning 'she had it out', as
some people say, with her lover. 'If I am to be
treated in this way you had better tell me so at once,'
she said.

'I know no better way of treating you,' said Mr.
Traffick.

'Dancing with that chit all night, turning her head,
and then walking with her all the next day! I will
not put up with such conduct.'

Mr. Traffick valued £120,000 very highly, as do
most men, and would have done much to keep it;
but he believed that the best way of making sure of
it would be by showing himself to be the master.
'My own one,' he said, 'you are really making an ass
of yourself.'

'Very well! Then I will write to papa, and let him
know that it must be all over.'

For three hours there was terrible trouble in the
apartments in the Palazzo Ruperti, during which
Mr. Traffick was enjoying himself by walking up and
down the Forum, and calculating how many Romans
could have congregated themselves in the space
which is supposed to have seen so much of the world's
doings.* During this time Augusta was very frequently in hysterics; but, whether in hysterics or out
of them, she would not allow Ayala to come near her.
She gave it to be understood that Ayala had interfered fatally, foully, damnably, with all her happiness. She demanded, from fit to fit, that telegrams
should be sent over to bring her father to Italy for her
protection. She would rave about Septimus, and
then swear that, under no consideration whatever,
would she ever see him again. At the end of three
hours she was told that Septimus was in the drawing-
room. Lady Tringle had sent half-a-dozen messengers after him, and at last he was found looking up
at the Arch of Titus.* 'Bid him go,' said Augusta.
'I never want to behold him again.' But within two

minutes she was in his arms, and before dinner she
was able to take a stroll with him on the Pincian.

He left, like a thriving lover, high in the good
graces of his beloved; but the anger which had fallen
on Ayala had not been removed. Then came a
rumour that the Marchesa, who was half English,
had called Ayala Cinderella, and the name had added
fuel to the fire of Augusta's wrath. There was much
said about it between Lady Tringle and her daughter,
the aunt really feeling that more blame was being
attributed to Ayala than she deserved. 'Perhaps she
gives herself airs,' said Lady Tringle, 'but really it is
no more.'

'She is a viper,' said Augusta.

Gertrude rather took Ayala's part, telling her
mother, in private, that the accusation about Mr.
Traffick was absurd. 'The truth is,' said Gertrude,
'that Ayala thinks herself very clever and very
beautiful, and Augusta will not stand it.' Gertrude
acknowledged that Ayala was upsetting and ungrateful. Poor Lady Tringle, in her husband's absence, did not know what to do about her niece.

Altogether, they were uncomfortable after Mr.
Traffick went and before Tom Tringle had come. On
no consideration whatsoever would Augusta speak
to her cousin. She declared that Ayala was a viper,
and would give no other reason. In all such quarrel-
ings the matter most distressing is that the evil
cannot be hidden. Everybody at Rome who knew
the Tringles, or who knew Ayala, was aware that
Augusta Tringle would not speak to her cousin.
When Ayala was asked she would shake her locks,
and open her eyes, and declare that she knew nothing
about it. In truth she knew very little about it. She
remembered that passage-at-arms about the going
upstairs at Glenbogie, but she could hardly understand that for so small an affront, and one so distant,
Augusta would now refuse to speak to her. That
Augusta had always been angry with her, and since
Mr. Traffick's arrival more angry than ever, she had

felt; but that Augusta was jealous in respect to her lover had never yet at all come home to Ayala. That she should have wanted to captivate Mr. Traffick,— she with her high ideas of some transcendental, more than human, hero!

But she had to put up with it, and to think of it. She had sense enough to know that she was no more than a stranger in her aunt's family, and that she must go if she made herself unpleasant to them. She was aware that hitherto she had not succeeded with her residence among them. Perhaps she might have to go. Some things she would bear, and in them she would endeavour to amend her conduct. In other matters she would hold her own, and go, if necessary. Though her young imagination was still full of her unsubstantial hero,—though she still had her castles in the air altogether incapable of terrestrial foundation, —still there was a common sense about her which told her that she must give and take. She would endeavour to submit herself to her aunt. She would be kind, —as she had always been kind,—to Gertrude. She would in all matters obey her uncle. Her misfortune with the Newfoundland dog had almost dwindled out of her mind. To Augusta she could not submit herself. But then Augusta, as soon as the next session of Parliament should be over, would be married out of the way. And, on her own part, she did think that her aunt was inclined to take her part in the quarrel with Augusta.

Thus matters were going on in Rome when there came up another and a worse cause for trouble.

## CHAPTER VII

### TOM TRINGLE IN EARNEST

TOM TRINGLE, though he had first appeared to his cousin Ayala as a Newfoundland dog which might perhaps be pleasantly playful, and then, as the same dog, very unpleasant because dripping with muddy water, was nevertheless a young man with so much manly truth about him as to be very much in love. He did not look like it; but then perhaps the young men who do fall most absolutely into love do not look like it. To Ayala her cousin Tom was as unloveable as Mr. Septimus Traffick. She could like them both well enough while they would be kind to her. But as to regarding cousin Tom as a lover,—the idea was so preposterous to her that she could not imagine that any one else should look upon it as real. But with Tom the idea had been real, and was, moreover, permanent. The black locks which would be shaken here and there, the bright glancing eyes which could be so joyous and could be so indignant, the colour of her face which had nothing in it of pink, which was brown rather, but over which the tell-tale blood would rush with a quickness which was marvellous to him, the lithe quick figure which had in it nothing of the weight of earth, the little foot which in itself was a perfect joy, the step with all the elasticity of a fawn,—these charms together had mastered him. Tom was not romantic or poetic, but the romance and poetry of Ayala had been divine to him. It is not always like to like in love. Titania loved the weaver Bottom with the ass's head.* Bluebeard, though a bad husband, is supposed to have been fond of his last wife.* The Beauty has always been beloved by the Beast. To Ayala the thing was monstrous;—but it was natural. Tom Tringle was determined to have his way, and when he started for Rome was more intent upon his love-making than all the glories of the Capitol and the Vatican.

When he first made his appearance before Ayala's eyes he was bedecked in a manner that was awful to her. Down at Glenbogie he had affected a rough attire, as is the custom with young men of ample means when fishing, shooting, or the like, is supposed to be the employment then in hand. The roughness had been a little overdone, but it had added nothing to his own uncouthness. In London he was apt to run a little towards ornamental gilding, but in London his tastes had been tempered by the ill-natured criticism of the world at large. He had hardly dared at Queen's Gate to wear his biggest pins; but he had taken upon himself to think that at Rome an Englishman might expose himself with all his jewelry. 'Oh, Tom, I never saw anything so stunning,' his sister Gertrude said to him. He had simply frowned upon her, and had turned himself to Ayala, as though Ayala, being an artist, would be able to appreciate something beautiful in art. Ayala had looked at him and had marvelled, and had ventured to hope that, with his Glenbogie dress, his Glenbogie manners and Glenbogie propensities would be changed.

At this time the family at Rome was very uncomfortable. Augusta would not speak to her cousin, and had declared to her mother and sister her determination never to speak to Ayala again. For a time Aunt Emmeline had almost taken her niece's part, feeling that she might best bring things back to a condition of peace in this manner. Ayala, she had thought, might thus be decoyed into a state of submission. Ayala, so instigated, had made her attempt. 'What is the matter, Augusta,' she had said, 'that you are determined to quarrel with me?' Then had followed a little offer that bygones should be bygones.

'I have quarrelled with you,' said Augusta, 'because you do not know how to behave yourself.' Then Ayala had flashed forth, and the little attempt led to a worse condition than ever, and words were spoken which even Aunt Emmeline had felt to be irrevocable, irremediable.

'Only that you are going away I would not consent to live here,' said Ayala. Then Aunt Emmeline had asked her where she would go to live should it please her to remove herself. Ayala had thought of this for a moment, and then had burst into tears. 'If I could not live I could die. Anything would be better than to be treated as she treats me.' So the matters were when Tom came to Rome with all his jewelry.

Lady Tringle had already told herself that, in choosing Ayala, she had chosen wrong. Lucy, though not so attractive as Ayala, was pretty, quiet, and ladylike. So she thought now. And as to Ayala's attractions, they were not at all of a nature to be serviceable to such a family as hers. To have her own girls outshone, to be made to feel that the poor orphan was the one person most worthy of note among them, to be subjected to the caprices of a pretty, proud, ill-conditioned minx;—thus it was that Aunt Emmeline was taught to regard her own charity and good-nature towards her niece. There was, she said, no gratitude in Ayala. Had she said that there was no humility she would have been more nearly right. She was entitled, she thought, to expect both gratitude and humility, and she was sorry that she had opened the Paradise of her opulent home to one so little grateful and so little humble as Ayala. She saw now her want of judgment in that she had not taken Lucy.

Tom, who was not a fool, in spite of his trinkets, saw the state of the case, and took Ayala's part at once. 'I think you are quite right,' he said to her, on the first occasion on which he had contrived to find himself alone with her after his arrival.

'Right about what?'

'In not giving up to Augusta. She was always like that when she was a child, and now her head is turned about Traffick.'

'I shouldn't grudge her her lover if she would only let me alone.'

'I don't suppose she hurts you much?'

'She sets my aunt against me, and that makes me unhappy. Of course I am wretched.'

'Oh, Ayala, don't be wretched.'

'How is one to help it? I never said an ill-natured word to her, and now I am so lonely among them!' In saying this,—in seeking to get one word of sympathy from her cousin, she forgot for a moment his disagreeable pretensions. But, no sooner had she spoken of her loneliness, than she saw that ogle in his eye of which she had spoken with so much ludicrous awe in her letters from Glenbogie to her sister.

'I shall always take your part,' said he.

'I don't want any taking of parts.'

'But I shall. I am not going to see you put upon. You are more to me, Ayala, than any of them.' Then he looked at her, whereupon she got up and ran away.

But she could not always run away, nor could she always refuse when he asked her to go with him about the show-places of the city. To avoid starting alone with him was within her power; but she found herself compelled to join herself to Gertrude and her brother in some of those little excursions which were taken for her benefit. At this time there had come to be a direct quarrel between Lady Tringle and the Marchesa, which, however, had arisen altogether on the part of Augusta. Augusta had forced her mother to declare that she was insulted, and then there was no more visiting between them. This had been sad enough for Ayala, who had struck up an intimacy with the Marchesa's daughters. But the Marchesa had explained to her that there was no help for it. 'It won't do for you to separate yourself from your aunt,' she had said. 'Of course we shall be friends, and at some future time you shall come and see us.' So there had been a division, and Ayala would have been quite alone had she declined the proffered companionship of Gertrude.

Within the walls and arches and upraised terraces of the Coliseum*they were joined one day by young Hamel, the sculptor, who had not, as yet, gone back to London,—and had not, as yet, met Lucy in the gardens at Kensington ; and with him there had been one Frank Houston, who had made acquaintance with Lady Tringle, and with the Tringles generally, since they had been at Rome. Frank Houston was a young man of family, with a taste for art, very good-looking, but not specially well off in regard to income.

He had heard of the good fortune of Septimus
Traffick in having prepared for himself a connection
with so wealthy a family as the Tringles, and had
thought it possible that a settlement in life might be
comfortable for himself. What few soft words he had
hitherto been able to say to Gertrude had been taken
in good part, and when, therefore, they met among
the walls of the Coliseum, she had naturally straggled
away to see some special wonder which he had a
special aptitude for showing. Hamel remained with
Ayala and Tom, talking of the old days at the bijou,
till he found himself obliged to leave them. Then
Tom had his opportunity.

'Ayala,' he said, 'all this must be altered.'

'What must be altered?'

'If you only knew, Ayala, how much you are to
me.'

'I wish you wouldn't, Tom. I don't want to be
anything to anybody in particular.'

'What I mean is, that I won't have them sit upon
you. They treat you as—as,—well, as though you
had only half a right to be one of them.'

'No more I have. I have no right at all.'

'But that's not the way I want it to be. If you
were my wife——'

'Tom, pray don't.'

'Why not? I'm in earnest. Why ain't I to speak
as I think? Oh, Ayala, if you knew how much I
think of you.'

'But you shouldn't. You haven't got a right.'

'I have got a right.'

'But I don't want it, Tom, and I won't have it.'
He had carried her away now to the end of the
terrace, or ruined tier of seats, on which they were
walking, and had got her so hemmed into a corner
that she could not get away from him. She was
afraid of him, lest he should put out his hand to take
hold of her,—lest something even more might be
attempted. And yet his manner was manly and
sincere, and had it not been for his pins and his

chains she could not but have acknowledged his goodness to her, much as she might have disliked his person. 'I want to get out,' she said. 'I won't stay here any more.' Mr. Traffick, on the top of St. Peter's, had been a much pleasanter companion.

'Don't you believe me when I tell you that I love you better than anybody?' pleaded Tom.

'No.'

'Not believe me? Oh, Ayala!'

'I don't want to believe anything. I want to get out. If you go on, I'll tell my aunt.'

Tell her aunt! There was a want of personal consideration to himself in this way of receiving his addresses which almost angered him. Tom Tringle was not in the least afraid of his mother,—was not even afraid of his father as long as he was fairly regular at the office in Lombard Street. He was quite determined to please himself in marriage, and was disposed to think that his father and mother would like him to be settled. Money was no object. There was, to his thinking, no good reason why he should not marry his cousin. For her the match was so excellent that he hardly expected she would reject him when she could be made to understand that he was really in earnest. 'You may tell all the world,' he said proudly. 'All I want is that you should love me.'

'But I don't. There are Gertrude and Mr. Houston, and I want to go to them.'

'Say one nice word to me, Ayala.'

'I don't know how to say a nice word. Can't you be made to understand that I don't like it?'

'Ayala.'

'Why don't you let me go away?'

'Ayala,—give me—one—kiss.' Then Ayala did go away, escaping by some kid-like manœuvre among the ruins, and running quickly, while he followed her, joined herself to the other pair of lovers, who probably were less in want of her society than she of theirs. 'Ayala, I am quite in earnest,' said Tom, as they were walking home, 'and I mean to go on with it.'

Ayala thought that there was nothing for it but to tell her aunt. That there would be some absurdity in such a proceeding she did feel,—that she would be acting as though her cousin were a naughty boy who was merely teasing her. But she felt also the peculiar danger of her own position. Her aunt must be made to understand that she, Ayala, was innocent in the matter. It would be terrible to her to be suspected even for a moment of a desire to inveigle the heir. That Augusta would bring such an accusation against her she thought probable. Augusta had said as much even at Glenbogie. She must therefore be on the alert, and let it be understood at once that she was, not leagued with her cousin Tom. There would be an absurdity;—but that would be better than suspicion.

She thought about it all that afternoon, and in the evening she came to a resolution. She would write a letter to her cousin and persuade him if possible to desist. If he should again annoy her after that she would appeal to her aunt. Then she wrote and sent her letter, which was as follows:—

' DEAR TOM,

' You don't know how unhappy you made me at the Coliseum to-day. I don't think you ought to turn against me when you know what I have to bear. It is turning against me to talk as you did. Of course it means nothing; but you shouldn't do it. It *never never* could mean anything. I hope you will be good-natured and kind to me, and then I shall be so much obliged to you. If you won't say anything more like that I will forget it altogether.

' Your affectionate cousin,
' AYALA.'

The letter ought to have convinced him. Those two underscored nevers should have eradicated from his mind the feeling which had been previously produced by the assertion that he had 'meant nothing.' But he was so assured in his own meanings that he paid no attention whatever to the nevers. The letter was a delight to him because it gave him the opportunity of a rejoinder,—and he wrote his rejoinder on a scented sheet of note-paper and copied it twice;—

'DEAREST AYALA,

'Why do you say that it means nothing? It means everything. No man was ever more in earnest in speaking to a lady than I am with you. Why should I not be in earnest when I am so deeply in love? From the first moment in which I saw you down at Glenbogie I knew how it was going to be with me.

'As for my mother I don't think she would say a word. Why should she? But I am not the sort of man to be talked out of my intentions in such a matter as this. I have set my heart upon having you and nothing will ever turn me off.

'Dearest Ayala, let me have one look to say that you will love me, and I shall be the happiest man in England. I think you so beautiful! I do, indeed. The governor has always said that if I would settle down and marry there should be lots of money. What could I do better with it than make my darling look as grand as the best of them?

'Yours, always meaning it,
'Most affectionately,
'T. TRINGLE.'

It almost touched her,—not in the way of love but of gratitude. He was still to her like Bottom with the ass's head, or the Newfoundland dog gambolling out of the water. There was the heavy face, and there were the big chains and the odious rings, and the great hands and the clumsy feet,—making together a creature whom it was impossible even to think of with love. She shuddered as she remembered the proposition which had been made to her in the Coliseum.

And now by writing to him she had brought down

upon herself this absolute love-letter. She had thought that by appealing to him as 'Dear Tom,' and by signing herself his affectionate cousin, she might have prevailed. If he could only be made to understand that it could never mean anything! But now, on the other hand, she had begun to understand that it did *mean* a great deal. He had sent to her a regular offer of marriage! The magnitude of the thing struck her at last. The heir of all the wealth of her mighty uncle wanted to make her his wife!

But it was to her exactly as though the heir had come to her wearing an ass's head on his shoulders. Love him! Marry him!—or even touch him? Oh, no. They might ill-use her; they might scold her; they might turn her out of the house; but no consideration would induce her to think of Tom Tringle as a lover.

And yet he was in earnest, and honest, and good. And some answer,—some further communication must be made to him. She did recognise some nobility in him, though personally he was so distasteful to her. Now his appeal to her had taken the guise of an absolute offer of marriage he was entitled to a discreet and civil answer. Romantic, dreamy, poetic, childish as she was, she knew as much as that. 'Go away, Tom, you fool, you,' would no longer do for the occasion. As she thought of it all that night it was borne in upon her more strongly than ever that her only protection would be in telling her aunt, and in getting her aunt to make Tom understand that there must be no more of it. Early on the following morning she found herself in her aunt's bedroom.

## CHAPTER VIII

### THE LOUT

'AUNT EMMELINE, I want you to read this letter.' So it was that Ayala commenced the interview. At this moment Ayala was not on much better terms with her aunt than she was with

her cousin Augusta. Ayala was a trouble to her,—
Lady Tringle,—who was altogether perplexed with
the feeling that she had burdened herself with an
inmate in her house who was distasteful to her and of
whom she could not rid herself. Ayala had turned
out on her hands something altogether different from
the girl she had intended to cherish and patronise.
Ayala was independent; superior rather than inferior
to her own girls; more thought of by others; apparently without any touch of that subservience
which should have been produced in her by her position. Ayala seemed to demand as much as though
she were a daughter of the house, and at the same
time to carry herself as though she were more gifted
than the daughters of the house. She was less
obedient even than a daughter. All this Aunt Emmeline could not endure with a placid bosom. She
was herself kind of heart. She acknowledged her
duty to her dead sister. She wished to protect and
foster the orphan. She did not even yet wish to
punish Ayala by utter desertion. She would protect
her in opposition to Augusta's more declared malig-
nity; but she did wish to be rid of Ayala, if she only
knew how.

She took her son's letter and read it, and as a
matter of course misunderstood the position. At
Glenbogie something had been whispered to her
about Tom and Ayala, but she had not believed
much in it. Ayala was a child, and Tom was to her
not much more than a boy. But now here was a
genuine love-letter,—a letter in which her son had
made a distinct proposition to marry the orphan.
She did not stop to consider why Ayala had brought
the letter to her, but entertained at once an idea that
the two young people were going to vex her very
soul by a lamentable love affair. How imprudent she
had been to let the two young people be together in
Rome, seeing that the matter had been whispered to
her at Glenbogie! 'How long has this been going
on?' she asked, severely.

'He used to tease me at Glenbogie, and now he is doing it again,' said Ayala.

'There must certainly be put an end to it. You must go away.'

Ayala knew at once that her aunt was angry with her, and was indignant at the injustice. 'Of course there must be put an end to it, Aunt Emmeline. He has no right to annoy me when I tell him not.'

'I suppose you have encouraged him.'

This was too cruel to be borne! Encouraged him! Ayala's anger was caused not so much by a feeling that her aunt had misappreciated the cause of her coming as that it should have been thought possible that she should have 'encouraged' such a lover. It was the outrage to her taste rather than to her conduct which afflicted her. 'He is a lout,' she said; 'a stupid lout!' thus casting her scorn upon the mother as well as on the son, and, indeed, upon the whole family. 'I have not encouraged him. It is untrue.'

'Ayala, you are very impertinent.'

'And you are very unjust. Because I want to put a stop to it I come to you, and you tell me that I encourage him. You are worse than Augusta.'

This was too much for the good nature even of Aunt Emmeline. Whatever may have been the truth as to the love affair, however innocent Ayala may have been in that matter, or however guilty Tom, such words from a niece to her aunt,—from a dependent to her superior,—were unpardonable. The extreme youthfulness of the girl, a peculiar look of childhood which she still had with her, made the feeling so much the stronger. 'You are worse than Augusta!'

And this was said to her who was specially conscious of her endeavours to mitigate Augusta's just anger. She bridled up, and tried to look big and knit her brows. At that moment she could not think what must be the end of it, but she felt that Ayala must be crushed. 'How dare you speak to me like that, Miss?' she said.

'So you are. It is very cruel. Tom will go on saying all this nonsense to me, and when I come to you you say I encourage him! I never encouraged him. I despise him too much. I did not think my own aunt could have told me that I encouraged any man. No, I didn't. You drive me to it, so that I have got to be impertinent.'

'You had better go to your room,' said the aunt. Then Ayala, lifting her head as high as she knew how, walked towards the door. 'You had better leave that letter with me.' Ayala considered the matter for a moment, and then handed the letter a second time to her aunt. It could be nothing to her who saw the letter. She did not want it. Having thus given it up she stalked off in silent disdain and went to her chamber.

Aunt Emmeline, when she was left alone, felt herself to be enveloped in a cloud of doubt. The desirableness of Tom as a husband first forced itself upon her attention, and the undesirableness of Ayala as a wife for Tom. She was perplexed at her own folly in not having seen that danger of this kind would arise when she first proposed to take Ayala into the house. Aunts and uncles do not like the marriage of cousins, and the parents of rich children do not, as a rule, approve of marriages with those which are poor. Although Ayala had been so violent, Lady Tringle could not rid herself of the idea that her darling boy was going to throw himself away. Then her cheeks became red with anger as she remembered that her Tom had been called a lout,—a stupid lout. There was an ingratitude in the use of such language which was not alleviated even by the remembrance that it tended against that matrimonial danger of which she was so much afraid. Ayala was behaving very badly. She ought not to have coaxed Tom to be her lover, and she certainly ought not to have called Tom a lout. And then Ayala had told her aunt that she was unjust and worse than Augusta! It was out of the question that such a state of things should be endured. Ayala must be made to go away.

Before the day was over Lady Tringle spoke to her son, and was astonished to find that the 'lout' was quite in earnest,—so much in earnest that he declared his purpose of marrying his cousin in opposition to his father and mother, in opposition even to Ayala herself. He was so much in earnest that he would not be roused to wrath even when he was told that Ayala had called him a lout. And then grew upon the mother a feeling that the young man had never been so little loutish before. For there had been, even in her maternal bosom, a feeling that Tom was open to the criticism expressed on him. Tom had been a hobble-de-hoy,* one of those over-grown lads who come late to their manhood, and who are regarded by young ladies as louts. Though he had spent his money only too freely when away, his sisters had sometimes said that he could not say 'bo to a goose' at home. But now,—now Tom was quite an altered young man. When his own letter was shown to him he simply said that he meant to stick to it. When it was represented to him that his cousin would be quite an unfit wife for him he assured his mother that his own opinion on that matter was very different. When his father's anger was threatened he declared that his father would have no right to be angry with him if he married a lady. At the word 'lout' he simply smiled. 'She'll come to think different from that before she's done with me,' he said, with a smile. Even the mother could not but perceive that the young man had been much improved by his love.

But what was she to do? Two or three days went on, during which there was no reconciliation between her and Ayala. Between Augusta and Ayala no word was spoken. Messages were taken to her by Gertrude, the object of which was to induce her to ask her aunt's pardon. But Ayala was of opinion that her aunt ought to ask her pardon, and could not be beaten from it. 'Why did she say that I encouraged him?' she demanded indignantly of Gertrude. 'I don't think she did encourage him,' said Gertrude to her mother. This might possibly be true, but not the less had she misbehaved. And though she might not yet have encouraged her lover it was only too probable that she might do so when she found that her lover was quite in earnest.

Lady Tringle was much harassed. And then there came an additional trouble. Gertrude informed her mother that she had engaged herself to Mr. Francis Houston, and that Mr. Houston was going to write to her father with the object of proposing himself as a son-in-law. Mr. Houston came also to herself, and told her, in the most natural tone in the world, that he intended to marry her daughter. She had not known what to say. It was Sir Thomas who managed all matters of money. She had an idea that Mr. Houston was very poor. But then so also had been Mr. Traffick, who had been received into the family with open arms. But then Mr. Traffick had a career, whereas Mr. Houston was lamentably idle. She could only refer Mr. Houston to Sir Thomas, and beg him not to come among them any more till Sir Thomas had decided. Upon this Gertrude also got angry, and shut herself up in her room. The apartments Ruperti were, therefore, upon the whole, an uncomfortable home to them.

Letters upon letters were written to Sir Thomas, and letters upon letters came. The first letter had been about Ayala. He had been much more tender towards Ayala than her aunt had been. He talked of calf-love, and said that Tom was a fool; but he had not at once thought it necessary to give imperative orders for Tom's return. As to Ayala's impudence, he evidently regarded it as nothing. It was not till Aunt Emmeline had spoken out in her third letter that he seemed to recognise the possibility of getting rid of Ayala altogether. And this he did in answer to a suggestion which had been made to him. 'If she

likes to change with her sister Lucy, and you like it,
I shall not object,' said Sir Thomas. Then there came
an order to Tom that he should return to Lombard
Street at once; but this order had been rendered
abortive by the sudden return of the whole family.
Sir Thomas, in his first letter as to Gertrude, had
declared that the Houston marriage would not do at
all. Then, when he was told that Gertrude and Mr.
Houston had certainly met each other more than
once since an order had been given for their separation, he desired the whole family to come back at
once to Merle Park.

The proposition as to Lucy had arisen in this wise.
Tom being in the same house with Ayala, of course
had her very much at advantage, and would carry on
his suit in spite of any abuse which she might lavish
upon him. It was quite in vain that she called him
lout. 'You'll think very different from that some of
these days, Ayala,' he said, more seriously.

'No, I shan't; I shall think always the same.'

'When you know how much I love you, you'll
change.'

'I don't want you to love me,' she said; 'and if you
were anything that is good you wouldn't go on after I
have told you so often. It is not manly of you. You
have brought me to all manner of trouble. It is your
fault, but they make me suffer.'

After that Ayala again went to her aunt, and on
this occasion the family misfortune was discussed in
more seemly language. Ayala was still indignant,
but she said nothing insolent. Aunt Emmeline was
still averse to her niece, but she abstained from
crimination. They knew each as enemies, but
recognised the wisdom of keeping the peace. 'As for
that, Aunt Emmeline,' Ayala said, 'you may be
quite sure that I shall never encourage him. I shall
never like him well enough.'

'Very well. Then we need say no more about that,
my dear. Of course, it must be unpleasant to us all,
being in the same house together.'

'It is very unpleasant to me, when he will go on bothering me like that. It makes me wish that I were anywhere else.'

Then Aunt Emmeline began to think about it very seriously. It was very unpleasant. Ayala had made herself disagreeable to all the ladies of the family, and only too agreeable to the young gentleman. Nor did the manifest favour of Sir Thomas do much towards raising Ayala in Lady Tringle's estimation. Sir Thomas had only laughed when Augusta had been requested to go upstairs for the scrap-book. Sir Thomas had been profuse with his presents even when Ayala had been most persistent in her misbehaviour. And then all that affair of the Marchesa, and even Mr. Traffick's infatuation! If Ayala wished that she were somewhere else would it not be well to indulge her wish! Aunt Emmeline certainly wished it. 'If you think so, perhaps some arrangement can be made,' said Aunt Emmeline, very slowly.

'What arrangement?'

'You must not suppose that I wish to turn you out.'

'But what arrangement?'

'You see, Ayala, that unfortunately we have not all of us hit it off nicely; have we?'

'Not at all, Aunt Emmeline. Augusta is always angry with me. And you,—you think that I have encouraged Tom.'

'I am saying nothing about that, Ayala.'

'But what arrangement is it, Aunt Emmeline?' The matter was one of fearful import to Ayala. She was prudent enough to understand that well. The arrangement must be one by which she would be banished from all the wealth of the Tringles. Her coming among them had not been a success. She had already made them tired of her by her petulance and independence. Young as she was she could see that, and comprehend the material injury she had done herself by her folly. She had been very wrong in telling Augusta to go upstairs. She had been wrong

in the triumph of her exclusive visits to the Marchesa.
She had been wrong in walking away with Mr.
Trafflck on the Pincian. She could see that. She had
not been wrong in regard to Tom,—except in calling
him a lout; but whether wrong or right she had been
most unfortunate. But the thing had been done, and
she must go.

At this moment the wealth of the Tringles seemed
to be more to her than it had ever been before,—and
her own poverty and destitution seemed to be more
absolute. When the word 'arrangement' was whispered to her there came upon her a clear idea of all
that which she was to lose. She was to be banished
from Merle Park, from Queen's Gate, and from
Glenbogie. For her there were to be no more carriages, and horses, and pretty trinkets;—none of that
abandon of the luxury of money among which the
Tringles lived. But she had done it for herself, and
she would not say a word in opposition to the fate
which was before her. 'What arrangement, aunt?'
she said again, in a voice which was intended to welcome any arrangement that might be made.

Then her aunt spoke very softly. 'Of course, dear
Ayala, we do not wish to do less than we at first
intended. But as you are not happy here——' Then
she paused, almost ashamed of herself.

'I am not happy here,' said Ayala, boldly.

'How would it be if you were to change,—with
Lucy?'

The idea which had been present to Lady Tringle
for some weeks past had never struck Ayala. The
moment she heard it she felt that she was more than
ever bound to assent. If the home from which she
was to be banished was good, then would that good
fall upon Lucy. Lucy would have the carriages and
the horses and the trinkets, Lucy, who certainly was
not happy at Kingsbury Crescent. 'I should be very
glad, indeed,' said Ayala.

Her voice was so brave and decided that, in itself,
it gave fresh offence to her aunt. Was there to be no

regret after so much generosity? But she misunderstood the girl altogether. As the words were coming from her lips,—'I should be very glad, indeed,'—Ayala's heart was sinking with tenderness as she remembered how much after all had been done for her. But as they wished her to go there should be not a word, not a sign of unwillingness on her part.

'Then perhaps it can be arranged,' said Lady Tringle.

'I don't know what Uncle Dosett may say. Perhaps they are very fond of Lucy now.'

'They wouldn't wish to stand in her way, I should think.'

'At any rate, I won't. If you, and my uncles, and Aunt Margaret, will consent, I will go whenever you choose. Of course I must do just as I'm told.'

Aunt Emmeline made a faint demur to this; but still the matter was held to be arranged. Letters were written to Sir Thomas, and letters came, and at last even Sir Thomas had assented. He suggested, in the first place, that all the facts which would follow the exchange should be explained to Ayala; but he was obliged after a while to acknowledge that this would be inexpedient. The girl was willing; and knew no doubt that she was to give up the great wealth of her present home. But she had proved herself to be an unfit participator, and it was better that she should go.

Then the departure of them all from Rome was hurried on by the indiscretion of Gertrude. Gertrude declared that she had a right to her lover. As to his having no income, what matter for that. Everyone knew that Septimus Traffick had no income. Papa had income enough for them all. Mr. Houston was a gentleman. Till this moment no one had known of how strong a will of her own Gertrude was possessed. When Gertrude declared that she would not consent to be separated from Mr. Houston then they were all hurried home.

## CHAPTER IX

### THE EXCHANGE

SUCH was the state of things when Mr. Dosett brought the three letters home with him to Kingsbury Crescent, having been so much disturbed by the contents of the two which were addressed to himself as to have found himself compelled to leave his office two hours before the proper time. The three letters were handed together by her uncle to Lucy, and she, seeing the importance of the occasion, read the two open ones before she broke the envelope of her own. That from Sir Thomas came first, and was as follows;—

'Lombard Street, January, 187–.

'MY DEAR DOSETT,

'I have had a correspondence with the ladies at Rome which has been painful in its nature, but which I had better perhaps communicate to you at once. Ayala has not got on as well with Lady Tringle and the girls as might have been wished, and they all think it will be better that she and Lucy should change places. I chiefly write to give my assent. Your sister will no doubt write to you. I may as well mention to you, should you consent to take charge of Ayala, that I have made some provision for her in my will, and that I shall not change it. I have to add on my own account that I have no complaint of my own to make against Ayala.

'Yours sincerely,

'T. TRINGLE.'

Lucy, when she had read this, proceeded at once to the letter from her aunt. The matter to her was one of terrible importance, but the importance was quite as great to Ayala. She had been allowed to go up alone into her own room. The letters were of such a nature that she could hardly have read them calmly in the presence of her Aunt Dosett. It was thus that her Aunt Emmeline had written;—

'Palazzo Ruperti, Rome, Thursday.
'MY DEAR REGINALD,

'I am sure you will be sorry to hear that we are in great trouble here. This has become so bad that we are obliged to apply to you to help us. Now you must understand that I do not mean to say a word against dear Ayala;—only she does not suit. It will occur sometimes that people who are most attached to each other do not suit. So it has been with dear Ayala. She is not happy with us. She has not perhaps accommodated herself to her cousins quite as carefully as she might have done. She is fully as sensible of this as I am, and is, herself, persuaded that there had better be a change.

'Now, my dear Reginald, I am quite aware that when poor Egbert died it was I who chose Ayala, and that you took Lucy partly in compliance with my wishes. Now I write to suggest that there should be a change. I am sure you will give me credit for a desire to do the best I can for both the poor dear girls. I did think that this might be best done by letting Ayala come to us. I now think that Lucy would do better with her cousins, and that Ayala would be more attractive without the young people around her.

'When I see you I will tell you everything. There has been no great fault. She has spoken a word or two to me which had been better unsaid, but I am well convinced that it has come from hot temper and not from a bad heart. Perhaps I had better tell you the truth. Tom has admired her. She has behaved very well; but she could not bear to be spoken to, and so there have been unpleasantnesses. And the girls certainly have not got on well together. Sir Thomas quite agrees with me that if you will consent there had better be a change.

'I will not write to dear Lucy herself because you and Margaret can explain it all so much better,—if you will consent to our plan. Ayala also will write to her sister. But pray tell her from me that I will love her very dearly if she will come to me. And indeed I have loved Ayala almost as though she were my own, only we have not been quite able to hit it off together.

'Of course neither has Sir Thomas nor have I any idea of escaping from a responsibility. I should be quite unhappy if I did not have one of poor dear Egbert's girls with me. Only I do think that Lucy would be the best for us; and Ayala thinks so too. I should be quite unhappy if I were doing this in opposition to Ayala.

'We shall be in England almost as soon as this letter, and I should be so glad if this could be decided at once. If a thing like this is to be done it is so much better for all parties that it should be done quickly. Pray give my best love to Margaret, and tell her that Ayala shall bring everything with her that she wants.

'Your most affectionate sister,

'EMMELINE TRINGLE.'

The letter, though it was much longer than her uncle's, going into details, such as that of Tom's unfortunate passion for his cousin, had less effect upon Lucy, as it did not speak with so much authority as that from Sir Thomas. What Sir Thomas said would surely be done; whereas Aunt Emmeline was only a woman, and her letter, unsupported, might not have carried conviction. But, if Sir Thomas wished it, surely it must be done. Then, at last, came Ayala's letter;—

'Rome, Thursday.

'DEAREST, DEAREST LUCY,

'Oh, I have such things to write to you! Aunt Emmeline has told it all to Uncle Reginald. You are to come and be the princess, and I am to go and be the milkmaid at home. I am quite content that it should be so because I know that it will be the best. You ought to be a princess and I ought to be a milkmaid.

' It has been coming almost ever since the first day that I came among them,—since I told Augusta to go upstairs for the scrap-book. I felt from the very moment in which the words were uttered that I had gone and done for myself. But I am not a bit sorry, as you will come in my place. Augusta will very soon be gone now, and Aunt Emmeline is not bad at all if you will only not contradict her. I always contradicted her, and I know that I have been a fool. But I am not a bit sorry, as you are to come instead of me.

' But it is not only about Augusta and Aunt Emmeline. There has been that oaf Tom. Poor Tom! I do believe that he is the most good-natured fellow alive. And if he had not so many chains I should not dislike him so very much. But he will go on saying horrible things to me. And then he wrote me a letter! Oh dear! I took the letter to Aunt Emmeline, and that made the quarrel. She said that I had—encouraged him! Oh, Lucy, if you will think of that! I was so angry that I said ever so much to her,—till she sent me out of the room. She had no business to say that I encouraged him. It was shameful! But she has never forgiven me, because I scolded her. So they have decided among them that I am to be sent away, and that you are to come in my place.

' My own darling Lucy, it will be ever so much better. I know that you are not happy in Kingsbury Crescent, and that I shall bear it very much better. I can sit still and mend sheets.' Poor Ayala, how little she knew herself! ' And you will make a beautiful grand lady, quiescent and dignified as a grand lady ought to be. At any rate it would be impossible that I should remain here. Tom is bad enough, but to be told that I encourage him is more than I can bear.

' I shall see you very soon, but I cannot help writing and telling it to you all. Give my love to Aunt Dosett. If she will consent to receive me I will endeavour to be good to her. In the meantime good-bye.

'Your most affectionate sister,
'AYALA.'

When Lucy had completed the reading of the letters she sat for a considerable time wrapped in thought. There was, in truth, very much that required thinking. It was proposed that the whole tenour of her life should be changed, and changed in a direction which would certainly suit her taste. She had acknowledged to herself that she had hated the comparative poverty of her Uncle Dosett's life, hating herself in that she was compelled to make such acknowledgment. But there had been more than the poverty which had been distasteful to her,—a something which she had been able to tell herself that she might be justified in hating without shame. There had been to her an absence of intellectual charm in the habits and manners of Kingsbury Crescent which she had regarded as unfortunate and depressing. There had been no thought of art delights. No one read poetry. No one heard music. No one looked at pictures. A sheet to be darned was the one thing of greatest importance. The due development of a leg of mutton, the stretching of a pound of butter, the best way of repressing the washerwoman's bills,— these had been the matters of interest. And they had not been made the less irritating to her by her aunt's extreme goodness in the matter. The leg of mutton was to be developed in the absence of her uncle,—if possible without his knowledge. He was to have his run of clean linen. Lucy did not grudge him anything, but was sickened by that partnership in economy which was established between her and her aunt. Undoubtedly from time to time she had thought of the luxuries which had been thrown in Ayala's way. There had been a regret,—not that Ayala should have them but that she should have missed them. Money she declared that she despised; —but the easy luxury of the bijou was sweet to her memory.

Now it was suggested to her suddenly that she was to exchange the poverty for the luxury, and to return to a mode of life in which her mind might be devoted

A.A.—6

to things of beauty. The very scenery of Glenbogie,
—what a charm it would have for her! Judging from
her uncle's manner, as well as she could during that
moment in which he handed to her the letter, she
imagined that he intended to make no great objection. Her aunt disliked her. She was sure that her
aunt disliked her in spite of the partnership. Only
that there was one other view of the case—how
happy might the transfer be. Her uncle was always
gentle to her, but there could hardly as yet have
grown up any strong affection for her. To him she was
grateful, but she could not tell herself that to part
from him would be a pang. There was, however,
another view of the case.

Ayala! How would it be with Ayala! Would
Ayala like the partnership and the economies?
Would Ayala be cheerful as she sat opposite to her
aunt for four hours at a time! Ayala had said that she
could sit still and mend sheets, but was it not manifest enough that Ayala knew nothing of the life of
which she was speaking? And would she, Lucy, be
able to enjoy the glories of Glenbogie while she
thought that Ayala was eating out her heart in the
sad companionship of Kingsbury Crescent? For
above an hour she sat and thought; but of one aspect
which the affair bore she did not think. She did not
reflect that she and Ayala were in the hands of Fate,
and that they must both do as their elders should
require of them.

At last there came a knock at the door, and her
aunt entered. She would sooner that it should have
been her uncle: but there was no choice but that the
matter should be now discussed with the woman
whom she did not love,—this matter that was so
dreadful to herself in all its bearings, and so dreadful
to one for whom she would willingly sacrifice herself
if it were possible! She did not know what she could
say to create sympathy with Aunt Dosett. 'Lucy,'
said Aunt Dosett, 'this is a very serious proposal.'

'Very serious,' said Lucy, sternly.

'I have not read the letters, but your uncle has told me about it.' Then Lucy handed her the two letters, keeping that from Ayala to herself, and she sat perfectly still while her aunt read them both slowly. 'Your Aunt Emmeline is certainly in earnest,' said Mrs. Dosett.

'Aunt Emmeline is very good-natured, and perhaps she will change her mind if we tell her that we wish it.'

'But Sir Thomas has agreed to it.'

'I am sure my uncle will give way if Aunt Emmeline will ask him. He says he has no complaint to make against Ayala. I think it is Augusta, and Augusta will be married, and will go away very soon.'

Then there came a change, a visible change, over the countenance of Aunt Dosett, and a softening of the voice,—so that she looked and spoke as Lucy had not seen or heard her before. There are people apparently so hard, so ungenial, so unsympathetic, that they who only half know them expect no trait of tenderness, think that features so little alluring cannot be compatible with softness. Lucy had acknowledged her Aunt Dosett to be good, but believed her to be incapable of being touched. But a word or two had now conquered her. The girl did not want to leave her,—did not seize the first opportunity of running from her poverty to the splendour of the Tringles! 'But, Lucy,' she said, and came and placed herself nearer to Lucy on the bed.

'Ayala——,' said Lucy, sobbing.

'I will be kind to her,—perhaps kinder than I have been to you.'

'You have been kind, and I have been ungrateful. I know it. But I will do better now, Aunt Dosett. I will stay, if you will have me.'

'They are rich and powerful, and you will have to do as they direct.'

'No! Who are they that I should be made to come and go at their bidding? They cannot make me leave you.'

'But they can rid themselves of Ayala. You see what your uncle says about money for Ayala.'

'I hate money.'

'Money is a thing which none of us can afford to hate. Do you think it will not be much to your Uncle Reginald to know that you are both provided for? Already he is wretched because there will be nothing to come to you. If you go to your Aunt Emmeline, Sir Thomas will do for you as he has done for Ayala. Dear Lucy, it is not that I want to send you away.' Then for the first time Lucy put her arm round her aunt's neck. 'But it had better be as is proposed, if your aunt still wishes it, when she comes home. I and your Uncle Reginald would not do right were we to allow you to throw away the prospects that are offered you. It is natural that Lady Tringle should be anxious about her son.'

'She need not, in the least,' said Lucy, indignantly.

'But you see what they say.'

'It is his fault, not hers. Why should she be punished?'

'Because he is Fortune's favourite, and she is not. It is no good kicking against the pricks, my dear. He is his father's son and heir, and everything must give way to him.'

'But Ayala does not want him. Ayala despises him. It is too hard that she is to lose everything because a young man like that will go on making himself disagreeable. They have no right to do it after having accustomed Ayala to such a home. Don't you feel that, Aunt Dosett?'

'I do feel it.'

'However it might have been arranged at first, it ought to remain now. Even though Ayala and I are only girls, we ought not to be changed about as though we were horses. If she had done anything wrong,—but Uncle Tom says she has done nothing wrong.'

'I suppose she has spoken to her aunt disrespectfully.'

'Because her aunt told her that she had encouraged
this man. What would you have a girl say when she
is falsely accused like that? Would you say it to me
merely because some horrid man would come and
speak to me?' Then there came a slight pang of
conscience as she remembered Isadore Hamel in
Kensington Gardens. If the men were not thought
to be horrid, then perhaps the speaking might be
a sin worthy of most severe accusation.

There was nothing more said about it that night,
nor till the following afternoon, when Mr. Dosett
returned home at the usual hour from his office.
Then Lucy was closeted with him for a quarter of an
hour in the drawing-room. He had been into the
City and seen Sir Thomas. Sir Thomas had been of
opinion that it would be much better that Lady
Tringle's wishes should be obeyed. It was quite true
that he himself had no complaint to make against
Ayala, but he did think that Ayala had been pert;
and, though it might be true that Ayala had not
encouraged Tom, there was no knowing what might
grow out of such a propensity on Tom's part. And
then it could not be pleasant to Lady Tringle or to
himself that their son should be banished out of their
house. When something was hinted as to the injustice of this, Sir Thomas endeavoured to put all
that right by declaring that, if Lady Tringle's wishes
could be attended to in this matter, provision would
be made for the two girls. He certainly would not
strike Ayala's name out of his will, and as certainly
would not take Lucy under his wing as his own child
without making some provision for her. Looking at
the matter in this light he did not think that Mr.
Dosett would be justified in robbing Lucy of the
advantages which were offered to her. With this
view Mr. Dosett found himself compelled to agree,
and with these arguments he declared to Lucy that
it was her duty to submit herself to the proposed
exchange.

Early in February all the Tringle family were in

Queen's Gate, and Lucy on her first visit to the house found that everyone, including Ayala, looked upon the thing as settled. Ayala, who under these circumstances was living on affectionate terms with all the Tringles, except Tom, was quite radiant. 'I suppose I had better go to-morrow, aunt?' she said, as though it were a matter of most trivial consequence.

'In a day or two, Ayala, it will be better.'

'It shall be Monday, then. You must come over here in a cab, Lucy.'

'The carriage shall be sent, my dear.'

'But then it must go back with me, Aunt Emmeline.'

'It shall, my dear.'

'And the horses must be put up, because Lucy and I must change all our things in the drawers.' Lucy at the time was sitting in the drawing-room, and Augusta, with most affectionate confidence, was singing to her all the praises of Mr. Traffick. In this way it was settled, and the change, so greatly affect-ing the fortunes of our two sisters, was arranged.

## CHAPTER X

### AYALA AND HER AUNT MARGARET

TILL the last moment for going Ayala seemed to be childish, triumphant, and indifferent. But, till that last moment, she was never alone with Lucy. It was the presence of her aunt and cousins which sustained her in her hardihood. Tom was never there,—or so rarely as not to affect her greatly. In London he had his own lodgings, and was not encouraged to appear frequently till Ayala should have gone. But Aunt Emmeline and Gertrude were perseveringly gracious, and even Augusta had somewhat relaxed from her wrath. With them Ayala was always good-humoured, but always brave. She affected to rejoice at the change which was to be made.

She spoke of Lucy's coming and of her own going as
an unmixed blessing. This she did so effectually as to
make Aunt Emmeline declare to Sir Thomas, with
tears in her eyes, that the girl was heartless. But
when, at the moment of parting, the two girls were
together, then Ayala broke down.

They were in the room, together, which one had
occupied and the other was to occupy, and their
boxes were still upon the floor. Though less than six
months had passed since Ayala had come among the
rich things and Lucy had been among the poor,
Ayala's belongings had become much more important than her sister's. Though the Tringles had been
unpleasant they had been generous. Lucy was sitting
upon the bed, while Ayala was now moving about
the room restlessly, now clinging to her sister, and
now sobbing almost in despair. 'Of course I know,'
she said. 'What is the use of telling stories about it
any longer?'

'It is not too late yet, Ayala. If we both go to
Uncle Tom he will let us change it.'

'Why should it be changed? If I could change it
by lifting up my little finger I could not do it. Why
should it not be you as well as me? They have tried
me, and,—as Aunt Emmeline says,—I have not
suited.'

'Aunt Dosett is not ill-natured, my darling.'

'No, I dare say not. It is I that am bad. It is bad
to like pretty things and money, and to hate poor
things. Or, rather, I do not believe it is bad at all,
because it is so natural. I believe it is all a lie as to
its being wicked to love riches. I love them, whether
it is wicked or not.'

'Oh, Ayala!'

'Do not you? Don't let us be hypocritical, Lucy,
now at the last moment. Did you like the way in
which they lived in Kingsbury Crescent?'

Lucy paused before she answered. 'I like it better
than I did,' she said. 'At any rate, I would willingly
go back to Kingsbury Crescent.'

'Yes,—for my sake.'

'Indeed I would, my pet.'

'And for your sake I would rather die than stay. But what is the good of talking about it, Lucy? You and I have no voice in it, though it is all about ourselves. As you say, we are like two tame birds, who have to be moved from one cage into another just as the owner pleases. We belong either to Uncle Tom or Uncle Dosett, just as they like to settle it. Oh, Lucy, I do so wish that I were dead.'

'Ayala, that is wicked.'

'How can I help it, if I am wicked? What am I to do when I get there? What am I to say to them? How am I to live? Lucy, we shall never see each other.'

'I will come across to you constantly.'

'I meant to do so, but I didn't. They are two worlds, miles asunder. Lucy, will they let Isadore Hamel come here?' Lucy blushed and hesitated. 'I am sure he will come.'

Lucy remembered that she had given her friend her address at Queen's Gate, and felt that she would seem to have done it as though she had known that she was about to be transferred to the other uncle's house. 'It will make no difference if he does,' she said.

'Oh, I have such a dream,—such a castle-in-the-air! If I could think it might ever be so, then I should not want to die.'

'What do you dream?' But Lucy, though she asked the question, knew the dream.

'If you had a little house of your own, oh, ever so tiny; and if you and he——?'

'There is no he.'

'There might be. And, if you and he would let me have any corner for myself, then I should be happy. Then I would not want to die. You would, wouldn't you?'

'How can I talk about it, Ayala? There isn't such a thing. But yet,—but yet; oh, Ayala, do you not know that to have you with me would be better than anything?'

'No;—not better than anything;—second best. He would be best. I do so hope that he may be "he." Come in.' There was a knock at the door, and Aunt Emmeline, herself, entered the room.

'Now, my dears, the horses are standing there, and the men are coming up for the luggage. Ayala, I hope we shall see you very often. And remember that, as regards anything that is unpleasant, by-gones shall be bygones.' Then there was a crowd of farewell kisses, and in a few minutes Ayala was alone in the carriage on her road up to Kingsbury Crescent.

The thing had been done so quickly that hitherto there had hardly been time for tears. To Ayala herself the most remarkable matter in the whole affair had been Tom's persistence. He had, at last, been allowed to bring them home from Rome, there having been no other gentleman whose services were available for the occasion. He had been watched on the journey very closely, and had had no slant in his favour, as the young lady to whom he was devoted was quite as anxious to keep out of his way as had been the others of the party to separate them. But he had made occasion, more than once, sufficient to express his intention. 'I don't mean to give you up, you know,' he had said to her. 'When I say a thing I mean it. I am not going to be put off by my mother. And as for the governor he would not say a word against it if he thought we were both in earnest.'

'But I ain't in earnest,' said Ayala; 'or rather, I am very much in earnest.'

'So am I. That's all I've got to say just at present.' From this there grew up within her mind a certain respect for the 'lout,' which, however, made him more disagreeable to her than he might have been had he been less persistent.

It was late in the afternoon, not much before dinner, when Ayala reached the house in Kingsbury Crescent. Hitherto she had known almost nothing

of her Aunt Dosett, and had never been intimate
even with her uncle. They, of course, had heard
much of her, and had been led to suppose that she
was much less tractable than the simple Lucy. This
feeling had been so strong that Mr. Dosett himself
would hardly have been led to sanction the change
had it not been for that promise from Sir Thomas
that he would not withdraw the provision he had
made for Ayala, and would do as much for Lucy if
Lucy should become an inmate of his family. Mrs.
Dosett had certainly been glad to welcome any
change, when a change was proposed to her. There
had grown up something of affection at the last
moment, but up to that time she had certainly disliked her niece. Lucy had appeared to her to be at
first idle and then sullen. The girl had seemed to
affect a higher nature than her own, and had been
wilfully indifferent to the little things which had
given to her life whatever interest it possessed.
Lucy's silence had been a reproach to her, though
she herself had been able to do so little to abolish
the silence. Perhaps Ayala might be better.

But they were both afraid of Ayala,—as they had
not been afraid of Lucy before her arrival. They
made more of preparation for her in their own minds,
and, as to their own conduct, Mr. Dosett was there
himself to receive her, and was conscious in doing so
that there had been something of failure in their
intercourse with Lucy. Lucy had been allowed to
come in without preparation, with an expectation
that she would fall easily into her place, and there
had been failure. There had been no regular consultation as to this new coming, but both Mr. and
Mrs. Dosett were conscious of an intended effort.

Lady Tringle and Mr. Dosett had always been
Aunt Emmeline and Uncle Reginald, by reason of
the nearness of their relationship. Circumstances of
closer intercourse had caused Sir Thomas to be
Uncle Tom. But Mrs. Dosett had never become more
than Aunt Dosett to either of the girls. This in itself

had been matter almost of soreness to her, and she
had intended to ask Lucy to adopt the more endearing form of her Christian name; but there had been
so little endearment between them that the moment
for doing so had never come. She was thinking of all
this up in her own room, preparatory to the reception
of this other girl, while Mr. Dosett was bidding her
welcome to Kingsbury Crescent in the drawing-room
below.

Ayala had been dissolved in tears during the drive
round by Kensington to Bayswater, and was hardly
able to repress her sobs as she entered the house.
'My dear,' said the uncle, 'we will do all that we can
to make you happy here.'

'I am sure you will; but—but—it is so sad coming
away from Lucy.'

'Lucy I am sure will be happy with her cousins.'
If Lucy's happiness were made to depend on her
cousins, thought Ayala, it would not be well assured.
'And my sister Emmeline is always good-natured.'

'Aunt Emmeline is very good, only——'

'Only what?'

'I don't know. But it is such a sudden change,
Uncle Reginald.'

'Yes, it is a very great change, my dear. They are
very rich and we are poor enough. I should hardly
have consented to this, for your sake, but that there
are reasons which will make it better for you both.'

'As to that,' said Ayala, stoutly, 'I had to come
away. I didn't suit.'

'You shall suit us, my dear.'

'I hope so. I will try. I know more now than I did
then. I thought I was to be Augusta's equal.'

'We shall all be equal here.'

'People ought to be equal, I think,—except old
people and young people. I will do whatever you and
my aunt tell me. There are no young people here, so
there won't be any trouble of that kind.'

'There will be no other young person, certainly.
You shall go upstairs now and see your aunt.'

Then there was the interview upstairs, which consisted chiefly in promises and kisses, and Ayala was left alone to unpack her boxes and prepare for dinner. Before she began her operations she sat still for a few moments, and with an effort collected her energies and made her resolution. She had said to Lucy in her passion that she would that she were dead. That that should have been wicked was not matter of much concern to her. But she acknowledged to herself that it had been weak and foolish. There was her life before her, and she would still endeavour to be happy though there had been so much to distress her. She had flung away wealth. She was determined to fling it away still when it should present itself to her in the shape of her cousin Tom. But she had her dreams,—her day-dreams,—those castles in the air* which it had been the delight of her life to construct, and in the building of which her hours had never run heavy with her. Isadore Hamel would, of course, come again, and would, of course, marry Lucy, and then there would be a home for her after her own heart. With Isadore as her brother, and her own Lucy close to her, she would not feel the want of riches and of luxury. If there were only some intellectual charm in her life, some touch of art, some devotion to things beautiful, then she could do without gold and silver and costly raiment. Of course, Isadore would come; and then—then—in the far distance, something else would come, something of which in her castle-building she had not yet developed the form, of which she did not yet know the bearing, or the manner of its beauty, or the music of its voice; but as to which she was very sure that its form would be beautiful and its voice full of music. It can hardly be said that this something was the centre of her dreams, or the foundation of her castles. It was the extreme point of perfection at which she would arrive at last, when her thoughts had become sublimated by the intensity of her thinking. It was the tower of the castle from which she could look down

upon the inferior world below,—the last point of the
dream in arranging which she would all but escape
from earth to heaven,—when in the moment of her
escape the cruel waking back into the world would
come upon her. But this she knew,—that this something, whatever might be its form or whatever its
voice, would be exactly the opposite of Tom Tringle.

She had fallen away from her resolution to her
dreams for a time, when suddenly she jumped up and
began her work with immense energy. Open went
one box after another, and in five minutes the room
was strewed with her possessions. The modest set of
drawers which was to supply all her wants was filled
with immediate haste. Things were deposited in whatever nooks might be found, and every corner was
utilised. Her character for tidiness had never stood
high. At the bijou Lucy, or her mother, or the
favourite maid, had always been at hand to make
good her deficiencies with a reproach which had
never gone beyond a smile or a kiss. At Glenbogie
and even on the journey there had been attendant
lady's maids. But here she was all alone.

Everything was still in confusion when she was
called to dinner. As she went down she recalled to
herself her second resolution. She would be good;—
whereby she intimated to herself that she would endeavour to do what might be pleasing to her Aunt
Dosett. She had little doubt as to her uncle. But she
was aware that there had been differences between
her aunt and Lucy. If Lucy had found it difficult to
be good how great would be the struggle required
from her!

She sat herself down at table a little nearer to her
aunt than her uncle, because it was specially her
aunt whom she wished to win, and after a few minutes
she put out her little soft hand and touched that of
Mrs. Dosett. 'My dear,' said that lady. 'I hope you
will be happy.'

'I am determined to be happy,' said Ayala, 'if you
will let me love you.'

Mrs. Dosett was not beautiful, nor was she romantic. In appearance she was the very reverse of Ayala. The cares of the world, the looking after shillings and their results, had given her that look of commonplace insignificance which is so frequent and so unattractive among middle-aged women upon whom the world leans heavily. But there was a tender corner in her heart which was still green, and from which a little rill of sweet water could be made to flow when it was touched aright. On this occasion a tear came to her eye as she pressed her niece's hand; but she said nothing. She was sure, however, that she would love Ayala much better than she had been able to love Lucy.

'What would you like me to do?' asked Ayala, when her aunt accompanied her that night to her bed-room.

'To do, my dear? What do you generally do?'

'Nothing. I read a little and draw a little, but I do nothing useful. I mean it to be different now.'

'You shall do as you please, Ayala.'

'Oh, but I mean it. And you must tell me. Of course things have to be different.'

'We are not rich like your uncle and aunt Tringle.'

'Perhaps it is better not to be rich, so that one may have something to do. But I want you to tell me as though you really cared for me.'

'I will care for you,' said Aunt Dosett, sobbing.

'Then first begin by telling me what to do. I will try and do it. Of course I have thought about it, coming away from all manner of rich things; and I have determined that it shall not make me unhappy. I will rise above it. I will begin to-morrow and do anything if you will tell me.' Then Aunt Dosett took her in her arms and kissed her, and declared that on the morrow they would begin their work together in perfect confidence and love with each other.

'I think she will do better than Lucy,' said Mrs. Dosett to her husband that night.

'Lucy was a dear girl too,' said Uncle Reginald.

'Oh, yes;—quite so. I don't mean to say a word against Lucy; but I think that I can do better with Ayala. She will be more diligent.' Uncle Reginald said nothing to this, but he could not but think that of the two Lucy would be the one most likely to devote herself to hard work.

On the next morning Ayala went out with her aunt on the round to the shopkeepers, and listened with profound attention to the domestic instructions which were given to her on the occasion. When she came home she knew much of which she had known nothing before. What was the price of mutton, and how much mutton she was expected as one of the family to eat per week; what were the necessities of the house in bread and butter, how far a pint of milk might be stretched,—with a proper understanding that her Uncle Reginald as head of the family was to be subjected to no limits. And before their return from that walk,—on the first morning of Ayala's sojourn,—Ayala had undertaken always to call Mrs. Dosett Aunt Margaret for the future.

## CHAPTER XI

### TOM TRINGLE COMES TO THE CRESCENT

DURING the next three months, up to the end of the winter and through the early spring, things went on without any change either in Queen's Gate or Kingsbury Crescent. The sisters saw each other occasionally, but not as frequently as either of them had intended. Lucy was not encouraged in the use of cabs, nor was the carriage lent to her often for the purpose of going to the Crescent. The reader may remember that she had been in the habit of walking alone in Kensington Gardens, and a walk across Kensington Gardens would carry her the greater part of the distance to Kingsbury Crescent. But Lucy, in her new circumstances, was not advised,—perhaps, I may say, was not allowed,—to walk alone. Lady Tringle, being a lady of rank and wealth, was afraid,

or pretended to be afraid, of the lions. Poor Ayala
was really afraid of the lions. Thus it came to pass
that the intercourse was not frequent. In her daily
life Lucy was quiet and obedient. She did not run
counter to Augusta, whose approaching nuptials
gave her that predominance in the house which is
always accorded to young ladies in her recognised
position. Gertrude was at this time a subject of
trouble at Queen's Gate. Sir Thomas had not been
got to approve of Mr. Frank Houston, and Gertrude
had positively refused to give him up. Sir Thomas
was, indeed, considerably troubled by his children.
There had been a period of disagreeable obstinacy
even with Augusta before Mr. Traffick had been
taken into the bosom of the family. Now Gertrude
had her own ideas, and so also had Tom. Tom had
become quite a trouble. Sir Thomas and Lady
Tringle, together, had determined that Tom must be
weaned; by which they meant that he must be cured
of his love. But Tom had altogether refused to be
weaned. Mr. Dosett had been requested to deny him
admittance to the house in Kingsbury Crescent, and
as this request had been fully endorsed by Ayala
herself orders had been given to the effect to the
parlour-maid. Tom had called more than once, and
had been unable to obtain access to his beloved. But
yet he resolutely refused to be weaned. He told his
father to his face that he intended to marry Ayala,
and abused his mother roundly when she attempted
to interfere. The whole family was astounded by his
perseverance, so that there had already sprung up
an idea in the minds of some among the Tringles that
he would be successful at last. Augusta was very
firm, declaring that Ayala was a viper. But Sir
Thomas, himself, began to inquire, within his own
bosom, whether Tom should not be allowed to settle
down in the manner desired by himself. In no consultation held at Queen's Gate on the subject was
there the slightest expression of an opinion that Tom
might be denied the opportunity of settling down as

he wished through any unwillingness on the part of Ayala.

When things were in this position, Tom sought an interview one morning with his father in Lombard Street. They rarely saw each other at the office, each having his own peculiar branch of business. Sir Thomas manipulated his millions in a little back room of his own, while Tom, dealing probably with limited thousands, made himself useful in an outer room. They never went to, or left, the office together, but Sir Thomas always took care to know that his son was or was not on the premises. 'I want to say a word or two, Sir, about—about the little affair of mine,' said Tom.

'What affair?' said Sir Thomas, looking up from his millions.

'I think I should like to—marry.'

'The best thing you can do, my boy; only it depends upon who the young lady may be.'

'My mind is made up about that, Sir; I mean to marry my cousin. I don't see why a young man isn't to choose for himself.' Then Sir Thomas preached his sermon, but preached it in the manner which men are wont to use when they know that they are preaching in vain. There is a tone of refusal, which, though the words used may be manifestly enough words of denial, is in itself indicative of assent. Sir Thomas ended the conference by taking a week to think over the matter, and when the week was over gave way. He was still inclined to think that marriages with cousins had better be avoided; but he gave way, and at last promised that if Tom and Ayala were of one mind an income should be forthcoming.

For the carrying out of this purpose it was necessary that the door of Uncle Dosett's house should be unlocked, and with the object of turning the key Sir Thomas himself called at the Admiralty. 'I find my boy is quite in earnest about this,' he said to the Admiralty clerk.

'Oh; indeed.'

'I can't say I quite like it myself.' Mr. Dosett could only shake his head. 'Cousins had better be cousins, and nothing more.'

'And then you would probably expect him to get money?'

'Not at all,' said Sir Thomas, proudly. 'I have got money enough for them both. It isn't an affair of money. To make a long story short, I have given my consent; and, therefore, if you do not mind, I shall be glad if you will allow Tom to call at the Crescent. Of course, you may have your own views; but I don't suppose you can hope to do better for the girl. Cousins do marry, you know, very often.' Mr. Dosett could only say that he could not expect to do anything for the girl nearly so good, and that, as far as he was concerned, his nephew Tom should be made quite welcome at Kingsbury Crescent. It was not, he added, in his power to answer for Ayala. As to this, Sir Thomas did not seem to have any doubts. The good things of the world, which it was in his power to offer, were so good, that it was hardly probable that a young lady in Ayala's position should refuse them.

'My dear,' said Aunt Margaret, the next morning, speaking in her most suasive tone, 'your Cousin Tom is to be allowed to call here.'

'Tom Tringle?'

'Yes, my dear. Sir Thomas has consented.'

'Then he had better not,' said Ayala, bristling up in hot anger. 'Uncle Tom has got nothing to do with it, either in refusing or consenting. I won't see him.'

'I think you must see him if he calls.'

'But I don't want. Oh, Aunt Margaret, pray make him not come. I don't like him a bit. We are doing so very well. Are we not, Aunt Margaret?'

'Certainly, my dear, we are doing very well;—at least, I hope so. But you are old enough now to understand that this is a very serious matter.'

'Of course it is serious,' said Ayala, who certainly

was not guilty of the fault of making light of her
future life. Those dreams of hers, in which were contained all her hopes and all her aspirations, were very
serious to her. This was so much the case that she
had by no means thought of her Cousin Tom in a
light spirit, as though he were a matter of no moment
to her. He was to her just what the Beast must have
been to the Beauty, when the Beast first began to be
in love. But her safety had consisted in the fact that
no one had approved of the Beast being in love with
her. Now she could understand that all the horrors
of oppression might fall upon her. Of course it was
serious; but not the less was she resolved that
nothing should induce her to marry the Beast.

'I think you ought to see him when he comes, and
to remember how different it will be when he comes
with the approval of his father. It is, of course, saying
that they are ready to welcome you as their daughter.'

'I don't want to be anybody's daughter.'

'But, Ayala, there are so many things to be thought
of. Here is a young man who is able to give you not
only every comfort but great opulence.'

'I don't want to be opulent.'

'And he will be a baronet.'

'I don't care about baronets, Aunt Margaret.'

'And you will have a house of your own in which
you may be of service to your sister.'

'I had rather she should have a house.'

'But Tom is not in love with Lucy.'

'He is such a lout! Aunt Margaret, I won't have
anything to say to him. I would a great deal sooner
die. Uncle Tom has no right to send him here. They
have got rid of me, and I am very glad of it; but it
isn't fair that he should come after me now that I'm
gone away. Couldn't Uncle Reginald tell him to stay
away?'

A great deal more was said, but nothing that was
said had the slightest effect on Ayala. When she was
told of her dependent position, and of the splendour
of the prospects offered, she declared that she would

rather go into the poor-house than marry her cousin. When she was told that Tom was good-natured, honest, and true, she declared that good-nature, honesty, and truth had nothing to do with it. When she was asked what it was that she looked forward to in the world she could merely sob and say that there was nothing. She could not tell even her sister Lucy of those dreams and castles. How, then, could she explain them to her Aunt Margaret? How could she make her aunt understand that there could be no place in her heart for Tom Tringle seeing that it was to be kept in reserve for some angel of light who would surely make his appearance in due season,—but who must still be there, present to her as her Angel of Light, even should he never show himself in the flesh. How vain it was to talk of Tom Tringle to her, when she had so visible before her eyes that Angel of Light with whom she was compelled to compare him!

But, though she could not be brought to say that she would listen patiently to his story, she was nevertheless made to understand that she must see him when he came to her. Aunt Margaret was very full on that subject. A young man who was approved of by the young lady's friends, and who had means at command, was, in Mrs. Dosett's opinion, entitled to a hearing. How otherwise were properly authorised marriages to be made up and arranged? When this was going on there was in some slight degree a diminished sympathy between Ayala and her aunt. Ayala still continued her household duties,—over which, in the privacy of her own room, she groaned sadly; but she continued them in silence. Her aunt, upon whom she had counted, was, she thought, turning against her. Mrs. Dosett, on the other hand, declared to herself that the girl was romantic and silly. Husbands with every immediate comfort, and a prospect of almost unlimited wealth, are not to be found under every hedge. What right could a girl so dependent as Ayala have to refuse an eligible match?

She therefore in this way became an advocate on behalf of Tom,—as did also Uncle Reginald, more mildly. Uncle Reginald merely remarked that Tom was attending to his business, which was a great thing in a young man. It was not much, but it showed Ayala that in this matter her uncle was her enemy. In this, her terrible crisis, she had not a friend, unless it might be Lucy.

Then a day was fixed on which Tom was to come, which made the matter more terrible by anticipation. 'What can be the good?' Ayala said to her aunt when the hour named for the interview was told her, 'as I can tell him everything just as well without his coming at all.' But all that had been settled. Aunt Margaret had repeated over and over again that such an excellent young man as Tom, with such admirable intentions, was entitled to a hearing from any young lady. In reply to this Ayala simply made a grimace, which was intended to signify the utter contempt in which she held her cousin Tom with all his wealth.

Tom Tringle, in spite of his rings and a certain dash of vulgarity, which was, perhaps, not altogether his own fault, was not a bad fellow. Having taken it into his heart that he was very much in love he was very much in love. He pictured to himself a happiness of a wholesome cleanly kind. To have the girl as his own, to caress her and foster her, and expend himself in making her happy; to exalt her, so as to have it acknowledged that she was, at any rate, as important as Augusta; to learn something from her, so that he, too, might become romantic, and in some degree poetical;—all this had come home to him in a not ignoble manner. But it had not come home to him that Ayala might probably refuse him. Hitherto Ayala had been very persistent in her refusals; but then hitherto there had existed the opposition of all the family. Now he had overcome that, and he felt therefore that he was entitled to ask and to receive.

On the day fixed, and at the hour fixed, he came in the plenitude of all his rings. Poor Tom! It was a pity that he should have had no one to advise him as to his apparel. Ayala hated his jewelry. She was not quite distinct in her mind as to the raiment which would be worn by the Angel of Light when he should come, but she was sure that he would not be chiefly conspicuous for heavy gilding; and Tom, moreover, had a waistcoat which would of itself have been suicidal. Such as he was, however, he was shown up into the drawing-room, where he found Ayala alone. It was certainly a misfortune to him that no preliminary conversation was possible. Ayala had been instructed to be there with the express object of listening to an offer of marriage. The work had to be done,—and should be done; but it would not admit of other ordinary courtesies. She was very angry with him, and she looked her anger. Why should she be subjected to this terrible annoyance? He had sense enough to perceive that there was no place for preliminary courtesy, and therefore rushed away at once to the matter in hand. 'Ayala!' he exclaimed, coming and standing before her as she sat upon the sofa.

'Tom!' she said, looking boldly up into his face.

'Ayala, I love you better than anything else in the world.'

'But what's the good of it?'

'Of course it was different when I told you so before. I meant to stick to it, and I was determined that the governor should give way. But you couldn't know that. Mother and the girls were all against us.'

'They weren't against me,' said Ayala.

'They were against our being married, and so they squeezed you out as it were. That is why you have been sent to this place. But they understand me now, and know what I am about. They have all given their consent, and the governor has promised to be liberal. When he says a thing he'll do it. There will be lots of money.'

'I don't care a bit about money,' said Ayala,
fiercely.

'No more do I,—except only that it is comfortable.
It wouldn't do to marry without money,—would it?'

'It would do very well if anybody cared for anybody.' The Angel of Light generally appeared 'in
formâ pauperis '* though there was always about him
a tinge of bright azure which was hardly compatible
with the draggle-tailed hue of everyday poverty.

'But an income is a good thing, and the governor
will come down like a brick.'

'The governor has nothing to do with it. I told
you before that it is all nonsense. If you will only go
away and say nothing about it I shall always think
you very good-natured.'

'But I won't go away,' said Tom speaking out
boldly. 'I mean to stick to it. Ayala, I don't believe
you understand that I am thoroughly in earnest.'

'Why shouldn't I be in earnest, too?'

'But I love you, Ayala. I have set my heart upon
it. You don't know how well I love you. I have
quite made up my mind about it.'

'And I have made up my mind.'

'But, Ayala——' Now the tenour of his face changed,
and something of the look of a despairing lover took
the place of that offensive triumph which had at first
sat upon his brow. 'I don't suppose you care for any
other fellow yet.'

There was the Angel of Light. But even though she
might be most anxious to explain to him that his suit
was altogether impracticable she could say nothing to
him about the angel. Though she was sure that the
angel would come, she was not certain that she would
ever give herself altogether even to the angel. The
celestial castle which was ever being built in her
imagination was as yet very much complicated. But
had it been ever so clear it would have been quite
impossible to explain anything of this to her cousin
Tom. 'That has nothing to do with it,' she said.

'If you knew how I love you!' This came from

him with a sob, and as he sobbed he went down before
her on his knees.

'Don't be a fool, Tom,—pray don't. If you won't
get up I shall go away. I must go away. I have
heard all that there is to hear. I told them that there
is no use in your coming.'

'Ayala!' with this there were veritable sobs.

'Then why don't you give it up and let us be good
friends?'

'I can't give it up. I won't give it up. When a
fellow means it as I do he never gives it up. Nothing
on earth shall make me give it up. Ayala, you've got
to do it, and so I tell you.'

'Nobody can make me,' said Ayala, nodding her
head, but somewhat tamed by the unexpected passion of the young man.

'Then you won't say one kind word to me?'

'I can't say anything kinder.'

'Very well. Then I shall go away and come again
constantly till you do. I mean to have you. When
you come to know how very much I love you I do
think you will give way at last.' With that he picked
himself up from the ground and hurried out of the
house without saying another word.


## CHAPTER XII

### 'WOULD YOU?'

THE scene described in the last chapter took place
in March. For three days afterwards there was
quiescence in Kingsbury Crescent. Then there came
a letter from Tom to Ayala, very pressing, full of love
and resolution, offering to wait any time,—even a
month,—if she wished it, but still persisting in his
declared intention of marrying her sooner or later;—
not by any means a bad letter had there not been
about it a little touch of bombast which made it
odious to Ayala's sensitive appreciation. To this
Ayala wrote a reply in the following words:

'When I tell you that I won't, you oughtn't to go on. It isn't manly. 'AYALA.'

'Pray do not write again for I shall never answer another.'

Of this she said nothing to Mrs. Dosett, though the arrival of Tom's letter must have been known to that lady. And she posted her own epistle without a word as to what she was doing.

She wrote again and again to Lucy imploring her sister to come to her, urging that as circumstances now were she could not show herself at the house in Queen's Gate. To these Lucy always replied; but she did not reply by coming, and hardly made it intelligible why she did not come. Aunt Emmeline hoped, she said, that Ayala would very soon be able to be at Queen's Gate. Then there was a difficulty about the carriage. No one would walk across with her except Tom; and walking by herself was forbidden. Aunt Emmeline did not like cabs. Then there came a third or fourth letter, in which Lucy was more explanatory, but yet not sufficiently so. During the Easter recess, which would take place in the middle of April, Augusta and Mr. Traffick would be married. The happy couple were to be blessed with a divided honeymoon. The interval between Easter and Whitsuntide would require Mr. Traffick's presence in the House, and the bride with her bridegroom were to return to Queen's Gate. Then they would depart again for the second holidays, and when they were so gone Aunt Emmeline hoped that Ayala would come to them for a visit. 'They quite understand,' said Lucy, 'that it will not do to have you and Augusta together.'

This was not at all what Ayala wanted. 'It won't at all do to have me and him together,' said Ayala to herself, alluding of course to Tom Tringle. But why did not Lucy come over to her? Lucy, who knew so well that her sister did not want to see any one of the Tringles, who must have been sure that any visit to

Queen's Gate must have been impossible, ought to
have come to her. To whom else could she say a word
in her trouble? It was thus that Ayala argued with
herself, declaring to herself that she must soon die
in her misery,—unless indeed that angel of light might
come to her assistance very quickly.

But Lucy had troubles of her own in reference to
the family at Queen's Gate, which did, in fact, make
it almost impossible to visit her sister for some weeks.
Sir Thomas had given an unwilling but a frank consent to his son's marriage,—and then expected
simply to be told that it would take place at such and
such a time, when money would be required. Lady
Tringle had given her consent,—but not quite frankly.
She still would have fain have forbidden the banns, had
any power of forbidding remained in her hands.
Augusta was still hot against the marriage, and still
resolute to prevent it. That proposed journey upstairs after the scrap-book at Glenbogie, that real
journey up to the top of St. Peter's, still rankled in
her heart. That Tom should make Ayala a future
baronet's wife; that Tom should endow Ayala with
the greatest share of the Tringle wealth; that Ayala
should become powerful in Queen's Gate, and domi-
nant probably at Merle Park and Glenbogie,—was
wormwood to her. She was conscious that Ayala was
pretty and witty, though she could affect to despise
the wit and the prettiness. By instigating her mother,
and by inducing Mr. Traffick to interfere when Mr.
Traffick should be a member of the family, she
thought that she might prevail. With her mother
she did in part prevail. Her future husband was at
present too much engaged with Supply and Demand
to be able to give his thoughts to Tom's affairs. But
there would soon be a time when he naturally would
be compelled to divide his thoughts. Then there was
Gertrude. Gertrude's own affairs had not as yet been
smiled upon, and the want of smiles she attributed
very much to Augusta. Why should Augusta have
her way and not she, Gertrude, nor her brother Tom?

She therefore leagued herself with Tom, and declared herself quite prepared to receive Ayala into the house. In this way the family was very much divided.

When Lucy first made her petition for the carriage, expressing her desire to see Ayala, both her uncle and her aunt were in the room. Objection was made,—some frivolous objection,—by Lady Tringle, who did not in truth care to maintain much connection between Queen's Gate and the Crescent. Then Sir Thomas, in his burly authoritative way, had said that Ayala had better come to them. That same evening he had settled or intended to settle it with his wife. Let Ayala come as soon as the Trafficks,—as they then would be,—should have gone. To this Lady Tringle had assented, knowing more than her husband as to Ayala's feelings, and thinking that in this way a breach might be made between them. Ayala had been a great trouble to her, and she was beginning to be almost sick of the Dormer connection altogether. It was thus that Lucy was hindered from seeing her sister for six weeks after that first formal declaration of his love made by Tom to Ayala. Tom had still persevered and had forced his way more than once into Ayala's presence, but Ayala's answers had been always the same. 'It's a great shame, and you have no right to treat me in this way.'

Then came the Traffick marriage with great éclat. There were no less than four Traffick bridesmaids, all of them no doubt noble, but none of them very young, and Gertrude and Lucy were bridesmaids,—and two of Augusta's friends. Ayala, of course, was not of the party. Tom was gorgeous in his apparel, not in the least depressed by his numerous repulses, quite confident of ultimate success, and proud of his position as a lover with so beautiful a girl. He talked of his affairs to all his friends, and seemed to think that even on this wedding-day his part was as conspicuous as that of his sister, because of his affair with his beautiful cousin. 'Augusta doesn't hit it off

with her,' he said to one of his friends, who asked why
Ayala was not at the wedding,—'Augusta is the
biggest fool out, you know. She's proud of her husband because he's the son of a lord. I wouldn't
change Ayala for the daughter of any duchess in
Europe;'—thus showing that he regarded Ayala
as being almost his own already. Lord Boardotrade
was there, making a semi-jocose speech, quite in the
approved way for a cognate paterfamilias. Perhaps
there was something of a thorn in this to Sir Thomas,
as it had become apparent at last that Mr. Traffick
himself did not purpose to add anything from his
own resources to the income on which he intended to
live with his wife. Lord Boardotrade had been
obliged to do so much for his eldest son that there
appeared to be nothing left for the member for Port
Glasgow. Sir Thomas was prepared with his £120,000,
and did not perhaps mind this very much. But a
man, when he pays his money, likes to have some
return for it, and he did not quite like the tone with
which the old nobleman, not possessed of very old
standing in the peerage, seemed to imply that he,
like a noble old Providence, had enveloped the whole
Tringle family in the mantle of his noble blood.* He
combined the jocose and the paternal in the manner
appropriate to such occasions; but there did run
through Sir Thomas's mind as he heard him an idea
that £120,000 was a sufficient sum to pay, and that it
might be necessary to make Mr. Traffick understand
that out of the income thenceforth coming he must
provide a house for himself and his wife. It had been
already arranged that he was to return to Queen's
Gate with his wife for the period between Easter and
Whitsuntide. It had lately,—quite lately,—been
hinted to Sir Thomas that the married pair would
run up again after the second holidays. Mr. Septimus
Traffick had once spoken of Glenbogie as almost all
his own, and Augusta had, in her father's hearing,
said a word intended to be very affectionate about
'dear Merle Park.' Sir Thomas was a father all over,

with all a father's feelings; but even a father does not
like to be done. Mr. Traffick, no doubt, was a member of Parliament and son of a peer;—but there
might be a question whether even Mr. Traffick had
not been purchased at quite his full value.

Nevertheless the marriage was pronounced to have
been a success. Immediately after it,—early, indeed,
on the following morning,—Sir Thomas inquired
when Ayala was coming to Queen's Gate. 'Is it
necessary that she should come quite at present?'
asked Lady Tringle.

'I thought it was all settled,' said Sir Thomas,
angrily. This had been said in the privacy of his own
dressing-room, but downstairs at the breakfast-table
in the presence of Gertrude and Lucy, he returned to
the subject. Tom, who did not live in the house, was
not there. 'I suppose we might as well have Ayala
now,' he said, addressing himself chiefly to Lucy.
'Do you go and manage it with her.' There was not
a word more said. Sir Thomas did not always have
his own way in his family. What man was ever
happy enough to do that? But he was seldom
directly contradicted. Lady Tringle when the order
was given pursed up her lips, and he, had he been
observant, might have known that she did not intend
to have Ayala if she could help it. But he was not
observant,—except as to millions.

When Sir Thomas was gone, Lady Tringle discussed the matter with Lucy. 'Of course, my dear,'
she said, 'if we could make dear Ayala happy——'

'I don't think she will come, Aunt Emmeline.'

'Not come!' This was not said at all in a voice of
anger, but simply as eliciting some further expression
of opinion.

'She's afraid of—Tom.' Lucy had never hitherto
expressed a positive opinion on that matter at
Queen's Gate. When Augusta had spoken of Ayala
as having run after Tom, Lucy had been indignant,
and had declared that the running had been all on
the other side. In a side way she had hinted that

Ayala, at any rate at present, was far from favourable to Tom's suit. But she had never yet spoken out her mind at Queen's Gate as Ayala had spoken it to her.

'Afraid of him?' said Aunt Emmeline.

'I mean that she is not a bit in love with him, and when a girl is like that I suppose she is—is afraid of a man, if everybody else wants her to marry him.'

"Why should everybody want her to marry Tom?' asked Lady Tringle, indignantly. 'I am sure I don't want her.'

'I suppose it is Uncle Tom, and Aunt Dosett, and Uncle Reginald,' said poor Lucy, finding that she had made a mistake.

'I don't see why anybody should want her to marry Tom. Tom is carried away by her baby face, and makes a fool of himself. As to everybody wanting her, I hope she does not flatter herself that there is anything of the kind.'

'I only meant that I think she would rather not be brought here, where she would have to see him daily.'

After this the loan of the carriage was at last made, and Lucy was allowed to visit her sister at the Crescent. 'Has he been there?' was almost the first question that Ayala asked.

'What he do you mean?'

'Isadore Hamel.'

'No; I have not seen him since I met him in the Park. But I do not want to talk about Mr. Hamel, Ayala. Mr. Hamel is nothing.'

'Oh, Lucy.'

'He is nothing. Had he been anything, he has gone, and there would be an end to it. But he is nothing.'

'If a man is true he may go, but he will come back.' Ayala had her ideas about the angel of light very clearly impressed upon her mind in regard to the conduct of the man, though they were terribly vague as to his personal appearance, his condition of life, his appropriateness for marriage, and many other

details of his circumstances. It had also often occurred to her that this Angel of Light, when he should
come, might not be in love with herself,—and that
she might have to die simply because she had seen
him and loved him in vain. But he would be a man
sure to come back if there were fitting reasons that
he should do so. Isadore Hamel was not quite an
Angel of Light, but he was nearly angelic,—at any
rate very good, and surely would come back.

'Never mind about Mr. Hamel, Ayala. It is not
nice to talk about a man who has never spoken a
word.'

'Never spoken a word! Oh, Lucy!'

'Mr. Hamel has never spoken a word, and I will
not talk about him. There! All my heart is open to
you, Ayala. You know that. But I will not talk
about Mr. Hamel. Aunt Emmeline wants you to
come to Queen's Gate.'

'I will not.'

'Or rather it is Sir Thomas who wants you to come.
I do like Uncle Tom. I do, indeed.'

'So do I.'

'You ought to come when he asks you.'

'Why ought I? That lout would be there,—of
course.'

'I don't know about his being a lout, Ayala.'

'He comes here, and I have to be perfectly brutal
to him. You can't guess the sort of things I say to
him, and he doesn't mind it a bit. He thinks that
he has to go on long enough, and that I must give
way at last. If I were to go to Queen's Gate it would
be just as much as to say that I had given way.'

'Why not?'

'Lucy!'

'Why not? He is not bad. He is honest, and true,
and kind-hearted. I know you can't be happy here.'

'No.'

'Aunt Dosett, with all her affairs, must be trouble
to you. I could not bear them patiently. How can
you?'

'Because they are better than Tom Tringle. I read somewhere about there being seven houses of the Devil,*each one being lower and worse than the other. Tom would be the lowest,—the lowest,—the lowest.'

'Ayala, my darling.'

'Do not tell me that I ought to marry Tom,' said Ayala, almost standing off in anger from the proferred kiss. 'Do you think that I could love him?'

'I think you could if you tried, because he is loveable. It is so much to be good, and then he loves you truly. After all, it is something to have everything nice around you. You have not been made to be poor and uncomfortable. I fear that it must be bad with you here.'

'It is bad.'

'I wish I could have stayed, Ayala. I am more tranquil than you, and could have borne it better.'

'It is bad. It is one of the houses,—but not the lowest. I can eat my heart out here, peaceably, and die with a great needle in my hand and a towel in my lap. But if I were to marry him I should kill myself the first hour after I had gone away with him. Things! What would things be with such a monster as that leaning over one? Would you marry him?' In answer to this, Lucy made no immediate reply. 'Why don't you say? You want me to marry him. Would you?'

'No.'

'Then why should I?'

'I could not try to love him.'

'Try! How can a girl try to love any man? It should come because she can't help it, let her try ever so. Trying to love Tom Tringle! Why can't you try?'

'He doesn't want me.'

'But if he did? I don't suppose it would make the least difference to him which it was. Would you try if he asked?'

'No.'

'Then why should I? Am I so much a poorer creature than you?'

'You are a finer creature. You know that I think so.'

'I don't want to be finer. I want to be the same.'

'You are free to do as you please. I am not—quite.'

'That means Isadore Hamel.'

'I try to tell you all the truth, Ayala; but pray do not talk about him even to me. As for you, you are free; and if you could——'

'I can't. I don't know that I am free, as you call it.' Then Lucy started, as though about to ask the question which would naturally follow. 'You needn't look like that, Lucy. There isn't any one to be named.'

'A man not to be named?'

'There isn't a man at all. There isn't anybody. But I may have my own ideas if I please. If I had an Isadore Hamel of my own I could compare Tom or Mr. Traffick, or any other lout to him, and could say how infinitely higher in the order of things was my Isadore than any of them. Though I haven't an Isadore can't I have an image? And can't I make my image brighter, even higher, than Isadore? You won't believe that, of course, and I don't want you to believe it yourself. But you should believe it for me. My image can make Tom Tringle just as horrible to me as Isadore Hamel can make him to you.' Thus it was that Ayala endeavoured to explain to her sister something of the castle which she had built in the air, and of the angel of light who inhabited the castle.

Then it was decided between them that Lucy should explain to Aunt Emmeline that Ayala could not make a prolonged stay at Queen's Gate. 'But how shall I say it?' asked Lucy.

'Tell her the truth, openly. "Tom wants to marry Ayala, and Ayala won't have him. Therefore, of course, she can't come, because it would look as though she were going to change her mind,—which she isn't." Aunt Emmeline will understand that, and will not be a bit sorry. She doesn't want to have me for a daughter-in-law. She had quite enough of me at Rome.'

All this time the carriage was waiting, and Lucy was obliged to return before half of all that was necessary had been said. What was to be Ayala's life for the future? How were the sisters to see each other? What was to be done when, at the end of the coming summer, Lucy should be taken first to Glenbogie and then to Merle Park? There is a support in any excitement, though it be in the excitement of sorrow only. At the present moment Ayala was kept alive by the necessity of her battle with Tom Tringle, but how would it be with her when Tom should have given up the fight? Lucy knew, by sad experience, how great might be the tedium of life in Kingsbury Crescent, and knew, also, how unfitted Ayala was to endure it. There seemed to be no prospect of escape in future. 'She knows nothing of what I am suffering,' said Ayala, 'when she gives me the things to do, and tells me of more things, and more, and more! How can there be so many things to be done in such a house as this?' But as Lucy was endeavouring to explain how different were the arrangements in Kingsbury Crescent from those which had prevailed at the bijou, the offended coachman sent up word to say that he didn't think Sir Thomas would like it if the horses were kept out in the rain any longer. Then Lucy hurried down, not having spoken of half the things which were down in her mind on the list for discussion.

## CHAPTER XIII

### HOW THE TRINGLES FELL INTO TROUBLE

AFTER the Easter holidays the Trafficks came back to Queen's Gate, making a combination of honeymoon and business which did very well for a time. It was understood that it was to be so. During honeymoon times the fashionable married couple is always lodged and generally boarded for nothing. That opening wide of generous hands, which exhibits itself in the joyous enthusiasm of a coming marriage, taking the shape of a houseful of presents, of a gorgeous and ponderous trousseau, of a splendid marriage feast, and not unfrequently of subsidiary presents from the opulent papa,—presents which are subsidiary to the grand substratum of settled dowry, —generously extends itself to luxurious provision for a month or two. That Mr. and Mrs. Traffick should come back to Queen's Gate for the six weeks intervening between Easter and Whitsuntide had been arranged, and arranged also that the use of Merle Park, for the Whitsun holidays, should be allowed to them. This last boon Augusta, with her sweetest kiss, had obtained from her father only two days before the wedding. But when it was suggested, just before the departure to Merle Park, that Mr. Traffick's unnecessary boots might be left at Queen's Gate, because he would come back there, then Sir Thomas, who had thought over the matter, said a word.

It was in this way. 'Mamma,' said Augusta, 'I suppose I can leave a lot of things in the big wardrobe. Jemima says I cannot take them to Merle Park without ever so many extra trunks.'

'Certainly, my dear. When anybody occupies the room, they won't want all the wardrobe. I don't know that any one will come this summer.'

This was only the thin end of the wedge, and, as Augusta felt, was not introduced successfully. The words spoken seemed to have admitted that a return to Queen's Gate had not been intended. The conversation went no further at the moment, but was recommenced the same evening. 'Mamma, I suppose Septimus can leave his things here?'

'Of course, my dear; he can leave anything,—to be taken care of.'

'It will be so convenient if we can come back,— just for a few days.'

Now, there certainly had been a lack of confidence between the married daughter and her mother as to a new residence. A word had been spoken, and Augusta had said that she supposed they would go to Lord Boardotrade when they left Queen's Gate, just to finish the season. Now, it was known that his lordship, with his four unmarried daughters, lived in a small house in a small street in Mayfair. The locality is no doubt fashionable, but the house was inconvenient. Mr. Traffick, himself, had occupied lodgings near the House of Commons, but these had been given up. 'I think you must ask your papa,' said Lady Tringle.

'Couldn't you ask him?' said the Honourable Mrs. Traffick. Lady Tringle was driven at last to consent, and then put the question to Sir Thomas,—beginning with the suggestion as to the unnecessary boots.

'I suppose Septimus can leave his things here?'

'Where do they mean to live when they come back to town?' asked Sir Thomas, sharply.

'I suppose it would be convenient if they could come here for a little time,' said Lady Tringle.

'And stay till the end of the season,—and then go down to Glenbogie, and then to Merle Park! Where do they mean to live?'

'I think there was a promise about Glenbogie,' said Lady Tringle.

'I never made a promise. I heard Traffick say that he would like to have some shooting,—though, as far as I know, he can't hit a haystack. They may come to Glenbogie for two or three weeks, if they like, but they shan't stay here during the entire summer.'

'You won't turn your own daughter out, Tom.'

'I'll turn Traffick out, and I suppose he'll take his wife with him,' said Sir Thomas, thus closing the conversation in wrath.

The Trafficks went and came back, and were admitted into the bed-room with the big wardrobe, and to the dressing-room where the boots were kept. On the very first day of his arrival Mr. Traffick was in the House at four, and remained there till four the next morning,—certain Irish Members having been very eloquent.* He was not down when Sir Thomas left the next morning at nine, and was again at the House when Sir Thomas came home to dinner. 'How long is it to be?' said Sir Thomas, that night, to his wife. There was a certain tone in his voice which made Lady Tringle feel herself to be ill all over. It must be said, in justice to Sir Thomas, that he did not often use this voice in his domestic circle, though it was well known in Lombard Street. But he used it now, and his wife felt herself to be unwell. 'I am not going to put up with it, and he needn't think it.'

'Don't destroy poor Augusta's happiness so soon.'

'That be d——d,' said the father, energetically. 'Who's going to destroy her happiness? Her happiness ought to consist in living in her husband's house. What have I given her all that money for?' Then Lady Tringle did not dare to say another word.

It was not till the third day that Sir Thomas and his son-in-law met each other. By that time Sir Thomas had got it into his head that his son-in-law was avoiding him. But on the Saturday there was no House. It was then just the middle of June,— Saturday, June 15*—and Sir Thomas had considered, at the most, that there would be yet nearly two months before Parliament would cease to sit and the time for Glenbogie would come. He had fed his anger warm, and was determined that he would not be done. 'Well, Traffick, how are you?' he said, encountering his son-in-law in the hall, and leading him into the dining-room. 'I haven't seen you since you've been back.'

'I've been in the House morning, noon, and night, pretty near.'

'I dare say. I hope you found yourself comfortable at Merle Park.'

'A charming house,—quite charming. I don't know whether I shouldn't build the stables a little further from——'

'Very likely. Nothing is so easy as knocking other people's houses about. I hope you'll soon have one to knock about of your own.'

'All in good time,' said Mr. Traffick, smiling.

Sir Thomas was one of those men who during the course of a successful life have contrived to repress their original roughnesses, and who make a not ineffectual attempt to live after the fashion of those with whom their wealth and successes have thrown them. But among such will occasionally be found one whose roughness does not altogether desert him, and who can on an occasion use it with a purpose. Such a one will occasionally surprise his latter-day associates by the sudden ferocity of his brow, by the hardness of his voice, and by an apparently unaccustomed use of violent words. The man feels that he must fight, and, not having learned the practice of finer weapons, fights in this way. Unskilled with foils or rapier he falls back upon the bludgeon with which his hand has not lost all its old familiarity. Such a one was Sir Thomas Tringle, and a time for such exercise had seemed to him to have come now. There are other men who by the possession of imperturbable serenity seem to be armed equally against rapier and bludgeon, whom there is no wounding with any weapon. Such a one was Mr. Traffick. When he was told of knocking about a house of his own, he quite took the meaning of Sir Thomas's words, and was immediately prepared for the sort of conversation which would follow. 'I wish I might; —a Merle Park of my own for instance. If I had gone into the city instead of to Westminster it might have come in my way.'

'It seems to me that a good deal has come in your way without very much trouble on your part.'

'A seat in the House is a nice thing,—but I work harder, I take it, than you do, Sir Thomas.'

'I never have had a shilling but what I earned. When you leave this where are you and Augusta going to live?'

This was a home question, which would have disconcerted most gentlemen in Mr. Traffick's position, were it not that gentlemen easily disconcerted would hardly find themselves there.

'Where shall we go when we leave this? You were so kind as to say something about Glenbogie when Parliament is up.'

'No, I didn't.'

'I thought I understood it.'

'You said something and I didn't refuse.'

'Put it any way you like, Sir Thomas.'

'But what do you mean to do before Parliament is up? The long and the short of it is, we didn't expect you to come back after the holidays. I like to be plain. This might go on for ever if I didn't speak out.'

'And a very comfortable way of going on it would be.' Sir Thomas raised his eyebrows in unaffected surprise, and then again assumed his frown. 'Of course I'm thinking of Augusta chiefly.'

'Augusta made up her mind no doubt to leave her father's house when she married.'

'She shows her affection for her parents by wishing to remain in it. The fact, I suppose, is, you want the rooms.'

'But even if we didn't? You're not going to live here for ever, I suppose?'

'That, Sir, is too good to be thought of, I fear. The truth is we had an idea of staying at my father's. He spoke of going down to the country and lending us the house. My sisters have made him change his mind and so here we are. Of course we can go into lodgings.'

'Or to an hotel.'

'Too dear! You see you've made me pay such a sum for insuring my life. I'll tell you what I'll do. If you'll let us make it out here till the 10th of July we'll go into an hotel then.' Sir Thomas, surprised at his own compliance, did at last give way. 'And then we can have a month at Glenbogie from the 12th.'*

'Three weeks,' said Sir Thomas, shouting at the top of his voice.

'Very well; three weeks. If you could have made it the month it would have been convenient; but I hate to be disagreeable.' Thus the matter was settled, and Mr. Traffick was altogether well pleased with the arrangement.

'What are we to do?' said Augusta, with a very long face. 'What are we to do when we are made to go away?'

'I hope I shall be able to make some of the girls go down by that time, and then we must squeeze in at my father's.'

This and other matters made Sir Thomas in those days irritable and disagreeable to the family. 'Tom,' he said to his wife, 'is the biggest fool that ever lived.'

'What is the matter with him now?' asked Lady Tringle, who did not like to have her only son abused.

'He's away half his time, and when he does come he'd better be away. If he wants to marry that girl why doesn't he marry her and have done with it?'

Now this was a matter upon which Lady Tringle had ideas of her own which were becoming every day stronger. 'I'm sure I should be very sorry to see it,' she said.

'Why should you be sorry? Isn't it the best thing a young man can do? If he's set his heart that way all the world won't talk him off. I thought all that was settled.'

'You can't make the girl marry him.'

'Is that it?' asked Sir Thomas, with a whistle. 'You used to say she was setting her cap at him.'

'She is one of those girls you don't know what she would be at. She's full of romance and nonsense, and isn't half as fond of telling the truth as she ought to be. She made my life a burden to me while she was with us, and I don't think she would be any better for Tom.'

'But he's still determined.'

'What's the use of that?' said Lady Tringle.

'Then he shall have her. I made him a promise and I'm not going to give it up. I told him that if he was in earnest he should have her.'

'You can't make a girl marry a young man.'

'You have her here, and then we'll take her to Glenbogie. Now when I say it I mean it. You go and fetch her, and if you don't I will. I'm not going to have her turned out into the cold in that way.'

'She won't come, Tom.' Then he turned round and frowned at her.

The immediate result of this was that Lady Tringle herself did drive across to Kingsbury Crescent accompanied by Gertrude and Lucy, and did make her request in form. 'My dear, your uncle particularly wants you to come to us for the next month.' Mrs. Dosett was sitting by. 'I hope Ayala may be allowed to come to us for a month.'

'Ayala must answer for herself,' said Mrs. Dosett, firmly. There had never been any warm friendship between Mrs. Dosett and her husband's elder sister.

'I can't,' said Ayala, shaking her head.

'Why not, my dear?' said Lady Tringle.

'I can't,' said Ayala.

Lady Tringle was not in the least offended or annoyed at the refusal. She did not at all desire that Ayala should come to Glenbogie. Ayala at Glenbogie would make her life miserable to her. It would, of course, lead to Tom's marriage, and then there would be internecine fighting between Ayala and Augusta. But it was necessary that she should take back to her husband some reply;—and this reply, if in the form of refusal, must come from Ayala herself. 'Your uncle has sent me,' said Lady Tringle, 'and I must give him some reason. As for expense, you know,'—then she turned to Mrs. Dosett with a smile, —'that of course would be our affair.'

'If you ask me,' said Mrs. Dosett, 'I think that as Ayala has come to us she had better remain with us. Of course things are very different, and she would be only discontented.' At this Lady Tringle smiled her sweetest smile,—as though acknowledging that things certainly were different,—and then turned to Ayala for a further reply.

'Aunt Emmeline, I can't,' said Ayala.

'But why, my dear? Can't isn't a courteous answer to a request that is meant to be kind.'

'Speak out, Ayala,' said Mrs. Dosett. 'There is nobody here but your aunts.'

'Because of Tom.'

'Tom wouldn't eat you,' said Lady Tringle, again smiling.

'It's worse than eating me,' said Ayala. 'He will go on when I tell him not. If I were down there he'd be doing it always. And then you'd tell me that I— encouraged him!'

Lady Tringle felt this to be unkind and undeserved. Those passages in Rome had been very disagreeable to every one concerned. The girl certainly, as she thought, had been arrogant and impertinent. She had been accepted from charity and had then domineered in the family. She had given herself airs and had gone out into company almost without authority, into company which had rejected her,— Lady Tringle. It had become absolutely necessary to get rid of an inmate so troublesome, so unbearable. The girl had been sent away,—almost ignominiously. Now she, Lady Tringle, the offended aunt, the aunt who had so much cause for offence, had been good enough, gracious enough, to pardon all this, and was again offering the fruition of a portion of her good things to the sinner. No doubt she was not anxious that the offer should be accepted, but not the less was it made graciously,—as she felt herself. In answer to this she had thrown back upon her the only hard word she had ever spoken to the girl! 'You wouldn't be told anything of the kind, but you needn't come if you don't like it.'

'Then I don't,' said Ayala, nodding her head.

'But I did think that after all that has passed, and when I am trying to be kind to you, you would have made yourself more pleasant to me. I can only tell your uncle that you say you won't.'

'Give my love to my uncle, and tell him that I am much obliged to him and that I know how good he is; but I can't—because of Tom.'

'Tom is too good for you,' exclaimed Aunt Emmeline, who could not bear to have her son depreciated even by the girl whom she did not wish to marry him.

'I didn't say he wasn't,' said Ayala, bursting into tears. 'The Archbishop of Canterbury would be too good for me, but I don't want to marry him.' Then she got up and ran out of the room in order that she might weep over her troubles in the privacy of her own chamber. She was thoroughly convinced that she was being ill-used. No one had a right to tell her that any man was too good for her unless she herself should make pretensions to the man. It was an insult to her even to connect her name with that of any man unless she had done something to connect it. In her own estimation her cousin Tom was infinitely beneath her,—worlds beneath her,—a denizen of an altogether inferior race, such as the Beast was to the Beauty! Not that Ayala had ever boasted to herself of her own face or form. It was not in that respect that she likened herself to the Beauty when she thought of Tom as the Beast. Her assumed superiority existed in certain intellectual or rather artistic and æsthetic gifts,—certain celestial gifts. But as she had boasted of them to no one, as she had never said that she and her cousin were poles asunder in their tastes, poles asunder in their feelings, poles asunder in their intelligence, was it not very, very cruel that she should be told, first that she encouraged him, and then that she was not good enough for him? Cinderella did not ask to have the Prince for her husband. When she had her own image of which no one could rob her, and was content with that, why should they treat her in this cruel way?

'I am afraid you are having a great deal of trouble with her,' said Lady Tringle to Mrs. Dosett.

'No, indeed. Of course she is romantic, which is very objectionable.'

'Quite detestable!' said Lady Tringle.

'But she has been brought up like that, so that it is not her fault. Now she endeavours to do her best.'

'She is so upsetting.'

'She is angry because her cousin persecutes her.'

'Persecutes her, indeed! Tom is in a position to ask any girl to be his wife. He can give her a home of her own, and a good income. She ought to be proud of the offer instead of speaking like that. But nobody wants her to have him.'

'He wants it, I suppose.'

'Just taken by her baby face;—that's all. It won't last, and she needn't think so. However, I've done my best to be kind, Mrs. Dosett, and there's an end of it. If you please I'll ring the bell for the carriage. Good-bye.' After that she swam out of the room and had herself carried back to Queen's Gate.

## CHAPTER XIV

### FRANK HOUSTON

THREE or four days afterwards Sir Thomas asked whether Ayala was to come to Glenbogie. 'She positively refused,' said his wife, 'and was so rude and impertinent that I could not possibly have her now.' Then Sir Thomas frowned and turned himself away, and said not a word further on that occasion.

There were many candidates for Glenbogie on this occasion. Among others there was Mr. Frank Houston, whose candidature was not pressed by himself,— as could not well have been done,—but was enforced by Gertrude on his behalf. It was now July. Gertrude and Mr. Houston had seen something of each other in Rome, as may be remembered, and since then had seen a good deal of each other in town. Gertrude was perfectly well aware that Mr. Houston was impecunious; but Augusta had been allowed to

have an impecunious lover, and Tom to throw himself at the feet of an impecunious love. Gertrude felt
herself to be entitled to her £120,000; did not for a
moment doubt but that she would get it. Why
shouldn't she give it to any young man she liked as
long as he belonged to decent people? Mr. Houston
wasn't a Member of Parliament,—but then he was
young and good-looking. Mr. Houston wasn't son to
a lord, but he was brother to a county squire, and
came of a family much older than that of those stupid
Boardotrade and Traffick people. And then Frank
Houston was very presentable, was not at all bald,
and was just the man for a girl to like as a husband.
It was dinned into her ears that Houston had no
income at all,—just a few hundreds a year on which
he never could keep himself out of debt. But he was
a generous man, who would be more than contented
with the income coming from £120,000. He would
not spunge upon the house at Queen's Gate. He
would not make use of Merle Park and Glenbogie.
He would have a house of his own for his old boots.
Four-per-cent* would give them nearly £5,000 a year.
Gertrude knew all about it already. They could have
a nice house near Queen's Gate;—say somewhere
about Onslow Gardens* There would be quite enough
for a carriage, for three months upon a mountain in
Switzerland, and three more among the art treasures
of Italy. It was astonishing how completely Gertrude had it all at her finger's-ends when she discussed the matter with her mother. Mr. Houston was
a man of no expensive tastes. He didn't want to
hunt. He did shoot, no doubt, and perhaps a little
shooting at Glenbogie might be nice before they went
to Switzerland. In that case two months on the top
of the mountain would suffice. But if he was not
asked he would never condescend to demand an entry
at Glenbogie as a part of his wife's dower. Lady
Tringle was thus talked over, though she did think
that at least one of her daughter's husbands ought
to have an income of his own. There was another

point which Gertrude put forward very frankly, and
which no doubt had weight with her mother. 'Mamma, I mean to have him,' she said, when Lady
Tringle expressed a doubt.

'But papa?'

'I mean to have him. Papa can scold, of course, if
he pleases.'

'But where would the income come from if papa
did not give it?'

'Of course he'll give it. I've a right to it as much
as Augusta.' There was something in Gertrude's face
as she said this which made her mother think that
she would have her way.

But Sir Thomas had hitherto declined. When
Frank Houston, after the manner of would-be sons-
in-law, had applied to Sir Thomas, Sir Thomas, who
already knew all about it, asked after his income, his
prospects, and his occupation. Fifty years ago young
men used to encounter the misery of such questions,
and to live afterwards often in the enjoyment of the
stern questioner's money and daughters. But there
used in those days to be a bad quarter of an hour
while the questions were being asked, and not unfrequently a bad six months afterwards, while the
stern questioner was gradually undergoing a softening process under the hands of the females of the
family. But the young man of to-day has no bad
quarter of an hour. 'You are a mercantile old brick,
with money and a daughter. I am a jeunesse dorée*
—gilded by blood and fashion, though so utterly impecunious! Let us know your terms. How much is
it to be, and then I can say whether we can afford to
live upon it.' The old brick surrenders himself more
readily and speedily to the latter than to the former
manner;—but he hardly surrenders himself quite at
once. Frank Houston, when inquired into, declared
at once, without blushing, that he had no income at
all to speak of in reference to matrimonial life. As to
family prospects he had none. His elder brother had
four blooming boys, and was likely to have more. As

for occupation, he was very fond of painting, very
fond of art all round, could shoot a little, and was
never in want of anything to do as long as he had a
book. But for the earning of money he had no turn
whatever. He was quite sure of himself that he could
never earn a shilling. But then on the other hand he
was not extravagant,—which was almost as good as
earning. It was almost incredible; but with his means,
limited as they were to a few hundreds, he did not
owe above a thousand pounds;—a fact which he
thought would weigh much with Sir Thomas in
regard to his daughter's future happiness.

Sir Thomas gave him a flat refusal. 'I think that I
may boast that your daughter's happiness is in my
charge,' said Frank Houston,

'Then she must be unhappy,' said Sir Thomas.
Houston shrugged his shoulders. 'A fool like that
has no right to be happy.'

'There isn't another man in the world by whom I
would allow her to be spoken of like that,' said
Houston.

'Bother!'

'I regard her as all that is perfect in woman, and
you must forgive me if I say that I shall not abandon
my suit. I may be allowed, at any rate, to call at the
house?'

'Certainly not.'

'That is a kind of thing that is never done nowadays;—never,' said Houston, shaking his head.

'I suppose my own house is my own.'

'Yours and Lady Tringle's, and your daughters',
no doubt. At any rate, Sir Thomas, you will think of
this again. I am sure you will think of it again. If
you find that your daughter's happiness depends
upon it——'

'I shall find nothing of the kind. Good morning.'

'Good morning, Sir Thomas.' Then Mr. Houston,
bowing graciously, left the little back room in Lombard Street, and, jumping into a cab had himself
taken straight away to Queen's Gate.

'Papa is always like that,' said Gertrude. On that day Mrs. Traffick, with all the boots, had taken herself away to the small house in Mayfair, and Gertrude, with her mother, had the house to herself. At the present moment Lady Tringle was elsewhere, so that the young lady was alone with her lover.

'But he comes round, I suppose.'

'If he doesn't have too much to eat,—which disagrees with him,—he does. He's always better down at Glenbogie because he's out of doors a good deal, and then he can digest things.'

'Then take him down to Glenbogie and let him digest it at once.'

'Of course we can't go till the 12th. Perhaps we shall start on the 10th, because the 11th is Sunday. What will you do, Frank?' There had been a whisper of Frank's going to the Tyrol in August, there to join the Mudbury Docimers, who were his far-away cousins. Imogene Docimer was a young lady of marvellous beauty,—not possessed indeed of £120,000,—of whom Gertrude had heard, and was already anxious that her Frank should not go to the Tyrol this year. She was already aware that her Frank had—just an artist's eye for feminine beauty in its various shapes, and thought that in the present condition of things he would be better at Glenbogie than in the Tyrol.

'I am thinking of wandering away somewhere;—perhaps to the Tyrol. The Mudbury Docimers are there. He's a pal of mine, besides being a cousin. Mrs. Docimer is a very nice woman.'

'And her sister?'

'A lovely creature. Such a turn of the neck! I've promised to make a study of her back head.'

'Come down to Glenbogie,' said Gertrude, sternly.

'How can I do that when your governor won't let me enter his house-door even in London?'

'But you're here.'

'Well,—yes;—I am here. But he told me not. I don't see how I'm to drive in at the gate at Glenbogie with all my traps, and ask to be shown my room. I have cheek enough for a good deal, my pet.'

'I believe you have, Sir;—cheek enough for anything. But mamma must manage it,—mamma and me, between us. Only keep yourself disengaged. You won't go to the Tyrol,—eh?' Then Frank Houston promised that he would not go to the Tyrol as long as there was a chance open that he might be invited to Glenbogie.

'I won't hear of it,' said Sir Thomas to his wife. On that occasion his digestion had perhaps failed him a little. 'He only wants to get my money.'

'But Gertrude has set her heart on it, and nothing will turn her away.'

'Why can't she set her heart on some one who has got a decent income? That man hasn't a shilling.'

'Nor yet has Mr. Traffick.'

'Mr. Traffick has, at any rate, got an occupation. Were it to do again, Mr. Traffick would never see a shilling of my money. By ——, those fellows, who haven't got a pound belonging to them, think that they're to live on the fat of the land out of the sweat of the brow of such men as me.'

'What is your money for, Tom, but for the children?'

'I know what it's for. I'd sooner build a hospital than give it to an idle fellow like that Houston. When I asked him what he did, he said he was fond of "picters"!* Sir Thomas would fall back from his usual modes of expression when he was a little excited.

'Of course he hasn't been brought up to work. But he is a gentleman, and I do think he would make our girl happy.'

'My money would make him happy,—till he had spent it.'

'Tie it up.'

'You don't know what you're talking about. How are you to prevent a man from spending his wife's income?'

'At any rate, if you have him down at Glenbogie you can see what sort of a man he is. You don't know him now.'

'As much as I wish to.'

'That isn't fair to the poor girl. You needn't give your consent to a marriage because he comes to Glenbogie. You have only to say that you won't give the money and then it must be off. They can't take the money from you.' His digestion could not have been very bad, for he allowed himself to be persuaded that Houston should be asked to Glenbogie for ten days. This was the letter of invitation;—

'MY DEAR MR. HOUSTON,

'We shall start for Glenbogie on the 10th of next month. Sir Thomas wishes you to join us on the 20th if you can, and stay till the end of the month. We shall be a little crowded at first, and therefore cannot name an earlier day.

'I am particularly to warn you that this means nothing more than a simple invitation. I know what passed between you and Sir Thomas, and he hasn't at all changed his mind. I think it right to tell you this. If you like to speak to him again when you are at Glenbogie of course you can.

'Very sincerely yours,

'EMMELINE TRINGLE.'

At the same time, or within a post of it, he got another letter, which was as follows;—

'DEAREST F,

'Papa, you see, hasn't cut up so very rough, after all. You are to be allowed to come and help to slaughter grouse, which will be better than going to that stupid Tyrol. If you want to draw somebody's back head you can do it there. Isn't it a joke papa's giving way like that all in a moment? He gets so fierce sometimes that we think he's going to eat everybody. Then he has to come down, and he gets eaten worse than anybody else.

' Of course, as you're asked to Glenbogie, you can
come here as often as you like. I shall ride on Thursday and Friday. I shall expect you exactly at six,
just under the Memorial. You can't come home to
dinner, you know, because he might flare up; but
you can turn in at lunch every day you please except
Saturday and Sunday. I intend to be so jolly down
at Glenbogie. You mustn't be shooting always.

'Ever your own,

'G.'

Frank Houston as he read this threw himself back
on the sofa and gave way to a soft sigh. He knew he
was doing his duty,—just as another man does who
goes forth from his pleasant home to earn his bread
and win his fortune in some dry, comfortless climate,
far from the delights to which he has been always
accustomed. He must do his duty. He could not
live always adding a hundred or two of debt to the
burden already round his neck. He must do his duty.
As he thought of this he praised himself mightily.
How beautiful was his far-away cousin, Imogene
Docimer, as she would twist her head round so as to
show the turn of her neck! How delightful it would
be to talk love to Imogene! As to marrying Imogene,
who hadn't quite so many hundreds as himself, that
he knew to be impossible. As for marriage, he wasn't
quite sure that he wanted to marry any one. Marriage, to his thinking, was 'a sort of grind' at the best.
A man would have to get up and go to bed with some
regularity. His wife might want him to come down
in a frock coat to breakfast. His wife would certainly
object to his drawing the back heads of other young
women. Then he thought of the provocation he had
received to draw Gertrude's back head. Gertrude
hadn't got any turn of a neck to speak of. Gertrude
was a stout, healthy girl; and, having £120,000, was
entitled to such a husband as himself. If he waited
longer he might be driven to worse before he found
the money which was so essentially necessary. He

was grateful to Gertrude for not being worse, and was determined to treat her well. But as for love, romance, poetry, art,—all that must for the future be out of the question. Of course, there would now be no difficulty with Sir Thomas, and therefore he must at once make up his mind. He decided that morning, with many soft regrets, that he would go to Glenbogie, and let those dreams of wanderings in the mountains of the Tyrol pass away from him. 'Dear, dearest Imogene!' He could have loved Imogene dearly had fates been more propitious. Then he got up and shook himself, made his resolution like a man, ate a large allowance of curried salmon for his breakfast,—and then wrote the following letter. 'Duty first!' he said to himself as he sat down to the table like a hero.

### Letter No. 1.

'DEAR LADY TRINGLE,

'So many thanks! Nothing could suit my book so well as a few days at Glenbogie just at the end of August. I will be there, like a book, on the 20th. Of course I understand all that you say. Fathers can't be expected to yield all at once, especially when suitors haven't got very much of their own. I shouldn't have dared to ask hadn't I known myself to be a most moderate man. Of course I shall ask again. If you will help me, no doubt I shall succeed. I really do think that I am the man to make Gertrude happy.

'Yours, dear Lady Tringle, ever so much,
'F. HOUSTON.'

### Letter No. 2.

'MY OWN ONE,

'Your governor is a brick. Of course, Glenbogie will be better than the Tyrol, as you are to be there. Not but what the Tyrol is a very jolly place, and we'll go and see it together some day. Ask Tom to let me know whether one can wear heavy boots in the Glenbogie mountains. They are much the best for the heather; but I have shot generally in Yorkshire, and there they are too hot. What number does he shoot with generally? I fancy the birds are wilder with you than with us.

'As for riding, I don't dare to sit upon a horse this weather. Nobody but a woman can stand it. Indeed, now I think of it, I sold my horse last week to pay the fellow I buy paints from. I've got the saddle and bridle, and if I stick them up upon a rail, under the trees, it would be better than any horse while the thermometer is near 80. All the ladies could come round and talk to one so nicely.

'I hate lunch, because it makes me red in the face, and nobody will give me my breakfast before eleven at the earliest. But I'll come in about three as often as you like to have me. I think I perhaps shall run over to the Tyrol after Glenbogie. A man must go somewhere when he has been turned out in that fashion. There are so many babies at Buncombe Hall!'※—Buncombe Hall is the family seat of the Houstons,—'and I don't like to see my own fate typified before the time.

'Can I do anything for you except riding or eating lunch,—which are simply feminine exercises? Always your own,                                       'FRANK.'

### Letter No. 3.

'DEAR COUSIN IM,

'How pleasant it is that a little strain of thin blood should make the use of that pretty name allowable! What a stupid world it is when the people who like each other best cannot get together because of proprieties, and marriages, and such balderdash as we call love. I do not in the least want to be in love with you,—but I do want to sit near you, and listen to you, and look at you, and to know that the whole air around is impregnated by the mysterious odour of your presence. When one is thoroughly satisfied with a woman there comes a scent as of sweet flowers, which does not reach the senses of those whose feelings are not so awakened.

'And now for my news! I suppose that G. T. will in a tremendously short period become Mistress F. H. "A long day, my Lord." But, if you are to be hung, better be hung at once. Père Tringle has not consented,—has done just the reverse,—has turned me out of his house, morally. That is, out of his London house. He asked of my "house and my home," as they did of Allan-a-Dale.*

> Queen's Gate and Glenbogie stand fair on the hill.
> "My home," quoth bold Houston, "shows gallanter still.
> 'Tis the garret up three pair——"

'Then he told me roughly to get me gone; but "I had laughed on the lass with my bonny black eye." So the next day I got an invite to Glenbogie, and at the appropriate time in August,

> She'll go to the mountains to hear a love tale,
> And the youth——

it will be told by is to be your poor unfortunate coz, Frank Houston. Who's going to whimper? Haven't I known all along what was to come? It has not been my lot in life to see a flower and pick it because I love it. But a good head of cabbage when you're hungry is wholesome food.—Your loving cousin, but not loving as he oughtn't to love,

'FRANK HOUSTON.'

'I shall still make a dash for the Tyrol when this episode at Glenbogie is over.'


## CHAPTER XV

### AYALA WITH HER FRIENDS

SOME few days after Lady Tringle had been at Kingsbury Crescent, two visitors, who knew little or nothing of each other, came to see Ayala. One was a lady and the other a gentleman, and the lady came first. The gentleman, however, arrived before the lady had gone. Mrs. Dosett was present while the lady remained; but when the gentleman came she was invited to leave him alone with her niece,—as shall be told.

The lady was the Marchesa Baldoni. Can the reader go so far back as to remember the Marchesa Baldoni? It was she who rather instigated Ayala to be naughty to the Tringles in Rome, and would have Ayala at her parties when she did not want the Tringles. The Marchesa was herself an English-woman, though she had lived at Rome all her life, and had married an Italian nobleman. She was now in London for a few weeks, and still bore in mind her friendship for Ayala, and a certain promise she had once made her. In Rome Lady Tringle, actuated by Augusta, who at the moment was very angry with everybody, including her own lover, had quarrelled with the Marchesa. The Marchesa had then told Ayala that she, Ayala, must stay with her aunt,—must, in fact, cease for the time to come to the Marchesa's apartments, because of the quarrel; but that a time would come in which they might again be friends. Soon afterwards the Marchesa had heard that the Tringle family had discarded poor Ayala,—that her own quarrel had, in fact, extended itself to Ayala, and that Ayala had been shunted off to a poor rela-tion, far away from all the wealth and luxuries which she had been allowed to enjoy for so short a time. Therefore, soon after her arrival in London, the Marchesa had made herself acquainted with the ad-dress of the Dosetts, and now was in Kingsbury Crescent in fulfilment of her promise made at Rome.

'So now you have got our friend Ayala,' said the Marchesa with a smile to Mrs. Dosett.

'Yes; we have her now. There has been a change. Her sister, Lucy, has gone to my husband's sister, Lady Tringle.'

The Marchesa made a pleasant little bow at each word. She seemed to Mrs. Dosett to be very gor-geously dressed. She was thoroughly well dressed,

and looked like a Marchesa ;—or perhaps, even, like
a Marchioness. She was a tall, handsome woman,
with a smile perhaps a little too continuously sweet,
but with a look conscious of her own position behind
it. She had seen in a moment of what nature was
Ayala, how charming, how attractive, how pretty,
how clever,—how completely the very opposite of
the Tringles! Ayala learned Italian so readily that
she could talk it almost at once. She could sing, and
play, and draw. The Marchesa had been quite willing
that her own daughter Nina should find a friend in
Ayala. Then had come the quarrel. Now she was
quite willing to renew the friendship, though Ayala's
position was so sadly altered. Mrs. Dosett was almost
frightened as the grand lady sat holding Ayala's
hand, and patting it. 'We used to know her so well
in Rome ;—did we not, Ayala ?'

'You were very kind to me.'

'Nina couldn't come, because her father would
make her go with him to the pictures. But now, my
dear, you must come to us just for a little time. We
have a furnished house in Brook Street,* near the
park, till the end of the season, and we have one
small spare room which will just do for you. I hope
you will let her come to us, for we really are old
friends,' said the Marchesa, turning to Mrs. Dosett.

Mrs. Dosett looked black. There are people who
always look black when such applications are made
to them,—who look black at any allusions to pleasures. And then there came across her mind serious
thoughts as to flowers and ribbons,—and then more
serious thoughts as to boots, dresses, and hats.
Ayala, no doubt, had come there less than six months
since with good store of everything; but Mrs. Dosett
knew that such a house as would be that of this lady
would require a girl to show herself with the newest
sheen on everything. And Ayala knew it too. The
Marchesa turned from the blackness of Mrs. Dosett's
face with her sweetest smile to Ayala. 'Can't we
manage it ?' said the Marchesa.

'I don't think we can,' said Ayala, with a deep sigh.

'And why not?'

Ayala looked furtively round to her aunt. 'I suppose I may tell, Aunt Margaret?' she said.

'You may tell everything, my dear,' said Mrs. Dosett.

'Because we are poor,' said Ayala.

'What does that matter?' said the Marchesa, brightening up. 'We want you because you are rich in good gifts and pretty ways.'

'But I can't get new frocks now as I used to do in Rome. Aunt Emmeline was cruel to me, and said things which I could not bear. But they let me have everything. Uncle Reginald gives me all that he has, and I am much happier here. But we cannot go out and buy things,—can we, Aunt Margaret?'

'No, my dear; we cannot.'

'It does not signify,' said the Marchesa. 'We are quite quiet, and what you have got will do very well. Frocks! The frocks you had in Rome are good enough for London. I won't have a word of all that. Nina has set her heart upon it, and so has my husband, and so have I. Mrs. Dosett, when we are at home we are the most homely people in the world. We think nothing of dressing. Not to come and see your old friends because of your frocks! We shall send for you the day after to-morrow. Don't you know, Mrs. Dosett, it will do her good to be with her young friend for a few days.' Mrs. Dosett had not succeeded in her remonstrances when Sir Thomas Tringle was shown into the room, and then the Marchesa took her leave. For Sir Thomas Tringle was the other visitor who came on that morning to see Ayala.

'If you wouldn't mind, Mrs. Dosett,' said Sir Thomas before he sat down, 'I should like to see Ayala alone.' Mrs. Dosett had not a word to say against such a request, and at once took her leave.

'My dear,' he began, coming and sitting opposite to Ayala, with his knees almost touching her, 'I have got something very particular to say to you.'

Ayala was at once much frightened. Her uncle had never before spoken to her in this way,—had never in truth said a word to her seriously. He had always been kind to her, making her presents, and allowing himself to be kissed graciously morning and evening. He had never scolded her, and, better than all, had never said a word to her, one way or the other, about Tom. She had always liked her uncle, because he had never caused her trouble when all the others in his house had been troublesome to her. But now she was afraid of him. He did not frown, but he looked very seriously at her, as he might look, perhaps, when he was counting out all his millions in Lombard Street. 'I hope you think that I have always wished to be kind to you, Ayala.'

'I am sure you have, Uncle Tom.'

'When you had come to us I always wished you to stay. I don't like changes of this sort. I suppose you didn't hit it off with Augusta. But she's gone now.'

'Aunt Emmeline said something.' That accusation, as to 'encouragement,' so rankled in her heart, that when she looked back at her grievances among the Tringles that always loomed the largest.

'I don't want to hear anything about it,' said Sir Thomas. 'Let bygones be bygones. Your aunt, I am sure, never meant unkindly by you. Now, I want you to listen to me.'

'I will, Uncle Tom.'

'Listen to me to the end, like a good girl.'

'I will.'

'Your Cousin Tom——.' Ayala gave a visible shudder, and uttered an audible groan, but as yet she did not say a word. Sir Thomas, having seen the shudder, and heard the groan, did frown as he began again. 'Your Cousin Tom is most truly attached to you.'

'Why won't he leave me alone, then?'

'Ayala, you promised to listen to me without speaking.'

'I will, Uncle Tom. Only——'

'Listen to me, and then I will hear anything you have to say.'

'I will,' said Ayala, screwing up her lips, so that no words should come out of them, let the provocation be what it might.

Sir Thomas began again. 'Your Cousin Tom is most truly attached to you. For some time I and his mother disapproved of this. We thought you were both too young, and there were other reasons which I need not now mention. But when I came to see how thoroughly he was in earnest, how he put his heart into it, how the very fact that he loved you had made a man of him; then how the fact that you would not return his love unmanned him,—when I saw all that, I gave my permission.' Here he paused, almost as though expecting a word; but Ayala gave an additional turn to the screw on her lips, and remained quite silent. 'Yes; we gave our permission, —I and your aunt. Of course, our son's happiness is all in all to us; and I do believe that you are so good that you would make him a good wife.'

'But——'

'Listen till I have done, Ayala.' Then there was another squeeze. 'I suppose you are what they call romantic. Romance, my dear, won't buy bread and butter. Tom is a very good young man, and he loves you most dearly. If you will consent to be his I will make a rich man of him. He will then be a respectable man of business, and will become a partner in the house. You and he can choose a place to live in almost where you please. You can have your own establishment and your carriage, and will be able to do a deal of good. You will make him happy, and you will be my dear child. I have come here to tell you that I will make you welcome into the family, and to promise that I will do everything I can to make you happy. Now you may say what you like; but, Ayala, think a little before you speak.'

Ayala thought a little;—not as to what she should say, but as to the words in which she might say it.

She was conscious that a great compliment was paid to her. And there was a certain pride in her heart as she thought that this invitation into the family had come to her after that ignominious accusation of encouragement had been made. Augusta had snubbed her about Tom, and her aunt; but now she was asked to come among them, and be one of them, with full observances. She was aware of all this, and aware, also, that such treatment required from her a gracious return. But not on that account could she give herself to the Beast. Not on that account could she be untrue to her image. Not on that account could she rob her bosom of that idea of love which was seated there. Not on that account could she look upon the marriage proposed to her with aught but a shuddering abhorrence. She sat silent for a minute or two, while her heavy eyes were fixed upon his. Then, falling on her knees before him, she put up her little hands to pray to him. 'Uncle Tom, I can't,' she said. And then the tears came running down her cheeks.

'Why can't you, Ayala? Why cannot you be sensible, as other girls are?' said Sir Thomas, lifting her up, and putting her on his knee.

'I can't,' she said. 'I don't know how to tell you.'

'Do you love some other man?'

'No; no; no!' To Uncle Tom, at any rate, she need say nothing of the image.

'Then why is it?'

'Because I can't. I don't know what I say, but I can't. I know how very, very, very good you are.'

'I would love you as my daughter.'

'But I can't, Uncle Tom. Pray tell him, and make him get somebody else. He would be quite happy if he could get somebody else.'

'It is you that he loves.'

'But what's the use of it, when I can't? Dear, dear Uncle Tom, do have it all settled for me. Nothing on earth could ever make me do it. I should die if I were to try.'

'That's nonsense.'

'I do so want not to make you angry, Uncle Tom. And I do so wish he would be happy with someone else. Nobody ought to be made to marry unless they like it;—ought they?'

'There is no talk of making,' said Sir Thomas, frowning.

'At any rate I can't,' said Ayala, releasing herself from her uncle's embrace.

It was in vain that even after this he continued his request, begging her to come down to Glenbogie, so that she might make herself used to Tom and his ways. If she could only once more, he thought, be introduced to the luxuries of a rich house, then she would give way. But she would not go to Glenbogie; she would not go to Merle Park; she would not consent to see Tom anywhere. Her uncle told her that she was romantic and foolish, endeavouring to explain to her over and over again that the good things of the world were too good to be thrown away for a dream. At last there was a touch of dignity in the final repetition of her refusal. 'I am sorry to make you angry, but I can't, Uncle Tom.' Then he frowned with all his power of frowning, and, taking his hat, left the room and the house almost without a word.

At the time fixed the Marchesa's carriage came, and Ayala with her boxes was taken away to Brook Street. Uncle Reginald had offered to do something for her in the way of buying a frock, but this she refused, declaring that she would not allow herself to become an expense merely because her friends in Rome had been kind to her. So she had packed up the best of what she had and started, with her heart in her mouth, fearing the grandeur of the Marchesa's house. On her arrival she was received by Nina, who at once threw herself into all her old intimacy. 'Oh, Ayala,' she said, 'this is so nice to have you again. I have been looking forward to this ever since we left Rome.'

'Yes,' said Ayala, 'it is nice.'

'But why did you tell mamma you would not come? What nonsense to talk to her about frocks! Why not come and tell me? You used to have everything at Rome, much more than I had.'

Then Ayala began to explain the great difference between Uncle Tom and Uncle Reginald,—how Uncle Tom had so many thousands that nobody could count them, how Uncle Reginald was so shorn in his hundreds that there was hardly enough to supply the necessaries of life. 'You see,' she said, 'when papa died Lucy and I were divided. I got the rich uncle, and Lucy got the poor one; but I made myself disagreeable, and didn't suit, and so we have been changed.'

'But why did you make yourself disagreeable?' said Nina, opening her eyes. 'I remember when we were at Rome your cousin Augusta was always quarrelling with you. I never quite knew what it was all about.'

'It wasn't only that,' said Ayala, whispering.

'Did you do anything very bad?'

Then it occurred to Ayala that she might tell the whole story to her friend, and she told it. She explained the nature of that great persecution as to Tom. 'And that was the real reason why we were changed,' said Ayala, as she completed her story.

'I remember seeing the young man,' said Nina.

'He is such a lout!'

'But was he very much in love?' asked Nina.

'Well, I don't know. I suppose he was after his way. I don't think louts like that can be very much in love to signify. Young men when they look like that would do with one girl as well as another.'

'I don't see that at all,' said Nina.

'I am sure he would if he'd only try. At any rate what's the good of his going on? They can't make a girl marry unless she chooses.'

'Won't he be rich?'

'Awfully rich,' said Ayala.

'Then I should think about it again,' said the young lady from Rome.

'Never,' said Ayala, with an impressive whisper. 'I will never think about it again. If he were made of diamonds I would not think about it again.'

'And is that why you were changed?' said Nina.

'Well, yes. No; it is very hard to explain. Aunt Emmeline told me that—that I encouraged him. I thought I should have rushed out of the house when she said that. Then I had to be changed. I don't know whether they could forgive me, but I could not forgive her.'

'And how is it now?'

'It is different now,' said Ayala, softly. 'Only that it can't make any real difference.'

'How different?'

'They'd let me come if I would, I suppose; but I shall never, never go to them any more.'

'I suppose you won't tell me everything?' said Nina, after a pause.

'What everything?'

'You won't be angry if I ask?'

'No, I will not be angry.'

'I suppose there is someone else you really care for?'

'There is no one,' said Ayala, escaping a little from her friend's embrace.

'Then why should you be so determined against that poor young man?'

'Because he is a lout and a beast,' said Ayala, jumping up. 'I wonder you should ask me;—as if that had anything to do with it. Would you fall in love with a lout because you had no one else? I would rather live for ever all alone, even in Kingsbury Crescent, than have to think of becoming the wife of my cousin Tom.' At this Nina shrugged her shoulders, showing that her education in Italy had been less romantic than that accorded to Ayala in London.

## CHAPTER XVI

### JONATHAN STUBBS

BUT, though Nina differed somewhat from Ayala as to their ideas as to life in general, they were close friends, and everything was done both by the Marchesa and by her daughter to make Ayala happy. There was not very much of going into grand society, and that difficulty about the dresses solved itself, as do other difficulties. There came a few presents, with entreaties from Ayala that presents of that kind might not be made. But the presents were, of course, accepted, and our girl was as prettily arrayed, if not as richly, as the best around her. At first there was an evening at the opera, and then a theatre,— diversions which are easy. Ayala, after her six dull months in Kingsbury Crescent, found herself well pleased to be taken to easy amusements. The carriage in the park was delightful to her, and delightful a visit which was made to her by Lucy. For the Tringle carriage could be spared for a visit in Brook Street, even though there was still a remembrance in the bosom of Aunt Emmeline of the evil things which had been done by the Marchesa in Rome. Then there came a dance,—which was not so easy. The Marchesa and Nina were going to a dance at Lady Putney's, and arrangements were made that Ayala should be taken. Ayala begged that there might be no arrangements, declared that she would be quite happy to see Nina go forth in her finery. But the Marchesa was a woman who always had her way, and Ayala was taken to Lady Putney's dance without a suspicion on the part of any who saw her that her ball-room apparatus was not all that it ought to be.

Ayala when she entered the room was certainly a little bashful. When in Rome, even in the old days at the bijou, when she did not consider herself to be quite out,* she had not been at all bashful. She had been able to enjoy herself entirely, being very fond of dancing, conscious that she could dance well, and always having plenty to say for herself. But now there had settled upon her something of the tedium, something of the silence, of Kingsbury Crescent, and she almost felt that she would not know how to behave herself if she were asked to stand up and dance before all Lady Putney's world. In her first attempt she certainly was not successful. An elderly gentleman was brought up to her,—a gentleman whom she afterwards declared to be a hundred, and who was, in truth, over forty, and with him she manœuvred gently through a quadrille. He asked her two or three questions to which she was able to answer only in monosyllables. Then he ceased his questions, and the manœuvres were carried on in perfect silence. Poor Ayala did not attribute any blame to the man. It was all because she had been six months in Kingsbury Crescent. Of course this aged gentleman, if he wanted to dance, would have a partner chosen for him out of Kingsbury Crescent. Conversation was not to be expected from a gentleman who was made to stand up with Kingsbury Crescent. Any powers of talking that had ever belonged to herself had of course evaporated amidst the gloom of Kingsbury Crescent. After this she was returned speedily to the wings of the Marchesa, and during the next dance sat in undisturbed peace. Then suddenly, when the Marchesa had for a moment left her, and when Nina had just been taken away to join a set, she saw the man of silence coming to her from a distance, with an evident intention of asking her to stand up again. It was in his eye, in his toe, as he came bowing forward. He had evidently learned to suppose that they two outcasts might lessen their miseries by joining them together. She was to dance with him because no one else would ask her! She had plucked up her spirit and resolved that, desolate as she might be, she would not descend so far as that, when, in a moment, another gentleman sprang in, as it were, between her and her enemy, and addressed her with free and easy speech as though he had known her all her life. 'You are Ayala Dormer, I am sure,' said he. She looked up into his face and nodded her head at him in her own peculiar way. She was quite sure that she had never set her eyes on him before. He was so ugly that she could not have forgotten him. So at least she told herself. He was very, very ugly, but his voice was very pleasant. 'I knew you were, and I am Jonathan Stubbs. So now we are introduced, and you are to come and dance with me.'

She had heard the name of Jonathan Stubbs. She was sure of that, although she could not at the moment join any facts with the name. 'But I don't know you,' she said, hesitating. Though he was so ugly he could not but be better than that ancient dancer whom she saw standing at a distance, looking like a dog that has been deprived of his bone.

'Yes, you do,' said Jonathan Stubbs, 'and if you'll come and dance I'll tell you about it. The Marchesa told me to take you.'

'Did she?' said Ayala, getting up, and putting her little hand upon his arm.

'I'll go and fetch her if you like; only she's a long way off, and we shall lose our place. She's my aunt.'

'Oh,' said Ayala, quite satisfied,—remembering now that she had heard her friend Nina boast of a Colonel cousin, who was supposed to be the youngest Colonel in the British army, who had done some wonderful thing,—taken a new province in India, or marched across Africa, or defended the Turks,—or perhaps conquered them. She knew that he was very brave,—but why was he so very ugly? His hair was ruby red, and very short; and he had a thick red beard: not silky, but bristly, with each bristle almost a dagger,—and his mouth was enormous. His eyes were very bright, and there was a smile about him, partly of fun, partly of good humour. But his mouth! And then that bristling beard! Ayala was half inclined to like him, because he was so completely master of himself, so unlike the unhappy ancient gentleman who was still hovering at a distance. But why was he so ugly? And why was he called Jonathan Stubbs?

'There now,' he said, 'we can't get in at any of the sets. That's your fault.'

'No, it isn't,' said Ayala.

'Yes, it is. You wouldn't stand up till you had heard all about me.'

'I don't know anything about you now.'

'Then come and walk about and I'll tell you. Then we shall be ready for a waltz. Do you waltz well?'

'Do you?'

'I'll back myself against any Englishman, Frenchman, German, or Italian, for a large sum of money. I can't come quite up to the Poles. The fact is, the honester the man is the worse he always dances. Yes; I see what you mean. I must be a rogue. Perhaps I am;—perhaps I'm only an exception. I knew your father.'

'Papa!'

'Yes, I did. He was down at Stalham with the Alburys once. That was five years ago, and he told me he had a daughter named Ayala. I didn't quite believe him.'

'Why not?'

'It is such an out-of-the-way name.'

'It's as good as Jonathan, at any rate.' And Ayala again nodded her head.

'There's a prejudice about Jonathan, as there is about Jacob and Jonah.* I never could quite tell why. I was going to marry a girl once with a hundred thousand pounds, and she wouldn't have me at last because she couldn't bring her lips to say Jonathan. Do you think she was right?'

'Did she love you?' said Ayala, looking up into his face.

'Awfully! But she couldn't bear the name; so within three months she gave herself and all her

money to Mr. Montgomery Talbot de Montpellier.
He got drunk, and threw her out of the window
before a month was over. That's what comes of
going in for sweet names.'

'I don't believe a word of it,' said Ayala.

'Very well. Didn't Septimus Traffick marry your
cousin?'

'Of course he did, about a month ago.'

'He is another friend of mine. Why didn't you go
to your cousin's marriage?'

'There were reasons,' said Ayala.

'I know all about it,' said the Colonel. 'You
quarrelled with Augusta down in Scotland, and you
don't like poor Traffick because he has got a bald
head.'

'I believe you're a conjuror,' said Ayala.

'And then your cousin was jealous because you
went to the top of St. Peter's, and because you would
walk with Mr. Traffick on the Pincian. I was in
Rome, and saw all about it.'

'I won't have anything more to do with you,' said
Ayala.

'And then you quarrelled with one set of uncles and
aunts, and now you live with another.'

'Your aunt told you that.'

'And I know your cousin, Tom Tringle.'

'You know Tom?' asked Ayala.

'Yes; he was ever so good to me in Rome about a
horse; I like Tom Tringle in spite of his chains.
Don't you think, upon the whole, if that young lady
had put up with Jonathan she would have done
better than marry Montpellier? But now they're
going to waltz, come along.'

Thereupon Ayala got up and danced with him for
the next ten minutes. Again and again before the
evening was over she danced with him; and although,
in the course of the night, many other partners had
offered themselves, and many had been accepted,
she felt that Colonel Jonathan Stubbs had certainly
been the partner of the evening. Why should he be

so hideously ugly? said Ayala to herself, as she wished him good night before she left the room with the Marchesa and Nina.

'What do you think of my nephew?' asked the Marchesa, when they were in the carriage together.

'Do tell us what you think of Jonathan,' said Nina.

'I thought he was very good-natured.'

'And very handsome?'

'Nina, don't be foolish. Jonathan is one of the most rising officers in the British service, and luckily he can be that without being beautiful to look at.'

'I declare,' said Nina, 'sometimes, when he is talking, I think him perfectly lovely. The fire comes out of his eyes, and he rubs his old red hairs about till they sparkle. Then he shines all over like a carbuncle, and every word he says makes me die of laughter.'

'I laughed too,' said Ayala.

'But you didn't think him beautiful,' said Nina.

'No, I did not,' said Ayala. 'I liked him very much, but I thought him very ugly. Was it true about the young lady who married Mr. Montgomery de Montpellier and was thrown out of a window a week afterwards?'

'There is one other thing I must tell you about Jonathan,' said Nina. 'You must not believe a word that he says.'

'That I deny,' said the Marchesa; 'but here we are. And now, girls, get out of the carriage and go up to bed at once.'

Ayala, before she went to sleep, and again when she woke in the morning, thought a great deal about her new friend. As to shining like a carbuncle,— perhaps he did, but that was not her idea of manly beauty. And hair ought not to sparkle. She was sure that Colonel Stubbs was very, very ugly. She was almost disposed to think that he was the ugliest man she had ever seen. He certainly was a great deal worse than her cousin Tom, who, after all, was not particularly ugly. But, nevertheless, she would very

much rather dance with Colonel Stubbs. She was
sure of that, even without reference to Tom's objectionable love-making. Upon the whole she liked
dancing with Colonel Stubbs, ugly as he was. Indeed,
she liked him very much. She had spent a very
pleasant evening because he had been there. 'It all
depends upon whether any one has anything to say.'
That was the determination to which she came when
she endeavoured to explain to herself how it had
come to pass that she had liked dancing with anybody so very hideous. The Angel of Light would of
course have plenty to say for himself, and would be
something altogether different in appearance. He
would be handsome,—or rather, intensely interesting, and his talk would be of other things. He would
not say of himself that he danced as well as though
he were a rogue, or declare that a lady had been
thrown out of a window the week after she was
married. Nothing could be more unlike an Angel of
Light than Colonel Stubbs,—unless, perhaps, it were
Tom Tringle. Colonel Stubbs, however, was completely unangelic,—so much so that the marvel was
that he should yet be so pleasant. She had no horror
of Colonel Stubbs at all. She would go anywhere
with Colonel Stubbs, and feel herself to be quite safe.
She hoped she might meet him again very often. He
was, as it were, the Genius of Comedy, without a
touch of which life would be very dull. But the
Angel of Light must have something tragic in his
composition,—must verge, at any rate, on tragedy.
Ayala did not know that beautiful description of a
'Sallow, sublime, sort of Werther-faced man,'*but I
fear that in creating her Angel of Light she drew a
picture in her imagination of a man of that kind.

Days went on, till the last day of Ayala's visit had
come, and it was necessary that she should go back
to Kingsbury Crescent. It was now August, and
everybody was leaving town. The Marchesa and
Nina were going to their relations, the Alburys, at
Stalham, and could not, of course, take Ayala with

them. The Dosetts would remain in town for another month, with a distant hope of being able to run down to Pegwell Bay for a fortnight in September. But even that had not yet been promised. Colonel Stubbs had been more than once at the house in Brook Street, and Ayala had come to know him almost as she might some great tame dog. It was now the afternoon of the last day, and she was sorry because she would not be able to see him again. She was to be taken to the theatre that night,—and then to Kingsbury Crescent and the realms of Lethe*early on the following morning.

It was very hot, and they were sitting with the shutters nearly closed, having resolved not to go out, in order that they might be ready for the theatre— when the door was opened and Tom Tringle was announced. Tom Tringle had come to call on his cousin.

'Lady Baldoni,' he said, 'I hope you won't think me intrusive, but I thought I'd come and see my cousin once whilst she is staying here.' The Marchesa bowed, and assured him that he was very welcome. 'It's tremendously hot,' said Tom.

'Very hot indeed,' said the Marchesa.

'I don't think it's ever so hot as this in Rome,' said Nina, fanning herself.

'I find it quite impossible to walk a yard,' said Tom, 'and therefore I've hired a hansom cab all to myself. The man goes home and changes his horse regularly when I go to dinner; then he comes for me at ten, and sticks to me till I go to bed. I call that a very good plan.' Nina asked him why he didn't drive the cab himself. 'That would be a grind,' said he, 'because it would be so hot all day, and there might be rain at night. Have you read what my brother-in-law, Traffick, said in the House last night, my Lady?'

'I'm afraid I passed it over,' said the Marchesa. 'Indeed, I am not very good at the debates.'

'They are dull,' said Tom, 'but when it's one's brother-in-law, one does like to look at it. I thought he made that very clear about the malt tax.'* The Marchesa smiled and bowed.

'What is—malt tax?' asked Nina.

'Well, it means beer,' said Tom. 'The question is whether the poor man pays it who drinks the beer, or the farmer who grows the malt. It is very interesting when you come to think of it.'

'But I fear I never have come to think of it,' said the Marchesa.

During all this time Ayala never said a word, but sat looking at her cousin, and remembering how much better Colonel Jonathan Stubbs would have talked if he had been there. Then, after a pause, Tom got up, and took his leave, having to content himself with simply squeezing his cousin's hand as he left the room.

'He is a lout,' said Ayala, as soon as she knew that the door was closed behind him.

'I don't see anything loutish at all,' said the Marchesa.

'He's just like most other young men,' said Nina.

'He's not at all like Colonel Stubbs,' said Ayala.

Then the Marchesa preached a little sermon. 'Colonel Stubbs, my dear,' she said, 'happens to have been thrown a good deal about the world, and has thus been able to pick up that easy mode of talking which young ladies like, perhaps because it means nothing. Your cousin is a man of business, and will probably have amassed a large fortune when my poor nephew will be a do-nothing old general on half-pay.* His chatter will not then have availed him quite so much as your cousin's habits of business.'

'Mamma,' said Nina, 'Jonathan will have money of his own.'

'Never mind, my dear. I do not like to hear a young man called a lout because he's more like a man of business than a man of pleasure.' Ayala felt herself to be snubbed, but was not a whit the less sure that Tom was a lout, and the Colonel an agreeable partner to dance with. But at the same time she remembered that neither the one nor the other was to be spoken of in the same breath, or thought of in the same spirit, as the Angel of Light.

When they were dressed, and just going to dinner, the ugly man with the red head was announced, and declared his purpose of going with them to the theatre. 'I've been to the office,' said he, 'and got a stall next to yours, and have managed it all. It now only remains that you should give me some dinner and a seat in the carriage.' Of course he was told that there was no dinner sufficient for a man to eat; but he put up with a feminine repast, and spent the whole of the evening sitting next to his aunt, on a back tier, while the two girls were placed in front. In this way, leaning forward, with his ugly head between them, he acted as a running chorus to the play during the whole performance. Ayala thoroughly enjoyed herself, and thought that in all her experience no play she'd seen had ever been so delightful. On their return home the two girls were both told to go to bed in the Marchesa's good-natured authoritative tone; but, nevertheless, Ayala did manage to say a word before she finally adjusted herself on her pillow. 'It is all very well, Nina, for your mamma to say that a young man of business is the best; but I do know a lout when I see him; and I am quite sure that my cousin Tom is a lout, and that Colonel Jonathan is not.'

'I believe you are falling in love with Colonel Jonathan,' said Nina.

'I should as soon think of falling in love with a wild bear;—but he's not a lout, and therefore I like him.'

## CHAPTER XVII

### LUCY IS VERY FIRM

IT was just before the Tringles had returned from Rome, during the winter, that Lucy Dormer had met Mr. Hamel in Kensington Gardens for the second time, had walked there with him perhaps for half-an-hour, and had then returned home with a conviction that she had done a wicked thing. But she had other convictions also, which were perhaps stronger. 'Now that we have met, am I to lose you again?' he had said. What could he mean by losing, except that she was the one thing which he desired to find? But she had not seen him since, or heard a word of his whereabouts, although, as she so well remembered, she had given him an address at her Aunt Emmeline's,—not knowing then that it would be her fate to become a resident in her Aunt Emmeline's house. She had told him that Ayala would live there, and that perhaps she might sometimes be found visiting Ayala. Now, she was herself filling Ayala's place, and might so easily have been found. But she knew nothing of the man who had once asked whether he was 'to lose her again.'

Her own feelings about Isadore Hamel were clear enough to herself now. Ayala in her hot humour had asked her whether she could give her hand and her heart to such a one as their cousin Tom, and she had found herself constrained to say that she could not do so, because she was not free,—not quite free,—to do as she pleased with her hand and her heart. She had striven hard not to acknowledge anything, even to Ayala,—even to herself. But the words had been forced from her, and now she was conscious, terribly conscious, that the words were true. There could be no one else now, whether Tom or another,—whether such as Tom or such as any other. It was just that little word that had won her. 'Am I to lose you again?' A girl loves most often because she is loved,

—not from choice on her part. She is won by the flattery of the man's desire. 'Am I to lose you again?' He had seemed to throw all his soul into his voice and into his eyes as he had asked the question. A sudden thrill had filled her, and, for his sake,—for his sake,— she had hoped that she might not be lost to him. Now she began to fear that he was lost to her.

Something has been told of the relations between Isadore Hamel and his father. They were both sculptors, the father having become a successful artist. The father was liberal, but he was essentially autocratic. If he supplied to his son the means of living,—and he was willing to supply the means of a very comfortable life,—he expected that his son should live to some extent in accordance with his fancies. The father wished his son to live in Rome, and to live after the manner of Romans. Isadore would prefer to live in London, and after the manner of Londoners. For a time he had been allowed to do so, and had achieved a moderate success. But a young artist may achieve a moderate success with a pecuniary result that shall be almost less than moderate. After a while the sculptor in Rome had told his son that if he intended to remain in London he ought to do so on the independent proceeds of his own profession. Isadore, if he would return to Rome, would be made welcome to join his affairs to those of his father. In other words, he was to be turned adrift if he remained in London, and petted with every luxury if he would consent to follow his art in Italy. But in Rome the father lived after a fashion which was distasteful to the son. Old Mr. Hamel had repudiated all conventions. Conventions are apt to go very quickly, one after another, when the first has been thrown aside. The man who ceases to dress for dinner soon finds it to be a trouble to wash his hands. A house is a bore. Calling is a bore. Church is a great bore. A family is a bore. A wife is an unendurable bore. All laws are bores, except those by which inferiors can be constrained to do their work. Mr.

Hamel had got rid of a great many bores, and had a strong opinion that bores prevailed more mightily in London than in Rome. Isadore was not a bore to him. He was always willing to have Isadore near to him. But if Isadore chose to enter the conventional mode of life he must do it at his own expense. It may be said at once that Isadore's present view of life was very much influenced by Lucy Dormer, and by a feeling that she certainly was conventional. A small house, very prettily furnished, somewhat near the Fulham Road, or perhaps verging a little towards South Kensington, with two maids, and perhaps an additional one as nurse in the process of some months, with a pleasant English breakfast and a pleasant English teapot in the evening, afforded certainly a very conventional aspect of life. But, at the present moment, it was his aspect, and therefore he could not go upon all fours with his father. In this state of things there had, during the last twelvemonth, been more than one journey made to Rome and back. Ayala had seen him at Rome, and Lady Tringle, remembering that the man had been intimate with her brother, was afraid of him. They had made inquiry about him, and had fully resolved that he should not be allowed into the house if he came after Ayala. He had no mother,—to speak of; and he had little brothers and sisters, who also had no mother,—to speak of. Mr. Hamel, the father, entertained friends on Sunday, with the express object of playing cards. That a Papist should do so was to be borne;—but Mr. Hamel was not a Papist, and, therefore, would certainly be ——. All this and much more had been learned at Rome, and therefore Lucy, though she herself never mentioned Mr. Hamel's name in Queen's Gate, heard evil things said of the man who was so dear to her.

It was the custom of her life to be driven out every day with her aunt and Gertrude. Not to be taken two or three times round the park would be to Lady Tringle to rob her of the best appreciated of all those

gifts of fortune which had come to her by reason of
the banker's wealth. It was a stern law;—and as
stern a law that Lucy should accompany her. Gertrude, as being an absolute daughter of the house,
and as having an almost acknowledged lover of her
own, was allowed some choice. But for Lucy there
was no alternative. Why should she not go and be
driven? Two days before they left town she was
being driven, while her aunt was sitting almost in a
slumber beside her, when suddenly a young man,
leaning over the railings, took off his hat so close to
Lucy that she could almost have put out her hand
to him. He was standing there all alone, and seemed
simply to be watching the carriages as they passed.
She felt that she blushed as she bowed to him, and
saw also that the colour had risen to his face. Then
she turned gently round to her aunt, whom she hoped
to find still sleeping; but Aunt Emmeline could
slumber with one eye open. 'Who was that young
man, my dear?' said Aunt Emmeline.

'It was Mr. Hamel.'

'Mr. Isadore Hamel!' said Aunt Emmeline, horrified. 'Is that the young man at Rome who has got
the horrible father?'

'I do not know his father,' said Lucy; 'but he does
live at Rome.'

'Of course, it's the Mr. Hamel I mean. He scraped
some acquaintance with Ayala, but I would not have
it for a moment. He is not at all the sort of person
any young girl ought to know. His father is a horrible
man. I hope he is no friend of yours, Lucy!'

'He is a friend of mine.' Lucy said this in a tone of
voice which was very seldom heard from her, but which,
when heard, was evidence that beneath the softness
of her general manner there lay a will of her own.

'Then, my dear, I hope that such friendship may
be discontinued as long as you remain with us.'

'He was a friend of papa's,' said Lucy.

'That's all very well. I suppose artists must know
artists, even though they are disreputable.'

'Mr. Hamel is not disreputable.'

Aunt Emmeline, as she heard this, could almost
fancy that she was renewing one of her difficulties
with Ayala. 'My dear,' she said,—and she intended
to be very impressive as she spoke,—'in a matter
such as this I must beg you to be guided by me. You
must acknowledge that I know the world better than
you do. Mr. Hamel is not a fit person to be acquainted with a young lady who occupies the place
of my daughter. I am sure that will be sufficient.'
Then she leant back in the carriage, and seemed
again to slumber; but she still had one eye open, so
that if Mr. Hamel should appear again at any corner
and venture to raise his hand she might be aware of
the impropriety. But on that day Mr. Hamel did not
appear again.

Lucy did not speak another word during the drive,
and on reaching the house went at once to her bed-
room. While she had been out with her aunt close
to her, and while it had been possible that the man
she loved should appear again, she had been unable
to collect her thoughts or to make up her mind what
she would do or say. One thing simply was certain
to her, that if Mr. Hamel should present himself again
to her she would not desert him. All that her aunt
had said to her as to improprieties and the like had
no effect at all upon her. The man had been welcomed at her father's house, had been allowed there
to be intimate with her, and was now, as she was well
aware, much dearer to her than any other human
being. Nor for all the Aunt Emmelines in the world
would she regard him otherwise than as her dearest
friend.

When she was alone she discussed the matter with
herself. It was repugnant to her that there should be
any secret on the subject between herself and her
aunt after what had been said,—much more that
there should be any deceit. Mr. Hamel is not fit to
be acquainted with a lady who occupies the position
of my daughter.' It was thus that her aunt had

spoken. To this the proper answer seemed to be,—
seemed at least to Lucy,—'In that case, my dear
aunt, I cannot for a moment longer occupy the position of your daughter, as I certainly am acquainted
and shall remain acquainted with Mr. Hamel.' But
to such speech as this on her own part there were two
impediments. In the first place it would imply that
Mr. Hamel was her lover,—for implying which Mr.
Hamel had given her no authority; and then what
should she immediately do when she had thus
obstinately declared herself to be unfit for that
daughter's position which she was supposed now to
occupy? With all her firmness of determination she
could not bring herself to tell her aunt that Mr. Hamel
was her lover. Not because it was not as yet true.
She would have been quite willing that her aunt
should know the exact truth, if the exact truth could
be explained. But how could she convey to such a
one as Aunt Emmeline the meaning of those words,
—'Am I to lose you again?' How could she make
her aunt understand that she held herself to be
absolutely bound, as by a marriage vow, by such
words as those,—words in which there was no
promise, even had they come from some fitting
suitor, but which would be regarded by Aunt Emmeline as being simply impertinent coming as they
did from such a one as Isadore Hamel. It was quite
out of the question to tell all that to Aunt Emmeline,
but yet it was necessary that something should be
told. She had been ordered to drop her acquaintance
with Isadore, and it was essential that she should
declare that she would do nothing of the kind. She
would not recognise such obedience as a duty on her
part. The friendship had been created by her father,
to whom her earlier obedience had been due. It
might be that, refusing to render such obedience, her
aunt and her uncle might tell her that there could be
no longer shelter for her in that house. They could
not cherish and foster a disobedient child. If it must
be so, it must. Though there should be no home left

to her in all the wide world she would not accept an
order which should separate her from the man she
loved. She must simply tell her aunt that she could
not drop Mr. Hamel's acquaintance,—because Mr.
Hamel was a friend.

Early on the next morning she did so. 'Are you
aware,' said Aunt Emmeline, with a severe face,
'that he is—illegitimate?' Lucy blushed, but made
no answer. 'Is he—is he—engaged to you?'

'No,' said Lucy, sharply.

'Has he asked you to marry him?'

'No,' said Lucy.

'Then what is it?' asked Lady Tringle, in a tone
which was intended to signify that as nothing of that
kind had taken place such a friendship could be a
matter of no consequence.

'He was papa's friend.'

'My dear, what can that matter? Your poor papa
has gone, and you are in my charge and your uncle's.
Surely you cannot object to choose your friends as we
should wish. Mr. Hamel is a gentleman of whom we
do not approve. You cannot have seen very much of
him, and it would be very easy for you, should he
bow to you again in the park, to let him see that you
do not like it.'

'But I do like it,' said Lucy with energy.

'Lucy!'

'I do like to see Mr. Hamel, and I feel almost sure
that he will come and call here now that he has seen
me. Last winter he asked me my address, and I gave
him this house.'

'When you were living with your Aunt Dosett?'

'Yes, I did, Aunt Emmeline. I thought Aunt
Margaret would not like him to come to Kingsbury
Crescent, and, as Ayala was to be here, I told him he
might call at Queen's Gate.'

Then Lady Tringle was really angry. It was not
only that her house should have been selected for so
improper a use but that Lucy should have shown a
fear and a respect for Mrs. Dosett which had not been

accorded to herself. It was shocking to her pride that that should have appeared to be easy of achievement at Queen's Gate which was too wicked to be attempted at Kingsbury Crescent. And then the thing which had been done seemed in itself to her to be so horrible! This girl, when living under the care of her aunt, had made an appointment with an improper young man at the house of another aunt! Any appointment made by a young lady with a young man must, as she thought, be wrong. She began to be aghast at the very nature of the girl who could do such a thing, and on reflecting that that girl was at present under her charge as an adopted daughter. 'Lucy,' she said, very impressively, 'there must be an end of this.'

'There cannot be an end of it,' said Lucy.

'Do you mean to say that he is to come here to this house whether I and your uncle like it or not?'

'He will come,' said Lucy; 'I am sure he will come. Now he has seen me he will come at once.'

'Why should he do that if he is not your lover?'

'Because,' said Lucy,—and then she paused; 'because——. It is very hard to tell you, Aunt Emmeline.'

'Why should he come so quickly?' demanded Aunt Emmeline again.

'Because——. Though he has said nothing to me such as that you mean,' stammered out Lucy, determined to tell the whole truth, 'I believe that he will.'

'And you?'

'If he did I should accept him.'

'Has he any means?'

'I do not know.'

'Have you any?'

'Certainly not.'

'And you would consent to be his wife after what I've told you?'

'Yes,' said Lucy, 'I should.'

'Then it must not be in this house. That is all. I will not have him here on any pretence whatsoever.'

'I thought not, Aunt Emmeline, and therefore I have told you.'

'Do you mean that you will make an appointment with him elsewhere?'

'Certainly not. I have not in fact ever made an appointment with him. I do not know his address. Till yesterday I thought that he was in Rome. I never had a line from him in my life, and of course have never written to him.' Upon hearing all this Lady Tringle sat in silence, not quite knowing how to carry on the conversation. The condition of Lucy's mind was so strange to her, that she felt herself to be incompetent to dictate. She could only resolve that under no circumstances should the objectionable man be allowed into her house. 'Now, Aunt Emmeline,' said Lucy, 'I have told you everything. Of course you have a right to order, but I also have some right. You told me I was to drop Mr. Hamel, but I cannot drop him. If he comes in my way I certainly shall not drop him. If he comes here I shall see him if I can. If you and Uncle Tom choose to turn me out, of course you can do so.'

'I shall tell your uncle all about it,' said Aunt Emmeline, angrily, 'and then you will hear what he says.' And so the conversation was ended.

At that moment Sir Thomas was, of course, in the City managing his millions, and as Lucy herself had suggested that Mr. Hamel might not improbably call on that very day, and as she was quite determined that Mr. Hamel should not enter the doors of the house in Queen's Gate, it was necessary that steps should be taken at once. Some hours afterwards Mr. Hamel did call and asked for Miss Dormer. The door was opened by a well-appointed footman, who, with lugubrious face,—with a face which spoke much more eloquently than his words,—declared that Miss Dormer was not at home. In answer to further inquiries he went on to express an opinion that Miss Dormer never would be at home;—from all which it may be seen that Aunt Emmeline had taken strong measures to carry out her purpose. Hamel, when he heard his fate thus plainly spoken from the man's mouth, turned away, not doubting its meaning. He had seen Lucy's face in the park, and had seen also Lady Tringle's gesture after his greeting. That Lady Tringle should not be disposed to receive him at her house was not matter of surprise to him.

When Lucy went to bed that night she did not doubt that Mr. Hamel had called, and that he had been turned away from the door.

## CHAPTER XVIII

### DOWN IN SCOTLAND

WHEN the time came, all the Tringles, together with the Honourable Mrs. Traffick, started for Glenbogie. Aunt Emmeline had told Sir Thomas all Lucy's sins, but Sir Thomas had not made so much of them as his wife had expected. 'It wouldn't be a bad thing to have a husband for Lucy,' said Sir Thomas.

'But the man hasn't got a sixpence.'

'He has a profession.'

'I don't know that he makes anything. And then think of his father! He is—illegitimate!' Sir Thomas seemed rather to sneer at this. 'And if you knew the way the old man lives in Rome! He plays cards all Sunday!' Again Sir Thomas sneered. Sir Thomas was fairly submissive to the conventionalities himself, but did not think that they ought to stand in the way of a provision for a young lady who had no provision of her own. 'You wouldn't wish to have him at Queen's Gate?' asked Lady Tringle.

'Certainly not, if he makes nothing by his profession. A good deal, I think, depends upon that.' Then nothing further was said, but Lucy was not told her uncle's opinion on the matter, as had been promised. When she went down to Glenbogie she

only knew that Mr. Hamel was considered to be by
far too black a sheep to be admitted into her aunt's
presence, and that she must regard herself as separated from the man as far as any separation could be
effected by her present protectors. But if he would
be true to her, as to a girl whom he had a short time
since so keenly rejoiced in 'finding again,' she was
quite sure that she could be true to him.

On the day fixed, the 20th of August, Mr. Houston
arrived at Glenbogie, with boots and stockings and
ammunition, such as Tom had recommended when
interrogated on those matters by his sister, Gertrude.
'I travelled down with a man I think you know,' he
said to Lucy ;—'at any rate your sister does, because
I saw him with her at Rome.' The man turned out to
be Isadore Hamel. 'I didn't like to ask him whether
he was coming here,' said Frank Houston.

'No ; he is not coming here,' said Aunt Emmeline.

'Certainly not,' said Gertrude, who was quite prepared to take up the cudgels on her mother's behalf
against Mr. Hamel.

'He said something about another man he used to
know at Rome, before you came. He was a nephew of
that Marchesa Baldoni.'

'She was a lady we didn't like a bit too well,' said
Gertrude.

'A very stuck-up sort of person, who did all she
could to spoil Ayala,' said Aunt Emmeline.

'Ayala has just been staying with her,' said Lucy.
'She has been very kind to Ayala.'

'We have nothing to do with that now,' said Aunt
Emmeline. 'Ayala can stay with whom she and her
aunt pleases. Is this Mr. Hamel, whom you saw, a
friend of the Marchesa's ? '

'He seemed to be a friend of the Marchesa's
nephew,' continued Houston ;—'one Colonel Stubbs.
We used to see him at Rome, and a most curious man
he is. His name is Jonathan, and I don't suppose
that any man was ever seen so red before. He is
shooting somewhere, and Hamel seems to be going

to join him. I thought he might have been coming here afterwards, as you all were in Rome together.'

'Certainly he is not coming here,' said Aunt Emmeline. 'And as for Colonel Stubbs, I never heard of him before.'

A week of the time allotted to Frank Houston had gone before he had repeated a word of his suit to Sir Thomas. But with Gertrude every opportunity had been allowed him, and by the rest of the family they had been regarded as though they were engaged. Mr. Traffick, who was now at Glenbogie, in accordance with the compact made with him, did not at first approve of Frank Houston. He had insinuated to Lady Tringle, and had said very plainly to Augusta, that he regarded a young man, without any employment and without any income, as being quite unfit to marry. 'If he had a seat in the House it would be quite a different thing,' he had said to Augusta. But his wife had snubbed him; telling him, almost in so many words, that if Gertrude was determined to have her way in opposition to her father she certainly would not be deterred by her brother-in-law. 'It's nothing to me,' Mr. Traffick had then said; 'the money won't come out of my pocket; but when a man has nothing else to do he is sure to spend all that he can lay his hands upon.' After that, however, he withdrew his opposition, and allowed it to be supposed that he was ready to receive Frank Houston as his brother-in-law, should it be so decided.

The time was running by both with Houston, the expectant son-in-law, and with Mr. Traffick, who had achieved his position, and both were aware that no grace would be allowed to them beyond that which had been promised. Frank had fully considered the matter, and was quite resolved that it would be unmanly in him to run after his cousin Imogene, in the Tyrol, before he had performed his business. One day, therefore, after having returned from the daily allowance of slaughter, he contrived to find Sir Thomas in the solitude of his own room, and again began to act the part of Allan-a-Dale. 'I thought, Mr. Houston,' said Sir Thomas, 'that we had settled that matter before.'

'Not quite,' said Houston.

'I don't know why you should say so. I intended to be understood as expressing my mind.'

'But you have been good enough to ask me down here.'

'I may ask a man to my house, I suppose, without intending to give him my daughter's hand.' Then he again asked the important question, to which Allan-a-Dale's answer was so unreasonable and so successful* 'Have you an income on which to maintain my daughter?'

'I cannot just say that I have, Sir Thomas,' said Houston, apologetically.

'Then you mean to ask me to furnish you with an income.'

'You can do as you please about that, Sir Thomas.'

'You can hardly marry her without it.'

'Well; no; not altogether. No doubt it is true that I should not have proposed myself had I not thought that the young lady would have something of her own.'

'But she has nothing of her own,' said Sir Thomas. And then that interview was over.

'You won't throw us over, Lady Tringle?' Houston said to Gertrude's mother that evening.

'Sir Thomas likes to have his own way,' said Lady Tringle.

'Somebody got round him about Septimus Traffick.'

'That was different,' said Lady Tringle. 'Mr. Traffick is in Parliament, and that gives him an employment. He is a son of Lord Boardotrade, and some of these days he will be in office.'

'Of course, you know that if Gertrude sticks to it she will have her own way. When a girl sticks to it her father has to give way. What does it matter to him whether I have any business or not? The money would be the same in one case as the other, only it does seem such an unnecessary trouble to have it put off.'

All this Lady Tringle seemed to take in good part, and half acknowledged that if Frank Houston were constant in the matter he would succeed at last. Gertrude, when the time for his departure had come, expressed herself as thoroughly disgusted by her father's sternness. 'It's all bosh,' she said to her lover. 'Who is Lord Boardotrade that that should make a difference? I have as much right to please myself as Augusta.' But there was the stern fact that the money had not been promised, and even Frank had not proposed to marry the girl of his heart without the concomitant thousands.

Before he left Glenbogie, on the evening of his departure, he wrote a second letter to Miss Docimer, as follows;—

'DEAR COUSIN IM,

'Here I am at Glenbogie, and here I have been for a week, without doing a stroke of work. The father still asks "of his house and his home," and does not seem to be at all affected by my reference to the romantic grandeur of my own peculiar residence. Perhaps I may boast so far as to say that I have laughed on the lass as successfully as did Allan-a-Dale. But what's the good of laughing on a lass* when one has got nothing to eat? Allan-a-Dale could pick a pocket or cut a purse, accomplishments in which I am altogether deficient. I suppose I shall succeed sooner or later, but when I put my neck into the collar I had no idea that there would be so much up-hill work before me. It is all very well joking, but it is not nice to be asked "of your house and your home" by a gentleman who knows very well you've got none, and is conscious of inhabiting three or four palaces himself. Such treatment must be described as being decidedly vulgar. And then he must know that it can be of no possible permanent use. The ladies are all on my side, but I am told by

Tringle mère that I am less acceptable than old
Traffick, who married the other girl, because I'm not
the son of Lord Boardotrade! Nothing astonishes me
so much as the bad taste of some people. Now, it
must all be put off till Christmas, and the cruel part
is, that one doesn't see how I'm to go on living.

'In the meantime I have a little time in which to
amuse myself, and I shall turn up in about three
weeks at Merle Park. I wish chiefly to beg that you
will not dissuade me from what I see clearly to be a
duty. I know exactly your line of argument. Following a girl for her money is, you will say, mercenary.
So, as far as I can see, is every transaction in the
world by which men live. The judges, the bishops, the
poets, the Royal academicians, and the Prime
Ministers, are all mercenary;—as is also the man who
breaks stones for 2s. 6d. a-day. How shall a man live
without being mercenary unless he be born to fortune? Are not girls always mercenary? Will she
marry me knowing that I have nothing? Will you
not marry some one whom you will probably like
much less simply because he will have something for
you to eat and drink? Of course I am mercenary,
and I don't even pretend to old Tringle that I am not
so. I feel a little tired of this special effort;—but if
I were to abandon it I should simply have to begin
again elsewhere. I have sighted my stag, and I must
go on following him, trying to get on the right side
of the wind till I bring him down. It is not nice, but
it is to me manifestly my duty,—and I shall do it.
Therefore, do not let there be any blowing up. I hate
to be scolded.

'Yours always affectionately,

'F. H.'

Gertrude, when he was gone, did not take the
matter quite so quietly as he did, feeling that, as she
had made up her mind, and as all her world would
know that she had made up her mind, it behoved her
to carry her purpose to its desired end. A girl who is

known to be engaged, but whose engagement is not allowed, is always in a disagreeable plight.

'Mamma,' she said, 'I think that papa is not treating me well.'

'My dear, your papa has always had his own way.'

'That is all very well;—but why am I to be worse used than Augusta? It turns out now that Mr. Traffick has not got a shilling of his own.'

'Your papa likes his being in Parliament.'

'All the girls can't marry Members of Parliament.'

'And he likes his being the son of Lord Boardotrade.'

'Lord Boardotrade! I call that very mean. Mr. Houston is a gentleman, and the Buncombe property has been for ever so many hundreds of years in the family. I think more of Frank as to birth and all that than I do of Lord Boardotrade and his mushroom peerage. Can't you tell papa that I mean to marry Mr. Houston at last, and that he is making very little of me to let me be talked about as I shall be?'

'I don't think I can, Gertrude.'

'Then I shall. What would he say if I were to run away with Frank?'

'I don't think Frank Houston would do that.'

'He would if I told him,—in a moment.' There Miss Tringle was probably in error. 'And unless papa consents I shall tell him. I am not going to be made miserable for ever.'

This was at Glenbogie, in Inverness-shire, on the south-eastern side of Loch Ness, where Sir Thomas Tringle possessed a beautiful mansion, with a deer-forest, and a waterfall of his own, and any amount of moors which the minds of sportsmen could conceive. Nothing in Scotland could be more excellent, unless there might be some truth in the remarks of those who said that the grouse were scarce, and that the deer were almost non-existent. On the other side of the lake, four miles up from the gates, on the edge of a ravine, down which rushed a little stream called the Caller, was an inconvenient rickety cottage, built

piecemeal at two or three different times, called
Drumcaller. From one room you went into another,
and from that into a third. To get from the sitting-
room, which was called the parlour, into another
which was called the den, you had to pass through
the kitchen, or else to make communication by a
covered passage out of doors which seemed to hang
over the margin of the ravine. Pine-trees enveloped
the place. Looking at the house from the outside any
one would declare it to be wet through. It certainly
could not with truth be described as a comfortable
family residence. But you might, perhaps, travel
through all Scotland without finding a more beautifully romantic spot in which to reside. From that
passage, which seemed to totter suspended over the
rocks, whence the tumbling rushing waters could
always be heard like music close at hand, the view
down over the little twisting river was such as filled
the mind with a conviction of realised poetry. Behind
the house across the little garden there was a high
rock where a little path had been formed, from which
could be seen the whole valley of the Caller and the
broad shining expanse of the lake beyond. Those who
knew the cottage of Drumcaller were apt to say that
no man in Scotland had a more picturesque abode, or
one more inconvenient. Even bread had to be carried
up from Callerfoot, as was called the little village
down on the lake side, and other provisions, such even
as meat, had to be fetched twenty miles, from the
town of Inverness.

A few days after the departure of Houston from
Glenbogie two men were seated with pipes in their
mouths on the landing outside the room called the
den to which the passage from the parlour ran. Here
a square platform had been constructed capable of
containing two arm-chairs, and here the owner of the
cottage was accustomed to sit, when he was disposed,
as he called it, to loaf away his time at Drumcaller.
This man was Colonel Jonathan Stubbs, and his companion at the present moment was Isadore Hamel.

'I never knew them in Rome,' said the Colonel. 'I never even saw Ayala there, though she was so much at my aunt's house. I was in Sicily part of the time, and did not get back till they had all quarrelled. I did know the nephew, who was a good-natured but a vulgar young man. They are vulgar people, I should say.'

'You could hardly have found Ayala vulgar?' asked Hamel.

'Indeed, no. But uncles and aunts and nephews and nieces are not at all bound to run together. Ayala is the daintiest little darling I ever saw.'

'I knew their father and mother, and certainly no one would have called them vulgar.'

'Sisters when they marry of course go off according to their husbands, and the children follow. In this case one sister became Tringlish after Sir Tringle, and the other Dormerish, after that most improvident of human beings, your late friend the artist. I don't suppose any amount of experience will teach Ayala how many shillings there are in a pound. No doubt the Honourable Mrs. Traffick knows all about it.'

'I don't think a girl is much improved by knowing how many shillings there are in a pound,' said Hamel.

'It is useful sometimes.'

'So it might be to kill a sheep and skin it, or to milk a cow and make cheese; but here, as in other things, one acquirement will drive out others. A woman, if she cannot be beautiful, should at any rate be graceful, and if she cannot soar to poetry, should at least be soft and unworldly.'

'That's all very well in its way, but I go in for roasting, baking, and boiling.

> I can bake and I can brew;
> I can make an Irish stew;
> Wash a shirt and iron it too.

That's the sort of girl I mean to go in for if ever I marry; and when you've got six children and a small income it's apt to turn out better than grace and poetry.'

'A little of both perhaps,' said Hamel.

'Well, yes; I don't mind a little Byron now and again, so there is no nonsense. As to Glenbogie, it's right over there across the lake. You can get a boat at Callerfoot, and a fellow to take you across and wait for you won't cost you more than three half-crowns. I suppose Glenbogie is as far from the lake on that side as my cottage is on this. How you'll get up except by walking I cannot say, unless you will write a note to Sir Thomas and ask him to send a horse down for you.'

'Sir Thomas would not accommodate me.'

'You think he will frown if you come after his niece?'

'I simply want to call on Miss Dormer,' said Hamel, blushing, 'because her father was always kind to me.'

'I don't mean to ask any questions,' said the Colonel.

'It is just so as I say. I do not like being in the neighbourhood without calling on Miss Dormer.'

'I daresay not.'

'But I doubt whether Sir Thomas or Lady Tringle would be at all inclined to make me welcome. As to the distance, I can walk that easily enough, and if the door is slammed in my face I can walk back again.'

Thus it was resolved that early on the following morning after breakfast Isadore Hamel should go across the lake and make his way up to Glenbogie.

## CHAPTER XIX

### ISADORE HAMEL IS ASKED TO LUNCH

ON the following morning, the morning of Monday, 2nd September, Isadore Hamel started on his journey. He had thought much about the journey before he made it. No doubt the door had been slammed in his face in London. He felt quite conscious of that, and conscious also that a man should not renew his attempt to enter a door when it

has been once slammed in his face. But he understood the circumstances nearly as they had happened,—except that he was not aware how far the
door had been slammed by Lady Tringle without
any concurrence on the part of Sir Thomas. But
the door had, at any rate, not been slammed by
Lucy. The only person he had really wished to
see within that house had been Lucy Dormer; and
he had hitherto no reason for supposing that she
would be unwilling to receive him. Her face had
been sweet and gracious when she saw him in the
Park. Was he to deny himself all hope of any future
intercourse with her because Lady Tringle had
chosen to despise him? He must make some attempt.
It was more than probable, no doubt, that this attempt would be futile. The servant at Glenbogie
would probably be as well instructed as the servant
in Queen's Gate. But still a man has to go on and
do something, if he means to do anything. There
could be no good in sitting up at Drumcaller, at one
side of the lake, and thinking of Lucy Dormer far
away, at the other side. He had not at all made up
his mind that he would ask Lucy to be his wife. His
professional income was still poor, and she, as he was
aware, had nothing. But he felt it to be incumbent
upon him to get nearer to her if it were possible, and
to say something to her if the privilege of speech
should be accorded to him.

He walked down to Callerfoot, refusing the loan of
the Colonel's pony carriage, and thence had himself
carried across the lake in a hired boat to a place called
Sandy's Quay. That, he was assured, was the spot
on the other side from whence the nearest road would
be found to Glenbogie. But nobody on the Callerfoot
side could tell him what would be the distance. At
Sandy's Quay he was assured that it was twelve
miles to Glenbogie House; but he soon found that
the man who told him had a pony for hire. 'Ye'll nae
get there under twelve mile,—or maybe saxteen, if
ye attampt to walk up the glin.' So said the owner of

the pony. But milder information came to him
speedily. A little boy would show him the way up
the glen for sixpence, and engage to bring him to the
house in an hour and a half. So he started with the
little boy, and after a hot scramble for about two
hours he found himself within the demesne. Poking
their way up through thick bushes from a ravine,
they showed their two heads,—first the boy and then
the sculptor,—close by the side of the private road,—
just as Sir Thomas was passing, mounted on his cob.
'It's his ain sell,' said the boy, dropping his head
again amongst the bushes.

Hamel, when he had made good his footing, had
first to turn round so that the lad might not lose his
wages. A dirty little hand came up for the sixpence,
but the head never appeared again. It was well
known in the neighbourhood,—especially at Sandy's
Quay, where boats were used to land,—that Sir
Thomas was not partial to visitors who made their
way into Glenbogie by any but the authorised road.
While Hamel was paying his debt, he stood still on
his steed waiting to see who might be the trespasser.
'That's not a high road,' said Sir Thomas, as the
young man approached him. As the last quarter of
an hour from the bottom of the ravine had been
occupied in very stiff climbing among the rocks the
information conveyed appeared to Hamel to have
been almost unnecessary. 'Your way up to the
house, if you are going there, would have been
through the lodge down there.'

'Perhaps you are Sir Thomas Tringle,' said Hamel.

'That is my name.'

'Then I have to ask your pardon for my mode of
ingress. I am going up to the house; but having
crossed the lake from Callerfoot I did not know my
way on this side, and so I have clambered up the
ravine.' Sir Thomas bowed, and then waited for
further tidings. 'I believe Miss Dormer is at the
house?'

'My niece is there.'

'My name is Hamel,—Isadore Hamel. I am a sculptor, and used to be acquainted with her father. I have had great kindness from the whole family, and so I was going to call upon her. If you do not object, I will go on to the house.'

Sir Thomas sat upon his horse speechless for a minute. He had to consider whether he did not object or not. He was well aware that his wife objected, —aware also that he had declined to coincide with his wife's objection when it had been pressed upon him. Why should not his niece have the advantage of a lover, if a proper sort of a lover came in her way? As to the father's morals or the son's birth, those matters to Sir Thomas were nothing. The young man, he was told, was good at making busts. Would any one buy the busts when they were made? That was the question. His wife would certainly be prejudiced,—would think it necessary to reject for Lucy any suitor she would reject for her own girls. And then, as Sir Thomas felt, she had not shown great judgment in selecting suitors for her own girls. 'Oh, Mr. Hamel, are you?' he said at last.

'Isadore Hamel.'

'You called at Queen's Gate once, not long ago?'

'I did,' said Hamel; 'but saw no one.'

'No, you didn't; I heard that. Well, you can go on to the house if you like, but you had better ask for Lady Tringle. After coming over from Callerfoot you'll want some lunch. Stop a moment. I don't mind if I ride back with you.' And so the two started towards the house, and Hamel listened whilst Sir Thomas expatiated on the beauties of Glenbogie.

They had passed through one gate and were approaching another, when, away among the trees, there was a young lady seen walking alone. 'There is Miss Dormer,' said Hamel; 'I suppose I may join her?' Sir Thomas could not quite make up his mind whether the meeting was to be allowed or not, but he could not bring himself at the spur of the moment to refuse his sanction. So Hamel made his way

across to Lucy, while Sir Thomas rode on alone to
the house.

Lucy had seen her uncle on the cob, and, being
accustomed to see him on the cob, knew of course
who he was. She had also seen another man with
him, but not in the least expecting that Hamel was
in those parts, had never dreamt that he was her
uncle's companion. It was not till Hamel was near
to her that she understood that the man was coming
to join herself; and then, when she did recognise the
man, she was lost in amazement. 'You hardly expected to see me here?' said he.

'Indeed; no.'

'Nor did I expect that I should find you in this
way.'

'My uncle knows it is you?' asked Lucy.

'Oh, yes. I met him as I came up from the ravine,
and he has asked me to go on to the house to lunch.'
Then there was silence for a few moments as they
walked on together. 'I hope you do not think that
I am persecuting you in making my way over here.'

'Oh, no; not persecuting!' Lucy when she heard
the sound of what she herself had said, was angry
with herself, feeling that she had almost declared
him guilty of some wrong in having come thither.
'Of course I am glad to see you,' she added, 'for
papa's sake, but I'm afraid——'

'Afraid of what, Miss Dormer?'

She looked him full in the face as she answered
him, collecting her courage to make the declaration
which seemed to be necessary. 'My Aunt Emmeline
does not want you to come.'

'Why should she not want me?'

'That I cannot tell. Perhaps if I did know I should
not tell. But it is so. You called at Queen's Gate,
and I know that you were not admitted, though I was
at home. Of course, Aunt Emmeline has a right to
choose who shall come. It is not as though I had a
house of my own.'

'But Sir Thomas asked me in.'

'Then you had better go in. After what Aunt Emmeline said, I do not think that you ought to remain with me.'

'Your uncle knows I am with you,' said Hamel. Then they walked on towards the house together in silence for a while. 'Do you mean to say,' he continued, 'that because your aunt objects you are never to see me again?'

'I hope I shall see you again. You were papa's friend, and I should be so very sorry not to see you again.'

'I suppose,' he said, slowly, 'I can never be more than your papa's friend.'

'You are mine also.'

'I would be more than that.' Then he paused as if waiting for a reply, but she of course had none to make. 'I would be so much more than that, Lucy.' Still she had no answer to give him. But there comes a time when no answer is as excellent eloquence as any words that can be spoken. Hamel, who had probably not thought much of this, was nevertheless at once informed by his instincts that it was so. 'Oh, Lucy,' he said, 'if you can love me say so.'

'Mr. Hamel,' she whispered.

'Lucy.'

'Mr. Hamel, I told you about Aunt Emmeline. She will not allow it. I ought not to have let you speak to me like this, while I am staying here.'

'But your uncle knows I am with you.'

'My aunt does not know. We must go to the house. She expressly desired that I would not speak to you.'

'And you will obey her—always?'

'No; not always. I did not say that I should obey her always. Some day, perhaps, I shall do as I think fit myself.'

'And then you will speak to me?'

'Then I will speak to you,' she said.

'And love me?'

'And love you,' she answered, again looking him full in the face. 'But now pray, pray let us go on.'

For he had stopped her awhile amidst the trees, and had put out his hand as though to take hers, and had opened his arms as though he would embrace her. But she passed on quickly, and hardly answered his further questions till they found themselves together in the hall of the house.

Then they met Lady Tringle, who was just passing into the room where the lunch was laid, and following her were Augusta, Gertrude, and the Honourable Septimus Traffick. For, though Frank Houston had found himself compelled to go at the day named, the Honourable Septimus had contrived to squeeze out another week. Augusta was indeed still not without hope that the paternal hospitality of Glenbogie might be prolonged till dear Merle Park should once again open her portals. Sir Thomas had already passed into the dining-room, having in a gruff voice informed his wife that he had invited Mr. Hamel to come in to lunch. 'Mr. Hamel!' she had exclaimed. 'Yes, Mr. Hamel. I could not see the man starving when he had come all this way. I don't know anything against him.' Then he had turned away, and had gone into the dining-room, and was now standing with his back to the empty fire-place, determined to take Mr. Hamel's part if any want of courtesy were shown to him.

It certainly was hard upon Lady Tringle. She frowned and was going to walk on without any acknowledgment, when Lucy timidly went through a form of introduction. 'Aunt Emmeline, this is Mr. Hamel. Uncle Tom met him somewhere in the grounds and has asked him to come to luncheon.' Then Lady Tringle curtseyed and made a bow. The curtsey and the bow together were sufficient to have crushed the heart of any young man who had not been comforted and exalted by such words as Isadore had heard from Lucy's lips not five minutes since. 'And love you,' she had said. After that Lady Tringle might curtsey and bow as she would, and he could still live uncrushed. After the curtsey and the how Lady Tringle passed on. Lucy fell into the rank behind Gertrude; and then Hamel afterwards took his place behind the Honourable Septimus. 'If you will sit there, Mr. Hamel,' said Lady Tringle, pointing to a chair, across the table, obliquely, at the greatest possible distance from that occupied by Lucy. There he was stationed between Mr. Traffick and Sir Thomas. But now, in his present frame of mind, his position at the table made very little difference to him.

The lunch was eaten in grim silence. Sir Thomas was not a man profuse with conversation at his meals, and at this moment was ill-inclined for any words except what he might use in scolding his wife for being uncivil to his guest. Lady Tringle sat with her head erect, hardly opening her mouth sufficiently to allow the food to enter it. It was her purpose to show her displeasure at Mr. Hamel, and she showed it. Augusta took her mother's part, thoroughly despising the two Dormer girls and any lover that they might have. Poor Gertrude had on that morning been violently persecuted by a lecture as to Frank Houston's impecuniosity. Lucy of course would not speak. The Honourable Septimus was anxious chiefly about his lunch,—somewhat anxious also to offend neither the master nor the mistress of Merle Park. Hamel made one or two little efforts to extract answers from Sir Thomas, but soon found that Sir Thomas would prefer to be left in silence. What did it signify to him? He had done all that he wanted, and much more than he had expected.

The rising and getting away from luncheon is always a difficulty,—so great a difficulty when there are guests that lunch should never be much a company festival. There is no provision for leaving the table as there is at dinner. But on this occasion Lady Tringle extemporised provision the first moment in which they had all ceased to eat. 'Mr. Hamel,' she said very loudly, 'would you like some cheese?' Mr. Hamel, with a little start, declared that he wanted no cheese. 'Then, my dears, I think we will go into my room. Lucy, will you come with me?' Upon this the four ladies all went out in procession, but her ladyship was careful that Lucy should go first so that there might be no possibility of escape. Augusta and Gertrude followed her. The minds of all the four were somewhat perturbed ; but among the four Lucy's heart was by far the lightest.

'Are you staying over with Stubbs at that cottage?' asked the Honourable Septimus. 'A very queer fellow is Stubbs.'

'A very good fellow,' said Hamel.

'I dare say. He hasn't got any shooting?'

'I think not.'

'Not a head. Glentower wouldn't let an acre of shooting over there for any money.' This was the Earl of Glentower, to whom belonged an enormous tract of country on the other side of the lake. 'What on earth does he do with himself stuck up on the top of those rocks?'

'He does shoot sometimes, I believe, when Lord Glentower is there.'

'That's a poor kind of fun, waiting to be asked for a day,' said the Honourable Septimus, who rarely waited for anything till he was asked. 'Does he get any fishing?'

'He catches a few trout sometimes in the tarns above. But I fancy that Stubbs isn't much devoted to shooting and fishing.'

'Then what the d—— does he do with himself in such a country as this?' Hamel shrugged his shoulders, not caring to say that what with walking, what with reading and writing, his friend could be as happy as the day was long in such a place as Drumcaller.

'Is he a Liberal?'

'A what?' asked Hamel. 'Oh, a Liberal? Upon my word I don't know what he is. He is chiefly given to poetry, tobacco, and military matters.' Then the Honourable Septimus turned up his nose in disgust,

and ceased his cross-examination as to the character
and pursuits of Colonel Jonathan Stubbs.

'Sir Thomas, I am very much obliged to you for
your kindness,' said Hamel, getting up suddenly.
'As it is a long way over to Drumcaller I think I will
make a start. I know my way down the Glen and
should be sure to miss it by any other route. Perhaps
you'll let me go back as I came.' Sir Thomas offered
him the loan of a horse, but this was refused, and
Hamel started on his return journey across the lake.

When he had gone a few steps from the portal he
turned to look at the house which contained one whom
he now regarded as belonging exclusively to himself;
perhaps he thought that he might catch some final
view of Lucy; or, not quite thinking it, fancied that
some such chance might at least be possible; but he
saw nothing but the uninteresting façade of the
grand mansion. Lucy was employed quite otherwise.
She was listening to a lecture in which her aunt was
describing to her how very badly Mr. Hamel had
behaved in obtruding himself on the shades of Glenbogie. The lecture was somewhat long, as Aunt
Emmeline found it necessary to repeat all the arguments which she had before used as to the miscreant's birth, as to his want of adequate means, and
as to the general iniquities of the miscreant's father.
All this she repeated more than once with an energy
that was quite unusual to her. The flood of her eloquence was so great that Lucy found no moment for
an interposing word till all these evils had been
denunciated twice and thrice. But then she spoke.
'Aunt Emmeline,' she said, 'I am engaged to Mr.
Hamel now.'

'What!'

'He has asked me to be his wife and I have
promised.'

'And that after all that I had said to you!'

'Aunt Emmeline, I told you that I should not drop
him. I did not bid him come here. Uncle Tom
brought him. When I saw him I would have avoided

him if I could. I told him he ought not to be here
because you did not wish it; and then he answered
that my uncle knew that he was with me. Of course
when he told me that he—loved me, I could not make
him any other answer.' Then Aunt Emmeline expressed the magnitude of her indignation simply by
silence, and Lucy was left to think of her lover in
solitude.

\*       \*       \*       \*       \*       \*

'And how have you fared on your day's journey?'
said the Colonel, when Hamel found him still seated
on the platform with a book in his hand.

'Much better than I thought. Sir Thomas gave me
luncheon.'

'And the young lady?'

'The young lady was gracious also; but I am afraid
that I cannot carry my praises of the family at Glenbogie any further. The three Tringle ladies looked at
me as I was sitting at table as though I certainly had
no business in their august society.'

## CHAPTER XX

### STUBBS UPON MATRIMONY

BEFORE that evening was over,—or in the course
of the night, it might be better said, as the two
men sat up late with their pipes,—Hamel told his
friend the Colonel exactly what had taken place that
morning over at Glenbogie. 'You went for the purpose, of course?' asked the Colonel.

'For an off chance.'

'I know that well enough. I never heard of a man's
walking twelve miles to call upon a young lady
merely because he knew her father; and when there
was to be a second call within a few weeks, the first
having not been taken in very good part by the
young lady's friends, my inquiring mind told me that
there was something more than old family friendship.'

'Your inquiring mind saw into the truth.'

'And now looks forward to further events. Can she bake and can she brew?'

'I do not doubt that she could if she tried.'

'And can she wash a shirt for a man? Don't suppose, my dear fellow, that I intend to say that your wife will have to wash yours. Washing a shirt, as read in the poem from which I am quoting, is presumed to be simply emblematic of household duties in general.'

'I take all you say in good part,—as coming from a friend.'

'I regard matrimony,' said the Colonel, 'as being altogether the happiest state of life for a man,— unless to be engaged to some lovely creature, in whom one can have perfect confidence, may be a thought happier. One can enjoy all the ecstatic mental reflection, all the delights of conceit which come from being loved, that feeling of superiority to all the world around which illumines the bosom of the favoured lover, without having to put one's hand into one's pocket, or having one's pipe put out either morally or physically. The next to this is matrimony itself, which is the only remedy for that consciousness of disreputable debauchery, a savour of which always clings, more or less strongly, to unmarried men in our rank of life. The chimes must be heard at midnight,* let a young man be ever so well given to the proprieties, and he must have just a touch of the swingebuckler about him, or he will seem to himself to be deficient in virility. There is no getting out of it until a man marry. But then——'

'Well; then?'

'Do you know the man whose long-preserved hat is always brushed carefully, whose coat is the pattern of neatness, but still a little threadbare when you look at it,—in the colour of whose cheek there is still some touch of juvenility, but whose step is ever heavy and whose brow is always sad? The seriousness of life has pressed the smiles out of him. He has learned hardly to want anything for himself but out-

ward decency and the common necessaries of life.
Such little personal indulgences as are common to
you and to me are as strange to him as ortolans*or
diamonds.'

'I do not think I do know him.'

'I do;—well. I have seen him in the regiment, I
have met him on the steps of a public office, I have
watched him as he entered his parsonage house. You
shall find him coming out of a lawyer's office, where
he has sat for the last nine hours, having supported
nature with two penny biscuits. He has always
those few thin hairs over his forehead, he has always
that well-brushed hat, he has always that load of
care on his brow. He is generally thinking whether
he shall endeavour to extend his credit with the
butcher, or resolve that the supply of meat may be
again curtailed without injury to the health of his
five daughters.'

'That is an ugly picture.'

'But is it true?'

'In some cases, of course, it is.'

'And yet not ugly all round,' said the meditative
Colonel, who had just replenished his pipe. 'There
are, on the other side, the five daughters, and the
partner of this load of cares. He knows it is well to
have the five daughters, rather than to live with
plenty of beef and mutton,—even with the ortolans
if you will,—and with no one to care whether his
body may be racked in this world or his spirit in the
next. I do not say whether the balance of good or
evil be on one side or the other; but when a man is
going to do a thing he should know what it is he is
going to do.'

'The reading of all this,' said Hamel, 'is, that if I
succeed in marrying Miss Dormer I must have thin
locks, and a bad hat, and a butcher's bill.'

'Other men do.'

'Some, instead, have balances at their bankers,
and die worth thirty, forty, or fifty thousand pounds,
to the great consolation of the five daughters.'

'Or a hundred thousand pounds! There is, of course, no end to the amount of thousands which a successful professional man may accumulate. You may be the man; but the question is, whether you should not have reasonable ground to suppose your-self the man, before you encumber yourself with the five daughters.'

'It seems to me,' said Hamel, 'that the need of such assurance is cowardly.'

'That is just the question which I am always debating with myself. I also want to rid myself of that swingebuckler flavour. I feel that for me, like Adam, it is not good that I should be alone.* I would fain ask the first girl, that I could love well enough to wish to make myself one with her, to be my wife, regardless of hats, butchers, and daughters. It is a plucky and a fine thing for a man to feel that he can make his back broad enough for all burdens. But yet what is the good of thinking that you can carry a sack of wheat when you are sure that you have not, in truth, strength to raise it from the ground?'

'Strength will come,' said Hamel.

'Yes, and the bad hat. And, worse than the bad hat, the soiled gown; and perhaps with the soiled gown the altered heart;—and perhaps with the altered heart an absence of all that tenderness which it is a woman's special right to expect from a man.'

'I should have thought you would have been the last to be so self-diffident.'

'To be so thoughtful, you mean,' said the Colonel. 'I am unattached now, and having had no special duty for the last three months I have given myself over to thinking in a nasty morbid manner. It comes, I daresay, partly from tobacco. But there is comfort in this,—that no such reflections falling out of one man's mouth ever had the slightest effect in influencing another man's conduct.'

Hamel had told his friend with great triumph of his engagement with Lucy Dormer, but the friend did not return the confidence by informing the sculp-

tor that during the whole of this conversation, and
for many days previous to it, his mind had been
concerned with the image of Lucy's sister. He was
aware that Ayala had been, as it were, turned out
from her rich uncle's house, and given over to the
comparative poverty of Kingsbury Crescent. He
himself, at the present moment, was possessed of
what might be considered a comfortable income for
a bachelor. He had been accustomed to live almost
more than comfortably; but, having so lived, was
aware of himself that he had not adapted himself for
straitened circumstances. In spite of that advice of
his as to the brewing, baking, and washing capabilities of a female candidate for marriage, he knew
himself well enough to be aware that a wife red with
a face from a kitchen fire would be distasteful to him.
He had often told himself that to look for a woman
with money would be still more distasteful. Therefore
he had thought that for the present, at least, it would
be well for him to remain as he was. But now he had
come across Ayala, and though in the pursuance of
his philosophy he had assured himself that Ayala
should be nothing to him, still he found himself so
often reverting to this resolution that Ayala, instead
of being nothing, was very much indeed to him.

Three days after this Hamel was preparing himself
for his departure immediately after breakfast. 'What
a beast you are to go,' said the Colonel, 'when there
can be no possible reason for your going.'

'The five daughters and the bad hat make it
necessary that a fellow should do a little work sometimes.'

'Why can't you make your images down here?'

'With you for a model, and mud out of the Caller
for clay.'

'I shouldn't have the slightest objection. In your
art you cannot perpetuate the atrocity of my colour,
as the fellow did who painted my portrait last winter.
If you will go, go, and make busts at unheard-of
prices, so that the five daughters may live for ever

on the fat of the land. Can I do any good for you by going over to Glenbogie?'

'If you could snub that Mr. Traffick, who is of all men the most atrocious.'

'The power doesn't exist,' said the Colonel, 'which could snub the Honourable Septimus. That man is possessed of a strength which I thoroughly envy,— which is perhaps more enviable than any other gift the gods can give. Words cannot penetrate that skin of his. Satire flows off him like water from a duck. Ridicule does not touch him. The fellest abuse does not succeed in inflicting the slightest wound. He has learnt the great secret that a man cannot be cut who will not be cut. As it is worth no man's while to protract an enmity with such a one as-he, he suffers from no prolonged enmities. He walks unassailable by any darts, and is, I should say, the happiest man in London.'

'Then I fear you can do nothing for me at Glenbogie. To mollify Aunt Emmeline would, I fear, be beyond your power. Sir Thomas, as far as I can see, does not require much mollifying.'

'Sir Thomas might give the young woman a thousand or two.'

'That is not the way in which I desire to keep a good hat on my head,' said Hamel, as he seated himself in the little carriage which was to take him down to Callerfoot.

The Colonel remained at Drumcaller till the end of September, when his presence was required at Aldershot,—during which time he shot a good deal, in obedience to the good-natured behests of Lord Glentower, and in spite of the up-turned nose of Mr. Traffick. He read much, and smoked much,—so that as to the passing of his time there was not need to pity him, and he consumed a portion of his spare hours in a correspondence with his aunt, the Marchesa, and with his cousin Nina. One of his letters from each shall be given,—and also one of the letters written to each in reply.

NINA TO HER COUSIN THE COLONEL

'MY DEAR JONATHAN,

' Lady Albury says that you ought to be here, and
so you ought. It is ever so nice. There is a Mr. Ponsonby here, and he and I can beat any other couple at
lawn tennis.* There is an awning over the ground,
which is such a lounge. Playing lawn tennis with a
parasol as those Melcombe girls did is stupid. They
were here, but have gone. One I am quite sure was
over head and ears in love with Mr. Ponsonby.
These sort of things are always all on one side, you
know. He isn't very much of a man, but he does play
lawn tennis divinely. Take it altogether, I don't
think there is anything out to beat lawn tennis. I
don't know about hunting,—and I don't suppose I
ever shall.

' We tried to have Ayala here, but I fear it will not
come off. Lady Albury was good-natured, but at
last she did not quite like writing to Mrs. Dosett.
So mamma wrote, but the lady's answer was very stiff.
She thought it better for Ayala to remain among her
own friends. Poor Ayala! It is clear that a knight
will be wanted to go in armour, and get her out of
prison. I will leave it to you to say who must be the
knight.

' I hope you will come for a day or two before you
go to Aldershot. We stay till the 1st of October.
You will be a beast if you don't. Lady Albury says
she never means to ask you again. "Oh, Stubbs!"
said Sir Harry; "Stubbs is one of those fellows who
never come if they're asked." Of course we all sat
upon him. Then he declared that you were the
dearest friend he had in the world, but that he never
dared to dream that you would ever come to Stalham
again. Perhaps if we can hit it off at last with Ayala,
then you would come. Mamma means to try again.
—Your affectionate cousin,

'                                    ' NINA.'

THE MARCHESA BALDONI TO HER NEPHEW,
COLONEL STUBBS

'MY DEAR JONATHAN,

'I did my best for my protégée, but I am afraid it
will not succeed. Her aunt Mrs. Dosett seems to
think that, as Ayala is fated to live with her, Ayala
had better take her fate as she finds it. The meaning
of that is, that if a girl is doomed to have a dull life
she had better not begin it with a little pleasure.
There is a good deal to be said for the argument, but
if I were the girl I should like to begin with the
pleasure and take my chance for the reaction. I
should perhaps be vain enough to think that during
the preliminary course I might solve all the difficulty
by my beaux yeux. I saw Mrs. Dosett once, and now
I have had a letter from her. Upon the whole, I am
inclined to pity poor Ayala.

'We are very happy here. The Marchese has gone
to Como to look after some property he has there.
Do not be ill-natured enough to say that the two
things go together;—but in truth he is never comfortable out of Italy. He had a slice of red meat put
before him the other day, and that decided him to
start at once.

'On the first of October we go back to London, and
shall remain till the end of November. They have
asked Nina to come again in November in order that
she may see a hunt. I know that means that she will
try to jump over something, and have her leg broken.
You must be here and not allow it. If she does come
here I shall perhaps go down to Brighton for a fortnight.

'Yes;—I do think Ayala Dormer is a very pretty
girl, and I do think, also, that she is clever. I quite
agree that she is ladylike. But I do not therefore
think that she is just such a girl as such a man as
Colonel Jonathan Stubbs ought to marry. She is one
of those human beings who seem to have been removed out of this world and brought up in another.

Though she knows ever so much that nobody else knows, she is ignorant of ever so much that everybody ought to know. Wandering through a grove, or seated by a brook, or shivering with you on the top of a mountain, she would be charming. I doubt whether she would be equally good at the top of your table, or looking after your children, or keeping the week's accounts. She would tease you with poetry, and not even pretend to be instructed when you told her how an army ought to be moved. I say nothing as to the fact that she hasn't got a penny, though you are just in that position which makes it necessary for a man to get some money with his wife. I therefore am altogether indisposed to any matrimonial outlook in that direction.—Your affectionate aunt,

'BEATRICE BALDONI.'


COLONEL STUBBS TO HIS COUSIN NINA

'DEAR NINA,

'Lady Albury is wrong; I ought not to be at Stalham. What should I do at Stalham at this time of year, who never shoot partridges, and what would be the use of attempting lawn tennis when I know I should be cut out by Mr. Ponsonby? If that day in November is to come off then I'll come and coach you across the country. You tell Sir Harry that I say so, and that I will bring three horses for one week. I think it very hard about poor Ayala Dormer, but what can any knight do in such a case? When a young lady is handed over to the custody of an uncle or an aunt, she becomes that uncle's and aunt's individual property. Mrs. Dosett may be the most noxious dragon that ever was created for the mortification and general misery of an imprisoned damsel, but still she is omnipotent. The only knight who can be of any service is one who will go with a ring in his hand, and absolutely carry the prisoner away by force of the marriage service. Your unfortunate cousin is so exclusively devoted to the duty of fighting

his country's battles that he has not even time to
think of a step so momentous as that.

'Poor Ayala! Do not be stupid enough to accuse me
of pitying her because I cannot be the knight to
release her; but I cannot but think how happy she
would be at Stalham, struggling to beat you and
Mr. Ponsonby at lawn tennis, and then risking a
cropper when the happy days of November should
come round.—Your loving cousin,

'J. S.'

COLONEL STUBBS TO THE MARCHESA BALDONI

'MY DEAR AUNT,

'Your letter is worthy of the Queen of Sheba, if,
as was no doubt the case, she corresponded with
King Solomon.* As for Ayala's fate, if it be her fate
to live with Mrs. Dosett, she can only submit to it.
You cannot carry her over to Italy, nor would the
Marchese allow her to divide his Italian good things
with Nina. Poor little bird! She had her chance of
living amidst diamonds and banknotes, with the
Tringle millionaires, but threw it away after some
fashion that I do not understand. No doubt she was
a fool, but I cannot but like her the better for it. I
hardly think that a fortnight at Stalham, with all
Sir Harry's luxuries around her, would do her much
service.

'As for myself and the top of my table, and the
future companion who is to be doomed to listen to my
military lucubrations, I am altogether inclined to
agree with you, seeing that you write in a pure spirit
of worldly good sense. No doubt the Queen of Sheba
gave advice of the same sort to King Solomon. I
never knew a woman to speak confidentially of
matrimony otherwise than as a matter of pounds,
shillings, and pence. In counsels so given, no word
of love has ever been known to creep in. Why should
it, seeing that love cannot put a leg of mutton into
the pot? Don't imagine that I say this in a spirit

either of censure or satire. Your ideas are my own, and should I ever marry I shall do so in strict accordance with your tenets, thinking altogether of the weekly accounts, and determined to eschew any sitting by the sides of brooks.

'I have told Nina about my plans. I will be at Stalham in November to see that she does not break her neck.—Yours always,                    ' J. S.'


## CHAPTER XXI

### AYALA'S INDIGNATION

PERHAPS Mrs. Dosett had some just cause for refusing her sanction for the proposed visit to Albury. If Fate did require that Ayala should live permanently in Kingsbury Crescent, the gaiety of a very gay house, and the wealth of a very wealthy house, would hardly be good preparation for such a life. Up to the time of her going to the Marchesa in Brook Street, Ayala had certainly done her best to suit herself to her aunt's manners,—though she had done it with pain and suffering. She had hemmed the towels and mended the sheets, and had made the rounds to the shops. She had endeavoured to attend to the pounds of meat and to sympathise with her aunt in the interest taken in the relics of the joints as they escaped from the hungry treatment of the two maidens in the kitchen. Ayala had been clever enough to understand that her aunt had been wounded by Lucy's indifference, not so much because she had desired to avail herself of Lucy's labours as from a feeling that that indifference had seemed to declare that her own pursuits were mean and vulgar. Understanding this she had struggled to make those pursuits her own,—and had in part succeeded. Her aunt could talk to her about the butter and the washing, matters as to which her lips had been closed in any conversation with Lucy. That Ayala was struggling Mrs. Dosett had been aware;—but she had

thought that such struggles were good and had not
been hopeless. Then came the visit to Brook Street,
and Ayala returned quite an altered young woman.
It seemed as though she neither could nor would
struggle any longer. 'I hate mutton-bones,' she said
to her aunt one morning soon after her return.

'No doubt we would all like meat joints the best,'
said her aunt, frowning.

'I hate joints too.'

'You have, I dare say, been cockered up* at the
Marchesa's with made dishes.'

'I hate dishes,' said Ayala, petulantly.

'You don't hate eating?'

'Yes, I do. It is ignoble. Nature should have
managed it differently. We ought to have sucked it
in from the atmosphere through our fingers and hairs,
as the trees do by their leaves. There should have
been no butchers, and no grease, and no nasty
smells from the kitchen,—and no gin.'

This was worse than all,—this allusion to the mild
but unfashionable stimulant to which Mr. Dosett had
been reduced by his good nature. 'You are flying in
the face of the Creator, Miss,' said Aunt Margaret, in
her most angry voice,—'in the face of the Creator
who made everything, and ordained what His creatures should eat and drink by His infinite wisdom.'

'Nevertheless,' said Ayala, 'I think we might have
done without boiled mutton.' Then she turned to
some articles of domestic needlework which were in
her lap so as to show that in spite of the wickedness
of her opinions she did not mean to be idle. But Mrs.
Dosett, in her wrath, snatched the work from her
niece's hands and carried it out of the room, thus
declaring that not even a pillow-case in her house
should owe a stitch to the hands of a girl so ungrateful
and so blasphemous.

The wrath wore off soon. Ayala, though not con-
trite was meek, and walked home with her aunt on
the following morning, patiently carrying a pound of
butter, six eggs, and a small lump of bacon in a

basket. After that the pillow-case was recommitted
to her. But there still was left evidence enough that
the girl's mind had been upset by the luxuries of
Brook Street,—evidence to which Aunt Margaret
paid very much attention, insisting upon it in her
colloquies with her husband. 'I think that a little
amusement is good for young people,' said Uncle
Reginald, weakly.

'And for old people too. No doubt about it, if they
can get it so as not to do them any harm at the same
time. Nothing can be good for a young woman which
unfits her for that state of life to which it has pleased
God to call her. Ayala has to live with us. No doubt
there was a struggle when she first came from your
sister, Lady Tringle, but she made it gallantly, and
I gave her great credit. She was just falling into a
quiet mode of life when there came this invitation
from the Marchesa Baldoni. Now she has come back
quite an altered person, and the struggle has to be
made all over again.' Uncle Reginald again expressed his opinion that young people ought to have
a little amusement, but he was not strong enough to
insist very much upon his theory. It certainly, however, was true that Ayala, though she still struggled,
had been very much disturbed by the visit.

Then came the invitation to Stalham. There was
a very pretty note from Lady Albury to Ayala herself, saying how much pleasure she would have in
seeing Miss Dormer at her house, where Ayala's old
friends the Marchesa and Nina were then staying.
This was accompanied by a long letter from Nina
herself, in which all the charms of Stalham, including
Mr. Ponsonby and lawn tennis, were set forth at full
length. Ayala had already heard much about Stalham and the Alburys from her friend Nina, who had
hinted in a whisper that such an invitation as this
might perhaps be forthcoming. She was ready
enough for the visit, having looked through her wardrobe, and resolved that things which had been good
enough for Brook Street would still be good enough

for Stalham. But the same post had brought a letter for Mrs. Dosett, and Ayala could see, that, as the letter was read, a frown came upon her aunt's brow, and that the look on her aunt's face was decidedly averse to Stalham. This took place soon after breakfast, when Uncle Reginald had just started for his office, and neither of them for a while said a word to the other of the letter that had been received. It was not till after lunch that Ayala spoke. 'Aunt,' she said, 'you have had a letter from Lady Albury?'

'Yes,' said Mrs. Dosett, grimly, 'I have had a letter from Lady Albury.'

Then there was another silence, till Ayala, whose mind was full of promised delights, could not refrain herself longer. 'Aunt Margaret,' she said; 'I hope you mean to let me go.' For a minute or two there was no reply, and Ayala again pressed her question. 'Lady Albury wants me to go to Stalham.'

'She has written to me to say that she would receive you.'

'And I may go?'

'I am strongly of opinion that you had better not,' said Mrs. Dosett, confirming her decree by a nod which might have suited Jupiter.

'Oh, Aunt Margaret, why not?'

'I think it would be most prudent to decline.'

'But why,—why,—why, Aunt Margaret?'

'There must be expense.'

'I have money enough for the journey left of my own from what Uncle Tom gave me,' said Ayala, pleading her cause with all her eloquence.

'It is not only the money. There are other reasons, —very strong reasons.'

'What reasons, Aunt Margaret?'

'My dear, it is your lot to have to live with us, and not with such people as the Marchesa Baldoni and Lady Albury.'

'I am sure I do not complain.'

'But you would complain after having for a time been used to the luxuries of Albury Park. I do not

say that as finding fault, Ayala. It is human nature
that it should be so.'

'But I won't complain. Have I ever complained?'

'Yes, my dear. You told me the other day that
you did not like bones of mutton, and you were disgusted because things were greasy. I do not say this
by way of scolding you, Ayala, but only that you
may understand what must be the effect of your
going from such a house as this to such a house as
Stalham, and then returning back from Stalham to
such a house as this. You had better be contented
with your position.'

'I am contented with my position,' sobbed Ayala.

'And allow me to write to Lady Albury refusing
the invitation.'

But Ayala could not be brought to look at the
matter with her aunt's eyes. When her aunt pressed
her for an answer which should convey her consent
she would give none, and at last left the room bitterly
sobbing. Turning the matter over in her own bosom
upstairs she determined to be mutinous. No doubt
she owed a certain amount of obedience to her aunt;
but had she not been obedient, had she not worked
hard and lugged about that basket of provisions, and
endeavoured to take an interest in all her aunt's
concerns? Was she so absolutely the property of
her aunt that she was bound to do everything her
aunt desired to the utter annihilation of all her hopes,
to the extermination of her promised joys? She felt
that she had succeeded in Brook Street. She had
met no Angel of Light, but she was associated with
people whom she had liked, and had been talked to
by those to whom it had been a pleasure to listen.
That colonel with the quaint name and the ugly face
was still present to her memory as he had leaned
over her shoulder at the theatre, making her now
laugh by his drollery, and now filling her mind with
interest by his description of the scenes which she
was seeing. She was sure that all this, or something
of the same nature, would be renewed for her delight

at Stalham. And was she to be robbed of this,—the only pleasure which seemed to remain to her in this world,—merely because her aunt chose to entertain severe notions as to duty and pleasure? Other girls went out when they were asked. At Rome, when that question of the dance at the Marchesa's had been discussed, she had had her own way in opposition to her Aunt Emmeline and her cousin Augusta. No doubt she had, in consequence partly of her conduct on that occasion, been turned out of her Uncle Tom's house; but of that she did not think at the present moment. She would be mutinous, and would appeal to her Uncle Reginald for assistance.

But the letter which contained the real invitation had been addressed to her aunt, and her aunt could in truth answer it as she pleased. The answer might at this moment be in the act of being written, and should it be averse Ayala knew very well that she could not go in opposition to it. And yet her aunt came to her in the afternoon consulting her again, quite unconquered as to her own opinion, but still evidently unwilling to write the fatal letter without Ayala's permission. Then Ayala assured herself that she had rights of her own, which her aunt did not care to contravene. 'I think I ought to be allowed to go,' she said, when her aunt came to her during the afternoon.

'When I think it will be bad for you?'

'It won't be bad. They are very good people. I think that I ought to be allowed to go.'

'Have you no reliance on those who are your natural guardians?'

'Uncle Reginald is my natural guardian,' said Ayala, through her tears.

'Very well! If you refuse to be guided by me as though I were not your aunt, and as you will pay no attention to what I tell you is proper for you and best, the question must be left till your uncle comes home. I cannot but be very much hurt that you should think so little of me. I have always endeavoured to do the best I could for you, just as though I were your mother.'

'I think that I ought to be allowed to go,' repeated Ayala.

As the first consequence of this, the replies to all the three letters were delayed for the next day's post. Ayala had considered much with what pretty words she might best answer Lady Albury's kind note, and she had settled upon a form of words which she had felt to be very pretty. Unless her uncle would support her, that would be of no avail, and another form must be chosen. To Nina she would tell the whole truth, either how full of joy she was,—or else how cruelly used and how thoroughly broken-hearted. But she could not think that her uncle would be unkind to her. Her uncle had been uniformly gentle. Her uncle, when he should know how much her heart was set upon it, would surely let her go.

The poor girl, when she tacitly agreed that her uncle should be the arbiter in the matter, thus pledging herself to abide by her uncle's decision, let it be what it might, did not think what great advantage her aunt would have over her in that discussion which would be held upstairs while the master of the house was washing his hands before dinner. Nor did she know of how much stronger will was her Aunt Margaret than her Uncle Reginald. While he was washing his hands and putting on his slippers, the matter was settled in a manner quite destructive of poor Ayala's hopes. 'I won't have it,' said Mrs. Dosett, in reply to the old argument that young people ought to have some amusement. 'If I am to be responsible for the girl I must be allowed my own way with her. It is trouble enough, and very little thanks I get for it. Of course she hates me. Nevertheless, I can endeavour to do my duty, and I will. It is not thanks, nor love, nor even gratitude, that I look for. I am bound to do the best I can by her because she is your niece, and because she has no other real friends. I knew what would come of it when she went to that house in Brook Street. I was soft then and gave way. The girl has moped about like a miserable creature ever since. If I am not to have my own way now I will have done with her altogether.' Having heard this very powerful speech, Uncle Reginald was obliged to give way, and it was settled that after dinner he should convey to Ayala the decision to which they had come.

Ayala, as she sat at the dinner-table, was all expectation, but she asked no question. She asked no question after dinner, while her uncle slowly, solemnly, and sadly sipped his one beaker of cold gin-and-water. He sipped it very slowly, no doubt because he was anxious to postpone the evil moment in which he must communicate her fate to his niece. But at last the melancholy glass was drained, and then, according to the custom of the family, Mrs. Dosett led the way up into the drawing-room, followed by Ayala and her husband. He, when he was on the stairs, and when the eyes of his wife were not upon him, tremulously put out his hand and laid it on Ayala's shoulder, as though to embrace her. The poor girl knew well that mark of affection. There would have been no need for such embracing had the offered joys of Stalham been in store for her. The tears were already in her eyes when she seated herself in the drawing-room, as far removed as possible from the arm-chair which was occupied by her aunt.

Then her uncle pronounced his judgment in a vacillating voice,—with a vacillation which was ineffectual of any good to Ayala. 'Ayala,' he said, 'your aunt and I have been talking over this invitation to Stalham, and we are of opinion, my dear, that you had better not accept it.'

'Why not, Uncle Reginald?'

'There would be expense.'

'I can pay for my own ticket.'

'There would be many expenses, which I need not explain to you more fully. The truth is, my dear, that poor people cannot afford to live with rich people, and had better not attempt it.'

'I don't want to live with them.'

'Visiting them is living with them for a time. I am sorry, Ayala, that we are not able to put you in a position in which you might enjoy more of the pleasures incidental to your age; but you must take the things as they are. Looking at the matter all round, I am sure that your aunt is right in advising that you should stay at home.'

'It isn't advice at all,' said Ayala.

'Ayala!' exclaimed her aunt, in a tone of indignation.

'It isn't advice,' repeated Ayala. 'Of course, if you won't let me go, I can't.'

'You are a very wicked girl,' said Mrs. Dosett, 'to speak to your uncle like that, after all that he has done for you.'

'Not wicked,' said the uncle.

'I say, wicked. But it doesn't matter. I shall at once write to Lady Albury, as you desire, and of course there will be no further question as to her going.' Soon after that Mrs. Dosett sat down to her desk, and wrote that letter to which the Marchesa had alluded in hers to her nephew. No doubt it was stern and hard, and of a nature to make such a woman as the Marchesa feel that Mrs. Dosett would not be a pleasant companion for a girl like Ayala. But it was written with a full conviction that duty required it; and the words, though hard and stiff, had been chosen with the purpose of showing that the doing of this disagreeable duty had been felt to be imperative.

When the matter had been thus decided, Ayala soon retreated to her own room. Her very soul was burning with indignation at the tyranny to which she thought herself subjected. The use of that weak word, advice, had angered her more than anything. It had not been advice. It had not been given as advice. A command had been laid upon her, a most cruel and unjust command, which she was forced to obey, because she lacked the power of escaping from her condition of slavery. Advice, indeed! Advice is a thing with which the advised one may or may not comply, as that advised one may choose. A slave must obey an order! Her own papa and her own mamma had always advised her, and the advice had always been followed, even when read only in the glance of an eye, in a smile, or a nod. Then she had known what it was to be advised. Now she was ordered,—as slaves are ordered; and there was no escape from her slavery!

She, too, must write her letter, but there was no need now of that pretty studied phrase, in which she had hoped to thank Lady Albury fitly for her great kindness. She found, after a vain attempt or two, that it was hopeless to endeavour to write to Lady Albury. The words would not come to her pen. But she did write to Nina:—

'DEAR, DEAREST NINA,

'They won't let me go! Oh, my darling, I am so miserable! Why should they not let me go, when people are so kind, so very kind, as Lady Albury and your dear mamma? I feel as though I should like to run from the house, and never come back, even though I had to die in the streets. I was so happy when I got your letter and Lady Albury's, and now I am so wretched! I cannot write to Lady Albury. You must just tell her, with many thanks from me, that they will not let me go!

'Your unhappy but affectionate friend,

'AYALA.'

## CHAPTER XXII

### AYALA'S GRATITUDE

THERE was much pity felt for Ayala among the folk at Stalham. The sympathies of them all should have been with Mrs. Dosett. They ought to have felt that the poor aunt was simply performing an unpleasant duty, and that the girl was impracticable if not disobedient. But Ayala was known to be very pretty, and Mrs. Dosett was supposed to be plain. Ayala was interesting, while Mrs. Dosett, from the nature of her circumstances, was most uninteresting. It was agreed on all sides, at Stalham, that so pretty a bird as Ayala should not be imprisoned for ever in so ugly a cage. Such a bird ought, at least, to be allowed its chance of captivating some fitting mate by its song and its plumage. That was Lady Albury's argument,—a woman very good-natured, a little given to match-making, a great friend to pretty girls,—and whose eldest son was as yet only nine, so that there could be no danger to herself or her own flock. There was much ridicule thrown on Mrs. Dosett at Stalham, and many pretty things said of the bird who was so unworthily imprisoned in Kingsbury Crescent. At last there was something like a conspiracy, the purport of which was to get the bird out of its cage in November.

In this conspiracy it can hardly be said that the Marchesa took an active part. Much as she liked Ayala, she was less prone than Lady Albury to think that the girl was ill-used. She was more keenly alive than her cousin,—or rather her cousin's wife,—to the hard necessities of the world. Ayala must be said to have made her own bed. At any rate there was the bed and she must lie on it. It was not the Dosetts' fault that they were poor. According to their means they were doing the best they could for their niece, and were entitled to praise rather than abuse. And then the Marchesa was afraid for her nephew. Colonel Stubbs, in his letter to her, had declared that he quite agreed with her views as to matrimony; but she was quite alive to her nephew's sarcasm. Her nephew, though he might in truth agree with her, nevertheless was sarcastic. Though he was sarcastic, still he might be made to accede to her views, because he did, in truth, agree with her. She was eminently an intelligent woman, seeing far into character, and she knew pretty well the real condition of her nephew's mind, and could foresee his conduct. He would marry before long, and might not improbably marry a girl with some money if one could be made to come in his way, who would at the same time suit his somewhat fastidious taste. But Ayala suited his taste, Ayala who had not a shilling, and the Marchesa thought it only too likely that if Ayala were released from her cage, and brought to Albury, Ayala might become Mrs. Jonathan Stubbs. That Ayala should refuse to become Mrs. Jonathan Stubbs did not present itself as a possibility to the Marchesa.

So the matters were when the Marchesa and Nina returned from Stalham to London, a promise having been given that Nina should go back to Stalham in November, and be allowed to see the glories of a hunt.* She was not to ride to hounds. That was a matter of course, but she was to be permitted to see what a pack of hounds was like, and of what like were the men in their scarlet coats, and how the huntsman's horn would sound when it should be heard among the woods and fields. It was already decided that the Colonel should be there to meet her, and the conspiracy was formed with the object of getting Ayala out of her cage at the same time. Stalham was a handsome country seat, in the county of Rufford, and Sir Harry Albury had lately taken upon himself the duties of Master of the Rufford and Ufford United Pack.* Colonel Stubbs was to be there with his horses in November, but had, in the meantime, been seen by Lady Albury, and had been instigated to do something for the release of Ayala.

But what could he do? It was at first suggested that he should call at Kingsbury Crescent, and endeavour to mollify the stony heart of Aunt Dosett. But, as he had said himself, he would be the worst person in the world to perform such an embassy. 'I am not an Adonis,* I know,' he said, 'nor do I look like a Lothario,* but still I am in some sort a young man, and therefore certain to be regarded as pernicious, as dangerous and damnable, by such a dragon of virtue as Aunt Dosett. I don't see how I could expect to have a chance.' This interview took place in London during the latter end of October, and it was at last decided that the mission should be made by Lady Albury herself, and made, not to Mrs. Dosett, at Kingsbury Crescent, but to Mr. Dosett at his office in Somerset House. 'I don't think I could stand Mrs. D.,' said Lady Albury.

Lady Albury was a handsome, fashionable woman, rather tall, always excellently dressed, and possessed of a personal assurance which nothing could daunt. She had the reputation of an affectionate wife and a good mother, but was nevertheless declared by some of her friends to be 'a little fast.' She certainly was fond of comedy,—those who did not like her were apt to say that her comedy was only fun,—and was much disposed to have her own way when she could get it. She was now bent upon liberating Ayala from her cage, and for this purpose had herself driven into the huge court belonging to Somerset House.

Mr. Dosett was dignified at his office with the use of a room to himself, a small room looking out upon the river, in which he spent six hours on six days of the week in arranging the indexes of a voluminous library of manuscript letter-books. It was rarely indeed that he was disturbed by the presence of any visitor. When, therefore, his door was opened by one of the messengers, and he was informed that Lady Albury desired to see him, he was for the moment a good deal disturbed. No option, however, was given to him as to refusing admission to Lady Albury. She

was in the room before the messenger had completed
his announcement, and had seated herself in one of
the two spare chairs which the room afforded as soon
as the door was closed. 'Mr. Dosett,' she said, 'I
have taken the great liberty of calling to say a few
words about your niece, Miss Ayala Dormer.'

When the lady was first announced, Mr. Dosett, in
his confusion, had failed to connect the name which
he had heard with that of the lady who had invited
Ayala to her house. But now he recognised it, and
knew who it was that had come to him. 'You were
kind enough,' he said, 'to invite my little girl to your
house some weeks ago.'

'And now I have come to invite her again.'

Mr. Dosett was now more disturbed than ever.
With what words was he to refuse the request which
this kind but very grand lady was about to make?
How could he explain to her all those details as to his
own poverty, and as to Ayala's fate in having to
share that poverty with him? How could he explain
the unfitness of Ayala's temporary sojourn with
people so wealthy and luxurious? And yet were he
to yield in the least how could he face his wife on his
return home to the Crescent? 'You are very kind,
Lady Albury,' he said.

'We particularly wish to have her about the end
of the first week in November,' said the lady. 'Her
friend Nina Baldoni will be there, and one or two
others whom she knows. We shall try to be a little
gay for a week or two.'

'I have no doubt it would be gay, and we at home
are very dull.'

'Do you not think a little gaiety good for young
people?' said her ladyship, using the very argument
which poor Mr. Dosett had so often attempted to
employ on Ayala's behalf.

'Yes; a little gaiety,' he said, as though deprecat-
ing the excessive amount of hilarity which he
imagined to prevail at Stalham.

'Of course you do,' said Lady Albury. 'Poor little

girl! I have heard so much about her, and of all your goodness to her. Mrs. Dosett, I know, is another mother to her; but still a little country air could not but be beneficial. Do say that she shall come to us, Mr. Dosett.'

Then Mr. Dosett felt that, disagreeable as it was, he must preach the sermon which his wife had preached to him, and he did preach it. He spoke timidly of his own poverty, and the need which there was that Ayala should share it. He spoke a word of the danger which might come from luxury, and of the discontent which would be felt when the girl returned to her own home. Something he added of the propriety of like living with like, and ended by praying that Ayala might be excused. The words came from him with none of that energy which his wife would have used,—were uttered in a low melancholy drone; but still they were words hard to answer, and called upon Lady Albury for all her ingenuity in finding an argument against them.

But Lady Albury was strong-minded, and did find an argument. 'You mustn't be angry with me,' she said, 'if I don't quite agree with you. Of course you wish to do the best you can for this dear child.'

'Indeed I do, Lady Albury.'

'How is anything then to be done for her if she remains shut up in your house? You do not, if I understand, see much company yourselves.'

'None at all.'

'You won't be angry with me for my impertinence in alluding to it.'

'Not in the least. It is the fact that we live altogether to ourselves.'

'And the happiest kind of life too for married people,' said Lady Albury, who was accustomed to fill her house in the country with a constant succession of visitors, and to have engagements for every night of the week in town. 'But for young people it is not quite so good. How is a young lady to get herself settled in life?'

'Settled?' asked Mr. Dosett, vaguely.

'Married,' suggested Lady Albury, more plainly. Mr. Dosett shook his head. No idea on the subject had ever flashed across his mind. To provide bread and meat, a bed and clothes, for his sister's child he had felt to be a duty,—but not a husband. Husbands came, or did not,—as the heavens might be propitious. That Ayala should go to Stalham for the sake of finding a husband was certainly beyond the extent of his providing care. 'In fact how is a girl to have a chance at all unless she is allowed to see some one? Of course I don't say this with reference to our house. There will be no young men there, or anything of that kind. But, taking a broad view, unless you let a girl like that have what chances come in her way how is she to get on? I think you have hardly a right to do it.'

'We have done it for the best.'

'I am sure of that, Mr. Dosett. And I hope you will tell Mrs. Dosett, with my compliments, how thoroughly I appreciate her goodness. I should have called upon her instead of coming here, only that I cannot very well get into that part of the town.'

'I will tell her what you are good enough to say.'

'Poor Ayala! I am afraid that her other aunt, Aunt Tringle, was not as good to her as your wife. I have heard about how all that occurred in Rome. She was very much admired there. I am told that she is perfectly lovely.'

'Pretty well.'

'A sort of beauty that we hardly ever see now,—and very, very clever.'

'Ayala is clever, I think.'

'She ought to have her chance. She ought indeed. I don't think you quite do your duty by such a girl as that unless you let her have a chance. She is sure to get to know people, and to be asked from one house to another. I speak plainly, for I really think you ought to let her come.'

All this sank deeply into the heart of Uncle Regi-

nald. Whether it was for good or evil it seemed to
him at the moment to be unanswerable. If there was
a chance of any good thing for Ayala, surely it could
not be his duty to bar her from that chance. A whole
vista of new views in reference to the treatment of
young ladies was opened to him by the words of his
visitor. Ayala certainly was pretty. Certainly she
was clever. A husband with an income would certainly be a good thing. Embryo husbands with incomes do occasionally fall in love with pretty girls.
But how can any pretty girl be fallen in love with
unless some one be permitted to see her? At Kingsbury Crescent there was not a man to be seen from
one end of the year to another. It occurred to him
now, for the first time, that Ayala by her present life
was shut out from any chance of marriage. It was
manifestly true that he had no right to seclude her in
that fashion. At last he made a promise, rashly, as
he felt at the very moment of making it, that he
would ask his wife to allow Ayala to go to Stalham.
Lady Albury of course accepted this as an undertaking that Ayala should come, and went away triumphant.

Mr. Dosett walked home across the parks with a
troubled mind, thinking much of all that had passed
between him and the lady of fashion. It was with
great difficulty that he could quite make up his mind
which was right,—the lady of fashion or his wife.
If Ayala was to live always as they lived at Kingsbury Crescent, if it should in process of time be her
fate to marry some man in the same class as themselves, if continued care as to small pecuniary needs
was to be her future lot, then certainly her comfort
would only be disturbed by such a visit as that now
proposed. And was it not probable that such would
be the destiny in store for her? Mr. Dosett knew the
world well enough to be aware that all pretty girls
such as Ayala cannot find rich husbands merely by
exhibiting their prettiness. Kingsbury Crescent, unalloyed by the dangers of Stalham, would certainly

be the most secure. But then he had been told that
Ayala now had special chances offered to her, and
that he had no right to rob her of those chances. He
felt this the more strongly, because she was not his
daughter,—only his niece. With a daughter he and
his wife might have used their own judgment without
check. But now he had been told that he had no
right to rob Ayala of her chances, and he felt that he
had not the right. By the time that he reached
Kingsbury Crescent he had, with many misgivings,
decided in favour of Stalham.

It was now some weeks since the first invitation
had been refused, and during those weeks life had not
been pleasant at the Crescent. Ayala moped and
pined as though some great misfortune had fallen
upon her. When she had first come to the Crescent
she had borne herself bravely, as a man bears a
trouble when he is conscious that he has brought it
on himself by his own act, and is proud of the act
which has done it. But when that excitement has
gone, and the trouble still remains, the pride wears
off, and the man is simply alive to his suffering. So
it had been with Ayala. Then had come the visit to
Brook Street. When, soon after that, she was invited
to Stalham, it seemed as though a new world was
being opened to her. There came a moment when she
could again rejoice that she had quarrelled with her
Aunt Emmeline. This new world would be a much
better world than the Tringle world. Then had come
the great blow, and it had seemed to her as though
there was nothing but Kingsbury Crescent before her
for the rest of her wretched life.

There was not a detail of all this hidden from the
eyes of Aunt Margaret. Stalham had decided that
Aunt Margaret was ugly and uninteresting. Stalham,
according to its own views, was right. Nevertheless
the lady in Kingsbury Crescent had both eyes to see
and a heart to feel. She was hot of temper, but she
was forgiving. She liked her own way, but she was
affectionate. She considered it right to teach her

niece the unsavoury mysteries of economy, but she
was aware that such mysteries must be distasteful
to one brought up as Ayala. Even when she had been
loudest in denouncing Ayala's mutiny, her heart had
melted in ruth because Ayala had been so unhappy.
She, too, had questioned herself again and again as
to the justness of her decision. Was she entitled to
rob Ayala of her chances? In her frequent discus-
sions with her husband she still persisted in declaring
that Kingsbury Crescent was safe, and that Stalham
would be dangerous. But, nevertheless, in her own
bosom she had misgivings. As she saw the poor girl
mope and weary through one day after another, she
could not but have misgivings.

'I have had that Lady Albury with me at the office
to-day, and have almost promised that Ayala shall
go to her on the 8th of November.' It was thus that
Mr. Dosett rushed at once into his difficulty as soon
as he found himself upstairs with his wife.

'You have?'

'Well, my dear, I almost did. She said a great
deal, and I could not but agree with much of it.
Ayala ought to have her chances.'

'What chances?' demanded Mrs. Dosett, who did
not at all like the expression.

'Well; seeing people. She never sees anybody
here.'

'Nobody is better than some people,' said Mrs.
Dosett, meaning to be severe on Lady Albury's
probable guests.

'But if a girl sees nobody,' said Mr. Dosett, 'she
can have no,—no,—no chances.'

'She has the chance of wholesome victuals,' said
Mrs. Dosett, 'and I don't know what other chances
you or I can give her.'

'She might see—a young man.' This Mr. Dosett
said very timidly.

'A young fiddlestick! A young man! Young men
should be waited for till they come naturally, and
never thought about if they don't come at all. I hate

this looking after young men. If there wasn't a young man for the next dozen years we should do better,—so as just to get out of the way of thinking about them for a time.' This was Mrs. Dosett's philosophy; but in spite of her philosophy she did yield, and on that night it was decided that Ayala after all was to be allowed to go to Stalham.

\* \* \* \* \*

To Mr. Dosett was deputed the agreeable task of telling Ayala on the next evening what was to befall her. If anything agreeable was to be done in that sombre house it was always deputed to the master.

'What!' said Ayala, jumping from her chair.

'On the eighth of November,' said Mr. Dosett.

'To Stalham?'

'Lady Albury was with me yesterday at the office, and your aunt has consented.'

'Oh, Uncle Reginald!' said Ayala, falling on her knees, and hiding her face on his lap. Heaven had been once more opened to her.

'I'll never forget it,' said Ayala, when she went to thank her aunt,—'never.'

'I only hope it may not do you a mischief.'

'And I beg your pardon, Aunt Margaret, because I was,—I was,—because I was——' She could not find the word which would express her own delinquency, without admitting more than she intended to admit,—'too self-asserting, considering that I am only a young girl.' That would have been her meaning could she have found appropriate words.

'We need not go back to that now,' said Aunt Margaret.

## CHAPTER XXIII

### STALHAM PARK

ON the day fixed Ayala went down to Stalham. A few days before she started there came to her a letter, or rather an envelope, from her uncle Sir Thomas, enclosing a cheque for £20. The Tringle women had heard that Ayala had been asked to Stalham, and had mentioned the visit disparagingly before Sir Thomas. ' I think it very wrong of my poor brother,' said Lady Tringle. 'She can't have a shilling even to get herself gloves.' This had an effect which had not been intended, and Sir Thomas sent the cheque for £20. Then Ayala felt not only that the heavens were opened to her but that the sweetest zephyrs were blowing her upon her course. Thoughts as to gloves had disturbed her, and as to some shoes which were wanting, and especially as to a pretty hat for winter wear. Now she could get hat, and shoes and gloves, and pay her fare, and go down to Stalham with money in her pocket. Before going she wrote a very pretty note to her Uncle Tom.

On her arrival she was made much of by everyone. Lady Albury called her the caged bird, and congratulated her on her escape from the bars. Sir Harry asked her whether she could ride to hounds. Nina gave her a thousand kisses. But perhaps her greatest delight was in finding that Jonathan Stubbs was at Albury. She had become so intimate with the Colonel that she regarded him quite like an old friend ; and when a girl has a male friend, though he may be much less loved, or not loved at all, he is always more pleasant, or at any rate more piquant, than a female friend. As for love with Colonel Stubbs that was quite out of the question. She was sure that he would never fall in love with herself. His manner to her was altogether unlike that of a lover. A lover would be smooth, soft, poetic, and flattering. He was always a little rough to her,—sometimes almost scolding her. But then he scolded her as she liked to be scolded,—with a dash of fun and a greatly predominating admixture of good-nature. He was like a bear,—but a bear who would always behave himself pleasantly. She was delighted when Colonel Stubbs congratulated her on her escape from Kingsbury Crescent, and felt that he was justified by his intimacy when he called Mrs. Dosett a mollified she-Cerberus.*

'Are you going to make one of my team?' said the Colonel to her on the morning after her arrival. It was a non-hunting morning, and the gentlemen were vacant about the house till they went out for a little shooting later in the day.

'What team?' said Ayala, feeling that she had suddenly received a check to her happiness. She knew that the Colonel was alluding to those hunting joys which were to be prepared for Nina, and which were far beyond her own reach. That question of riding gear is terrible to young ladies who are not properly supplied. Even had time admitted she would not have dared to use her uncle's money for such a purpose, in the hope that a horse might be lent to her. She had told herself that it was out of the question, and had declared to herself that she was too thankful for her visit to allow any regret on such a matter to cross her mind. But when the Colonel spoke of his team there was something of a pang. How she would have liked to be one of such a team!

'My pony team. I mean to drive two. You mustn't think that I am taking a liberty when I say that they are to be called Nina and Ayala.'

There was no liberty at all. Had he called her simply Ayala she would have felt it to be no more than pleasant friendship, coming from him. He was so big, and so red, and so ugly, and so friendly! Why should he not call her Ayala? But as to that team,—it could not be. 'If it's riding,' she said demurely, 'I can't be one of the ponies.'

'It is riding,—of course. Now the Marchesa is not here, we mean to call it hunting in a mild way.'

'I can't,' she said.

'But you've got to do it, Miss Dormer.'

'I haven't got anything to do it with. Of course, I don't mind telling you.'

'You are to ride the sweetest little horse that ever was foaled,—just bigger than a pony. It belongs to Sir Harry's sister who is away, and we've settled it all. There never was a safer little beast, and he can climb through a fence without letting you know that it's there.'

'But I mean—clothes,' said Ayala. Then she whispered, 'I haven't got a habit, or anything else anybody ought to have.'

'Ah,' said the Colonel; 'I don't know anything about that. I should say that Nina must have managed that. The horse department was left to me, and I have done my part. You will find that you will have to go out next Tuesday and Friday. The hounds will be here on Tuesday, and they will be at Rufford on Friday. Rufford is only nine miles from here, and it's all settled.'

Before the day was over the difficulty had vanished. Miss Albury's horse was not only called into requisition but Miss Albury's habit also. Ayala had a little black hat of her own, which Lady Albury assured her would do excellently well for the hunting field. There was some fitting and some trying on, and perhaps a few moments of preliminary despair; but on the Tuesday morning she rode away from the hall door at eleven o'clock mounted on Sprite, as the little horse was called, and felt herself from head to foot to be one of Colonel Stubbs's team. When at Glenbogie she had ridden a little, and again in Italy, and being fearless by nature, had no trepidation to impair the fulness of her delight.

Hunting from home coverts rarely exacts much jumping from ladies. The woods are big, and the gates are numerous. It is when the far-away homes of wild foxes are drawn,—those secluded brakes and gorses where the noble animal is wont to live at a distance from carriage-roads and other weak refuges of civilisation,—that the riding capacities of ladies must be equal to those of their husbands and brothers.* This present moment was an occasion for great delight,—at least, so it was found by both Nina and Ayala. But it was not an opportunity for great glory. Till it was time for lunch one fox after another ran about the big woods of Albury in a fashion that seemed perfect to the two girls, but which nearly broke the heart of old Tony,* who was still huntsman to the Ufford and Rufford United Hunt. 'Darm their nasty ways,' said Tony to Mr. Larry Twentyman, who was one of the popular habitués of the hunt; 'they runs one a top of another's brushes, till there ain't a 'ound living knows t'other from which. There's always a many on 'em at Albury, but I never knew an Albury fox worth his grub yet.' But there was galloping along roads and through gates, and long strings of horsemen followed each other up and down the rides, and an easy coming back to the places from which they started, which made the girls think that the whole thing was divine. Once or twice there was a little bank, and once or twice a little ditch,—just sufficient to make Ayala feel that no possible fence would be a difficulty to Sprite. She soon learnt that mode of governing her body which leaping requires, and when she was brought into lunch at about two she was sure that she could do anything which the art of hunting required. But at lunch an edict went forth as to the two girls, against further hunting for that day. Nina strove to rebel, and Ayala attempted to be eloquent by a supplicating glance at the Colonel. But they were told that as the horses would be wanted again on Friday they had done enough. In truth, Tony had already trotted off with the hounds to Pringle's Gorse, a distance of five miles, and the gentlemen who had lingered over their lunch had to follow him at their best pace. 'Pringle's Gorse is not just the place for young ladies,' Sir Harry said, and so the matter had been decided against Nina and Ayala.

At about six Sir Harry, Colonel Stubbs, and the other gentlemen returned, declaring that nothing quicker than their run from Pringle's Gorse had ever been known in that country. 'About six miles, straight on end in forty minutes,' said the Colonel, 'and then a kill in the open.'

'He was laid up under a bank,' said young Gosling.

'He was so beat that he couldn't carry on a field farther,' said Captain Batsby, who was staying in the house.

'I call that the open,' said Stubbs.

'I always think I kill a fox in the open,' said Sir Harry, 'when the hounds run into him, because he cannot run another yard with the country there before him.' Then there was a long discussion, as they stood drinking tea before the fire, as to what 'the open' meant, from which they went to other hunting matters. To all this Ayala listened with attentive ears, and was aware that she had spent a great day. Oh, what a difference was there between Stalham and Kingsbury Crescent!

The next two days were almost equally full of delight. She was taken into the stables to see her horse, and as she patted his glossy coat she felt that she loved Sprite with all her heart. Oh, what a world of joy was this;—how infinitely superior even to Queen's Gate and Glenbogie! The gaudy magnificence of the Tringles had been altogether unlike the luxurious comfort of Stalham, where everybody was at his ease, where everybody was good-natured, where everybody seemed to acknowledge that pleasure was the one object of life! On the evening before the Friday she was taken out to dinner by Captain Batsby. She was not sure that she liked Captain Batsby, who made little complimentary speeches to her. But her neighbour on the other side was

Colonel Stubbs, and she was quite sure that she liked Colonel Stubbs.

'I know you'll go like a bird to-morrow,' said Captain Batsby.

'I shouldn't like that, because there would be no jumping,' said Ayala.

'But you'd be such a beautiful bird.' The Captain, as he drawled out his words, made an eye at her, and she was sure that she did not like the Captain.

'At what time are we to start to-morrow?' she said, turning to the Colonel.

'Ten, sharp. Mind you're ready. Sir Harry takes us on the drag, and wouldn't wait for Venus, though she wanted five minutes more for her back hair.'

'I don't suppose she ever wants any time for her back hair. I wouldn't if I were a goddess.'

'Then you'd be a very untidy goddess, that's all. I wonder whether you are untidy.'

'Well;—yes;—sometimes.'

'I hate untidy girls.'

'Thank you, Colonel Stubbs.'

'What I like is a nice prim little woman, who never had a pin in the wrong place in her life. Her cuffs and collars are always as stiff as steel, and she never rubs the sleeves of her dresses by leaning about, like some young ladies.'

'That's what I do.'

'My young woman never sits down lest she should crease her dress. My young woman never lets her ribbons get tangled. My young woman can dress upon £40 a year, and always look as though she came out of a band-box.'

'I don't believe you've got a young woman, Colonel Stubbs.'

'Well; no; I haven't,—except in my imagination.'

If so, he too must have his Angel of Light! 'Do you ever dream about her?'

'Oh dear, yes. I dream that she does scold so awfully when I have her to myself. In my dreams, you know, I'm married to her, and she always wants

me to eat hashed mutton. Now, if there is one thing
that makes me more sick than another it is hashed
mutton. Of course I shall marry her in some of my
waking moments, and then I shall have to eat
hashed mutton for ever.'

Then Captain Batsby put in another word. 'I
should so like to be allowed to give you a lead to-
morrow.'

'Oh, thank you,—but I'd rather not have it,' said
Ayala, who was altogether in the dark, thinking that
'a lead' might be some present which she would not
wish to accept from Captain Batsby.

'I mean that I should like to show you a line if we
get a run.'

'What is a line?' asked Ayala.

'A line? Why a line is just a lead;—keep your
eye on me and I'll take the fences where you can
follow without coming to grief.'

'Oh,' said Ayala, 'that's a lead, is it? Colonel
Stubbs is going to give my friend and me a lead, as
long as we stay here.'

'No man ever ought to coach more than one lady
at once,' said the Captain, showing his erudition.
'You're sure to come on top of one another if there
are two.'

'But Colonel Stubbs is especially told by the
Marchesa to look after both of us,' said Ayala almost
angrily. Then she turned her shoulder to him, and
was soon intent upon further instructions from the
Colonel.

The following morning was fine, and all the ladies
in the house were packed on to the top of Sir Harry's
drag* The Colonel sat behind Sir Harry on the plea
that he was wanted to take care of the two girls.
Captain Batsby and three other gentlemen were put
inside, where they consoled themselves with unlimited tobacco. In this way they were driven to a
spot called Rufford Cross Roads, where they found
Tony Tappett sitting perfectly quiescent on his old
mare, while the hounds were seated around him on

the grassy sides of the roads. With him was talking a stout, almost middle-aged gentleman, in a scarlet coat, and natty pink top boots, who was the owner of all the country around. This was Lord Rufford,* who a few years since was known as one of the hardest riders in those parts; but he had degenerated into matrimony, was now the happy father of half-a-dozen babies, and was hardly ever seen to jump over a fence. But he still came out when the meets were not too distant, and carefully performed that first duty of an English country gentleman,—the preservation of foxes. Though he did not ride much, no one liked a little hunting gossip better than Lord Rufford. It was, however, observed that even in regard to hunting he was apt to quote the authority of his wife.

'Oh, yes, my Lord,' said Tony, 'there'll sure to be a fox at Dillsborough. But we'll find one afore we get to Rufford, my Lord.'

'Lady Rufford says there hasn't been a fox seen in the home woods this week.'

'Her ladyship will be sure to know,' said Tony.

'Do you remember that fence where poor Major Caneback got his fall six years ago?' asked the Lord.

'Seven years next Christmas, my Lord,' said Tony. 'He never put a leg across a saddle again, poor fellow! I remember him well, my Lord; a man who could 'andle a 'orse wonderful, though he didn't know 'ow to ride to 'ounds; not according to my idea. To get your animal to carry you through, never mind 'ow long the thing is; that's my idea of riding to 'ounds, my Lord. The major was for always making a 'orse jump over everything. I never wants 'em to jump over nothing I can't help;*—I don't, my Lord.'

'That's just what her ladyship is always saying to me,' said Lord Rufford, 'and I do pretty much what her ladyship tells me.'

On this occasion Lady Rufford had been quite right about the home covers. No doubt she generally was right in any assertion she made as to her husband's affairs. After drawing them Tony trotted on towards Dillsborough, running his hounds through a few little springs, which lay near his way. As they went Colonel Stubbs rode between the two girls. 'Whenever I see Rufford,' said the Colonel, 'he does me a world of good.'

'What good can a fat man like that do you?' said Nina.

'He is a continual sermon against marriage. If I could see Rufford once a week I know that I should be safe.'

'He seems to me to be a very comfortable old gentleman,' said Ayala.

'Old! Seven years ago he was acknowledged to be the one undisputed paragon of a young man in this county. No one else dreamed of looking at a young lady if he chose to turn his eyes in that direction. He was handsome as Apollo——'

'He an Apollo!' said Nina.

'The best Apollo there then was in these parts, and every one knew that he had forty thousand a-year to spend. Now he is supposed to be the best hand in the house at rocking the cradle.'

'Do you mean to say that he nurses the babies?' asked Ayala.

'He looks as if he did at any rate. He never goes ten miles away from his door without having Lady Rufford with him, and is always tucked up at night just at half-past ten by her ladyship's own maid. Ten years ago he would generally have been found at midnight with cards in his hand and a cigar in his mouth. Now he is allowed two cigarettes a-day. Well, Mr. Twentyman, how are you getting on?' This he said to a good-looking better sort of farmer, who came up, riding a remarkably strong horse, and dressed in pink and white cords.

'Thank ye, Colonel, pretty well, considering how hard the times are. A man who owns a few acres and tries to farm them must be on the road to ruin nowadays. That's what I'm always telling my wife, so that she may know what she has got to expect.' Mr. Twentyman had been married just twelve months.

'She isn't much frightened, I daresay,' said the Colonel.

'She's young, you see,' continued the farmer, 'and hasn't settled herself down yet to the sorrows of life.' This was that Mr. Lawrence Twentyman*who married Kate Masters, the youngest daughter of old Masters, the attorney at Dillsborough, and sister of Mrs. Morton, wife of the squire of Bragton. 'By the holy,' said Twentyman suddenly, 'the hounds have put a fox out of that little spinney.'

## CHAPTER XXIV

### RUFFORD CROSS-ROADS

AYALA, who had been listening attentively to the conversation of Mr. Twentyman, and been feeling that she was being initiated every moment into a new phase of life,—who had been endeavouring to make some connection in her mind between the new charms of the world around her and that world of her dreams that was ever present to her, and had as yet simply determined that neither could Lord Rufford or Mr. Twentyman have ever been an Angel of Light,—at once straightened herself in her saddle, and prepared herself for the doing of something memorable. It was evident to her that Mr. Twentyman considered that the moment for action had come. He did not gallop off wildly, as did four or five others, but stood still for a moment looking intently at a few hounds who, with their tails feathering in the air and with their noses down, seemed at the same time to be irresolute and determined, knowing that the scent was there but not yet quite fixed as to its line. 'Half a moment, Colonel,' he said, standing up in his stir-rups, with his left hand raised, while his right held his reins and his whip close down on his horse's neck. 'Half a moment!' He only whispered, and then shook his head angrily, as he heard the ill-timed shouting of one or two men who had already reached the other side of the little skirting of trees. 'I wish Fred Botsey's tongue were tied to his teeth,' he said, still whispering. 'Now, Colonel, they have it. There's a little lane to the right, and a gate. After that the country's open, and there's nothing which the ladies' nags can't do. I know the country so well, you'd perhaps better come with me for a bit.'

'He knows all about it,' said the Colonel to Ayala. 'Do as he tells you.'

Ayala and Nina both were quick enough to obey. Twentyman dashed along the lane, while the girls followed him with the Colonel after them. When they were at the hunting-gate already spoken of, old Tony Tappett was with them, trotting, impatient to get to the hounds, courteously giving place to the ladies,—whom, however, in his heart, he wished at home in bed,—and then thrusting himself through the gate in front of the Colonel. 'D—— their pig-headed folly,' he said, as he came up to his friend Twentyman—'they knows no more about it than if they'd just come from be'ind a counter,—'olloaing, 'olloaing, 'olloaing,—as if 'olloaing 'd make a fox break! 'Owsomever 'e's off now, and they've got Cranbury Brook between them and his line!' This he said in a squeaking little voice, intended to be jocose and satirical, shaking his head as he rode. This last idea seemed to give him great consolation.

It was the consideration, deep and well-founded, as to the Cranbury which had induced Larry Twentyman to pause on the road when he had paused, and then to make for the lane and the gate. The direction had hardly seemed to be that of the hounds, but Larry knew the spinney, knew the brook,—knew the fox, perhaps,—and was aware of the spot at which the brute would cross the water if he did cross it. The brute did cross the water, and therefore there was Cranbury Brook between many of the forward riders and his line.

Sir Harry was then with them, and two or three other farmers. But Larry had a lead, and the two girls were with him. Tony Tappett, though he had got up to his hounds, did not endeavour to ride straight to them as did Larry Twentyman. He was old and unambitious, very anxious to know where his hounds were, so that he might be with them should they want the assistance of his voice and counsel, anxious to be near enough to take their fox from them should they run into him, but taking no glory in jumping over a fence if he could avoid it, creeping about here and there, knowing from experience nearly every turn in the animal's mind, aware of every impediment which would delay him, riding fast only when the impediments were far between, taking no amusement to himself out of the riding, but with his heart cruelly, bloodily, ruthlessly set upon killing the animal before him. To kill his fox he would imperil his neck, but for the glory of riding he would not soil his boots if he could help it. After the girls came the Colonel, somewhat shorn of his honour in that he was no longer giving them a lead, but doing his best to maintain the pace, which Twentyman was making very good. 'Now, young ladies,' said Twentyman, 'give them their heads, and let them do it just as they please,—alongside of each other, and not too near to me.' It was a brook,—a confluent of Cranbury Brook, and was wide enough to require a good deal of jumping. It may be supposed that the two young ladies did not understand much of the instructions given to them. To hold their breath and be brave was the only idea present to them. The rest must come from instinct and chance. The other side of the brook was heaven; —this would be purgatory. Larry, fearing perhaps that the order as to their not being too near might not be obeyed, added a little to his own pace so as to be clear of them. Nevertheless they were only a few strides behind, and had Larry's horse missed his footing there would have been a mess. As it was they took the brook side by side close to each other, and landed full of delight and glory on the opposite bank. 'Bravo! young ladies,' shouted Twentyman.

'Oh, Nina, that is divine,' said Ayala. Nina was a little too much out of breath for answering, but simply threw up her eyes to Heaven and made a flourish with her whip, intended to be expressive of her perfect joy.

Away went Larry and away went the girls with him, quite unconscious that the Colonel's horse had balked the brook and then jumped into it,—quite unconscious that Sir Harry, seeing the Colonel's catastrophe, had followed Tony a quarter of a mile up the brook to a ford. Even in the soft bosoms of young ladies 'the devil take the hindmost' will be the motto most appropriate for hunting. Larry Twentyman, of whom they had never heard before, was now the god of their idolatry. Where Larry Twentyman might go it was manifestly their duty to follow, even though they should never see the poor Colonel again. They recked nothing of the fox or of the hounds or of the master or even of the hunts-man. They had a man before them to show them the way, and as long as they could keep him in sight each was determined to be at any rate as good as the other. To give Larry his due it must be acknowledged that he was thoroughly thoughtful of them. At every fence encountered he studied the spot at which they would be least likely to fall. He had to remember, also, that there were two of them together, and that he had made himself in a way responsible for the safety of both. All this he did, and did well, because he knew his business. With the exception of the water-jump, the country over which they passed was not difficult. For a time there was a run of gates, each of which their guide was able to open for them, and as they came near to Dillsborough Wood there were gaps in most of the fences; but it seemed to the girls that they had galloped over monstrous hedges and leapt over walls which it would almost take a strong man to climb. The brook, however,—the river as it seemed to them,—had been the crowning glory. Ayala was sure that that brook would never be forgotten by her. Even the Angel of Light was hardly more heavenly than the brook.

That the fox was running for Dillsborough Wood was a fact well known both to Tony Tappett and Mr. Larry Twentyman. A fox crossing the brook from the Rufford side would be sure to run to Dillsborough Wood. When Larry, with the two girls, were just about to enter the ride, there was old Tony standing up on his horse at the corner, looking into the covert. And now also a crowd of horsemen came rushing up, who had made their way along the road, and had passed up to the wood through Mr. Twentyman's farmyard; for, as it happened, here it was that Mr. Twentyman lived and farmed his own land. Then came Sir Harry, Colonel Stubbs, and some others who had followed the line throughout,—the Colonel with his boots full of water, as he had been forced to get off his horse in the bed of the brook. Sir Harry, himself, was not in the best of humours,—as will sometimes be the case with masters when they fail to see the cream of a run. 'I never saw such riding in my life,' said Sir Harry, as though some great sin had been committed by those to whom he was addressing himself. Larry turned round, and winked at the two girls, knowing that, if sin had been committed, they three were the sinners. The girls understood nothing about it, but still thought that Larry Twentyman was divine.

While they were standing about on the rides, Tony was still at his work. The riding was over, but the fox had to be killed, and Dillsborough Wood was a covert in which a fox will often require a large amount of killing. No happier home for the vulpine deity exists among the shires of England! There are earths there deep, capacious, full of nurseries; but these, on the present occasion, were debarred from the poor stranger by the wicked ingenuity of man.

A.A —;2

But there were deep dells, in which the brambles
and bracken were so thick that no hound careful of
his snout would penetrate them. The undergrowth of
the wood was so interwoven that no huntsman could
see through its depths. There were dark nooks so
impervious that any fox ignorant of the theory of his
own scent must have wondered why a hound should
have been induced to creep into spaces so narrow.
From one side to another of the wood the hunted
brute would traverse, and always seem to have at
last succeeded in putting his persecutors at fault.
So it was on this occasion. The run, while it lasted,
had occupied, perhaps, three-quarters of an hour,
and during a time equally long poor old Tony was to
be seen scurrying from one side of the wood to another, and was to be heard loudly swearing at his
attendant whips because the hounds did not follow
his footsteps as quickly as his soul desired.

'I never mean to put on a pair of top-boots again,
as long as I live,' said the Colonel. At this time a
little knot of horsemen was stationed in a knoll in the
centre of the wood, waiting till they should hear the
fatal whoop. Among them were Nina, Ayala, the
Colonel, Larry Twentyman, and Captain Batsby.

'Give up top-boots?' said Larry. 'You don't
mean to say you'll ride in black!'

'Top-boots, black boots, spurs, breeches, and red
coat, I renounce them all from this moment. If ever
I'm seen in a hunting field again it will be in a pair of
trousers with overalls.'

'Now, you're joking, Colonel,' said Larry.

'Why won't you wear a red coat any more?' said
Ayala.

'Because I'm disgraced for ever. I came out to
coach two young women, and give them a lead,
and all I've done was to tumble into a brook, while
a better man has taken my charge away from
me.'

'Oh, Jonathan, I am so sorry,' said Nina, 'particularly about your getting into the water.'

'Oh, Colonel Stubbs, we ought to have stopped,' said Ayala.

'It was my only comfort to see how very little I was wanted,' said the Colonel. 'If I had broke my neck instead of wetting my feet it would have been just the same to some people.'

'Oh, Jonathan!' said Nina, really shocked.

'We ought to have stopped. I know we ought to have stopped,' said Ayala, almost crying.

'Nobody ever stops for any one out hunting,' said Twentyman, laying down a great law.

'I should think not,' said Captain Batsby, who had hardly been off the road all the time.

'I am sure the Colonel will not be angry with me because I took the young ladies on,' said Larry.

'The Colonel is such a muff,' said the Colonel himself, 'that he will never presume to be angry with anybody again. But if my cousin and Miss Dormer are not very much obliged to you for what you have done for them there will be nothing of gratitude left in the female British bosom. You have probably given to them the most triumphant moment of their existence.'

'It was their own riding, Colonel; I had nothing to do with it.'

'I am so much obliged to you, Sir,' said Nina.

'And so am I,' said Ayala, 'though it was such a pity that Colonel Stubbs got into the water.'

At that moment came the long expected call. Tony Tappett had killed his fox, after crossing and re-crossing through the wood half a score of times. 'Is it all over?' asked Ayala, as they hurried down the knoll and scurried down the line to get to the spot outside the wood to which Tony was dragging the carcase of his defeated enemy.

'It's all over him,' said Larry. 'A good fox he was, but he'll never run again. He is one of them bred at Littlecotes. The foxes bred at Littlecotes always run.'

'And is he dead?' asked Nina. 'Poor fellow! I

wish it wasn't necessary to kill them.' Then they stood by till they saw the body of the victim thrown up into the air, and fall amongst the blood-smirched upturned noses of the expectant pack.

'I call that a pretty little run, Sir Harry,' said Larry Twentyman.

'Pretty well,' said Sir Harry; 'the pace wasn't very great, or that pony of mine which Miss Dormer is riding could not have lived with it.'

'Horses, Sir Harry, don't want so much pace, if they are allowed to go straight. It's when a man doesn't get well away, or has made a mess with his fences, that he needs an extra allowance of pace to catch the hounds. If you're once with them and can go straight you may keep your place without such a deal of legs.' To this Sir Harry replied only by a grunt, as on the present occasion he had 'made a mess with his fences,' as Larry Twentyman had called it.

'And now, young ladies,' said Larry, 'I hope you'll come in and see my missus and her baby, and have a little bit of lunch, such as it is.'

Nina asked anxiously whether there would not be another fox. Ayala also was anxious lest in accepting the proffered hospitality she should lose any of the delights of the day. But it was at length arranged that a quarter of an hour should be allowed before Tony took his hounds over to the Bragton coverts. Immediately Larry was off his horse, rushing into the house and ordering everyone about it to come forth with bread and cheese and sherry and beer. In spite of what he had said of his ruin it was known that Larry Twentyman was a warm man, and that no man in Rufford gave what he had to give with a fuller heart. His house was in the middle of the Rufford and Ufford hunting country, and the consumption there during the hunting months of bread and cheese, sherry and beer, must have been immense. Everyone seemed to be intimate with him, and all called for what they wanted as if they were on their own premises. On such occasions as these

Larry was a proud man; for no one in those parts carried a lighter heart or was more fond of popularity.

The parlour inside was by no means big enough to hold the crowding guests, who therefore munched their bread and cheese and drank their beer round the front door, without dismounting from their horses; but Nina and Ayala with their friend the Colonel were taken inside to see Mrs. Twentyman and her baby. 'Now, Larry, what sort of a run was it?' said the young mother. 'Where did you find him, and what line did he take?'

'I'll tell you all about it when I come back; there are two young ladies for you now to look after.' Then he introduced his wife and the baby which was in her arms. 'The little fellow is only six weeks old, and yet she wanted to come to the meet. She'd have been riding to hounds if I'd let her.'

'Why not?' said Mrs. Twentyman. 'At any rate I might have gone in the pony carriage and had baby with me.'

'Only six weeks old!' said Nina, stooping down and kissing the child.

'He is a darling!' said Ayala. 'I hope he'll go out hunting some day.'

'He'll want to go six times a week if he's anything like his father,' said Mrs. Twentyman.

'And seven times if he's like his mother,' said Larry. Then again they mounted their nags, and trotted off across the high roads to the Bragton coverts. Mrs. Twentyman with her baby in her arms walked down to the gate at the high road and watched them with longing eyes, till Tony and the hounds were out of sight.

Nothing further in the way of hunting was done that day which requires to be recorded. They drew various coverts and found a fox or two, but the scent, which had been so strong in the morning, seemed to have gone, and the glory of the day was over. The two girls and the Colonel remained companions during the afternoon, and succeeded in making themselves merry over the incident of the brook. The Colonel was in truth well pleased that Larry Twenty-man should have taken his place, though he probably would not have been gratified had he seen Captain Batsby assume his duties. It had been his delight to see the two girls ride, and he had been near enough to see them. He was one of those men who, though fond of hunting, take no special glory in it, and are devoid of the jealousy of riding. Not to have a good place in a run was no worse to him than to lose a game of billiards or a rubber of whist. Let the reader understand that this trait in his character is not mentioned with approbation. 'Always to excel and to go ahead of everbody' should, the present writer thinks, be in the heart of every man who rides to hounds. There was in our Colonel a philosophical way of looking into the thing which perhaps became him as a man, but was deleterious to his character as a sportsman.*

'I do hope you've enjoyed yourself, Ayala!' he said, as he lifted her from her horse.

'Indeed,—indeed, I have!' said Ayala, not notic-ing the use of her Christian name. 'I have been so happy, and I'm so much obliged to you!'

## CHAPTER XXV

### 'YOU ARE NOT HE.'

AYALA had been a week at Stalham, and according to the understanding which had existed she should now have returned to Kingsbury Crescent. She had come for a week, and she had had her week. Oh, what a week it had been, so thoroughly happy, without a cloud, filled full with ecstatic pleasures! Jonathan Stubbs had become to her the pleasantest of friends. Lady Albury had covered her with caresses and little presents. Nina was the most perfect of friends. Sir Harry had never been cross, except for that one moment in the wood. And as for

Sprite,—Sprite had nearly realised her idea of an
Angel of Light. Oh, how happy she had been! She
was to return on the Monday, having thus comprised
two Sundays within her elongated week. She knew
that her heaven was to be at an end; but she was
grateful, and was determined in her gratitude to be
happy and cheerful to the close. But early on this
Sunday morning Colonel Stubbs spoke a word to
Lady Albury. 'That little girl is so thoroughly happy
here. Cannot you prolong it for her just for another
three days?'

'Is it to be for her,—or for Colonel Stubbs, who is
enamoured of the little girl?' asked Lady Albury.

'For both,' said the Colonel, rather gravely.

'Are you in earnest?'

'What do you call in earnest? I do love to see a
pretty creature enjoy herself thoroughly as she does.
If you will make her stay till Thursday Albury will
let her ride the little horse again at Star Cross on
Wednesday.

'Of course she shall stay,—all the season if you
wish it. She is indeed a happy girl if you are in
earnest.'

Then it was settled, and Lady Albury in her
happiest manner informed Ayala that she was not
to be allowed to take her departure till after she had
ridden Sprite once again. 'Sir Harry says that you
have given the little horse quite a name, and that
you must finish off his character for him at Star
Cross.' As was the heart of the Peri when the gate of
Paradise was opened for her*so was the heart of
Ayala. There were to be four days, with the fourth
as a hunting-day, before she need think of going!
There was an eternity of bliss before her.

'But Aunt Margaret!' she said, not, however,
doubting for a moment that she would stay. Who
cares for a frowning aunt at the distance of an
eternity. I fear that in the ecstasy of her joy she had
forgotten the promise made, that she would always
remember her aunt's goodness to her. 'I will write

a note to Mrs. Dosett, and make it all straight,' said
Lady Albury. The note was written, and, whether
matters were straight or crooked at Kingsbury
Crescent, Ayala remained at Albury.

Colonel Stubbs had thought about the matter, and
determined that he was quite in earnest. He had, he
told himself, enough for modest living,—for modest
living without poverty. More would come to him
when old General Stubbs, his uncle, should die. The
general was already past seventy. What was the use
of independence if he could not allow himself to have
the girl whom he really loved? Had any human
being so perfectly lovely as Ayala ever flashed before
his eyes before? Was there ever a sweeter voice
heard from a woman's mouth? And then all her
little ways and motions,—her very tricks,—how full
of charm they were! When she would open her eyes
and nod her head, and pout with her lips, he would
declare to himself that he could no longer live without her. And then every word that fell from her lips
seemed to have something in it of pretty humour. In
fact the Colonel was in love, and had now resolved
that he would give way to his love in spite of his
aunt, the Marchesa, and in spite of his own philosophy.

He felt by no means sure of success, but yet he
thought that he might succeed. From the moment
in which, as the reader may remember, he had accosted her at the ball, and desired her to dance with
him in obedience to his aunt's behests, it had been
understood by everyone around him that Ayala had
liked him. They had become fast friends. Ayala
allowed him to do many little things which, by some
feminine instinct of her own, would have been put
altogether beyond the reach of Captain Batsby. The
Colonel knew all this, and knew at the same time that
he should not trust to it only. But still he could not
but trust to it in some degree. Lady Albury had told
him that Ayala would be a happy girl if he were in
earnest, and he himself was well aware of Ayala's
dependent position, and of the discomforts of Kings-

bury Crescent. Ayala had spoken quite openly to him
of Kingsbury Crescent as to a confidential friend.
But on all that he did not lean much as being in his
favour. He could understand that such a girl as
Ayala would not accept a husband merely with the
object of avoiding domestic poverty. Little qualms
of doubt came upon him as he remembered the nature
of the girl, so that he confessed to himself that Lady
Albury knew nothing about it. But, nevertheless, he
hoped. His red hair and his ugly face had never yet
stood against him among the women with whom he
had lived. He had been taught by popularity to
think himself a popular man;—and then Ayala had
shown so many signs of her friendship!

There was shooting on Saturday, and he went out
with the shooters, saying nothing to any one of an
intended early return; but at three o'clock he was
back at the house. Then he found that Ayala was
out in the carriage, and he waited. He sat in the
library pretending to read, till he heard the sounds of
the carriage-wheels, and then he met the ladies in
the hall. 'Are they all home from shooting?' asked
Lady Albury. The Colonel explained that no one
was home but himself. He had missed three cock-
pheasants running, and had then come away in disgust. 'I am the most ignominious creature in existence,' he said laughing; 'one day I tumble into a
ditch three feet wide——'

'It was ten yards at least,' said Nina, jealous as to
the glory of her jump.

'And to-day I cannot hit a bird. I shall take to
writing a book and leave the severer pursuit of sport
to more enterprising persons.' Then suddenly turning round he said to Ayala, 'Are you good-natured
enough to come and take a walk with me in the
shrubbery?'

Ayala, taken somewhat by surprise at the request,
looked up into Lady Albury's face. 'Go with him,
my dear, if you are not tired,' said Lady Albury.
'He deserves consolation after all his good deeds to

you.' Ayala still doubted. Though she was on terms
of pleasant friendship with the man, yet she felt
almost awestruck at this sudden request that she
should walk alone with him. But not to do so,
especially after Lady Albury's injunction, would
have been peculiar. She certainly was not tired, and
had such a walk come naturally it would have been
an additional pleasure to her; but now, though she
went she hesitated, and showed her hesitation.

'Are you afraid to come with me?' he said, as soon
as they were out on the gravel together.

'Afraid! Oh, dear no, I should not be afraid to go
anywhere with you, I think; only it seems odd that
you did not ask Nina too.'

'Shall I tell you why?'

'Why was it?'

'Because I have something to say to you which I
do not wish Nina to hear just at this moment. And
then I thought that we were such friends that you
would not mind coming with me.'

'Of course we are,' said Ayala.

'I don't know why it should be so, but I seem to
have known you years instead of days.'

'Perhaps that is because you knew papa.'

'More likely because I have learnt to know your
papa's daughter.'

'Do you mean Lucy?'

'I mean Ayala.'

'That is saying the same thing twice over. You
know me because you know me.'

'Just that. How long do you suppose I have
known that Mrs. Gregory, who sat opposite to us
yesterday?'

'How can I tell?'

'Just fifteen years. I was going to Harrow when
she came as a young girl to stay with my mother.
Her people and my people had known each other for
the last fifty years. Since that I have seen her constantly, and of course we are very intimate.'

'I suppose so.'

' I know as much about her after all that as if we
had lived in two different hemispheres and couldn't
speak a word of each other's language. There isn't
a thought or a feeling in common between us. I ask
after her husband and her children, and then tell her
it's going to rain. She says something about the old
General's health, and then there is an end of everything between us. When next we meet we do it all
over again.'

'How very uninteresting!' said Ayala.

'Very uninteresting. It is because there are so
many Mrs. Gregorys about that I like to go down to
Drumcaller and live by myself. Perhaps you're a
Mrs. Gregory to somebody.'

'Why should I be a Mrs. Gregory? I don't think
I am at all like Mrs. Gregory.'

'Not to me, Ayala.' Now she heard the 'Ayala,'
and felt something of what it meant. There had been
moments at which she had almost disliked to hear
him call her Miss Dormer; but now,—now she wished
that he had not called her Ayala. She strove to assume a serious expression of face, but having done so
she could not dare to turn it up towards him. The
glance of her little anger, if there was any, fell only
upon the ground. 'It is because you are to me a
creature so essentially different from Mrs. Gregory
that I seem to know you so well. I never want to go
to Drumcaller if you are near me;—or, if I think of
Drumcaller, it is that I might be there with you.'

'I am sure the place is very pretty, but I don't
suppose I shall ever see it.'

'Do you know about your sister and Mr. Hamel?'

'Yes,' said Ayala, surprised. 'She has told me all
about it. How do you know?'

'He was staying at Drumcaller,—he and I together
with no one else,—when he went over to ask her. I
never saw a man so happy as when he came back
from Glenbogie. He had got all that he wanted in
the world.'

'I do so love him because he loves her.'

'And I love her—because she loves you.'

'It is not the same, you know,' said Ayala, trying to think it all out.

'May I not love her?'

'He is to be my brother. That's why I love him. She can't be your sister.' The poor girl, though she had tried to think it all out, had not thought very far.

'Can she not?' he said.

'Of course not. Lucy is to marry Mr. Hamel.'

'And whom am I to marry?' Then she saw it all. 'Ayala,—Ayala,—who is to be my wife?'

'I do not know,' she said,—speaking with a gruff voice, but still in a whisper, with a manner altogether different,—thinking how well it would be that she should be taken at once back into the house.

'Do you know whom I would fain have as my wife?' Then he felt that it behoved him to speak out plainly. He was already sure that she would not at once tell him that it should be as he would have it,— that she would not instantly throw herself into his arms. But he must speak plainly to her, and then fight his cause as best he might. 'Ayala, I have asked you to come out with me that I might ask you to be my wife. It is that that I did not wish Nina to hear at once. If you will put out your hand and say that it shall be so, Nina and all the world shall know it. I shall be as proud then as Hamel, and as happy,— happier, I think. It seems to me that no one can love as I do now, Ayala; it has grown upon me from hour to hour as I have seen you. When I first took you away to that dance it was so already. Do you remember that night at the theatre,—when I had come away from everything and striven so hard that I might be near to you before you went back to your home? Ayala, I loved you then so dearly;—but not as I love you now. When I saw you riding away from me yesterday, when I could not get over the brook, I told myself that unless I might catch you at last, and have you all to myself, I could never again be happy. Do you remember when you stooped down

and kissed that man's baby at the farmhouse? Oh,
Ayala, I thought then that if you would not be my
wife,—if you would not be my wife,—I should never
have wife, never should have baby, never should
have home of my own.' She walked on by his side,
listening, but she had not a word to say to him. It
had been easy enough to her to reject and to rebuke
and to scorn Tom Tringle, when he had persisted in
his suit; but she knew not with what words to reject
this man who stood so high in her estimation, who
was in many respects so perfect, whom she so
thoroughly liked,—but whom, nevertheless, she
must reject. He was not the Angel of Light. There
was nothing there of the azure wings upon which
should soar the all but celestial being to whom she
could condescend to give herself and her love. He was
pleasant, good, friendly, kind-hearted,—all that a
friend or a brother should be; but he was not the
Angel of Light. She was sure of that. She told herself that she was quite sure of it, as she walked
beside him in silence along the path. 'You know
what I mean, Ayala, when I tell you that I love you,'
he continued. But still she made no answer. 'I have
seen at last the one human being with whom I feel
that I can be happy to spend my life, and, having
seen her, I ask her to be my wife. The hope has been
dwelling with me and growing since I first met you.
Shall it be a vain hope? Ayala, may I still hope?'

'No,' she said, abruptly.

'Is that all?'

'It is all that I can say.'

'Is that one "no" to be the end of everything between us?'

'I don't know what else I ought to say to you,
Colonel Stubbs.'

'Do you mean that you can never love me?'

'Never,' she said.

'That is a hard word,—and hardly friendly. Is
there to be no more than one hard word between you
and me? Though I did not venture to think that

you could tell me that you loved me, I looked for
something kinder, something gentler than that.'

'From such a sharp and waspish word as "no,"
To pluck the sting!'*

Ayala did not know the lines I have quoted, but
the idea conveyed in them was present clearly to her
mind. She would fain have told him, had she known
how to do so, that her heart was very gentle towards
him, was very kind, gentle and kind as a sister's;—
but that she could not love him, so as to become his
wife. 'You are not he,—not he, not that Angel of
Light, which must come to me, radiant with poetry,
beautiful to the eye, full of all excellences of art,
lifted above the earth by the qualities of his mind,—
such a one as must come to me if it be that I am ever
to confess that I love. You are not he, and I cannot
love you. But you shall be the next to him in my
estimation, and you are already so dear to me that I
would be tender to you, would be gentle,—if only I
knew how.' It was all there, clear enough in her
mind, but she had not the words. 'I don't know what
it is that I ought to say,' she exclaimed through her
sobs.

'The truth, at any rate,' he answered sternly, 'but
not the truth, half and half, after the fashion of some
young ladies. Do not think that you should palter
with the truth either because it may not be palatable
to me, or seem decorous to yourself. To my happiness
this matter is all important, and you are something to
my happiness, if only because I have risked it on your
love. Tell me;—why cannot you love me?'

The altered tone of his voice, which now had in it
something of severity, seemed to give her more
power.

'It is because——' Then she paused.

'Because why? Out with it, whatever it is. If it
be something that a man may remedy I will remedy
it. Do not fear to hurt me. Is it because I am ugly?
That I cannot remedy.' She did not dare to tell
him that it was so, but she looked up at him, not

dissenting by any motion of her head. 'Then God help me, for ugly I must remain.'

'It is not that only.'

'Is it because my name is Stubbs—Jonathan Stubbs?' Now she did assent, nodding her head at him. He had bade her tell him the truth, and she was so anxious to do as he bade her! 'If it be so, Ayala, I must tell you that you are wrong,—wrong and foolish; that you are carried away by a feeling of romance, which is a false romance. Far be it from me to say that I could make you happy, but I am sure that your happiness cannot be made and cannot be marred by such accidents as that. Do you think that my means are not sufficient?'

'No;—no,' she cried; 'I know nothing of your means. If I could love you I would not condescend to ask,—even to hear.'

'There is no other man, I think?'

'There is no other man.'

'But your imagination has depicted to you something grander than I am,'—then she assented quickly, turning round and nodding her head to him,—'some one who shall better respond to that spirit of poetry which is within you?' Again she nodded her head approvingly, as though to assure him that now he knew the whole truth. 'Then, Ayala, I must strive to soar till I can approach your dreams. But, if you dare to desire things which are really grand, do not allow yourself to be mean at the same time. Do not let the sound of a name move you, or I shall not believe in your aspirations. Now, shall I take you back to the house?'

Back to the house they went, and there was not another word spoken between them. By those last words of his she had felt herself to be rebuked. If it were possible that he could ask her again whether that sound, Jonathan Stubbs, had anything to do with it, she would let him know now, by some signal, that she no longer found a barrier in the name. But there were other barriers,—barriers which he himself had not pretended to call vain. As to his ugliness, that he had confessed he could not remedy; calling on God to pity him because he was so. And as for that something grander which he had described, and for which her soul sighed, he had simply said that he would seek for it. She was sure that he would not find it. It was not to such as he that the something grander,—which was to be the peculiar attribute of the Angel of Light,—could be accorded. But he ad owned that the something grander might exist.

## CHAPTER XXVI

### 'THE FINEST HERO THAT I EVER KNEW.'

THE Colonel and Ayala returned to the house without a word. When they were passing through the hall she turned to go at once up the stairs to her own room. As she did so he put out his hand to her, and she took it. But she passed on without speaking, and when she was alone she considered it over all in her own mind. There could be no doubt that she was right. Of that she was quite sure. It was certainly a fixed law that a girl should not marry a man unless she loved him. She did not love this man, and therefore she ought not to marry him. But there were some qualms at her heart as to the possible reality of the image which she had created for her own idolatry. And she had been wounded when he told her that she should not allow herself to be mean amidst her soarings. She had been wounded, and yet she knew that he had been right. He had intended to teach her the same lesson when he told her the absurd story of the woman who had been flung out of the window. She could not love him; but that name of his should never again be a reason for not doing so. Let the Angel of Light come to her with his necessary angelic qualities, and no want of euphony in a sound should be a barrier to him. Nor in truth could any outside appearance be an attribute of angelic light. The Angel of Light might be there even with red hair. Something as to the truth of this also came across her, though the Colonel had not rebuked her on that head.

But how should she carry herself now during the four days which remained to her at Stalham Park? All the loveliness seemed to depart from her prospect. She would hardly know how to open her mouth before her late friend. She suspected that Lady Albury knew with what purpose the Colonel had taken her out in the shrubbery, and she would not dare to look Lady Albury in the face. How should she answer Nina if Nina were to ask her questions about the walk. The hunt for next Wednesday was no longer a delight to which she could look forward. How would it be possible that Colonel Stubbs should direct her now as to her riding, and instruct her as to her conduct in the hunting-field? It would be better for her that she should return at once to Kingsbury Crescent.

As she thought of this there did come upon her a reflection that had she been able to accept Colonel Stubbs's offer there would have been an end for ever to the miseries of her aunt's house. She would have been lifted at once into the mode of life in which the man lived. Instead of being a stranger admitted by special grace into such an Elysium as that of Stalham Park, she would become one of those to whom such an Elysium belonged almost of right. By her own gifts she would have won her way into that upper and brighter life which seemed to her to be all smiles and all joy. As to his income she thought nothing and cared nothing. He lived with men who had horses and carriages, and who spent their time in pleasurable pursuits. And she would live amidst ladies who were always arrayed in bright garments, who, too, had horses and carriages at their command, and were never troubled by these sordid cares which made life at Kingsbury Crescent so sad and tedious. One little word would have done it all for her, would have enabled her to take the step by which she would be placed among the bright ones of the earth.

But the remembrance of all this only made her firmer in her resolution. If there was any law of right and wrong fixed absolutely in her bosom, it was this,—that no question of happiness or unhappiness, of suffering or joy, would affect her duty to the Angel of Light. She owed herself to him should he come to seek her. She owed herself to him no less, even should he fail to come. And she owed herself equally whether he should be rich or poor. As she was fortifying herself with these assurances, Nina came to ask her whether she would not come down to tea. Ayala pleaded headache, and said that she would rest till dinner. 'Has anything happened?' asked Nina. Ayala simply begged that she might be asked no questions then, because her head was aching. 'If you do not tell me everything, I shall think you are no true friend,' said Nina, as she left the room.

As evening drew on she dressed for dinner, and went down into the drawing-room. In doing so it was necessary to pass through the billiard-room, and there she found Colonel Stubbs, knocking about the balls. 'Are you dressed for dinner?' he exclaimed; 'I haven't begun to think of it yet, and Sir Harry hates a man when he comes in late. That wretch Batsby has beaten me four games.' With that he rushed off, putting down the cue with a rattle, and seeming to Ayala to have recovered altogether from the late prostration of his spirits.

In the drawing-room Ayala was for a few minutes alone, and then, as she was glad to see, three or four ladies all came in at once, so that no question could be asked her by Lady Albury. They went into dinner without the Colonel, who was in truth late, and she was taken in by Mr. Gosling, whose pretty little wife was just opposite to her. On the other side of her sat Lord Rufford, who had come to Stalham with his wife for a day or two, and who immediately began

to congratulate her on the performance of the day
before. 'I am told you jumped the Cranbury Brook,'
he said. 'I should as soon think of jumping the
Serpentine.'

'I did it because somebody told me.'

'Ah,' said Lord Rufford, with a sigh, 'there is
nothing like ignorance, innocence, and youth combined. But why didn't Colonel Stubbs get over
after you?'

'Because Colonel Stubbs couldn't,' said that
gentleman, as he took his seat in the vacant chair.

'It may be possible,' said Sir Harry, 'that a gentleman should not be able to jump over Cranbury
Brook; but any gentleman, if he will take a little
trouble, may come down in time for dinner.'

'Now that I have been duly snubbed right and
left,' said the Colonel, 'perhaps I may eat my soup.'

Ayala, who had expected she hardly knew what
further troubles, and who had almost feared that
nobody would speak to her because she had misbehaved herself, endeavoured to take heart of grace
when she found that all around her, including the
Colonel himself, were as pleasant as ever. She had
fancied that Lady Albury had looked at her specially
when Colonel Stubbs took his seat, and she had
specially noticed the fact that his chair had not been
next her own. These little matters she was aware Lady
Albury managed herself, and was aware also that in
accordance with the due rotation of things she and
the Colonel should have been placed together. She
was glad that it was not so, but at the same time she
was confident that Lady Albury knew something of
what had passed between herself and her suitor. The
evening, however, went off easily, and nothing occurred to disturb her except that the Colonel had called
her by her Christian name, when as usual he brought
to her a cup of tea in the drawing-room. Oh, that he
would continue to do so, and yet not demand from
her more than their old friendship!

The next morning was Sunday, and they all went

to church. It was a law at Stalham that every one
should go to church on Sunday morning. Sir Harry
himself, who was not supposed to be a peculiarly
religious man, was always angry when any male
guest did not show himself in the enormous family
pew. 'I call it d—— indecent,' he has been heard to
say. But nobody was expected to go twice,—and
consequently nobody ever did go twice. Lunch was
protracted later than usual. The men would roam
about the grounds with cigars in their mouths, and
ladies would take to reading in their own rooms, in
following which occupation they would spend a considerable part of the afternoon asleep. On this afternoon Lady Albury did not go to sleep, but contrived
to get Ayala alone upstairs into her little sitting-
room. 'Ayala,' she said, with something between a
smile and a frown, 'I am afraid I am going to be
angry with you.'

'Please don't be angry, Lady Albury.'

'If I am right in what I surmise, you had an offer
made to you yesterday which ought to satisfy the
heart of almost any girl in England.' Here she
paused, but Ayala had not a word to say for herself.
'If it was so, the best man I know asked you to share
his fortune with him.'

'Has he told you?'

'But he did?'

'I shall not tell,' said Ayala, proudly.

'I know he did. I knew that it was his intention
before. Are you aware what kind of man is my
cousin, Jonathan Stubbs? Has it occurred to you
that in truth and gallantry, in honour, honesty,
courage and real tenderness, he is so perfect as to be
quite unlike to the crowd of men you see?'

'I do know that he is good,' said Ayala.

'Good! Where will you find any one good like
him? Compare him to the other men around him,
and then say whether he is good! Can it be possible
that you should refuse the love of such a man as
that?'

'I don't think I ought to be made to talk about it,' said Ayala, hesitating.

'My dear, it is for your own sake and for his. When you go away from here it may be so difficult for him to see you again.'

'I don't suppose he will ever want,' said Ayala.

'It is sufficient that he wants it now. What better can you expect for yourself?'

'I expect nothing,' said Ayala, proudly. 'I have got nothing, and I expect nothing.'

'He will give you everything, simply because he loves you. My dear, I should not take the trouble to tell you all this, did I not know that he is a man who ought to be accepted when he asks such a request as that. Your happiness would be safe in his hands.' She paused, but Ayala had not a word to say. 'And he is not a man likely to renew such a request. He is too proud for that. I can conceive no possible reason for such a refusal unless it be that you are engaged. If there be some one else, then of course there must be an end of it.'

'There is no one else.'

'Then, my dear, with your prospects it is sheer folly. When the General dies he will have over two thousand a year.'

'As if that had anything to do with it!' said Ayala, holding herself aloft in her wrath, and throwing angry glances at the lady.

'It is what I call romance,' said Lady Albury. 'Romance can never make you happy.'

'At any rate it is not riches. What you call romance may be what I like best. At any rate if I do not love Colonel Stubbs I am sure I ought not to marry him;—and I won't.'

After this there was nothing further to be said. Ayala thought that she would be turned out of the room,—almost out of the house, in disgrace. But Lady Albury, who was simply playing her part, was not in the least angry. 'Well, my dear,' she said, 'pray,—pray, think better of it. I am in earnest, of

course, because of my cousin,—because he seems to
have put his heart upon it. He is just the man to be
absolutely in love when he is in love. But I would
not speak as I do unless I were sure that he would
make you happy. My cousin Jonathan is to me the
finest hero that I know. When a man is a hero he
shouldn't be broken-hearted for want of a woman's
smiles,—should he?'

'She ought not to smile unless she loves him,' said
Ayala, as she left the room.

The Monday and Tuesday went very quietly.
Lady Albury said nothing more on the great subject,
and the Colonel behaved himself exactly as though
there had been no word of love at all. There was
nothing special said about the Wednesday's hunt
through the two days, till Ayala almost thought that
there would be no hunt for her. Nor, indeed, did
she much wish for it. It had been the Colonel
who had instigated her to deeds of daring, and
under his sanction that she had ventured to ride.
She would hardly know how to go through the
Wednesday,—whether still to trust him, or whether
to hold herself aloof from him. When nothing was
said on the subject till late on the evening of the
Tuesday, she had almost resolved that she would not
put on her habit when the morning came. But just
as she was about to leave the drawing-room with her
bed-candle Colonel Stubbs came to her. 'Most of us
ride to the meet to-morrow,' he said; 'but you and
Nina shall be taken in the waggonette so as to save
you a little. It is all arranged.' She bowed and
thanked him, going to bed almost sorry that it should
have been so settled. When the morning came Nina
could not ride. She had hurt her foot, and, coming
early into Ayala's room, declared with tears that she
could not go. 'Then neither shall I,' said Ayala,
who was at that moment preparing to put on her
habit.

'But you must. It is all settled, and Sir Harry
would be offended if you did not go. What has

Jonathan done that you should refuse to ride with him because I am lame?'

'Nothing,' said Ayala.

'Oh, Ayala, do tell me. I should tell you everything. Of course you must hunt whatever it is. Even though he should have offered and you refused him, of course you must go.'

'Must I?' said Ayala.

'Then you have refused him?'

'I have. Oh, Nina, pray do not speak of it. Do not think of it if you can help it. Why should everything be disturbed because I have been a fool?'

'Then you think you have been a fool?'

'Other people think so; but if so I shall at any rate be constant to my folly. What I mean is, that it has been done, and should be passed over as done with. I am quite sure that I ought not to be scolded; but Lady Albury did scold me.' Then they went down together to breakfast, Ayala having prepared herself properly for the hunting-field.

In the waggonette there were with her Lady Albury, Mrs. Gosling, and Nina, who was not prevented by her lameness from going to the meet. The gentlemen all rode, so that there was no immediate difficulty as to Colonel Stubbs. But when she had been put on her horse by his assistance and found herself compelled to ride away from the carriage, apparently under his especial guidance, her heart misgave her, and she thoroughly wished that she was at home in the Crescent. Though she was specially under his guidance there were at first others close around her, and, while they were on the road going to the covert which they were to draw, conversation was kept up so that it was not necessary for her to speak;—but what should she do when she should find herself alone with him as would certainly be the case? It soon was the case. The hounds were at work in a large wood in which she was told they might possibly pass the best part of the day, and it was not long before the men had dispersed themselves, some on this side some on that, and she found herself with no one near her but the Colonel. 'Ayala,' he said, 'of course you know it is my duty to look after you, and to do it better if I can than I did on Friday.'

'I understand,' she said.

'Do not let any remembrance of that walk on Saturday interfere with your happiness to-day. Who knows when you may be out hunting again?'

'Never!' she said; 'I don't suppose I shall ever hunt again.'

'Carpe diem,' he said laughing. 'Do you know what 'carpe diem' means?'

'It is Latin perhaps.'

'Yes; and therefore you are not supposed to understand it. This is what it means. As an hour for joy has come, do not let any trouble interfere with it. Let it all be, for this day at least, as though there had been no walk in the Stalham Woods. There is Larry Twentyman. If I break down as I did on Friday you may always trust to him. Larry and you are old friends now.'

'Carpe diem,'*she said to herself. 'Oh, yes; if it were only possible. How is one to "carpe diem" with one's heart full of troubles?' And it was the less possible because this man whom she had rejected was so anxious to do everything for her happiness. Lady Albury had told her that he was a hero,—that he was perfect in honour, honesty, and gallantry; and she felt inclined to own that Lady Albury was almost right. Yet,—yet how far was he from that image of manly perfection which her daily thoughts had created for her! Could she have found an appropriate word with which to thank him she would have done so; but there was no such word; and Larry Twentyman was now with them, taking off his hat and overflowing with compliments. 'Oh, Miss Dormer, I am so delighted to see you out again.'

'How is the baby, Mr. Twentyman?'

'Brisk as a bee, and hungry as a hunter.'

'And how is Mrs. Twentyman?'

'Brisker and hungrier than the baby. What do you think of the day, Colonel?'

'A very good sort of day, Twentyman, if we were anywhere out of these big woods.' Larry shook his head solemnly. The Mudcombe Woods in which they were now at work had been known to occupy Tony Tappett and his whole pack from eleven o'clock till the dusk of evening. 'We've got to draw them, of course,' continued the Colonel. Then Mr. Twentyman discoursed at some length on the excellence of Mudcombe Woods. What would any county be without a nursery for young foxes? Gorse-coverts, hedgerows, and little spinneys would be of no avail unless there were some grandly wild domain in which maternal and paternal foxes could roam in comparative security. All this was just as Ayala would have it, because it enabled her to ask questions, and saved her from subjects which might be painful to her.

The day, in truth, was not propitious to hunting even. Foxes were found in plenty, and two of them were killed within the recesses of the wood; but on no occasion did they run a mile into the open. For Ayala it was very well, because she was galloping hither and thither, and because before the day was over, she found herself able to talk to the Colonel in her wonted manner; but there was no great glory for her as had been the glory of Little Cranbury Brook.

On the next morning she was taken back to London and handed over to her aunt in Kingsbury Crescent without another word having been spoken by Colonel Stubbs in reference to his love.

## CHAPTER XXVII

### LADY ALBURY'S LETTER

' I HAVE had a letter from Lady Albury,' said Aunt Margaret, almost as soon as Ayala had taken off her hat and cloak.

'Yes, I know, Aunt Margaret. She wrote to ask that I might stay for four more days. I hope it was not wrong.'

'I have had another letter since that, on Monday, about it; I have determined to show it you. There it is. You had better read it by yourself, and I will come to you again in half-an-hour.' Then, very solemnly, but with no trace of ill-humour, Mrs. Dosett left the room. There was something in her tone and gait so exceedingly solemn that Ayala was almost frightened. Of course, the letter must be about Colonel Stubbs, and, of course, the writer of it would find fault with her. She was conscious that she was adding one to her terribly long list of sins in not consenting to marry Colonel Stubbs. It was her misfortune that all her friends found fault with everything that she did. Among them there was not one, not even Nina, who fully sympathised with her. Not even to Lucy could she expatiate with a certainty of sympathy in regard to the Angel of Light. And now, though her aunt was apparently not angry,— only solemn,—she felt already sure that she was to be told that it was her duty to marry Colonel Stubbs. It was only the other day that her aunt was preaching to her as to the propriety of marrying her cousin Tom. It seemed, she said to herself, that people thought that a girl was bound to marry any man who could provide a house for her, and bread to eat, and clothes to wear. All this passed through her mind as she slowly drew Lady Albury's letter from the envelope and prepared to read it. The letter was as follows:—

'Albury, Monday, 18th November, 18—.

'DEAR MADAM,

'Your niece will return to you, as you request, on Thursday, but before she reaches you I think it my duty to inform you of a little circumstance which has occurred here. My cousin, Colonel Jonathan Stubbs, who is also the nephew of the Marchesa Baldoni, has made Miss Dormer an offer. I am bound to add that I did not think it improbable that it would be so, when I called on your husband, and begged him to allow your niece to come to us. I did not then know my cousin's intention as a fact. I doubt whether he knew it himself; but from what I had heard I thought it probable, and, as I conceive that any young lady would be fortunate in becoming my cousin's wife, I had no scruple.

'He has proposed to her, and she has rejected him. He has set his heart upon the matter, and I am most anxious that he should succeed, because I know him to be a man who will not easily brook disappointment where he has set his heart. Of all men I know he is the most steadfast in his purpose.

'I took the liberty of speaking to your niece on the subject, and am disposed to think that she is deterred by some feeling of foolish romance, partly because she does not like the name, partly because my cousin is not a handsome man in a girl's eyes;— more probably, however, she has built up to herself some poetic fiction, and dreams of she knows not what. If it be so, it is a pity that she should lose an opportunity of settling herself well and happily in life. She gave as a reason that she did not love him. My experience is not so long as yours, perhaps, but such as I have has taught me to think that a wife will love her husband when she finds herself used well at all points. Mercenary marriages are, of course, bad; but it is a pity, I think, that a girl, such as your niece, should lose the chance of so much happiness by a freak of romance.

'Colonel Stubbs, who is only twenty-eight years of age, has a staff appointment at Aldershot. He has private means of his own, on which alone he would be justified in marrying. On the death of his uncle, General Stubbs, he will inherit a considerable accession of fortune. He is not, of course, a rich man; but he has ample for the wants of a family. In all other good gifts, temper, manliness, truth, and tenderness, I know no one to excel him. I should trust any young friend of my own into his hands with perfect safety.

' I have thought it right to tell you this. You will use your own judgment in saying what you think fit to your niece. Should she be made to understand that her own immediate friends approve of the offer, she would probably be induced to accept it. I have not heard my cousin say what may be his future plans. I think it possible that, as he is quite in earnest, he will not take one repulse. Should he ask again, I hope that your niece may receive him with altered views.

' Pray believe me to be, my dear Madam,

' Yours sincerely,

' ROSALINE ALBURY.'

Ayala read the letter twice over before her aunt returned to her, and, as she read it, felt something of a feeling of renewed kindness come upon her in reference to the writer of it; —not that she was in the least changed in her own resolution, but that she liked Lady Albury for wishing to change her. The reasons given, however, were altogether impotent with her. Colonel Stubbs had the means of keeping a wife! If that were a reason then also ought she to marry her cousin, Tom Tringle. Colonel Stubbs was good and true; but so also very probably was Tom Tringle. She would not compare the two men. She knew that her cousin Tom was altogether distasteful to her, while she took delight in the companionship of the Colonel. But the reasons for marrying one were to her thinking as strong as for marrying the other. There could be only one valid excuse for marriage,—that of adoring the man;—and she was quite sure that she did not adore Colonel Jonathan Stubbs. Lady Albury had said in her letter, that a girl would be sure to love a man who treated her well after marriage; but that would not suffice for her. Were she to marry at all, it would be necessary that she should love the man before her marriage.

'Have you read the letter, my dear?' said Mrs. Dosett; as she entered the room and closed the door carefully behind her. She spoke almost in a whisper, and seemed to be altogether changed by the magnitude of the occasion.

'Yes, Aunt Margaret, I have read it.'

'I suppose it is true?'

'True! It is true in part.'

'You did meet this Colonel Stubbs?'

'Oh, yes; I met him.'

'And you had met him before?'

'Yes, Aunt Margaret. He used to come to Brook Street. He is the Marchesa's nephew.'

'Did he——' This question Aunt Margaret asked in a very low whisper, and her most solemn voice. 'Did he make love to you in Brook Street?'

'No,' said Ayala sharply.

'Not at all?'

'Not at all. I never thought of such a thing. I never dreamed of such a thing when he began talking to me out in the woods at Stalham on Saturday.'

'Had you been—been on friendly terms with him?'

'Very friendly terms. We were quite friends, and used to talk about all manner of things. I was very fond of him, and never afraid of anything that he said to me. He was Nina's cousin and seemed almost to be my cousin too.'

'Then you do like him?'

'Of course I do. Everybody must like him. But that is no reason why I should want to marry him.'

Upon this Mrs. Dosett sat silent for a while turning the great matter over in her thoughts. It was quite clear to her that every word which Ayala had spoken was true; and probable also that Lady Albury's words were true. In her inmost thoughts she regarded Ayala as a fool. Here was a girl who had not a shilling of her own, who was simply a burden on relatives whom she did not especially love, who was doomed to a life which was essentially distasteful to her;—for all this in respect to herself and her house Mrs. Dosett had sense enough to acknowledge,—who seemed devoted to the society of rich and gay people, and yet would not take the opportunities that were offered her of escaping what she disliked and going to that which she loved! Two offers had now been made to her, both of them thoroughly eligible, to neither of which would objection have been made by any of the persons concerned. Sir Thomas had shown himself to be absolutely anxious for the success of his son. And now it seemed that the grand relations of this Colonel Stubbs were in favour of the match. What it was in Ayala that entitled her to such promotion Mrs. Dosett did not quite perceive. To her eyes her niece was a fantastic girl, pretty indeed, but not endowed with that regular tranquil beauty which she thought to be of all feminine graces the most attractive. Why Tom Tringle should have been so deeply smitten with Ayala had been a marvel to her; and now this story of Colonel Stubbs was a greater marvel. 'Ayala,' she said, 'you ought to think better of it.'

'Think better of what, Aunt Margaret?'

'You have seen what this Lady Albury says about her cousin, Colonel Stubbs.'

'What has that to do with it?'

'You believe what she says? If so why should you not accept him?'

'Because I can't,' said Ayala.

'Have you any idea what is to become of your future life?' said Mrs. Dosett, very gravely.

'Not in the least,' said Ayala. But that was a fib, because she had an idea that in the fullness of time it would be her heavenly fate to put her hand into that of the Angel of Light.

'Gentlemen won't come running after you always, my dear.'

This was almost as bad as being told by her Aunt Emmeline that she had encouraged her cousin Tom. 'It's a great shame to say that. I don't want anybody to run after me. I never did.'

'No, my dear; no. I don't think that you ever did.' Mrs. Dosett, who was justice itself, did acknowledge to herself that of any such fault as that suggested, Ayala was innocent. Her fault was quite in the other direction, and consisted of an unwillingness to settle herself and to free her relations of the burden of maintaining her when proper opportunities arose for doing so. 'I only want to explain to you that people must,—must,—must make their hay while the sun shines. You are young now.'

'I am not one-and-twenty yet,' said Ayala, proudly.

'One-and-twenty is a very good time for a girl to marry,—that is to say if a proper sort of gentleman asks her.'

'I don't think I ought to be scolded because they don't seem to me to be the proper sort. I don't want anybody to come. Nobody ought to be talked to about it at all. If I cared about any one that you or Uncle Reginald did not approve, then you might talk to me. But I don't think that anything ought to be said about anybody unless I like him myself.' So the conversation was over, and Mrs. Dosett felt that she had been entirely vanquished.

Lady Albury's letter was shown to Mr. Dosett, but he refused to say a word to his niece on the subject. In the argument which followed between him and his wife he took his niece's part, opposing altogether that idea that hay should be made while the sun shines. 'It simply means selling herself,' declared Mr. Dosett.

'That is nonsense, Reginald. Of course such a girl as Ayala has to do the best she can with her good looks. What else has she to depend upon?'

'My brother-in-law will do something for her.'

' I hope he will,—though I do not think that a very safe reed to depend upon as she has twice offended him. But of course a girl thinks of marrying. Ayala would be very much disgusted if she were told that she was to be an old maid, and live upon £100 a year supplied by Sir Thomas's bounty. It might have been that she would have to do it;—but now that chances are open she ought to take them. She should choose between her cousin Tom and this Colonel Stubbs; and you should tell her that, if she will not, you will no longer be responsible for her.'

To this Mr. Dosett turned altogether a deaf ear. He was quite sure that his responsibility must be continued till Ayala should marry, or till he should die, and he would not make a threat which he would certainly be unable to carry out. He would be very glad if Ayala could bring herself to marry either of the young men. It was a pity that she should feel herself compelled to refuse offers so excellent. But it was a matter for her own judgment, and one in which he would not interfere. For two days this almost led to a coldness between the man and his wife, during which the sufferings of poor Mrs. Dosett were heartrending.

Not many days after Ayala's return her sister Lucy came to see her. Certain reasons had caused Lady Tringle to stay at Glenbogie longer than usual, and the family was now passing through London on their way to Merle Park. Perhaps it was the fact that the Trafficks had been effectually extruded from Glenbogie, but would doubtless turn up at Merle Park, should Lady Tringle take up her residence there before the autumn was over. That they should spend their Christmas at Merle Park was an acknowledged thing;—to mamma Tringle an acknowledged benefit, because she liked to have her daughter with her; to papa Tringle an acknowledged evil, because he could not endure to be made to give more than he intended to give. That they should remain there afterwards through January, and till the meeting of Parliament, was to be expected. But it was hoped that they might be driven to find some home for themselves if they were left homeless by Sir Thomas for a while. The little plan was hardly successful, as Mr. Traffick had put his wife into lodgings at Hastings, ready to pounce down on Merle Park as soon as Lady Tringle should have occupied the house a few days. Lady Tringle was now going there with the rest of the family, Sir Thomas having been in town for the last six weeks.

Lucy took advantage of the day which they passed in London, and succeeded in getting across to the Crescent. At this time she had heard nothing of Colonel Stubbs, and was full indeed of her own troubles.

'You haven't seen him?' she said to her sister.

'Seen who?' asked Ayala, who had two 'hims' to her bow,—and thought at the moment rather of her own two 'hims' than of Lucy's one.

'Isadore. He said that he would call here.' Ayala explained that she had not seen him, having been absent from town during the last ten days,—during which Mr. Hamel had in fact called at the house. 'Ayala,' concluded Lucy, 'what am I to do?'

'Stick to him,' said Ayala, firmly.

'Of course I shall. But Aunt Emmeline thinks that I ought to give him up or——'

'Or what?'

'Or go away,' said Lucy, very gravely.

'Where would you go to?'

'Oh, where indeed? Of course he would have me, but it would be ruin to him to marry a wife without a penny when he earns only enough for his own wants. His father has quarrelled with him altogether. He says that nobody can prevent our being married if we please, and that he is quite ready to make a home for me instantly; but I know that last year he hardly earned more than two hundred pounds after paying all his expenses, and were I to take him at his word I should ruin him.'

'Would Uncle Tom turn you out?'

'He has been away almost ever since Mr. Hamel came to Glenbogie, and I do not know what he will say. Aunt Emmeline declares that I can only stay with them just as though I were her daughter, and that a daughter would be bound to obey her.'

'Does Gertrude obey her about Mr. Houston?'

'Gertrude has her own way with her mother altogether. And of course a daughter cannot really be turned out. If she tells me to go I suppose I must go.'

'I should ask Uncle Tom,' said Ayala. 'She could not make you go out into the street. When she had to get rid of me, she could send me here in exchange; but she can't say now that you don't suit, and have me back again.'

'Oh, Ayala, it is so miserable. I feel that I do not know what to do with myself.'

'Nor do I,' said Ayala, jumping up from the bed on which she was sitting. 'It does seem to be so crossgrained. Nobody will let you marry, and everybody will make me.'

'Do they still trouble you about Tom?'

'It is not Tom now, Lucy. Another man has come up.'

'As a lover?'

'Oh, yes; quite so. His name is,—such a name, Lucy,—his name is Colonel Jonathan Stubbs.'

'That is Isadore's friend,—the man who lives at Drumcaller.'

'Exactly. He told me that Mr. Hamel was at Drumcaller with him. And now he wants me to be his wife.'

'Do you not like him?'

'That is the worst part of it all, Lucy. If I did not like him I should not mind it half so much. It is just because I like him so very much that I am so very unhappy. His hair is just the colour of Aunt Emmeline's big shawl.'

'What does that signify?'

'And his mouth stretches almost from ear to ear.'

'I shouldn't care a bit for his mouth.'

'I don't think I do much, because he does look so good-natured when he laughs. Indeed he is always the most good-natured man that ever lived.'

'Has he got an income enough for marriage?' asked Lucy, whose sorrows were already springing from that most fertile source of sorrowing.

'Plenty they tell me,—though I do not in the least know what plenty means.'

'Then, Ayala, why should you not have him?'

'Because I can't,' said Ayala. 'How is a girl to love a man if she does not love him? Liking has nothing to do with it. You don't think liking ought to have anything to do with it?'

This question had not been answered when Aunt Margaret came into the room, declaring that the Tringle manservant, who had walked across the park with Miss Dormer, was waxing impatient. The sisters, therefore, were separated, and Lucy returned to Queen's Gate.

## CHAPTER XXVIII*

### MISS DOCIMER

' I TELL you fairly that I think you altogether wrong;—that it is cowardly, unmanly, and disgraceful. I don't mean, you see, to put what you call a fine point upon it.'

'No, you don't.'

'It is one of those matters on which a person must speak the truth or not speak at all. I should not have spoken unless you forced it upon me. You don't care for her in the least.'

'That's true. I do not know that I am especially quick at what you call caring for young ladies. If I care for anybody it is for you.'

'I suppose so; but that may as well be dropped for

the present. You mean to marry this girl simply because she has got a lot of money?'

'Exactly that;—as you before long will marry some gentleman only because he has got money.'

'You have no right to say so because I am engaged to no man. But if I were so it is quite different. Unless I marry I can be nobody. I can have no existence that I can call my own. I have no other way of pushing myself into the world's notice. You are a man.'

'You mean to say that I could become a merchant or a lawyer,—be a Lord Chancellor in time, or perhaps an Archbishop of Canterbury.'

'You can live and eat and drink and go where you wish without being dependent on any one. If I had your freedom and your means do you think that I would marry for money?'

In this dialogue the main part was taken by Mr. Frank Houston, whose ambition it was to marry Miss Gertrude Tringle, and the lady's part by his cousin and intimate friend, Miss Imogene Docimer. The scene was a walk through a pine-forest on the southern slopes of the Tyrolean Alps, and the occasion had been made a little more exhilarating than usual by the fact that Imogene had been strongly advised both by her brother, Mr. Mudbury Docimer, and by her sister-in law, Mrs. Mudbury Docimer, not to take any more distant rambles with her far-away cousin Frank Houston. In the teeth of that advice this walk was taken, and the conversation in the pine-wood had at the present moment arrived at the point above given.

'I do not know that any two persons were ever further asunder in an argument than you and I in this,' said Frank, not in the least disconcerted by the severe epithets which had been applied to him. 'I conceive that you are led away by a desire to deceive yourself, whereas hypocrisy should only be used with the object of deceiving others.'

'How do I deceive myself?'

' In making believe that men are generally different from what they are;—in trying to suppose that I ought to be, if I am not, a hero. You shall not find a man whose main object is not that of securing an income. The clergyman who preaches against gold licks the ground beneath the minister's feet in order that he may become a bishop. The barrister cares not with what case he may foul his hands so long as he may become rich. The man in trade is so aware of his own daily dishonesty that he makes two separate existences for himself, and endeavours to atone for his rascality in the City by his performance of all duties at the West End. I regard myself to be so infinitely cleaner in my conscience than other men that I could not bring myself to be a bishop, an attorney-general, or a great merchant. Of all the ways open to me this seems to me to be the least sordid. I give her the only two things which she desires,—myself and a position. She will give me the only thing I desire, which is some money. When you marry you'll make an equally fine bargain,—only your wares will be your beauty.'

'You will not give her yourself;—not your heart.'

'Yes, I shall. I shall make the most of her, and shall do so by becoming as fond of her as I can. Of course I like breeding. Of course I like beauty. Of course I like that aroma of feminine charm which can only be produced by a mixture of intellect, loveliness, taste, and early association. I don't pretend to say that my future would not be much sweeter before me with you as my wife,—if only either of us had a sufficiency of income. I acknowledge that. But then I acknowledge also that I prefer Miss Tringle, with £100,000, to you with nothing; and I do not think that I ought to be called unmanly, disgraceful, and a coward, because I have courage enough to speak the truth openly to a friend whom I trust. My theory of life shocks you, not because it is uncommon, but because it is not commonly declared.'

They were silent for a while as they went on through the path, and then Miss Docimer spoke to him in an altered voice. 'I must ask you not to speak to me again as one who by any possibility could have been your wife.'

'Very well. You will not wish me to abandon the privilege of thinking of past possibilities?'

'I would—if it were possible.'

'Quite impossible! One's thoughts, I imagine, are always supposed to be one's own.'

'You know what I mean. A gentleman will always spare a woman if he can do so; and there are cases, such as have been ours, in which it is a most imperative duty to do so. You should not have followed us when you had made up your mind about this young lady.'

'I took care to let you know, beforehand, that I intended it.'

'You should not have thrown the weight upon me. You should not even have written to me.'

'I wonder what you would have said then,—how loudly you would have abused me,—had I not written! Would you not have told me then that I had not the courage to be open with you?' He paused for an answer, but she made none. 'But I do recognize the necessity of my becoming subject to abuse in this state of affairs. I have been in no respect false, nor in any way wanting in affection. When I suggested to you that £600 a-year between us, with an increasing family, and lodgings in Marylebone, would be uncomfortable, you shuddered at the prospect. When I explained to you that you would have the worst of it because my club would be open to me, you were almost angry with me because I seemed to imply that there could be any other than one decision.'

'There could only be one decision,—unless you were man enough to earn your bread.'

'But I wasn't. But I ain't. You might as well let that accident pass, sans dire. Was there ever a moment in which you thought that I should earn my bread?'

'Never for a moment did I endow you with the power of doing anything so manly.'

'Then why throw it in my teeth now? That is not fair. However, I do own that I have to be abused. I don't see any way in which you and I are to part without it. But you need not descend to Billingsgate.'

'I have not descended to Billingsgate,* Mr. Houston.'

'Upper-world Billingsgate! Cowardice, as an accusation from a woman to a man, is upper-world Billingsgate. But it doesn't matter. Of course I know what it means. Do you think your brother wants me to go away at once?'

'At once,' she said.

'That would be disagreeable and absurd. You mean to sit to me for that head?'

'Certainly not.'

'I cannot in the least understand why not. What has a question of art to do with marriage or giving in marriage? And why should Mrs. Docimer be so angry with me, when she has known the truth all along?'

'There are questions which it is of no avail to answer. I have come out with you now because I thought it well that we should have a final opportunity of understanding each other. You understand me at any rate.'

'Perfectly,' he said. 'You have taken especial care on this occasion to make yourself intelligible.'

'So I intended. And as you do understand me, and know how far I am from approving your philosophy, you can hardly wish to remain with us longer.' Then they walked on together in absolute silence for above a mile. They had come out of the wood, and were descending, by a steep and narrow path, to the village in which stood the hotel at which the party was staying. Another ten minutes would take them down to the high road. The path

here ran by the side of a rivulet, the course of which
was so steep that the waters made their way down in
a succession of little cataracts.* From the other side
of the path was a fence, so close to it, that on this
particular spot there was room only for one to walk.
Here Frank Houston stepped in front of his companion, so as to stop her. 'Imogene,' he said, 'if it
is intended that I am to start by the diligence for
Innspruck this evening, you had better bid me farewell at once.'

'I have bidden you farewell,' she said.

'Then you have done it in so bitter a mood that
you had better try your hand at it again. Heaven
only knows in what manner you or I may meet again.'

'What does it matter?' she asked.

'I have always felt that the hearts of men are
softer than the hearts of women. A woman's hand is
soft, but she can steel her heart when she thinks it
necessary, as no man can do. Does it occur to you at
this moment that there has been some true affection
between you and me in former days?'

'I wish it did not.'

'It may be so that I wish it also; but there is the
fact. No wishing will enable me to get rid of it. No
wishing will save me from the memory of early
dreams and sweet longings and vain triumphs.
There is the remembrance of bright glory made very
sad to me by the meanness of the existing truth. I do
not say but that I would obliterate it if I could; but
it is not to be obliterated; the past will not be made
more pleasant to me by any pretence of present
indignation. I should have thought that it would
have been the same with you.'

'There has been no glory,' she said, 'though I quite
acknowledge the meanness.'

'There has been at any rate some love.'

'Misplaced. You had better let me pass on. I
have, as you say, steeled myself. I will not condescend to any tenderness. In my brother's presence
and my sister's I will wish you good-bye and express

a hope that you may be successful in your enter-
prises. Here, by the brook-side, out upon the
mountain-path, where there is no one to hear us
but our two selves, I will bid you no farewell softer
than that already spoken. Go and do as you propose. You have my leave. When it shall have been
done there shall never be a word spoken by me
against it. But, when you ask me whether you are
right, I will only say that I think you to be wrong.
It may be that you owe nothing to me; but you owe
something to her, and something also to yourself.
Now, Mr. Houston, I shall be glad to pass on.'

He shrugged his shoulders and then stepped out of
the path, thinking as he did so how ignorant he had
been, after all that had passed, of much of the
character of Imogene Docimer. It could not be, he
had thought, but that she would melt into softness
at last. 'I will not condescend to any tenderness,'
she had said, and it seemed that she would be as good
as her word. He then walked down before her in
silence, and in silence they reached the inn.

'Mr. Houston,' said Mrs. Docimer, before they sat
down to dinner together, 'I thought it was understood that you and Imogene should not go out alone
together again.'

'I have taken my place to Innspruck by the diligence this evening,' he answered.

'Perhaps it will be better so, though both Mudbury
and I will be sorry to lose your company.'

'Yes, Mrs. Docimer, I have taken my place. Your
sister seemed to think that there would be great
danger if I waited till to-morrow morning when I
could have got a pleasant lift in a return carriage.
I hate travelling at night and I hate diligences. I
was quite prepared to post all the way, though it
would have ruined me,—only for this accursed
diligence.'

'I am sorry you should be inconvenienced.'

'It does not signify. What a man without a wife
may suffer in that way never does signify. It's just

fourteen hours. You wouldn't like Docimer to ome
with me.'

'That's nonsense. You needn't go the whole way
unless you like. You could sleep at Brunecken.'

'Brunecken is only twelve miles, and it might be
dangerous.'

'Of course you choose to turn everything into
ridicule.'

'Better that than tears, Mrs. Docimer. What's the
good of crying? I can't make myself an elder son.
I can't endow Imogene with a hundred thousand
pounds. She told me just now that I might earn my
bread, but she knows that I can't. It's very sad.
But what can be got by being melancholy?'

'At any rate you had better be away from her.'

'I am going,—this evening. Shall I walk on, half
a stage, at once, without any dinner? I wish you had
heard the kind of things she said to me. You would
not have thought that I had gone to walk with her
for my own pleasure.'

'Have you not deserved them?'

'I think not;—but nevertheless I bore them. A
woman, of course, can say what she pleases. There's
Docimer,—I hope he won't call me a coward.'

Mr. Docimer came out on the terrace, on which the
two were standing, looking as sour as death. 'He is
going by the diligence to Innspruck this afternoon,'
said Mrs. Docimer.

'Why did he come? A man with a grain of feeling
would have remained away.'

'Now, Docimer,' said Frank, 'pray do not make
yourself unpleasant. Your sister has been abusing
me all the morning like a pickpocket, and your wife
looks at me as though she would say just as much if
she dared. After all, what is it I have done that you
think so wicked?'

'What will everybody think at home,' said Mrs.
Docimer, 'when they know that you're with us
again? What chance is she to have if you follow her
about in this way?'

'I shall not follow her very long,' said Frank. 'My wings will soon be cut, and then I shall never fly again.' They were at this time walking up and down the terrace together, and it seemed for a while that neither of them had another word to say in the matter of the dispute between them. Then Houston went on again in his own defence. 'Of course it is all bad,' he said. 'Of course we have all been fools. You knew it, and allowed it; and have no right to say a word to me.'

'We thought that when your uncle died there would have been money,' said Docimer, with a subdued growl.

'Exactly; and so did I. You do not mean to say that I deceived either you or her?'

'There should have been an end of it when that hope was over.'

'Of course there should. There should never have been a dream that she or I could marry on six hundred a year. Had not all of us been fools, we should have taken our hats off and bade each other farewell for ever when the state of the old man's affairs was known. We were fools; but we were fools together; and none of us have a right to abuse the others. When I became acquainted with this young lady at Rome, it had been settled among us that Imogene and I must seek our fortunes apart.'

'Then why did you come after her?' again asked Mr. Docimer.

At this moment Imogene herself joined them on the terrace. 'Mary,' she said to her sister-in-law, 'I hope you are not carrying on this battle with Mr. Houston. I have said what there was to be said.'

'You should have held your tongue and said nothing,' growled her brother.

'Be that as it may I have said it, and he quite understands what I think about it. Let us eat our dinner in peace and quietness, and then let him go on his travels. He has the world free before him, which he no doubt will open like an oyster, though

he does not carry a sword."* Soon after this they did
dine, and contented themselves with abusing the
meat and the wine, and finding fault with Tyrolese
cookery, just as though they had no deeper cares
near their hearts. Precisely at six the heavy diligence stopped before the hotel door, and Houston,
who was then smoking with Docimer on the terrace,
got up to bid them adieu. Mrs. Docimer was kind
and almost affectionate, with a tear in her eye.
'Well, old fellow,' said Docimer, 'take care of yourself. Perhaps everything will turn up right some of
these days.' 'Good-bye, Mr. Houston,' said Imogene,
just giving him her hand to touch in the lightest
manner possible. 'God bless you, Imogene,' said he.
And there was a tear also in his eye. But there was
none in hers, as she stood looking at him while he
prepared himself for his departure; nor did she say
another word to him as he went. 'And now,' said she,
when the three of them were left upon the terrace, 'I
will ask a great favour of you both. I will beg you
not to let there be another word about Mr. Houston
among us.' After that she rambled out by herself,
and was not seen again by either of them that
evening.

When she was alone she too shed her tears, though
she felt impatient and vexed with herself as they
came into her eyes. It was not perhaps only for her
lost love that she wept. Had no one known that her
love had been given and then lost she might have
borne it without weeping. But now, in carrying on
this vain affair of hers, in devoting herself to a lover
who had, with her own consent, passed away from
her, she had spent the sweet fresh years of her youth,
and all those who knew her would know that it had
been so. He had told her that it would be her fate to
purchase for herself a husband with her beauty. It
might be so. At any rate she did not doubt her own
beauty. But, if it were to be so, then the romance
and the charm of her life were gone. She had quite
agreed that six hundred a year, and lodgings in

Marylebone, would be quite unendurable; but what
was there left for her that would be endurable? He
could be happy with the prospect of Gertrude
Tringle's money. She could not be happy, looking
forward to that unloved husband who was to be
purchased by her beauty.

## CHAPTER XXIX

### AT MERLE PARK. NO. 1

SIR THOMAS took the real holiday of the year at
Glenbogie,—where he was too far removed from
Lombard Street to be drawn daily into the vortex of
his millions. He would stay usually six weeks at
Glenbogie,—which were by no means the happiest
weeks of the year. Of all the grand things of the
world which his energy and industry had produced
for him, he loved his millions the best. It was not
because they were his,—as indeed they were not. A
considerable filing off them,—what he regarded as
his percentage,—annually became his own; but it
was not this that he loved. In describing a man's
character it is the author's duty to give the man his
due. Sir Thomas liked his own wealth well enough.
Where is the rich man who does not?—or where is
the poor man who does not wish that he had it to
like? But what he loved were the millions with
which Travers and Treason dealt. He was Travers
and Treason, though his name did not even appear
in the firm, and he dealt with the millions. He could
affect the rate of money throughout Europe, and
emissaries from national treasuries would listen to
his words. He had been Governor and Deputy-
Governor of the Bank of England. All the City
respected him, not so much because he was rich, as
that he was one who thoroughly understood millions.
If Russia required to borrow some infinite number of
roubles, he knew how to arrange it, and could tell to
a rouble at what rate money could be made by it,

and at what rate money would certainly be lost.* He liked his millions, and was therefore never quite comfortable at Glenbogie. But at Merle Park he was within easy reach of London. At Merle Park he was not obliged to live, from week's end to week's end, without a sight of Lombard Street. The family might be at Merle Park, while he might come down on a Friday and remain till Tuesday morning. That was the plan proposed for Merle Park. As a fact he would spend four days in town, and only two down in the country. Therefore, though he spent his so-named holiday at Glenbogie, Merle Park was the residence which he loved.

In this autumn he went up to London long before his family, and then found them at Merle Park on the Saturday after their arrival there. They had gone down on the previous Wednesday. On the Saturday, when he entered the house, the first thing he saw was Mr. Traffick's hat in the hall. This was Saturday, 23rd November, and there would be three months before Parliament would meet! A curse was not muttered, but just formed between his teeth, as he saw the hat. Sir Thomas, in his angriest mood, never went so far as quite to mutter his curses. Will one have to expiate the anathemas which are well kept within the barrier of the teeth, or only those which have achieved some amount of utterance? Sir Thomas went on, with a servant at his heels, chucking about the doors rather violently, till he found Mr. Traffick alone in the drawing-room. Mr. Traffick had had a glass of sherry and bitters brought in for his refreshment and Sir Thomas saw the glass on the mantelpiece. He never took sherry and bitters himself. One glass of wine, with his two o'clock mutton chop, sufficed him till dinner. It was all very well to be a Member of Parliament, but, after all, Members of Parliament never do anything. Men who work don't take sherry and bitters! Men who work don't put their hats in other people's halls without leave from the master of the house! 'Where's your mis-

tress?' said Sir Thomas, to the man, without taking
any notice of his son-in-law. The ladies had only just
come in from driving, were very cold, and had gone
up to dress. Sir Thomas went out of the room,
again banging the door, and again taking no notice
of Mr. Traffick. Mr. Traffick put his hand up to the
mantelpiece, and finished his sherry and bitters.

'My dear,' said Mr. Traffick to his wife, up in her
bed-room, 'your father has come down in one of his
tantrums.'

'I knew he would,' said Augusta.

'But it does not signify the least. Give him a kiss
when you see him, and don't seem to notice it.
There is not a man in the world has a higher regard
for me than your father, but if any one were to see
him in one of his tantrums they would suppose he
meant to be uncivil.'

'I hope he won't be downright unkind, Septimus,'
said his wife.

'Never fear! The kindest-hearted man in the
world is your father.'

'So he's here!' That was the first word of greeting
which Sir Thomas addressed to his wife in her bed-
room.

'Yes, Tom;—they're here.'

'When did they come?'

'Well;—to tell the truth, we found them here.'

'The ——!' But Sir Thomas restrained the word
on the right, or inside, of the teeth.

'They thought we were to be here a day sooner,
and so they came on the Wednesday morning. They
were to come, you know.'

'I wish I knew when they were to go.'

'You don't want to turn your own daughter out
of your own house?'

'Why doesn't he get a house of his own for her?
For her sake why doesn't he do it? He has the
spending of £6,000 a year of my money, and yet I am
to keep him! No;—I don't want to turn my daughter
out of my house; but it'll end in my turning him out.'

When a week had passed by Mr. Traffick had not
been as yet turned out. Sir Thomas, when he came
back to Merle Park on the following Friday, condescended to speak to his son-in-law, and to say
something to him as to the news of the day; but this
he did in an evident spirit of preconceived hostility.
'Everything is down again,' he said.

'Fluctuations are always common at this time of
the year,' said Traffick; 'but I observe that trade
always becomes brisk a little before Christmas.'

'To a man with a fixed income like you, it doesn't
much matter,' said Sir Thomas.

'I was looking at it in a public light.'

'Exactly. A man who has an income, and never
spends it, need not trouble himself with private views
as to the money market.' Mr. Traffick rubbed his hands,
and asked whether the new buildings at the back of
the Lombard Street premises were nearly finished.

Mr. Traffick's economy had a deleterious effect upon
Gertrude, which she, poor girl, did not deserve. Sir
Thomas, deeply resolving in his mind that he would,
at some not very distant date, find means by which
he would rid himself of Mr. Traffick, declared to
himself that he would not, at any rate, burden himself with another son-in-law of the same kind. Frank
Houston was, to his thinking, of the same kind,
and therefore he hardened his heart against Frank
Houston. Now Frank Houston, could he have got
his wife with £6,000 a year,—as Mr. Traffick had
done,—would certainly not have troubled the
Tringle mansions with too much of his presence. It
would have been his object to remove himself as far
as possible from the Tringles, and to have enjoyed
his life luxuriously with the proceeds of his wife's
fortune. But his hopes in this respect were unjustly
impeded by Mr. Traffick's parsimony. Soon after
leaving the hotel in the Tyrol at which we lately saw
him, Frank Houston wrote to his lady-love, declaring
the impatience of his ardour, and suggesting that it
would be convenient if everything could be settled

before Christmas. In his letter he declared to Gertrude how very uncomfortable it was to him to have to discuss money matters with her father. It was so disagreeable that he did not think that he could bring himself to do it again. But, if she would only be urgent with her father, she would of course prevail. Acting upon this Gertrude determined to be urgent with her father on his second coming to Merle Park, when, as has been explained, Sir Thomas was in a frame of mind very much opposed to impecunious sons-in-law. Previous to attacking her father Gertrude had tried her hand again upon her mother, but Lady Tringle had declined. 'If anything is to be done you must do it yourself,' Lady Tringle had said.

'Papa,' said Gertrude, having followed him into a little sitting-room where he digested and arranged his telegrams when at Merle Park, 'I wish something could be settled about Mr. Houston.'

Sir Thomas at this moment was very angry. Mr. Traffick had not only asked for the loan of a carriage to take him into Hastings, but had expressed a wish that there might be a peculiar kind of claret served at dinner with which he was conversant and to which he was much attached. 'Then,' said he, 'you may as well have it all settled at once.'

'How, papa?'

'You may understand for good and all that I will have nothing to do with Mr. Houston.'

'Papa, that would be very cruel.'

'My dear, if you call me cruel I will not allow you to come and talk to me at all. Cruel indeed! What is your idea of cruelty?'

'Everybody knows that we are attached to each other.'

'Everybody knows nothing of the kind. I know nothing of the kind. And you are only making a fool of yourself. Mr. Houston is a penniless adventurer and is only attached to my money. He shall never see a penny of it.'

'He is not an adventurer, papa. He is much less like an adventurer than Mr. Traffick. He has an income of his own, only it is not much.'

'About as much as would pay his bill at the club for cigars and champagne. You may make your mind at rest, for I will not give Mr. Houston a shilling. Why should a man expect to live out of my earnings who never did a day's work in his life?'

Gertrude left the room despondently, as there was nothing more to be done on the occasion. But it seemed to her as though she were being used with the utmost cruelty. Augusta had been allowed to marry her man without a shilling, and had been enriched with £120,000. Why should she be treated worse than Augusta? She was very strongly of opinion that Frank Houston was very much better than Septimus Traffick. Mr. Traffick's aptitude for saving his money was already known to the whole household. Frank would never wish to save. Frank would spend her income for her like a gentleman. Frank would not hang about Glenbogie or Merle Park till he should be turned out. Everybody was fond of Frank. But she, Gertrude, had already learnt to despise Mr. Traffick, Member of Parliament though he was. She had already begun to think that having been chosen by Frank Houston, who was decidedly a man of fashion, she had proved herself to be of higher calibre than her sister Augusta. But her father's refusal to her had been not only very rough but very decided. She would not abandon her Frank. Such an idea never for a moment crossed her mind. But what step should she next take? Thinking over it during the whole of the day she did at last form a plan. But she greatly feared that the plan would not recommend itself to Mr. Frank Houston. She was not timid, but he might be so. In spite of her father's anger and roughness she would not doubt his ultimate generosity; but Frank might doubt it. If Frank could be induced to come and carry her off from Merle Park and marry her in some manner approved for such occasions, she would stand the risk of getting the money afterwards. But she was greatly afraid that the risk would be too much for Frank. She did not, however, see any other scheme before her. As to waiting patiently till her father's obdurate heart should be softened by the greater obduracy of her own love, there was a tedium and a prolonged dulness in such a prospect which were anything but attractive to her. Had it been possible she would have made a bargain with her father. ' If you won't give us £120,000 let us begin with £60,000.' But even this she feared would not altogether be agreeable to Frank. Let her think of it how she would, that plan of being run away with seemed alone to be feasible—and not altogether disagreeable.

It was necessary that she should answer her lover's letter. No embargo had as yet been put upon her correspondence, and therefore she could send her reply without external difficulty:

'Dear Frank,' she said, 'I quite agree with you about Christmas. It ought to be settled. But I have very bad news to send to you. I have been to papa as you told me, but he was very unkind. Nothing could be worse. He said that you ought to earn your bread, which is, of course, all humbug. He didn't understand that there ought to be some gentlemen who never earn their bread. I am sure, if you had been earning your bread by going to Lombard Street every day, I shouldn't have ever cared for you.

'He says that he will not give a single shilling. I think he is angry because Augusta's husband will come and live here always. That is disgusting, of course. But it isn't my fault. It is either that, or else some money has gone wrong;—or perhaps he had a very bad fit of indigestion. He was, however, so savage, that I really do not know how to go to him again. Mamma is quite afraid of him, and does not dare say a word, because it was she who managed about Mr. Traffick.

'What ought to be done? Of course, I don't like to

think that you should be kept waiting. I am not sure that I quite like it myself. I will do anything you propose, and am not afraid of running a little risk. If we could get married without his knowing anything about it, I am sure he would give the money afterwards,—because he is always so good-natured in the long run, and so generous. He can be very savage, but he would be sure to forgive.

'How would it be if I were to go away? I am of age, and I believe that no one could stop me. If you could manage that we should get married in that way, I would do my best. I know people can get themselves married at Ostend. I do not see what else is to be done. You can write to me at present here, and nothing wrong will come of it. But Augusta says that if papa were to begin to suspect anything about my going away he would stop my letters.—Dear Frank, I am yours always, and always most lovingly,

'GERTRUDE.

'You needn't be a bit afraid but that I should be quite up to going off if you could arrange it.'

'I believe, papa,' said Mrs. Traffick, on the afternoon of the day on which this was written, 'that Gertrude is thinking of doing something wrong, and therefore I feel it to be my duty to bring you this letter.' Augusta had not been enabled to read the letter, but had discussed with her sister the propriety of eloping. 'I won't advise it,' she had said, 'but, if you do, Mr. Houston should arrange to be married at Ostend. I know that can be done.' Some second thought had perhaps told her that any such arrangement would be injurious to the noble blood of the Traffick family, and she had therefore 'felt it to be her duty' to extract the letter from the family letter-box, and to give it to her father. A daughter who could so excellently do her duty would surely not be turned out before Parliament met.

Sir Thomas took the letter and said not a word to

his elder child. When he was alone he doubted. He was half-minded to send the letter on. What harm could the two fools do by writing to each other? While he held the strings of the purse there could be no marriage. Then he bethought himself of his paternal authority, of the right he had to know all that his daughter did,—and he opened the letter. 'There ought to be gentlemen who don't earn their bread!' 'Ought there?' said he to himself. If so, these gentlemen ought not to come to him for bread. He was already supporting one such, and that was quite enough. 'Mamma is quite afraid of him, and doesn't dare say a word.' That he rather liked. 'I am sure he would give the money afterwards.' 'I am sure he would do no such thing,' he said to himself, and he reflected that in such a condition he should rather be delighted than otherwise in watching the impecunious importunities of his baffled son-in-law. The next sentence reconciled his girl to him almost entirely. 'He is always so good-natured in the long run, and so generous!' For 'good-natured' he did not care much, but he liked to be thought generous. Then he calmly tore the letter in little bits, and threw them into the waste-paper basket.*

He sat for ten minutes thinking what he had better do, finding the task thus imposed upon him to be much more difficult than the distribution of a loan. At last he determined that, if he did nothing, things would probably settle themselves. Mr. Houston, when he received no reply from his lady-love, would certainly be quiescent, and Gertrude, without any assent from her lover, could hardly arrange her journey to Ostend. Perhaps it might be well that he should say a word of caution to his wife; but as to that he did not at present quite make up his mind, as he was grievously disturbed while he was considering the subject.

'If you please, Sir Thomas,' said the coachman, hurrying into the room almost without the ceremony of knocking,—'if you please, Phoebe mare has been

brought home with both her knees cut down to the
bone.'

'What!' exclaimed Sir Thomas, who indulged himself in a taste for horseflesh, and pretended to know
one animal from another.

'Yes, indeed, Sir Thomas, down to the bone,' said
the coachman, who entertained all that animosity
against Mr. Traffick which domestics feel for habitual
guests who omit the ceremony of tipping. 'Mr.
Traffick brought her down on Windover Hill, Sir
Thomas, and she'll never be worth a feed of oats
again. I didn't think a man was born who could throw
that mare off her feet, Sir Thomas.' Now Mr. Traffick,
when he had borrowed the phaeton and pair of
horses that morning to go into Hastings, had dis-
pensed with the services of a coachman, and had insisted on driving himself.

## CHAPTER XXX

### AT MERLE PARK. NO. 2

HAS any irascible reader,—any reader who thoroughly enjoys the pleasure of being in a rage,—
encountered suddenly some grievance which, heavy
as it may be, has been more than compensated by
the privilege it has afforded of blowing-up the
offender? Such was the feeling of Sir Thomas as he
quickly followed his coachman out of the room. He
had been very proud of his Phoebe mare, who could
trot with him from the station to the house at the
rate of twelve miles an hour. But in his present
frame of mind he had liked the mare less than he
disliked his son-in-law. Mr. Traffick had done him
this injury, and he now had Mr. Traffick on the hip.
There are some injuries for which a host cannot
abuse his guest. If your best Venetian decanter be
broken at table you are bound to look as though you
liked it. But if a horse be damaged a similar amount

of courtesy is hardly required. The well-nurtured gentleman, even in that case, will only look unhappy and not say a word. Sir Thomas was hardly to be called a well-nurtured gentleman; and then it must be remembered that the offender was his son-in-law. 'Good heavens!' he exclaimed, hurrying into the yard. 'What is this?'

The mare was standing out on the pavement with three men around her, of whom one was holding her head, another was down on his knees washing her wounds, and the third was describing the fatal nature of the wounds which she had received. Traffick was standing at a little distance, listening in silence to the implied rebukes of the groom. 'Good heavens, what is this?' repeated Sir Thomas, as he joined the conclave.

'There are a lot of loose stones on that hill,' said Traffick, 'and she tripped on one and came down, all in a lump, before you could look at her. I'm awfully sorry, but it might have happened to any one.'

Sir Thomas knew how to fix his darts better than by throwing them direct at his enemy. 'She has utterly destroyed herself,' said he, addressing himself to the head-groom, who was busily employed with the sponge in his hand.

'I'm afraid she has, Sir Thomas. The joint-oil will be sure to run on both knees; the gashes is so mortal deep.'

'I've driven that mare hundreds of times down that hill,' said Sir Thomas, 'and I never knew her to trip before.'

'Never, Sir Thomas,' said the groom.

'She'd have come down with you to-day,' said Mr. Traffick, defending himself.

'It was my own fault, Bunsum. That's all that can be said about it.' Bunsum the groom, kneeling as he was, expressed, by his grimaces, his complete agreement with this last opinion of his master. 'Of course I ought to have known that he couldn't drive,' said Sir Thomas.

'A horse may fall down with anybody,' said Mr. Traffick.

'You'd better take her and shoot her,' said Sir Thomas, still addressing the groom. 'She was the best thing we had in the stable, but now she is done for.' With that he turned away from the yard without having as yet addressed a word to his son-in-law.

This was so intolerable that even Mr. Traffick could not bear it in silence. 'I have told you that I am very sorry,' said he, following Sir Thomas closely, 'and I don't know what a man can do more.'

'Nothing,—unless it be not to borrow a horse again.'

'You may be sure I will never do that.'

'I'm not sure of it at all. If you wanted another to-morrow you'd ask for him if you thought you could get him.'

'I call that very uncivil, Sir Thomas,—and very unkind.'

'Bother!' said Sir Thomas. 'It is no good in being kind to a fellow like you. Did you ever hear what the cabman did who had a sovereign given to him for driving a mile? He asked the fool who gave it him to make it a guinea. I am the fool, and, by George, you are the cabman!' With this Sir Thomas turned into the house by a small door, leaving his son-in-law to wander round to the front by himself.

'Your father has insulted me horribly,' he said to his wife, whom he found up in her bed-room.

'What is the matter now, Septimus?'

'That little mare of his, which I have no doubt has come down half a score of times before, fell with me and cut her knees.'

'That's Phoebe,' said Augusta. 'She was his favourite.'

'It's a kind of thing that might happen to anyone, and no gentleman thinks of mentioning it. He said such things to me that upon my word I don't think I can stop in the house any longer.'

'Oh, yes, you will,' said the wife.

'Of course, it is a difference coming from one's father-in-law. It's almost the same as from one's father.'

'He didn't mean it, Septimus.'

'I suppose not. If he had, I really couldn't have borne it. He does become very rough sometimes, but I know that at bottom he has a thorough respect for me. It is only that induces me to bear it.' Then it was settled between husband and wife that they should remain in their present quarters, and that not a word further should be said, at any rate by them, about the Phoebe mare. Nor did Sir Thomas say another word about the mare, but he added a note to those already written in the tablets of his memory*as to his son-in-law, and the note declared that no hint, let it be ever so broad, would be effectual with Mr. Traffick.

The next day was a Sunday, and then another trouble awaited Sir Thomas. At this time it was not customary with Tom to come often to Merle Park. He had his own lodgings in London and his own club, and did not care much for the rural charms of Merle Park. But on this occasion he had condescended to appear, and on the Sunday afternoon informed his father that there was a matter which he desired to discuss with him. 'Father,' said he, 'I am getting confoundedly sick of all this.'

'Confounded,' said Sir Thomas, 'is a stupid foolish word, and it means nothing.'*

'There is a sort of comfort in it, Sir,' said Tom; 'but if it's objectionable I'll drop it.'

'It is objectionable.'

'I'll drop it, Sir. But nevertheless I am very sick of it.'

'What are you sick of, Tom?'

'All this affair with my cousin.'

'Then, if you take my advice, you'll drop that too.'

'I couldn't do that, father. A word is all very well. A man can drop a word; but a girl is a different sort of thing. One can't drop a girl, even if one tries.'

'Have you tried, Tom?'

'Yes, I have. I've done my best to try. I put it out of my mind for a fortnight and wouldn't think of her. I had a bottle of champagne every day at dinner and then went to the theatre. But it was all of no use. I have set my heart on it and I can't give her up. I'll tell you what I'd like to do. I'd like to give her a diamond necklace.'

'It wouldn't be the slightest use,' said Sir Thomas, shaking his head.

'Why not? It's what other men do. I mean it to be something handsome;—about three hundred pounds.'

'That's a large sum of money for a necklace.'

'Some of them cost a deal more than that.'

'And you'd only throw away your money.'

'If she took it, she'd take me too. If she didn't,— why I should still have the diamonds. I mean to try any way.'

'Then it's of no use your coming to me.'

'I thought you'd let me have the money. It's no good running into debt for them. And then if you'd add something of your own,—a locket, or something of that kind,—I think it would have an effect. I have seen a necklace at Ricolay's, and if I could pay ready money for it I could have 20 per cent. off it. The price named is three hundred guineas. That would make it £254 5s. £250 would buy it if the cheque was offered.'

There was a spirit about the son which was not displeasing to the father. That idea that the gift, if accepted, would be efficacious, or if not that it would be rejected,—so that Tom would not lose his hopes and his diamonds together,—seemed to be sound. Sir Thomas, therefore, promised the money, with the distinct understanding that if the gift were not accepted by Ayala it should be consigned to his own hands. But as for any present from himself, he felt that this would not be the time for it. He had called upon his niece and solicited her himself, and she had been deaf to his words. After that he could not condescend to send her gifts. 'Should she become my promised daughter-in-law then I would send her presents,' said Sir Thomas.

The poor man certainly received less pleasure from his wealth than was credited to him by those who knew his circumstances. Yet he endeavoured to be good to those around him, and especially good to his children. There had been present to him ever since the beginning of his successes,—ever since his marriage,—a fixed resolution that he would not be a curmudgeon with his money, that he would endeavour to make those happy who depended on him, and that he would be liberal in such settlements for his children as might be conducive to their happiness and fortunes in life. In this way he had been very generous to Mr. Traffick. The man was a Member of Parliament, the son of a peer, and laborious. Why should he expect more? Money was wanting, but he could supply the money. So he had supplied it, and had been content to think that a good man should be propped up in the world by his means. What that had come to the reader knows. He thoroughly detested his son-in-law, and would have given much to have had his money back again,—so that Mr. Traffick should have had no share in it.

Then there was his second daughter! What should be done with Gertrude? The money should be forthcoming for her too if the fitting man could be found. But he would have nothing further to do with a penniless lover, let his position in the world of fashion, or even in the world of politics, be what it might. The man should either have wealth of his own, or should be satisfied to work for it. Houston had been unfortunate in the moment of his approaches. Sir Thomas had been driven by his angry feelings to use hard, sharp words, and now was forced to act up to his words. He declared roughly that Mr. Houston should not have a shilling of his money,—as he had certainly been justified for doing; and his daughter, who had always been indulged in every kind of luxury, had at once concocted a plot for running away from her home! As he thought of the plot it seemed to be wonderful to him that she should be willing to incur such a danger,—to be ready without a penny to marry a penniless man,—till he confessed to himself that, were she to do so, she would certainly have the money sooner or later. He was capable of passion, capable of flying out and saying a very severe thing to Septimus Traffick or another when his temper was hot; but he was incapable of sustained wrath. He was already aware that if Mr. Traffick chose to stay he would stay;—that if Mr. Houston were brave enough to be persistent he might have both the money and the girl. As he thought of it all he was angry with himself, wishing that he were less generous, less soft, less forgiving.

And now here was Tom,—whom at the present moment he liked the best of all his children, who of the three was the least inclined to run counter to him,—ready to break his heart, because he could not get a little chit of a girl of whom he would probably be tired in twelve months after he possessed her! Remembering what Tom had been, he was at a loss to understand how such a lad should be so thoroughly in love. At the present moment, had Ayala been purchaseable, he would have been willing to buy her at a great price, because he would fain have pleased Tom had it been possible. But Ayala, who had not a penny in the world,—who never would have a penny unless he should give it her,—would not be purchased, and would have nothing to do with Tom! The world was running counter to him, so that he had no pleasure in his home, no pleasure in his money, no pleasure in his children. The little back-parlour in Lombard Street was sweeter to him than Merle Park, with all its charms. His daughter Gertrude wanted to run away from him, while by no inducement could he get Mr. Traffick to leave the house.

While he was in this humour he met his niece Lucy

roaming about the garden. He knew the whole story of Lucy's love, and had been induced by his wife to acknowledge that her marriage with the sculptor was not to be sanctioned. He had merely expressed his scorn when the unfortunate circumstances of Hamel's birth had been explained to him again and again. He had ridiculed the horror felt by his wife at the equally ill-born brothers and sisters in Rome. He had merely shaken his head when he was told that Hamel's father never went inside any place of worship. But when it was explained to him that the young man had, so to say, no income at all, then he was forced to acknowledge that the young man ought not to be allowed to marry his niece.

To Lucy herself he had as yet said nothing on the subject since he had asked the lover in to lunch at Glenbogie. He heard bad accounts of her. He had been told by his wife, on different occasions,—not in the mere way of conversation, but with premeditated energy of fault-finding,—that Lucy was a disobedient girl. She was worse than Ayala. She persisted in saying that she would marry the penniless artist as soon as he should profess himself to be ready. It had been different, she had tried to explain to her aunt, before she had been engaged to him. Now she considered herself to be altogether at his disposal. This had been her plea, but her plea had been altogether unacceptable to Aunt Emmeline. 'She can do as she pleases, of course,' Sir Thomas had said. That might be all very well; but Aunt Emmeline was strongly of opinion that an adopted daughter of Queen's Gate, of Glenbogie, and Merle Park, ought not to be allowed to do as she pleased with herself. A girl ought not to be allowed to have the luxuries of palatial residences, and the luxuries of free liberty of choice at the same time. More than once it had occurred to Sir Thomas that he would put an end to all these miseries by a mere scratch of his pen. It need not be £120,000, or £100,000, as with a daughter. A few modest thousands would do it. And then this man Hamel, though the circumstances of his birth had been unfortunate, was not an idler like Frank Houston. As far as Sir Thomas could learn, the man did work, and was willing to work. The present small income earned would gradually become more. He had a kindly feeling towards Lucy, although he had been inclined to own that her marriage with Hamel was out of the question. 'My dear,' he said to her, 'why are you walking about alone?' She did not like to say that she was walking alone because she had no one to walk with her,—no such companion as Isadore would be if Isadore were allowed to come to Merle Park; so she simply smiled, and went on by her uncle's side. 'Do you like this place as well as Glenbogie?' he asked.

'Oh; yes.'

'Perhaps you will be glad to get back to London again?'

'Oh; no.'

'Which do you like best, then?'

'They are all so nice, if——'

'If what, Lucy?'

'Caelum non animum mutant qui trans mare currunt,'*Lucy might have said, had she known the passage. As it was she put the same feeling into simpler words, 'I should like one as well as the other, Uncle Tom, if things went comfortably.'

'There's a great deal in that,' he said. ' I suppose the meaning is, that you do not get on well with your aunt?'

'I am afraid she is angry with me, Uncle Tom.'

'Why do you make her angry, Lucy? When she tells you what is your duty, why do you not endeavour to do it?'

'I cannot do what she tells me,' said Lucy; 'and, as I cannot, I think I ought not to be here.'

'Have you anywhere else to go to?' To this she made no reply, but walked on in silence. 'When you say you ought not to be here, what idea have you formed in your own mind as to the future?'

'That I shall marry Mr. Hamel, some day.'

'Do you think it would be well to marry any man without an income to live upon? Would it be a comfort to him seeing that he had just enough to maintain himself, and no more?' These were terrible questions to her,—questions which she could not answer, but yet as to which her mind entertained an easy answer. A little help from him, who was willing to indulge her with so many luxuries while she was under his roof, would enable her to be an assistance rather than a burden to her lover. But of this she could not utter a word. 'Love is all very well,' continued Sir Thomas, in his gruffest voice; 'but love should be regulated by good sense. It is a crime when two beggars think of marrying each other,—two beggars who are not prepared to live as beggars do.'

'He is not a beggar,' said Lucy, indignantly. 'He has begged nothing; nor have I.'

'Pshaw!' said Sir Thomas; 'I was laying down a general rule. I did not mean to call anybody a beggar. You shouldn't take me up like that.'

'I beg your pardon, Uncle Tom,' she said piteously.

'Very well; very well; that will do.' But still he went on walking with her, and she felt she could not leave him till he gave her some signal that she was to go. They continued in this way till they had come nearly round the large garden; when he stopped, as he was walking, and addressed her again. 'I suppose you write to him sometimes.'

'Yes,' said Lucy, boldly.

'Write to him at once, and tell him to come and see me in Lombard Street on Tuesday, at two o'clock. Give me the letter, and I will take care it is sent to him directly I get to town. Now you had better go in, for it is getting very cold.'

## CHAPTER XXXI

### THE DIAMOND NECKLACE

TOM went up to London intent upon his diamonds. To tell the truth he had already made the purchase subject to some question of ready money. He now paid for it after considerable chaffering as to the odd pounds, which he succeeded in bringing to a successful termination. Then he carried the necklace away with him, revolving in his mind the different means of presentation. He thought that a letter might be best if only he was master of the language in which such a letter should properly be written. But he entirely doubted his own powers of composition. He was so modest in this respect that he would not even make an attempt. He knew himself well enough to be aware that he was in many respects ignorant. He would have endeavoured to take the necklace personally to Ayala had he not been conscious that he could not recommend his present with such romantic phrases and touches of poetry as would be gratifying to her fine sense. Were he to find himself in her presence with the necklace he must depend on himself for his words; but a letter might be sent in his own handwriting, the poetry and romance of which might be supplied by another.

Now it had happened that Tom had formed a marvellous friendship in Rome with Colonel Stubbs. They had been hunting together in the Campagna, and Tom had been enabled to accommodate the Colonel with the loan of a horse when his own had been injured. They had since met in London, and Stubbs had declared to more than one of his friends that Tom, in spite of his rings and his jewelry, was a very good fellow at bottom. Tom had been greatly flattered by the intimacy, and had lately been gratified by an invitation to Aldershot in order that the military glories of the camp might be shown to him. He had accepted the invitation, and a day in the present week had been fixed. Then it occurred to him suddenly that he knew no one so fitted to write such a letter as that demanded as his friend Colonel Jonathan Stubbs. He had an idea that the Colonel, in spite of his red hair and in spite of a certain aptitude for drollery which pervaded him, had a romantic side to his character; and he felt confident that, as to the use of language, the Colonel was very great indeed. He therefore, when he went to Aldershot, carefully put the bracelet in his breast-pocket and determined to reveal his secret and to ask for aid.

The day of his arrival was devoted to the ordinary pursuits of Aldershot and the evening to festivities, which were prolonged too late into the night to enable him to carry out his purpose before he went to bed. He arranged to leave on the next morning by a train between ten and eleven, and was told that three or four men would come in to breakfast at half-past nine. His project then seemed to be all but hopeless. But at last with great courage he made an effort. 'Colonel,' said he, just as they were going to bed, 'I wonder if you could give me half-an-hour before breakfast. It is a matter of great importance.' Tom, as he said this, assumed a most solemn face.

'An hour if you like, my dear boy. I am generally up soon after six, and am always out on horseback before breakfast as soon as the light serves.'

'Then if you'll have me called at half-past seven I shall be ever so much obliged to you.'

The next morning at eight the two were closeted together, and Tom immediately extracted the parcel from his pocket and opened the diamonds to view. 'Upon my word that is a pretty little trinket,' said the Colonel, taking the necklace in his hand.

'Three hundred guineas!' said Tom, opening his eyes very wide.

'I daresay.'

'That is, it would have been three hundred guineas unless I had come down with the ready. I made the fellow give me twenty per cent. off. You should always remember this when you are buying jewelry.'

A.A.—15

'And what is to be done with this pretty thing? I suppose it is intended for some fair lady's neck.'

'Oh, of course.'

'And why has it been brought down to Aldershot? There are plenty of fellows about this place who will get their hands into your pocket if they know that you have such a trinket as that about you.'

'I will tell you why I brought it,' said Tom, very gravely. 'It is, as you say, for a young lady. I intend to make that young lady my wife. Of course this is a secret, you know.'

'It shall be as sacred as the Pope's toe,' said Stubbs.

'Don't joke about it, Colonel, if you please. It's life and death to me.'

'I'll keep your secret and will not joke. Now what can I do for you?'

'I must send this as a present with a letter. I must first tell you that she has,—well, refused me.'

'That never means much the first time, old boy.'

'She has refused me half-a-dozen times, but I mean to go on with it. If she refuses me two dozen times I'll try her a third dozen.'

'Then you are quite in earnest?'

'I am. It's a kind of thing I know that men laugh about, but I don't mind telling you that I am downright in love with her. The governor approves of it.'

'She has got money, probably?'

'Not a shilling;—not as much as would buy a pair of gloves. But I don't love her a bit the less for that. As to income, the governor will stump up like a brick. Now I want you to write the letter.'

'It's a kind of thing a third person can't do,' said the Colonel, when he had considered the request for a moment.

'Why not? Yes, you can.'

'Do it yourself, and say just the simplest words as they come up. They are sure to go further with any girl than what another man may write. It is impossible that another man should be natural on such a task as that.'

'Natural! I don't know about natural,' said Tom, who was anxious now to explain the character of the lady in question. 'I don't know that a letter that was particularly natural would please her. A touch of poetry and romance would go further than anything natural.'

'Who is the lady?' asked the Colonel, who certainly was by this time entitled to be so far inquisitive.

'She is my cousin,—Ayala Dormer.'

'Who?'

'Ayala Dormer;—my cousin. She was at Rome, but I do not think you ever saw her there.'

'I have seen her since,' said the Colonel.

'Have you? I didn't know.'

'She was with my aunt, the Marchesa Baldoni.'

'Dear me! So she was. I never put the two things together. Don't you admire her?'

'Certainly I do. My dear fellow, I can't write this letter for you.' Then he put down the pen which he had taken up as though he had intended to comply with his friend's request. 'You may take it as settled that I cannot write it.'

'No?'

'Impossible. One man should never write such a letter for another man. You had better give the thing in person,—that is, if you mean to go on with the matter.'

'I shall certainly go on with it,' said Tom, stoutly.

'After a certain time, you know, reiterated offers do, you know,—do,—do,—partake of the nature of persecution.'

'Reiterated refusals are the sort of persecution I don't like.'

'It seems to me that Ayala,—Miss Dormer, I mean,—should be protected by a sort of feeling,—feeling of—of what I may perhaps call her dependent position. She is peculiarly,—peculiarly situated.'

'If she married me she would be much better situated. I could give her everything she wants.'

'It isn't an affair of money, Mr. Tringle.'

Tom felt, from the use of the word Mister, that he was in some way giving offence; but felt also that there was no true cause for offence. 'When a man offers everything,' he said, 'and asks for nothing, I don't think he should be said to persecute.'

'After a time it becomes persecution. I am sure Ayala would feel it so.'

'My cousin can't suppose that I am ill-using her,' said Tom, who disliked the 'Ayala' quite as much as he did the 'Mister.'

'Miss Dormer, I meant. I can have nothing further to say about it. I can't write the letter, and I should not imagine that Ayala,—Miss Dormer,—would be moved, in the least by any present that could possibly be made to her. I must go out now, if you don't mind, for half-an-hour; but I shall be back in time for breakfast.'

Then Tom was left alone with the necklace lying on the table before him. He knew that something was wrong with the Colonel, but could not in the least guess what it might be. He was quite aware that early in the interview the Colonel had encouraged him to persevere with the lady, and had then, suddenly, not only advised him to desist, but had told him in so many words that he was bound to desist out of consideration for the lady. And the Colonel had spoken of his cousin in a manner that was distasteful to him. He could not analyse his feelings. He did not exactly know why he was displeased, but he was displeased. The Colonel, when asked for his assistance, was, of course, bound to talk about the lady,—would be compelled, by the nature of the confidence, to mention the lady's name;—would even have been called on to write her Christian name. But this he should have done with a delicacy; —almost with a blush. Instead of that Ayala's name had been common on his tongue. Tom felt himself to be offended, but hardly knew why. And then, why had he been called Mister Tringle? The breakfast, which was eaten shortly afterwards in the company of three or four other men, was not eaten in comfort; —and then Tom hurried back to London and to Lombard Street.

After this failure Tom felt it to be impossible to go to another friend for assistance. There had been annoyance in describing his love to Colonel Stubbs, and pain in the treatment he had received. Even had there been another friend to whom he could have confided the task, he could not have brought himself to encounter the repetition of such treatment. He was as firmly fixed as ever in his conviction that he could not write the letter himself. And, as he thought of the words with which he should accompany a personal presentation of the necklace, he reflected that in all probability he might not be able to force his way into Ayala's presence. Then a happy thought struck him. Mrs. Dosett was altogether on his side. Everybody was on his side except Ayala herself, and that pigheaded Colonel. Would it not be an excellent thing to entrust the necklace to the hands of his Aunt Dosett, in order that she might give it over to Ayala with all the eloquence in her power? Satisfied with this project he at once wrote a note to Mrs. Dosett.

'My DEAR AUNT,

'I want to see you on *most important business*. If I shall not be troubling you, I will call upon you tomorrow at ten o'clock, before I go to my place of business.

'Yours affectionately,
'T. TRINGLE, Junior.'

On the following morning he apparelled himself with all his rings. He was a good-hearted, well-intentioned young man, with excellent qualities; but he must have been slow of intellect when he had not as yet learnt the deleterious effect of all those rings. On this occasion he put on his rings, his chains, and his bright waistcoat, and made himself a thing disgusting to be looked at by any well-trained female.

As far as his aunt was concerned he would have been
altogether indifferent as to his appearance, but there
was present to his mind some small hope that he
might be allowed to see Ayala, as the immediate
result of the necklace. Should he see Ayala, then
how unfortunate it would be that he should present
himself before the eyes of his mistress without those
adornments which he did not doubt would be grateful to her. He had heard from Ayala's own lips that
all things ought to be pretty. Therefore he endeavoured to make himself pretty. Of course he
failed,—as do all men who endeavour to make themselves pretty,—but it was out of the question that
he should understand the cause of his failure.

'Aunt Dosett, I want you to do me a very great
favour,' he began, with a solemn voice.

'Are you going to a party, Tom?' she said.

'A party! No,—who gives a party in London at
this time of the day? Oh, you mean because I have
just got a few things on. When I call anywhere I
always do. I have got another lady to see, a lady of
rank, and so I just made a change.' But this was a fib.

'What can I do for you, Tom?'

'I want you to look at that.' Then he brought out
the necklace, and, taking it out of the case, displayed
the gems tastefully upon the table.

'I do believe they are diamonds,' said Mrs. Dosett.

'Yes; they are diamonds. I am not the sort of
fellow to get anything sham. What do you think
that little thing cost, Aunt Dosett?'

'I haven't an idea. Sixty pounds, perhaps!'

'Sixty pounds! Do you go into a jeweller's shop
and see what you could do among diamonds with
sixty pounds!'

'I never go into jewellers' shops, Tom.'

'Nor I, very often. It's a sort of place where a
fellow can drop a lot of money. But I did go into one
after this. It don't look much, does it?'

'It is very pretty.'

'I think it is pretty. Well, Aunt Dosett, the

price for that little trifle was three—hundred— guineas!' As he said this he looked into his aunt's face for increased admiration.

'You gave three hundred guineas for it!'

'I went with ready money in my hand, when I tempted the man with a cheque to let me have it for two hundred and fifty pounds. In buying jewelry you should always do that.'

'I never buy jewelry,' said Mrs. Dosett, crossly.

'If you should, I mean. Now, I'll tell you what I want you to do. This is for Ayala.'

'For Ayala!'

'Yes, indeed. I am not the fellow to stick at a trifle when I want to carry my purpose. I bought this the other day and gave ready money for it,—two hundred and fifty pounds,—on purpose to give it to Ayala. In naming the value,—of course you'll do that when you give it her,—you might as well say three hundred guineas. That was the price on the ticket. I saw it myself,—so there won't be any untruth you know.'

'Am I to give it her?'

'That's just what I want. When I talk to her she flares up, and, as likely as not, she'd fling the necklace at my head.'

'She wouldn't do that, I hope.'

'It would depend upon how the thing went. When I do talk to her it always seems that nothing I say can be right. Now, if you will give it her you can put in all manner of pretty things.'

'This itself will be the prettiest thing,' said Mrs. Dosett.

'That's just what I was thinking. Everybody agrees that diamonds will go further with a girl than anything else. When I told the governor he quite jumped at the idea.'

'Sir Thomas knows you are giving it?'

'Oh, dear, yes. I had to get the rhino from him. I don't go about with two hundred and fifty pounds always in my own pocket.'

'If he had sent the money to Ayala how much better it would have been,' said poor Mrs. Dosett.

'I don't think that at all. Who ever heard of making a present to a young lady in money? Ayala is romantic, and that would have been the most unromantic thing out. That would not have done me the least good in the world. It would simply have gone to buy boots and petticoats and such like. A girl would never be brought to think of her lover merely by putting on a pair of boots. When she fastens such a necklace as this round her throat he ought to have a chance. Don't you think so, Aunt Dosett?'

'Tom, shall I tell you something?' said the aunt.

'What is it, Aunt Dosett?'

'I don't believe that you have a chance.'

'Do you mean that?' he asked, sorrowfully.

'I do.'

'You think that the necklace will do no good?'

'Not the least. Of course I will offer it to her if you wish it, because her uncle and I quite approve of you as a husband for Ayala. But I am bound to tell you the truth. I do not think the necklace will do you any good.' Then he sat silent for a time, meditating upon his condition. It might be imprudent;— it might be a wrong done to his father to jeopardise the necklace. How would it be if Ayala were to take the necklace and not to take him? 'Am I to give it?' she asked.

'Yes,' said he, bravely, but with a sigh; 'give it her all the same.'

'From you or from Sir Thomas?'

'Oh, from me;—from me. If she were told it came from the governor she'd keep it whether or no. I am sure I hope she will keep it,' he said, trying to remove the bad impression which his former words might perhaps have left.

'You may be sure she will not keep it,' said Mrs. Dosett, 'unless she should intend to accept your hand. Of that I can hold out no hope to you. There is a matter, Tom, which I think I should tell you as you are so straightforward in your offer. Another gentleman has asked her to marry him.'

'She has accepted him!' exclaimed Tom.

'No, she has not accepted him. She has refused him.'

'Then I'm just where I was,' said Tom.

'She has refused him, but I think that she is in a sort of way attached to him; and though he too has been refused I imagine that his chance is better than yours.'

'And who the d—— is he?' said Tom, jumping up from his seat in great excitement.

'Tom!' exclaimed Mrs. Dosett.

'I beg your pardon; but you see this is very important. Who is the fellow?'

'He is one Colonel Jonathan Stubbs.'

'Who?'

'Colonel Jonathan Stubbs.'

'Impossible! It can't be Colonel Stubbs. I know Colonel Stubbs.'

'I can assure you it is true, Tom. I have had a letter from a lady,—a relative of Colonel Stubbs,—telling me the whole story.'

'Colonel Stubbs!' he said. 'That passes anything I ever heard. She has refused him?'

'Yes, she has refused him.'

'And has not accepted him since?'

'She certainly has not accepted him yet.'

'You may give her the necklace all the same,' said Tom, hurrying out of the room. That Colonel Stubbs should have made an offer to Ayala, and yet have accepted his, Tom Tringle's confidence!

## CHAPTER XXXII

### TOM'S DESPAIR

THE reader will understand that the fate of the necklace was very soon decided. Ayala declared that it was very beautiful. She had, indeed, a pretty taste for diamonds, and would have been proud enough to call this necklace her own; but, as she

declared to her aunt, she would not accept Tom
though he were made of diamonds from head to foot.
Accept Tom, when she could not even bring herself
to think of becoming the wife of Jonathan Stubbs!
If Colonel Stubbs could not be received by her
imagination as an Angel of Light, how immeasurably
distant from anything angelic must be Tom Tringle!
'Of course it must go back,' she said, when the
question had to be decided as to the future fate of the
necklace. As a consequence poor Mr. Dosett was
compelled to make a special journey into the City,
and to deposit a well-sealed parcel in the hands of
Tom Tringle himself. 'Your cousin sends her kind
regards,' he said, 'but cannot bring herself to accept
your magnificent present.'

Tom had been very much put about since his visit
to the Crescent. Had his aunt merely told him that
his present would be inefficacious, he would have
taken that assurance as being simply her opinion,
and would have still entertained some hopes in the
diamonds. But these tidings as to another lover
crushed him altogether. And such a lover! The very
man whom he had asked to write his letter for him!
Why had not Colonel Stubbs told him the truth when
thus his own secret had become revealed by an
accident? He understood it all now,—the 'Ayala,'
and the 'Mister,' and the reason why the Colonel
could not write the letter. Then he became very
angry with the Colonel, whom he bitterly accused of
falsehood and treason. What right had the Colonel
to meddle with his cousin at all? And how false he
had been to say nothing of what he himself had done
when his rival had told him everything! In this way
he made up his mind that it was his duty to hate
Colonel Stubbs, and if possible to inflict some personal punishment upon him. He was reckless of himself now, and, if he could only get one good blow at
the Colonel's head with a thick stick, would be indifferent as to what the law might do with him afterwards. Or perhaps he might be able to provoke

Colonel Stubbs to fight with him. He had an idea that duels at present were not in fashion.* But nevertheless, in such a case as this, a man ought to fight. He could at any rate have the gratification of calling the Colonel a coward if he should refuse to fight.

He was the more wretched because his spirit within him was cowed by the idea of the Colonel. He did acknowledge to himself that his chance could be but bad while such a rival as Colonel Stubbs stood in his way. He tried to argue with himself that it was not so. As far as he knew, Colonel Stubbs was and would remain a very much less rich man than himself. He doubted very much whether Colonel Stubbs could keep a carriage in London for his wife, while it had been already arranged that he was to be allowed to do so should he succeed in marrying Ayala. To be a partner in the house of Travers and Treason was a much greater thing than to be a Colonel. But, though he assured himself of all this again and again, still he was cowed. There was something about the Colonel which did more than redeem his red hair and ugly mouth. And of this something poor Tom was sensible. Nevertheless, if occasion should arise he thought that he could 'punch the Colonel's head';— not without evil consequence to himself;—but still that he could 'punch the Colonel's head,' not minding the consequences.

Such had been his condition of mind when he left the Crescent, and it was not improved by the receipt of the parcel. He hardly said a word when his uncle put it into his hands, merely muttering something and consigning the diamonds to his desk. He did not tell himself that Ayala must now be abandoned. It would have been better for him if he could have done so. But all real, springing, hopeful hope departed from his bosom. This came from the Colonel, rather than from the rejected necklace.

'Did you send that jewelry?' his father asked him some days afterwards.

'Yes; I sent it.'

'And what has now become of it?'

'It is in my desk there.'

'Did she send it back again?'

'It came back. My Uncle Dosett brought it. I do not want to say anything more about it, if you please.'

'I am sorry for that, Tom;—very sorry. As you had set your heart upon it I wish it could have been as you would have it. But the necklace should not be left there.' Tom shook his head in despair.

'You had better let me have the necklace. It is not that I should grudge it to you, Tom, if it could do you any good.'

'You shall have it, Sir.'

'It will be better so. That was the understanding.' Then the necklace was transferred to some receptacle belonging to Sir Thomas himself, the lock of which might probably be more secure than that of Tom's desk, and there it remained in its case, still folded in the various papers in which Mrs. Dosett had encased it.

Then Tom found it necessary to adopt some other mode of life for his own consolation and support. He had told his father on one occasion that he had devoted himself for a fortnight to champagne and the theatres. But this had been taken as a joke. He had been fairly punctual at his place of business and had shown no symptoms of fast living. But now it occurred to him that fast living would be the only thing for him. He had been quite willing to apply himself to marriage and a steady life; but fortune had not favoured him. If he drank too much now, and lay in bed, and became idle, it was not his fault. There came into his head an idea that Ayala and Colonel Stubbs between them must look to that. Could he meet Ayala he would explain to her how his character as a moral man had been altogether destroyed by her conduct;—and should he meet Colonel Stubbs he would explain something to him also.

A new club had been established in London lately called the Mountaineers,* which had secured for itself handsome lodgings in Piccadilly, and considered itself to be, among clubs, rather a comfortable institution than otherwise. It did not as yet affect much fashion, having hitherto secured among its members only two lords,—and they were lords by courtesy. But it was a pleasant, jovial place, in which the delights of young men were not impeded by the austerity of their elders. Its name would be excused only on the plea that all other names available for a club had already been appropriated in the metropolis. There was certainly nothing in the club peculiarly applicable to mountains. But then there are other clubs in London with names which might be open to similar criticism. It was the case that many young men engaged in the City had been enrolled among its members, and it was from this cause, no doubt, that Tom Tringle was regarded as being a leading light among the Mountaineers. It was here that the champagne had been drunk to which Tom had alluded when talking of his love to his father. Now, in his despair, it seemed good to him to pass a considerable portion of his time among the Mountaineers.

'You'll dine here, Faddle?' he said one evening to a special friend of his, a gentleman also from the City, with whom he had been dining a good deal during the last week.

'I suppose I shall,' said Faddle, 'but ain't we coming it a little strong? They want to know at the Gardens what the deuce it is I'm about.' The Gardens was a new row of houses, latterly christened Badminton Gardens, in which resided the father and mother of Faddle.

'I've given up all that kind of thing,' said Tom.

'Your people are not in London.'

'It will make no difference when they do come up. I call an evening in the bosom of one's family about the slowest thing there is. The bosom must do without me for the future.'

'Won't your governor cut up rough?'

'He must cut up as he pleases. But I rather fancy he knows all about it. I shan't spend half as much money this way as if I had a house and wife and family,—and what we may call a bosom of one's own.' Then they had dinner and went to the theatre, and played billiards, and had supper, and spent the night in a manner very delightful, no doubt, to themselves, but of which their elder friends could hardly have approved.

There was a good deal of this following upon the episode of the necklace, and it must be told with regret that our young hero fell into certain exploits which were by no means creditable to him. More than one good-humoured policeman had helped him home to his lodgings; but alas, on Christmas Eve, he fell into the hands of some guardian of the peace who was not quite sufficiently good-natured, and Tom passed the night and the greater part of the following morning, recumbent, he in one cell, and his friend Faddle in the next, with an intimation that they would certainly be taken before a magistrate on the day after Christmas Day.

Oh, Ayala! Ayala! It must be acknowledged that you were in a measure responsible;—and not only for the lamentable condition of your lover, but also of that of his friend. For, in his softer moments, Tom had told everything to Faddle, and Faddle had declared that he would be true to the death to a friend suffering such unmerited misfortune. Perhaps the fidelity of Faddle may have owed something to the fact that Tom's pecuniary allowances were more generous than those accorded to himself. To Ayala must be attributed the occurrence of these misfortunes. But Tom in his more fiery moments,—those moments which would come between the subsidence of actual sobriety and the commencement of intoxication,—attributed all his misfortunes to the Colonel. 'Faddle,' he would say in these moments, 'of course I know that I'm a ruined man. Of course

I'm aware that all this is only a prelude to some ignominious end. I have not sunk to this kind of thing without feeling it.' 'You'll be right enough some day, old fellow,' Faddle would reply. 'I shall live to be godfather to the first boy.' 'Never, Faddle!' Tom replied. 'All those hopes have vanished. You'll never live to see any child of mine. And I know well where to look for my enemy. Stubbs indeed! I'll Stubbs him. If I can only live to be revenged on that traitor then I shall die contented. Though he shot me through the heart, I should die contented.'

This had happened a little before that unfortunate Christmas Eve. Up to this time Sir Thomas, though he had known well that his son had not been living as he should do, had been mild in his remonstrances, and had said nothing at Merle Park to frighten Lady Tringle. But the affair of Christmas Eve came to his ears with all its horrors. A policeman whom Tom had struck with his fist in the pit of the stomach had not been civil enough to accept this mark of familiarity with good humour. He had been much inconvenienced by the blow, and had insisted upon giving testimony to this effect before the magistrate. There had been half-an-hour, he said, in which he had hung dubious between this world and the next, so great had been the violence of the blow, and so deadly its direction! The magistrate was one of those just men who find a pleasure and a duty in protecting the police of the metropolis. It was no case, he declared, for a fine. What would be a fine to such a one as Thomas Tringle, junior! And Tom,—Tom Tringle, the only son of Sir Thomas Tringle, the senior partner in the great house of Travers and Treason,—was ignominiously locked up for a week. Faddle, who had not struck the blow, was allowed to depart with a fine and a warning. Oh, Ayala, Ayala, this was thy doing!

When the sentence was known Sir Thomas used all his influence to extricate his unfortunate son, but in vain. Tom went through his penalty, and, having no help from champagne, doubtless had a bad time of it. Ayala, Stubbs, the policeman, and the magistrate, seemed to have conspired to destroy him. But the week at last dragged itself out, and then Tom found himself confronted with his father in the back-parlour of the house in Queen's Gate. 'Tom,' he said, 'this is very bad!'

'It is bad, Sir,' said Tom.

'You have disgraced me, and your mother, and yourself. You have disgraced Travers and Treason!' Poor Tom shook his head. 'It will be necessary, I fear, that you should leave the house altogether.' Tom stood silent without a word. 'A young man who has been locked up in prison for a week for maltreating a policeman can hardly expect to be entrusted with such concerns as those of Travers and Treason. I and your poor mother cannot get rid of you and the disgrace which you have entailed upon us. Travers and Treason can easily get rid of you.' Tom knew very well that his father was, in fact, Travers and Treason, but he did not yet feel that an opportunity had come in which he could wisely speak a word. 'What have you got to say for yourself, Sir?' demanded Sir Thomas.

'Of course, I'm very sorry,' muttered Tom.

'Sorry, Tom! A young man holding your position in Travers and Treason ought not to have to be sorry for having been locked up in prison for a week for maltreating a policeman! What do you think must be done, yourself?'

'The man had been hauling me about in the street.'

'You were drunk, no doubt.'

'I had been drinking. I am not going to tell a lie about it. But he needn't have done as he did. Faddle knows that, and can tell you.'

'What can have driven you to associate with such a young man as Faddle? That is the worst part of it. Do you know what Faddle and Company are,—stock jobbers, who ten years ago hadn't a thousand pounds in the way of capital among them! They've been connected with a dozen companies, none of which are floating now, and have made money out of them all! Do you think that Travers and Treason will accept a young man as a partner who associates with such people as that?'

'I have seen old Faddle's name and yours on the same prospectus*together, Sir.'

'What has that to do with it? You never saw him inside our counter. What a name to appear along with yours in such an affair as this! If it hadn't been for that, you might have got over it. Young men will be young men. Faddle! I think you will have to go abroad for a time, till it has been forgotten.'

'I should like to stay, just at present, Sir,' said Tom.

'What good can you do?'

'All the same, I should like to stay, Sir.'

'I was thinking that, if you were to take a tour through the United States, go across to San Francisco, then up to Japan, and from thence through some of the Chinese cities down to Calcutta and Bombay, you might come back by the Euphrates Valley to Constantinople, see something of Bulgaria and those countries, and so home by Vienna and Paris. The Euphrates Valley Railway will be finished by that time, perhaps, and Bulgaria will be as settled as Hertfordshire. You'd see something of the world, and I could let it be understood that you were travelling on behalf of Travers and Treason. By the time that you were back, people in the City would have forgotten the policeman, and if you could manage to write home three or four letters about our trade with Japan and China, they would be willing to forget Faddle.'

'But, Sir——'

'Shouldn't you like a tour of that kind?'

'Very much indeed, Sir;—only——'

'Only what, Tom?'

'Ayala!' said Tom, hardly able to suppress a sob as he uttered the fatal name.

'Tom, don't be a fool. You can't make a young

woman have you if she doesn't choose. I have done all that I could for you, because I saw that you'd set your heart upon it. I went to her myself, and then I gave two hundred and fifty pounds for that bauble. I am told I shall have to lose a third of the sum in getting rid of it.'

'Ricolay told me that he'd take it back at two hundred and twenty,' said Tom, whose mind, prostrate as it was, was still alive to consideration of profit and loss.

'Never mind that for the present,' said Sir Thomas. 'Don't you remember the old song ?—" If she will, she will, you may depend on't. And if she won't, she won't; and there's an end on't."* You ought to be a man and pluck up your spirits. Are you going to allow a little girl to knock you about in that way?' Tom only shook his head, and looked as if he was very ill. In truth, the champagne, and the imprisonment, and Ayala together, had altogether altered his appearance. 'We've done what we could about it, and now it is time to give it over. Let me hear you say that you will give it over.' Tom stood speechless before his father. 'Speak the word, and the thing will be done,' continued Sir Thomas, endeavouring to encourage the young man.

'I can't,' said Tom, sighing.

'Nonsense!'

'I have tried, and I can't.'

'Tom, do you mean to say that you are going to lose everything because a chit of a girl like that turns up her nose at you?'

'It's no use my going while things are like this,' said Tom. 'If I were to get to New York, I should come back by the next ship. As for letters about business, I couldn't settle my mind to anything of the kind.'

'Then you're not the man I took you to be,' said the father.

'I could be man enough,' said Tom, clenching his fist, 'if I could get hold of Colonel Stubbs.'

'Colonel who?'

'Stubbs! Jonathan Stubbs! I know what I'm talking about. I'm not going to America, nor China, nor anything else, till I've polished him off. It's all very well your abusing me, but you don't know what it is I have suffered. As for being called a man I don't care about it. What I should like best would be to get Ayala on one side and Stubbs on the other, and then all three to go off the Duke of York's Column together.* It's no good talking about Travers and Treason. I don't care for Travers and Treason as I am now. If you'll get Ayala to say that she'll have me, I'll go to the shop every morning at eight and stay till nine; and as for the Mountaineers it may all go to the d—— for me.' Then he rushed out of the room, banging the door after him.

Sir Thomas, when he was thus left, stood for a while with his hands in his trousers' pockets, contemplating the condition of his son. It was wonderful to him that a boy of his should be afflicted in this manner. When he had been struck by the juvenile beauties of Emmeline Dosett he had at once asked the young lady to share his fortunes with him, and the young lady had speedily acceded to his request. Then he had been married, and that was all he had ever known of the troubles of love. He could not but think, looking back at it as he did now from a distance, that had Emmeline been hard-hearted he would have endured the repulse and have passed on speedily to some other charmer. But Tom had been wounded after a fashion which seemed to him to have been very uncommon. It might be possible that he should recover in time, but while undergoing recovery he would be ruined;—so great were the young man's sufferings! Now Sir Thomas, though he had spoken to Tom with all the severity which he had been able to assume, though he had abused Faddle, and had vindicated the injured dignity of Travers and Treason with all his eloquence; though he had told Tom it was unmanly to give way to his love, yet, of living creatures,

Tom was at this moment the dearest to his heart. He had never for an instant entertained the idea of expelling Tom from Travers and Treason because of the policeman, or because of Faddle. What should he do for the poor boy now? Was there any argument, any means of persuasion, by which he could induce that foolish little girl to accept all the good things which he was ready to do for her? Could he try yet once again himself, with any chance of success?

Thinking of all this, he stood there for an hour alone with his hands in his trousers' pockets.

## CHAPTER XXXIII

### ISADORE HAMEL IN LOMBARD STREET

IN following the results of Tom's presentation of the necklace we have got beyond the period which our story is presumed to have reached. Tom was in durance during the Christmas week, but we must go back to the promise which had been made by her uncle, Sir Thomas, to Lucy about six weeks before that time. The promise had extended only to an undertaking on the part of Sir Thomas to see Isadore Hamel if he would call at the house in Lombard Street at a certain hour on a certain day. Lucy was overwhelmed with gratitude when the promise was made. A few moments previously she had been indignant because her uncle had appeared to speak of her and her lover as two beggars,—but Sir Thomas had explained and in some sort apologised, and then had come the promise which to Lucy seemed to contain an assurance of effectual aid. Sir Thomas would not have asked to see the lover had he intended to be hostile to the lover. Something would be done to solve the difficulty which had seemed to Lucy to be so grave. She would not any longer be made to think that she should give up either her lover or her home under her uncle's roof. This had been terribly dis-

tressing to her because she had been well aware that
on leaving her uncle's house she could be taken in only
by her lover, to whom an immediate marriage would
be ruinous. And yet she could not undertake to give
up her lover. Therefore her uncle's promise had made
her very happy, and she forgave the ungenerous
allusion to the two beggars.

The letter was written to Isadore in high spirits.
'I do not know what Uncle Tom intends, but he
means to be kind. Of course you must go to him, and
if I were you I would tell him everything about
everything. He is not strict and hard like Aunt
Emmeline. She means to be good too, but she is
sometimes so very hard. I am happier now because
I think something will be done to relieve you from
the terrible weight which I am to you. I sometimes
wish that you had never come to me in Kensington
Gardens, because I have become such a burden to
you.'

There was much more in which Lucy no doubt
went on to declare that, burden as she was, she intended to be persistent. Hamel, when he received
this letter, was resolved to keep the appointment
made for him, but his hopes were not very high. He
had been angry with Lady Tringle,—in the first
place, because of her treatment of himself at Glenbogie, and then much more strongly, because she
had been cruel to Lucy. Nor did he conceive himself
to be under any strong debt of gratitude to Sir
Thomas, though he had been invited to lunch. He
was aware that the Tringles had despised him, and
he repaid the compliment with all his heart by despising the Tringles. They were to him samples of the
sort of people which he thought to be of all the most
despicable. They were not only vulgar and rich, but
purse-proud and conceited as well. To his thinking
there was nothing of which such people were entitled
to be proud. Of course they make money,—money
out of money, an employment which he regarded as
vile,—creating nothing either useful or beautiful. To

A.A.—16

create something useful was, to his thinking, very
good. To create something beautiful was almost
divine. To manipulate millions till they should breed
other millions was the meanest occupation for a
life's energy. It was thus, I fear, that Mr. Hamel
looked at the business carried on in Lombard Street,
being as yet very young in the world and seeing
many things with distorted eyes.

He was aware that some plan would be proposed
to him which might probably accelerate his marriage,
but was aware also that he would be very unwilling
to take advice from Sir Thomas. Sir Thomas, no
doubt, would be coarse and rough, and might perhaps offer him pecuniary assistance in a manner
which would make it impossible for him to accept it.
He had told himself a score of times that, poor as he
was, he did not want any of the Tringle money.
His father's arbitrary conduct towards him had
caused him great misery. He had been brought up in
luxury, and had felt it hard enough to be deprived of
his father's means because he would not abandon the
mode of life that was congenial to him. But having
been thus, as it were, cast off by his father, he had
resolved that it behoved him to depend only on himself. In the matter of his love he was specially prone
to be indignant and independent. No one had a right
to dictate to him, and he would follow the dictation of
none. To Lucy alone did he acknowledge any debt,
and to her he owed everything. But even for her
sake he could not condescend to accept Sir Thomas's
money, and with his money his advice. Lucy had
begged him in her letter to tell everything to her
uncle. He would tell Sir Thomas everything as to
his income, his prospects, and his intentions, because
Sir Thomas as Lucy's uncle would be entitled to such
information. But he thought it very improbable
that he should accept any counsel from Sir Thomas.

Such being the condition of Hamel's mind it was
to be feared that but little good would come from his
visit to Lombard Street. Lucy had simply thought

that her uncle, out of his enormous stores, would provide an adequate income. Hamel thought that Sir Thomas, out of his enormous impudence, would desire to dictate everything. Sir Thomas was, in truth, anxious to be good-natured, and to do a kindness to his niece; but was not willing to give his money without being sure that he was putting it into good hands.

'Oh, you're Hamel,' said a young man to him, speaking to him across the counter in the Lombard Street office. This was Tom, who, as the reader will remember, had not yet got into his trouble on account of the policeman.

Tom and Hamel had never met but once before, for a few moments in the Coliseum at Rome, and the artist, not remembering him, did not know by whom he was accosted in this familiar manner. 'That is my name, Sir,' said Hamel. 'Here is my card. Perhaps you will do me the kindness to take it to Sir Thomas Tringle.'

'All right, old fellow; I know all about it. He has got Puxley with him from the Bank of England just at this moment. Come through into this room. He'll soon have polished off old Puxley.' Tom was no more to Hamel than any other clerk, and he felt himself to be aggrieved; but he followed Tom into the room as he was told, and then prepared to wait in patience for the convenience of the great man. 'So you and Lucy are going to make a match of it,' said Tom.

This was terrible to Hamel. Could it be possible that all the clerks in Lombard Street talked of his Lucy in this way, because she was the niece of their senior partner? Were all the clerks, as a matter of course, instructed in the most private affairs of the Tringle family? 'I am here in obedience to directions from Sir Thomas,' said Hamel, ignoring altogether the impudent allusion which the young man had made.

'Of course you are. Perhaps you don't know who I am?'

'Not in the least,' said Hamel.

'I am Thomas Tringle, junior,' said Tom, with a little accession of dignity.

'I beg your pardon; I did not know,' said Hamel.

'You and I ought to be thick,' rejoined Tom, 'because I'm going in for Ayala. Perhaps you've heard that before?'

Hamel had heard it and was well aware that Tom was to Ayala an intolerable burden, like the old man of the sea. He had heard of Tom as poor Ayala's pet aversion,—as a lover not to be shaken off though he had been refused a score of times. Ayala was to the sculptor only second in sacredness to Lucy. And now he was told by Tom himself that he was—'going in for Ayala.' The expression was so distressing to his feelings that he shuddered when he heard it. Was it possible that any one should say of him that he was 'going in' for Lucy? At that moment Sir Thomas opened the door, and grasping Hamel by the hand led him away into his own sanctum.

'And now, Mr. Hamel,' said Sir Thomas, in his cheeriest voice, 'how are you?' Hamel declared that he was very well, and expressed a hope that Sir Thomas was the same. 'I am not so young as I was, Mr. Hamel. My years are heavier and so is my work. That's the worst of it. When one is young and strong one very often hasn't enough to do. I daresay you find it so sometimes.'

'In our profession,' said Hamel, 'we go on working, though very often we do not sell what we do.'

'That's bad,' said Sir Thomas.

'It is the case always with an artist before he has made a name for himself. It is the case with many up to the last day of a life of labour. An artist has to look for that, Sir Thomas.'

'Dear me! That seems very sad. You are a sculptor, I belive?'

'Yes, Sir Thomas.'

'And the things you make must take a deal of room and be very heavy.' At this Mr. Hamel only smiled. 'Don't you think if you were to call an

auction you'd get something for them?' At this
suggestion the sculptor frowned but condescended to
make no reply. Sir Thomas went on with his suggestion. 'If you and half-a-dozen other beginners made
a sort of gallery among you, people would buy them
as they do those things in the Marylebone Road*and
stick them up somewhere about their grounds. It
would be better than keeping them and getting
nothing.' Hamel had in his studio at home an alle-.
gorical figure of Italia United, and another of a
Prostrate Roman Catholic Church,* which in his
mind's eye he saw for a moment stuck here or there
about the gardens of some such place as Glenbogie!
Into them had been infused all the poetry of his
nature and all the conviction of his intelligence. He
had never dreamed of selling them. He had never
dared to think that any lover of Art would encourage
him to put into marble those conceptions of his
genius which now adorned his studio, standing there
in plaster of Paris. But to him they were so valuable,
they contained so much of his thoughts, so many of
his aspirations, that even had the marble counter-
parts been ordered and paid for nothing would have
induced him to part with the originals. Now he was
advised to sell them by auction in order that he might
rival those grotesque tradesmen whose business it is
to populate the gardens of wealthy but tasteless
Britons! It was thus that the idea represented itself
to him. He simply smiled; but Sir Thomas did not
fail to appreciate the smile.

'And now about this young lady?' said Sir
Thomas, not altogether in so good a humour as he
had been when he began his suggestion. 'It's a bad
look out for her when, as you say, you cannot sell
your work when you've done it.'

'I think you do not quite understand the matter,
Sir Thomas.'

'Perhaps not. It certainly does seem unintelligible
that a man should lumber himself up with a lot of
things which he cannot sell. A tradesman would

know that he must get into the bankruptcy court if
he were to go on like that. And what is sauce for the
goose will be sauce for the gander also.' Mr. Hamel
again smiled but held his tongue. 'If you can't sell
your wares how can you keep a wife?'

'My wares, as you call them, are of two kinds.
One, though no doubt made for sale, is hardly sale-
able. The other is done to order. Such income as I
make comes from the latter.'

'Heads,' suggested Sir Thomas.

'Busts they are generally called.'

'Well, busts. I call them heads. They are heads.
A bust, I take it, is——well, never mind.' Sir Thomas
found a difficulty in defining his idea of a bust. 'A
man wants to have something more or less like some
one to put up in a church and then he pays you.'

'Or perhaps in his library. But he can put it where
he likes when he has bought it.'

'Just so. But there ain't many of those come in
your way, if I understand right.'

'Not as many as I would wish.'

'What can you net at the end of the year? That's
the question.'

Lucy had recommended him to tell Sir Thomas
everything; and he had come there determined to
tell at any rate everything referring to money. He
had not the slightest desire to keep the amount of his
income from Sir Thomas. But the questions were
put to him in so distasteful a way that he could not
bring himself to be confidential. 'It varies with
various circumstances, but it is very small.'

'Very small? Five hundred a year?' This was ill-
natured, because Sir Thomas knew that Mr. Hamel
did not earn five hundred a year. But he was
becoming acerbated by the young man's manner.

'Oh dear, no,' said Hamel.

'Four hundred?'

'Nor four hundred,—nor three. I have never
netted three hundred in one year after paying the
incidental expenses.'

'That seems to me to be uncommonly little for a young man who is thinking of marrying. Don't you think you had better give it up?'

'I certainly think nothing of the kind.'

'Does your father do anything for you?'

'Nothing at all.'

'He also makes heads?'

'Heads,—and other things.'

'And sells them when he has made them.'

'Yes, Sir Thomas; he sells them. He had a hard time once, but now he is run after. He refuses more orders than he can accept.'

'And he won't do anything for you.'

'Nothing. He has quarrelled with me.'

'That is very bad. Well now, Mr. Hamel, would you mind telling me what your ideas are?' Sir Thomas, when he asked the question, still intended to give assistance, was still minded that the young people should by his assistance be enabled to marry. But he was strongly of opinion that it was his duty, as a rich and protecting uncle, to say something about imprudence, and to magnify difficulties. It certainly would be wrong for an uncle, merely because he was rich, to give away his money to dependent relatives without any reference to those hard principles which a possessor of money always feels it to be his business to inculcate. And up to this point Hamel had done nothing to ingratiate himself. Sir Thomas was beginning to think that the sculptor was an impudent prig, and to declare to himself that, should the marriage ever take place, the young couple would not be made welcome at Glenbogie or Merle Park. But still he intended to go on with his purpose, for Lucy's sake. Therefore he asked the sculptor as to his ideas generally.

'My idea is that I shall marry Miss Dormer, and support her on the earnings of my profession. My idea is that I shall do so before long, in comfort. My idea also is, that she will be the last to complain of any discomfort which may arise from my straitened

circumstances at present. My idea is that I am preparing for myself a happy and independent life.
My idea also is,—and I assure you that of all my
ideas this is the one to which I cling with the fondest
assurance,—that I will do my very best to make her
life happy when she comes to grace my home.'

There was a manliness in this which would have
touched Sir Thomas had he been in a better humour,
but, as it was, he had been so much irritated by the
young man's manner, that he could not bring himself
to be just. 'Am I to understand that you intend to
marry on something under three hundred a year?'

Hamel paused for a moment before he made his
reply. 'How am I to answer such a question,' he
said, at last, 'seeing that Miss Dormer is in your
hands, and that you are unlikely to be influenced by
anything that I may say?'

'I shall be very much influenced,' said Sir Thomas.

'Were her father still alive, I think we should have
put our heads together, and between us decided on
what might have been best for Lucy's happiness.'

'Do you think that I'm indifferent to her happiness?' demanded Sir Thomas.

'I should have suggested to him,' continued
Hamel, not noticing the last question, 'that she
should remain in her own home till I could make one
for her worthy of her acceptance. And then we
should have arranged among us what would have
been best for her happiness. I cannot do this with
you. If you tell her to-morrow that she must give up
either your protection or her engagement with me,
then she must come to me, and make the best of all
the little that I can do for her.'

'Who says that I'm going to turn her out?' said
Sir Thomas, rising angrily from his chair.

'I do not think that any one has said this of you.'

'Then why do you throw it in my teeth?'

'Because your wife has threatened it.'

Then Sir Thomas boiled over in his anger. 'No
one has threatened it. It is untrue. You are guilty

both of impertinence and untruth in saying so.' Here Hamel rose from his chair, and took up his hat. 'Stop, young man, and hear what I have to say to you. I have done nothing but good to my niece.'

'Nevertheless, it is true, Sir Thomas, that she has been told by your wife that she must either abandon me or the protection of your roof. I find no fault with Lady Tringle for saying so. It may have been the natural expression of a judicious opinion. But when you ask after my intentions in reference to your niece I am bound to tell you that I propose to subject her to the undoubted inconveniences of my poor home, simply because I find her to be threatened with the loss of another.'

'She has not been threatened, Sir.'

'You had better ask your wife, Sir Thomas. And, if you find that what I have said is true, I think you will own that I have been obliged to explain as I have done. As you have told me to my face that I have been guilty of untruth, I shall now leave you.' With this he walked out of the room, and the words which Sir Thomas threw after him had no effect in recalling him.

It must be acknowledged that Hamel had been very foolish in referring to Aunt Emmeline's threat. Who does not know that words are constantly used which are intended to have no real effect? Who does not know that an angry woman will often talk after this fashion? But it was certainly the fact that Aunt Emmeline had more than once declared to Lucy that she could not be allowed to remain one of that family unless she would give up her lover. Lucy, in her loyal endeavours to explain to her lover her own position, had told him of the threat, and he, from that moment, had held himself prepared to find a home for his future wife should that threat be carried into execution. Sir Thomas was well aware that such words had been spoken, but he knew his wife, and knew how little such words signified. His wife, without his consent, would not have the power to turn a

dog from Merle Park. The threat had simply been
an argument intended to dissuade Lucy from her
choice; and now it had been thrown in his teeth just
when he had intended to make provision for this
girl, who was not, in truth, related to him, in order
that he might ratify her choice! He was very angry
with the young prig who had thus rushed out of his
presence. He was angry, too, with his wife, who had
brought him into his difficulty by her foolish threat.
But he was angry, also, with himself, knowing that
he had been wrong to accuse the man of a falsehood.

## CHAPTER XXXIV

### 'I NEVER THREATENED TO TURN YOU OUT.'

THEN there were written the following letters,
which were sent and received before Sir Thomas
went to Merle Park, and therefore, also, before he
again saw Lucy:

'DEAREST, DEAREST LOVE,

'I have been, as desired, to Lombard Street, but I
fear that my embassy has not led to any good. I
know myself to be about as bad an ambassador as
any one can send. An ambassador should be soft and
gentle,—willing to make the best of everything, and
never prone to take offence, nor should he be addicted
specially to independence. I am ungentle, and apt to
be suspicious,—especially if anything be said deroga-
tory to my art. I am proud of being an artist, but I
am often ashamed of myself because I exhibit my
pride. I may say the same of my spirit of independence. I am determined to be independent if I
live,—but I find my independence sometimes kicking
up its heels, till I hate it myself.

'From this you will perceive that I have not had
a success in Lombard Street. I was quite willing to
answer your uncle any questions he could ask about
money. Indeed, I had no secret from him on any
subject. But when he subjected me to cross-
examination, forcing me into a bathos of poverty, as

he thought, I broke down. "Not five hundred a-
year!" "Not four!!" "Not three!!!" "Oh, heavens!
and you propose to take a wife!" You will understand how I writhed and wriggled under the scorn.

'And then there came something worse than this,
—or rather, if I remember rightly, the worst thing
came first. You were over in my studio, and will
remember, perhaps, some of my own abortive
treasures, those melancholy but soul-inspiring creations of which I have thought so much, and others
have thought so little? That no one else should
value them is natural, but to me it seems unnatural,
almost cruel, that any one should tell me to my face
that they were valueless. Your uncle, of course, had
never seen them, but he knew that sculptors are
generally burdened with these "wares," as he called
them; and he suggested that I should sell them by
auction for what they might fetch,—in order that
the corners which they occupy might be vacant. He
thought that, perhaps, they might do for country
gentlemen to stick about among their shrubs. You,
knowing my foolish soreness on the subject, will
understand how well I must have been prepared by
this to endure your uncle's cross-examination.

'Then he asked me as to my ideas,—not art ideas,
but ideas as to bread and cheese for the future.
told him as exactly as I could. I explained to him
that if you were left in possession of a comfortable
home, such as would have been that of your father,
I should think it best for your sake to delay our
marriage till I should be prepared to do something
better for you than I can at present; but that I hold
myself ready to give you all that I have to give at a
moment's notice, should you be required to leave his
house. And, Lucy, speaking in your name, I said
something further, and declared my belief that you,
for my sake, would bear the inconveniences of so
poor a home without complaining.

'Then there arose anger both on his side and on
mine; and I must say, insult on his. He told me that

I had no business to suggest that you would be
expelled from his house. I replied that the threat
had come, if not from him, then from Lady Tringle.
Upon this he accused me of positive falsehood,
asserting that your aunt had said nothing of the kind.
I then referred him to Lady Tringle herself, but refused to stay any longer in the room with him,
because he had insulted me.

'So you will see that I did less than nothing by my
embassy. I told myself that it would be so as I
descended into the underground cavern at the
Gloucester Road Station.* You are not to suppose
that I blame him more, or, indeed, so much as I do
myself. It was not to be expected that he should
behave as a gentleman of fine feeling. But, perhaps,
it ought to have been expected that I should
behave like a man of common sense. I ought
to have taken his advice about the auction, apparently, in good part. I ought not to have writhed
when he scorned my poor earnings. When he asked
as to my ideas, I should not have alluded to your
aunt's threat as to turning you out. I should have
been placid and humble; and then his want of generous
feeling would have mattered nothing. But spilt milk
and broken eggs are past saving. Whatever good things
may have come from your uncle's generosity had I
brushed his hair for him aright, are now clean gone,
seeing that I scrubbed him altogether the wrong way.

'For myself, I do not know that I should regret it
very much. I have an idea that no money should be
sweet to a man except that which he earns. And I have
enough belief in myself to be confident that sooner or
later I shall earn a sufficiency. But, dearest, I own that
I feel disgusted with myself when I think that I have
diminished your present comfort, or perhaps lessened
for the future resources which would have been yours
rather than mine. But the milk has been spilt, and
now we must only think what we can best do without
it. It seems to me that only two homes are possible
for you,—one with Sir Thomas as his niece, and the

other with me as my wife. I am conceited enough to
think that you will prefer the latter even with many
inconveniences. Neither can your uncle or your
aunt prevent you from marrying at a very early day,
should you choose to do so. There would be some
preliminary ceremony, of the nature of which I am
thoroughly ignorant, but which could, I suppose, be
achieved in a month. I would advise you to ask your
aunt boldly whether she wishes you to go or to stay
with her, explaining, of course, that you intend to
hold to your engagement, and explaining at the same
time that you are quite ready to be married at once,
if she is anxious to be quit of you. That is my advice.

'And now, dear, one word of something softer! For
did any lover ever write to the lady of his heart so
long a letter so abominably stuffed with matters of
business? How shall I best tell you how dearly I love
you? Perhaps I may do it by showing you that as
far as I myself am concerned I long to hear that your
Aunt Emmeline and your Uncle Tom are more
hard-hearted and obdurate than were ever uncle and
aunt before them. I long to hear that you have been
turned out into the cold, because I know that then
you must come to me, though it be even less than
three hundred a-year. I wish you could have seen
your uncle's face as those terribly mean figures
reached his ears. I do not for a moment fear that we
should want. Orders come slow enough, but they
come a little quicker than they did. I have never for
a moment doubted my own ultimate success, and if
you were with me I should be more confident than
ever. Nevertheless, should your aunt bid you to
stay, and should you think it right to comply with
her desire, I will not complain.

'Adieu! This comes from one who is altogether
happy in his confidence that at any rate before long
you will have become his wife.

'ISADORE HAMEL.

'I quite expect to be scolded for my awkwardness.
Indeed I shall be disappointed if I am not.'

The same post which brought Hamel's long letter to Lucy brought also a short but very angry scrawl from Sir Thomas to his wife. No eyes but those of Lady Tringle saw this epistle, and no other eyes shall see it. But the few words which it contained were full of marital wrath. Why had she threatened·to turn her own niece out of his doors? Why had she subjected him to the necessity of defending her by a false assertion? Those Dormer nieces of hers were giving him an amount of·trouble and annoyance which he certainly had not deserved. Lucy, though not a word was said to her of this angry letter, was conscious that something had been added to her aunt's acerbity. Indeed, for the last day or two her aunt's acerbity towards her had been much diminished. Lady Tringle had known that her husband intended to do something by which the Hamel marriage would be rendered possible; and she, though she altogether disapproved of the Hamel marriage, would be obliged to accede to it if Sir Thomas acceded to it and encouraged it by his money. Let them be married, and then, as far as the Tringles were concerned, let there be an end of these Dormer troubles for ever. To that idea Lady Tringle had reconciled herself as soon as Sir Thomas had declared his purpose, but now,—as she declared to herself,—'all the fat was again in the fire.' She received Lucy's salutations on that morning with a very bad grace.

But she had been desired to give no message, and therefore she was silent on the subject to Lucy. To the Honourable Mrs. Traffick she said a few words. 'After all Ayala was not half as bad as Lucy,' said Lady Tringle.

'There, mamma, I think you are wrong,' said the Honourable Mrs. Traffick. 'Of all the upsetting things I ever knew Ayala was the worst. Think of her conduct with Septimus.' Lady Tringle made a little grimace, which, however, her daughter did not see. 'And then with that Marchesa!'

'That was the Marchesa's fault.'

'And with Tom!'

'I don't think she was so much to blame with Tom. If she were, why doesn't she take him now she can have him? He is just as foolish about her as ever. Upon my word I think Tom will make himself ill about it.'

'You haven't heard it all, mamma.'

'What haven't I heard?'

'Ayala has been down with the Alburys at Stalham.'

'I did hear that.'

'And another man has turned up. What on earth they see in her is what I can't understand.'

'Another man has offered to her! Who is he?'

'There was a Colonel Stubbs down there. Septimus heard it all from young Batsby at the club. She got this man to ride about the country with her everywhere, going to the meets with him and coming home. And in this way she got him to propose to her. I don't suppose he means anything; but that is why she won't have anything to do with Tom now. Do you mean to say she didn't do all she could to catch Tom down at Glenbogie, and then at Rome? Everybody saw it. I don't think Lucy has ever been so bad as that.'

'It's quite different, my dear.'

'She has come from a low father,' said the Honourable Mrs. Traffick, proudly, 'and therefore she has naturally attached herself to a low young man. There is nothing to be wondered at in that. I suppose they are fond of each other, and the sooner they are married the better.'

'But he can't marry her because he has got nothing.'

'Papa will do something.'

'That's just what your papa won't. The man has been to your father in the City and there has been ever such a row. He spoke ill of me because I endeavoured to do my duty by the ungrateful girl. I am sure I have got a lesson as to taking up other people's children. I endeavoured to do an act of charity, and see what has come of it. I don't believe in charity.'

'That is wicked, mamma. Faith, Hope, and Charity!*But you've got to be charitable before you begin the others.'

'I don't think it is wicked. People would do best if they were made to go along on what they've got of their own.' This seemed to Augusta to be a direct blow at Septimus and herself. 'Of course I know what you mean, mamma.'

'I didn't mean anything.'

'But, if people can't stay for a few weeks in their own parents' houses, I don't know where they are to stay.'

'It isn't weeks, Augusta; it's months. And as to parents, Lord Boardotrade is Mr. Traffick's parent. Why doesn't he go and stay with Lord Boardotrade?' Then Augusta got up and marched with stately step out of the room. After this it was not possible that Lucy would find much immediate grace in her aunt's eyes.

From the moment that Lucy had received her letter there came upon her the great burden of answering it. She was very anxious to do exactly as Hamel had counselled her. She was quite alive to the fact that Hamel had been imprudent in Lombard Street; but not the less was she desirous to do as he bade her,—thinking it right that a woman should obey some one, and that her obedience could be due only to him. But in order to obey him she must consult her aunt. 'Aunt Emmeline,' she said that afternoon, 'I want to ask you something.'

'What is it now?' said Aunt Emmeline, crossly.

'About Mr. Hamel.'

'I don't want to hear any more about Mr. Hamel. I have heard quite enough of Mr. Hamel.'

'Of course I am engaged to him, Aunt Emmeline.'

'So I hear you say. I do not think it very dutiful

of you to come and talk to me about him, knowing as
you do what I think about him.'

'What I want to ask is this. Ought I to stay here
or ought I to go away?'

'I never heard such a girl! Where are you to go
to? What makes you ask the question?'

'Because you said that I ought to go if I did not
give him up.'

'You ought to give him up.'

'I cannot do that, aunt.'

'Then you had better hold your tongue and say
nothing further about it. I don't believe he earns
enough to give you bread to eat and decent clothes to
wear. What would you do if children were to come
year after year? If you really love him I wonder how
you can think of being such a millstone round a
man's neck!'

This was very hard to bear. It was so different
from the delicious comfort of his letter. 'I do not for
a moment believe that we should want.' 'I have
never for one moment doubted my own ultimate
success.' But after all was there not more of truth
in her aunt's words, hard and cruel as they were?
And on these words, such as they were, she must
found her answer to her lover; for he had bade her
ask her aunt what she was to do as to staying or
preparing herself for an immediate marriage. Then,
before the afternoon was over, she wrote to Hamel
as follows:—

'DEAR ISADORE,

'I have got ever so much to say, but I shall begin by
doing as you told me in your postscript. I won't
quite scold you, but I do think you might have been
a little gentler with poor Uncle Tom. I do not say
this because I at all regret anything which perhaps
he might have done for us. If you do not want
assistance from him certainly I do not. But I do
think that he meant to be kind; and, though he may
not be quite what you call a gentleman of fine feeling,

yet he has taken me into his house when I had no other to go to, and in many respects has been generous to me. When he said that you were to go to him in Lombard Street, I am sure that he meant to be generous. And, though it has not ended well, yet he meant to be kind to both of us.

'There is what you will call my scolding; though, indeed, dearest, I do not intend to scold at all. Nor am I in the least disappointed except in regard to you. This morning I have been to Aunt Emmeline, as you desired, and I must say that she was very cross. Of course I know that it is because she is my own aunt that Uncle Tom has me here at all; and I feel that I ought to be very grateful to her. But, in spite of all that you say, laughing at Uncle Tom because he wants you to sell your grand work by auction, he is much more good-natured than Aunt Emmeline. I am quite sure my aunt never liked me, and that she will not be comfortable till I am gone. But when I asked her whether I ought to stay, or to go, she told me to hold my tongue, and say nothing further about it. Of course, by this, she meant that I was to remain, at any rate for the present.

'My own dearest, I do think this will be best, though I need not tell you how I look forward to leaving this, and being always with you. For myself I am not a bit afraid, though Aunt Emmeline said dreadful things about food and clothes, and all the rest of it. But I believe much more in what you say, that success will be sure to come. But still will it not be wise to wait a little longer? Whatever I may have to bear here, I shall think that I am bearing it for your dear sake; and then I shall be happy.

'Believe me to be always and always your own
'LUCY.'

This was written and sent on a Wednesday, and nothing further was said either by Lucy herself, or by her aunt, as to the lover, till Sir Thomas came down to Merle Park on the Saturday evening. On his arrival he seemed inclined to be gracious to the whole household, even including Mr. Traffick, who received any attention of that kind exactly as though the most amicable arrangements were always existing between him and his father-in-law. Aunt Emmeline, when it seemed that she was to encounter no further anger on account of the revelation which Hamel had made in Lombard Street, also recovered her temper, and the evening was spent as though there were no causes for serious family discord. In this spirit, on the following morning, they all went to church, and it was delightful to hear the flattering words with which Mr. Traffick praised Merle Park, and everything belonging to it, during the hour of lunch. He went so far as to make some delicately laudatory hints in praise of hospitality in general, and especially as to that so nobly exercised by London merchant-princes. Sir Thomas smiled as he heard him, and, as he smiled, he resolved that, as soon as the Christmas festivities should be over, the Honourable Septimus Traffick should certainly be turned out of that house.

After lunch there came a message to Lucy by a page-boy, who was supposed to attend generally to the personal wants of Aunt Emmeline, saying that her uncle would be glad of her attendance for a walk. 'My dear,' said he, 'have you got your thick boots on? Then go and put 'em on. We will go down to the Lodge, and then come home round by Windover Hill.' She did as she was bade, and then they started. 'I want to tell you,' said he, 'that this Mr. Hamel of yours came to me in Lombard Street.'

'I know that, Uncle Tom.'

'He has written to you, then, and told you all about it?'

'He has written to me, certainly, and I have answered him.'

'No doubt. Well, Lucy, I had intended to be kind to your Mr. Hamel, but, as you are probably aware, I was not enabled to carry out my intentions. He seems to be a very independent sort of young man.'

'He is independent, I think.'

'I have not a word to say against it. If a man can be independent it is so much the better. If a man can do everything for himself, so as to require neither to beg nor to borrow, it will be much better for him. But, my dear, you must understand that a man cannot be independent with one hand, and accept assistance with the other, at one and the same time.'

'That is not his character, I am sure,' said Lucy, striving to hide her indignation while she defended her lover's character.

'I do not think it is. Therefore he must remain independent, and I can do nothing for him.'

'He knows that, Uncle Tom.'

'Very well. Then there's an end of it. I only want to make you understand that I was willing to assist him, but that he was unwilling to be assisted. I like him all the better for it, but there must be an end of it.'

'I quite understand, Uncle Tom.'

'Then there's one other thing I've got to say. He accused me of having threatened to turn you out of my house. Now, my dear——' Hereupon Lucy struggled to say a word, hardly knowing what word she ought to say, but he interrupted her,—'Just hear me out till I've done, and then there need not be another word about it. I never threatened to turn you out.'

'Not you, Uncle Tom,' she said, endeavouring to press his arm with her hand.

'If your aunt said a word in her anger you should not have made enough of it to write and tell him.'

'I thought she meant me to go, and then I didn't know whom else to ask.'

'Neither I nor she, nor anybody else, ever intended to turn you out. I have meant to be kind to you both,—to you and Ayala; and if things have gone wrong I cannot say that it has been my fault. Now, you had better stay here, and not say a word more about it till he is ready to take you. That can't be yet for a long time. He is making, at present, not more than two hundred a year. And I am sure it must be quite as much as he can do to keep a coat on his back with such an income as that. You must make up your mind to wait,—probably for some years. As I told you before, if a man chooses to have the glory of independence he must also bear the inconvenience. Now, my dear, let there be an end of this, and never say again that I want to turn you out of my house.'

## CHAPTER XXXV

### TOM TRINGLE SENDS A CHALLENGE

THE next six weeks went on tranquilly at Merle Park without a word spoken about Hamel. Sir Thomas, who was in the country as little as possible, showed his scorn to his son-in-law simply by the paucity of his words, speaking to him, when he did speak to him, with a deliberate courtesy which Mr. Traffick perfectly understood. It was that dangerous serenity which so often presages a storm. 'There is something going to be up with your father,' he said to Augusta. Augusta replied that she had never seen her father so civil before. 'It would be a great convenience,' continued the Member of Parliament, 'if he could be made to hold his tongue till Parliament meets; but I'm afraid that's too good to expect.' In other respects things were comfortable at Merle Park, though they were not always comfortable up in London. Tom, as the reader knows, was misbehaving himself sadly at the Mountaineers. This was the period of unlimited champagne, and of almost total absence from Lombard Street. It was seldom that Sir Thomas could get hold of his son, and when he did that broken-hearted youth would reply to his expostulations simply by asserting that if his father would induce Ayala to marry him everything should

go straight in Lombard Street. Then came the final
blow. Tom was of course expected at Merle Park on
Christmas Eve, but did not make his appearance
either then or on Christmas Day. Christmas fell on
a Wednesday, and it was intended that the family
should remain in the country till the following Monday. On the Thursday Sir Thomas went up to town
to make inquiries respecting his heir, as to whom
Lady Tringle had then become absolutely unhappy.
In London he heard the disastrous truth. Tom, in
his sportive mood, had caused serious inconvenience
to a most respectable policeman, and was destined to
remain another week in the hands of the Philistines.*
Then, for a time, all the other Tringle troubles were
buried and forgotten in this great trouble respecting
Tom. Lady Tringle was unable to leave her room
during the period of incarceration. Mr. Traffick
promised to have the victim liberated by the direct
interference of the Secretary of State, but failed to
get anything of the kind accomplished. The girls
were completely cowed by the enormity of the misfortune; so that Tom's name was hardly mentioned
except in sad and confidential whispers. But of all
the sufferers Sir Thomas suffered the most. To him
it was a positive disgrace, weighing down every
moment of his life. At Travers and Treason he could
not hold up his head boldly and open his mouth
loudly as had always been his wont. At Travers and
Treason there was not a clerk who did not know that
'the governor' was an altered man since this misfortune had happened to the hope of the firm. What
passed between Sir Thomas and his son on the
occasion has already been told in a previous chapter.
That Sir Thomas, on the whole, behaved with indulgence must be acknowledged; but he felt that his
son must in truth absent himself from Lombard
Street for a time.

Tom had been advised by his father to go forth
and see the world. A prolonged tour had been proposed to him which to most young men might seem

to have great attraction. To him it would have had attraction enough, had it not been for Ayala. There would have been hardly any limit to the allowance made to him, and he would have gone forth armed with introductions, which would have made every port a happy home to him. But as soon as the tour was suggested he resolved at once that he could not move himself to a distance from Ayala. What he expected,—what he even hoped,—he could not tell himself. But while Ayala was in London, and Ayala was unmarried, he could not be made to take himself far away.

He was thoroughly ashamed of himself. He was not at all the man who could bear a week of imprisonment and not think himself disgraced. For a day or two he shut himself up altogether in his lodgings, and never once showed himself at the Mountaineers. Faddle came to him, but he snubbed Faddle at first, remembering all the severe things his father had said about the Faddles in general. But he soon allowed that feeling to die away when the choice seemed to be between Faddle and solitude. Then he crept out in the dark and ate his dinners with Faddle at some tavern, generally paying the bill for both of them. After dinner he would play half-a-dozen games of billiards with his friend at some unknown billiard-room, and then creep home to his lodgings,—a blighted human being!

At last, about the end of the first week in January, he was induced to go down to Merle Park. There Mr. and Mrs. Traffick were still sojourning, the real grief which had afflicted Sir Thomas having caused him to postpone his intention in regard to his son-in-law. At Merle Park Tom was cosseted and spoilt by the women very injudiciously. It was not perhaps the fact that they regarded him as a hero simply because he had punched a policeman in the stomach and then been locked up in vindication of the injured laws of his country; but that incident in combination with his unhappy love did seem to make him heroic. Even

Lucy regarded him with favour because of his constancy to her sister; whereas the other ladies measured their admiration for his persistency by the warmth of their anger against the silly girl who was causing so much trouble. His mother told him over and over again that his cousin was not worth his regard; but then, when he would throw himself on the sofa in an agony of despair,—weakened perhaps as much by the course of champagne as by the course of his love,—then she, too, would bid him hope, and at last promised that she herself would endeavour to persuade Ayala to look at the matter in a more favourable light. 'It would all be right if it were not for that accursed Stubbs,' poor Tom would say to his mother. 'The man whom I called my friend! The man I lent a horse to when he couldn't get one anywhere else! The man to whom I confided everything, even about the necklace! If it hadn't been for Stubbs I never should have hurt that policeman! When I was striking him I thought that it was Stubbs!' Then the mother would heap feminine maledictions on the poor Colonel's head, and so together they would weep and think of revenge.

From the moment Tom had heard Colonel Stubbs's name mentioned as that of his rival he had meditated revenge. It was quite true when he said that he had been thinking of Stubbs when he struck the policeman. He had consumed the period of his confinement in gnashing his teeth, all in regard to our poor friend Jonathan. He told his father that he could not go upon his long tour because of Ayala. But in truth his love was now so mixed up with ideas of vengeance that he did not himself know which prevailed. If he could first have slaughtered Stubbs then perhaps he might have started! But how was he to slaughter Stubbs? Various ideas occurred to his mind. At first he thought that he would go down to Aldershot with the biggest cutting-whip he could find in any shop in Piccadilly; but then it occurred to him that at Aldershot he would have all the British army against

him, and that the British army might do something
to him worse even than the London magistrate.
Then he would wait till the Colonel could be met
elsewhere. He ascertained that the Colonel was still
at Stalham, where he had passed the Christmas, and
he thought how it might be if he were to attack the
Colonel in the presence of his friends, the Alburys.
He assured himself that, as far as personal injury
went, he feared nothing. He had no disinclination to
be hit over the head himself, if he could be sure of
hitting the Colonel over the head. If it could be managed that they two should fly at each other with their
fists, and be allowed to do the worst they could to
each other for an hour, without interference, he
would be quite satisfied. But down at Stalham that
would not be allowed. All the world would be
against him, and nobody there to see that he got fair
play. If he could encounter the man in the streets of
London it would be better; but were he to seek the
man down at Stalham he would probably find himself in the County Lunatic Asylum. What must he
do for his revenge? He was surely entitled to it. By
all the laws of chivalry, as to which he had his own
ideas, he had a right to inflict an injury upon a
successful—even upon an unsuccessful—rival. Was it
not a shame that so excellent an institution as duel-
ling should have been stamped out? Wandering
about the lawns and shrubberies at Merle Park he
thought of all this, and at last he came to a resolution.

The institution had been stamped out, as far as
Great Britain was concerned.* He was aware of that.
But it seemed to him that it had not been stamped
out in other more generous countries. He had happened to notice that a certain enthusiastic politician
in France had enjoyed many duels, and had never
been severely repressed by the laws of his country.
Newspaper writers were always fighting in France,
and were never guillotined. The idea of being hanged
was horrible to him,—so distasteful that he saw at a
glance that a duel in England was out of the ques-

tion. But to have his head cut off, even if it should
come to that, would be a much less affair. But in
Belgium, in Italy, in Germany, they never did cut
off the heads of the very numerous gentlemen who
fought duels. And there were the Southern States of
the American Union, where he fancied that men
might fight duels as they pleased. He would be ready
to go even to New Orleans at a day's notice if only he
could induce Colonel Stubbs to meet him there. And
he thought that, if Colonel Stubbs really possessed
half the spirit which seemed to be attributed to him
by the British army generally, he would come, if
properly invoked, and fight such a duel as this,
whether at New Orleans or at some other well-chosen
blood-allowing spot on the world's surface. Tom was
prepared to go anywhere for blood.

But the invocation must be properly made. When
he had wanted another letter of another kind to be
written for him, the Colonel himself was the man to
whom he had gone for assistance. And, had his
present enemy been any other than the Colonel himself, he would have gone to the Colonel in preference
to any one else for aid in this matter. There was no
one, in truth, in whom he believed so thoroughly as
in the Colonel. But that was out of the question.
Then he reflected what friend might now stand him
in stead. He would have gone to Houston, who
wanted to marry his sister; but Houston seemed to
have disappeared, and he did not know where he
might be found. There was his brother-in-law,
Traffick,—but he feared lest Traffick might give him
over once more into the hands of the police. He
thought of Hamel, as being in a way connected with
the family; but he had seen so little of Hamel, and
had so much disliked what he had seen, that he was
obliged to let that hope go by. There was no one left
but Faddle whom he could trust. Faddle would do
anything he was told to do. Faddle would carry the
letter, no doubt, or allow himself to be named as a
proposed second. But Faddle could not write the

letter. He felt that he could write the letter himself better than Faddle.

He went up to town, having sent a mysterious letter to Faddle, bidding his friend attend him in his lodgings. He did not yet dare to go to the Mountaineers, where Faddle would have been found. But Faddle came, true to the appointment. 'What is it, now?' said the faithful friend. 'I hope you are going back to Travers and Treasons'. That is what I should do, and walk in just as though nothing had happened.'

'Not if you were me, you wouldn't.'

'That makes a difference, of course.'

'There is something else to be done before I can again darken the doors of Travers and Treason;—if I should ever do so!'

'Something particular?'

'Something very particular. Faddle, I do think you are a true friend.'

'You may say that. I have stuck to you always,—though you don't know the kind of things my people say to me about it. They say I am going to ruin myself because of you. The governor threatened to put me out of the business altogether. But I'm a man who will be true to my friend, whatever happens. I think you have been a little cool to me, lately; but even that don't matter.'

'Cool! If you knew the state that I'm in you wouldn't talk of a fellow being cool! I'm so knocked about it all that I don't know what I'm doing.'

'I do take that into consideration.'

'Now, I'll tell you what I'm going to do.' Then he stood still, and looked Faddle full in the face. Faddle, sitting awe-struck on his chair, returned the gaze. He knew that a moment of supreme importance was at hand. 'Faddle, I'll shoot that fellow down like a dog.'

'Will you, indeed?'

'Like a dog;—if I can get at him. I should have no more compunction in taking his life than a mere worm. Why should I, when I know that he has sapped the very juice of my existence?'

'Do you mean,—do you mean,—that you would—murder him?'

'It would not be murder. Of course it·might be that he would shoot me instead. Upon the whole, I think I should like that best.'

'Oh; a duel!' said Faddle.

'That's what I mean. Murder him! Certainly not. Though I should like nothing half so well as to thrash him within an inch of his life. I would not murder him. My plan is this,—I shall write to him a letter inviting him to meet me in any corner of the globe that he may select. Torrid zone or Arctic circle will be all the same to me. You will have to accompany me as my second.' Faddle shivered with excitement and dread of coming events. Among other ideas there came the thought that it might be difficult to get back from the Arctic circle without money if his friend Tom should happen to be shot dead in that locality. 'But first of all,' continued Tom, 'you will have to carry a letter.'

'To the Colonel?' suggested Faddle.

'Of course. The man is now staying with friends of his named Albury at a place called Stalham. From what I hear they are howling swells. Sir Harry Albury is Master of the Hounds, and Lady Albury when she is up in London has all the Royal Family constantly at her parties. Stubbs is a cousin of his; but you must go right away up to him among 'em all, and deliver the letter into his hands without minding 'em a bit.

'Couldn't it go by post?'

'No; this kind of letter mustn't go by post. You have to be able to swear that you delivered it yourself into his own hands. And then you must wait for an answer. Even though he should want a day to think of it, you must wait.'

'Where am I to stay, Tom?'

'Well; it may be they'll ask you to the house, be-

cause, though you carry the letter for me, you are not
supposed to be his enemy. If so, put a jolly face on
it, and enjoy yourself as well as you can. You must
seem, you know, to be just as big a swell as anybody
there. But if they don't ask you, you must go to the
nearest inn. I'll pay the bill.'

'Shall I go to-day?' asked Faddle.

'I've got to write the letter first. It'll take a little
time, so that you'd better put it off till to-morrow.
If you will leave me now I'll write it, and if you will
come back at six we'll go and have a bit of dinner at
Bolivia's.' This was an eating-house in the neighbourhood of Leicester Square, to which the friends
had become partial during this troubled period of
their existence.

'Why not come to the Mountaineers, old boy?'
Tom shook his head, showing that he was not yet up
to such festivity as that; and then Faddle took his
departure.

Tom at once got out his pen and paper, and began
to write his letter. It may be imagined that it was
not written off-hand, or without many struggles.
When it was written it ran as follows:—

'SIR,

'You will not, I think, be surprised to hear from me
in anything but a friendly spirit. I went down to you
at Aldershot as to a friend whom I could trust with
my bosom's dearest secret, and you have betrayed
me. I told you of my love, a love which has long
burned in my heart, and you received my confidence
with a smile, knowing all the time that you were my
rival. I leave it to you to say what reply you can
make as to conduct so damning, so unmanly, so
dastardly,—and so very unlike a friend as this!

'However, there is no place here for words. You
have offered me the greatest insult and the greatest
injury which one man can inflict upon another!
There is no possibility of an apology, unless you are
inclined to say that you will renounce for ever your

claim upon the hand of Miss Ayala Dormer. This I
do not expect, and, therefore, I call upon you to give
me that satisfaction which is all that one gentleman
can offer to another. After the injury you have done
me I think it quite impossible that you should refuse.

'Of course, I know that duels cannot be fought in
England because of the law. I am sorry that the law
should have been altered, because it allows so many
cowards to escape the punishment they deserve.' Tom,
as he wrote this, was very proud of the keenness of the
allusion. 'I am quite sure, however, that a man who
bears the colours of a colonel in the British army
will not try to get off by such a pretext.' He was
proud, too, about the colours. 'France, Belgium,
Italy, the United States, and all the world, are open! I
will meet you wherever you may choose to arrange a
meeting. I presume that you will prefer pistols.

'I send this by the hands of my friend, Mr. Faddle,
who will be prepared to make arrangements with you
or with any friend on your behalf. He will bring
back your reply, which no doubt will be satisfactory.
—I am, Sir, your most obedient servant,

'THOMAS TRINGLE, junior.'

When, after making various copies, Tom at last
read the letter as finally prepared, he was much
pleased with it, doubting whether the Colonel himself could have written it better, had the task been
confided to his hands. When Faddle came, he read it
to him with much pride, and then committed it to his
custody. After that they went out and ate their dinner
at Bolivia's with much satisfaction, but still with a
bearing of deep melancholy, as was proper on such
an occasion.

## CHAPTER XXXVI

### TOM TRINGLE GETS AN ANSWER

FADDLE as he went down into the country made up his mind that the law which required such letters to be delivered by hand was an absurd law. The post would have done just as well, and would have saved a great deal of trouble. These gloomy thoughts were occasioned by a conviction that he could not carry himself easily or make himself happy among such 'howling swells' as these Alburys. If they should invite him to the house the matter would be worse that way than the other. He had no confidence in his dress coat, which he was aware had been damaged by nocturnal orgies. It is all very well to tell a fellow to be as 'big a swell' as anybody else, as Tom had told him. But Faddle acknowledged to himself the difficulty of acting up to such advice. Even the eyes of Colonel Stubbs turned upon him after receipt of the letter would oppress him.

Nevertheless he must do his best, and he took a gig at the station nearest to Albury. He was careful to carry his bag with him, but still he lived in hope that he would be able to return to London the same day. When he found himself within the lodges of Stalham Park he could hardly keep himself from shivering, and, when he asked the footman at the door whether Colonel Stubbs was there, he longed to be told that Colonel Stubbs had gone away on the previous day to some—he did not care what—distant part of the globe. But Colonel Stubbs had not gone away. Colonel Stubbs was in the house.

Our friend the Colonel had not suffered as Tom had suffered since his rejection;—but nevertheless he had been much concerned. He had set his heart upon Ayala before he had asked her, and could not bring himself to change his heart because she had refused him. He had gone down to Aldershot and had performed his duties, abstaining for the present from

repeating his offer. The offer of course must be
repeated, but as to the when, the where, and the how,
he had not as yet made up his mind. Then Tom
Tringle had come to him at Aldershot communicating
to him the fact that he had a rival;—and also the
other fact that the other rival like himself had hitherto been unsuccessful. It seemed improbable to him
that such a girl as Ayala should attach herself to
such a man as her cousin Tom. But nevertheless he
was uneasy. He regarded Tom Tringle as a miracle
of wealth, and felt certain that the united efforts of
the whole family would be used to arrange the match.
Ayala had refused him also, and therefore, up to the
present moment, the chances of the other man were
no better than his own. When Tom left him at
Aldershot he hardly remembered that Tom knew
nothing of his secret, whereas Tom had communicated
to him his own. It never for a moment occurred to
him that Tom would quarrel with him; although
he had seen that the poor fellow had been disgusted
because he had refused to write the letter.

On Christmas Eve he had gone down to Stalham, and there he had remained discussing the
matter of his love with Lady Albury. To no one else
in the house had the affair been mentioned, and by
Sir Harry he was supposed to remain there only for
the sake of the hunting. With Sir Harry he was of all
guests the most popular, and thus it came to pass
that his prolonged presence at Stalham was not
matter of special remark. Much of his time he did
devote to hunting, but there were half hours devoted
in company with Lady Albury to Ayala's perfection
and Ayala's obstinacy.

Lady Albury was almost inclined to think that
Ayala should be given up. Married ladies seldom
estimate even the girls they like best at their full
value. It seems to such a one as Lady Albury almost
a pity that such a one as Colonel Stubbs should
waste his energy upon anything so insignificant as
Ayala Dormer. The speciality of the attraction is

of course absent to the woman, and unless she has considered the matter so far as to be able to clothe her thoughts in male vestments, as some women do, she cannot understand the longing that is felt for so small a treasure. Lady Albury thought that young ladies were very well, and that Ayala was very well among young ladies; but Ayala in getting Colonel Stubbs for a husband would, as Lady Albury thought, have received so much more than her desert that she was now almost inclined to be angry with the Colonel. 'My dear friend,' he said to her one day, 'you might as well take it for granted. I shall go after my princess with all the energy which a princess merits.'

'The question is whether she be a princess,' said Lady Albury.

'Allow me to say that that is a point on which I cannot admit a doubt. She is a princess to me, and just at present I must be regarded as the only judge in the matter.'

'She shall be a goddess, if you please,' said Lady Albury.

'Goddess, princess, pink, or pearl;—any name you please supposed to convey perfection shall be the same to me. It may be that she is in truth no better, or more lovely, or divine, than many another young lady who is at the present moment exercising the heart of many another gentleman. You know enough of the world to be aware that every Jack has his Gill. She is my Gill, and that's an end of it.'

'I hope then that she may be your Gill.'

'And, in order that she may, you must have her here again. I should absolutely not know how to go to work were I to find myself in the presence of Aunt Dosett in Kingsbury Crescent.' In answer to this Lady Albury assured him that she would be quite willing to have the girl again at Stalham if it could be managed. She was reminding him, however, how difficult it had been on a previous occasion to overcome the scruples of Mrs. Dosett, when a servant

brought in word to Colonel Stubbs that there was
a man in the hall desirous of seeing him immediately
on particular business. Then the servant presented
our friend Faddle's card.

MR. SAMUEL FADDLE,

1, Badminton Gardens.

'Yes, Sir;' said the servant. 'He says he has a
letter which he must put into your own particular
hands.'

'That looks like a bailiff,' said Lady Albury,
laughing. Colonel Stubbs, declaring that he had no
special reason to be afraid of any bailiff, left the room
and went down into the hall.

At Stalham the real hall of the house was used as a
billiard-room, and here, leaning against the billiard
table, the Colonel found poor Faddle. When a man
is compelled by some chance circumstance to address
another man whom he does not know, and whom by
inspection he feels he shall never wish to know, he
always hardens his face, and sometimes also his
voice. So it was with the Colonel when he looked at
Faddle. A word he did say, not in words absolutely
uncivil, as to the nature of the business in hand.
Then Faddle, showing his emotion by a quaver in his
voice, suggested that as the matter was one of extreme
delicacy some more private apartment might be provided. Upon this Stubbs led the way into a little
room which was for the most part filled with hunting-
gear, and offered the stranger one of the three chairs
which it contained. Faddle sat down, finding himself so compelled, though the Colonel still remained
standing, and then extracted the fatal epistle from
his pocket. 'Colonel Stubbs,' said he, handing up the
missive, 'I am directed by my friend, Mr. Thomas
Tringle, junior, to put this letter into your own hand.
When you have read it I shall be ready to consult
with you as to its contents.' These few words he had
learnt by heart on his journey down, having practised them continually.

The Colonel took the letter, and turning to the window read it with his back to the visitor. He read it twice from beginning to end in order that he might have time to resolve whether he would laugh aloud at both Faddle and Tringle, or whether it might not be better to endeavour to soften the anger of poor Tom by a message which should be at any rate kindly worded. 'This is from my friend, Tom Tringle,' he said.

'From Mr. Thomas Tringle, junior,' said Faddle, proudly.

'So I perceive. I am sorry to think that he should be in so much trouble. He is one of the best fellows I know, and I am really grieved that he should be unhappy. This, you know, is all nonsense.'

'It is not nonsense at all, Colonel Stubbs.'

'You must allow me to be the judge of that, Mr. Faddle. It is at any rate nonsense to me. He wants me to go somewhere and fight a duel,—which I should not do with any man under any circumstances. Here there is no possible ground for any quarrel whatsoever,—as I will endeavour to explain, myself, to my friend, Mr. Tringle. I shall be sure to write to him at once,—and so I will bid you good afternoon.'

But this did not at all suit poor Faddle after so long a journey. 'I thought it probable that you would write, Colonel Stubbs, and therefore I am prepared to wait. If I cannot be accommodated here I will wait,—will wait elsewhere.'

'That will not be at all necessary. We have a post to London twice a day.'

'You must be aware, Colonel Stubbs, that letters of this sort should not be sent by post.'

'The kind of letter I shall write may be sent by post very well. It will not be bellicose, and therefore there can be no objection.'

'I really think, Colonel Stubbs, that you are making very little of a very serious matter.'

'Mr. Faddle, I really must manage my own affairs after my own way. Would you like a glass of sherry?

If not, I need hardly ask you to stay here any longer.'
Upon that he went out into the billiard-room and
rang the bell. Poor Faddle would have liked the
glass of sherry, but he felt that it would be incom-
patible with the angry dignity which he assumed,
and he left the house without another word or even a
gesture of courtesy. Then he returned to London,
having taken his bag and dress coat all the way to
Stalham for nothing.

Tom's letter was almost too good to be lost, but
there was no one to whom the joke could be made
known except Lady Albury. She, he was sure, would
keep poor Tom's secret as well as his own, and to her
he showed the letter. 'I pity him from the bottom
of my heart,' he said. Lady Albury declared that
the writer of such a letter was too absurd for pity.
'Not at all. Unless he really loved her he wouldn't
have been so enraged. I suppose he does think that
I injured him. He did tell me his story, and I didn't
tell him mine. I can understand it all, though I
didn't imagine he was such a fool as to invite me to
travel all round the world because of the harsh laws
of Great Britain. Nevertheless, I shall write to him
quite an affectionate letter, remembering that,
should I succeed myself, he will be my first cousin
by marriage.'

Before he went to bed that night he wrote his
letter, and the reader may as well see the whole
correspondence:—

' MY DEAR TRINGLE,

' If you will think of it all round you will see that
you have got no cause of quarrel with me any more
than I have with you. If it be the case that we are
both attached to your cousin, we must abide her
decision whether it be in favour of either of us, or,
as may be too probably the case, equally adverse to
both of us. If I understand your letter rightly, you
think that I behaved unfairly when I did not tell you
of my own affairs upon hearing yours from your own

lips. Why should I? Why should I have been held
to be constrained to tell my secret because you, for
your own sake, had told me yours? Had I been
engaged to your cousin,—which I regret to say is
very far from the case,—I should have told you,
naturally. I should have regarded the matter as
settled, and should have acquainted you with a fact
which would have concerned you. But as such was
not a fact, I was by no means bound to tell you how
my affairs stood. This ought to be clear to you, and
I hope will be when you have read what I say.

'I may as well go on to declare that under no
circumstances should I fight a duel with you. If I
thought I had done wrong in the matter I would beg
your pardon. I can't do that as it is,—though I am
most anxious to appease you,—because I have done
you no wrong.

'Pray forget your animosity,—which is in truth un-
founded,—and let us be friends as we were before.

'Yours very sincerely,    JONATHAN STUBBS.'

Faddle reached London the evening before the
Colonel's letter, and again dined with his friend at
Bolivia's. At first they were both extremely angry,
acerbating each other's wrath. Now that he was safe
back in London Faddle thought that he would have
enjoyed an evening among the 'swells' of Stalham,
and felt himself to be injured by the inhospitable
treatment he had received—'after going all the way
down there, hardly to be asked to sit down!'

'Not asked to sit down!'

'Well, yes, I was;—on a miserable cane-bottomed
chair in a sort of cupboard. And he didn't sit down.
You may call them swells, but I think your Colonel
Stubbs is a very vulgar sort of fellow. When I told
him the post isn't the proper thing for such a letter,
he only laughed. I suppose he doesn't know what
is the kind of thing among gentlemen.'

'I should think he does know,' said Tom.

'Then why doesn't he act accordingly? Would you

believe it; he never so much as asked me whether I
had a mouth on. It was just luncheon time, too.'

'I suppose they lunch late.'

'They might have asked me. I shouldn't have
taken it. He did say something about a glass of
sherry, but it was in that sort of tone which tells a
fellow that he is expected not to take it. And then he
pretended to laugh. I could see that he was shaking
in his shoes at the idea of having to fight. He go to
the torrid zone! He would much rather go to a
police office if he thought that there was any fighting
on hand. I should dust his jacket with a stick if I
were you.'

Later on in the evening Tom declared that this
was what he would do, but, before he came to that,
a third bottle of Signor Bolivia's champagne had
been made to appear. The evening passed between
them not without much enjoyment. On the opening
of that third cork the wine was declared to be less
excellent than what had gone before, and Signor
Bolivia was evoked in person. A gentleman named
Walker, who looked after the establishment, made
his appearance, and with many smiles, having been
induced to swallow a bumper of the compound himself, declared, with a knowing shake of the head and
an astute twinkle of the eye, that the wine was not
equal to the last. He took a great deal of trouble, he
assured them, to import an article which could not be
surpassed, if it could be equalled, in London, always
visiting Epernay* himself once a year for the purpose
of going through the wine-vaults. Let him do what
he would an inferior bottle,—or, rather, a bottle
somewhat inferior,—would sometimes make its way
into his cellar. Would Mr. Tringle let him have the
honour of drawing another cork, so that the exact
amount of difference might be ascertained? Tom
gave his sanction; the fourth cork was drawn; and
Mr. Walker, sitting down and consuming the wine
with his customers, was enabled to point out to a
hair's breadth the nature and the extent of the varia-

tion. Tringle still thought that the difference was considerable. Faddle was, on the whole, inclined to agree with Signor Bolivia. It need hardly be said that the four bottles were paid for,—or rather scored against Tringle, who at the present time had a little account at the establishment.

'Show a fellar fellar's letters morrer.' Such or something like it was Faddle's last request to his friend as they bade each other farewell for the night in Pall Mall. But Faddle was never destined to see the Colonel's epistle. On his attempting to let himself in at Badminton Gardens, he was kidnapped by his father in his night-shirt and dressing-gown; and was sent out of London on the following morning by long sea down to Aberdeen,* whither he was intrusted to the charge of a stern uncle. Our friend Tom saw nothing more of his faithful friend till years had rolled over both their heads.

By the morning post, while Tom was still lying sick with headache,—for even with Signor Bolivia's wine the pulling of many corks is apt to be dangerous, —there came the letter from the Colonel. Bad as Tom was, he felt himself constrained to read it at once, and learned that neither the torrid zone or Arctic circle would require his immediate attendance. He was very sick, and perhaps, therefore, less high in courage than on the few previous days. Partly, perhaps, from that cause, but partly, also, from the Colonel's logic, he did find that his wrath was somewhat abated. Not but what it was still present to his mind that if two men loved the same girl as ardently, as desperately, as eternally as he loved Ayala, the best thing for them would be to be put together like the Kilkenny cats,* till whatever remnant should be left of one might have its chance with the young lady. He still thought that it would be well that they should fight to the death, but a glimmering of light fell upon his mind as to the Colonel's abnegation of all treason in the matter. 'I suppose it wasn't to be expected that he should tell,' he said to himself.

'Perhaps I shouldn't have told in the same place. But as to forgetting animosity that is out of the question! How is a man to forget his animosity when two men want to marry the same girl?'

About three o'clock on that day he dressed himself, and sat waiting for Faddle to come to him. He knew how anxious his friend would be to see the Colonel's letter. But Faddle by this time had passed the Nore, and had added sea-sickness to his other maladies. Faddle came to him no more, and the tedious hours of the afternoon wore themselves away in his lodgings till he found his solitude to be almost more unbearable than his previous misfortunes. At last came the time when he must go out for his dinner. He did not dare to attempt the Mountaineers. And as for Bolivia, Bolivia with his corks, and his eating-house, and his vintages, was abominable to him. About eight o'clock he slunk into a quiet little house on the north side of Oxford Street, and there had two mutton chops, some buttered toast, and some tea. As he drank his tea he told himself that on the morrow he would go back to his mother at Merle Park, and get from her such consolation as might be possible.

## CHAPTER XXXVII

### GERTRUDE IS UNSUCCESSFUL

IT was now the middle of January, and Gertrude Tringle had received no reply from her lover to the overture which she had made him. Nor, indeed, had she received any letter from him since that to which this overture had been a reply. It was now two months since her proposition had been made, and during that time her anger had waxed very hot against Mr. Houston. After all, it might be a question whether Mr. Houston was worth all the trouble which she, with her hundred thousand pounds, was taking on his behalf. She did not like the idea of abandoning

him, because, by doing so, she would seem to yield
to her father. Having had a young man of her own,
it behoved her to stick to her young man in spite of
her parents. But what is a girl to do with a lover
who, at the end of two months, has made no reply
to an offer from herself that he should run away with
her, and take her to Ostend? She was in this frame
of mind when, lo and behold, she found her own letter,
still inclosed in her own envelope,—but opened, and
thrust in among her father's papers* It was evident
enough that the letter had never passed from out of
the house. There had been treachery on the part of
some servant;—or perhaps her father might have
condescended to search the little box;—or, more
probable still, Augusta had betrayed her! Then
she reflected that she had communicated her purpose
to her sister, that her sister had abstained from any
questions since the letter had been written, and that
her sister, therefore, no doubt, was the culprit.
There, however, was the letter, which had never
reached her lover's hands, and, as a matter of course,
her affections returned with all their full ardour to
the unfortunate ill-used man. That her conduct was
now watched would, she thought, be a matter of
course. Her father knew her purpose, and, like stern
parents in general, would use all his energies to
thwart it. Sir Thomas had, in truth, thought but
little about the matter since he had first thrust the
letter away. Tom's troubles, and the disgrace
brought by them upon Travers and Treason generally,
had so occupied his mind that he cared but little for
Gertrude and her lover. But Gertrude had no doubt
that she was closely watched, and in these circumstances was driven to think how she could best use
her wits so as to countermine her father. To run
away from Queen's Gate would, she thought, be
more difficult, and more uncomfortable, than to
perform the same operation at Merle Park. It was
intended that the family should remain in the
country, at any rate, till Easter, and Gertrude re-

solved that there might yet be time for another effort
before Easter should be past, if only she could avoid
those hundred Argus eyes,* which were, no doubt,
fixed upon her from all sides.

She prepared another letter to her lover, which
she addressed to him at his club in London. In this
she told him nothing of her former project, except
that a letter written by her in November had fallen
into the hands of enemies. Then she gave him to
understand that there was need of the utmost caution; but that, if adequate caution were used, she did
not doubt they might succeed. She said nothing
about her great project, but suggested to him that
he should run down into Sussex, and meet her at a
certain spot indicated, outside the Park palings, half-
an-hour after dusk. It might be, she said, impossible
that the meeting should be effected, but she thought
that she could so manage as to leave the house un-
watched at the appointed hour. With the object of
being especially safe she began and concluded her
letter without any names, and then managed to
deposit it herself in the box of the village post-
office.

Houston, when he received this letter, at once
made up his mind that he would not be found on the
outer side of the Park palings on the evening named.
He told himself that he was too old for the romance
of love-making, and that should he be received, when
hanging about in the dark, by some custodian with a
cudgel, he would have nothing to thank but his own
folly. He wrote back therefore to say that he regarded the outside of the Park palings as indiscreet,
but that he would walk up through the lodge-gate to
the house at three o'clock in the afternoon of the day
named, and he would take it as an additional mark
of her favour if she would meet him on the road.
Gertrude had sent him a mysterious address; he was
to direct the letter to 'O.P.Q., Post Office, Hastings,'
and she was prepared to hire a country boy to act as
Love's messenger on the occasion. But of this in-

struction Frank took no notice, addressing the letter to Merle Park in the usual way.

Gertrude received her letter without notice from any one. On that occasion Argus, with all his eyes, was by chance asleep. She was very angry with her lover,—almost determined to reject him altogether, almost disposed to yield to her angry parents and look out for some other lover who might be accepted in better part; but still, when the day came she put on her hat and walked down the road towards the lodge.

As Fortune had it,—Fortune altogether unfavourable to those perils for which her soul was longing,— no one watched her, no one dogged her steps, no one took any notice of her, till she met Frank Houston when he had passed about a hundred yards through the gates. 'And so you have come,' she said.

'Oh, yes; I have come. I was sure to come when I said so. No man is more punctual than I am in these matters. I should have come before,—only I did not get your letter.'

'Oh, Frank!'

'Well, my darling. You are looking uncommonly well, and I am so glad to see you. How are they all?'

'Frank!'

'What is it?'

'Oh, Frank, what are we to do?'

'The governor will give way at last, I should say.'

'Never;—that is while we are as we are now. If we were married——'

'Ah,—I wish we were! Wouldn't it be nice?'

'Do you really think so?'

'Of course I do. I'm ready to-morrow for the matter of that.'

'But could you do something great?'

'Something great! As to earning my bread, you mean? I do not think I could do that. I didn't turn my hand to it early enough.'

'I wasn't thinking of—your bread.'

'You said,—could I do something great?'

'Frank, I wrote you a letter and described it all. How I got the courage to do it I do not know. I feel as though I could not bring myself to say it now. I wonder whether you would have the courage.'

'I should say so. I don't know quite what sort of thing it is; but I generally have pluck enough for anything in a common way.'

'This is something in an uncommon way.'

'I couldn't break open Travers and Treason, and get at the safe, or anything in that way.'

'It is another sort of safe of which you must break the lock, Frank; another treasure you must steal. Do you not understand me?'

'Not in the least.'

'There is Tom,' said Gertrude. 'He is always wandering about the place now like a ghost. Let us go back to the gate.' Then Frank turned. 'You heard, I suppose, of that dreadful affair about the policeman.'

'There was a row, I was told.'

'Did you feel that the family were disgraced?'

'Not in the least. He had to pay five shillings,— hadn't he,—for telling a policeman to go about his business?'

'He was—locked up,' said Gertrude, solemnly.

'It's just the same. Nobody thinks anything about that kind of thing. Now, what is it I have got to do? We had better turn back again as soon as we can, because I must go up to the house before I go.'

'You will?'

'Certainly. I will not leave it to your father to say that I came skulking about the place, and was ashamed to show my face. That would not be the way to make him give you your money.'

'I am sure he'd give it,—if we were once married.'

'If we were married without having it assured beforehand we should look very blue if things went wrong afterwards.'

'I asked you whether you had courage.'

'Courage enough, I think, when my body is concerned; but I am an awful coward in regard to money. I wouldn't mind hashed mutton and baked potatoes for myself, but I shouldn't like to see you eating them, dearest, after all the luxuries to which you have been accustomed.'

'I should think nothing of it.'

'Did you ever try? I never came absolutely to hashed mutton, but I've known how very uncomfortable it is not to be able to pay for the hot joints. I'm willing to own honestly that married life without an income would not have attractions for me.'

'But if it was sure to come?'

'Ah, then indeed,—with you! I have just said how nice it would be.'

'Have you ever been at Ostend?' she asked, suddenly.

'Ostend. Oh, yes. There was a man there who used to cheat horribly at écarté. He did me out of nearly a hundred pounds one night.'

'But there's a clergyman there, I'm told.'

'I don't think this man was in orders. But he might have been. Parsons come out in so many shapes! This man called himself a count. It was seven years ago.'

'I am speaking of to-day.'

'I've not been there since.'

'Would you like to go there,—with me?'

'It isn't a nice sort of place, I should say, for a honeymoon. But you shall choose. When we are married you shall go where you like.'

'To be married!' she exclaimed.

'Married at Ostend! Would your mother like that?'

'Mother! Oh, dear!'

'I'll be shot if I know what you're after, Gertrude. If you've got anything to say you'd better speak out. I want to go up to the house now.'

They had now taken one or two turns between the lodge and a point in the road from which the house could be observed, and at which Tom could still be

seen wandering about, thinking no doubt of Ayala.
Here Frank stopped as though determined not to
turn to the lodge again. It was wonderful to
Gertrude that he should not have understood what
she had already said. When he talked of her mother
going with them to the Ostend marriage she was
almost beside herself. This lover of hers was a man
of the world and must have heard of elopements.
But now had come a time in which she must be plain,
unless she made up her mind to abandon her plan
altogether. 'Frank,' she said, 'if you were to run
away with me, then we could be married at Ostend.'

'Run away with you!'

'It wouldn't be the first time that such a thing has
been done.'

'The commonest thing in the world, my dear,
when a girl has got her money in her own hands.
Nothing I should like so much.'

'Money! It's always money. It's nothing but the
money, I believe.'

'That's unkind, Gertrude.'

'Ain't you unkind? You won't do anything I ask.'

'My darling, that hashed mutton and those baked
potatoes are too clear before my eyes.'

'You think of nothing, I believe, but your dinner.'

'I think, unfortunately, of a great many other
things. Hashed mutton is simply symbolical. Under
the head of hashed mutton I include poor lodgings,
growlers when we get ourselves asked to eat a dinner
at somebody's table, limited washing-bills, table-
napkins rolled up in their dirt every day for a week,
antimacassars to save the backs of the chairs, a
picture of you darning my socks while I am reading
a newspaper hired at a halfpenny from the public-
house round the corner, a pint of beer in the pewter
between us,—and perhaps two babies in one cradle
because we can't afford to buy a second.'

'Don't, Sir.'

'In such an emergency I am bound to give you the
advantage both of my experience and imagination.'

'Experience!'

'Not about the cradles! That is imagination. My darling, it won't do. You and I have not been brought up to make ourselves happy on a very limited income.'

'Papa would be sure to give us the money,' she said, eagerly.

'In such a matter as this, where your happiness is concerned, my dear, I will trust no one.'

'My happiness!'

'Yes, my dear, your happiness! I am quite willing to own the truth. I am not fitted to make you happy, if I were put upon the hashed mutton régime as I have described to you. I will not run the risk,—for your sake.'

'For your own, you mean,' she aid.

'Nor for my own, if you wish me to add that also.'

Then they walked up towards the house for some little way in silence. 'What is it you intend, then?' she asked.

'I will ask your father once again.'

'He will simply turn you out of the house,' she said. Upon this he shrugged his shoulders, and they walked on to the hall-door in silence.

Sir Thomas was not at Merle Park, nor was he expected home that evening. Frank Houston could only therefore ask for Lady Tringle, and her he saw together with Mr. and Mrs. Traffick. In presence of them all nothing could be said of love affairs; and, after sitting for half-an-hour, during which he was not entertained with much cordiality, he took his leave, saying that he would do himself the honour of calling on Sir Thomas in the City. While he was in the drawing-room Gertrude did not appear. She had retired to her room, and was there resolving that Frank Houston was not such a lover as would justify a girl in breaking her heart for him.

And Frank as he went to town brought his mind to the same way of thinking. The girl wanted something romantic to be done, and he was not disposed

to do anything romantic for her. He was not in the
least angry with her, acknowledging to himself that
she had quite as much a right to her way of looking
at things as he had to his. But he felt almost sure
that the Tringle alliance must be regarded as impossible. If so, should he look out for another heiress,
or endeavour to enjoy life, stretching out his little
income as far as might be possible;—or should he
assume altogether a new character, make a hero of
himself, and ask Imogene Docimer to share with him
a little cottage in whatever might be the cheapest
spot to be found in the civilised parts of Europe? If
it was to be hashed mutton and a united cradle, he
would prefer Imogene Docimer to Gertrude Tringle
for his companion.

But there was still open to him the one further
chance with Sir Thomas; and this chance he could
try with the comfortable feeling that he might be
almost indifferent as to what Sir Thomas might say.
To be prepared for either lot is very self-assuring
when any matter of difficulty has to be taken in hand.
On arriving at the house in Lombard Street he soon
found himself ushered once more into Sir Thomas's
presence. 'Well, Mr. Houston, what can I do for
you to-day?' asked the man of business, with a
pleasant smile.

'It is the old story, Sir Thomas.'

'Don't you think, Mr. Houston, that there is
something,—a little,—unmanly shall I call it, in
coming so often about the same thing?'

'No, Sir Thomas, I do not. I think my conduct
has been manly throughout.'

'Weak, perhaps, would have been a better word.
I do not wish to be uncourteous, and I will therefore
withdraw unmanly. Is it not weak to encounter so
many refusals on the same subject?'

'I should feel myself to have been very strong if
after so many refusals I were to be successful at
last.'

'There is not the least chance of it.'

'Why should there be no chance if your daughter's happiness depends upon it?'

'There is no chance, because I do not believe that my daughter's happiness does depend upon it. She is foolish, and has made a foolish proposition to you.'

'What proposition?' asked Houston, in surprise, having heard nothing of that intercepted letter.

'That journey to Ostend, with the prospect of finding a good-natured clergyman in the town! I hardly think you would be fool enough for that.'

'No, Sir Thomas, I should not do that. I should think it wrong.' This he said quite gravely, asking no questions; but was very much at a loss to know where Sir Thomas had got his information.

'I am sure you would think it foolish: and it would be foolish. I pledge you my word, that were you to do such a thing I should not give you a shilling. I should not let my girl starve; but I should save her from suffering in such a manner as to let you have no share of the sustenance I provided for her.'

'There is no question of that kind,' said Frank, angrily.

'I hope not;—only as I know that the suggestion has been made I have thought it well to tell you what would be my conduct if it were carried out.'

'It will not be carried out by me,' said Frank.

'Very well; I am glad to hear it. To tell the truth, I never thought that you would run the risk. A gentleman of your sort, when he is looking for a wife with money, likes to have the money quite certain.'

'No doubt,' said Frank, determined not to be browbeaten.

'And now, Mr. Houston, let me say one word more to you and then we may part, as I hope, good friends. I do not mean my daughter Gertrude to marry any man such as you are;—by that I mean an idle gentleman without means. Should she do so in my teeth she would have to bear the punishment of sharing that poor gentleman's idleness and poverty. While I lived she would not be allowed absolutely

to want, and when I died there would be some trifle
for her, sufficient to keep the wolf from the door.
But I give you my solemn word and honour that she
shall never be the means of supplying wealth and
luxury to such a husband as you would be. I have
better purposes for my hard-earned money. Now,
good-day.' With that he rose from his chair and put
out his hand. Frank rose also from his chair, took
the hand that was offered him, and stepped out of
Travers and Treason into Lombard Street, with no
special desire to shake the dust off his feet as he did
so. He felt that Sir Thomas had been reasonable,—
and he felt also that Gertrude Tringle would perhaps
have been dear at the money.

Two or three days afterwards he despatched the
following little note to poor Gertrude at Merle Park:—

'DEAR GERTRUDE,

'I have seen your father again, and found him to be
absolutely obdurate. I am sure he is quite in earnest
when he tells me that he will not give his daughter to
an impoverished idle fellow such as I am. Who shall
say that he is wrong? I did not dare to tell him so,
anxious as I was that he should change his purpose.

'I feel myself bound in honour, believing, as I do,
that he is quite resolved in his purpose, to release you
from your promise. I should feel that I was only
doing you an injury were I to ask you to be bound by
an engagement which could not, at any rate for many
years, be brought to a happy termination.

'As we may part as sincere friends I hope you will
consent to keep the little token of my regard which
I gave you.

'FRANK HOUSTON.'

## CHAPTER XXXVIII

### FRANK HOUSTON IS PENITENT

' AND now the Adriatic's free to wed another,"said Houston to himself, as he put himself into a cab, and had himself carried to his club. There he wrote that valedictory letter to Gertrude which is given at the end of the last chapter. Had he reason to complain of his fate, or to rejoice? He had looked the question of an establishment full in the face,—an establishment to be created by Sir Thomas Tringle's money, to be shared with Sir Thomas Tringle's daughter, and had made up his mind to accept it, although the prospects were not, as he told himself, 'altogether rosy.' When he first made up his mind to marry Gertrude,—on condition that Gertrude should bring with her, at any rate, not less than three thousand a-year,—he was quite aware that he would have to give up all his old ways of life, and all his little pleasures. He would become son-in-law to Sir Thomas Tringle, with a comfortable house to live in; with plenty to eat and drink, and, probably, a horse or two to ride. If he could manage things at their best, perhaps he might be able to settle himself at Pau, or some other place of the kind, so as to be as far away as possible from Tringle influences. But his little dinners at one club, his little rubbers of whist at the other club, his evenings at the opera, the pleasant smiles of the ladies, whom he loved in a general way,—these would be done with for ever! Earn his own bread! Why, he was going to earn his bread, and that in a most disagreeable manner. He would set up an establishment, not because such an establishment would have any charms for him, but because he was compelled by lack of money to make some change in his present manner of life. And yet the time had been when he had looked forward to a marriage as the happiest thing that could befall him. As far as his nature could love, he had loved Imogene

Docimer. There had come a glimpse upon him of something better than the little dinners and the little rubbers. There had been a prospect of an income,—not ample, as would have been that forthcoming from Sir Thomas,—but sufficient for a sweet and modest home, in which he thought that it would have sufficed for his happiness to paint a few pictures, and read a few books, and to love his wife and children. Even as to that there had been a doubt. There was a regret as to the charms of London life. But, nevertheless, he had made up his mind,—and she, without any doubt, had made up hers. Then that wicked uncle had died, and was found to have expended on his own pursuits the money which was to have been left to his nephew. Upon that there was an explanation between Frank and Imogene; and it was agreed that their engagement should be over, while a doubtful and dangerous friendship was to be encouraged between them.

Such was the condition of things when Frank first met Gertrude Tringle at Rome, now considerably more than twelve months since. When Gertrude had first received his proposition favourably he had written to Imogene a letter in that drolling spirit common to him, in which he declared his purpose ;—or rather, not his purpose, but his untoward fate, should the gods be unkind to him. She had answered him after the same fashion, saying, that in regard to his future welfare she hoped that the gods would prove unkind. But had he known how to read all that her letter expressed between the lines, he would have perceived that her heart was more strongly moved than his own. Since that time he had learned the lesson. There had been a letter or two ; and then there had been that walk in the wood on the Italian side of the Tyrolese Alps. The reader may remember how he was hurried away in the diligence for Innspruck, because it was considered that his further sojourn in the same house with Imogene was dangerous. He had gone, and even as he went had attempted to make a joke of the whole affair. But it

had not been quite a joke to him even then. There
was Imogene's love and Imogene's anger,—and together with these an aversion towards the poor girl
whom he intended to marry,—which became the
stronger the more strongly he was convinced both
of Imogene's love and of her anger.

Nevertheless, he persevered,—not with the best
success, as has already been told. Now, as he left the
house in Lombard Street, and wrote what was intended to be his last epistle to Gertrude, he was
driven again to think of Miss Docimer. Indeed, he
had in his pocket, as he sat at his club, a little note
which he had lately received from that lady, which,
in truth, had disturbed him much when he made
his last futile efforts at Merle Park and in Lombard
Street. The little note was as follows:—

'DEAR FRANK,

'One little friendly word in spite of our storm on the
Tyrolese hill-side! If Miss Tringle is to be the arbiter
of your fate;—why, then, let there be an end of everything between us. I should not care to be called upon
to receive such a Mrs. Frank Houston as a dear
friend. But if Tringle père should at the last moment
prove hard-hearted, then let me see you again.—
Yours,                                                       'I.'

With this letter in his pocket he had gone down to
Merle Park, determined to put an end to the Tringle
affair in one way or the other. His duty, as he had
planned it to himself, would not be altered by
Imogene's letter; but if that duty should become impracticable,—why, then, it would be open to him to
consider whatever Imogene might have to say to him.

The Docimers were now in London, where it was
their custom to live during six months of the year;
but Houston had not been at their house since he had
parted from them in the Tyrol. He had spent but
little of his time in London since the autumn, and,
when there, had not been anxious to see people who
had, at any rate, treated him somewhat roughly.

But now it would be necessary that he should answer
Imogene's letter. What should be the nature of such
answer he certainly had not as yet decided; nor could
he have decided before those very convincing assurances of Sir Thomas Pringle. That matter was at
any rate over, and now the 'Adriatic might wed
another,'—if the Adriatic thought well to do so.
The matter, however, was one which required a good
deal of consideration. He gave to it ten minutes of
intense thought, during which he consumed a cup of
coffee and a cigarette; and then, throwing away the
burnt end of the paper, he hurried into the morning-
room, and wrote to the lady as follows:—

' DEAR IMOGENE,

'You will not have to press to your bosom as my
wife the second daughter of Sir Thomas Tringle,
Bart. The high honour of that alliance has at last
been refused by him in very plain language. Had she
become Mrs. Frank Houston, I do not doubt but you
would have done your duty to your own cousin.
That lot, however, has not been written for me in the
Book of Fates. The father is persistent in looking
upon me as an idle profligate adventurer; and though
he has been kind enough to hint more than once that
it might be possible for me to achieve the young lady,
he has succeeded in convincing me that I never
should achieve anything beyond the barren possession of her beauty. A wife and family on my present
very moderate income would be burdensome; and,
therefore, with infinite regrets, I have bade adieu to
Miss Tringle.

'I have not hitherto been to see either you or your
brother or Mrs. Docimer because I have been altogether unaware whether you or your brother or Mrs.
Docimer would be glad to see me. As you say yourself, there was a storm on the Tyrolese hill-side,—in
which there was more than one wind blowing at the
same time. I do not find fault with anybody,—
perhaps a storm was needed to clear the air. But I

hate storms. I do not pretend to be a very grand
fellow, but I do endeavour not to be disagreeable.
Your brother, if you remember, was a little hard.
But, in truth, I say this only to account for my
apparent incivility.

'And, perhaps, with another object;—to gain a
little time before I plunge into the stern necessity of
answering all that you say in your very comprehensive letter of five lines. The first four lines I have
answered. There will be no such Mrs. Frank Houston
as that suggested. And then, as to the last line. Of
course, you will see me again, and that very speedily.
So it would seem that the whole letter is answered.

'But yet it is not answered. There is so much in
it that whole sheets would not answer it. A quire of
notepaper stuffed full would hardly contain all that
I might find to say in answer to it,—on one side and
the other. Nay, I might fill as many reams of folio
as are required for a three-volume novel. And then I
might call it by one of two names, "The Doubts of
Frank Houston," or "The Constancy of Imogene
Docimer,"—as I should at last bring my story to one
ending or the other. But the novel would contain
that fault which is so prevalent in the novels of the
present day. The hero would be a very namby-
pamby sort of a fellow, whereas the heroine would
be too perfect for human nature.

'The hero would be always repeating to himself a
certain line out of a Latin poet,*which, of all lines, is
the most heart-breaking:—

> The better course I see and know;—
> The worser one is where I go.

But then in novels the most indifferent hero comes
out right at last. Some god comes out of a theatrical
cloud*and leaves the poor devil ten thousand a-year
and a title. He isn't much of a hero when he does go
right under such inducements, but he suffices for the
plot, and everything is rose-coloured. I would be
virtuous at a much cheaper rate;—if only a young
man with his family might have enough to eat and

drink. What is your idea of the lowest income at which a prudent,—say not idiotically-quixotic hero,—might safely venture to become heroic?

'Now I have written to you a long letter, and think that I have indicated to you the true state of my feelings. Whatever may turn up I do not think I shall go fortune-hunting again. If half-a-million in female hands were to throw itself at my head, there is no saying whether I might not yield. But I do not think that I shall again make inquiry, as to the amount of booty supposed to be within the walls of a city, and then sit down to besiege the city with regular lines of approach. It is a disgusting piece of work. I do not say but what I can lie, and did lie foully on the last siege operation; but I do not like it. And then to be told that one is unmanly by the father, and a coward by the young lady, as occurred to me in this affair, is disheartening. They were both right, though I repudiated their assertions. This might be borne as a prelude to success; but, as part of a failure, it is disgusting. At the present moment I am considering what economy might effect as to a future bachelor life, and am meditating to begin with a couple of mutton chops and half-a-pint of sherry for my dinner to-day. I know I shall break down and have a woodcock and some champagne.

' I will come to you about three on Sunday. If you can manage that your brother should go out and make his calls, and your sister attend divine service in the afternoon, it would be a comfort.

'Your always,       F. HOUSTON.'

It was a long rambling letter, without a word in it of solid clearly-expressed meaning; but Imogene, as she read it, understood very well its real purport. She understood more than its purport, for she could see by it,—more clearly than the writer did himself,—how far her influence over the man had been restored, and how far she might be able to restore it. But was it well that she should regain her influence? Her influence regained would simply mean a renewed engagement. No doubt the storm on the hill-side had come from the violence of true love on her part! No doubt her heart had been outraged by the idea that he should give himself up to another woman after all that had passed between them. She had been devoted to him altogether; but yet she had been taught by him to regard her love as a passion which of its nature contained something of the ridiculous. He had never ceased gently to laugh at himself, even in her presence, because he had subjected himself to her attraction. She had caught up the same spirit,—or at any rate the expression of spirit, —and, deceived by that, he had thought that to relieve herself from the burden of her love would be as easy to her as to him. In making this mistake he had been ignorant of the intrinsic difference in the nature of a man's and of a woman's heart, and had been unaware that that, which to a man at his best can only be a part of his interest in his life's concerns, will to a woman be everything. She had attempted to follow his lead when it did not seem that by doing so she would lose anything. But when the moment of trial came she had not in truth followed his lead at all. She made the attempt, and in making the attempt gave him her permission to go from her; but when she realised the fact that he was gone,—or going,—then she broke down utterly. Then there came these contentions between her and her brother, and that storm on the hill-side.

After that she passed some months of wretchedness. There was no possibility for her to droll away her love. She had taught herself to love the man whether he were good or whether he were bad,— whether he were strong-hearted or whether he were fickle,—and the thing was there present to her, either as a permanent blessing, or, much more probably, a permanent curse. As the months went on she learned, though she never saw Frank himself, that his purpose of marrying Gertrude Tringle was

not likely to be carried out. Then at last she wrote
that comprehensive letter of five lines,—as Houston
had called it. It had been intended to be comprehensive, and did, in fact, contain much more than
it seemed to say. 'If you can bring yourself to return
to me, and to endure whatever inconveniences may
be incidental to your doing so, I hereby declare that
I will do the same; and I declare also that
I can find for myself no other content in the world
except what may come to me from such an agreement between us.' It was this that she said in that
last line, in which she had begged him to come to her,
if at the last moment 'Tringle père' should prove to
be hard-hearted. All troubles of poverty, all the
lingering annoyance of waiting, all her possible
doubts as to his future want of persistency, would be
preferable to the great loss which she found herself
unable to endure.

Yes; it would be very well that both her brother
and her sister-in-law should be absent when he came
to her. To neither of them had she said a word of her
last correspondence;—to neither of them a word of
her renewed hopes. For the objections which might
be raised by either of them would she care little if
she could succeed with Frank. But while that
success was still doubtful it would be well to get at
any rate the assistance of her sister-in-law. On the
Sunday afternoon Mr. Docimer would certainly be
away from the house. It was his custom to go off
among his friends almost immediately after lunch,
and his absence might be counted on as assured. But
with his wife it was different. The project of sending
her to church was quite out of the question. Mrs.
Docimer generally went to church of a Sunday morning, and then always considered herself to have performed the duties of the day. Nor did Imogene like
the idea of this appointment with her lover without a
word spoken about it to her sister-in-law. 'Mary,'
she said, 'Frank Houston is coming here on Sunday.'

'Frank!' exclaimed Mrs. Docimer. 'I thought we

were to consider ourselves as altogether separated from that fortunate youth.'

'I don't see why.'

'Well; he left us not with the kindest possible feelings in the Tyrol; and he has allowed ever so many months to pass by without coming to see us. I asked Mudbury whether we should have him to dinner one day last week, and he said it would be better to let him go his own way.'

'Nevertheless, he is coming here on Sunday.'

'Has he written to you?'

'Yes, he has written to me,—in answer to a line from me. I told him that I wished to see him.'

'Was that wise?'

'Wise or not, I did so.'

'Why should you wish to see him?'

'Am I to tell you the truth or a lie?'

'Not a lie, certainly. I will not ask for the truth if the truth be unpalatable to you.'

'It is unpalatable;—but yet I might as well tell it you. I wrote to ask him to come and see me, because I love him so dearly.'

'Oh, Imogene!'

'It is the truth.'

'Did you tell him so?'

'No; I told him nothing. I merely said, that, if this match was over between him and that girl of Sir Thomas Tringle, then he might come and see me again. That was all that I said. His letter was very much longer, but yet it did not say much. However, he is to come, and I am prepared to renew our engagement should he declare that he is willing to do so.'

'What will Mudbury say?'

'I do not care very much what he says. I do not know that I am bound to care. If I have resolved to entangle myself with a long engagement, and Mr. Houston is willing to do the same, I do not think that my brother should interfere. I am my own mistress, and am dealing altogether with my own happiness.

'Imogene, we have discussed this so often before.'

'Not a doubt; and with such effect that with my permission Frank was enabled to ask this young woman with a lot of money to marry him. Had it been arranged, I should have had no right to find fault with him, however sore of heart I might have been. All that has fallen through, and I consider myself quite entitled to renew my engagement again. I shall not ask him, you may be sure of that.'

'It comes to the same thing, Imogene.'

'Very likely. It often happens that ladies mean that to be expressed which it does not become them to say out loud. So it may be with me on this occasion. Nevertheless, the word, if it have to be spoken, will have to be spoken by him. What I want you to do now is to let me have the drawing-room alone at three o'clock on Sunday. If anything has to be said it will have to be said without witnesses.'

With some difficulty Mrs. Docimer was induced to accede to the request, and to promise that, at any rate for the present, nothing should be said to her husband on the subject.

## CHAPTER XXXIX

### CAPTAIN BATSBY

IN the meantime, poor Ayala, whose days were running on in a very melancholy manner under her aunt's wings in Kingsbury Crescent, was creating further havoc and disturbing the bosom of another lover. At Stalham she had met a certain Captain Batsby, and had there attracted his attention. Captain Batsby had begged her to ride with him on one of those hunting-days, and had offered to give her a lead,—having been at the moment particularly jealous of Colonel Stubbs. On that day both Ayala and Nina had achieved great honour;—but this, to the great satisfaction of Captain Batsby, had not been achieved under the leadership of Colonel Stubbs. Larry Twentyman, long famous among the riding-men of the Ufford and Rufford United Hunt, had been the hero of the hour. Thus Captain Batsby's feelings had been spared, and after that he had imagined that any kindly feelings which Ayala might have had for the Colonel had sunk into abeyance. Then he had sought some opportunity to push himself into Ayala's favour, but hitherto his success in that direction had not been great.

Captain Batsby was regarded by the inhabitants of Stalham as a nuisance,—but as a nuisance which could not be avoided. He was half-brother to Sir Harry, whose mother had married, as her second husband, a certain opulent Mr. Batsby out of Lancashire. They were both dead now, and nothing of them remained but this Captain. He was good-natured, simple, and rich, and in the arrangement of the Albury-cum-Batsby affairs, which took place after the death of Mrs. Batsby, made himself pleasant to everybody concerned. Sir Harry, who certainly had no particular affection for his half-brother, always bore with him on this account; and Lady Albury was equally gracious, mindful of the wisdom of keeping on good terms with a rich relation. It was as yet quite on the cards that the Batsby money might come to some of the Albury scions.

But the Captain was anxious to provide himself with a wife who might be the mother of scions of his own. In fact he had fallen fearfully in love with Ayala, and was quite resolved to ask her to be his wife when he found that she was just on the point of flying from Stalham. He had intended to be quicker in his operations, but had lacked opportunity. On that last hunting-day the Colonel had always been still in his way, and circumstances had never seemed to favour him when he endeavoured to have a few words in private with the young lady. Then she was gone, and he could only learn respecting her that she lived with her aunt, Mrs. Dosett, in Kingsbury Crescent.

'I'm blessed if Benjamin isn't smitten with that girl!' Benjamin was Captain Batsby, and that girl

A.A.—19

was of course Ayala Dormer. The man who blessed
himself was Sir Harry Albury, and the observation
was addressed to his wife. This took place within an
hour of Ayala's departure from Stalham.

'Benjamin in love with Ayala Dormer! I don't
believe a word of it,' said Lady Albury. It was not
surprising that she should not believe it. There was
her special favourite, Colonel Stubbs, infatuated by
the same girl; and, as she was aware, Tom Tringle,
the heir of Travers and Treason, was in the same
melancholy condition. And, after all, according to
her thinking, there was nothing in the girl to justify
all this fury. In her eyes Ayala was pretty, but no
more. She would have declared that Ayala had
neither bearing, nor beauty, nor figure. A bright
eye, a changing colour, and something of vivacity
about her mouth, was all of which Ayala had to
boast. Yet here were certainly the heir of the man of
millions, and that Crichton* of a Colonel, both
knocked off their legs. And now she was told that
Captain Batsby, who always professed himself hard
to please in the matter of young ladies, was in the
same condition. 'Do you mean to say he told you?'
she asked.

'No,' said Sir Harry; 'he is not at all the man to do
that. In such a matter he is sure to have a great
secret, and be sure also to let his secret escape in
every word that he speaks. You will find that what
I say is truth.'

Before the day was out Lady Albury did find her
husband to be correct. Captain Batsby, though he
was very jealous of his secret, acknowledged to himself the necessity of having one confidant. He could
hardly, he thought, follow Ayala without some
assistance. He knew nothing of Mrs. Dosett, nothing
of Kingsbury Crescent, and very little as to Ayala
herself. He regarded Lady Albury as his chosen
friend, and generally communicated to her whatever
troubles he might have. These had consisted chiefly
of the persecutions to which he had been subjected by

the mothers of portionless young ladies. How not to get married off against his will had been the difficulty of his life. His half-sister-in-law had hitherto preserved him, and therefore to her he now went for assistance in this opposite affair. 'Rosalind,' he said in his gravest voice, 'what do you think I have to tell you?'

Lady Albury knew what was coming, but of course she hid her knowledge. 'I hope Mrs. Motherly has not written to you again,' she said. Mrs. Motherly was a lady who had been anxious that her daughter should grace Captain Batsby's table, and had written to him letters, asking him his intentions.

'Oh, dear; nothing of that kind. I do not care a straw for Mrs. Motherly or the girl either. I never said a word to her that any one could make a handle of. But I want to say a word to somebody now.'

'What sort of a word is it to be, Ben?'

'Ah,' he groaned. 'Rosalind, you must understand that I never was so much in earnest in my life!'

'You are always in earnest.'

Then he sighed very deeply. 'I shall expect you to help me through this matter, Rosalind.'

'Do I not always help you?'

'Yes; you do. But you must stick to me now like wax. What do you think of that young lady, Miss Dormer?'

'I think she is a pretty girl; and the gentlemen tell me that she rides bravely.'

'Don't you consider her divine?' he asked.

'My dear Ben, one lady never considers another to be divine. Among ourselves we are terribly human, if not worse. Do you mean to tell me that you are in love with Ayala Dormer?'

'You have guessed it,' said he. 'You always do guess everything.'

'I generally do guess as much as that, when young gentlemen find young ladies divine. Do you know anything about Miss Dormer?'

'Nothing but her beauty;—nothing but her wit;—

nothing but her grace! I know all that, and I don't seem to want to know any more.'

'Then you must be in love! In the first place she hasn't got a sixpence in the world.'

'I don't want sixpences,' said the Captain, proudly.

'And in the next place I am not at all sure that you would like her people. Father and mother she has none.'

'Then I cannot dislike them.'

'But she has uncles and aunts, who are, I am afraid, objectionable. She lives with a Mr. Dosett, who is a clerk in Somerset House,—a respectable man, no doubt, but one whom you would not perhaps want at your house very often.'

'I don't care about uncles and aunts,' said Captain Batsby. 'Uncles and aunts can always be dropped much easier than fathers and mothers. At any rate I am determined to go on, and I want you to put me in the way. How must I find her?'

'Go to No. 10, Kingsbury Crescent, Bayswater. Ask for Mrs. Dosett and tell her what you've come about. When she knows that you are well off she will not turn a deaf ear to you. What the girl may do it is beyond me to say. She is very peculiar.'

'Peculiar?' said the Captain with another sigh.

Lady Albury did, in truth, think Ayala was very peculiar, seeing that she had refused two such men as Tom Tringle in spite of his wealth, and Colonel Stubbs in spite of his position. This she had done though she had no prospects of her own before her, and no comfortable home at the present! Might it not be more than probable that she would also refuse Captain Batsby, who was less rich than the one and certainly less known to the world than the other? But as to this it was not necessary that she should say anything. To assist Colonel Stubbs she was bound by true affection for the man. In regard to her husband's half-brother she was only bound to seem to assist him. 'I can write a line to Mrs. Dosett, if you wish it,' she said, 'or to Miss Dormer.'

'I wish you would. It would be best to the aunt, and just tell her that I am fairly well off. She'll tell Ayala I could make quite a proper settlement on her. That kind of thing does go a long way with young ladies.'

'It ought to do at any rate,' said Lady Albury. 'It certainly does with the old ladies.' Then the matter was settled. She was to write to Mrs. Dosett and inform that lady that Captain Batsby intended to call at Kingsbury Crescent in the form of a suitor for Miss Ayala Dormer's hand. She would go on to explain that Captain Batsby was quite in a position to marry and maintain a wife.

'And if she should accept me you'll have her down here, Rosalind?' Here was a difficulty, as it was already understood that Ayala was to be again brought down to Stalham on the Colonel's account; but Lady Albury could make the promise, as, should the Captain be accepted, no harm would in that case be done to the Colonel. She was, however, tolerably sure that the Captain would not be accepted. 'And, if she shouldn't take me all at once, still you might have her,' suggested the lover. As to this, which was so probable, there would be a great difficulty. Ayala was to be seduced into coming again to Stalham if possible,—but specially on the Colonel's behoof. In such a case it must be done behind the Captain's back. Lady Albury saw the troubles which were coming, but nevertheless she promised that she would see what could be done. All this having been settled, Captain Batsby took his leave and went off to London.

Mrs. Dosett, when she received Lady Albury's letter, was very much surprised. She too failed to understand what there was in Ayala to produce such a multiplicity of suitors, one after another. When Lucy came to her and had begun to be objectionable, she had thought that she might some day be relieved from her troubles by the girl's marriage. Lucy, to her eyes, was beautiful, and mistress of a manner likely to be winning in a man's eyes, though ungracious to herself. But in regard to Ayala she had expressed nothing of the kind. Ayala was little, and flighty, and like an elf,—as she had remarked to her husband. But now, within twelve months, three lovers had appeared, and each of them suitable for matrimonial purposes. She could only tell her husband, and then tell Ayala.

'Captain Batsby! I don't believe it!' said Ayala, almost crying. If Colonel Stubbs could not be made to assume the garb of an Angel of Light what was she to think of Captain Batsby?

'You can read Lady Albury's letter.'

'I don't want to read Lady Albury's letter. I won't see him. I don't care what my uncle says. I don't care what anybody says. Yes, I do know him. I remember him very well. I spoke to him once or twice, and I did not like him at all.'

'You said the same of Colonel Stubbs.'

'I didn't say the same of Colonel Stubbs. He is a great deal worse than Colonel Stubbs.'

'And you said just the same of Tom.'

'He is the same as Tom;—just as bad. It is no good going on about him, Aunt Margaret. I won't see him. If I were locked up in a room with him I wouldn't speak a word to him. He has no right to come.'

'A gentleman, my dear, has always a right to ask a lady to be his wife if he has got means.'

'You always say so, Aunt Margaret, but I don't believe it. There should be,—there should have been,—I don't know what; but I am quite sure the man has no right to come to me, and I won't see him.' To this resolution Ayala clung, and, as she was very firm about it, Mrs. Dosett, after consultation with her husband, at last gave way, and consented to see Captain Batsby herself.

In due time Captain Batsby came. At any knock heard at the door during this period Ayala flew out of the drawing-room into her own chamber; and at the

Captain's knock she flew with double haste, feeling sure that his was the special knock. The man was shown up, and in a set speech declared his purpose to Mrs. Dosett, and expressed a hope that Lady Albury might have written on the subject. Might he be allowed to see the young lady?

'I fear that would be of no service, Captain Batsby.'

'Of no service?'

'On receiving Lady Albury's letter I was of course obliged to tell my niece the honour you proposed to do her.'

'I am quite in earnest, you know,' said the Captain.

'So I suppose, as Lady Albury would not have written, nor would you have come on such a mission. But so is my niece in earnest.'

'She will, at any rate, hear what I have got to say.'

'She would rather not,' said Mrs. Dosett. 'She thinks that it would only be painful to both of you. As she has quite made up her mind that she cannot accept the honour you propose to do her, what good would it serve?'

'Is Miss Dormer at home?' asked the Captain, suddenly. Mrs. Dosett hesitated for a while, anxious to tell a lie on the matter, but fearing to do so. 'I suppose she is at home,' continued the urgent lover.

'Miss Dormer is at present in her own chamber.'

'Then I think I ought to see her,' continued the Captain. 'She can't know at present what is my income.'

'Lady Albury has told us that it is sufficient.'

'But that means nothing. Your niece cannot be aware that I have a very pretty little place of my own down in Berkshire.'

'I don't think it would make a difference,' said Mrs. Dosett.

'Or that I shall be willing to settle upon her a third of my income. It is not many gentlemen who will do as much as that for a young lady, when the young lady has nothing of her own.'

'I am sure you are very generous.'

'Yes, I am. I always was generous. And I have no impediments to get rid of; not a trouble of that kind in all the world. And I don't owe a shilling. Very few young men, who have lived as much in the world as I have, can say that.'

'I am sure your position is all that is desirable.'

'That's just it. No position could be more desirable. I should give up the service immediately as soon as I was married.' At that Mrs. Dosett bowed, not knowing what words to find for further conversation. 'After that,' continued the Captain, 'do you mean to say that I am not to be allowed to see the young lady?'

'I cannot force her to come down, Captain Batsby.'

'I would if I were you.'

'Force a young lady?'

'Something ought to be done,' said he, beginning almost to whine. 'I have come here on purpose to see her, and I am quite prepared to do what is handsome. My half-sister, Lady Albury, had her down at Stalham, and is quite anxious to have her there again. I suppose you have no objection to make to me, Mrs. Dosett?'

'Oh, dear no.'

'Or Mr. Dosett?'

'I do not say that he has, Captain Batsby; but this is a matter in which a young lady's word must be paramount. We cannot force her to marry you, or even to speak to you.' The Captain still went on with entreaties, till Mrs. Dosett found herself so far compelled to accede to him as to go up to Ayala's room and beg her to come down and answer this third suitor with her own voice. But Ayala was immovable. When her aunt came near her she took hold of the bed as though fearing an attempt would be made to drag her out of the room. She again declared that if she were forced into the room below nothing could oblige her to speak even a word.

'As for thanking him,' she said, 'you can do that

yourself, Aunt Margaret, if you like. I am not a bit obliged to him; but, if you choose to say so, you may; only pray do tell him to go away,—and tell him never, never to come back any more.' Then Mrs. Dosett returned to the drawing-room, and declared that her embassy had been quite in vain.

'In all my life,' said Captain Batsby, as he took his leave, 'I never heard of such conduct before.' Nevertheless, as he went away he made up his mind that Lady Albury should get Ayala again down to Stalham. He was very angry, but his love remained as hot as ever.

'As I did not succeed in seeing her,' he said, in a letter to his half-sister, 'of course I do not know what she might have said to me herself. I might probably have induced her to give me another hearing. I put it all down to that abominable aunt, who probably has some scheme of her own, and would not let Miss Dormer come down to me. If you will have her again at Stalham, everything may be made to go right.'

\* \* \* \* \* \*

At home, in Kingsbury Crescent, when Ayala had gone to bed, both Mr. and Mrs. Dosett expressed themselves as much troubled by the peculiarity of Ayala's nature. Mrs. Dosett declared her conviction that that promised legacy from Uncle Tom would never be forthcoming, because he had been so much offended by the rejection of his own son. And even should the legacy remain written in Sir Thomas's will, where would Ayala find a home if Mr. Dosett were to die before the baronet? This rejection of suitors,—of fit, well-to-do, unobjectionable suitors,—was held by Mrs. Dosett to be very wicked, and a direct flying in the face of Providence. 'Does she think,' said Mrs. Dosett, urging the matter with all her eloquence to her husband, 'that young men with incomes are to be coming after her always like this?' Mr. Dosett shook his head and scratched it at the same time, which was always a sign with him that he

was not at all convinced by the arguments used, but
that he did not wish to incur further hostility by
answering them. 'Why shouldn't she see an eligible
man when he comes recommended like this?'

'I suppose, my dear, she didn't think him nice
enough.'

'Nice! pshaw! I call it a direct flying in the face
of Providence. If he were ever so nasty and twice
as old she ought to think twice about it in her position. There is poor Tom, they say, absolutely ill.
The housekeeper was over here from Queen's Gate
the other day, and she declares that that affair about
the policeman all came from his being in love. And
now he has left the business and has gone to Merle
Park, because he is so knocked in a heap that he
cannot hold up his head.'

'I don't see why love should make a man punch
a policeman's breath out of him,' said Mr. Dosett.

'Of course Tom was foolish; but he would do very
well if she would have him. Of course your sister,
and Sir Thomas, and all of them, will be very furious.
What right will she have to expect money after that?'

'Tom is an ass,' said Mr. Dosett.

'I suppose Colonel Stubbs is an ass too. What I
want to know is what it is she looks for. Like any
other girl, she expects to get married some day, I
suppose; but she has been reading poetry, and novels,
and trash, till she has got her head so full of nonsense
that she doesn't know what it is she does want. I
should like to shake her till I shook all the romance
out of her. If there is anything I do hate it is
romance, while bread and meat, and coals, and
washing, are so dear.' With this Mrs. Dosett took
herself and her troubles up to her bedroom.

Mr. Dosett sat for a while gazing with speculative
eyes at the embers of the fire. He was conscious in
his heart that some part of that attack upon romance
in general was intended for himself. Though he did
not look to be romantic, especially when seated at
his desk in Somerset House, with his big index-book

before him, still there was left about him some touch
of poetry, and an appreciation of the finer feelings
of our nature. Though he could have wished that
Ayala should have been able to take one of these
three well-to-do suitors, who were so anxious to
obtain her hand, still he could not bring himself not
to respect her, still he was unable not to love her,
because she was steadfastly averse to accept as a
husband a man for whom she had no affection. As he
looked at the embers he asked himself how it ought
to be. Here was a girl whose only gift in life was her
own personal charm. That that charm must be
powerful was evident from the fact that she could
attract such men as these. Of the good things of the
world, of a pleasant home, of ample means, and of all
that absence of care which comes from money, poor
Mr. Dosett had by no means a poor appreciation.
That men are justified in seeking these good things
by their energy, industry, and talents, he was quite
confident. How was it with a girl who had nothing
else but her beauty,—or, perhaps, her wit,—in lieu
of energy and industry? Was she justified in carrying
her wares also into the market, and making the most
of them? The embers had burned so low, and he had
become so cold before he had settled the question
in his own mind, that he was obliged to go up to bed,
leaving it unsettled.

## CHAPTER XL

### AUNT EMMELINE'S NEW PROPOSITION

A FEW days after this, just as the bread and cheese
had been put on the table for the modest mid-day
meal at Kingsbury Crescent, there came a most unwonted honour on Mrs. Dosett. It was a call from
no less a person than Lady Tringle herself, who had
come all the way up from Merle Park on purpose. It
was a Saturday. She had travelled by herself and
intended to go back on the same day with her husband.

This was an amount of trouble which she very seldom
gave herself, not often making a journey to London
during the periods of her rural sojourn; and, when
she began by assuring her sister-in-law that she
made the journey with no object but that of coming
to Kingsbury Crescent, Mrs. Dosett was aware that
something very important was to be communicated.
Mrs. Dosett and Ayala were together in the dining-
room when Lady Tringle appeared, and the embrac-
ings were very affectionate. They were particularly
affectionate towards Ayala, who was kissed as though
nothing had ever happened to interfere with the
perfect love existing between the aunt and the niece.
They were more than friendly, almost sisterly, towards Mrs. Dosett, whom in truth Lady Tringle met
hardly more than once in a year. It was very manifest that Aunt Emmeline wanted to have something
done. 'Now, my darling,' she said, turning to Ayala,
'if you would not mind going away for ten minutes,
I could say a few words on very particular business
to your aunt.' Then she gave her niece a tender little
squeeze and assumed her sweetest smile.

It will be as well to go back a little and tell the
cause which had produced this unexpected visit.
There had been very much of real trouble at Merle
Park. Everything was troublesome. Gertrude had
received her final letter from her lover, had declared
herself to be broken-hearted, and was evincing her
sorrow by lying in bed half the day, abstaining from
her meals, and relieving herself from famine by sly
visits to the larder. It was supposed that her object
was to bend the stony heart of her father, but the
process added an additional trouble to her mother.
Then the Trafficks were a sore vexation. It was now
nearly the end of January and they were still at
Merle Park. There had been a scene in which Sir
Thomas had been very harsh. 'My dear,' he had said
to his wife, 'I find that something must be done to
the chimney of the north room. The workmen must
be in it by the first of February. See and have all

the furniture taken out before they come.' Now the north room was the chamber in which the Trafficks slept, and the Trafficks were present when the order was given. No one believed the story of the chimney. This was the mode of expulsion which Sir Thomas had chosen on the spur of the moment. Mr. Traffick said not a word, but in the course of the morning Augusta expostulated with her mother. This was also disagreeable. Then the condition of Tom was truly pitiable. All his trust in champagne, all his bellicose humour, had deserted him. He moped about the place the most miserable of human beings, spending hour after hour in imploring his mother's assistance. But Lucy with her quiet determination, and mute persistency in waiting, was a source of almost greater annoyance to her aunt than even her own children. That Lucy should in any degree have had her way with Mr. Hamel, had gone against the grain with her. Mr. Hamel, to her thinking, was a person to be connected with whom would be a disgrace. She was always speaking of his birth, of his father's life, and of those Roman iniquities. She had given way for a time when she had understood that her husband intended to give the young people money enough to enable them to marry. In that case Lucy would at once be taken away from the house. But now all that had come to an end. Sir Thomas had given no money, and had even refused to give any money. Nevertheless he was peacefully indulgent to Lucy, and was always scolding his wife because she was hostile to Lucy's lover.

In this emergency she induced him to accede to a proposition, by which one of her miseries would be brought to an end and another might perhaps be remedied. A second exchange should be made. Lucy should be sent back to Kingsbury Crescent, and Ayala should once more be brought into favour at Merle Park, Queen's Gate, and Glenbogie. 'Your brother will never put up with it,' said Sir Thomas. Lady Tringle was not afraid of her brother, and thought that by soft words she might even talk over her sister-in-law. Ayala, she knew, had been troublesome in Kingsbury Crescent. She was sure, she said, Ayala's whims would of their nature be more troublesome to such a woman as Mrs. Dosett than Lucy's obstinacy. Ayala had no doubt been pert and disobedient at Glenbogie and at Rome, but there had been an unbending obduracy about Lucy which had been more distasteful to Aunt Emmeline than even Ayala's pert disobedience. 'It will be the only way,' she had said to Sir Thomas, 'to put Tom on his legs again. If the girl comes back here she will be sure to have him at last.' There was much in this which to Sir Thomas was weak and absurd. That prolonged journey round by San Francisco, Japan, and Pekin, was the remedy which recommended itself to him. But he was less able to despatch Tom at once to Japan than the elder Faddle had been to send off the younger Faddle to the stern realities of life in Aberdeen. He was quite willing that Tom should marry Ayala if it could be arranged, and therefore he gave his consent.

So armed, Lady Tringle had come up to Kingsbury Crescent, and was now about to undertake a task, which she acknowledged to herself to be difficult. She, in the first place, had had her choice and had selected a niece. Then she had quarrelled with her own selection, and had changed nieces. This had been done to accommodate her own fancy; and now she wanted to change the nieces back again! She felt aware that her request was unreasonable, and came, therefore, determined to wrap it up in her blandest smiles.

When Ayala had left the room Mrs. Dosett sat mute in attention. She was quite aware that something very much out of the ordinary way was to be asked of her. In her ordinary way Lady Tringle never did smile when she came to Kingsbury Crescent. She would be profuse in finery, and would seem to throw off sparks of wealth at every word she spoke. Now even her dress had been toned down to her humbler manner, and there was no touch of her husband's purse in her gait. 'Margaret,' she said, 'I have a proposition of great importance to make to you.' Mrs. Dosett opened her eyes wider and sat still mute. 'That poor girl is not,—is not,—is not doing perhaps the very best for herself here at Kingsbury Crescent.'

'Why is she not doing the best for herself?' asked Mrs. Dosett, angrily.

'Do not for a moment suppose that I am finding fault either with you or my brother.'

'You'd be very wrong if you did.'

'No doubt;—but I am not finding fault. I know how very generous you have both been. Of course Sir Thomas is a rich man, and what he gives to one of the girls comes to nothing. Of course it is different with you. It is hard upon my brother to have any such burden put upon him; and it is very good both in him and you to bear it.'

'What is it you want us to do now, Emmeline?'

'Well;—I was going to explain. I do think it a great pity that Tom and Ayala should not become man and wife. If ever any young man ever did love a girl I believe that he loves her.'

'I think he does.'

'It is dreadful. I never saw anything like it. He is just for all the world like those young men we read of who do all manner of horrible things for love,— smothering themselves and their young women with charcoal, or throwing them into the Regent's Canal. I am constantly afraid of something happening. It was all because of Ayala that he got into that terrible row at the police court,—and then we were afraid he was going to take to drink. He has given all that up now.'

'I am very glad he has given drink up. That wouldn't do him any good.'

'He is quite different now. The poor fellow hardly takes anything. He will sit all the afternoon smoking cigarettes and sipping tea. It is quite sad to see him. Then he comes and talks to me, and is always asking me to make Ayala have him.'

'I don't think that anybody can ever make Ayala do anything.'

'Not quite by talking to her. I dare say not. I did not mean to say a word to her about it just now.'

'We can do nothing, I fear,' said Mrs. Dosett.

'I was going to suggest something. But I wanted first to say a word or two about poor Lucy.' They were just at present all 'poor' to Lady Tringle,— Ayala, Lucy, Tom, and Gertrude. Even Augusta was poor because she was to be turned out of her bedroom.

'Is she in trouble?'

'Oh, dear, yes. But,' she added, thinking well to correct herself, so that Mrs. Dosett might not imagine that she would have to look forward to troubles with Lucy, 'she could arrange her affairs, no doubt, if she were not with us. She is engaged to that Mr. Isadore Hamel, the sculptor.'

'So I have heard.'

'He does not earn very much just at present, I fear. Sir Thomas did offer to help him, but he was perhaps a little hoity-toity, giving himself airs. That, however, did not come off, and there they are, waiting. I don't mean to say a word against poor Lucy. I think it a pity, you know; but perhaps it was natural enough. He isn't what I should have liked for a niece who was living with me just as though she was my daughter; but I couldn't help that.'

'But what are we to do, Emmeline?'

'Let them just change places again.'

'Change again! Ayala go to you and Lucy come back here!'

'Just that. If Ayala were with us she would be sure to get used to Tom at last. And then Lucy could manage her affairs with Mr. Hamel so much better if she were with you.'

'Why should she manage her affairs better if she were with us?'

Lady Tringle was aware that this was the weak part of her case. On the poor Ayala and poor Tom side of the question there was a good deal which might be said. Then, though she might not convince, she might be eloquent. But, touching Lucy, she could say nothing which did not simply signify that she wanted to get rid of the girl. Now, Mrs. Dosett had also wanted to get rid of Lucy when the former exchange had been made. 'What I mean is, that, if she were away, Sir Thomas would be more likely to do something for her.' This was an invention at the spur of the moment.

'Do you not feel that the girls should not be chucked about like balls from a battledore?' asked Mrs. Dosett.

'For their own good, Margaret. I only propose it for their own good. You can't but think it would be a good thing for Ayala to be married to our Tom.'

'If she liked him.'

'Why shouldn't she like him? You know what that means. Poor Ayala is young, and a little romantic. She would be a great deal happier if all that could be knocked out of her. She has to marry somebody, and the sooner she settles down the better. Sir Thomas will do anything for them;—a horse and carriage, and anything she could set her heart upon! There is nothing Sir Thomas would not do for Tom so as to get him put upon his legs again.'

'I don't think Ayala would go.'

'She must, you know,' whispered Lady Tringle, 'if we both tell her.'

'And Lucy?'

'She must too,' again whispered Lady Tringle. 'If they are told they are to go, what else can they do? Why shouldn't Ayala wish to come?'

'There were quarrels before.'

'Yes;—because of Augusta. Augusta is married now.' Lady Tringle could not quite say that Augusta was gone.

'Will you speak to Ayala?'

'Perhaps it would come better from you, Margaret, if you agree with me.'

'I am not sure that I do. I am quite sure that your brother would not force her to go, whether she wished it or not. No doubt we should be glad if the marriage could be arranged. But we cannot force a girl to marry, and her aversion in this case is so strong——'

'Aversion!'

'Aversion to being married, I mean. It is so strong that I do not think she will go of her own accord to any house where she is likely to meet her cousin. I dare say she may be a fool. I say nothing about that. Of course, she shall be asked; and, if she wishes to go, then Lucy can be asked too. But of course it must all depend upon what your brother says.'

Then Lady Tringle took her leave without again seeing Ayala herself, and as she went declared her intention of calling at Somerset House. She would not think it right, she said, in a matter of such importance, to leave London without consulting her brother. It might be possible, she thought, that she would be able to talk her brother over; whereas his wife, if she had the first word, might turn him the other way.

'Is Aunt Emmeline gone?' asked Ayala, when she came down. 'I am glad she has gone, because I never know how to look when she calls me dear. I know she hates me.'

'I hope not, Ayala.'

'I am sure she does, because I hated Augusta. I do hate Augusta, and my aunt hates me. The only one of the lot I like is Uncle Tom.'

Then the proposition was made, Ayala sitting with her mouth wide open as the details, one after another, were opened out to her. Her aunt did it with exquisite fairness, abstaining from opening out some of the details which might be clear enough to Ayala without any explanation. Her Aunt Emmeline

was very anxious to have her back again;—the only
reason for her former expulsion having been the
enmity of Augusta. Her Uncle Tom and her aunt,
and, no doubt, Gertrude, would be very glad to
receive her. Not a word was said about Tom. Then
something was urged as to the material comforts of
the Tringle establishments, and of the necessary
poverty of Kingsbury Crescent.

'And Lucy is to have the poverty?' said Ayala,
indignantly.

'I think it probable, my dear, that before long
Lucy will become the wife of Mr. Hamel.'

'And you want to get rid of me?' demanded Ayala.

'No, my dear; not so. You must not think that
for a moment. The proposition has not originated
with me at all. I am endeavouring to do my duty by
explaining to you the advantages which you would
enjoy by going to your Aunt Emmeline, and which
you certainly cannot have if you remain here. And
I must tell you, that, if you return to Sir Thomas,
he will probably provide for you. You know what
I mean by providing for you?'

'No, I don't,' said Ayala, who had in her mind
some dim idea that her cousin Tom was supposed to
be a provision. She was quite aware that her Aunt
Margaret, in her explanation as hitherto given, had
not mentioned Tom's name, and was sure that it had
not been omitted without reason.

'By providing, I mean that if you are living in his
house he will leave you something in his will;—as
would be natural that he should do for a child
belonging to him. Your Uncle Reginald'—this she
said in a low and very serious tone——'will, I fear,
have nothing to leave to you.' Then there was silence
for some minutes, after which Mrs. Dosett asked the
important question, 'Well, Ayala, what do you think
about it?'

'Must I go?' said Ayala. 'May I stay?'

'Yes, my dear; you may certainly stay if you
wish it.'

'Then I will stay,' said Ayala, jumping up on to her feet. 'You do not want to turn me out, Aunt Margaret?' Then she went down on her knees, and, leaning on her aunt's lap, looked up into her face. 'If you will keep me I will try to be good.'

'My dear, you are good. I have nothing to complain of. Of course we will keep you. Nobody has thought for a moment of bidding you go. But you should understand that when your aunt made the proposition I was bound to tell it you.' Then there was great embracing and kissing, and Ayala felt that she was relieved from a terrible danger. She had often declared that no one could make her marry her cousin Tom; but it had seemed to her for a moment that if she were given up bodily to the Tringles no mode of escape would be open to her short of suicide. There had been a moment almost of regret that she had never brought herself to regard Jonathan Stubbs as an Angel of Light.

At Somerset House Lady Tringle made her suggestion to her brother with even more flowery assurance of general happiness than she had used in endeavouring to persuade his wife. Ayala would, of course, be married to Tom in the course of the next six months, and during the same period Lucy, no doubt, would be married to that very enterprising but somewhat obstinate young man, Mr. Hamel. Thus there would be an end to all the Dormer troubles; 'and you, Reginald,' she said, 'will be relieved from a burden which never ought to have been laid upon your shoulder.'

'We will think of it,' he said very gravely, over and over again. Beyond that 'we will think of it' he could not be induced to utter a word.

## CHAPTER XLI

### 'A COLD PROSPECT!'

THREE days were allowed to Frank Houston to consider within his own mind what he would say for himself and what he would propose finally to do when he should see Miss Docimer on the appointed Sunday. He was called upon to decide whether, after so many resolutions made to the contrary, he would now at last bring himself to encounter poverty and a family,—genteel poverty with about seven hundred and fifty pounds a-year between himself and his wife. He had hitherto been very staunch on the subject, and had unfortunately thought that Imogene Docimer had been as firmly fixed in her determination. His theory had in itself been good. If two people marry they are likely, according to the laws of nature, to have very soon more than two. In the process of a dozen years they may not improbably become ever so many more than two. Funds which were barely enough, if enough, for two, would certainly fail to be enough for half-a-dozen. His means were certainly not enough for himself, as he had hitherto found them. Imogene's means were less even than his own. Therefore, it was clear that he and Imogene ought not to marry and encounter the danger of all those embryo mouths. There was a logic about it which had seemed to him to be unanswerable. It was a logic which applied to his case above all others. The man who had a hope of earning money need not be absolutely bound by it. To him the money might come as quickly as the mouths. With the cradles would arrive the means of buying the cradles. And to the man who had much more than enough for himself,—to such a man as he had expected to be while he was looking forward to the coffin of that iniquitous uncle,—the logic did not apply at all. In defending himself, both to himself and to Imogene, he was very strong upon that point.

A man who had plenty and would not divide his
plenty with another might with truth be called
selfish. Rich old bachelors might with propriety be
called curmudgeons. But was it right that a man
should be abused,—even by a young lady to whom,
under more propitious circumstances, he had offered
his heart,—when he declared himself unwilling to
multiply suffering by assisting to bring into the
world human beings whom he would be unable to
support? He had felt himself to be very strong in his
logic, and had unfortunately made the mistake of
supposing that it was as clear to Imogene as to
himself.

Then he had determined to rectify the inconvenience of his position. It had become manifest to
him whilst he was waiting for his uncle's money that
not only were his own means insufficient for married
life but even for single comfort. It would always
come to pass that when he had resolved on two
mutton chops and half-a-pint of sherry the humble
little meal would spread itself into woodcock and
champagne. He regarded it as an unkindness in
Providence that he should not have been gifted with
economy. Therefore, he had to look about him for a
remedy; and, as Imogene was out of the question, he
found a remedy in Gertrude Tringle. He had then
believed that everything was settled for him,—not,
indeed, in a manner very pleasant, but after a fashion
that would make life possible to him. Sir Thomas
had given one of his daughters, with a large sum of
money, to such a man as Septimus Traffick,—a man
more impecunious than himself, one whom Frank
did not hesitate to pronounce to be much less of a
gentleman. That seat in the House of Commons was
to him nothing. There were many men in the House
of Commons to whom he would hardly condescend to
speak. To be the younger son of a latter-day peer was
to him nothing. He considered himself in all respects
to be a more eligible husband than Septimus Traffick.
Therefore he had entertained but little doubt when

he found himself accepted by Gertrude herself and her mother. Then by degrees he had learned to know something of the young lady to whom he intended to devote himself; and it had come to pass that the better he had known the less he had liked her. Nevertheless he had persevered, groaning in spirit as he thought of the burden with which he was about to inflict himself. Then had come the release. Sir Thomas had explained to him that no money would be forthcoming; and the young lady had made to him a foolish proposition, which, as he thought, fully justified him in regarding the match as at an end.

And then he had three days in which to make up his mind. It may be a question whether three days are ever much better than three minutes for such a purpose. A man's mind will very generally refuse to make itself up until it be driven and compelled by emergency. The three days are passed not in forming but in postponing judgment. In nothing is procrastination so tempting as in thought. So it came to pass, that through the Thursday, the Friday, and the Saturday, Frank Houston came to no conclusion, though he believed that every hour of the time was devoted to forming one. Then, as he ate his dinner on Saturday night at his club, a letter was brought to him, the handwriting of which was familiar to him. This letter assisted him little in thinking.

The letter was from Gertrude Tringle, and need not be given in its entirety. There was a good deal of reproach, in that he had been so fickle as to propose to abandon her at the first touch of adversity. Then she had gone on to say, that, knowing her father a great deal better than he could do, she was quite satisfied that the money would be all right. But the last paragraph of the letter shall be given. 'Papa has almost yielded already. I have been very ill;'—here the extent of her malady was shown by the strength of the underscoring with which the words were made significant;—'very ill indeed,' she went on to say, 'as you will understand if you have ever really loved me. I have kept my bed almost ever since I got your cruel letter.' Bed and cruel were again strenuously underscored. 'It has made papa very unhappy, and, though he has said nothing to myself, he has told mamma that if I am really in earnest he will do something for us.' The letter was long, but this is all the reader need see of it. But it must be explained that the young lady had greatly exaggerated her mother's words, and that her mother had exaggerated those which Sir Thomas had spoken. 'She is a stupid idiot,' Sir Thomas had said to his wife. 'If she is obedient, and does her duty, of course I shall do something for her some day.' This had been stretched to that promise of concession which Gertrude communicated to her lover.

This was the assistance which Frank Houston received in making up his mind on Saturday night. If what the girl said was true, there was still open to him the manner of life which he had prepared for himself; and he did believe the announcement to be true. Though Sir Thomas had been so persistent in his refusals, his experience in life had taught him to believe that a parent's sternness is never a match for a daughter's obstinacy. Had there been a touch of tenderness in his heart to the young lady herself he would not have abandoned her so easily. But he had found his consolation when giving up his hope of Sir Thomas's money. Now, should he again take to the girl, and find his consolation in accepting the money? Should he resolve upon doing so, this would materially affect any communication which he might make to Imogene on the following day.

While thus in doubt he went into the smoking-room and there he found any thinking to be out of the question. A great question was being debated as to club law. One man had made an assertion. He had declared that another man had been seen playing cards in a third man's company. A fourth man had, thereupon, put his hat on his head, and had declared contumaciously that the 'assertion was not

true.' Having so declared he had contumaciously
stalked out of the room, and had banged the door
after him,—very contumaciously indeed. The question was whether the contumacious gentleman had
misbehaved himself in accordance with the rules of
the club, and, if so, what should be done to him.
Not true is as bad as 'false.' 'False,' applied to a
gentleman in a club, must be matter either of an
apology or expulsion. The objectionable word had,
no doubt, been said in defence of an absent man, and
need not, perhaps, have been taken up had the
speaker not at once put on his hat and stalked out
of the room, and banged the door. It was asserted
that a lie may be given by the way in which a door is
banged. And yet no club punishes the putting on of
hats, or stalking off, or the banging of doors. It was
a difficult question, and occupied Frank Houston till
two o'clock in the morning, to the exclusion of
Gertrude Tringle and Imogene Docimer.

On the Sunday morning he was not up early, nor
did he go to church. The contumacious gentleman
was a friend of his, whom he knew that no arguments
would induce to apologise. He believed also that
gentleman No. 3 might have been seen playing cards
with gentleman No. 2,—so that there was no valid
excuse for the banging of the door. He was much
exercised by the points to be decided, so that when
he got into a cab to be taken to Mrs. Docimer's house
he had hardly come to any other conclusion than
that one which had arisen to him from a comparison
between the two young ladies. Imogene was nearly
perfect, and Gertrude was as nearly the reverse as
a young lady could be with the proper number of
eyes in her head and a nose between them. The style
of her letter was abominable to him. 'Very ill indeed;—as you will understand, if you ever really
loved me!' There was a mawkish clap-trap about it
which thoroughly disgusted him. Everything from
Imogene was straightforward and downright whether
it were love or whether it were anger. But then to be

A.A.—20

settled with an income of £3,000 a year would relieve
him from such a load of care!

'And so Tringle père does not see the advantage of
such a son-in-law,' said Imogene, after the first
greetings were over between them. The greetings
had been very simple,—just a touch of the hand, just
a civil word,—civil, but not in the least tender, just
an inclination of the head, and then two seats
occupied with all the rug between them.

'Yes, indeed!' said Frank. 'The man is a fool,
because he will probably get somebody who will
behave less well to his daughter, and make a worse
use of his money.'

'Just so. One can only be astonished at his folly.
Is there no hope left?'

'A glimmer there is.'

'Oh, indeed!'

'I got a letter last night from my lady-love, in
which she tells me that she is very ill, and that her
sickness is working upon her father's bowels.'

'Frank!'

'It is the proper language;—working upon her
father's bowels of compassion. Fathers always have
bowels of compassion at last.'

'You will return then, of course?'

'What do you say?'

'As for myself,—or as for you?'

'As a discreet and trusty counsellor. To me you
have always been a trusty counsellor.'

'Then I should put a few things into a bag, go
down to Merle Park, and declare that, in spite of all
the edicts that ever came from a father's mouth, you
cannot absent yourself while you know that your
Gertrude is ill.'

'And so prepare a new cousin for you to press to
your bosom.'

'If you can endure her for always, why should not
I for an hour or two, now and again?'

'Why not, indeed? In fact, Imogene, this enduring, and not enduring,—even this living, and not

living,—is, after all, but an affair of the imagination. Who can tell but that, as years roll on, she may be better-looking even than you?'

'Certainly.'

'And have as much to say for herself?'

'A great deal more that is worth hearing.'

'And behave herself as a mother of a family with quite as much propriety?'

'In all that I do not doubt that she would be my superior.'

'More obedient I am sure she would be.'

'Or she would be very disobedient.'

'And then she can provide me and my children with ample comforts.'

'Which I take it is the real purpose for which a wife should be married.'

'Therefore,' said he,—and then he stopped.

'And therefore there should be no doubt.'

'Though I hate her,' he said, clenching his fist with violence as he spoke, 'with every fibre of my heart,—still you think there should be no doubt?'

'That, Frank, is violent language,—and foolish.'

'And though I love you so intensely that whenever I see her the memory of you becomes an agony to me.'

'Such language is only more violent and more foolish.'

'Surely not, if I have made up my mind at last, that I never will willingly see Miss Tringle again.' Here he got up, and walking across the rug, stood over her, and waited as though expecting some word from her. But she, putting her two hands up to her head, and brushing her hair away from her forehead, looked up to him for what further words might come to him. 'Surely not,' he continued, 'if I have made up my mind at last, that nothing shall ever again serve to rob me of your love,—if I may still hope to possess it.'

'Oh, Frank!' she said, 'how mean I am to be a creature obedient to the whistle of such a master as you!'

'But are you obedient?'

'You know that well enough. I have had no
Gertrude with whom I have vacillated, whether for
the sake of love or lucre. Whatever you may be,—
whether mean or noble,—you are the only man with
whom I can endure to live, for whom I would endure
to die. Of course I had not expected that your love
should be like mine. How should it be so, seeing that
you are a man and that I am but a woman.' Here he
attempted to seat himself by her on the sofa, which
she occupied, but she gently repulsed him, motioning
him towards the chair which he had occupied. 'Sit
there, Frank,' she said, 'so that we may look into
each other's faces and talk seriously. Is it to come to
this then, that I am to ruin you at last?'

'There will be no ruin.'

'But there will, if we are married now. Shall I tell
you the kind of life which would satisfy me?'

'Some little place abroad?' he asked.

'Oh, dear, no! No place to which you would be
confined at all. If I may remain as I am, knowing
that you intend to marry no one else, feeling confident that there is a bond binding us together even
though we should never become man and wife, I
should be, if not happy, at least contented.'

'That is a cold prospect.'

'Cold;—but not ice-cold, as would have been the
other. Cold, but not wretchedly cold, as would be
the idea always present to me that I had reduced you
to poverty. Frank, I am so far selfish that I cannot
bear to abandon the idea of your love. But I am
not so far selfish as to wish to possess it at the expense
of your comfort. Shall it be so?'

'Be how?' said he, speaking almost in anger.

'Let us remain just as we are. Only you will
promise me, that as I cannot be your wife there shall
be no other. I need hardly promise you that there
will be no other husband.' Now he sat frowning at
her, while she, still pressing back her hair with her
hands, looked eagerly into his face. 'If this will be
enough for you,' she said, 'it shall be enough for me.'

'No, by G—d!'

'Frank!'

'It will certainly not be enough for me. I will have nothing to do with so damnable a compact.'

'Damnable!'

'Yes; that is what I call it. That is what any man would call it,—and any woman too, who would speak her mind.'

'Then, Sir, perhaps you will be kind enough to make your proposition. I have made mine, such as it is, and am sorry that it should not have been received at any rate with courtesy.' But as she said this there was a gleam of a bright spirit in her eyes, such as he had not seen since first the name of Gertrude had been mentioned to her.

'Yes,' said he. 'You have made your proposition, and now it is only fair that I should make mine. Indeed, I made it already when I suggested that little place abroad. Let it be abroad or at home, or of what nature it may,—so that you shall be there, and I with you, it shall be enough for me. That is my proposition; and, if it be not accepted, then I shall return to Miss Tringle and all the glories of Lombard Street.'

'Frank——' she said. Then, before she could speak another word, he had risen from his seat, and she was in his arms. 'Frank,' she continued, pushing back his kisses, 'how impossible it is that I should not be obedient to you in all things! I know,—I know that I am agreeing to that which will cause you some day to repent.'

'By heavens, no!' said he. 'I am changed in all that.'

'A man cannot change at once. Your heart is soft, but your nature remains the same. Frank, I could be so happy at this moment if I could forget the picture which my imagination points to me of your future life. Your love, and your generous words, and the look out of your dear eyes, are sweet to me now, as when I was a child, whom you first made so proud by telling her that she owned your heart. If I could only revel in the return of your affections——'

'It is no return,' said he. 'There has never been a moment in which my affections have not been the same.'

'Well, then,—in these permitted signs of your affection,—if it were not that I cannot shut out the future! Don ot press me to name any early day, because no period of my future life will be so happy to me as this.'

    \*        \*        \*        \*        \*        \*

'Is there any reason why I should not intrude?' said Mrs. Docimer, opening the door when the above conversation had been extended for perhaps another hour.

'Not in the least, as far as I'm concerned,' said Frank. 'A few words have been spoken between us, all of which may be repeated to you if Imogene can remember them.'

'Every one of them,' said Imogene; 'but I hardly think that I shall repeat them.'

'I suppose they have been very much a matter of course,' said Mrs. Docimer;—'the old story repeated between you two for the fourth or fifth time. Considering all things, do you think that I should congratulate you?'

'I ask for no congratulation,' said Imogene.

'You may certainly congratulate me,' said Frank. After that the conversation became tame, and the happy lover soon escaped from the house into the street. When there he found very much to occupy his mind. He had certainly made his resolution at last, and had done so in a manner which would now leave him no power of retrogression. The whole theory of his life had,—with a vengeance,—been thrown to the winds. 'The little place abroad,'—or elsewhere,—was now a settled certainty. He had nearly got the better of her. He had all but succeeded in putting down his own love and hers by a little gentle ridicule, and by a few half-wise phrases which she at the moment had been unable to answer; but she now had in truth vanquished him by the absolute sincerity of her love.

## CHAPTER XLII

### ANOTHER DUEL

FRANK HOUSTON on that Sunday afternoon became an altered man. The reader is not to suppose
by this that he is declared to have suddenly thrown
off all his weaknesses, and to have succeeded in
clothing himself in an armour of bright steel, proof
for the rest of his life against all temptations. Such
suits of armour are not to be had at a moment's
notice; nor, as I fear, can a man ever acquire one
quite perfect at all points who has not begun to make
it for himself before Houston's age. But he did on
that day dine off the two mutton chops, and comforted himself with no more than the half-pint of
sherry. It was a great beginning. Throughout the
whole evening he could not be got for a moment to join
any of the club juntas which were discussing the great
difficulty of the contumacious gentleman. 'I think
he must really be going to be married at last!' one
club pundit said when a question was asked as to
Houston's singular behaviour on the occasion.

He was indeed very sober,—so sober that he left
the smoking-room as soon as his one silent cigar was
finished, and went out alone in order that he might
roam the streets in thoughtful solitude. It was a
clear frosty night, and as he buttoned his greatcoat
around him he felt that the dry cold air would do him
good, and assist his meditations. At last then everything was arranged for him, and he was to encounter
exactly that mode of life which he had so often told
himself to be most unfit for him. There were to be
the cradles always full, and his little coffer so nearly
empty! And he had done it all for himself. She,
Imogene, had proposed a mode of life to him which
would at any rate have saved him from this; but it
had been impossible that he should accept a plan so
cruel to her when the proposition came from herself.
It must all soon be done now. She had asked that a

distant day might be fixed for their marriage. Even that request, coming from her, made it almost imperative upon him to insist upon an early day. It would be well for him to look upon to-morrow, or a few morrows whose short distance would be immaterial, as the time fixed.

No;—there should be no going back now! So he declared to himself, endeavouring to prepare the suit of armour for his own wearing. Pau might be the best place,—or perhaps one of those little towns in Brittany. Dresden would not do, because there would be society at Dresden, and he must of course give up all ideas of society. He would have liked Rome; but Rome would be far too expensive, and then residents in Rome require to be absent three or four months every year. He and his wife and large family,—he had no doubt in life as to the large family,—would not be able to allow themselves any recreation such as that. He thought he had heard that the ordinary comforts of life were cheap in the west of Ireland,—or, if not cheap, unobtainable, which would be the same thing. Perhaps Castlebar might be a good locality for his nursery. There would be nothing to do at Castlebar,—no amusement whatever for such a one as himself, no fitting companion for Imogene. But then amusement for himself and companions for Imogene must of course be out of the question. He thought that perhaps he might turn his hand to a little useful gardening,—parsnips instead of roses,—while Imogene would be at work in the nursery. He would begin at once and buy two or three dozen pipes, because tobacco would be so much cheaper than cigars. He knew a shop at which were to be had some very pretty new-fashioned meerschaums, which, he had been told, smokers of pipes found to be excellent. But, whether it should be Pau or whether it should be Castlebar, whether it should be pipes, or whether, in regard to economy, no tobacco at all, the question now was at any rate settled for him. He felt rather proud of his gallantry, as he took himself home to bed, declaring to himself that he would answer that last letter from Gertrude in a very few words and in a very decided tone.

There would be many little troubles. On the Monday morning he got up early thinking that as a family man such a practice would be necessary for him. When he had disturbed the house and nearly driven his own servant mad by demanding breakfast at an altogether unaccustomed hour, he found that he had nothing to do. There was that head of Imogene for which she had only once sat, and at which he had occasionally worked from memory because of her refusal to sit again; and he thought for a moment that this might be good employment for him now. But his art was only an expense to him. He could not now afford for himself paint and brushes and canvas, so he turned the half-finished head round upon his easel. Then he took out his banker's book, a bundle of bills and some blotted scraps of ruled paper, with which he set himself to work to arrange his accounts. When he did this he must certainly have been in earnest. But he had not as yet succeeded in seeing light through his figures when he was interrupted by the arrival of a letter which altogether arrested his attention. It was from Mudbury Docimer, and this was the letter;—

'DEAR HOUSTON,

'Of course I think that you and Imogene are two fools. She has told me what took place here yesterday, and I have told her the same as I tell you. I have no power to prevent it; but you know as well as I do that you and she cannot live together on the interest of sixteen thousand pounds. When you've paid everything that you owe I don't suppose there will be so much as that. It had been arranged between you that everything should be over; and if I had thought that anything of the kind would have occurred again I would have told them not to let you into the house. What is the good of two such people

as you making yourselves wretched for ever, just to
satisfy the romance of a moment? I call it wicked.
So I told Imogene, and so I tell you.

'You have changed your mind so often that of
course you may change it again. I am sure that Imogene expects that you will. Indeed I can hardly believe
that you intend to be such a Quixote. But at any
rate I have done my duty. She is old enough to look
after herself, but as long as she lives with me as my
sister I shall tell her what I think; and until she
becomes your wife,—which I hope she never will
be,—I shall tell you the same.

'Yours truly,

'MUDBURY DOCIMER.'

'He always was a hard, unfeeling fellow,' said
Frank to himself. Then he put the letter by with a
crowd of others, assuring himself that it was one
which required no answer.

On the afternoon he called at the house, as he did
again on the Tuesday; but on neither day did he
succeed in seeing Imogene. This he thought to be
hard, as the pleasure of her society was as sweet to
him as ever, though he was doubtful as to his wisdom
in marrying her. On the Wednesday morning he
received a note from her asking him not to come at
once, because Mudbury had chosen to put himself
into a bad humour. Then a few words of honey were
added; 'Of course you know that nothing that he
can say will make a change. I am too well satisfied
to allow of any change that shall not come from you
yourself.' He was quite alive to the sweetness of the
honey, and declared to himself that Mudbury
Docimer's ill-humour was a matter to him of no
concern whatever.

But on the Wednesday there came also another
letter,—in regard to which it will be well that we
should travel down again to Merle Park. An answer
altogether averse to the proposed changes as to the
nieces had been received from Mrs. Dosett. 'As
Ayala does not wish it, of course nothing can be

done.' Such was the decision as conveyed by
Mrs. Dosett. It seemed to Lady Tringle that this
was absurd. It was all very well extending charity
to the children of her deceased sister, Mrs. Dormer;
but all the world was agreed that beggars should not
be choosers. 'As Ayala does not wish it.' Why
should not Ayala wish it? What a fool must Ayala be
not to wish it! Why should not Ayala be made to do
as she was told, whether she wished it or not? Such
were the indignant questions which Lady Tringle
asked of her husband. He was becoming sick of the
young ladies altogether,—of her own girls as well as
the Dormer girls. 'They are a pack of idiots together,' he said, 'and Tom is the worst of the lot.'
With this he rushed off to London, and consoled
himself with his millions.

Mrs. Dosett's letter had reached Merle Park on the
Tuesday morning, Sir Thomas having remained down
in the country over the Monday. Gertrude, having
calculated the course of the post with exactness, had
hoped to get a reply from Frank to that last letter of
hers,—dated from her sick bed, but written in truth
after a little surreptitious visit to the larder after the
servants' dinner,—on the Sunday morning. This
had been possible, and would have evinced a charming alacrity on the part of her lover. But this she had
hardly ventured to expect. Then she had looked
with anxiety to the arrival of letters on the Monday
afternoon, but had looked in vain. On the Tuesday
morning she had felt so certain that she had contrived to open the post-bag herself in spite of illness;
—but there had been nothing for her. Then she sent
the dispatch which reached Frank on the Wednesday
morning, and immediately afterwards took to her
bed again with such a complication of disorders that
the mare with the broken knees was sent at once
into Hastings for the doctor.

'A little rice will be the best thing for her,' said the
doctor.

'But the poor child takes nothing,—literally

nothing,' said Lady Tringle, who was frightened for
her child. Then the doctor went on to say that
arrowroot would be good, and sago, but offered no
other prescription. Lady Tringle was disgusted by
his ignorance, and thought that it might be well to
send up to London for some great man. The doctor
bowed, and made up his mind that Lady Tringle was
an ass. But, being an honest man, and also tender-
hearted, he contrived to get hold of Tom before he
left the house.

'Your sister's health is generally good?' he said.
Tom assented. As far as he knew, Gertrude had
always been as strong as a horse. 'Eats well?' asked
the doctor. Tom, who occasionally saw the family at
lunch, gave a description of his sister's general
performance.

'She is a fine healthy young lady,' said the doctor.
Tom gave a brother's ready adhesion to the word
healthy, but passed over the other epithet as being
superfluous. 'Now, I'll tell you what it is,' said the
doctor. 'Of course I don't want to inquire into any
family secrets.'

'My father, you know,' said Tom, 'won't agree
about the man she's engaged to.'

'That is it? I knew there was some little trouble,
but I did not want to ask any questions. Your
mother is unnecessarily frightened, and I have not
wished to disturb her. Your sister is taking plenty
of nourishment?'

'She does not come to table, nor yet have it in her
own room.'

'She gets it somehow. I can say that it is so. Her
veins are full, and her arms are strong. Perhaps she
goes into the kitchen. Have a little tray made ready
for her, with something nice. She will be sure to find
it, and when she has found it two or three times she
will know that she has been discovered. If Lady
Tringle does send for a physician from London you
could perhaps find an opportunity of telling him
what I have suggested. Her mamma need know

nothing about it.' This took place on the Tuesday, and on the Wednesday morning Gertrude knew that she had been discovered,—at any rate by Tom and the doctor. 'I took care to keep a wing for you,' said Tom; 'I carved them myself at dinner.' As he so addressed her he came out from his hiding-place in the kitchen about midnight, and surprised her in the larder. She gave a fearful scream, which, however, luckily was not heard through the house. 'You won't tell mamma, Tom, will you?' Tom promised that he would not, on condition that she would come down to breakfast on the following morning. This she did, and the London physician was saved a journey.

But, in the meantime, Gertrude's second letter had gone up to Frank, and also a very heartrending epistle from Lady Tringle to her husband. 'Poor Gertrude is in a very bad state. If ever there was a girl really broken-hearted on account of love, she is one. I did not think she would ever set her heart upon a man with such violent affection. I do think you might give way when it becomes a question of life and death. There isn't anything really against Mr. Houston.' Sir Thomas, as he read this, was a little shaken. He had hitherto been inclined to agree with Rosalind, 'That men have died from time to time, and worms have eaten them, but not for love.'* But now he did not know what to think about it. There was Tom undoubtedly in a bad way, and here was Gertrude brought to such a condition, simply by her love, that she refused to take her meals regularly! Was the world come to such a pass that a father was compelled to give his daughter with a large fortune to an idle adventurer, or else to be responsible for his daughter's life? Would Augusta have pined away and died had she not been allowed to marry her Traffick? Would Lucy pine and die unless money were given to her sculptor? Upon the whole, Sir Thomas thought that the cares of his family were harder to bear than those of his millions. In regard

to Gertrude, he almost thought that he would give
way, if only that he might be rid of that trouble.

It must be acknowledged that Frank Houston,
when he received the young lady's letter, was less
soft-hearted than her father. The letter was, or
should have been, heart-rending:—

'YOU CRUEL MAN,

'You must have received my former letter, and
though I told you that I was ill and almost dying you
have not heeded it! Three posts have come, and I
have not had a line from you. In your last you were
weak enough to say that you were going to give it
all up because you could not make papa do just what
you wanted all at once. Do you know what it is to
have taken possession of a young lady's heart; or is
it true, as Augusta says of you, that you care for
nothing but the money? If it is so, say it at once
and let me die. As it is I am so very ill that I cannot
eat a mouthful of anything, and have hardly strength
left to me to write this letter.

'But I cannot really believe what Augusta says,
though I daresay it may have been so with Mr.
Traffick. Perhaps you have not been to your club,
and so you have not got my former letter. Or it may
be that you are ill yourself. If so, I do wish that I
could come and nurse you, though indeed I am so ill
that I am quite unable to leave my bed.

'At any rate, pray write immediately;—and do
come! Mamma seems to think that papa will give
way because I am so ill. If so, I shall think my
illness the luckiest thing in the world.—You must
believe, dearest Frank, that I am now, as ever, yours
most affectionately,

'GERTRUDE.'


Frank Houston was less credulous than Sir
Thomas, and did not believe much in the young
lady's sickness. It was evident that the young lady
was quite up to the work of deceiving her father and

mother, and would no doubt be willing to deceive himself if anything could be got by it. But, whether she were ill or whether she were well, he could offer her no comfort. Nevertheless, he was bound to send her some answer, and with a troubled spirit he wrote as follows:—

'MY DEAR MISS TRINGLE,

'It is to me a matter of inexpressible grief that I should have to explain again that I am unable to persist in seeking the honour of your hand in opposition to the absolute and repeated refusals which I have received from your father. It is so evident that we could not marry without his consent that I need not now go into that matter. But I think myself bound to say that, considering the matter in all its bearing, I must regard our engagement as finally at an end. Were I to hesitate in saying this very plainly I think I should be doing you an injury.

'I am sorry to hear that you are unwell, and trust that you may soon recover your health.

'Your sincere friend,

'FRANK HOUSTON.'

On the next morning Gertrude was still in her bed, having there received her letter, when she sent a message to her brother. Would Tom come and see her? Tom attended to her behest, and then sat down by her bedside on being told in a mysterious voice that she had to demand from him a great service. 'Tom,' she said, 'that man has treated me most shamefully and most falsely.'

'What man?'

'What man? Why, Frank Houston. There has never been any other man. After all that has been said and done he is going to throw me over.'

'The governor threw him over,' said Tom.

'That amounts to nothing. The governor would have given way, of course, and if he hadn't that was no matter of his. After he had had my promise he was bound to go on with it. Don't you think so?'

'Perhaps he was,' said Tom, dubiously.

'Of course he was. What else is the meaning of a promise? Now I'll tell you what you must do. You must go up to London and find him out. You had better take a stick with you, and then ask him what he means to do.'

'And if he says he'll do nothing?'

'Then, Tom, you should call him out. It is just the position in which a brother is bound to do that kind of thing for his sister. When he has been called out, then probably he'll come round, and all will be well.'

The prospect was one which Tom did not at all like. He had had one duel on his hands on his own account, and had not as yet come through it with flying colours. There were still moments in which he felt that he would be compelled at last to take to violence in reference to Colonel Stubbs. He was all but convinced that were he to do so he would fall into some great trouble, but still it was more than probable that his outraged feelings would not allow him to resist. But this second quarrel was certainly unnecessary. 'That's all nonsense, Gertrude,' he said, 'I can do nothing of the kind.'

'You will not?'

'Certainly not. It would be absurd. You ask Septimus and he will tell you that it is so.'

'Septimus, indeed!'

'At any rate, I won't. Men don't call each other out now-a-days. I know what ought to be done in these kind of things, and such interference as that would be altogether improper.'

'Then, Tom,' said she, raising herself in bed, and looking round upon him, 'I will never call you my brother again!'

## CHAPTER XLIII

### ONCE MORE!

'PROBABLY you are not aware, Sir, that I am not at present the young lady's guardian.' This was said at the office in Lombard Street by Sir Thomas, in answer to an offer made to him by Captain Batsby for Ayala's hand. Captain Batsby had made his way boldly into the great man's inner room, and had there declared his purpose in a short and business-like manner. He had an ample income of his own, he said, and was prepared to make a proper settlement on the young lady. If necessary, he would take her without any fortune;—but it would, of course, be for the lady's comfort and for his own if something in the way of money were forthcoming. So much he added, having heard of this uncle's enormous wealth, and having also learned the fact that if Sir Thomas were not at this moment Ayala's guardian he had been not long ago. Sir Thomas listened to him with patience, and then replied to him as above.

'Just so, Sir Thomas. I did hear that. But I think you were once; and you are still her uncle.'

'Yes; I am her uncle.'

'And when I was so ill-treated in Kingsbury Crescent I thought I would come to you. It could not be right that a gentleman making an honourable proposition,—and very liberal, as you must acknowledge,—should not be allowed to see the young lady. It was not as though I did not know her. I had been ten days in the same house with her. Don't you think, Sir Thomas, I ought to have been allowed to see her?'

'I have nothing to do with her,' said Sir Thomas; —'that is, in the way of authority.' Nevertheless, before Captain Batsby left him, he became courteous to that gentleman, and though he could not offer any direct assurance he acknowledged that the application was reasonable. He was, in truth, becoming tired of Ayala, and would have been glad to find a husband whom she would accept, so that she might be out of Tom's way. He had been quite willing that Tom should marry the girl if it were possible, but he began to be convinced that it was impossible. He had offered again to open his house to her, with all its wealth, but she had refused to come into it. His wife had told him that, if Ayala could be brought back in place of Lucy, she would surely yield. But Ayala would not allow herself to be brought back. And there was Tom as bad as ever. If Ayala were once married then Tom could go upon his travels, and come back, no doubt, a sane man. Sir Thomas thought it might be well to make inquiry about this Captain, and then see if a marriage might be arranged. Mrs. Dosett, he told himself, was a hard, stiff woman, and would never get the girl married unless she allowed such a suitor as this Captain Batsby to have access to the house. He did make inquiry, and before the week was over had determined that if Ayala would become Mrs. Batsby there might probably be an end to one of his troubles.

As he went down to Merle Park he arranged his plan. He would, in the first place, tell Tom that Ayala had as many suitors as Penelope,*and that one had come up now who would probably succeed. But when he reached home he found that his son was gone. Tom had taken a sudden freak, and had run up to London. 'He seemed quite to have got a change,' said Lady Tringle.

'I hope it was a change for the better as to that stupid girl.' Lady Tringle could not say that there had been any change for the better, but she thought that there had been a change about the girl. Tom had, as she said, quite 'brisked up,' had declared that he was not going to stand this thing any longer, had packed up three or four portmanteaus, and had had himself carried off to the nearest railway station in time for an afternoon train up to London. 'What is he going to do when he gets there?' asked Sir Thomas. Lady Tringle had no idea what her son intended to do, but thought that something special was intended in regard to Ayala.

'He is an ass,' said the father

'You always say he is an ass,' said the mother, complaining.

'No doubt I do. What else am I to call him?' Then he went on and developed his scheme. 'Let Ayala be asked to Merle Park for a week,—just for a week,—and assured that during that time Tom would not be there. Then let Captain Batsby also be invited.' Upon this there followed an explanation as to Captain Batsby and his aspirations. Tom must be relieved after some fashion, and Sir Thomas declared that no better fashion seemed to present itself. Lady Tringle received her orders with sundry murmurings, still grieving for her son's grief;—but she assented, as she always did assent, to her husband's propositions.

Now we will accompany Tom up to London. The patient reader will perhaps have understood the condition of his mind when in those days of his sharpest agony he had given himself up to Faddle and champagne. By these means he had brought himself into trouble and disgrace, of which he was fully conscious. He had fallen into the hands of the police and had been harassed during the whole period by headache and nausea. Then had come the absurdity of his challenge to Colonel Stubbs, the folly of which had been made plain to him by the very letter which his rival had written to him. There was good sense enough about the poor fellow to enable him to understand that the police court, and the prison, that Faddle and the orgies at Bolivia's, that his challenge and the reply to it, were alike dishonourable to him. Then had come a reaction, and he spent a miserable fortnight down at Merle Park, doing nothing, resolving on nothing, merely moping about and pouring the oft-repeated tale of his woes into his mother's bosom. These days at Merle Park gave him back at any rate his health, and rescued him from the intense wretchedness of his condition on the day after the comparison of Bolivia's wines. In this improved state he told himself that it behoved him even yet to do something as a man, and he came suddenly to the bold resolution of having,—as he called it to himself,—another 'dash at Ayala.'

How the 'dash' was to be made he had not determined when he left home. But to this he devoted the whole of the following Sunday. He had received a lachrymose letter from his friend Faddle, at Aberdeen, in which the unfortunate youth had told him that he was destined to remain in that wretched northern city for the rest of his natural life. He had not as yet been to the Mountaineers since his mishap with the police, and did not care to show himself there at present. He was therefore altogether alone, and, walking all alone the entire round of the parks, he at last formed his resolution.

On the following morning when Mr. Dosett entered his room at Somerset House, a little after half-past ten o'clock, he found his nephew Tom there before him, and waiting for him. Mr. Dosett was somewhat astonished, for he too had heard of Tom's misfortunes. Some ill-natured chronicle of Tom's latter doings had spread itself among the Tringle and Dosett sets, and Uncle Reginald was aware that his nephew had been forced to relinquish his stool in Lombard Street. The vices of the young are perhaps too often exaggerated, so that Mr. Dosett had heard of an amount of champagne consumed and a number of policemen wounded, of which his nephew had not been altogether guilty. There was an idea at Kingsbury Crescent that Tom had gone nearly mad, and was now kept under paternal care at Merle Park. When, therefore, he saw Tom blooming in health, and brighter than usual in general appearance, he was no doubt rejoiced, but also surprised, at the change. 'What, Tom!' he said; 'I'm glad to see you looking so well. Are you up in London again?'

'I'm in town for a day or two,' said Tom.

'And what can I do for you?'

'Well, Uncle Reginald, you can do a great deal for me if you will. Of course you've heard of all those rows of mine?'

'I have heard something.'

'Everybody has heard,' said Tom, mournfully. 'I don't suppose anybody was ever knocked so much about as I've been for the last six months.'

'I'm sorry for that, Tom.'

'I'm sure you are, because you're always good-natured. Now I wonder if you will do a great thing to oblige me.'

'Let us hear what it is,' said Uncle Reginald.

'I suppose you know that there is only one thing in the world that I want.' Mr. Dosett thought that it would be discreet to make no reply to this, but, turning his chair partly round, he prepared to listen very attentively to what his nephew might have to say to him. 'All this about the policeman and the rest of it has simply come from my being so unhappy about Ayala.'

'It wouldn't be taken as a promise of your being a good husband, Tom, when you get into such a mess as that.'

'That's because people don't understand,' said Tom. 'It is because I am so earnest about it, and because I can't bear the disappointment! There isn't one at Travers and Treason who doesn't know that if I'd married Ayala I should have settled down as quiet a young man as there is in all London. You ask the governor else himself. As long as I thought there was any hope I used to be there steady as a rock at half-past nine. Everybody knew it. So I should again, if she'd only come round.'

'You can't make a young lady come round, as you call it.'

'Not make her; no. Of course you can't make a girl. But persuading goes a long way. Why shouldn't she have me? As to all these rows, she ought to feel at any rate that they're her doing. And what she's

done it stands to reason she could undo if she would.
It only wants a word from her to put me all right
with the governor,—and to put me all right with
Travers and Treason too. Nobody can love her as
I do.'

'I do believe that nobody could love her better,'
said Mr. Dosett, who was beginning to be melted
by his nephew's earnestness.

'Oughtn't that to go for something? And then she
would have everything that she wishes. She might
live anywhere she pleased,—so that I might go to
the office every day. She would have her own
carriage, you know.'

'I don't think that would matter much with Ayala.'

'It shows that I'm in a position to ask her,' said
Tom. 'If she could only bring herself not to hate
me——'

'There is a difference, Tom, between hating and
not loving.'

'If she would only begin to make a little way, then
I could hope again. Uncle Reginald, could you not
tell her that at any rate I would be good to her?'

'I think you would be good to her,' he said.

'Indeed, I would. There is nothing I would not do
for her. Now will you let me see her just once again,
and have one other chance?'

This was the great thing which Tom desired from
his uncle, and Mr. Dosett was so much softened by
his nephew's earnestness that he did promise to do
as much as this;—to do as much as this, at least, if it
were in his power. Of course, Ayala must be told.
No good could be done by surprising her by a visit.
But he would endeavour so to arrange it that, if
Tom were to come to him on the following afternoon,
they two should go to the Crescent together, and
then Tom should remain and dine there,—or go
away before dinner, as he might please, after the
interview. This was settled, and Tom left Somerset
House, rejoicing greatly at his success. It seemed to
him that now at last a way was open to him.

Uncle Reginald, on his return home, took his niece aside and talked to her very gently and very kindly. 'Whether you like him or whether you do not, my dear, he is so true to you that you are bound to see him again when he asks it.' At first she was very stout, declaring that she would not see him. Of what good could it be, seeing that she would rather throw herself into the Thames than marry him? Had she not told him so over and over again, as often as he had spoken to her? Why would he not just leave her alone? But against all this her uncle pleaded gently but persistently. He had considered himself bound to promise so much on her behalf, and for his sake she must do as he asked. To this, of course, she yielded. And then he said many good things of poor Tom. His constancy was a great virtue. A man so thoroughly in love would no doubt make a good husband. And then there would be the assent of all the family, and an end, as far as Ayala was concerned, of all pecuniary trouble. In answer to this she only shook her head, promising, however, that she would be ready to give Tom an audience when he should be brought to the Crescent on the following day.

Punctually at four Tom made his appearance at Somerset House, and started with his uncle as soon as the index-books had been put in their places. Tom was very anxious to take his uncle home in a cab, but Mr. Dosett would not consent to lose his walk. Along the Embankment they went, and across Charing Cross into St. James's Park, and then by Green Park, Hyde Park, and Kensington Gardens, all the way to Notting Hill. Mr. Dosett did not walk very fast, and Tom thought they would never reach Kingsbury Crescent. His uncle would fain have talked about the weather, of politics, or the hardships of the Civil Service generally; but Tom would not be diverted from his one subject. Would Ayala be gracious to him? Mr. Dosett had made up his mind to say nothing on the subject. Tom must plead

his own cause. Uncle Reginald thought that he knew
such pleading would be useless, but still would not
say a word to daunt the lover. Neither could he say
a word expressive of hope. As they were fully an
hour-and-a-half on their walk, this reticence was
difficult.

Immediately on his arrival, Tom was taken up
into the drawing-room. This was empty, for it had
been arranged that Mrs. Dosett should be absent till
the meeting was over. 'Now I'll look for this child,'
said Uncle Reginald, in his cheeriest voice as he left
Tom alone in the room. Tom, as he looked round at
the chairs and tables, remembered that he had never
received as much as a kind word or look in the room,
and then great drops of perspiration broke out all over
his brow. All that he had to hope for in the world
must depend upon the next five minutes;—might
depend perhaps upon the very selection of the words
which he might use.

Then Ayala entered the room and stood before him.

'Ayala,' he said, giving her his hand.

'Uncle Reg. says that you would like to see me
once again.'

'Of course I want to see you once, and twice,—and
always. Ayala, if you could know it! If you could
only know it!' Then he clasped his two hands high
upon his breast, not as though appealing to her
heart, but striking his bosom in very agony. 'Ayala,
I feel that, if I do not have you as my own, I can
only die for the want of you. Ayala, do you believe
me?'

'I suppose I believe you, but how can I help it?'

'Try to help it! Try to try and help it! Say a
word that you will perhaps help it by-and-bye.'
Then there came a dark frown upon her brow,—not,
indeed, from anger, but from a feeling that so terrible
a task should be thrown upon her. 'I know you think
that I am common.'

'I have never said a word, Tom, but that I could
not love you.'

'But I am true,—true as the sun. Would I come again after all if it were not that I cannot help coming? You have heard that I have been,—been misbehaving myself?'

'I have not thought about that.'

'It has been so because I have been so wretched. Ayala, you have made me so unhappy. Ayala, you can make me the happiest man there is in London this day. I seem to want nothing else. As for drink, or clubs, or billiards, and all that, they are nothing to me,—unless when I try to forget that you are so—so unkind to me!'

'It is not unkind, not to do as you ask me.'

'To do as I ask you,—that would be kind. Oh, Ayala, cannot you be kind to me?' She shook her head, still standing in the place which she had occupied from the beginning. 'May I come again? Will you give me three months, and then think of it? If you would only say that, I would go back to my work and never leave it.' But she still shook her head. 'Must I never hope?'

'Not for that, Tom. How can I help it?'

'Not help it?'

'No. How can I help it? One does not fall in love by trying,—nor by trying prevent it.'

'By degrees you might love me,—a little.' She had said all that she knew how to say, and again shook her head. 'It is that accursed Colonel,' he exclaimed, forgetting himself as he thought of his rival.

'He is not accursed,' said Ayala, angrily.

'Then you love him?'

'No! But you should not ask. You have no right to ask. It is not proper.'

'You are not engaged to him?'

'No; I am not engaged to him. I do not love him. As you will ask, I tell you. But you should not ask; and he is not accursed. He is better than you,—though I do not love him. You should not have driven me to say this. I do not ask you questions.'

'There is none that I would not answer. Stay,

A.A.—2 J

Ayala,' for now she was going to leave the room. 'Stay yet a moment. Do you know that you are tearing my heart in pieces? Why is it that you should make me so wretched? Dear Ayala;—dearest Ayala;— stay yet a moment.'

'Tom, there is nothing more that I can say. I am very, very sorry if you are unhappy. I do think that you are good and true; and if you will shake hands with me, there is my hand. But I cannot say what you want me to say.' Tom took her by the hand and tried to hold her, without, however, speaking to her again. But she slid away from him and left the room, not having for a moment sat down in his presence.

When the door was closed he stood awhile looking round him, trying to resolve what he might do or what he might say next. He was now at any rate in the house with her, and did not know whether such an opportunity as that might ever occur to him again. He felt that there were words within his bosom which, if he could only bring them up to his mouth, would melt the heart of a stone. There was his ineffable love, his whole happiness at stake, his purpose,—his holy purpose,—to devote himself, and all that he had, to her well-being. Of all this he had a full conception within his own heart, if only he could express it so that others should believe him! But of what use was it now? He had had this further liberty of speech accorded to him, and in it he had done nothing, made no inch of progress. She had hardly spoken a dozen words to him, but of those she had spoken two remained clear upon his memory. He must never hope, she had said; and she had said also that that other man was better than he. Had she said that he was dearer, the word would hardly have been more bitter. All the old feeling came upon him of rage against his rival, and of a desire that something desperate should be done by which he might wreak his vengeance.

But there he was standing alone in Mrs. Dosett's drawing-room, and it was necessary that he should carry himself off. As for dining in that house, sitting down to eat and drink in Ayala's presence after such a conversation as that which was past, that he felt to be quite out of the question. He crammed his hat upon his head, left the room, and hurried down the stairs towards the door.

In the passage he was met by his uncle, coming out of the dining-room. 'Tom,' he said, 'you'll stay and eat your dinner?'

'No, indeed,' said Tom, angrily.

'You shouldn't let yourself be disturbed by little trifles such as these,' said his uncle, trying to put a good face upon the matter.

'Trifles!' said Tom Tringle. 'Trifles!' And he banged the door after him as he left the house.

## CHAPTER XLIV

### IN THE HAYMARKET

IT was now the beginning of February. As Tom and his uncle had walked from Somerset House the streets were dry and the weather fine; but, as Mr. Dosett had remarked, the wind was changing a little out of the east and threatened rain. When Tom left the house it was already falling. It was then past six, and the night was very dark. He had walked there with a top coat and umbrella, but he had forgotten both as he banged the door after him in his passion; and, though he remembered them as he hurried down the steps, he would not turn and knock at the door and ask for them. He was in that humour which converts outward bodily sufferings almost into a relief. When a man has been thoroughly ill-used in greater matters it is almost a consolation to him to feel that he has been turned out into the street to get wet through without his dinner,—even though he may have turned himself out.

He walked on foot, and as he walked became damp and dirty, till he was soon wet through. As soon as he reached Lancaster Gate he went into the park;

and under the doubtful glimmer of the lamps trudged
on through the mud and slush, not regarding his
path, hardly thinking of the present moment in the
full appreciation of his real misery. What should he
do with himself? What else was there now left to
him? He had tried everything and had failed. As he
endeavoured to count himself up, as it were, and tell
himself whether he were worthy of a happier fate
than had been awarded to him, he was very humble,
—humble, though so indignant! He knew himself to
be a poor creature in comparison with Jonathan
Stubbs. Though he could not have been Stubbs had
he given his heart for it, though it was absolutely
beyond him to assume one of those tricks of bearing,
one of those manly, winning ways, which in his eyes
was so excellent in the other man, still he saw them
and acknowledged them, and told himself that they
would be all powerful with such a girl as Ayala.
Though he trusted to his charms and his rings, he
knew that his charms and his rings were abominable,
as compared with that outside look and natural
garniture which belonged to Stubbs, as though of
right,—as though it had been born with him. Not
exactly in those words, but with a full inward sense
of the words, he told himself that Colonel Stubbs was
a gentleman,—whereas he acknowledged himself to
be a cad. How could he have hoped that Ayala
should accept such a one, merely because he would
have a good house of his own and a carriage? As he
thought of all this, he hardly knew which he hated
most,—himself or Jonathan Stubbs.

He went down to the family house in Queen's Gate,
which was closed and dark,—having come there with
no special purpose, but having found himself there,
as though by accident, in the neighbourhood. Then
he knocked at the door, which, after a great undoing
of chains, was opened by an old woman, who with
her son had the custody of the house when the family
were out of town. Sir Thomas in these days had
rooms of his own in Lombard Street in which he

loved to dwell, and would dine at a city club, never leaving the precincts of the city throughout the week. The old woman was an old servant, and her son was a porter at the office. 'Mr. Tom! Be that you? Why you are as wet as a mop!' He was wet as any mop, and much dirtier than a mop should be. There was no fire except in the kitchen, and there he was taken. He asked for a greatcoat, but there was no such thing in the house, as the young man had not yet come home. Nor was there any food that could be offered him, or anything to drink; as the cellar was locked up, and the old woman was on board wages. But he sat crouching over the fire, watching the steam as it came up from his damp boots and trousers. 'And ain't you had no dinner, Mr. Tom?' said the old woman. Tom only shook his head. 'And ain't you going to have none?' The poor wretch again shook his head. 'That's bad, Mr. Tom.' Then she looked up into his face. 'There is something wrong I know, Mr. Tom. I hears that from Jem. Of course he hears what they do be saying in Lombard Street.'

'What is it they say, Mrs. Tapp?'

'Well;—that you ain't there as you used to be. Things is awk'ard, and Sir Thomas, they say, isn't best pleased. But of course it isn't no affair of mine, Mr. Tom.'

'Do they know why?' he asked.

'They do say it's some'at about a young lady.'

'Yes; by heavens!' said Tom, jumping up out of his chair. 'Oh, Mrs. Tapp, you can't tell the condition I'm in. A young lady indeed! D—— the fellow!'

'Don't 'ee now, Mr. Tom.'

'D—— the fellow! But there's no good in my standing here cursing. I'll go off again. You needn't say that I've been here, Mrs. Tapp?'

'But you won't go out into the rain, Mr. Tom?'

'Rain,—what matters the rain?' Then he started again, disregarding all her prayers, and went off eastward on foot, disdaining the use of a cab because he had settled in his mind on no place to which he would go.

Yes; they knew all about it, down to the very porters at the office. Everyone had heard of his love for Ayala; and everyone had heard also that Ayala had scorned him. Not a man or woman connected by ever so slight a tie to the establishment was unaware that he had been sent away from his seat because of Ayala! All this might have been borne easily had there been any hope; but now he was forced to tell himself that there was none. He saw no end to his misery,—no possibility of escape. Where was he to go in this moment of his misery for any shred of comfort? The solitude of his lodgings was dreadful to him; nor had he heart enough left to him to seek companionship at his club.

At about ten o'clock he found himself, as it were, by accident, close to Mr. Bolivia's establishment. He was thoroughly wet through, jaded, wretched, and in want of sustenance. He turned in, and found the place deserted. The diners had gone away, and the hour had not come at which men in quest of later refreshment were wont to make their appearance. But there were still one or two gas-lights burning; and he threw himself wearily into a little box or partition nearest to the fire. Here Signor Bolivia himself came to him, asking in commiserating accents what had brought him thither in so wretched a plight. 'I have left my coat and umbrella behind,' said Tom, trying to pluck up a little spirit,—'and my dinner too.'

'No dinner, Mr. Tringle; and you wet through like that! What shall I get you, Mr. Tringle?' But Tom declared that he would have no dinner. He was off his appetite altogether, he said. He would have a bottle of champagne and a devilled biscuit. Mr. Walker, who, as we are aware, put himself forward to the world generally as Signor Bolivia, felt for the moment a throb of pity, which overcame in his heart the innkeeper's natural desire to make the most he could of his customer. 'Better have a mutton chop and a little drop of brandy-and-water hot.'

'I ain't up to it, Bolivia,' said the young man. 'I couldn't swallow it if I had it. Give us the bottle of champagne and the devilled biscuit.' Then Mr. Walker,—for Bolivia was in truth Walker,—fetched the wine and ordered the biscuit; and poor Tom was again brought back to the miserable remedy to which he had before applied himself in his misfortune. There he remained for about an hour, during a part of which he slept; but before he left the house he finished the wine. As he got up to take his departure Mr. Walker scanned his gait and bearing, having a friendly feeling for the young man, and not wishing him to fall again into the hands of the police. But Tom walked forth apparently as sober as a judge, and as melancholy as a hangman. As far as Mr. Walker could see the liquor had made no impression on him. 'If I were you, Mr. Tringle,' said the keeper of the eating-house, 'I'd go home at once, because you are so mortal wet.'

'All right,' said Tom, going out into the pouring rain.

It was then something after eleven, and Tom instead of taking the friendly advice which had been offered to him, walked, as fast as he could, round Leicester Square; and as he walked the fumes of the wine mounted into his head. But he was not drunk, —not as yet so drunk as to misbehave himself openly. He did not make his way round the square without being addressed, but he simply shook off from him those who spoke to him. His mind was still intent upon Ayala. But now he was revengeful rather than despondent. The liquor had filled him once again with a desire to do something. If he could destroy himself and the Colonel by one and the same blow, how fitting a punishment would that be for Ayala! But how was he to do it? He would throw himself down from the top of the Duke of York's column, but that would be nothing unless he could force the Colonel to take the jump with him! He had called the man out and he wouldn't come! Now, with the alcohol in his brain, he again thought that the man was a coward for not coming. Had not such a meeting been from time immemorial the resource of gentlemen injured as he now was injured? The Colonel would not come when called,—but could he not get at him so as to strike him? If he could do the man a real injury he would not care what amount of punishment he might be called upon to bear.

He hurried at last out of the square into Coventry Street and down the Haymarket. His lodgings were in Duke Street, turning out of Piccadilly,—but he could not bring himself to go home to his bed. He was unutterably wretched, but yet he kept himself going with some idea of doing something, or of fixing some purpose. He certainly was tipsy now, but not so drunk as to be unable to keep himself on his legs. He gloried in the wet, shouting inwardly to himself that he in his misery was superior to all accidents of the weather. Then he stood for awhile watching the people as they came out of the Haymarket Theatre. He was at this time a sorry sight to be seen. His hat was jammed on to his head and had been almost smashed in the jamming. His coat reeking wet through was fastened by one button across his chest. His two hands were thrust into his pockets, and the bottle of champagne was visible in his face. He was such a one,—to look at,—that no woman would have liked to touch nor any man to address. In this guise he stood there amidst the crowd, foremost among those who were watching the ladies as they got into their vehicles. 'And she might be as good as the best of them, and I might be here to hand her into her own carriage,'—said he to himself,—'if it were not for that intruder!'

At that moment the intruder was there before him, and on his arm was a lady whom he was taking across to a carriage, at the door of which a servant in livery was standing. They were followed closely by a pretty young girl who was picking her steps after them alone. These were Lady Albury and Nina, whom Colonel Stubbs had escorted to the play.

'You will be down by the twentieth?' said the elder lady.

'Punctual as the day comes,' said the Colonel.

'And mind you have Ayala with you,' said the younger.

'If Lady Albury can manage it with her aunt of course I will wait upon her,' said the Colonel. Then the door of the carriage was shut, and the Colonel was left to look for a cab. He had on an overcoat and an opera hat, but otherwise was dressed as for dinner. On one side a link-boy was offering him assistance, and on another a policeman tendering him some service. He was one of those who by their outward appearance always extort respect from those around them.

As long as the ladies had been there,—during the two minutes which had been occupied while they got into the carriage,—Tom had been restrained by their presence. He had been restrained by their presence even though he had heard Ayala's name and had understood the commission given to the man whom he hated. Had Colonel Stubbs luckily followed the ladies into the carriage Tom, in his fury, would have taken himself off to his bed. But now,— there was his enemy within a yard of him! Here was the opportunity the lack of which seemed, a few moments since, to be so grievous to him! He took two steps out from the row in which he stood and struck his rival high on his breast with his fist. He had aimed at the Colonel's face but in his eagerness had missed his mark. 'There,' said he, 'there! You would not fight me, and now you have got it.' Stubbs staggered, and would have fallen but for the policeman. Tom, though no hero, was a strong young man, and had contrived to give his blow with all his force. The Colonel did not at first see from whom the outrage had come, but at once claimed the policeman's help.

'We've got him, Sir;—we've got him,' said the policeman.

'You've got me,' said Tom, 'but I've had my revenge.' Then, though two policemen and one waterman were now holding him, he stretched himself up to his full height and glared at his enemy in the face.

'It's the chap who gave that hawful blow to Thompson in the bow'ls!' said one of the policemen, who by this time had both Tom's arms locked behind his own.

Then the Colonel knew who had struck him. 'I know him,' said the Colonel to the policeman. 'It is a matter of no consequence.'

'So do we, Sir. He's Thomas Tringle, junior.'

'He's a friend of mine,' said the Colonel. 'You must let him come with me.'

'A friend, is he?' said an amateur attendant. The policeman, who had remembered the cruel onslaught made on his comrade, looked very grave, and still held Tom tight by the arms. 'A very hugly sort of friend,' said the amateur. Tom only stretched himself still higher, but remained speechless.

'Tringle,' said the Colonel, 'this was very foolish, you know,—a most absurd thing to do! Come with me, and we will talk it all over.'

'He must come along with us to the watch-house just at present,' said the policeman. 'And you, Sir, if you can, had better please to come with us. It ain't far across to Vine Street, but of course you can have a cab if you like it.' This was ended by two policemen walking off with Tom between them, and by the Colonel following in a cab, after having administered divers shillings to the amateur attendants. Though the journey in the cab did not occupy above five minutes, it sufficed him to determine what step he should take when he found himself before the night officers of the watch.

When he found himself in the presence of the night officer he had considerable difficulty in carrying out his purpose. That Tom should be locked up for the night, and be brought before the police magistrate next morning to answer for the outrage he had committed, seemed to the officers to be a matter of course. It was long before the Colonel could persuade the officer that this little matter between him and Mr. Tringle was a private affair, of which he at least wished to take no further notice. 'No doubt,' he said, 'he had received a blow on his chest, but it had not hurt him in the least.'

''E 'it the gen'leman with all his might and main,' said the policeman.

'It is quite a private affair,' said the Colonel. 'My name is Colonel Stubbs; here is my card. Sir —— is a particular friend of mine.' He named a pundit of the peace, very high in the estimation of all policemen. 'If you will let the gentleman come away with me I will be responsible for him to-morrow, if it should be necessary to take any further step in the matter.' This he said very eagerly, and with all the authority which he knew how to use. Tom, in the meantime, stood perfectly motionless, with his arms folded akimbo on his breast, wet through, muddy, still tipsy, a sight miserable to behold.

The card and the Colonel's own name, and the name of the pundit of the peace together, had their effect, and after a while Tom was dismissed in the Colonel's care. The conclusion of the evening's affair was, for the moment, one which Tom found very hard to bear. It would have been better for him to have been dragged off to a cell, and there to have been left to his miserable solitude. But as he went down through the narrow ways leading from the police-office out into the main street he felt that he was altogether debarred from making any further attack upon his protector. He could not strike him again, as he might have done had he escaped from the police by his own resources. His own enemy had saved him from durance, and he could not, therefore, turn again upon his enemy.

'In heaven's name, my dear fellow,' said the Colonel, 'what good do you expect to get by that? You have hit me a blow when you knew that I was unprepared, and, therefore, unarmed. Was that manly?' To this Tom made no reply. 'I suppose you have been drinking?' And Stubbs, as he asked this question, looked into his companion's face. 'I see you have been drinking. What a fool you are making of yourself!'

'It is that girl,' said Tom.

'Does that seem to you to be right? Can you do yourself any good by that? Will she be more likely to listen to you when she hears that you have got drunk, and have assaulted me in the street? Have I done you any harm?'

'She says that you are better than me,' replied Tom.

'If she does, is that my doing? Come, old fellow, try to be a man. Try to think of this thing rightly. If you can win the girl you love, win her; but, if you cannot, do not be such an ass as to suppose that she is to love no one because she will not love you. It is a thing which a man must bear if it comes in his way. As far as Miss Dormer is concerned, I am in the same condition as you. But do you think that I should attack you in the street if she began to favour you to-morrow?'

'I wish she would; and then I shouldn't care what you did.'

'I should think you a happy fellow, certainly; and for a time I might avoid you, because your happiness would remind me of my own disappointment; but I should not come behind your back and strike you! Now, tell me where you live, and I will see you home.' Then Tom told him where he lived, and in a few minutes the Colonel had left him within his own hall door.

## CHAPTER XLV

### THERE IS SOMETHING OF THE ANGEL ABOUT HIM

THE little accident which was recorded at the close of the last chapter occurred on a Tuesday night. On the following afternoon Tom Tringle, again very much out of spirits, returned to Merle Park. There was now nothing further for him to do in London. He had had his last chance with Ayala, and the last chance had certainly done him no good. Fortune, whether kindly or unkindly, had given him an opportunity of revenging himself upon the Colonel; he had taken advantage of the opportunity, but did not find himself much relieved by what he had done. His rival's conduct had caused him to be thoroughly ashamed of himself. It had at any rate taken from him all further hope of revenge. So that now there was nothing for him but to take himself back to Merle Park. On the Wednesday he heard nothing further of the matter; but on the Thursday Sir Thomas came down from London, and, showing to poor Tom a paragraph in one of the morning papers, asked whether he knew anything of the circumstance to which reference was made. The paragraph was as follows:—

'That very bellicose young City knight who at Christmas time got into trouble by thrashing a policeman within an inch of his life in the streets, and who was then incarcerated on account of his performance, again exhibited his prowess on Tuesday night by attacking Colonel ——, an officer than whom none in the army is more popular,—under the portico of the Haymarket theatre. We abstain from mentioning the officer's name,—which is, however, known to us. The City knight again fell into the hands of the police and was taken to the watchhouse. But Colonel ——, who knew something of his family, accompanied him, and begged his assailant off. The officer on duty was most unwilling to

let the culprit go; but the Colonel used all his influence and was successful. This may be all very well
between the generous Colonel and the valiant knight.
But if the young man has any friends thay had better
look to him. A gentleman with such a desire for the
glories of battle must be restrained if he cannot control his propensities when wandering about the
streets of the metropolis.'

'Yes,' said Tom,—who scorned to tell a lie in any
matter concerning Ayala. 'It was me. I struck
Colonel Stubbs, and he got me off at the police
office.'

'And you're proud of what you've done?'

'No, Sir, I'm not. I'm not proud of anything.
Whatever I do or whatever I say seems to go
against me.'

'He didn't go against you as you call it.'

'I wish he had with all my heart. I didn't ask
him to get me off. I struck him because I hated
him; and whatever might have happened I would
sooner have borne it than be like this.'

'You would sooner have been locked up again in
prison?'

'I would sooner anything than be as I am.'

'I tell you what it is, Tom,' said the father. 'If
you remain here any longer with this bee in your
bonnet you will be locked up in a lunatic asylum,
and I shall not be able to get you out again. You
must go abroad.' To this Tom made no immediate
answer. Lamentable as was his position, he still was
unwilling to leave London while Ayala was living
there. Were he to consent to go away for any
lengthened period, by doing so he would seem to
abandon his own claim. Hope he knew there was
none; but yet, even yet, he regarded himself as one
of Ayala's suitors. 'Do you think it well,' continued
the father, 'that you should remain in London while
such paragraphs as these are being written about
you?'

'I am not in London now,' said Tom.

'No, you are not in London while you are at Merle Park,—of course. And you will not go up to London without my leave. Do you understand that?' Here Tom again was silent. 'If you do,' continued his father, 'you shall not be received down here again, nor at Queen's Gate, nor will the cheques for your allowance be honoured any longer at the bank. In fact if you do not obey me I will throw you off altogether. This absurdity about your love has been carried on long enough.' And so it came to be understood in the family that Tom was to be kept in mild durance at Merle Park till everything should have been arranged for his extended tour about the world. To this Tom himself gave no positive assent, but it was understood that when the time came he would yield to his father's commands.

It had thus come to pass that the affray at the door of the Haymarket became known to so much of the world at large as interested itself in the affairs either of Colonel Stubbs or of the Tringles. Other paragraphs were written in which the two heroes of the evening were designated as Colonel J—— S—— and as T—— T——, junior, of the firm of T—— and T——, in the City. All who pleased could read these initials, and thus the world was aware that our Colonel had received a blow, and had resented the affront only by rescuing his assailant from the hands of the police. A word was said at first which seemed to imply that the Colonel had not exhibited all the spirit which might have been expected from him. Having been struck should he not have thrashed the man who struck him;—or at any rate have left the ruffian in the hands of the policemen for proper punishment? But many days had not passed over before the Colonel's conduct had been viewed in a different light, and men and women were declaring that he had done a manly and a gallant thing. The affair had in this way become sufficiently well known to justify the allusion made to it in the following letter from Lady Albury to Ayala:—

'Stalham, Tuesday, 11th February, 18—.

'MY DEAR AYALA,

'It is quite indispensable for the happiness of everybody, particularly that of myself and Sir Harry, that you should come down here on the twentieth. Nina will be here on her farewell visit before her return to her mother. Of course you have heard that it is all arranged between her and Lord George Bideford, and this will be the last opportunity which any of us will have of seeing her once again before her martyrdom. The world is to be told that he is to follow her to Rome, where they are to be married,— no doubt by the Pope himself under the dome of St. Peter's. But my belief is that Lord George is going to travel with her all the way. If he is the man I take him to be he will do so, but of course it would be very improper.

'You, however, must of course come and say pretty things to your friend; and, as you cannot go to Rome to see her married, you must throw your old shoe after her when she takes her departure from Stalham. I have written a line to your aunt to press my request for this visit. This she will no doubt show to you, and you, if you please, can show her mine in return.

'And now, my dear, I must explain to you one or two other arrangements. A certain gentleman will *certainly* not be here. It was not my fault that a certain gentleman went to Kingsbury Crescent. The certain gentleman is, as you are aware, a great friend of ours, and was entitled to explain himself if it so seemed good to him; but the certain gentleman was not favoured in that enterprise by the Stalham interest. At any rate, the certain gentleman will not be at Stalham on this occasion. So much for the certain gentleman.

'Colonel Stubbs will be here, and, as he will be coming down on the twentieth, would be glad to travel by the same train, so that he may look after

your ticket and your luggage, and be your slave for
the occasion. He will leave the Paddington Station
by the 4 P.M. train if that will suit you.

'We all think that he behaved beautifully in that
little affair at the Haymarket theatre. I should not
mention it only that everybody has heard of it.
Almost any other man would have struck the poor
fellow again; but he is one of the very few who always know what to do at the moment without
taking time to think of it.

'Mind you come like a good girl.—Your affectionate friend,                    'ROSALINE ALBURY.'

It was in this way that Ayala heard what had
taken place between her cousin Tom and Colonel
Stubbs. Some hint of a fracas between the two men
had reached her ears; but now she asked various
questions of her aunt, and at last elicited the truth.
Tom had attacked her other lover in the street,—
had attacked Colonel Stubbs because of his injured
love, and had grossly misbehaved himself. As a
consequence he would have been locked up by the
police had not the Colonel himself interfered on his
behalf. This to Ayala seemed to be conduct worthy
almost of an Angel of Light.

Then the question of the proposed visit was discussed,—first with her aunt, and then with herself.
Mrs. Dosett was quite willing that her niece should
go to Stalham. To Mrs. Dosett's thinking, a further
journey to Stalham would mean an engagement with
Colonel Stubbs. When she had read Lady Albury's
letter she was quite sure that that had been Lady
Albury's meaning. Captain Batsby was not to receive the Stalham interest;—but that interest was
to be used on the part of Colonel Stubbs. She had
not the slightest objection. It was clear to her that
Ayala would have to be married before long. It was
out of the question that one man after another should
fall in love with her violently, and that nothing
should come of it. Mrs. Dosett had become quite

despondent about Tom. There was an amount of dislike which it would be impossible to overcome. And as for Captain Batsby there could be no chance for a man whom the young lady could not be induced even to see. But the other lover, whom the lady would not admit that she loved,—as to whom she had declared that she could never love him,—was held in very high favour. 'I do think it was so noble not to hit Tom again,' she had said. Therefore, as Colonel Stubbs had a sufficient income, there could be no reason why Ayala should not go again to Stalham. So it was that Mrs. Dosett argued with herself, and such was the judgment which she expressed to Ayala.

But there were difficulties. Ayala's little stock of cash was all gone. She could not go to Stalham without money, and that money must come out of her Uncle Reginald's pocket. She could not go to Stalham without some expenditure, which, as she well knew, it would be hard for him to bear. And then there was that terrible question of her clothes! When that suggestion had been made of a further transfer of the nieces a cheque had come from Sir Thomas. 'If Ayala comes to us she will want a few things,' Sir Thomas had said in a note to Mrs. Dosett. But Mr. Dosett had chosen that the cheque should be sent back when it was decided that the further transfer should not take place. The cheque had been sent back, and there had been an end of it. There must be a morning dress, and there must be another hat, and there must be boots. So much Mrs. Dosett acknowledged. Let them do what they might with the old things, Mrs. Dosett acknowledged that so much as that would at least be necessary. 'We will both go to work,' Mrs. Dosett said, 'and we will ask your uncle what he can do for us.' I think she felt that she had received some recompense when Ayala kissed her.

It was after this that Ayala discussed the matter with herself. She had longed to go once again to

Stalham,—' dear Stalham,' as she called it to herself.
And as she thought of the place she told herself that
she loved it because Lady Albury had been so kind
to her, and because of Nina, and because of the
hunting, and because of the general pleasantness and
luxury of the big comfortable house. And yes; there
was something to be said, too, of the pleasantness of
Colonel Stubbs. Till he had made love to her he had
been, perhaps, of all these fine new friends the
pleasantest. How joyous his voice had sounded to
her! How fraught with gratification to her had been
his bright ugly face! How well he had known how
to talk to her, and to make her talk, so that everything had been easy with her! How thoroughly she
remembered all his drollery on that first night at
the party in London,—and all his keen sayings at the
theatre ;—and the way he had insisted that she should
hunt! She thought of little confidences she had had
with him, almost as though he had been her brother!
And then he had destroyed it all by becoming her
lover!

Was he to be her lover still; and if so would it be
right that she should go again to Stalham, knowing
that she would meet him there? Would it be right
that she should consent to travel with him,—under
his special escort? Were she to do so would she not
be forced to do more,—if he should again ask her?
It was so probable that he would not ask her again!
It was so strange that such a one should have asked
her!

But if he did ask her? Certainly he was not like
that Angel of Light whom she had never seen, but
of whom the picture in her imagination was as clearly
drawn as though she were in his presence daily.
No ;—there was a wave of hair and a shape of brow,
and a peculiarity of the eye, with a nose and mouth
cut as sharp as chisel could cut them out of
marble, all of which graced the Angel but none of
which belonged to the Colonel. Nor were these the
chief of the graces which made the Angel so glorious

to her. There was a depth of poetry about him, deep and clear, pellucid as a lake among grassy banks, which made all things of the world mean when compared to it. The Angel of Light lived on the essence of all that was beautiful, altogether unalloyed by the grossness of the earth. That such a one should come in her way! Oh, no; she did not look for it! But, having formed such an image of an angel for herself, would it be possible that she should have anything less divine, less beautiful, less angelic?

Yes; there was something of the Angel about him; even about him, Colonel Jonathan Stubbs. But he was so clearly an Angel of the earth, whereas the other one, though living upon the earth, would be of the air, and of the sky, of the clouds, and of the heaven, celestial. Such a one she knew she had never seen. She partly dreamed that she was dreaming. But if so had not her dream spoilt her for all else? Oh, yes; indeed he was good, this red-haired ugly Stubbs. How well had he behaved to Tom! How kind he had been to herself! How thoughtful of her he was! If it were not a question of downright love, —of giving herself up to him, body and soul, as it were,—how pleasant would it be to dwell with him! For herself she would confess that she loved earthly things,—such as jumping over the brook with Larry Twentyman before her to show her the way. But for her love, it was necessary that there should be an Angel of Light. Had she not read that angels had come from heaven and taken in marriage the daughters of men?*

But was it right that she should go to Stalham, seeing that there were two such strong reasons against it? She could not go without costing her uncle money, which he could ill afford; and if she did go would she—would she not confess that she had abandoned her objection to the Colonel's suit? She, too, understood something of that which had made itself so plain to her aunt. 'Your uncle thinks it is right that you should go,' her aunt said to her in the drawing-room that evening; 'and we will set to work to-morrow and do the best that we can to make you smart.'

Her uncle was sitting in the room at the time, and Ayala felt herself compelled to go to him and kiss him, and thank him for all his kindness. 'I am so sorry to cost you so much money, Uncle Reginald,' she said.

'It will not be very much, my dear,' he answered. 'It is hard that young people should not have some amusement. I only hope they will make you happy at Stalham.'

'They always make people happy at Stalham,' said Ayala, energetically.

'And now, Ayala,' said her aunt, 'you can write your letter to Lady Albury before we go out to-morrow. Give her my compliments, and tell her that as you are writing I need not trouble her.'

Ayala, when she was alone in her bedroom, felt almost horrified as she reflected that in this manner the question had been settled for her. It had been impossible for her to reject her uncle's liberal offer when it had been made. She could not find the courage at that moment to say that she had thought better of it all, and would decline the visit. Before she was well aware of what she was doing she had assented, and had thus, as it were, thrown over all the creations of her dream. And yet, as she declared herself, not even Lady Albury could make her marry this man, merely because she was at her house. She thought that, if she could only avoid that first journey with Colonel Stubbs in the railway, still she might hold her own. But, were she to travel with him of her own accord, would it not be felt that she would be wilfully throwing herself in his way? Then she made a little plan for herself, which she attempted to carry out when writing her letter to Lady Albury on the following morning. What was the nature of her plan, and how she effected it, will be seen in the letter which she wrote:—

'Kingsbury Crescent, Thursday.

'DEAR LADY ALBURY,

'It is so very good of you to ask me again, and
I shall be so happy to visit Stalham once more! I
should have been very sorry not to see dear Nina
before her return to Italy. I have written to congratulate her of course, and have told her what a
happy girl I think she is. Though I have not seen
Lord George I take all that from her description. As
she is going to be his wife immediately, I don't at
all see why he should not go back with her to Rome.
As for being married by the Pope, I don't think he
ever does anything so useful as that. I believe he sits
all day and has his toe kissed.* That is what they
told me at Rome.

'I am very glad of what you tell me about the
certain gentleman, because I don't think I could
have been happy at Stalham if he had been there.
It surprised me so much that I could not think that
he meant it in earnest. We never hardly spoke to
each other when we were in the house together.

'Perhaps, if you don't mind, and I shan't be in the
way,'—here she began to display the little plan
which she had made for her own protection,—' I will
come down by an earlier train than you mention.
There is one at 2.15, and then I need not be in the
dark all the way. You need not say anything about
this to Colonel Stubbs, because I do not at all mind
travelling by myself.—Yours affectionately,

'AYALA.'

This was her little plan. But she was very innocent
when she thought that Lady Albury would be blind
to such a scheme as that. She got three words from
Lady Albury, saying that the 2.15 train would do
very well, and that the carriage would be at the
station to meet her. Lady Albury did not also say
in her note that she had communicated with Colonel
Stubbs on the subject, and informed him that he

must come up from Aldershot earlier than he intended in order that he might adapt himself to
Ayala's whims. 'Foolish little child!' said Lady
Albury to herself. 'As if that would make any
difference!' It was clear to Lady Albury that Ayala
must surrender now that she was coming to Stalham
a second time, knowing that the Colonel would be
there.

## CHAPTER XLVI

### AYALA GOES AGAIN TO STALHAM

THE correspondence between Lady Albury and
Colonel Stubbs was close and frequent, the friendship between them being very close. Ayala had
sometimes asked herself why Lady Albury should
have been so kind and affectionate to her, and had
failed to find any sufficient answer. She had been
asked to Stalham at first,—so far as she knew,—
because she had been intimate at Rome with the
Marchesa Baldoni. Hence had apparently risen Lady
Albury's great friendship, which had seemed even
to herself to be strange. But in truth the Marchesa
had had very little to do with it,—nor had Lady
Albury become attached to Ayala for Ayala's own
sake. To Lady Albury Colonel Stubbs was,—as she
declared to herself very often,—'her own real
brother.' She had married a man very rich, well
known in the world, whom she loved very well; and
she was not a woman who in such a position would
allow herself to love another man. That there might
certainly be no danger of this kind she was continually impressing on her friend the expediency of
marriage,—if only he could find some one good
enough to marry. Then the Colonel had found Ayala.
Lady Albury at the beginning of all this was not
inclined to think that Ayala was good enough.
Judging at first from what she heard and then from
what she saw, she had not been very favourable to

Ayala. But when her friend had insisted,—had declared that his happiness depended on it,—had shown by various signs that he certainly would carry out his intentions, if not at Stalham then elsewhere, Lady Albury had yielded herself to him, and had become Ayala's great friend. If it was written in the book that Ayala was to become Mrs. Stubbs then it would certainly be necessary that she and Ayala should be friends. And she herself had such confidence in Jonathan Stubbs as a man of power, that she did not doubt of his success in any matter to which he might choose to devote himself. The wonder had been that Ayala should have rejected the chance when it had come in her way. The girl had been foolish, allowing herself to be influenced by the man's red hair and ill-sounding name,—not knowing a real pearl when she saw it. So Lady Albury had thought,—having only been partially right in so thinking,—not having gone to the depth of Ayala's power of dreaming. She was very confident, however, that the girl, when once again at Stalham, would yield herself easily; and therefore she went to work, doing all that she could to smoothen love's road for her friend Jonathan. Her woman's mind had seen all those difficulties about clothes, and would have sent what was needful herself had she not feared to offend both the Dosetts and Ayala. Therefore she prepared a present which she could give to the girl at Stalham without offence. If it was to be the girl's high fate to become Mrs. Jonathan Stubbs, it would be proper that she should be adorned and decked, and made beautiful among others of her class,—as would become the wife of such a hero.

Of all that passed between her and Ayala word was sent down to Aldershot. 'The stupid little wretch will throw you out, I know,' wrote Lady Albury, 'by making you start two hours before you have done your work. But you must let your work do itself for this occasion. There is nothing like a little journey together to make people understand each other.'

The Colonel was clearly determined to have the little journey together. Whatever might be the present military duties at Aldershot, the duties of love were for the nonce in the Colonel's mind more imperative. Though his Royal Highness had been coming that afternoon to inspect all the troops, still he would have resolved so to have arranged matters as to travel down with Ayala to Stalham. But not only was he determined to do this, but he found it necessary also to arrange a previous meeting with Lady Albury before that important twentieth of the month. This he did by making his friend believe that her presence in London for a few hours would be necessary for various reasons. She came up as he desired, and there he met her at her hotel in Jermyn Street. On his arrival here he felt that he was almost making a fool of himself by the extent of his anxiety. In his nervousness about this little girl he was almost as insane as poor Tom Tringle, who, when she despised his love, was altogether unable to control himself. 'If I cannot persuade her at last, I shall be knocking somebody over the head, as he did.' It was thus he was talking to himself as he got out of the cab at the door of the hotel.

'And now, Jonathan,' said Lady Albury, 'what can there possibly be to justify you in giving me all this trouble?'

'You know you had to come up about that cook's character.'

'I know that I have given that as a reason to Sir Harry; but I know also that I should have gone without a cook for a twelvemonth had you not summoned me.'

'The truth is I could not get down to Stalham and back without losing an additional day, which I cannot possibly spare. With you it does not very much matter how many days you spare.'

'Nor how much money I spend, nor how much

A.A.—22

labour I take, so that I obey all the commands of Colonel Jonathan Stubbs! What on earth is there that I can say or do for you more?'

'There are one or two things,' said he, 'that I want you to understand. In the first place, I am quite in earnest about this.'

'Don't I know that you're in earnest?'

'But perhaps you do not understand the full extent of my earnestness. If she were to refuse me ultimately I should go away.'

'Go away! Go where?'

'Oh; that I have not at all thought of;—probably to India, as I might manage to get a regiment there. But in truth it would matter very little.'

'You are talking like a goose.'

'That is very likely, because in this matter I think and feel like a goose. It is not a great thing in a man to be turned out of his course by some undefined feeling which he has as to a young woman. But the thing has occurred before now, and will occur again, in my case, if I am thrown over.'

'What on earth is there about the girl?' asked Lady Albury. 'There is that precious brother-in-law of ours going to hang himself incontinently because she will not look at him. And that unfortunate friend of yours, Tom Tringle, is, if possible, worse than Ben Batsby or yourself.'

'If two other gentlemen are in the same condition it only makes it the less singular that I should be the third. At any rate, I am the third.'

'You do not mean to liken yourself to them?'

'Indeed I do. As to our connection with Miss Dormer, I can see no difference. We are all in love with her, and she has refused us all. It matters little whether a man's ugliness or his rings or his natural stupidity may have brought about this result.'

'You are very modest, Jonathan.'

'I always was, only you never could see it. I am modest in this matter; but not for that reason the less persistent in doing the best I can for myself. My

object now in seeing you is to let you understand
that it is—well, not life and death, because she will
not suffice either to kill me or to keep me alive,—
but one of those matters which, in a man's career,
are almost as important to him as life and death.
She was very decided in her refusal.'

'So is every girl when a first offer is made to her.
How is any girl so to arrange her thoughts at a
moment's notice as to accept a man off-hand?'

'Girls do do so.'

'Very rarely, I think; and when they do they are
hardly worth having,' said Lady Albury, laying
down the law on the matter with great precision.
'If a girl accept a man all at once when she has had,
as it were, no preparation for such a proposal, she
must always surely be in a state of great readiness
for matrimonial projects. When there has been a
prolonged period of spooning then of course it is
quite a different thing. The whole thing has in fact
been arranged before the important word has been
spoken.'

'What a professor in the art you are!' said he.

'The odd thing is, that such a one as you should
be so ignorant. Can't you understand that she would
not come to Stalham if her mind were made up
against you? I said nothing of you as a lover, but
I took care to let her know that you were coming.
You are very ready to put yourself in the same boat
with poor Ben Batsby or that other unfortunate
wretch. Would she, do you think, have consented
to come had she known that Ben would have been
there, or your friend Tom Tringle?'

There was much more of it, but the upshot was,—
as the Colonel had intended that it should be,—that
Lady Albury was made to understand that Ayala's
good-will was essential to his happiness. 'Of course
I will do my best,' she said, as he parted from her.
'Though I am not quite as much in love with her
myself as you are, yet I will do my best.' Then when
she was left alone, and was prosecuting her inquiries

about the new cook, and travelling back in the afternoon to Stalham, she again considered how wonderful a thing it was such a girl as Ayala, so small,
apparently so unimportant, so childish in her
manner, with so little to say for herself, should
become a person of such terrible importance.

The twentieth came, and at ten minutes before
two Ayala was at the Paddington Railway Station.
The train, which was to start at 2.15, had been
chosen by herself so that she might avoid the Colonel,
and there she was, with her aunt, waiting for it.
Mrs. Dosett had thought it to be her duty to see her
off, and had come with her in the cab. There were
the two boxes laden with her wardrobe, such as it
was. Both she and her aunt had worked hard; for
though,—as she had declared to herself,—there was
no special reason for it, still she had wished to look
her best. As she saw the boxes put into the van, and
had told herself how much shabbier they were than
the boxes of other young ladies who went visiting to
such houses as Stalham, she rejoiced that Colonel
Stubbs was not there to see them. And she considered whether it was possible that Colonel Stubbs
should recognise a dress which she had worn at
Stalham before, which was now to appear in a quite
altered shape. She wondered also whether it would
be possible that Colonel Stubbs should know how
poor she was. As she was thinking of all this there
was Colonel Stubbs on the platform.

She had never doubted but that her little plan would
be efficacious. Nor had her aunt doubted,—who had
seen through the plan, though not a word had been
spoken between them on the subject. Mrs. Dosett
had considered it to be impossible that a Colonel
engaged on duties of importance at Aldershot should
run away from them to wait upon a child like Ayala,
—even though he had professed himself to be in love
with the child. She had never seen the Colonel, and
on this occasion did not expect to see him. But there
he was, all suddenly, shaking hands with Ayala.

'My aunt, Mrs. Dosett,' whispered Ayala. Then the Colonel began to talk to the elder lady as though the younger lady were a person of very much less importance. Yes; he had run up from Aldershot a little earlier than he had intended. There had been nothing particular to keep him down at Aldershot. It had always been his intention to go to Stalham on this day, and he was glad of the accident which was bringing Miss Dormer there just at the same time. He spent a good deal of his time at Stalham because Sir Harry and he, who were in truth cousins, were as intimate as brothers. He always lived at Stalham when he could get away from duty and was not in London. Stalham was a very nice place certainly; one of the most comfortable houses he knew in England. So he went on till he almost made Mrs. Dosett believe, and did make Ayala believe, that his visit to Stalham had nothing to do with herself. And yet Mrs. Dosett knew that the offer had been made. Ayala bethought herself that she did not care so much for the re-manufactured frock after all, nor yet for the shabby appearance of the boxes. The real Angel of Light would not care for her frock nor for her boxes; and certainly would not be indifferent after the fashion of,—of,—! Then she began to reflect that she was making a fool of herself.

She was put into the carriage, Mr. Dosett having luckily decided against the use of the second class. Going to such a house as Stalham Ayala ought, said Mr. Dosett, to go as any other lady would. Had it been himself or his wife it would have been very different; but for Ayala, on such an occasion as this, he would be extravagant. Ayala was therefore put into her seat while the Colonel stood at the door outside, still talking to Mrs. Dosett. 'I don't think she will be let to come away at the end of a week,' said the Colonel. 'Sir Harry doesn't like people to come away very soon.' Ayala heard this, and thought that she remembered that Sir Harry himself was very indifferent as to the coming and going of the visitors. 'They go up to London about the end of March,' said the Colonel, 'and if Miss Dormer were to return about a week before it would do very well.'

'Oh, no,' said Ayala, putting her head out of the window; 'I couldn't think of staying so long as that.' Then the last final bustle was made by the guard; the Colonel got in, the door was shut, and Mrs. Dosett, standing on the platform, nodded her head for the last time.

There were only four persons in the carriage. In the opposite corner there were two old persons, probably a husband and wife, who had been very careful as to a foot-warming apparatus, and were muffled up very closely in woollen and furs. 'If you don't mind shutting the door, Sir,' said the old gentleman, rather testily, 'because my wife has a pain in her face.' The door absolutely was shut when the words were spoken, but the Colonel made some sign of closing all the apertures. But there was a ventilator above, which the old lady spied. 'If you don't mind shutting that hole up there, Sir, because my husband is very bad with neuralgia.' The Colonel at once got up and found that the ventilator was fast closed, so as not to admit a breath of air. 'There are draughts come in everywhere,' said the old gentleman. 'The Company ought to be prosecuted.' 'I believe the more people they kill the better they like it,' said the old lady. Then the Colonel looked at Ayala with a very grave face, with no hint at a smile, with a face which must have gratified even the old lady and gentleman. But Ayala understood the face, and could not refrain from a little laugh. She laughed only with her eyes,—but the Colonel saw it.

'The weather has been very severe all day,' said the Colonel, in a severe voice.

Ayala protested that she had not found it cold at all. 'Then, Miss, I think you must be made of granite,' said the old lady. 'I hope you'll remember that other people are not so fortunate.' Ayala again smiled, and the Colonel made another effort as though to prevent any possible breath of air from making its way into the interior of the vehicle.

There was silence among them for some minutes, and then Ayala was quite surprised by the tone in which her friend addressed her. 'What an ill-natured girl you must be,' said he, 'to have put me to such a terrible amount of trouble all on purpose.'

'I didn't,' said Ayala.

'Yes, you did. Why wouldn't you come down by the four o'clock train as I told you? Now I've left everything undone, and I shouldn't wonder if I get into such a row at the Horse Guards that I shall never hear the end of it. And now you are not a bit grateful.'

'Yes, I am grateful; but I didn't want you to come at all,' she said.

'Of course I should come. I didn't think you were so perverse.'

'I'm not perverse, Colonel Stubbs.'

'When young persons are perverse, it is my opinion they oughtn't to be encouraged,' said the old lady from her corner.

'My dear, you know nothing about it,' said the old gentleman.

'Yes, I do,' said the old lady. 'I know all about it. Whatever she does a young lady ought not to be perverse. I do hate perversity. I am sure that hole up there must be open, Sir, for the wind does come in so powerful.' Colonel Stubbs again jumped up and poked at the ventilator.

In the meantime Ayala was laughing so violently that she could with difficulty prevent herself from making a noise, which, she feared, would bring down increased wrath upon her from the old lady. That feigned scolding from the Colonel at once brought back upon her the feeling of sudden and pleasant intimacy which she had felt when he had first come and ordered her to dance with him at the ball in

London. It was once again with her as though she knew this man almost more intimately, and certainly more pleasantly, than any of her other acquaintances. Whatever he said she could answer him now, and pretend to scold him, and have her joke with him as though no offer had ever been made. She could have told him now all the story of that turned dress, if that subject had come naturally to her, or have laughed with him at her own old boxes, and confided to him any other of the troubles of her poverty, as if they were jokes which she could share at any rate with him. Then he spoke again. 'I do abominate a perverse young woman,' he said. Upon this Ayala could no longer constrain herself, but burst into loud laughter.

After a while the two old people became quite familiar, and there arose a contest, in which the lady took part with the Colonel, and the old man protected Ayala. The Colonel spoke as though he were quite in earnest, and went on to declare that the young ladies of the present time were allowed far too much licence. 'They never have their own bread to earn,' he said, 'and they ought to make themselves agreeable to other people who have more to do.'

'I quite agree with you, Sir,' said the old lady. 'They should run about and be handy. I like to see a girl that can jump about the house and make herself useful.'

'Young ladies ought to be young ladies,' said the old man, putting his mouth for a moment up out of his comforter.

'And can't a young lady be useful and yet be a young lady?' said the Colonel.

'It is her special province to be ornamental,' said the old gentleman. 'I like to see young ladies ornamental. I don't think young ladies ought to be scolded, even if they are a little fractious.'

'I quite agree with you, Sir,' said Ayala. And so the fight went on with sundry breaks and changes in the matter under discussion till the station for

Stalham had been reached. The old gentleman, indeed, seemed to lose his voice before the journey was half over, but the lady persevered, so that she and the Colonel became such fast friends that she insisted on shaking hands with him when he left the carriage.

'How could you be so wicked as to go on hoaxing her like that?' said Ayala, as soon as they were on the platform.

'There was no hoax at all. I was quite in earnest. Was not every word true that I said? Now come and get into the carriage quickly, or you will be as bad as the old gentleman himself.'

Ayala did get into the carriage quickly, where she found Nina.

The two girls were full of conversation as they went to Stalham; but through it all Ayala could not refrain from thinking how the Jonathan Stubbs of to-day had been exactly like that Jonathan Stubbs she had first known,—and how very unlike a lover.

## CHAPTER XLVII

### CAPTAIN BATSBY AT MERLE PARK

WHEN Ayala went to Stalham Captain Batsby went to Merle Park. They had both been invited by Lady Tringle, and when the letter was written to Ayala she was assured that Tom should not be there. At that time Tom's last encounter with the police had not as yet become known to the Tringles, and the necessity of keeping Tom at the house in the country was not manifest. The idea had been that Captain Batsby should have an opportunity of explaining himself to Ayala. The Captain came; but, as to Ayala, Mrs. Dosett sent word to say that she had been invited to stay some days just at that time with her friend Lady Albury at Stalham.

What to do with Captain Batsby had been felt to be a difficulty by Lady Albury. It was his habit to

come to Stalham some time in March and there
finish the hunting season. It might be hoped that
Ayala's little affair might be arranged early in
March, and then, whether he came or whether he
did not, it would be the same to Ayala. But the
Captain himself would be grievously irate when he
should hear the trick which would have been played
upon him. Lady Albury had already desired him
not to come till after the first week in March, having
fabricated an excuse. She had been bound to keep
the coast clear both for Ayala's sake and the
Colonel's; but she knew that when her trick should
be discovered there would be unmeasured wrath.
'Why the deuce don't you let the two men come,
and then the best man may win!' said Sir Harry,
who did not doubt but that, in such a case, the
Colonel would prove to be the best man. Here too
there was another difficulty. When Lady Albury
attempted to explain that Ayala would not come
unless she were told that she would not meet the
Captain, Sir Harry declared that there should be no
such favour. 'Who the deuce is this little girl,' he
asked, 'that everybody should be knocked about in
this way for her?' Lady Albury was able to pacify
the husband, but she feared that any pacifying of
the Captain would be impossible. There would be a
family quarrel;—but even that must be endured for
the Colonel's sake.

In the meantime the Captain was kept in absolute
ignorance of Ayala's movements, and went down to
Merle Park hoping to meet her there. He must have
been very much in love, for Merle Park was by no
means a spot well adapted for hunting. Hounds
there were in the neighbourhood, but he turned up
his nose at the offer when Sir Thomas suggested that
he might bring down a hunter. Captain Batsby,
when he went on hunting expeditions, never stirred
without five horses, and always confined his operations to six or seven favoured counties. But Ayala
just at present was more to him than hunting, and

therefore, though it was now the end of February, he went to Merle Park.

'It was all Sir Thomas's doing.' It was thus that Lady Tringle endeavoured to console herself when discussing the matter with her daughters. The Honourable Septimus Traffick had now gone up to London, and was inhabiting a single room in the neighbourhood of the House. Augusta was still at Merle Park, much to the disgust of her father. He did not like to tell her to be gone; and would indeed have been glad enough of her presence had it not been embittered by the feeling that he was being 'done.' But there she remained, and in discussing the affairs of the Captain with her mother and Gertrude was altogether averse to the suggested marriage for Ayala. To her thinking Ayala was not entitled to a husband at all. Augusta had never given way in the affair of Tom;—had declared her conviction that Stubbs had never been in earnest; and was of opinion that Captain Batsby would be much better off at Merle Park without Ayala than he would have been in that young lady's presence. When he arrived nothing was said to him at once about Ayala. Gertrude, who recovered from the great sickness occasioned by Mr. Houston's misconduct, though the recovery was intended only to be temporary, made herself as pleasant as possible. Captain Batsby was made welcome, and remained three days before he sought an opportunity of asking a question about Ayala.

During this time he found Gertrude to be a very agreeable companion, but he made Mrs. Traffick his first confidant. 'Well, you know, Captain Batsby, to tell you the truth, we are not very fond of our cousin.'

'Sir Thomas told me she was to be here.'

'So we know. My father is perhaps a little mistaken about Ayala.'

'Was she not asked?' demanded Captain Batsby, beginning to think that he had been betrayed.

'Oh, yes; she was asked. She has been asked very often, because she is mamma's niece, and did live with us once for a short time. But she did not come. In fact she won't go anywhere, unless——'

'Unless what?'

'You know Colonel Stubbs?'

'Jonathan Stubbs. Oh dear, yes; very intimately. He is a sort of connection of mine. He is my half-brother's second cousin by the father's side.'

'Oh indeed! Does that make him very near?'

'Not at all. I don't like him, if you mean that. He always takes everything upon himself down at Stalham.'

'What we hear is that Ayala is always running after him.'

'Ayala running after Jonathan?'

'Haven't you heard of that?' asked Mrs. Traffick. 'Why;—she is at Stalham with the Alburys this moment, and I do not doubt that Colonel Stubbs is there also. She would not have gone had she not been sure of meeting him.'

This disturbed the Captain so violently that for two or three hours he kept himself apart, not knowing what to do with himself or where to betake himself. Could this be true about Jonathan Stubbs? There had been moments of deep jealousy down at Stalham; but then he had recovered from that, having assured himself that he was wrong. It had been Larry Twentyman and not Jonathan Stubbs who had led the two girls over the brook,—into which Stubbs had simply fallen, making himself an object of pity. But now again the Captain believed it all. It was on this account, then, that his half-sister-in-law, Rosaline, had desired him to stay away from Stalham for the present! He knew well how high in favour with Lady Albury was that traitor Stubbs; how it was by her favour that Stubbs, who was no more than a second cousin, was allowed to do just what he pleased in the stables, while Sir Harry himself, the master of the hounds, confined

himself to the kennel! He was determined at first
to leave Merle Park and start instantly for Stalham,
and had sent for his servant to begin the packing of
his things; but as he thought of it more maturely he
considered that his arrival at Stalham would be very
painful to himself as well as to others. For the others
he did not much care, but he saw clearly that the
pain to himself would be very disagreeable. No one
at Stalham would be glad to see him. Sir Harry
would be disturbed, and the other three persons with
whom he was concerned,—Lady Albury, Stubbs, and
Ayala,—would be banded together in hostility
against him. What chance would he have under
such circumstances? Therefore he determined that
he would stay at Merle Park yet a little longer.

And, after all, was Ayala worth the trouble which
he had proposed to take for her? How much had he
offered her, how scornfully had his offer been received, and how little had she to give him in return!
And now he had been told that she was always
running after Jonathan Stubbs! Could it be worth
his while to run after a girl who was always running
after Jonathan Stubbs? Was he not much higher
in the world than Jonathan Stubbs, seeing that he
had, at any rate, double Stubbs's income? Stubbs
was a red-haired, ugly, impudent fellow, who made
his way wherever he went simply by 'cheek'! Upon
reflection, he found that it would be quite beneath
him to run after any girl who could so demean herself as to run after Jonathan Stubbs. Therefore he
came down to dinner on that evening with all his
smiles, and said not a word about Ayala to Sir
Thomas, who had just returned from London.

'Is he very much provoked?' Sir Thomas asked his
wife that evening.

'Provoked about what?'

'He was expressly told that he would meet Ayala
here.'

'He seems to be making himself very comfortable,
and hasn't said a word to me about Ayala. I am sick

of Ayala. Poor Tom is going to be really ill.' Then
Sir Thomas frowned, and said nothing more on that
occasion.

Tom was certainly in an uncomfortable position,
and never left his bed till after noon. Then he would
mope about the place, moping even worse than he
did before, and would spend the evening all alone in
the housekeeper's room, with a pipe in his mouth,
which he seemed hardly able to take the trouble to keep
alight. There were three or four other guests in the
house, including two honourable Miss Trafficks, and
a couple of young men out of the City, whom Lady
Tringle hoped might act as antidotes to Houston and
Hamel. But with none of them would Tom associate.
With Captain Batsby he did form some little intimacy; driven to it, no doubt, by a community of
interest. 'I believe you were acquainted with my
cousin, Miss Dormer, at Stalham?' asked Tom. At
that moment the two were sitting over the fire in the
housekeeper's room, and Captain Batsby was smoking a cigar, while Tom was sucking an empty pipe.

'Oh, yes,' said Captain Batsby, pricking up his
ears, 'I saw a good deal of her.'

'A wonderful creature!' ejaculated Tom.

'Yes, indeed!'

'For a real romantic style of beauty, I don't suppose that the world ever saw her like before. Did
you?'

'Are you one among your cousin's admirers?'
demanded the Captain.

'Am I?' asked Tom, surprised that there should
be anybody who had not as yet heard his tragic
story. 'Am I one of her admirers? Why,—rather!
Haven't you heard about me and Stubbs?'

'No, indeed.'

'I thought that everybody had heard that. I
challenged him, you know.'

'To fight a duel?'

'Yes; to fight a duel. I sent my friend Faddle
down with a letter to Stalham, but it was of no use.

Why should a man fight a duel when he has got such a girl as Ayala to love him?'

'That is quite true, then?'

'I fear so! I fear so! Oh, yes; it is too true. Then you know;'—and as he came to this portion of his story he jumped up from his chair and frowned fiercely;—'then, you know, I met him under the portico of the Haymarket, and struck him.'

'Oh,—was that you?'

'Indeed it was.'

'And he did not do anything to you?'

'He behaved like a hero,' said Tom. 'I do think that he behaved like a hero,—though of course I hate him.' The bitterness of expression was here very great. 'He wouldn't let them lock me up. Though, in the matter of that, I should have been best pleased if they would have locked me up for ever, and kept me from the sight of the world. Admire that girl, Captain Batsby! I don't think that I ever heard of a man who loved a girl as I love her. I do not hesitate to say that I continue to walk the world, —in the way of not committing suicide, I mean,— simply because there is still a possibility while she has not as yet stood at the hymeneal altar with another man. I would have shot Stubbs willingly, though I knew I was to be tried for it at the Old Bailey,—and hung! I would have done it willingly, —willingly; or any other man.' After that Captain Batsby thought it might be prudent not to say anything especial as to his own love.

And how foolish would it be for a man like himself, with a good fortune of his own, to marry any girl who had not a sixpence! The Captain was led into this vain thought by the great civility displayed to him by the ladies of the house. With Lucy, whom he knew to be Ayala's sister, he had not prospered very well. It came to his ears that she was out of favour with her aunt, and he therefore meddled with her but little. The Tringle ladies, however, were very kind to him,—so kind that he was tempted to think

less than ever of one who had been so little courteous
to him as Ayala. Mrs. Traffick was of course a
married woman, and it amounted to nothing. But
Gertrude——! All the world knew that Septimus
Traffick without a shilling of his own had become the
happy possessor of a very large sum of money. He,
Batsby, had more to recommend him than Traffick!
Why should not he also become a happy possessor?
He went away for a week's hunting into North-
amptonshire, and then, at Lady Tringle's request,
came back to Merle Park.

At this time Miss Tringle had quite recovered her
health. She had dropped all immediate speech as to
Mr. Houston. Had she not been provoked, she would
have allowed all that to drop into oblivion. But a
married sister may take liberties. 'You are well rid
of him, I think,' said Augusta. Gertrude heaved a
deep sigh. She did not wish to acknowledge herself
to be rid of him until another string were well fitted
to her bow. 'After all, a man with nothing to do in
the world, with no profession, no occupation, with
no money——'

'Mr. Traffick had not got very much money of his
own.'

'He has a seat in Parliament, which is very much
more than fortune, and will undoubtedly be in power
when his party comes in. And he is a man of birth.
But Frank Houston had nothing to recommend him.'

'Birth!' said Gertrude, turning up her nose.

'The Queen, who is the fountain of honour, made
his father a nobleman, and that constitutes birth.'
This the married sister said with stern severity of
manner, and perfect reliance on the constitutional
privileges of her Sovereign.

'I don't know that we need talk about it,' said
Gertrude.

'Not at all. Mr. Houston has behaved very badly,
and I suppose there is an end of him as far as this
house is concerned. Captain Batsby seems to me to
be a very nice young man, and I suppose he has got

money. A man should certainly have got money,—
or an occupation.'

'He has got both,' said Gertrude, which, however,
was not true, as Captain Batsby had left the service.

\* \* \* \* \* \*

'Have you forgotten my cousin so soon?' Gertrude
asked one day, as she was walking with the happy
Captain in the park. The Captain, no doubt, had
been saying soft things to her.

'Do you throw that in my teeth as an offence?'

'Inconstancy in men is generally considered as an
offence,' said Gertrude. What it might be in women
she did not just then declare.

'After all I have heard of your cousin since I have
been here, I should hardly have thought that it
would be reckoned so in this case.'

'You have heard nothing against her from me.'

'I am told that she has treated your brother very
badly.'

'Poor Tom!'

'And that she is flirting with a man I particularly
dislike.'

'I suppose she does make herself rather peculiar
with that Colonel Stubbs.'

'And, after all, only think how little I saw of her!
She is pretty.'

'So some people think. I never saw it myself,' said
Gertrude. 'We always thought her a mass of affec-
tation. We had to turn her out of the house once, you
know. She was living here, and then it was that her
sister had to come in her place. It is not their fault
that they have got nothing;—poor girls! They
are mamma's nieces, and so papa always has one of
them.' After that forgiveness was accorded to the
Captain on account of his fickle conduct, and Gertrude consented to accept of his services in the guise
of a lover. That this was so Mrs. Traffick was well
aware. Nor was Lady Tringle very much in the dark.
Frank Houston was to be considered as good as gone,

and if so it would be well that her daughter should
have another string. She was tired of the troubles
of the girls around her, and thought that as Captain
Batsby was supposed to have an income he would do
as a son-in-law. But she had not hitherto been consulted by the young people, who felt among themselves that there still might be a difficulty. The
difficulty lay with Sir Thomas. Sir Thomas had
brought Captain Batsby there to Merle Park as
Ayala's lover, and as he had been very little at home
was unaware of the changes which had taken place.
And then Gertrude was still supposed to be engaged
to Mr. Houston, although this lover had been so
violently rejected by himself. The ladies felt that,
as he was made of sterner stuff than they, so would it
be more difficult to reconcile him to the alterations
which were now proposed in the family arrangements. Who was to bell the cat? 'Let him go to
papa in the usual way, and ask his leave,' said Mrs.
Traffick.

'I did suggest that,' said Gertrude, 'but he seems
not to like to do it quite yet.'

'Is he such a coward as that?'

'I do not know that he is more a coward than anybody else. I remember when Septimus was quite
afraid to go near papa. But then Benjamin has got
money of his own, which does make a difference.'

'It's quite untrue saying that Septimus was ever
afraid of papa. Of course he knows his position as a
Member of Parliament too well for that. I suppose
the truth is, it's about Ayala.'

'It is a little odd about Ayala,' said Gertrude,
resuming her confidential tone. 'It is so hard to
make papa understand about these kind of things.
I declare I believe he thinks that I never ought to
speak to another man because of that scoundrel
Frank Houston.'

All this was in truth so strange to Sir Thomas that
he could not understand any of the existing per-
plexities. Why did Captain Batsby remain as a guest

at Merle Park? He had no special dislike to the man, and when Lady Tringle had told him that she had asked the Captain to prolong his visit he had made no objection. But why should the man remain there, knowing as he did now that there was no chance of Ayala's coming to Merle Park? At last, on a certain Saturday evening, he did make inquiry on the subject. 'What on earth is that man staying here for?' he said to his wife.

'I think he likes the place.'

'Perhaps he likes the place as well as Septimus Traffick, and means to live here always!' Such allusions as these were constant with Sir Thomas, and were always received by Lady Tringle with dismay and grief. 'When does he mean to go away?' asked Sir Thomas, gruffly.

Lady Tringle had felt that the time had come in which some word should be said as to the Captain's intentions; but she feared to say it. She dreaded to make the clear explanation to her husband. 'Perhaps,' said she, 'he is becoming fond of some of the young ladies.'

'Young ladies! What young ladies? Do you mean Lucy?'

'Oh dear no!' said Lady Tringle.

'Then what the deuce do you mean? He came here after Ayala, because I wanted to have all that nonsense settled about Tom. Ayala is not here, nor likely to be here; and I don't know why he should stay here philandering away his time. I hate men in a country-house who are thorough idlers. You had better take an opportunity of letting him know that he has been here long enough.'

All this was repeated by Lady Tringle to Mrs. Traffick, and by Mrs. Traffick to Gertrude. Then they felt that this was no time for Captain Batsby to produce himself to Sir Thomas as a suitor for his youngest daughter.

## CHAPTER XLVIII

### THE JOURNEY TO OSTEND

'NO doubt it will be very hard to make papa understand.' This was said by Gertrude to her new lover a few days after that order had been given that the lover should be sent away from Merle Park. The purport of the order in all its severity had not been conveyed to Captain Batsby. The ladies had felt,—Gertrude had felt very strongly,—that were he informed that the master of the house demanded his absence he would take himself off at once. But still something had to be said,—and something done. Captain Batsby was, just at present, in a matrimonial frame of mind. He had come to Merle Park to look for a wife, and, as he had missed one, was, in his present mood, inclined to take another. But there was no knowing how long this might last. Augusta had hinted that 'something must be done, either with papa's consent or without it.' Then there had come the conversation in which Gertrude acknowledged the existing difficulty. 'Papa, too, probably, would not consent quite at once.'

'He must think it very odd that I am staying here,' said the Captain.

'Of course it is odd. If you could go to him and tell him everything!' But the Captain, looking at the matter all round, thought that he could not go to Sir Thomas and tell him anything. Then she began gently to introduce the respectable clergyman at Ostend. It was not necessary that she should refer at length to the circumstances under which she had studied the subject, but she gave Captain Batsby to understand that it was one as to which she had picked up a good deal of information.

But the money! 'If Sir Thomas were made really angry, the consequences would be disastrous,' said the Captain. But Gertrude was of a different way of thinking. Her father was, no doubt, a man who could be very imperious, and would insist upon having his own way as long as his own way was profitable to him. But he was a man who always forgave.

'If you mean about the money,' said Gertrude, 'I am quite sure that it would all come right.' He did mean about the money, and was evidently uneasy in his mind when the suggested step was made manifest to him. Gertrude was astonished to see how long and melancholy his face could become. 'Papa was never unkind about money in his life,' said Gertrude. 'He could not endure to have any of us poor.'

On the next Saturday Sir Thomas again came down, and still found his guest at Merle Park. We are now a little in advance of our special story, which is, or ought to be, devoted to Ayala. But, with the affairs of so many lovers and their loves, it is almost impossible to make the chronicle run at equal periods throughout. It was now more than three weeks since Ayala went to Stalham, and Lady Albury had written to the Captain confessing something of her sin, and begging to be forgiven. This she had done in her anxiety to keep the Captain away. He had not answered his sister-in-law's letter, but, in his present frame of mind, was not at all anxious to finish up the hunting-season at Stalham. Sir Thomas, on his arrival, was very full of Tom's projected tour. He had arranged everything,—except in regard to Tom's own assent. He had written to New York, and had received back a reply from his correspondent assuring him that Tom should be made most heartily welcome. It might be that Tom's fighting propensities had not been made known to the people of New York. Sir Thomas had taken a berth on board of one of the Cunard boats, and had even gone so far as to ask the Captain to come down for a day or two to Merle Park. He was so much employed with Tom that he could hardly afford time and consideration to Captain Batsby and his affairs. Nevertheless he did ask a question, and received an answer with which he seemed to be satisfied. 'What on earth is that man staying here for?' he said to his wife.

'He is going on Friday,' replied Lady Tringle, doubtingly;—almost as though she thought that she would be subjected to further anger because of this delay. But Sir Thomas dropped the subject, and passed on to some matter affecting Tom's outfit. Lady Tringle was very glad to change the subject, and promised that everything should be supplied befitting the hottest and coldest climates on the earth's surface.

'She sails on the nineteenth of April,' said Sir Thomas to his son.

'I don't think I could go as soon as that, Sir,' replied Tom, whining.

'Why not? There are more than three weeks yet, and your mother will have everything ready for you. What on earth is there to hinder you?'

'I don't think I could go—not on the nineteenth of April.'

'Well then, you must. I have taken your place, and Firkin expects you at New York. They'll do everything for you there, and you'll find quite a new life. I should have thought you'd have been delighted to get away from your wretched condition here.'

'It is wretched,' said Tom; 'but I'd rather not go quite so soon.'

'Why not?'

'Well, then——'

'What is it, Tom? It makes me unhappy when I see you such a fool.'

'I am a fool! I know I am a fool!'

'Then make a new start of it. Cut and run, and begin the world again. You're young enough to forget all this.'

'So I would, only——'

'Only what?'

'I suppose she is engaged to that man Stubbs! If I knew it for certain then I would go. If I went before,

I should only come back as soon as I got to New York.
If they were once married and it were all done with
I think I could make a new start.'

In answer to this his father told him that he must
go on the nineteenth of April, whether Ayala were
engaged or disengaged, married or unmarried;—that
his outfit would be bought, his cabin would be ready,
circular notes for his use would be prepared, and
everything would be arranged to make his prolonged
tour as comfortable as possible; but that if he did not
start on that day all the Tringle houses would be
closed against him, and he would be turned penniless out into the world. 'You'll have to learn that I'm
in earnest,' said Sir Thomas, as he turned his back
and walked away. Tom took himself off to reflect
whether it would not be a grand thing to be turned
penniless out into the world,—and all for love!

By the early train on Monday Sir Thomas re-
turned to London, having taken little or no heed of
Captain Batsby during his late visit to the country.
Even at Merle Park Captain Batsby's presence was
less important than it would otherwise have been to
Lady Tringle and Mrs. Traffick, because of the seri-
ous nature of Sir Thomas's decision as to his son.
Lady Tringle perhaps suspected something. Mrs.
Traffick, no doubt, had her own ideas as to her sister's
position; but nothing was said and nothing was done.
Both on the Wednesday and on the Thursday Lady
Tringle went up to town to give the required orders
on Tom's behalf. On the Thursday her elder daughter
accompanied her, and returned with her in the evening. On their arrival they learnt that neither Captain
Batsby nor Miss Gertrude had been seen since ten
o'clock; that almost immediately after Lady Tringle's
departure in the morning Captain Batsby had caused
all his luggage to be sent into Hastings; and that it
had since appeared that a considerable number of
Miss Gertrude's things were missing. There could be
no doubt that she had caused them to be packed up
with the Captain's luggage. 'They have gone to

Ostend, mamma,' said Augusta. 'I was sure of it, because I've heard Gertrude say that people can always get themselves married at Ostend. There is a clergyman there on purpose to do it.'

It was at this time past seven o'clock, and Lady Tringle when she heard the news was so astounded that she did not at first know how to act. It was not possible for her to reach Dover that night before the night-boat for Ostend should have started,—even could she have done any good by going there. Tom was in such a condition that she hardly dared to trust him; but it was settled at last that she should telegraph at once to Sir Thomas, in Lombard Street, and that Tom should travel up to London by the night train.

On the following morning Lady Tringle received a letter from Gertrude, posted by that young lady at Dover as she passed through on her road to Ostend. It was as follows:—

'DEAR MAMMA,

'You will be surprised on your return from London to find that we have gone. After much thinking about it we determined it would be best, because we had quite made up our mind *not to be kept separated*. Ben was so eager about it that I was obliged to yield. We were afraid that if we asked papa at once he would not have given his consent. Pray give him my most dutiful love, and tell him that I am sure he will never have occasion to be ashamed of his son-in-law. I don't suppose he knows, but it is the fact that Captain Batsby has about three thousand a year of his own. It is very different from having nothing, like that wretch Frank Houston, or, for that matter, Mr. Traffick. Ben was quite in a position to ask papa, but things had happened which made us both feel that papa would not like it just at present. We mean to be married at Ostend, and then will come back as soon as you and papa say that you will receive us. In the meantime I wish you would send some of my clothes after me. Of course I had to come away with very little luggage, because I was obliged to have my things mixed up with Ben's. I did not dare to have my boxes brought down by the servants. Could you send me the green silk in which I went to church the last two Sundays, and my pink gauze, and the grey poplin? Please send two or three flannel petticoats, as I could not put them among his things, and as many cuffs and collars as you can cram in. I suppose I can get boots at Ostend, but I should like to have the hat with the little brown feather. There is my silk jacket with the fur trimming; I should like to have that. I suppose I shall have to be married without any regular dress, but I am sure papa will make up my trousseau to me afterwards. I lent a little lace fichu to Augusta; tell her I shall so like to have it.

'Give papa my best love, and Augusta, and poor Tom, and accept the same from your affectionate daughter,

'GERTRUDE.

'I suppose I must not add the other name yet.'

Sir Thomas did not receive the telegram till eleven o'clock, when he returned from dinner, and could do nothing that night. On the next morning he was disturbed soon after five o'clock by Tom, who had come on the same errand. 'Idiots!' exclaimed Sir Thomas, 'What on earth can they have gone to Ostend for? And what can you do by coming up?'

'My mother thought that I might follow them to Ostend.'

'They wouldn't care for you. No one will care for you until you have got rid of all this folly. I must go. Idiots! Who is to marry them at Ostend? If they are fools enough to want to be married, why shouldn't they get married in England?'

'I suppose they thought you wouldn't consent.'

'Of course I shan't consent. But why should I consent a bit more because they have gone to Ostend?

A.A.—23

I don't suppose anybody ever had such a set of fools about him as I have.' This would have been hard upon Tom had it not been that he had got beyond the feeling of any hardness from contempt or contumely. As he once said of himself, all sense of other injury had been washed out of him by Ayala's unkindness.

On that very day Sir Thomas started for Ostend, and reached the place about two o'clock. Captain Batsby and Gertrude had arrived only during the previous night, and Gertrude, as she had been very sick, was still in bed. Captain Batsby was not in bed. Captain Batsby had been engaged since an early hour in the morning looking for that respectable clergyman of the Church of England of whose immediate services he stood in need. By the time that Sir Thomas had reached Ostend he had found that no such clergyman was known in the place. There was a regular English clergyman who would be very happy to marry him,—and to accept the usual fees,—after the due performance of certain preliminaries as ordained by the law, and as usual at Ostend. The lady, no doubt, could be married at Ostend, after such preliminaries,—as she might have been married also in England. All this was communicated by the Captain to Gertrude,—who was still very unwell,—at her bedroom door. Her conduct during this trying time was quite beyond reproach,— and also his,—as Captain Batsby afterwards took an opportunity of assuring her father.

'What on earth, Sir, is the meaning of all this?' said Sir Thomas, encountering the man who was not his son-in-law in the sitting-room of the hotel.

'I have just run away with your daughter, Sir Thomas. That is the simple truth.'

'And I have got the trouble of taking her back again.'

'I have behaved like a gentleman through it all, Sir Thomas,' said the Captain, thus defending his own character and the lady's.

'You have behaved like a fool. What on earth am I to think of it, Sir? You were asked down to my house because you gave me to understand that you proposed to ask my niece, Miss Dormer, to be your wife; and now you have run away with my daughter. Is that behaviour like a gentleman?'

'I must explain myself.'

'Well, Sir?' Captain Batsby found the explanation very difficult; and hummed and hawed a great deal. 'Do you mean to say that it was a lie from beginning to end about Miss Dormer?' Great liberties of speech are allowed to gentlemen whose daughters have been run away with, and whose hospitality has been outraged.

'Oh dear no. What I said then was quite true. It was my intention. But—but—.' The perspiration broke out upon the unhappy man's brow as the great immediate trouble of his situation became clear to him. 'There was no lie,—no lie at all. I beg to assure you, Sir Thomas, that I am not a man to tell a lie.'

'How has it all been, then?'

'When I found how very superior a person your daughter was!'

'It isn't a month since she was engaged to somebody else,' said the angry father, forgetting all propriety in his indignation.

'Gertrude?' demanded Captain Batsby.

'You are two fools. So you gave up my niece?'

'Oh dear yes, altogether. She didn't come to Merle Park, you know. How was I to say anything to her when you didn't have her there?'

'Why didn't you go away then, instead of remaining under a false pretence? Or why, at any rate, didn't you tell me the truth?'

'And what would you have me to do now?' asked Captain Batsby.

'Go to the d———,' said Sir Thomas, as he left the room, and went to his daughter's chamber.

Gertrude had heard that her father was in the

house, and endeavoured to hurry herself into her
clothes while the interview was going on between
him and her father. But she was not yet perfectly
arrayed when her father burst into her room. 'Oh,
papa,' she said, going down on her knees, 'you do
mean to forgive us?'

'I mean to do nothing of the kind. I mean to
carry you home and have you locked up.'

'But we may be married!'

'Not with my leave. Why didn't you come and
ask if you wanted to get yourselves married? Why
didn't you tell me?'

'We were ashamed.'

'What has become of Mr. Houston, whom you
loved so dearly?'

'Oh, papa!'

'And the Captain was so much attached to
Ayala!'

'Oh, papa!'

'Get up, you stupid girl. Why is it that my children
are so much more foolish than other people's? I
don't suppose you care for the man in the least.'

'I do, I do. I love him with all my heart.'

'And as for him,—how can he care for you when
it is but the other day he was in love with your
cousin?'

'Oh, papa!'

'What he wants is my money, of course.'

'He has got plenty of money, papa.'

'I can understand him, fool as he is. There is
something for him to get. He won't get it, but he
might think it possible. As for you, I cannot understand you at all. What do you expect? It can't be
for love of a hatchet-faced fellow like that, whom
you had never seen a fortnight ago.'

'It is more than a month ago, papa.'

'Frank Houston was, at any rate, a manly-looking
fellow.'

'He was a scoundrel,' said Gertrude, now standing up for the first time.

'A good-looking fellow was Frank Houston; that at least may be said for him,' continued the father, determined to exasperate his daughter to the utmost. 'I had half a mind to give way about him, because he was a manly, outspoken fellow, though he was such an idle dog. If you'd gone off with him, I could have understood it;—and perhaps forgiven it,' he added.

'He was a scoundrel!' screamed Gertrude, remembering her ineffectual attempts to make her former lover perform this same journey.

'But this fellow! I cannot bring myself to believe that you really care for him.'

'He has a good income of his own, while Houston was little better than a beggar.'

'I'm glad of that,' said Sir Thomas, 'because there will be something for you to live upon. I can assure you that Captain Batsby will never get a shilling of my money. Now, you had better finish dressing yourself, and come down and eat your dinner with me if you've got any appetite. You will have to go back to Dover by the boat to-night.'

'May Ben dine with us?' asked Gertrude, timidly.

'Ben may go to the d——. At any rate he had better not show himself to me again,' said Sir Thomas.

The lovers, however, did get an opportunity of exchanging a few words, during which it was settled between them that as the young lady must undoubtedly obey her father's behests, and return to Dover that night, it would be well for Captain Batsby to remain behind at Ostend. Indeed, he spoke of making a little tour as far as Brussels, in order that he might throw off the melancholy feelings which had been engendered. 'You will come to me again, Ben,' she said. Upon this he looked very grave. 'You do not mean to say that after all this you will desert me?'

'He has insulted me so horribly!'

'What does that signify? Of course he is angry. If you could only hear how he has insulted me.'

'He says that you were in love with somebody else not a month since.'

'So were you, Ben, for the matter of that.' He did, however, before they parted, make her a solemn promise that their engagement should remain an established fact, in spite both of father and mother.

Gertrude, who had now recovered the effects of her sea-sickness,—which, however, she would have to encounter again so very quickly,—contrived to eat a hearty dinner with her father. There, however, arose a little trouble. How should she contrive to pack up the clothes which she had brought with her, and which had till lately been mixed with the Captain's garments? She did, however, at last succeed in persuading the chamber-maid to furnish her with a carpet-bag, with which in her custody she arrived safely on the following day at Merle Park.

## CHAPTER XLIX

### THE NEW FROCK

AYALA'S arrival at Stalham was full of delight to her. There was Nina with all her new-fledged hopes and her perfect assurance in the absolute superiority of Lord George Bideford to any other man either alive or dead. Ayala was quite willing to allow this assurance to pass current, as her Angel of Light was as yet neither alive nor dead. But she was quite certain,—wholly certain,—that when the Angel should come forth he would be superior to Lord George. The first outpourings of all this took place in the carriage as Nina and Ayala were driven from the station to the house, while the Colonel went home alone in a dog-cart. It had been arranged that nothing should be said to Ayala about the Colonel, and in the carriage the Colonel's name was not mentioned. But when they were all in the hall at Stalham, taking off their cloaks and depositing their wraps, standing in front of the large fire, Colonel

Stubbs was there. Lady Albury was present also, welcoming her guests, and Sir Harry, who had already come home from hunting, with one or two other men in red coats and top breeches, and a small bevy of ladies who were staying in the house. Lady Albury was anxious to know how her friend had sped with Ayala, but at such a moment no question could be asked. But Ayala's spirits were so high that Lady Albury was at a loss to understand whether the whole thing had been settled by Jonathan with success,—or whether, on the other hand, Ayala was so happy because she had not been troubled by a word of love.

'He has behaved so badly, Lady Albury,' said Ayala.

'What;—Stubbs?' asked Sir Harry, not quite understanding all the ins and outs of the matter.

'Yes, Sir Harry. There was an old lady and an old gentleman. They were very funny and he would laugh at them.'

'I deny it,' said the Colonel.

'Why shouldn't he laugh at them if they were funny?' asked Lady Albury.

'He knew it would make me laugh out loud. I couldn't help myself, but he could be as grave as a judge all the time. So he went on till the old woman scolded me dreadfully.'

'But the old man took your part,' said the Colonel.

'Yes;—he did. He said that I was ornamental.'

'A decent and truth-speaking old gentleman,' said one of the sportsmen in top boots.

'Quite so;—but then the old lady said that I was perverse, and Colonel Stubbs took her part. If you had been there, Lady Albury, you would have thought that he had been in earnest.'

'So I was,' said the Colonel.

All this was very pleasant to Ayala. It was a return to the old joyousness when she had first discovered the delight of having such a friend as

Colonel Stubbs. Had he flattered her, paid her compliments, been soft and delicate to her,—as a lover might have been,—she would have been troubled in spirit and heavy at heart. But now it seemed as though all that love-making had been an episode which had passed away, and that the old pleasant friendship still remained. As yet, while they were standing there in the hall, there had come no moment for her to feel whether there was anything to regret in this. But certainly there had been comfort in it. She had been able to appear before all her Stalham friends, in the presence even of the man himself, without any of that consciousness which would have oppressed her had he come there simply as her acknowledged lover, and had she come there conscious before all the guests that it was so.

Then they sat for a while drinking tea and eating buttered toast in the drawing-room. A supply of buttered toast fully to gratify the wants of three or four men just home from hunting has never yet been created by the resources of any establishment. But the greater marvel is that the buttered toast has never the slightest effect on the dinner which is to follow in an hour or two. During this period the conversation turned chiefly upon hunting,—which is of all subjects the most imperious. It never occurs to a hunting-man to suppose that either a lady, or a bishop, or a political economist, can be indifferent to hunting. There is something beyond millinery,— beyond the interests of the church,—beyond the price of wheat,—in that great question whether the hounds did or did not change their fox in Gobblegoose Wood. On the present occasion Sir Harry was quite sure that the hounds did carry their fox through Gobblegoose Wood, whereas Captain Glomax,* who had formerly been master of the pack which now obeyed Sir Harry, was perfectly certain that they had got upon another animal, who went away from Gobblegoose as fresh as paint. He pretended even to ridicule Sir Harry for supposing that any fox could have run at that pace up Buddlecombe Hill who had travelled all the way from Stickborough Gorse. To this Sir Harry replied resentfully that the Captain did not know what were the running powers of a dog-fox in March. Then he told various stories of what had been done in this way at this special period of the year. Glomax, however, declared that he knew as much of a fox as any man in England, and that he would eat both the foxes, and the wood, and Sir Harry, and, finally, himself, if the animal which had run up Buddlecombe Hill was the same which they brought with them from Stickborough Gorse into Gobblegoose Wood. So the battle raged, and the ladies no doubt were much interested;—as would have been the bishop had he been there, or the political economist.

After this Ayala was taken up into her room, and left to sit there by herself for a while till Lady Albury should send her maid. 'My dear,' said Lady Albury, 'there is something on the bed which I expect you to wear to-night. I shall be broken-hearted if it doesn't fit you. The frock is a present from Sir Harry; the scarf comes from me. Don't say a word about it. Sir Harry always likes to make presents to young ladies.' Then she hurried out of the room while Ayala was still thanking her. Lady Albury had at first intended to say something about the Colonel as they were sitting together over Ayala's fire, but she had made up her mind against this as soon as she saw their manner towards each other on entering the house. If Ayala had accepted him at a word as they were travelling together, then there would be need of no further interference in the matter. But if not, it would be better that she should hold her peace for the present.

Ayala's first instinct was to look at the finery which had been provided for her. It was a light grey silk, almost pearl colour, as to which she thought she had never seen anything so lovely before. She measured the waist with her eye, and knew at once that

it would fit her. She threw the gauzy scarf over her
shoulders and turned herself round before the large
mirror which stood near the fire-place. 'Dear Lady
Albury!' she exclaimed; 'dear Lady Albury!' It
was impossible that she should have understood that
Lady Albury's affection had been shown to Jonathan
Stubbs much rather than to her when those presents
were prepared.

She got rid of her travelling dress and her boots,
and let down her hair, and seated herself before the
fire, that she might think of it all in her solitude.
Was she or was she not glad,—glad in sober earnest,
glad now the moment of her mirth had passed by,
the mirth which had made her return to Stalham so
easy for her,—was she or was she not glad that this
change had come upon the Colonel, this return to his
old ways? She had got her friend again, but she had
lost her lover. She did not want the lover. She was
sure of that. She was still sure that if a lover would
come to her who would be in truth acceptable,—such
a lover as would enable her to give herself up to him
altogether, and submit herself to him as her lord and
master,—he must be something different from Jonathan Stubbs. That had been the theory of her life
for many months past, a theory on which she had
resolved to rely with all her might from the moment
in which this man had spoken to her of his love.
Would she give way and render up herself and all her
dreams simply because the man was one to be liked?
She had declared to herself again and again that it
should not be so. There should come the Angel of
Light or there should come no lover for her. On that
very morning as she was packing up her boxes at
Kingsbury Crescent she had arranged the words in
which, should he speak to her on the subject in the
railway train, she would make him understand that
it could never be. Surely he would understand if
she told him so simply, with a little prayer that his
suit might not be repeated. His suit had not been
repeated. Nothing apparently had been further from

his intention. He had been droll, pleasant, friendly,
—just like his old dear self. For in truth the pleasantness and the novelty of his friendship had made
him dear to her. He had gone back of his own
accord to the old ways, without any little prayer from
her. Now was she contented? As the question
would thrust itself upon her in opposition to her own
will, driving out the thoughts which she would fain
have welcomed, she gazed listlessly at the fire. If it
were so, then for what purpose, then for what reason,
had Lady Albury procured for her the pale grey
pearl-coloured dress?

And why were all these grand people at Stalham
so good to her,—to her, a poor little girl, whose
ordinary life was devoted to the mending of linen and
to the furtherance of economy in the use of pounds of
butter and legs of mutton? Why was she taken out
of her own sphere and petted in this new luxurious
world? She had a knowledge belonging to her,—if
not quite what we may call common sense,—which
told her that there must be some cause. Of some
intellectual capacity, some appreciation of things
and words which were divine in their beauty, she
was half conscious. It could not be, she felt, that
without some such capacity she should have imaged
to herself that Angel of Light. But not for
such capacity as that had she been made welcome at Stalham. As for her prettiness, her beauty
of face and form, she thought about them not at all,
—almost not at all. In appearing in that pale-pearl
silk, with that gauzy scarf upon her shoulders, she
would take pride. Not to be shamed among other
girls by the poorness of her apparel was a pride to
her. Perhaps to excel some others by the prettiness
of her apparel might be a pride to her. But of
feminine beauty, as a great gift bestowed upon her,
she thought not at all. She would look in the mirror
for the effect of the scarf, but not for the effect of
the neck and shoulders beneath it. Could she have
looked in any mirror for the effect of the dreams she

had thus dreamed,—ah! that would have been the mirror in which she would have loved yet feared to look!

Why was Lady Albury so kind to her? Perhaps Lady Albury did not know that Colonel Stubbs had changed his mind. She would know it very soon, and then, maybe, everything would be changed. As she thought of this she longed to put the pearl silk dress aside, and not to wear it as yet,—to put it aside so that it might never be worn by her if circumstances should so require. It was to be hoped that the man had changed his mind,—and to be hoped that Lady Albury would know that he had done so. Then she would soon see whether there was a change. Could she not give a reason why she should not wear the dress this night? As she sat gazing at the fire a tear ran down her cheek. Was it for the dress she would not wear, or for the lover whom she would not love?

The question as to the dress was settled for her very soon. Lady Albury's maid came into the room, —not a chit of a girl without a thought of her own except as to her own grandness in being two steps higher than the kitchen-maid,—but a well-grown, buxom, powerful woman, who had no idea of letting such a young lady as Ayala do anything in the matter of dress but what she told her. When Ayala suggested something as to the next evening in reference to the pale-pearl silk the buxom powerful woman pooh-poohed her down in a moment. What;—after Sir Harry had taken so much trouble about having it made; having actually inquired about it with his own mouth. 'To-night, Miss; you must wear it to-night! My lady would be quite angry!' 'My lady not know what you wear! My lady knows what all the ladies wear,—morning, noon, and night.' That little plan of letting the dress lie by till she should know how she should be received after Colonel Stubbs's change of mind had been declared, fell to the ground altogether under the hands of the buxom powerful woman.

When she went into the drawing-room*some of the guests were assembled. Sir Harry and Lady Albury were there, and so was Colonel Stubbs. As she walked in Sir Harry was standing well in front of the fire, in advance of the rug, so as to be almost in the middle of the room. Captain Glomax was there also, and the discussion about the foxes was going on. It had occurred to Ayala that as the dress was a present from Sir Harry she must thank him. So she walked up to him and made a little curtsey just before him. 'Am I nice, Sir Harry?' she said.

'Upon my word,' said Sir Harry, 'that is the best spent ten-pound-note I ever laid out in my life.' Then he took her by the hand and gently turned her round, so as to look at her and her dress.

'I don't know whether I am nice, but you are,' she said, curtseying again. Everybody felt that she had had quite a little triumph as she subsided into a seat close by Lady Albury, who called her. As she seated herself she caught the Colonel's eye, who was looking at her. She fancied that there was a tear in it. Then he turned himself and looked away into the fire.

'You have won his heart for ever,' said Lady Albury.

'Whose heart?' asked Ayala, in her confusion.

'Sir Harry's heart. As for the other, cela va sans dire. You must go on wearing it every night for a week or Sir Harry will want to know why you have left it off. If the woman had made it on you it couldn't have fitted better. Baker,'——Baker was the buxom female,——'said that she knew it was right. You did that very prettily to Sir Harry. Now go up and ask Colonel Stubbs what he thinks of it.'

'Indeed, I won't,' said Ayala. Lady Albury, a few minutes afterwards, when she saw Ayala walking away towards the drawing-room leaning on the Colonel's arm, acknowledged to herself that she did at last understand it. The Colonel had been able to see it all, even without the dress, and she confessed in her mind that the Colonel had eyes with which to see, and ears with which to hear, and a judgment with which to appreciate. 'Don't you think that girl very lovely?' she said to Lord Rufford, on whose arm she was leaning.

'Something almost more than lovely,' said Lord Rufford, with unwonted enthusiasm.

It was acknowledged now by everybody. 'Is it true about Colonel Stubbs and Miss Dormer?' whispered Lady Rufford to her hostess in the drawing-room.

'Upon my word, I never inquire into those things,' said Lady Albury. 'I suppose he does admire her. Everybody must admire her.'

'Oh yes;' said Lady Rufford. 'She is certainly very pretty. Who is she, Lady Albury?' Lady Rufford had been a Miss Penge, and the Penges were supposed to be direct descendants from Boadicea.

'She is Miss Ayala Dormer. Her father was an artist, and her mother was a very handsome woman. When a girl is as beautiful as Miss Dormer, and as clever, it doesn't much signify who she is.' Then the direct descendant from Boadicea withdrew, holding an opinion much at variance with that expressed by her hostess.

'Who is that young lady who sat next to you?' asked Captain Glomax of Colonel Stubbs, after the ladies had gone.

'She is a Miss Ayala Dormer.'

'Did I not see her out hunting with you once or twice early in the season?'

'You saw her out hunting, no doubt, and I was there. I did not specially bring her. She was staying here, and rode one of Albury's horses.'

'Take her top and bottom, and all round,' said Captain Glomax, 'she is the prettiest little thing I've seen for many a day. When she curtseyed to Sir Harry in the drawing-room I almost thought that I should like to be a marrying man myself.' Stubbs did not carry on the conversation, having felt displeased rather than otherwise by the admiration expressed.

'I didn't quite understand before,' said Sir Harry to his wife that night, 'what it was that made Jonathan so furious about that girl; but I think I see it now.'

'Fine feathers make fine birds,' said his wife, laughing.

'Feathers ever so fine,' said Sir Harry, 'don't make well-bred birds.'

'To tell the truth,' said Lady Albury, 'I think we shall all have to own that Jonathan has been right.'

This took place upstairs, but before they left the drawing-room Lady Albury whispered a few words to her young friend. 'We have had a terrible trouble about you, Ayala.'

'A trouble about me, Lady Albury? I should be so sorry.'

'It is not exactly your fault;—but we haven't at all known what to do with that unfortunate man.'

'What man?' asked Ayala, forgetful at the moment of all men except Colonel Stubbs.

'You naughty girl! Don't you know that my brother-in-law is broken-hearted about you?'

'Captain Batsby!' whispered Ayala, in her faintest voice.

'Yes; Captain Batsby. A Captain has as much right to be considered as a Colonel in such a matter as this.' Here Ayala frowned, but said nothing. 'Of course, I can't help it, who may break his heart, but poor Ben is always supposed to be at Stalham just at this time of the year, and now I have been obliged to tell him one fib upon another to keep him away. When he comes to know it all, what on earth will he say to me?'

'I am sure it has not been my fault,' said Ayala.

'That's what young ladies always say when gentlemen break their hearts.'

When Ayala was again in her room, and had got rid of the buxom female who came to assist her in taking off her new finery, she was aware of having passed the evening triumphantly. She was conscious of admiration. She knew that Sir Harry had been pleased by her appearance. She was sure that Lady Albury was satisfied with her, and she had seen something in the Colonel's glance that made her feel that he had not been indifferent. But in their conversation at the dinner table he had said nothing which any other man might not have said, if any other man could have made himself as agreeable. Those hunting days were all again described with their various incidents, with the great triumph over the brook, and Twentyman's wife and baby, and fat Lord Rufford, who was at the moment sitting there opposite to them; and the ball in London, with the lady who was thrown out of the window; and the old gentleman and the old lady of to-day who had been so peculiar in their remarks. There had been nothing else in their conversation, and it surely was not possible that a man who intended to put himself forward as a lover should have talked in such fashion as that! But then there were other things which occurred to her. Why had there been that tear in his eye? And that 'cela va sans dire' which had come from Lady Albury in her railing mood;— what had that meant? Lady Albury, when she said that, could not have known that the Colonel had changed his purpose.

But, after all, what is a dress, let it be ever so pretty? The Angel of Light would not care for her dress, let her wear what she might. Were he to seek her because of her dress, he would not be the Angel of Light of whom she had dreamed. It was not by any dress that she could prevail over him. She did rejoice because of her little triumph;—but she knew that she rejoiced because she was not an Angel of Light herself. Her only chance lay in this, that the angels of yore did come down from heaven to ask for love and worship from the daughters of men.

As she went to bed, she determined that she would still be true to her dream. Not because folk admired a new frock would she be ready to give herself to a man who was only a man,—a man of the earth really; who had about him no more than a few of the real attributes of an Angel of Light.

## CHAPTER L

### GOBBLEGOOSE WOOD ON SUNDAY

THE next two days were not quite so triumphant to Ayala as had been the evening of her arrival. There was hunting on both of those days, the gentlemen having gone on the Friday away out of Sir Harry's country to the Brake hounds. Ayala and the Colonel had arrived on the Thursday. Ayala had not expected to be asked to hunt again,—had not even thought about it. It had been arranged before on Nina's account, and Nina now was not to hunt any more. Lord George did not altogether approve of it, and Nina was quite in accord with Lord George,— though she had held up her whip and shaken it in triumph when she jumped over the Cranbury Brook. And the horse which Ayala had ridden was no longer in the stables. 'My dear, I am so sorry; but I'm afraid we can't mount you,' Lady Albury said. In answer to this Ayala declared that she had not thought of it for a moment. But yet the days seemed to be dull with her. Lady Rufford was,—well,—perhaps a little patronising to her, and patronage such as that was not at all to Ayala's taste. 'Lady Albury seems to be quite a kind friend to you,' Lady Rufford said. Nothing could be more true. The idea implied was true also,—the idea that such a one as Ayala was much in luck's way to find such a friend as Lady Albury. It was true no doubt; but, nevertheless, it was ungracious, and had to be resented. 'A very kind friend, indeed. Some people only make friends of those who are as grand as themselves.'

'I am sure we should be very glad to see you at Rufford if you remain long in the country,' said Lady

Rufford, a little time afterwards. But even in this
there was not a touch of that cordiality which might
have won Ayala's heart. 'I am not at all likely to
stay,' said Ayala. 'I live with my uncle and aunt at
Notting Hill; and I very rarely go away from home.'
Lady Rufford, however, did not quite understand it.
It had been whispered to her that morning that
Ayala was certainly going to marry Colonel Stubbs;
and, if so, why should she not come to Rufford?

On that day, the Friday, she was taken in to
dinner by Captain Glomax. 'I remember quite as if
it were yesterday,' said the Captain. 'It was the day
we rode the Cranbury Brook.'

Ayala looked up into his face, also remembering
everything as well as it were yesterday. 'Mr.
Twentyman rode over it,' she said, 'and Colonel
Stubbs rode into it.'

'Oh, yes; Stubbs got a ducking; so he did.' The
Captain had not got a ducking, but then he had gone
round by the road. 'It was a good run that.'

'I thought so.'

'We haven't been lucky since Sir Harry has had
the hounds somehow. There doesn't seem to be the
dash about 'em there used to be when I was here.
I had them before Sir Harry, you know.' All this
was nearly in a whisper.

'Were you Master?' asked Ayala, with a tone of
surprise which was not altogether pleasing to the
Captain.

'Indeed I was, but the fag of it was too great, and
the thanks too small, so I gave it up. They used to
get four days a week out of me.' During the two
years that the Captain had had the hounds, there had
been, no doubt, two or three weeks in which he had
hunted four days.

Ayala liked hunting, but she did not care much for
Captain Glomax, who, having seen her once or twice
on horseback, would talk to her about nothing else.
A little away on the other side of the table Nina was
sitting next to Colonel Stubbs, and she could hear

their voices and almost their words. Nina and Jonathan were first cousins, and, of course, could be happy together without giving her any cause for jealousy;—but she almost envied Nina. Yet she had hoped that it might not fall to her lot to be taken out again that evening by the Colonel. Hitherto she had not even spoken to him during the day. They had started to the meet very early, and the gentlemen had almost finished their breakfast before she had come down. If there had been any fault it was her fault, but yet she almost felt that there was something of a disruption between them. It was so evident to her that he was perfectly happy whilst he was talking to Nina.

After dinner it seemed to be very late before the men came into the drawing-room, and then they were still engaged upon that weary talk about hunting, till Lady Rufford, in order to put a stop to it, offered to sing. 'I always do,' she said, 'if Rufford ventures to name a fox in the drawing-room after dinner.' She did sing, and Ayala thought that the singing was more weary than the talk about hunting.

While this was going on, the Colonel had got himself shut up in a corner of the room. Lady Albury had first taken him there, and afterwards he had been hemmed in when Lady Rufford sat down to the piano. Ayala had hardly ventured even to glance at him, but yet she knew all that he did, and heard almost every word that he spoke. The words were not many, but still when he did speak his voice was cheerful. Nina now and again had run up to him, and Lady Rufford had asked him some questions about the music. But why didn't he come and speak to her? thought Ayala. Though all that nonsense about love was over, still he ought not to have allowed a day to pass at Stalham without speaking to her. He was the oldest friend there in that house except Nina. It was indeed no more than nine months since she had first seen him, but still it seemed to her that he was an old friend. She did feel, as she endeavoured to answer the questions that Lord Rufford was asking her, that Jonathan Stubbs was treating her unkindly.

Then came the moment in which Lady Albury marshalled her guests out of the room towards their chambers. 'Have you found yourself dull without the hunting?' the Colonel said to Ayala.

'Oh dear no; I must have a dull time if I do, seeing that I have only hunted three days in my life.' There was something in the tone of her voice which, as she herself was aware, almost expressed dissatisfaction. And yet not for worlds would she have shown herself to be dissatisfied with him, could she have helped it.

'I thought that perhaps you might have regretted the little pony,' he said.

'Because a thing has been very pleasant, it should not be regretted because it cannot be had always.'

'To me a thing may become so pleasant, that unless I can have it always my life must be one long regret.'

'The pony is not quite like that,' said Ayala, smiling, as she followed the other ladies out of the room.

On the next morning the meet was nearer, and some of the ladies were taken there in an open carriage. Lady Rufford went, and Mrs. Gosling, and Nina and Ayala. 'Of course there is a place for you,' Lady Albury had said to her. 'Had I wanted to go I would have made Sir Harry send the drag; but I've got to stop at home and see that the buttered toast is ready by the time the gentlemen all come back.' The morning was almost warm, so that the sportsmen were saying evil things of violets and primroses, as is the wont of sportsmen on such occasions, and at the meet the ladies got out of the carriage and walked about among the hounds, making civil speeches to old Tony. 'No, my lady,' said Tony, 'I don't like these sunshiny mornings at all; there ain't no kind of scent, and I goes riding about these big woods, up and down, till my shirt is as wet on my back with the sweat as though I'd been pulled through the river.' Then Lady Rufford walked away and did not ask Tony any more questions.

Ayala was patting one of the hounds when the Colonel, who had given his horse to a groom, came and joined her. 'If you don't regret that pony,' said he, 'somebody else does.'

'I do regret him in one way, of course. I did like it very much; but I don't think it nice, when much has been done for me, to say that I want to have more done.'

'Of course I knew what you meant.'

'Perhaps you would go and tell Sir Harry, and then he would think me very ungrateful.'

'Ayala,' he said, 'I will never say anything of you that will make anybody think evil of you. But, between ourselves, as Sir Harry is not here, I suppose I may confess that I regret the pony.'

'I should like it, of course,' whispered Ayala.

'And so should I,—so much! I suppose all these men here would think me an ass if they knew how little I care about the day's work,—whether we find, or whether we run, or whether we kill,—just because the pony is not here. If the pony were here I should have that feeling of expectation of joy, which is so common to girls when some much-thought-of ball or promised pleasure is just before them.' Then Tony went off with his hounds, and Jonathan, mounting his horse, followed with the ruck.

Ayala knew very well what the pony meant, as spoken of by the Colonel. When he declared that he regretted the pony, it was because the pony might have carried herself. He had meant her to understand that the much-thought-of ball or promised pleasure would have been the delight of again riding with herself. And then he had again called her Ayala. She could remember well every occasion on which he had addressed her by her Christian name. It had been but seldom. Once, however, it had occurred in the full flow of their early intimacy, before that love-making had been begun. It had struck her as being almost wrong, but still as very pleasant. If it might be made right by some feeling of brotherly friendship, how pleasant would it be! And now she would like it again, if only it might be taken as a sign of friendship rather than of love. It never occurred to her to be angry as she would have been angry with any other man. How she would have looked at Captain Batsby had he dared to call her Ayala! Colonel Stubbs should call her Ayala as long as he pleased,—if it were done only in friendship.

After that they were driven about for a while, seeing what Tony did with the hounds, as tidings came to them now and again that one fox had broken this way and another had gone the other. But Ayala, through it all, could not interest herself about the foxes. She was thinking only of Jonathan Stubbs. She knew that she was pleased because he had spoken to her, and had said kind, pleasant words to her. She knew that she had been displeased while he had sat apart from her, talking to others. But yet she could not explain to herself why she had been either pleased or displeased. She feared that there was more than friendship,—than mere friendship, in that declaration of his that he did in truth regret the pony. His voice had been, oh, so sweet as he had said it! Something told her that men do not speak in mere friendship after that fashion. Not even in the softness of friendship between a man and a woman will the man's voice become as musical as that! Young as she was, child as she was, there was an instinct in her breast which declared to her that it was so. But then, if it were so, was not everything again wrong with her? If it were so, then must that condition of things be coming back which it had been, and still was, her firm resolve to avoid. And yet, as the carriage was being driven about, and as the frequent exclamations came that the fox had traversed this way or that, her pride was gratified and she was happy.

'What was Colonel Stubbs saying to you?' asked Nina, when they were at home at the house after lunch.

'He was talking about the dear pony which I used to ride.'

'About nothing else?'

'No;—about nothing else.' This Ayala said with a short, dry manner of utterance which she would assume when she was determined not to have a subject carried on.

'Ayala, why do you not tell me everything? I told you everything as soon as it happened.'

'Nothing has happened.'

'I know he asked you,' said Nina.

'And I answered him.'

'Is that to be everything?'

'Yes;—that is to be everything,' said Ayala, with a short, dry manner of utterance. It was so plain, that even Nina could not pursue the subject.

There was nothing done on that day in the way of sport. Glomax thought that Tony had been idle, and had made a holiday of the day from the first. But Sir Harry declared that there had not been a yard of scent. The buttered toast, however, was eaten, and the regular sporting conversation was carried on. Ayala, however, was not there to hear it. Ayala was in her own room dreaming.

She was taken in to dinner by a curate in the neighbourhood,—to whom she endeavoured to make herself very pleasant, while the Colonel sat at her other side. The curate had a good deal to say as to lawn tennis. If the weather remained as it was, it was thought that they could all play lawn tennis on the Tuesday,—when there would be no hunting. The curate was a pleasant young fellow, and Ayala devoted herself to him and to their joint hopes for next Tuesday. Colonel Stubbs never once attempted to interfere with the curate's opportunity. There was

Lady Rufford on the other side of him, and to Lady
Rufford he said all that he did say during dinner. At
one period of the repast she was more than generally
lively, because she felt herself called upon to warn her
husband that an attack of the gout was imminent,
and would be certainly produced instantaneously
if he could not deny himself the delight of a certain
dish which was going the round of the table. His
lordship smiled and denied himself,—thinking, as he
did so, whether another wife, plus the gout, would or
would not have been better for him. All this either
amused Colonel Stubbs sufficiently, or else made him
so thoughtful, that he made no attempt to interfere with the curate. In the evening there was again
music,—which resulted in a declaration made upstairs by Sir Harry to his wife that that wife of
Rufford's was a confounded bore. 'We all knew that,
my dear, as soon as he married her,' said Lady Albury.

'Why did he marry a bore?'

'Because he wanted a wife to look after himself,
and not to amuse his friends. The wonder used to be
that he had done so well.'

Not a word had there been,—not a word, since that
sound of 'Ayala' had fallen upon her ears. No;—
he was not handsome, and his name was Jonathan
Stubbs;—but surely no voice so sweet had ever
fallen from a man's lips! So she sat and dreamed far
into the night. He, the Angel of Light, would certainly have a sweeter voice! That was an attribute
without which no angel could be angelic! As to the
face and the name, that would not perhaps signify.
But he must have an intellect high soaring, a soul
tuned to music, and a mind versed in nothing but
great matters. He might be an artist, or more
probably a poet;—or perhaps a musician. Yet she
had read of poets, artists, and musicians, who had
misused their wives, been fond of money, and had
perhaps been drunkards. The Angel of Light must
have the gifts, and must certainly be without the
vices.

The next day was Sunday and they all went to church. In the afternoon they, as many of them as pleased, were to walk as far as Gobblegoose Wood, which was only three miles from the house. They could not hunt and therefore they must go to the very scene of the late contest and again discuss it there. Sir Harry and the Captain would walk and so would Ayala and Nina and some others. Lord Rufford did not like walking, and Lady Rufford would stay at home to console him. Ayala used her little wiles to keep herself in close company with Nina; but the Colonel's wiles were more effective;— and then, perhaps, Nina assisted the Colonel rather than Ayala. It came to pass that before they had left Gobblegoose Wood Ayala and the Colonel were together. When it was so he did not beat about the bush for a moment longer. He had fixed his opportunity for himself and he put it to use at once.

'Ayala,' he said, 'am I to have any other answer?'

'What answer?'

'Nay, my dearest,—my own, own dearest as I fain would have you,—who shall say what answer but you? Ayala, you know that I love you!'

'I thought you had given it up.'

'Given it up. Never,—never! Does a man give up his joy,—the pride of his life,—the one only delight on which his heart has set itself! No, my darling, I have not given it up. Because you would not have it as I wished when I first spoke to you, I have not gone on troubling you. I thought I would wait till you were used again to the look of me, and to my voice. I shall never give it up, Ayala. When you came into the room that night with your new frock on——' Then he paused, and she glanced round upon him, and saw that a tear again was in his eye. 'When you came in and curtseyed to Sir Harry I could hardly keep within myself because I thought you were so beautiful.'

'It was the new gown which he had given me.'

'No, my pet;—no! You may add a grace to a

A.A.—24

dress, but it can do but little for you. It was the little motion, the little word, the light in your eye! It twinkles at me sometimes when you glance about, so that I do not know whether it is meant for me or not. I fear that it is never meant for me.'

'It is meant for nothing,' said Ayala.

'And yet it goes into my very bosom. When you were talking to that clergyman at dinner I could see every sparkle that came from it. Then I wonder to myself whether you can ever be thinking of me as I am always thinking of you.' She knew that she had been thinking of him every waking moment since she had been at Albury and through many of her sleeping moments also. 'Ayala, one little word, one other glance from your eyes, one slightest touch from your hand upon my arm, shall tell me,—shall tell me,—shall tell me that I am the happiest, the proudest man in all the world.' She walked on steadfastly, closing her very teeth against a word, with her eyes fixed before her so that no slightest glance should wander. Her two hands were in her little muff, and she kept them with her fingers clasped together, as though afraid lest one might rebel, and fly away, and touch the sleeve of his coat. 'Ayala, how is it to be with me?'

'I cannot,' she said sternly. And her eyes were still fixed before her, and her fingers were still bound in one with another. And yet she loved him. Yet she knew that she loved him. She could have hung upon his arm and smiled up into his face, and frowned her refusal only with mock anger as he pressed her to his bosom,—only that those dreams were so palpable to her and so dear, had been to her so vast a portion of her young life! 'I cannot,' she said again. 'I cannot.'

'Is that to be your answer for ever?' To this she made no immediate reply. 'Must it be so, Ayala?'

'I cannot,' she said. But the last little word was so impeded by the sobs which she could not restrain as almost to be inaudible.

'I will not make you unhappy, Ayala.' Yes, she was unhappy. She was unhappy because she knew that she could not rule herself to her own happiness; because, even at this moment, she was aware that she was wrong. If she could only release part of herself from the other, then could she fly into his arms and tell him that that spirit which had troubled her had flown. But the spirit was too strong for her, and would not fly. 'Shall we go and join them?' he asked her in a voice altered, but still so sweet to her ears.

'If you think so,' she replied.

'Perhaps it will be best, Ayala. Do not be angry with me now. I will not call you so again.' Angry! Oh, no! She was not angry with him! But it was very bitter to her to be told that she should never hear the word again from his lips.

'The hunted fox never went up Buddlecombe Hill;—never. If he did I'll eat every fox in the Rufford and Offord country.' This was heard, spoken in most angry tones by Captain Glomax, as the Colonel and Ayala joined the rest of the party.

## CHAPTER LI

### 'NO!'

AYALA, on her return from the walk to the wood, spent the remainder of the afternoon in tears. During the walk she kept close to Sir Harry, pretending to listen to the arguments about the fox, but she said nothing. Her ears were really intent on endeavouring to catch the tones of her lover's voice as he went on in front of them talking to Nina. Nothing could be more pleasant than the sound as he said a word or two now and again, encouraging Nina in her rhapsodies as to Lord George and all Lord George's family. But Ayala learned nothing from that. She had come to know the man well enough to be aware that he could tune his voice to the

occasion, and could hide his feelings let them be ever
so strong. She did not doubt his love now. She did
not doubt but that at this moment his heart was
heavy with rejected love. She quite believed in him.
But nevertheless his words were pleasant and kind
as he encouraged Nina.

Nor did she doubt her own love. She was alone in
her room that afternoon till she told herself at last
the truth. Oh, yes; she loved him. She was sure of
that. But now he was gone! Why had she been so
foolish? Then it seemed as though at that moment
the separation took place between herself and the
spirit which had haunted her. She seemed to know
now,—now at this very moment,—that the man was
too good for her. The knowledge had been coming
to her. It had almost come when he had spoken to
her in the wood. If it could only have been that
he should have delayed his appeal to her for yet
another day or two! She thought now that if he
could have delayed it but for a few hours the cure
would have been complete. If he had talked to her as
he so well knew how to talk while they were in the
wood together, while they were walking home,—so
as to have exorcised the spirit from her by the sweetness of his words,—and then have told her that there
was his love to have if she chose to have it, then she
thought she would have taken it. But he had come
to her while those words which she had prepared
under the guidance of the spirit were yet upon her
tongue. 'I cannot,' she had said. 'I cannot.' But
she had not told him that she did not love him.

'I did love him,' she said to herself, almost acknowledging that the spirit had been wholly exorcised.
The fashion of her mind was altogether different
from that which had so strongly prevailed with her.
He was an honest, noble man, high in the world's
repute, clever, a gentleman, a man of taste, and
possessed of that gentle ever-present humour which
was so inexpressibly delightful to her. She never
again spoke to herself even in her thoughts of that

Angel of Light,—never comforted herself again with the vision of that which was to come! There had appeared to her a man better than all other men, and when he had asked her for her hand she had simply said,—'I cannot.' And yet she had loved him all the time. How foolish, how false, how wicked she had been! It was thus that she thought of it all as she sat there alone in her bedroom through the long hours of the afternoon. When they sent up for her asking her to come down, she begged that she might be allowed to remain there till dinner-time, because she was tired with her walk.

He would not come again now. Oh, no,—he was too proud, too firm, too manly for that. It was not for such a one as he to come whining after a girl,— like her cousin Tom. Would it be possible that she should even yet tell him? Could she say to him one little word, contradicting that which she had so often uttered in the wood? 'Now I can,' once whispered in his ear, would do it all. But as to this she was aware that there was no room for hope. To speak such a word, low as it might be spoken, simple and little as it might be, was altogether impossible. She had had her chance and had lost it,—because of those idle dreams. That the dreams had been all idle she declared to herself,—not aware that the Ayala whom her lover had loved would not have been an Ayala to be loved by him, but for the dreams. Now she must go back to her uncle and aunt and to Kingsbury Crescent, with the added sorrow that the world of dreams was closed to her for ever. When the maid came to her she consented to have the frock put on, the frock which Sir Harry had given her, boldly resolving to struggle through her sorrow till Lady Albury should have dismissed her to her home. Nobody would want her now at Stalham, and the dismissal would soon come.

While she had been alone in her room the Colonel had been closeted with Lady Albury. They had at least been thus shut up together for some half-hour

during which he had told his tale. 'I have to own,'
said he, half-laughing as he began his tale, 'that I
thoroughly respect Miss Dormer.'

'Why is she to be called Miss Dormer?'

'Because she has shown herself worthy of my
respect.'

'What is it that you mean, Jonathan?'

'She knew her own mind when she told me at first
that she could not accept the offer which I did myself the honour of making her, and now she sticks to
her purpose. I think that a young lady who will do
that should be respected.'

'She has refused you again?'

'Altogether.'

'As how?'

'Well, I hardly know that I am prepared to explain the "as how" even to you. I am about as
thick-skinned a man in such matters as you may find
anywhere, but I do not know that even I can bring
myself to tell the "as how." The "as how" was very
clear in one respect. It was manifest that she knew
her own mind, which is a knowledge not in the
possession of all young ladies. She told me that she
could not marry me.'

'I do not believe it.'

'Not that she told me so?'

'Not that she knew her own mind. She is a little
simple fool, who with some vagary in her brain is
throwing away utterly her own happiness, while she
is vexing you.'

'As to the vexation you are right.'

'Cross-grained little idiot!'

'An idiot she certainly is not; and as to being cross-
grained I have never found it. A human being with
the grains running more directly all in the same way
I have never come across.'

'Do not talk to me, Jonathan, like that,' she said.
'When I call her cross-grained I mean that she is
running counter to her own happiness.'

'I cannot tell anything about that. I should have

endeavoured, I think, to make her happy. She has certainly run counter to my happiness.'

'And now?'

'What;—as to this very moment! I shall leave Stalham to-morrow.'

'Why should you do that? Let her go if one must go.'

'That is just what I want to prevent. Why should she lose her little pleasure?'

'You don't suppose that we can make the house happy to her now! Why should we care to do so when she will have driven you away?' He sat silent for a minute or two looking at the fire, with his hands on his two knees. 'You must acknowledge, Jonathan,' continued she, 'that I have taken kindly to this Ayala of yours.'

'I do acknowledge it.'

'But it cannot be that she should be the same to us simply as a young lady, staying here as it were on her own behalf, as she was when we regarded her as your possible wife. Then every little trick and grace belonging to her endeared itself to us because we regarded her as one who was about to become one of ourselves. But what are her tricks and graces to us now?'

'They are all the world to me,' said the Colonel.

'But you must wipe them out of your memory,—unless, indeed, you mean to ask her again.'

'Ah!—that is it.'

'You will ask her again?'

'I do not say so; but I do not wish to rob myself of the chance. It may be that I shall. Of course I should to-morrow if I thought there was a hope. To-morrow there would be none,—but I should like to know, that I could find her again in hands so friendly as yours, if at the end of a month I should think myself strong enough to encounter the risk of another refusal. Would Sir Harry allow her to remain here for another month?'

'He would say, probably, nothing about it.'

'My plan is this,' he continued; 'let her remain here, say, for three weeks or a month. Do you continue all your kindness to her,—if not for her sake then for mine. Let her feel that she is made one of yourselves, as you say.'

'That will be hard,' said Lady Albury.

'It would not be hard if you thought that she was going to become so at last. Try it, for my sake. Say not a word to her about me,—though not shunning my name. Be to her as though I had told you nothing of this. Then when the period is over I will come again, —if I find that I can do so. If my love is still stronger than my sense of self-respect, I shall do so.' All this Lady Albury promised to do, and then the interview between them was over.

'Colonel Stubbs is going to Aldershot to-morrow,' said she to Ayala in the drawing-room after dinner. 'He finds now that he cannot very well remain away.' There was no hesitation in her voice as she said this, and no look in her eye which taught Ayala to suppose that she had heard anything of what had occurred in the wood.

'Is he indeed?' said Ayala, trying, but in vain, to be equally undemonstrative.

'It is a great trouble to us, but we are quite unable to prevent it,—unless you indeed can control him.'

'I cannot control him,' said Ayala, with that fixed look of resolution with which Lady Albury had already become familiar.

That evening before they went to bed the Colonel bade them all good-bye, as he intended to start early in the morning. 'I never saw such a fellow as you are for sudden changes,' said Sir Harry.

'What is the good of staying here for hunting when the ground and Tony's temper are both as hard as brick-bats? If I go now I can get another week further on in March if the rain should come.' With this Sir Harry seemed to be satisfied; but Ayala felt sure that Tony's temper and the rain had had nothing to do with it.

'Good-bye, Miss Dormer,' he said, with his pleasantest smile, and his pleasantest voice.

'Good-bye,' she repeated. What would she not have given that her voice should be as pleasant as his, and her smile! But she failed so utterly that the little word was inaudible,—almost obliterated by the choking of a sob. How bitterly severe had that word, Miss Dormer, sounded from his mouth! Could he not have called her Ayala for the last time,——even though all the world should have heard it? She was wide awake in the morning and heard the wheels of his cart as he was driven off. As the sound died away upon her ear she felt that he was gone from her for ever. How had it been that she had said, 'I cannot,' so often, when all her heart was set upon 'I can?'

And now it remained to her to take herself away from Stalham as fast as she might. She understood perfectly all those ideas which Lady Albury had expressed to her well-loved friend. She was nothing to anybody at Stalham, simply a young lady staying in the house;—as might be some young lady connected with them by blood, or some young lady whose father and mother had been their friends. She had been brought there to Stalham, now this second time, in order that Jonathan Stubbs might take her as his wife. Driven by some madness she had refused her destiny, and now nobody would want her at Stalham any longer. She had better begin to pack up at once,—and go. The coldness of the people, now that she had refused to do as she had been asked, would be unbearable to her. And yet she must not let it appear that Stalham was no longer dear to her merely because Colonel Stubbs had left it. She would let a day go by, and then say with all the ease she could muster that she would take her departure on the next. After that her life before her would be a blank. She had known up to this,—so at least she told herself,—that Jonathan Stubbs would afford her at any rate another chance. Now there could be no other chance.

. The first blank day passed away, and it seemed
to her almost as though she had no right to speak to
any one. She was sure that Lady Rufford knew what
had occurred, because nothing more was said as to
the proposed visit. Mrs. Colonel Stubbs would have
been welcome anywhere, but who was Ayala Dormer?
Even though Lady Albury bade her come out in the
carriage, it seemed to her to be done as a final effort
of kindness. Of course they would be anxious to be
rid of her. That evening the buxom woman did not
come to help her dress herself. It was an accident.
The buxom woman was wanted here and there till
it was too late, and Ayala had left her room. Ayala,
in truth, required no assistance in dressing. When
the first agonizing moment of the new frock had been
passed over, she would sooner have arrayed herself
without assistance. But now it seemed as though the
buxom woman was running away because she, Ayala,
was thought to be no longer worthy of her services.

On the next morning she began her little speech
to Lady Albury. 'Going away to-morrow?' said
Lady Albury.

'Or perhaps the next day,' suggested Ayala.

'My dear, it has been arranged that you should
stay here for another three weeks.'

'No.'

'I say it was arranged. Everybody understood it.
I am sure your aunt understood it. Because one
person goes, everybody else isn't to follow so as to
break up a party. Honour among thieves!'

'Thieves!'

'Well;—anything else you like to call us all. The
party has been made up. And to tell the truth I
don't think that young ladies have the same right
of changing their minds and rushing about as men
assume. Young ladies ought to be more steady.
Where am I to get another young lady at a moment's
notice to play lawn tennis with Mr. Greene? Compose yourself and stay where you are like a good
girl.'

'What will Sir Harry say?'

'Sir Harry will probably go on talking about the Stillborough fox and quarrelling with that odious Captain Glomax. That is, if you remain here. If you go all of a sudden, he will perhaps hint——'

'Hint what, Lady Albury?'

'Never mind. He shall make no hints if you are a good girl.' Nothing was said at the moment about the Colonel,—nothing further than the little allusion made above. Then there came the lawn tennis, and Ayala regained something of her spirits as she contrived with the assistance of Sir Harry to beat Nina and the curate. But on the following day Lady Albury spoke out more plainly. 'It was because of Colonel Stubbs that you said that you would go away.'

Ayala paused for a moment, and then answered stoutly, 'Yes, it was because of Colonel Stubbs.'

'And why?'

Ayala paused again and the stoutness almost deserted her. 'Because——'

'Well, my dear?'

'I don't think I ought to be asked,' said Ayala.

'Well, you shall not be asked. I will not be cruel to you. But do you not know that if I ask anything it is with a view to your own good?'

'Oh, yes,' said Ayala.

'But though I may not ask I suppose I may speak.' To this Ayala made no reply, either assenting or dissenting. 'You know, do you not, that I and Colonel Stubbs love each other like brother and sister,—more dearly than many brothers and sisters?'

'I suppose so.'

'And that therefore he tells me everything. He told me what took place in the wood,—and because of that he has gone away.'

'Of course you are angry with me;—because he has gone away.'

'I am sorry that he has gone,—because of the cause of it. I always wish that he should have everything that he desires; and now I wish that he should have this thing because he desires it above all other things.' Does he desire it above all other things?—thought Ayala to herself. And, if it be really so, cannot I now tell her that he shall have it? Cannot I say that I too long to get it quite as eagerly as he longs to have it? The suggestion rushed quickly to her mind; but the answer to it came as quickly. No;—she would not do so. No offer of the kind would come from her. By what she had said must she abide,—unless, indeed, he should come to her again. 'But why should you go, Ayala, because he has gone? Why should you say aloud that you had come here to listen to his offer, and that you had gone away as soon as you had resolved that, for this reason or that, it was not satisfactory to you?'

'Oh, Lady Albury.'

'That would be the conclusion drawn. Remain here with us, and see if you can like us well enough to be one of us.'

'Dear Lady Albury, I do love you dearly.'

'What he may do I cannot say. Whether he may bring himself to try once again I do not know,—nor will I ask you whether there might possibly be any other answer were he to do so.'

'No!' said Ayala, driven by a sudden fit of obstinacy which she could not control.

'I ask no questions about it, but I am sure it will be better for you to remain here for a few weeks. We will make you happy if we can, and you can learn to think over what has passed without emotion.' Thus it was decided that Ayala should prolong her visit into the middle of March. She could not understand her own conduct when she again found herself alone. Why had she ejaculated that sudden 'No,' when Lady Albury had suggested to her the possibility of changing her purpose? She knew that she would fain change it if it were possible; and yet when the idea was presented to her she replied with a sudden denial of its possibility. But

still there was hope, even though the hope was faint.
'Whether he may bring himself to try again I do not
know.' So it was that Lady Albury had spoken of
him, and of what Lady Albury said to her she now
believed every word. 'Whether he could bring himself!' Surely such a one as he would not condescend
so far as that. But if he did one word should be
sufficient. By no one else would she allow it to be
thought, for an instant, that she would wish to
reverse her decision. It must still be No to any other
person from whom such suggestion might come. But
should he give her the chance she would tell him
instantly the truth of everything. 'Can I love you!
Oh, my love, it is impossible that I should not love
you!' It would be thus that the answer should be
given to him, should he allow her the chance of
making it.

## CHAPTER LII

### 'I CALL IT FOLLY.'

THREE weeks passed by, and Ayala was still at
Stalham. Colonel Stubbs had not as yet appeared, and very little had been said about him. Sir
Henry would sometimes suggest that if he meant to
see any more hunting he had better come at once,
but this was not addressed to Ayala. She made up
her mind that he would not come, and was sure that
she was keeping him away by her presence. He could
not—'bring himself to try over again,' as Lady
Albury had put it! Why should he—'bring himself'—
to do anything on behalf of one who had treated him
so badly? It had been settled that she should remain
to the 25th of March, when the month should be up
from the time in which Lady Albury had decided
upon that as the period of her visit. Of her secret
she had given no slightest hint. If he ever did come
again it should not be because she had asked for
his coming. As far as she knew how to carry out

such a purpose, she concealed from Lady Albury anything like a feeling of regret. And she was so far successful that Lady Albury thought it expedient to bring in other assistance to help her cause,—as will be seen by a letter which Ayala received when the three weeks had passed by.

In the meantime there had been at first dismay, then wonder, and lastly, some amusement, at the condition of Captain Batsby. When Captain Batsby had first learned at Merle Park that Ayala and Jonathan Stubbs were both at Stalham, he wrote very angrily to Lady Albury. In answer to this his sister-in-law had pleaded guilty,—but still defending herself. How could she make herself responsible for the young lady,—who did not indeed seem ready to bestow her affections on any of her suitors? But still she acknowledged that a little favour was being shown to Colonel Stubbs,—wishing to train the man to the idea that, in this special matter, Colonel Stubbs must be recognised as the Stalham favourite. Then no further letters were received from the Captain, but there came tidings that he was staying at Merle Park. Ayala heard continually from her sister, and Lucy sent some revelations as to the Captain. He seemed to be very much at home at Merle Park, said Lucy; and then, at last, she expressed her own opinion that Captain Batsby and Gertrude were becoming very fond of each other. And yet the whole story of Gertrude and Mr. Houston was known, of course, to Lucy, and through Lucy to Ayala. To Ayala these sudden changes were very amusing, as she certainly did not wish to retain her own hold on the Captain, and was not specially attached to her cousin Gertrude. From Ayala the tidings went to Lady Albury, and in this way the fears which had been entertained as to the Captain's displeasure were turned to wonder and amusement. But up to this period nothing had been heard of the projected trip to Ostend.

Then came the letter to Ayala, to which allusion has been made, a letter from her old friend the Marchesa, who was now at Rome. It was ostensibly in answer to a letter from Ayala herself, but was written in great part in compliance with instructions received from Lady Albury. It was as follows:—

'DEAR AYALA,—

'I was glad to get your letter about Nina. She is very happy, and Lord George is here. Indeed, to tell the truth, they arrived together,—which was not at all proper; but everything will be made proper on Tuesday, 8th April, which is the day at last fixed for the wedding. I wish you could have been here to be one of the bridesmaids. Nina says that you will have it that the Pope is to marry her. Instead of that it is going to be done by Lord George's uncle, the Dean of Dorchester, who is coming for this purpose. Then they are going up to a villa they have taken on Como, where we shall join them some time before the spring is over. After that they seem to have no plans,— except plans of connubial bliss, which is never to know any interruption.

'Now that I have come to connubial bliss, and feel so satisfied as to Nina's prospects, I have a word or two to say about the bliss of somebody else. Nina is my own child, and of course comes first. But one Jonathan Stubbs is my nephew, and is also very near to my heart. From all that I hear, I fancy that he has set his mind also on connubial bliss. Have you not heard that it is so?

'A bird has whispered to me that you have not been kind to him. Why should it be so? Nobody knows better than I do that a young lady is entitled to the custody of her own heart, and that she should not be compelled, or even persuaded, to give her hand in opposition to her own feelings. If your feelings and your heart are altogether opposed to the poor fellow, of course there must be an end of it. But I had thought that from the time you first met him he had been a favourite of yours;—so much so that there was a moment in which I feared that you

. might think too much of the attentions of a man
who has ever been a favourite with all who have
known him. But I have found that in this I was
altogether mistaken. When he came that evening to
see the last of you at the theatre, taking, as I knew
he did, considerable trouble to release himself from
other engagements, I was pretty sure how it was
going to be. He is not a man to be in love with a girl
for a month and then to be in love with another the
next month. When once he allowed himself to think
that he was in love, the thing was done and fixed
either for his great delight,—or else to his great
trouble.

. 'I knew how it was to be, and so it has been. Am I
not right in saying that on two occasions, at considerable intervals, he has come to you and made
distinct offers of his hand? I fear, though I do not
actually know it, that you have just as distinctly
rejected those offers. I do not know it, because none
but you and he can know the exact words with which
you received from him the tender of all that he had
to give you. I can easily believe that he, with all his
intelligence, might be deceived by the feminine reserve and coyness of such a girl as you. If it be so,
I do pray that no folly may be allowed to interfere
with his happiness and with yours.

'I call it folly, not because I am adverse to feminine
reserve, not because I am prone to quarrel even with
what I call coyness; but because I know his nature
so well, and feel that he would not bear rebuffs of
which many another man would think nothing; that
he would not bring himself to ask again, perhaps
even for a seventh time, as they might do. And, if it
be that by some frequent asking his happiness and
yours could be insured, would it not be folly that such
happiness should be marred by childish disinclination on your part to tell the truth?

'As I said before, if your heart be set against
him, there must be an end of it. I can understand
that a girl so young as you should fail to see the

great merit of such a man. I therefore write as I do, thinking it possible that in this respect you may be willing to accept from my mouth something as to the man which shall be regarded as truth. It is on the inner man, on his nature and disposition, that the happiness of a wife must depend. A more noble nature, a more truthful spirit than his, I have never met. He is one on whom in every phase of life you may depend,—or I may depend,—as on a rock. He is one without vacillation, always steady to his purpose, requiring from himself in the way of duty and conduct infinitely more than he demands from those around him. If ever there was a man altogether manly, he is one. And yet no woman, no angel, ever held a heart more tender within his bosom. See him with children! Think of his words when he has spoken to yourself! Remember the estimation in which those friends hold him who know him best, —such as I and your friend, Lady Albury, and Sir Harry, and his cousin Nina. I could name many others, but these are those with whom you have seen him most frequently. If you can love such a man, do you not think that he would make you happy? And if you cannot, must there not be something wrong in your heart,—unless indeed it be already predisposed to some one else? Think of all this, dear Ayala, and remember that I am always

'Your affectionate friend,<br>'JULIA BALDONI.'

Ayala's first feeling as she read the letter was a conviction that her friend had altogether wasted her labour in writing it. Of what use was it to tell her of the man's virtues,—to tell her that the man's heart was as tender as an angel's, his truth as assured as a god's, his courage that of a hero,—that he was possessed of all those attributes which should by right belong to an Angel of Light? She knew all that without requiring the evidence of a lady from Rome,— having no need of any evidence on that matter from any other human being. Of what use could any evidence be on such a subject from the most truthful lips that ever spoke? Had she not found it all out herself would any words from others have prevailed with her? But she had found it out herself. It was already her gospel. That he was tender and true, manly, heroic,—as brightly angelic as could be any Angel of Light,—was already an absolute fact to her. No!— her heart had never been predisposed to any one else. It was of him she had always dreamed even long before she had seen him. He was the man, perfect in all good things, who was to come and take her with him; —if ever man should come and take her. She wanted no Marchesa Baldoni now to tell her that the angel had in truth come and realised himself before her in all his glory.

But she had shown herself to be utterly unfit for the angel. Though she recognised him now, she had not recognised him in time;—and even when she had recognised him she had been driven by her madness to reject him. Feminine reserve and coyness! Folly! Yes, indeed; she knew all that, too, without need of telling from her elders. The kind of coyness which she had displayed had been the very infatuation of feminine imbecility. It was because nature had made her utterly unfit for such a destiny that she had been driven by coyness and feminine reserve to destroy herself! It was thus that Ayala conversed with herself.

'I know his nature so well, and feel that he would not bear rebuffs of which many another man would think nothing.' Thus, she did not doubt, the Marchesa had spoken very truly. But of what value was all that now? She could not recall the rebuff. She could not now eradicate the cowardice which had made her repeat those wicked fatal words,—'I cannot.' 'I cannot.' 'I cannot.' The letter had come too late, for there was nothing she could do to amend her doom. She must send some answer to her friend in Italy, but there could be nothing in her answer to her to assist her. The feminine reserve and coyness had become odious to her,—as it had been displayed by herself to him. But it still remained in full force as to any assistance from others. She could not tell another to send him back to her. She could not implore help in her trouble. If he would come himself,—himself of his own accord,—himself impelled once more by his great tenderness of heart,—himself once more from his real, real love; then there should be no more coyness. 'If you will still have me,—oh yes!'

But there was the letter to be written. She so wrote it that by far the greater part of it,—the larger part at least,—had reference to Nina and her wedding. 'I will think of her on the 8th of April,' she said. 'I shall then be at home at Kingsbury Crescent, and I shall have nothing else to think of.' In that was her first allusion to her own condition with her lover. But on the last side of the sheet it was necessary that she should say more than that. Something must be said thoughtfully, carefully, and gratefully in reply to so much thought, and care, and friendship, as had been shown to her. But it must be so written that nothing of her secret should be read in it. The task was so troublesome that she was compelled to recopy the whole of her long letter, because the sentences as first written did not please her. 'I am so much obliged to you,' she said, 'by your kindness about Colonel Stubbs. He did do me the honour of asking me to be his wife. And I felt it so. You are not to suppose that I did not understand that. It is all over now, and I cannot explain to you why I felt that it would not do. It is all over, and therefore writing about it is no good. Only I want you to be sure of two things,—that there is no one else, and that I do love you so much for all your kindness. And you may be sure of a third thing, too,—that it is all over. I do hope that he will still let me be his friend. As a friend I have always liked him so much.' It was brave and bold, she thought, in answer to such words as the Marchesa's; but she did not know how to do it any better.

On Tuesday, the 25th of March, she was to return to Kingsbury Crescent. Various little words were said at Stalham indicating an intended break in the arrangement. 'The Captain certainly won't come now,' said Lady Albury, alluding to the arrangement as though it had been made solely with the view of saving Ayala from an encounter with her objectionable lover. 'Croppy has come back,' said Sir Harry one day;—Croppy being the pony which Ayala had ridden. 'Miss Dormer can have him now for what little there is left of the hunting.' This was said on the Saturday before she was to go. How could she ride Croppy for the rest of the hunting when she would be at Kingsbury Crescent? On neither of these occasions did she say a word, but she assumed that little look of contradiction which her friends at Stalham already knew how to read. Then, on the Sunday morning, there came a letter for Lady Albury. 'What does he say?' asked Sir Harry, at breakfast. 'I'll show it you before you go to church,' answered his wife. Then Ayala knew that the letter was from Colonel Stubbs.

But she did not expect that the letter should be shown to her,—which, however, came to be the case. When she was in the library, waiting to start to church, Lady Albury came in and threw the letter to her across the table. 'That concerns you,' she said, 'you had better read it.' There was another lady in the room, also waiting to start on their walk across the park, and therefore it was natural that nothing else should be said at the moment. Ayala read the letter, returned it to the envelope, and then handed it back to Lady Albury,—so that there was no word spoken about it before church. The letter, which was very short, was as follows:—

'I shall be at Stalham by the afternoon train on Sunday, 30th,—in time for dinner, if you will send the dog-cart. I could not leave this most exigeant of all places this week. I suppose Albury will go on in the woodlands for a week or ten days in April, and I must put up with that. I hear that Batsby is altogether fixed by the fascinations of Merle Park. I hope that you and Albury will receive consolation in the money.' Then there was a postscript. 'If Croppy can be got back again, Miss Dormer might see me tumble into another river.'

It was evident that Lady Albury did not expect anything to be said at present. She put the letter into her pocket, and there, for the moment, was the end of it. It may be feared that Ayala's attention was not fixed that morning so closely as it should have been on the services of the Church. There was so much in that little letter which insisted upon having all her attention! Had there been no postscript, the letter would have been very different. In that case the body of the letter itself would have intended to have no reference to her,—or rather it would have had a reference altogether opposite to that which the postscript gave it. In that case it would have been manifest to her that he had intentionally postponed his coming till she had left Stalham. Then his suggestion about the hunting would have had no interest for her. Everything would have been over. She would have been at Kingsbury Crescent, and he would have been at Stalham. But the postscript declared his intention of finding her still in the old quarters. She would not be there,—as she declared to herself. After this there would be but one other day, and then she would be gone. But even this allusion to her and to the pony made the letter something to her of intense interest. Had it not been so Lady Albury would not have shown it to her. As it was, why had Lady Albury shown it to her in that quiet, placid, friendly way,—as though it were natural that any letter from Colonel Stubbs to Stalham should be shown to her?

At lunch Sir Harry began about the pony at once. 'Miss Dormer,' he said, 'the pony will hardly be fit to-morrow, and the distances during the rest of the

week are all too great for you; you had better wait
till Monday week, when Stubbs will be here to look
after you.'

'But I am going home on Tuesday,' said Ayala.

'I've had the pony brought on purpose for you,'
said Sir Harry.

'You are not going at all,' said Lady Albury. 'All
that has to be altered. I'll write to Mrs. Dosett.'

'I don't think——' began Ayala.

'I shall take it very much amiss,' said Sir Harry,
'if you go now. Stubbs is coming on purpose.'

'I don't think——' began Ayala again.

'My dear Ayala, it isn't a case for thinking,' said
Lady Albury. 'You most positively will not leave
this house till some day in April, which will have to
be settled hereafter. Do not let us have a word more
about it.' Then, on that immediate occasion, no
further word about it was spoken. Ayala was quite
unable to speak as she sat attempting to eat her lunch.

## CHAPTER LIII

### HOW LUCY'S AFFAIRS ARRANGED THEMSELVES

WE must go again to Merle Park, where the
Tringle family was still living,—and from
which Gertrude had not as yet been violently abducted at the period to which the reader has been
brought in the relation which has been given of the
affairs at Stalham. Jonathan Stubbs's little note to
Lady Albury was received on Sunday, 23rd March,
and Gertrude was not abducted till the 29th. On
Sunday, the 30th, she was brought back,—not in
great triumph. At that time the house was considerably perturbed. Sir Thomas was very angry
with his daughter Augusta, having been led to believe that she had been privy to Gertrude's escapade,
—so angry that very violent words had been spoken
as to her expulsion from the house. Tom also was

ill, absolutely ill in bed, with a doctor to see him,—
and all from love, declaring that he would throw
himself over the ship's side and drown himself while
there was yet a chance left to him for Ayala. And
in the midst of this Lady Tringle herself was by no
means exempt from the paternal wrath. She was
told that she must have known what was going on
between her daughter and that idiot Captain,—that
she encouraged the Trafficks to remain,—that she
coddled up her son till he was sick from sheer lacka-
daisical idleness. The only one in the house who
seemed to be exempt from the wrath of Sir Thomas
was Lucy,—and therefore it was upon Lucy's head
that fell the concentrated energy of Aunt Emmeline's revenge. When Captain Batsby was spoken
of with contumely in the light of a husband,—this
being always done by Sir Thomas,—Lady Tringle
would make her rejoinder to this, when Sir Thomas
had turned his back, by saying that a captain in Her
Majesty's army, with good blood in his veins and a
competent fortune, was at any rate better than a
poor artist, who had, so to say, no blood, and was unable to earn his bread; and when Tom was ridiculed
for his love for Ayala she would go on to explain,—
always after Sir Thomas's back had been turned,—
that poor Tom had been encouraged by his father,
whereas Lucy had taken upon herself to engage herself in opposition to her pastors and masters. And
then came the climax. It was all very well to say
that Augusta was intruding,—but there were people
who intruded much worse than Augusta, without
half so much right. When this was said the poor
sore-hearted woman felt her own cruelty, and endeavoured to withdraw the harsh words; but the
wound had been given, and the venom rankled so
bitterly that Lucy could no longer bear her existence
among the Tringles. 'I ought not to remain after
that,' she wrote to her lover. 'Though I went into
the poor-house I ought not to remain.'

'I wrote to Mr. Hamel,' she said to her aunt, 'and

told him that as you did not like my being here I had better,—better go away.'

'But where are you to go? And I didn't say that I didn't like you being here. You oughtn't to take me up in that way.'

'I do feel that I am in the way, aunt, and I think that I had better go.'

'But where are you to go? I declare that everybody says everything to break my heart. Of course you are to remain here till he has got a house to keep you in.' But the letter had gone and a reply had come telling Lucy that whatever might be the poorhouse to which she would be destined he would be there to share it with her.

Hamel wrote this with high heart. He had already resolved, previous to this, that he would at once prepare a home for his coming bride, though he was sore distressed by the emergency of his position. His father had become more and more bitter with him as he learned that his son would in no respect be guided by him. There was a sum of money which he now declared to be due to him, and which Isadore acknowledged to have been lent to him. Of this the father demanded repayment. 'If,' said he, 'you acknowledge anything of the obedience of a son, that money is at your disposal,—and any other that you may want. But, if you determine to be as free from my control and as deaf to my advice as might be any other young man, then you must be to me as might be any other young man.' He had written to his father saying that the money should be repaid as soon as possible. The misfortune had come to him at a trying time. It was, however, before he had received Lucy's last account of her own misery at Merle Park, so that when that was received he was in part prepared.

Our Colonel, in writing to Lady Albury, had declared Aldershot to be a most exigeant place,—by which he had intended to imply that his professional cares were too heavy to allow his frequent absence;

but nevertheless he would contrive occasionally to
fly up to London for a little relief. Once when doing
so he had found himself sitting in the sculptor's
studio, and there listening to Hamel's account of
Lucy's troubles at Merle Park. Hamel said nothing
as to his own difficulties, but was very eager in explaining the necessity of removing Lucy from the
tyranny to which she was subjected. It will perhaps
be remembered that Hamel down in Scotland had
declared to his friend his purpose of asking Lucy
Dormer to be his wife, and also the success of his
enterprise after he had gone across the lake to Glenbogie. It will be borne in mind also that should the
Colonel succeed in winning Ayala to his way of
thinking the two men would become the husbands of
the two sisters. Each fully sympathised with the
other, and in this way they had become sincere and
intimate friends.

'Is she like her sister?' asked the Colonel, who was
not as yet acquainted with Lucy.

'Hardly like her, although in truth there is a
family likeness. Lucy is taller, with perhaps more
regular features, and certainly more quiet in her
manner.'

'Ayala can be very quiet too,' said the lover.

'Oh, yes,—because she varies in her moods. I
remember her almost as a child, when she would
remain perfectly still for a quarter of an hour, and
then would be up and about the house everywhere,
glancing about like a ray of the sun reflected from a
mirror as you move it in your hand.'

'She has grown steadier since that,' said the
Colonel.

'I cannot imagine her to be steady,—not as Lucy
is steady. Lucy, if it be necessary, can sit and fill
herself with her own thoughts for the hour together.'

'Which of them was most like their father?'

'They were both of them like him in their thorough
love for things beautiful;—but they are both of them
unlike him in this, that he was self-indulgent, while

they, like women in general, are always devoting themselves to others.' She will not devote herself to me, thought Jonathan Stubbs to himself, but that may be because, like her father, she loves things beautiful. 'My poor Lucy,' continued Hamel, 'would fain devote herself to those around her if they would only permit it.'

'She would probably prefer devoting herself to you,' said the Colonel.

'No doubt she would,—if it were expedient. If I may presume that she loves me, I may presume also that she would wish to live with me.'

'Is it not expedient?' asked the other.

'It will be so, I trust, before long.'

'But it seems to be so necessary just at present.' To this the sculptor at the moment made no reply. 'If,' continued Stubbs, 'they treat her among them as you say, she ought at any rate to be relieved from her misery.'

'She ought to be relieved certainly. She shall be relieved.'

'But you say that it is not expedient.'

'I only meant that there were difficulties;—difficulties which will have to be got over. I think that all difficulties are got over when a man looks at them steadily.'

'This, I suppose, is an affair of money.'

'Well, yes. All difficulties seem to me to be an affair of money. A man, of course, would wish to earn enough before he marries to make his wife comfortable. I would struggle on as I am, and not be impatient, were it not that I fear she is more uncomfortable as she is now than she would be here in the midst of my poverty.'

'After all, Hamel, what is the extent of the poverty? What are the real circumstances? As you have gone so far you might as well tell me everything.' Then after considerable pressure the sculptor did tell him everything. There was an income of less than three hundred a year,—which would probably

become about four within the next twelvemonth.
There were no funds prepared with which to buy the
necessary furniture for the incoming of a wife, and
there was that debt demanded by his father.

'Must that be paid?' asked the Colonel.

'I would starve rather than not pay it,' said
Hamel, 'if I alone were to be considered. It would
certainly be paid within the next six months if I
were alone, even though I should starve.'

Then his friend told him that the debt should be
paid at once. It amounted to but little more than a
hundred pounds. And then, of course, the conversation was carried further. When a friend inquires as to
the pecuniary distresses of a friend he feels himself as
a matter of course bound to relieve him. He would
supply also the means necessary for the incoming
of the young wife. With much energy, and for a
long time, Hamel refused to accept the assistance
offered to him; but the Colonel insisted in the first
place on what he considered to be due from himself to
Ayala's sister, and then on the fact that he doubted
not in the least the ultimate success which would
attend the professional industry of his friend. And
so before the day was over it was settled among
them. The money was to be forthcoming at once,
so that the debt might be paid and the preparations
made, and Hamel was to write to Lucy and declare
that he should be ready to receive her as soon as
arrangements should be made for their immediate
marriage. Then came the further outrage,—that
cruel speech as to intruders, and Lucy wrote to her
lover, owning that it would be well for her that she
should be relieved.

The news was, of course, declared to the family at
Merle Park. 'I never knew anything so hard,' said
Aunt Emmeline. 'Of course you have told him that
it was all my fault.' When Lucy made no answer to
this, she went on with her complaint. 'I know that
you have told him that I have turned you out,—
which is not true.'

'I told him it was better I should go, as you did not like my being here.'

'I suppose Lucy was in a little hurry to have the marriage come off,' said Augusta,—who would surely have spared her cousin if at the moment she had remembered the haste which had been displayed by her sister.

'I thought it best,' said Lucy.

'I'm sure I don't know how it is to be done,' said Aunt Emmeline. 'You must tell your uncle yourself. I don't know how you are to be married from here, seeing the trouble we are in.'

'We shall be up in London before that,' said Gertrude.

'Or from Queen's Gate either,' continued Aunt Emmeline.

'I don't suppose that will much signify. I shall just go to the church.'

'Like a servant-maid?' asked Gertrude.

'Yes;—like a servant-maid,' said Lucy. 'That is to say, a servant-maid would, I suppose, simply walk in and be married; and I shall do the same.'

'I think you had better tell your uncle,' said Aunt Emmeline. 'But I am sure I did not mean that you were to go away like this. It will be your own doing, and I cannot help it if you will do it.'

Then Lucy did tell her uncle. 'And you mean to live upon three hundred a year!' exclaimed Sir Thomas. 'You don't know what you are talking about.'

'I think Mr. Hamel knows.'

'He is as ignorant as a babe unborn;—I mean about that kind of thing. I don't doubt he can make things in stone as well as anybody.'

'In marble, Uncle Tom.'

'Marble is stone, I suppose;—or in iron.'

'Bronze, Uncle Tom.'

'Very well. There is iron in bronze, I suppose. But he doesn't know what a wife will cost. Has he bought any furniture?'

'He is going to buy it,—just a little;—what will do.'

'Why should you want to bring him into this?' Lucy looked wistfully up into his face. He himself had been personally kind to her, and she found it to be impossible to complain to him of her aunt. 'You are not happy here?'

'My aunt and cousins think that I am wrong; but I must be married to him now, Uncle Tom.'

'Why did he kick up his heels when I wanted to help him?' Nevertheless, he gave his orders on the subject very much in Lucy's favour. She was to be married from Queen's Gate, and Gertrude must be her bridesmaid. Ayala no doubt would be the other. When his wife expostulated, he consented that the marriage should be very quiet, but still he would have it as he had said. Then he bestowed a cheque upon Lucy,—larger in amount than Stubbs's loan,—saying that after what had passed in Lombard Street he would not venture to send money to so independent a person as Mr. Isadore Hamel; but adding that Lucy, perhaps, would condescend to accept it. There was a smile in his eye as he said the otherwise ill-natured word, so that Lucy, without any wound to her feelings, could kiss him and accept his bounty.

'I suppose I am to have nothing to do in settling the day,' said Aunt Emmeline. It was, however, settled between them that the marriage should take place on a certain day in May. Upon this Lucy was of course overjoyed, and wrote to her lover in a full flow of spirits. And she sent him the cheque, having written her name with great pride on the back of it. There was a little trouble about this as a part of it had to come back as her trousseau, but still the arrangement was pleasantly made. Then Sir Thomas again became more kind to her, in his rough manner,—even when his troubles were at the worst after the return of Gertrude. 'If it will not be altogether oppressive to his pride you may tell him that I shall make you an allowance of a hundred a year as my niece,—just for your personal expenses.'

'I don't know that he is so proud, Uncle Tom.'

"He seemed so to me. But if you say nothing to him about it, and just buy a few gowns now and again, he will perhaps be so wrapt up in the higher affairs of his art as not to take any notice.'

'I am sure he will notice what I wear,' said Lucy. However she communicated her uncle's intentions to her lover, and he sent back his grateful thanks to Sir Thomas. As one effect of all this the Colonel's money was sent back to him, with an assurance that as things were now settling themselves such pecuniary assistance was not needed. But this was not done till Ayala had heard what the Angel of Light had done on her sister's behalf. But as to Ayala's feelings in that respect we must be silent here, as otherwise we should make premature allusion to the condition in which Ayala found herself before she had at last managed to escape from Stalham Park.

'Papa,' said Gertrude, to her father one evening, 'don't you think you could do something for me too now?' Just at this time Sir Thomas, greatly to his own annoyance, was coming down to Merle Park every evening. According to their plans as at present arranged, they were to stay in the country till after Easter, and then they were to go up to town in time to despatch poor Tom upon his long journey round the world. But poor Tom was now in bed, apparently ill, and there seemed to be great doubt whether he could be made to go on the appointed day in spite of the taking of his berth and the preparation of his outfit. Tom, if well enough, was to sail on the nineteenth of April, and there now wanted not above ten days to that time. 'Don't you think you could do something for me now?' asked Gertrude. Hitherto Sir Thomas had extended no sign of pardon to his youngest daughter, and never failed to allude to her and to Captain Batsby as 'those two idiots' whenever their names were mentioned before him.

'Yes, my dear; I will endeavour to do a good deal for you if you will behave yourself.'

'What do you call behaving myself, papa?'

'In the first place telling me that you are very sorry for your misbehaviour with that idiot.'

'Of course I am sorry if I have offended you.'

'Well, that shall go for something. But how about the idiot?'

'Papa!' she exclaimed.

'Was he not an idiot? Would any one but an idiot have gone on such an errand as that?'

'Gentlemen and ladies have done it before, papa.'

'I doubt it,' he said. 'Gentlemen have run away with young ladies before, and generally have behaved very badly when they have done so. He behaved very badly indeed, because he had come to my house, with my sanction, with the express purpose of expressing his affection for another young lady. But I think that his folly in this special running away was worse even than his conduct. How did he come to think that he could get himself married merely by crossing over the sea to Ostend? I should be utterly ashamed of him as a son-in-law,—chiefly because he has shown himself to be an idiot.'

'But, papa, you will accept him, won't you?'

'No, my dear, I will not.'

'Not though I love him?'

'If I were to give you a choice which would you take, him or Mr. Houston?'

'Houston is a scoundrel.'

'Very likely; but then he is not an idiot. My choice would be altogether in favour of Mr. Houston. Shall I tell you what I will do, my dear? I will consent to accept Captain Batsby as my son-in-law if he will consent to become your husband without having a shilling with you.'

'Would that be kind, papa?'

'I do not think I could show you any greater kindness than to protect you from a man who I am quite sure does not care a farthing about you. He has, you tell me, an ample income of his own.'

'Oh yes, papa.'

'Then he can afford to marry you without a fortune. Poor Mr. Houston could not have done so, because he had nothing of his own. I declare, as I think of it all, I am becoming very tender-hearted towards Mr. Houston. Don't you think we had better have Mr. Houston back again? I suppose he would come if you were to send for him.' Then she burst into tears and went away and hid herself.

## CHAPTER LIV

### TOM'S LAST ATTEMPT

WHILE Gertrude was still away on her ill-omened voyage in quest of a parson, Lady Tringle was stirred up to a great enterprise on behalf of her unhappy son. There wanted now little more than a fortnight before the starting of the ship which his father still declared should carry him out across the world, and he had progressed so far in contemplating the matter as to own to himself that it would be best for him to obey his father if there was no hope. But his mind was still swayed by a theory of love and constancy. He had heard of men who had succeeded after a dozen times of asking. If Stubbs, the hated but generous Stubbs, were in truth a successful rival, then indeed the thing would be over; —then he would go, the sooner the better; and, as he told his mother half-a-dozen times a day, it would matter nothing to him whether he were sent to Japan, or the Rocky Mountains, or the North Pole. In such a case he would be quite content to go, if only for the sake of going. But how was he to be sure? He was, indeed, nearly sure in the other direction. If Ayala were in truth engaged to Colonel Stubbs it would certainly be known through Lucy. Then he had heard, through Lucy, that, though Ayala was staying at Stalham, the Colonel was not there. He had gone, and Ayala had remained week after week without him. Then, towards the end of

March, he wrote a letter to his Uncle Reginald, which was very piteous in its tone:—

'DEAR UNCLE REGINALD,' the letter said,

'I don't know whether you have heard of it, but I have been very ill—and unhappy. I am now in bed, and nobody here knows that I am sending this letter to you. It is all about Ayala, and I am not such a fool as to suppose that you can do anything for me. If you could I think you would,—but of course you can't. She must choose for herself,—only I do so wish that she should choose me. Nobody would ever be more kind to her. But you can tell me really how it is. Is she engaged to marry Colonel Stubbs? I know that she refused him, because he told me so himself. If she is not engaged to him I think that I would have another shy at it. You know what the poet says,—"Faint heart never won fair lady."* Do tell me if she is or is not engaged. I know that she is with those Alburys, and that Colonel Stubbs is their friend. But they can't make her marry Colonel Stubbs any more than my friends can make her marry me. I wish they could. I mean my friends, not his.

'If she were really engaged I would go away and hide myself in the furthermost corner of the world. Siberia or Central Africa would be the same to me. They would have little trouble in getting rid of me if I knew that it was all over with me. BUT I WILL NEVER STIR FROM THESE REALMS TILL I KNOW MY FATE!—Therefore, waiting your reply, I am your affectionate nephew,

'THOMAS TRINGLE, junior,'

Mr. Dosett, when he received this letter, consulted his wife before he replied to it, and then did so very shortly:—

'MY DEAR TOM,

'As far as I know, or her aunt, your cousin Ayala is not engaged to marry any one. But I should deceive you if I did not add my belief that she is resolved not to accept the offer you have done her the honour to make her.

'Your affectionate uncle,
'REGINALD DOSETT.'

The latter portion of this paragraph had no influence whatsoever on Tom. Did he not know all that before? Had he ever attempted to conceal from his relations the fact that Ayala had refused him again and again? Was not that as notorious to the world at large as a minister's promise that the income-tax should be abolished?* But the income-tax was not abolished,—and, as yet, Ayala was not married to any one else. Ayala was not even engaged to any other suitor. Why should she not change her mind as well as the minister? Certainly he would not go either to the North Pole or to New York as long as there should be a hope of bliss for him in England. Then he called his mother to his bedside.

'Go to Stalham, my dear!' said his mother.

'Why not? They can't eat you. Lady Albury is no more than a Baronet's wife,—just the same as you.'

'It isn't about eating me, Tom. I shouldn't know what to say to them.'

'You need not tell them anything. Say that you had come to call upon your niece.'

'But it would be such an odd thing to do. I never do call on Ayala,—even when I am in London.'

'What does it matter being odd? You could learn the truth at any rate. If she does not care for any one else why shouldn't she have me? I could make her a baronet's wife,—that is, some day when the governor——'

'Don't, Tom;—don't talk in that way.'

'I only mean in the course of nature. Sons do come after their fathers, you know. And as for money, I suppose the governor is quite as rich as those Alburys.'

'I don't think that would matter.'

'It does count, mother. I suppose Ayala is the same as other girls in that respect. I am sure I don't know why it is that she should have taken such an aversion to me. I suppose it is that she doesn't think me so much,—quite such a swell as some other men.'

'One can't account for such things, Tom.'

'No;—that is just it. And therefore she might come round without accounting for it. At any rate, you might try. You might tell her that it is ruining me;—that I shall have to go about wandering over all the world because she is so hard-hearted.'

'I don't think I could, my dear,' said Lady Tringle, after considering the matter for a while.

'Why not? Is it because of the trouble?'

'No, my dear; a mother does not think what trouble she may take for her child, if any good may be done. It is not the trouble. I would walk all round England to get her for you if that would do it.'

'Why not, then? At any rate you might get an answer from her. She would tell you something of her intention. Mother, I shall never go away till I know more about it than I do now. The governor says that he will turn me out. Let him turn me out. That won't make me go away.'

'Oh, Tom, he doesn't mean it.'

'But he says it. If I knew that it was all over,— that every chance was gone, then I would go away.'

'It is not the Alburys that I am afraid of,' said Lady Tringle.

'What then?'

'It is your father. I cannot go if he will not let me.' Nevertheless she promised before she left his bedside that she would ask Sir Thomas when he came home whether he would permit her to make the journey. All this occurred while Sir Thomas was away in quest of his daughter. And it may be imagined that immediately after his return he was hardly in a humour to yield to any such request as that which had been suggested. He was for the moment

almost sick of his children, sick of Merle Park, sick
of his wife, and inclined to think that the only comfort to be found in the world was to be had among
his millions, in that little back parlour in Lombard
Street.

It was on a Sunday that he returned, and on that
day he did not see his son. On the Monday morning
he went into the room, and Tom was about to press
upon him the prayer which he had addressed to his
mother when his lips were closed by his father's
harshness. 'Tom,' he said, 'you will be pleased to
remember that you start on the nineteenth.'

'But, father——'

'You start on the nineteenth,' said Sir Thomas.
Then he left the room, closing the door behind him
with none of the tenderness generally accorded to an
invalid.

'You have not asked him?' Tom said to his
mother shortly afterwards.

'Not yet, my dear. His mind is so disturbed by
this unfortunate affair.'

'And is not my mind disturbed? You may tell
him that I will not go, though he should turn me out
a dozen times, unless I know more about it than I
do now.'

Sir Thomas came home again that evening, very
sour in temper, and nothing could be said to him.
He was angry with everybody, and Lady Tringle
hardly dared to go near him, either then or on the
following morning. On the Tuesday evening, however, he returned somewhat softened in his demeanour. The millions had perhaps gone right,
though his children would go so wrong. When he
spoke either to his younger daughter or of her he did
so in that jeering tone which he afterwards always
assumed when allusion was made to Captain Batsby,
and which, disagreeable as it was, seemed to imply
something of forgiveness. And he ate his dinner, and
drank his glass of wine, without making any allusion
to the parsimonious habits of his son-in-law, Mr.

Traffick. Lady Tringle, therefore, considered that she might approach him with Tom's request.

'You go to Stalham!' he exclaimed.

'Well, my dear, I suppose I could see her?'

'And what could you learn from her?'

'I don't suppose I could learn much. She was always a pig-headed, stiff-necked creature. I am sure it wouldn't be any pleasure to me to see her.'

'What good would it do?' demanded Sir Thomas.

'Well, my dear; he says that he won't go unless he can get a message from her. I am sure I don't want to go to Stalham. Nothing on earth could be so disagreeable. But perhaps I could bring back a word or two which would make him go upon his journey.'

'What sort of word?'

'Why;—if I were to say that she were engaged to this Colonel Stubbs, then he would go. He says that he would start at once if he knew that his cousin were really engaged to somebody else.'

'But if she be not?'

'Perhaps I could just colour it a little. It would be such a grand thing to get him away, and he in this miserable condition! If he were once on his travels, I do think he would soon begin to forget it all.'

'Of course he would,' said Sir Thomas.

'Then I might as well try. He has set his heart upon it, and if he thinks that I have done his bidding then he will obey you. As for turning him out, Tom, of course you do not really mean that!'

In answer to this Sir Thomas said nothing. He knew well enough that Tom couldn't be turned out. That turning out of a son is a difficult task to accomplish, and one altogether beyond the power of Sir Thomas. The chief cause of his sorrow lay in the fact that he, as the head of Travers and Treason, was debarred from the assistance and companionship of his son. All Travers and Treason was nothing to him, because his son would run so far away from the right path. There was nothing he would not do to bring him back. If Ayala could have been bought by any reasonable, or even unreasonable, amount of thousands, he would have bought her willingly for his boy's delight. It was a thing wonderful to him that Tom should have been upset so absolutely by his love. He did appreciate the feeling so far that he was willing to condone all those follies already committed if Tom would only put himself in the way of recovery. That massacreing of the policeman, those ill-spent nights at the Mountaineers and at Bolivia's, that foolish challenge, and the almost more foolish blow under the portico at the Haymarket, should all be forgiven if Tom would only consent to go through some slight purgation which would again fit him for Travers and Treason. And the purgation should be made as pleasant as possible. He should travel about the world with his pocket full of money and with every arrangement for luxurious comfort. Only he must go. There was no other way in which he could be so purged as to be again fit for Travers and Treason. He did not at all believe that Ayala could now be purchased. Whether pig-headed or not, Ayala was certainly self-willed. No good such as Tom expected would come from this projected visit to Stalham. But if he would allow it to be made in obedience to Tom's request,—then perhaps some tidings might be brought back which, whether strictly true or not, might induce Tom to allow himself to be put on board the ship. Arguing thus with himself, Sir Thomas at last gave his consent.

It was a most disagreeable task which the mother thus undertook. She could not go from Merle Park to Stalham and back in one day. It was necessary that she should sleep two nights in London. It was arranged, therefore, that she should go up to London on the Thursday; then make her journey down to Stalham and back on the Friday, and get home on the Saturday. There would then still remain nearly a fortnight before Tom would have to leave Merle Park. After much consideration it was decided that a note should be written to Ayala apprising her of her aunt's coming. 'I hope Lady Albury will not be surprised at my visit,' said the note, 'but I am so anxious to see you, just for half-an-hour, upon a matter of great importance, that I shall run my chance.' She would prefer to have seen the girl without any notice; but then, had no notice been given, the girl would perhaps have been out of the way. As it was a telegram was received back in reply. 'I shall be at home. Lady Albury will be very glad to see you at lunch. She says there shall be a room all ready if you will sleep.'

'I certainly shall not stay there,' Lady Tringle said to Mrs. Traffick, 'but it is as well to know that they will be civil to me.'

'They are stuck-up sort of people I believe,' said Augusta; 'just like that Marchesa Baldoni, who is one of them. But, as to their being civil, that is a matter of course. They would hardly be uncivil to any one connected with Lord Boardotrade!'

Then came the Thursday on which the journey was to be commenced. As the moment came near Lady Tringle was very much afraid of the task before her. She was afraid even of her niece Ayala, who had assumed increased proportions in her eyes since she had persistently refused not only Tom but also Colonel Stubbs and Captain Batsby, and then in spite of her own connexion with Lord Boardotrade, —of whom since her daughter's marriage she had learned to think less than she had done before,—she did feel that the Alburys were fashionable people, and that Ayala as their guest had achieved something for herself. Stalham was, no doubt, superior in general estimation to Merle Park, and with her there had been always a certain awe of Ayala which she had not felt in reference to Lucy. Ayala's demand that Augusta should go upstairs and fetch the scrapbook had had its effect,—as had also her success in going up St. Peter's and to the Marchesa's dance; and then there would be Lady Albury herself,—and all the Alburys! Only that Tom was very anxious, she would even now have abandoned the undertaking.

'Mother,' said Tom, on the last morning, 'you will do the best you can for me.'

'Oh, yes, my dear.'

'I do think that, if you would make her understand the real truth, she might have me yet. She wouldn't like that a fellow should die.'

'I am afraid that she is hard-hearted, Tom.'

'I do not believe it, mother. I have seen her when she wouldn't kill even a fly. If she could only be made to see all the good she could do.'

'I am afraid she won't care for that unless she can bring herself really to love you.'

'Why shouldn't she love me?'

'Ah, my boy; how am I to tell you? Perhaps if you hadn't loved her so well it might have been different. If you had scorned her——'

'Scorn her! I couldn't scorn her. I have heard of that kind of thing before, but how is one to help oneself? You can't scorn a friend just because you choose to say so to yourself. When I see her she is something so precious to me that I could not be rough to her to save my life. When she first came it wasn't so. I could laugh at her then. But now——! They talk about goddesses, but I am sure she is a goddess to me.'

'If you had made no more than a woman of her it might have been better, Tom.' All that was too late now. The doctrine which Lady Tringle was enunciating to her son, and which he repudiated, is one that has been often preached and never practised. A man when he is conscious of the presence of a mere woman, to whom he feels that no worship is due, may for his own purpose be able to tell a lie to her, and make her believe that he acknowledges a divinity in her presence. But, when he feels the goddess, he cannot carry himself before her as though she were a mere woman, and, as such, inferior to himself in her

attributes. Poor Tom had felt the touch of something divine, and had fallen immediately prostrate
before the shrine with his face to the ground. His
chance with Ayala could in no circumstances have
been great; but she was certainly not one to have
yielded to a prostrate worshipper.

'Mother!' said Tom, recalling Lady Tringle as she
was leaving the room.

'What is it, my dear? I must really go now or I
shall be too late for the train.'

'Mother, tell her, tell her,—tell her that I love
her.' His mother ran back, kissed his brow, and then
left the room.

Lady Tringle spent that evening in Queen's Gate,
where Sir Thomas remained with her. The hours
passed heavily, as they had not much present to
their mind with which to console each other. Sir
Thomas had no belief whatever in the journey except
in so far as it might help to induce his son to
proceed upon his travels;—but his wife had been so
far softened by poor Tom's sorrows as to hope a little,
in spite of her judgment, that Ayala might yet
relent. Her heart was soft towards her son, so that
she felt that the girl would deserve all manner of
punishment unless she would at last yield to Tom's
wishes. She was all but sure that it could not be so,
and yet, in spite of her convictions, she hoped.

On the next morning the train took her safely to
the Stalham Road Station, and as she approached
the end of her journey her heart became heavier
within her. She felt that she could not but fail to
give any excuse to the Alburys for such a journey,—
unless, indeed, Ayala should do as she would have
her. At the station she found the Albury carriage,
with the Albury coachman, and the Albury footman,
and the Albury liveries, waiting for her. It was a
closed carriage, and for a moment she thought that
Ayala might be there. In that case she could have
performed her commission in the carriage, and then
have returned to London without going to the house

at all. But Ayala was not there. Lady Tringle was driven up to the house, and then taken through the hall into a small sitting-room, where for a moment she was alone. Then the door opened, and Ayala, radiant with beauty, in all the prettiness of her best morning costume, was in a moment in her arms. She seemed in her brightness to be different from that Ayala who had been known before at Glenbogie and in Rome. 'Dear Aunt,' said Ayala, 'I am so delighted to see you at Stalham!'

## CHAPTER LV

### IN THE CASTLE THERE LIVED A KNIGHT

AYALA was compelled to consent to remain at Stalham. The 'I don't think' which she repeated so often was, of course, of no avail to her. Sir Harry would be angry, and Lady Albury would be disgusted, were she to go,—and so she remained. There was to be a week before Colonel Stubbs would come, and she was to remain not only for the week but also for some short time afterwards,—so that there might be yet a few days left of hunting under the Colonel. It could not, surely, have been doubtful to her after she had read that letter,—with the postscript,—that if she remained her happiness would be insured! He would not have come again and insisted on her being there to receive him if nothing were to come of it. And yet she had fought for permission to return to Kingsbury Crescent after her little fashion, and had at last yielded, as she told Lady Albury,— because Sir Harry seemed to wish it. 'Of course he wishes it,' said Lady Albury. 'He has got the pony on purpose, and nobody likes being disappointed when he has done a thing so much as Sir Harry.' Ayala, delighted as she was, did not make her secret known. She was fluttered, and apparently uneasy,— so that her friend did not know what to make of it, or which way to take it. Ayala's secret was to herself a secret still to be maintained with holy reticence. It might still be possible that Jonathan Stubbs should never say another word to her of his love. If he did, —why then all the world might know. Then there would be no secret. Then she could sit and discuss her love, and his love, all night long with Lady Albury, if Lady Albury would listen to her. In the meantime the secret must be a secret. To confess her love, and then to have her love disappointed,—that would be death to her!

And thus it went on through the whole week, Lady Albury not quite knowing what to make of it. Once she did say a word, thinking that she would thus extract the truth, not as yet understanding how potent Ayala could be to keep her secret. 'That man has, at any rate, been very true to you,' she said. Ayala frowned, and shook her head, and would not say a word upon the subject. 'If she did not mean to take him now, surely she would have gone,' Lady Albury said to her husband.

'She is a pretty little girl enough,' said Sir Harry, 'but I doubt whether she is worth all the trouble.'

'Of course she is not. What pretty little girl ever was ? But as long as he thinks her worth it the trouble has to be taken.'

'Of course she'll accept him ?'

'I am not at all so sure of it. She has been made to believe that you wanted her to stay, and therefore she has stayed. She is quite master enough of herself to ride out hunting with him again and then to refuse him.' And so Lady Albury doubted up to the Sunday, and all through the Sunday,—up to the very moment when the last preparations were to be made for the man's arrival.

The train reached the Stalham Road Station at 7 P.M., and the distance was five miles. On Sundays they usually dined at Stalham at 7.30. The hour fixed was to be 8 on this occasion,—and even with this there would be some bustling. The house was now nearly empty, there being no visitors there except Mr. and Mrs. Gosling and Ayala. Lady Albury gave many thoughts to the manner of the man's reception, and determined at last that Jonathan should have an opportunity of saying a word to Ayala immediately on his arrival if he so pleased. 'Mind you are down at half-past seven,' she said to Ayala, coming to her in her bedroom.

'I thought we should not dine till eight.'

'There is no knowing. Sir Harry is so fussy. I shall be down, and I should like you to be with me.' Then Ayala promised. 'And mind you have his frock on.'

'You'll make me wear it out before any one else sees it,' she said, laughing. But again she promised. She got a glimmer of light from it all, nearly understanding what Lady Albury intended. But against such intentions as these she had no reason to fight. Why should she not be ready to see him? Why should she not have on her prettiest dress when he came? If he meant to say the word,—then her prettiest dress would be all too poor, and her readiest ears not quick enough to meet so great a joy. If he were not to say the other word,—then should she shun him by staying behind, or be afraid of the encounter? Should she be less gaily attired because it would be unnecessary to please his eye?

Oh, no! 'I'll be there at half-past seven,' she said. 'But I know the train will be late, and Sir Harry won't get his dinner till nine.'

'Then, my dear, great as the Colonel is, he may come in and get what is left for him in the middle. Sir Harry will not wait a minute after eight.'

The buxom woman came and dressed her. The buxom woman probably knew what was going to happen;—was perhaps more keenly alive to the truth than Lady Albury herself. 'We have taken great care of it, haven't we, Miss?' she said, as she fastened the dress behind. 'It's just as new still.'

'New!' said Ayala. 'It has got to be new with me for the next two years.'

'I don't know much about that, Miss. Somebody will have to pay for a good many more new dresses before two years are over, I take it.' To this Ayala made no answer, but she was quite sure that the buxom woman intended to imply that Colonel Stubbs would have to pay for the new dresses.

Punctually at half-past seven she was in the drawing-room, and there she remained alone for a few minutes. She endeavoured to sit down and be quiet, but she found it impossible to compose herself. Almost immediately he would be there, and then,—as she was quite sure,—her fate would be known to her instantly. She knew that the first moment of his presence in the room with her would tell her everything. If that were told to her which she desired to hear, everything should be re-told to him as quickly. But, if it were otherwise, then she thought that when the moment came she would still have strength enough to hide her sorrow. If he had come simply for the hunting,—simply that they two might ride a-hunting together so that he might show to her that all traces of his disappointment were gone,—then she would know how to teach him to think that her heart towards him was as it had ever been. The thing to be done would be so sad as to call from her tears almost of blood in her solitude; but it should be so done that no one should know that any sorrow such as this had touched her bosom. Not even to Lucy should this secret be told.

There was a clock on the mantelpiece to which her eye was continually turned. It now wanted twenty minutes to eight, and she was aware that if the train was punctual he might now be at the hall-door. At this moment Lady Albury entered the room. 'Your knight has come at last,' she said; 'I hear his wheels on the gravel.'

'He is no knight of mine,' said Ayala, with that peculiar frown of hers.

'Whose ever knight he is, there he is. Knight or not, I must go and welcome him.' Then Lady Albury

hurried out of the room and Ayala was again alone.
The door had been left partly open, so that she could
hear the sound of voices and steps across the inner
hall or billiard-room. There were the servants waiting
upon him, and Sir Harry bidding him to go up and
dress at once so as not to keep the whole house
waiting, and Lady Albury declaring that there was
yet ample time as the dinner certainly would not be
on the table for half-an-hour. She heard it all, and
heard him to whom all her thoughts were now given
laughing as he declared that he had never been so
cold in his life, and that he certainly would not
dress himself till he had warmed his fingers. She
was far away from the door, not having stirred from
the spot on which she was standing when Lady
Albury left her; but she fancied that she heard the
murmur of some slight whisper, and she told herself
that Lady Albury was telling him where to seek her.
Then she heard the sound of the man's step across
the billiard-room, she heard his hand upon the door,
and there he was in her presence!'

When she thought of it all afterwards, as she did so
many scores of times, she never could tell how it had
occurred. When she accused him in her playfulness,
telling him that he had taken for granted that of
which he had had no sign, she never knew whether
there had been aught of truth in her accusation. But
she did know that he had hardly closed the door behind him when she was in his arms, and felt the burning love of his kisses upon her cheeks. There had
been no more asking whether he was to have any
other answer. Of that she was quite sure. Had there
been such further question she would have answered
him, and some remembrance of her own words
would have remained with her. She was quite sure
that she had answered no question. Some memory
of mingled granting and denying, of repulses and
assents all quickly huddled upon one another, of
attempts to escape while she was so happy to remain,
and then of a deluge of love terms which fell upon

her ears,—'his own one, his wife, his darling, his
Ayala, at last his own sweet Ayala,'—this was what
remained to her of that little interview. She had not
spoken a word. She thought she was sure of that.
Her breath had left her,—so that she could not speak.
And yet it had been taken for granted,—though on
former occasions he had pleaded with slow piteous
words! How had it been that he had come to know
the truth so suddenly? Then she became aware that
Lady Albury was speaking to Mrs. Gosling in the
billiard-room outside, detaining her other guest till
the scene within should be over. At that moment she
did speak a word which she remembered afterwards.
'Go;—go; you must go now.' Then there had been
one other soft repulse, one other sweet assent, and
the man had gone. There was just a moment for her,
in which to tell herself that the Angel of Light had
come for her, and had taken her to himself.

Mrs. Gosling, who was a pretty little woman, crept
softly into the room, hiding her suspicion if she had
any. Lady Albury put out her hand to Ayala behind
the other woman's back, not raising it high, but just
so that her young friend might touch it if she pleased.
Ayala did touch it, sliding her little fingers into the
offered grasp. 'I thought it would be so,' whispered
Lady Albury. 'I thought it would be so.'

'What the deuce are you all up to?' said Sir Harry,
bursting into the room. 'It's eight now, and that
man has only just gone up to his room.'

'He hasn't been in the house above five minutes
yet,' said Lady Albury, 'and I think he has been very
quick.' Ayala thought so too.

During dinner and afterwards they were very full
of hunting for the next day. It was wonderful to
Ayala that there should be thought for such a trifle
when there was such a thing as love in the world.
While there was so much to fill her heart, how could
there be thoughts of anything else? But Jonathan,—
he was Jonathan to her now, her Jonathan, her Angel
of Light,—was very keen upon the subject. There

was but one week left. He thought that Croppy might manage three days as there was to be but one week. Croppy would have leisure and rest enough afterwards. 'It's a little sharp,' said Sir Harry.

'Oh, pray don't,' said Ayala.

But Lady Albury and Jonathan together silenced Sir Harry, and Mrs. Gosling proved the absurdity of the objection by telling the story of a pony who had carried a lady three days running. 'I should not have liked to be either the pony, or the owner, or the lady,' said Sir Harry. But he was silenced. What did it matter though the heavens fell, so that Ayala was pleased? What is too much to be done for a girl who proves herself to be an angel by accepting the right man at the right time?

She had but one moment alone with her lover that night. 'I always loved you,' she whispered to him as she fled away. The Colonel did not quite understand the assertion, but he was contented with it as he sat smoking his cigar with Sir Harry and Mr. Gosling.

But, though she could have but one word that night with her lover, there were many words between her and Lady Albury before they went to bed. 'And so, like wise people, you have settled it all between you at last,' said Lady Albury.

'I don't know whether he is wise.'

'We will take that for granted. At any rate he has been very true.'

'Oh, yes.'

'And you,—you knew all about it.'

'No;—I knew nothing. I did not think he would ever ask again. I only hoped.'

'But why on earth did you give him so much trouble?'

'I can't tell you,' said Ayala, shaking her head.

'Do you mean that there is still a secret?'

'No, not that. I would tell you anything that I could tell, because you have been so very, very good to me. But I cannot tell. I cannot explain even to myself. Oh, Lady Albury, why have you been so good to me?'

'Shall I say because I have loved you?'

'Yes;—if it be true.'

'But it is not true.'

'Oh, Lady Albury!'

'I do love you dearly. I shall always love you now. I do hope I shall love you now, because you will be his wife. But I have not been kind to you as you call it because I loved you.'

'Then why?'

'Because I loved him. Cannot you understand that? Because I was anxious that he should have all that he wanted. Was it not necessary that there should be some house in which he might meet you? Could there have been much of a pleasant time for wooing between you in your aunt's drawing-room in Kingsbury Crescent?'

'Oh, no,' said Ayala.

'Could he have taken you out hunting unless you had been here? How could he and you have known each other at all unless I had been kind to you? Now you will understand.'

'Yes,' said Ayala, 'I understand now. Did he ask you?'

'Well,—he consulted me. We talked you all over, and made up our minds, between us, that if we petted you down here that would be the best way to win you. Were we not right?'

'It was a very nice way. I do so like to be petted.'

'Sir Harry was in the secret, and he did his petting by buying the frock. That was a success too, I think.'

'Did he care about that, Lady Albury?'

'What he?'

'Jonathan,' said Ayala, almost stumbling over the word, as she pronounced it aloud for the first time.

'I think he liked it. But whether he would have persevered without it you must ask yourself. If he tells you that he would never have said another word

A.A.—26

to you only for this frock, then I think you ought to
thank Sir Harry, and give him a kiss.'

'I am sure he will not tell me that,' said Ayala,
with mock indignation.

'And now, my dear, as I have told you all my
secret, and have explained to you how we laid our
heads together, and plotted against you, I think you
ought to tell me your secret. Why was it that you refused him so pertinaciously on that Sunday when
you were out walking, and yet you knew your mind
about it so clearly as soon as he arrived to-day?'

'I can't explain it,' said Ayala.

'You must know that you liked him.'

'I always liked him.'

'You must have more than liked on that Sunday.'

'I adored him.'

'Then I don't understand you.'

'Lady Albury, I think I fell in love with him the
first moment I saw him. The Marchesa took me to a
party in London, and there he was.'

'Did he say anything to you then?'

'No. He was very funny,—as he often is. Don't
you know his way? I remember every word he said
to me. He came up without any introduction and
ordered me to dance with him.'

'And you did?'

'Oh yes. Whatever he told me I should have done.
Then he scolded me because I did not stand up
quick enough. And he invented some story about a
woman who was engaged to him and would not marry
him because he had red hair and his name was
Jonathan. I knew it was all a joke, and yet I hated
the woman.'

'That must have been love at first sight.'

'I think it was. From that day to this I have
always been thinking about him.'

'And yet you refused him twice over?'

'Yes.'

'At ever so long an interval?' Ayala bobbed her
head at her companion. 'And why?'

'Ah;—that I can't tell. I shall try to tell him some day, but I know that I never shall. It was because ——. But, Lady Albury, I cannot tell it. Did you ever picture anything to yourself in a waking dream?'

'Build castles in the air?' suggested Lady Albury.

'That's just it.'

'Very often. But they never come true.'

'Never have come true,—exactly. I had a castle in the air, and in the castle lived a knight.' She was still ashamed to say that the inhabitant of the castle was an Angel of Light. 'I wanted to find out whether he was the knight who lived there. He was.'

'And you were not quite sure till to-day?'

'I have been sure a long time. But when we walked out on that Sunday I was such an idiot that I did not know how to tell him. Oh, Lady Albury, I was such a fool! What should I have done if he hadn't come back?'

'Sent for him.'

'Never;—never! I should have been miserable always! But now I am so happy.'

'He is the real knight?'

'Oh, yes; indeed. He is the real,—real knight, that has always been living in my castle.'

Ayala's promotion was now so firmly fixed that the buxom female came to assist her off with her clothes when Lady Albury had left her. From this time forth it was supposed that such assistance would be necessary. 'I take it, Miss,' said the buxom female, 'there will be a many new dresses before the end of this time two years.' From which Ayala was quite sure that everybody in the house knew all about it.

*       *       *       *       *       *

But it was now, now when she was quite alone, that the great sense of her happiness came to her. In the fulness of her dreams there had never been more than the conviction that such a being, and none other, could be worthy of her love. There had

never been faith in the hope that such a one would
come to her,—never even though she would tell herself that angels had come down from heaven and
had sought in marriage the hands of the daughters
of men. Her dreams had been to her a barrier against
love rather than an encouragement. But now he
that she had in truth dreamed of had come for her.
Then she brought out the Marchesa's letter and read
that description of her lover. Yes; he was all that;
true, brave, tender,—a very hero. But then he was
more than all that,—for he was in truth the very
'Angel of Light.'

## CHAPTER LVI

### GOBBLEGOOSE WOOD AGAIN

THE Monday was devoted to hunting. I am not at
all sure that riding about the country with a pack
of hounds is an amusement specially compatible
with that assured love entertainment which was now
within the reach of Ayala and her Angel. For the
rudiments of love-making, for little endearing attentions, for a few sweet words to be whispered with
shortened breath as one horse gallops beside another,
perhaps for a lengthened half-hour together, amidst
the mazes of a large wood when opportunities are no
doubt given for private conversation, hunting may
be very well. But for two persons who are engaged,
with the mutual consent of all their friends, a comfortable sofa is perhaps preferable. Ayala had heard as
yet but very little of her lover's intentions;—was
acquainted only with that one single intention which
he had declared in asking her to be his wife. There
were a thousand things to be told,—the how, the
where, and the when. She knew hitherto the why,
and that was all. Nothing could be told her while she
was galloping about a big wood on Croppy's back.
'I am delighted to see you again in these parts, Miss,'
said Larry Twentyman, suddenly.

'Oh, Mr. Twentyman; how is the baby?'

'The baby is quite well, Miss. His mamma has been out ever so many times.'

'I ought to have asked for her first. Does baby come out too?'

'Not quite. But when the hounds are near mamma comes for an hour or so. We have had a wonderful season,—quite wonderful. You have heard, perhaps, of our great run from Dillsborough Wood. We found him there, close to my place, you know, and run him down in the Brake country after an hour and forty minutes. There were only five or six of them. You'd have been one, Miss, to a moral, if you'd have been here on the pony. I say we never changed our fox.'

Ayala was well disposed towards Larry Twentyman, and was quite aware that, according to the records and established usages of that hunt, he was a man with whom she might talk safely. But she did not care about the foxes so much as she had done before. There was nothing now for which she cared much, except Jonathan Stubbs. He was always riding near her throughout the day, so that he might be with her should there arise anything special to be done; but he was not always close to her,—as she would have had him. He had gained his purpose, and he was satisfied. She had entered in upon the fruition of positive bliss, but enjoyed it in perfection only when she heard the sound of his voice, or could look into his eyes as she spoke to him. She did not care much about the great run from Dillsborough, or even for the compliment with which Mr. Twentyman finished his narrative. They were riding about the big woods all day, not without killing a fox, but with none of the excitement of a real run. 'After that Croppy will be quite fit to come again on Wednesday,' suggested the Colonel on their way home. To which Sir Harry assented.

'What do you folks mean to do to-day?' asked Lady Albury at breakfast on the following morning. Ayala had her own little plan in her head, but did not dare to propose it publicly. 'Will you choose to be driven, or will you choose to walk?' said Lady Albury, addressing herself to Ayala. Ayala, in her present position, was considered to be entitled to special consideration. Ayala thought she would prefer to walk. At last there came a moment in which she could make her request to the person chiefly concerned. 'Walk with me to the wood with that absurd name,' suggested Ayala.

'Gobblegoose Wood,' suggested the Colonel. Then that was arranged according to Ayala's wishes.

A walk in a wood*is perhaps almost as good as a comfortable seat in a drawing-room, and is, perhaps, less liable to intrusion. They started and walked the way which Ayala remembered so well when she had trudged along, pretending to listen to Sir Harry and Captain Glomax as they carried on their discussion about the hunted fox, but giving all her ears to the Colonel, and wondering whether he would say anything to her before the day was over. Then her mind had been in a perturbed state which she herself had failed to understand. She was sure that she would say 'No' to him, should he speak, and yet she desired that it should be 'Yes.' What a fool she had been, she told herself as she walked along now, and how little she had deserved all the good that had come to her!

The conversation was chiefly with him as they went. He told her much now of the how, and the when, and the where. He hoped there might be no long delay. He would live, he said, for the next year or two at Aldershot, and would be able to get a house fit for her on condition that they should be married at once. He did not explain why the house could not be taken even though their marriage were delayed two or three months,—but as to this she asked no questions. Of course they must be married in London if Mrs. Dosett wished it; but if not it might be arranged that the wedding should take place at Stalham. Upon all this and many other things he had much to propose, and all that he said Ayala accepted as gospel. As the Angel of Light had appeared,—as the knight who was lord of the castle had come forth,—of course he must be obeyed in everything. He could hardly have made a suggestion to which she would not have acceded. When they had entered the wood Ayala in her own quiet way led him to the very spot in which on that former day he had asked her his question. 'Do you remember this path?' she asked.

'I remember that you and I were walking here together,' he said.

'Ay, but this very turn? Do you remember this branch?'

'Well, no; not the branch.'

'You put your hand on it when you said that "never—never," to me.'

'Did I say "never,—never"?'

'Yes, you did;—when I was so untrue to you.'

'Were you untrue?' he asked.

'Jonathan, you remember nothing about it. It has all passed away from you just as though you were talking to Captain Glomax about the fox.'

'Has it, dear?'

'I remember every word of it. I remember how you stood and how you looked, even to the hat you wore and the little switch you held in your hand,—when you asked for one little word, one glance, one slightest touch. There, now;—you shall have all my weight to bear.' Then she leant upon him with both her hands, turned round her arm, glanced up into his face, and opened her lips as though speaking that little word. 'Do you remember that I said I thought you had given it all up?'

'I remember that, certainly.'

'And was not that untrue? Oh, Jonathan, that was such a story. Had I thought so I should have been miserable.'

'Then why did you swear to me so often that you could not love me?'

'I never said so,' replied Ayala; 'never.'

'Did you not?' he asked.

'I never said so. I never told you such a story as that. I did love you then, almost as well as I do now. Oh, I had loved you for so long a time!'

'Then why did you refuse me?'

'Ah; that is what I would explain to you now,— here on this very spot,—if I could. Does it not seem odd that a girl should have all that she wants offered to her, and yet not be able to take it?'

'Was it all that you wanted?'

'Indeed it was. When I was in church that morning I told myself that I never, never could be happy unless you came to me again.'

'But when I did come you would not have me.'

'I knew how to love you,' she said, 'but I did not know how to tell you that I loved you. I can tell you now; cannot I?' and then she looked up at him and smiled. 'Yes, I think I shall never be tired of telling you now. It is sweet to hear you say that you love me, but it is sweeter still to be always telling you. And yet I could not tell you then. Suppose you had taken me at my word?'

'I told you that I should never give you up.'

'It was only that that kept me from being altogether wretched. I think that I was ashamed to tell you the truth when I had once refused to do as you would have me. I had given you so much trouble all for nothing. I think that if you had asked me on that first day at the ball in London I should have said yes, if I had told the truth.'

'That would have been very sudden. I had never seen you before that.'

'Nevertheless it was so. I don't mind owning it to you now, though I never, never, would own it to any one else. When you came to us at the theatre I was sure that no one else could ever have been so good. I certainly did love you then.'

'Hardly that, Ayala.'

'I did,' she said. 'Now I have told you everything,

and if you choose to think I have been bad,—why you must think so, and I must put up with it.'

'Bad, my darling?'

'I suppose it was bad to fall in love with a man like that; and very bad to give him the trouble of coming so often. But now I have made a clean breast of it, and if you want to scold me you must scold me now. You may do it now, but you must never scold me afterwards,—because of that.' It may be left to the reader to imagine the nature of the scolding which she received.

Then on their way home she thanked him for all the good that he had done to all those belonging to her. 'I have heard it all from Lucy;—how generous you have been to Isadore.'

'That has all come to nothing,' he said.

'How come to nothing? I know that you sent him the money.'

'I did offer to lend him something, and, indeed, I sent him a cheque; but two days afterwards he returned it. That tremendous uncle of yours——'

'Uncle Tom?'

'Yes, your Uncle Tom; the man of millions! He came forward and cut me out altogether. I don't know what went on down there in Sussex, but when he heard that they intended to be married shortly he put his hand into his pocket, as a magnificent uncle, overflowing with millions, ought to do.'

'I did not hear that.'

'Hamel sent my money back at once.'

'And poor Tom! You were so good to poor Tom.'

'I like Tom.'

'But he did behave badly.'

'Well; yes. One gentleman shouldn't strike another, even though he be ever so much in love. It's an uncomfortable proceeding, and never has good results. But then, poor fellow, he has been so much in earnest.'

'Why couldn't he take a No when he got it?'

'Why didn't I take a No when I got it?'

'That was very different. He ought to have taken it. If you had taken it you would have been very wrong, and have broken a poor girl's heart. I am sure you knew that all through.'

'Did I?'

'And then you were too good-natured. That was it. I don't think you really love me;—not as I love you. Oh, Jonathan, if you were to change your mind now! Suppose you were to tell me that it was a mistake! Suppose I were to awake and find myself in bed at Kingsbury Crescent?'

'I hope there may be no such waking as that!'

'I should go mad,—stark mad. Shake me till I find out whether it is real waking, downright, earnest. But, Jonathan, why did you call me Miss Dormer when you went away? That was the worst of all. I remember when you called me Ayala first. It went through and through me like an electric shock. But you never saw it;—did you?'

On that afternoon when she returned home she wrote to her sister Lucy, giving a sister's account to her sister of all her happiness. 'I am sure Isadore is second best, but Jonathan is best. I don't want you to say so; but if you contradict me I shall stick to it. You remember my telling you that the old woman in the railway said that I was perverse. She was a clever old woman, and knew all about it, for I was perverse. However, it has come all right now, and Jonathan is best of all. Oh, my man,—my man! Is it not sweet to have a man of one's own to love?' If this letter had been written on the day before,—as would have been the case had not Ayala been taken out hunting,—it would have reached Merle Park on the Wednesday, the news would have been made known to Aunt Emmeline, and so conveyed to poor Tom, and that disagreeable journey from Merle Park to Stalham would have been saved. But there was no time for writing on the Monday. The letter was sent away in the Stalham post-bag on the Tuesday evening, and

did not reach Merle Park till the Thursday, after
Lady Tringle had left the house. Had it been known
on that morning that Ayala was engaged to Colonel
Stubbs that would have sufficed to send Tom away
upon his travels without any more direct messenger
from Stalham.

On the Wednesday there was more hunting, and
on this day Ayala, having liberated her mind to her
lover in Gobblegoose Wood, was able to devote herself more satisfactorily to the amusement in hand.
Her engagement was now an old affair. It had already become matter for joking to Sir Harry, and
had been discussed even with Mrs. Gosling. It was,
of course, 'a joy for ever,'*—but still she was beginning to descend from the clouds and to walk the
earth,—no more than a simple queen. When, therefore, the hounds went away and Larry told her that
he knew the best way out of the wood, she collected
her energies and rode 'like a little brick,' as Sir Harry
said when they got back to Stalham. On that afternoon she received the note from her aunt and replied to it by telegram.

On the Thursday she stayed at home and wrote
various letters. The first was to the Marchesa, and
then one to Nina,—in both of which much had to be
said about 'Jonathan.' To Nina also she could repeat
her idea of the delight of having a man to love. Then
there was a letter to Aunt Margaret,—which certainly
was due, and another to Aunt Emmeline,—which
was not however received until after Lady Tringle's
visit to Stalham. There was much conversation between her and Lady Albury as to the possible
purpose of the visit which was to be made on the
morrow. Lady Albury was of opinion that Lady
Tringle had heard of the engagement, and was coming with the intention of setting it on one side on
Tom's behalf. 'But she can't do that, you know,'
said Ayala, with some manifest alarm. 'She is
nothing to me now, Lady Albury. She got rid of me,
you know. I was changed away for Lucy.'

'If there had been no changing away, she could do nothing,' said Lady Albury.

About a quarter of an hour before the time for lunch on the following day Lady Tringle was shown into the small sitting-room which has been mentioned in a previous chapter, and Ayala, radiant with happiness and beauty, appeared before her. There was a look about her of being at home at Stalham, as though she were almost a daughter of the house, that struck her aunt with surprise. There was nothing left of that submissiveness which, though Ayala herself had not been submissive, belonged, as of right, to girls so dependent as she and her sister Lucy. 'I am so delighted to see you at Stalham,' said Ayala, as she embraced her aunt.

'I am come to you,' said Lady Tringle, 'on a matter of very particular business.' Then she paused, and assumed a look of peculiar solemnity.

'Have you got my letter?' demanded Ayala.

'I got your telegram, and I thought it very civil of Lady Albury. But I cannot stay. Your poor cousin Tom is in such a condition that I cannot leave him longer than I can help.'

'But you have not got my letter?'

'I have had no letter from you, Ayala.'

'I have sent you such news,—oh, such news, Aunt Emmeline!'

'What news, my dear?' Lady Tringle as she asked the question seemed to become more solemn than ever.

'Oh, Aunt Emmeline——; I am——'

'You are what, Ayala?'

'I am engaged to be married to Colonel Jonathan Stubbs.'

'Engaged!'

'Yes, Aunt Emmeline;—engaged. I wrote to you on Tuesday to tell you all about it. I hope you and Uncle Tom will approve. There cannot possibly be any reason against it,—except only that I have nothing to give him in return; that is in the way of money. Colonel Stubbs, Aunt Emmeline, is not what Uncle Tom will call a rich man, but everybody here says that he has got quite enough to be comfortable. If he had nothing in the world it could not make any difference to me. I don't understand how anybody is to love any one or not to love him just because he is rich or poor.'

'But you are absolutely engaged!' exclaimed Lady Tringle.

'Oh dear yes. Perhaps you would like to ask Lady Albury about it. He did want it before, you know.'

'But now you are engaged to him?' In answer to this Ayala thought it sufficient simply to nod her head. 'It is all over then?'

'All over!' exclaimed Ayala. 'It is just going to begin.'

'All over for poor Tom,' said Lady Tringle.

'Oh yes. It was always over for him, Aunt Emmeline. I told him ever so many times that it never could be so. Don't you know, Aunt Emmeline, that I did?'

'But you said that to this man just the same.'

'Aunt Emmeline,' said Ayala, putting on all the serious dignity which she knew how to assume, 'I am engaged to Colonel Stubbs, and nothing on earth that anybody can say can change it. If you want to hear all about it, Lady Albury will tell you. She knows that you are my aunt, and therefore she will be quite willing to talk to you. Only nothing that anybody can say can change it.'

'Poor Tom!' ejaculated the rejected lover's mother.

'I am very sorry if my cousin is displeased.'

'He is ill,—terribly ill. He will have to go away and travel all about the world, and I don't know that ever he will come back again. I am sure this Stubbs will never love you as he has done.'

'Oh, aunt, what is the use of that?'

'And then Tom will have twice as much. But, however——' Ayala stood silent, not seeing that any good could be done by addition to her former assurances. 'I will go and tell him, my dear, that's all. Will you not send him some message, Ayala?'

'Oh, yes; any message that I can that shall go along with my sincere attachment to Colonel Stubbs. You must tell him that I am engaged to Colonel Stubbs. You will tell him, Aunt Emmeline?'

'Oh, yes; if it must be so.'

'It must,' said Ayala. 'Then you may give him my love, and tell him that I am very unhappy that I should have been a trouble to him, and that I hope he will soon be well, and come back from his travels.' By this time Aunt Emmeline was dissolved in tears. 'I could not help it, Aunt Emmeline, could I?' Her aunt had once terribly outraged her feelings by telling her that she had encouraged Tom. Ayala remembered at this moment the cruel words and the wound which they had inflicted on her; but, nevertheless, she behaved tenderly, and endeavoured to be respectful and submissive. 'I could not help it,—could I, Aunt Emmeline?'

'I suppose not, my dear.'

After that Lady Tringle declared that she would return to London at once. No;—she would rather not go in to lunch. She would rather go back at once to the station if they would take her. She had been weeping, and did not wish to show her tears. Therefore, at Ayala's request, the carriage came round again,—to the great disgust, no doubt, of the coachman,—and Lady Tringle was taken back to the station without having seen any of the Albury family.

## CHAPTER LVII

### CAPTAIN BATSBY IN LOMBARD STREET

IT was not till Colonel Stubbs had been three or four days at Stalham, basking in the sunshine of Ayala's love, that any of the Stalham family heard of the great event which had occurred in the life of

Ayala's third lover. During that walk to and from Gobblegoose Wood something had been said between the lovers as to Captain Batsby,—something, no doubt, chiefly in joke. The idea of the poor Captain having fallen suddenly into so melancholy a condition was droll enough. 'But he never spoke to me,' said Ayala. 'He doesn't speak very much to any one,' said the Colonel, 'but he thinks a great deal about things. He has had ever so many affairs with ever so many ladies, who generally, I fancy, want to marry him because of his money. How he has escaped so long nobody knows.' A man when he has just engaged himself to be married is as prone as ever to talk of other men 'escaping,' feeling that, though other young ladies were no better than evils to be avoided, his young lady is to be regarded as almost a solitary instance of a blessing. Then, two days afterwards, arrived the news of the trip to Ostend. Sir Harry received a letter from a friend in which an account was given of his half-brother's adventure. 'What do you think has happened?' said Sir Harry, jumping up from his chair at the breakfast table.

'What has happened?' asked his wife.

'Benjamin has run off to Ostend with a young lady.'

'Benjamin,—with a young lady!' exclaimed Lady Albury. Ayala and Stubbs were equally astonished, each of them knowing that the Captain had been excluded from Stalham because of the ardour of his unfortunate love for Ayala. 'Ayala, that is your doing!'

'No!' said Ayala. 'But I am very glad if he's happy.'

'Who is the young lady?' asked Stubbs.

'It is that which makes it so very peculiar,' said Sir Harry, looking at Ayala. He had learned something of the Tringle family, and was aware of Ayala's connection with them.

'Who is it, Harry?' demanded her ladyship.

'Sir Thomas Tringle's younger daughter.'

'Gertrude!' exclaimed Ayala, who also knew of the engagement with Mr. Houston.

'But the worst of it is,' continued Sir Harry, 'that he is not at all happy. The young lady has come back, while nobody knows what has become of Benjamin.'

'Benjamin never will get a wife,' said Lady Albury. Thus all the details of the little event became known at Stalham,—except the immediate condition and whereabouts of the lover.

Of the Captain's condition and whereabouts something must be told. When the great disruption came, and he had been abused and ridiculed by Sir Thomas at Ostend, he felt that he could neither remain there where the very waiters knew what had happened, nor could he return to Dover in the same vessel with Sir Thomas and his daughter. He therefore took the first train and went to Brussels.

But Brussels did not offer him many allurements in his present frame of mind. He found nobody there whom he particularly knew, and nothing particular to do. Solitude in a continental town with no amusements beyond those offered by the table d'hôte and the theatre is oppressing. His time he endeavoured to occupy with thinking of the last promise he had made to Gertrude. Should he break it or should he keep it? Sir Thomas Tringle was, no doubt, a very rich man,—and then there was the fact which would become known to all the world, that he had run off with a young lady. Should he ultimately succeed in marrying the young lady the enterprise would bear less of an appearance of failure than it would do otherwise. But then, should the money not be forthcoming, the consolation coming from the possession of Gertrude herself would hardly suffice to make him a happy man. Sir Thomas, when he came to consider the matter, would certainly feel that his daughter had compromised herself by the journey, and that it would be good for her to be married to the man who had taken her. It might be that Sir Thomas would yield, and consent to make, at any rate, some compromise. A rumour had reached his ears that Traffick had received £200,000 with the elder daughter. He would consent to take half that sum. After a week spent amidst the charms of Brussels he returned to London, without any public declaration of his doing so,—'sneaked back,' as a friend of his said of him at the club;—and then went to work to carry out his purpose as best he might. All that was known of it at Stalham was that he had returned to his lodgings in London.

On Friday, the 11th of April, when Ayala was a promised bride of nearly two weeks' standing, and all the uncles and aunts were aware that her lot in life had been fixed for her, Sir Thomas was alone in the back-room in Lombard Street, with his mind sorely diverted from the only joy of his life. The whole family were now in town, and Septimus Traffick with his wife was actually occupying a room in Queen's Gate. How it had come to pass Sir Thomas hardly knew. Some word had been extracted from him signifying a compliance with a request that Augusta might come to the house for a night or two until a fitting residence should be prepared for her. Something had been said of Lord Boardotrade's house being vacated for her and her husband early in April. An occurrence to which married ladies are liable was about to take place with Augusta, and Sir Thomas certainly understood that the occurrence was to be expected under the roof of the coming infant's noble grandfather. Something as to ancestral halls had been thrown out in the chance way of conversation. Then he certainly had assented to some minimum of London hospitality for his daughter,—as certainly not including the presence of his son-in-law; and now both of them were domiciled in the big front spare bed-room at Queen's Gate! This perplexed him sorely. And then Tom had been brought up from the country still as an invalid, his mother moaning and groaning over him as though

he were sick almost past hope of recovery. And yet
the nineteenth of the month, now only eight days
distant, was still fixed for his departure. Tom, on
the return of his mother from Stalham, had to a
certain extent accepted as irrevocable the fact of
which she bore the tidings. Ayala was engaged to
Stubbs, and would, doubtless, with very little delay,
become Mrs. Jonathan Stubbs. 'I knew it,' he said;
'I knew it. Nothing could have prevented it unless
I had shot him through the heart. He told me that
she had refused him; but no man could have looked
like that after being refused by Ayala.' Then he
never expressed a hope again. It was all over for him
as regarded Ayala. But he still refused to be well, or
even, for a day or two, to leave his bed. He had
allowed his mother to understand that if the fact of
her engagement were indubitably brought home to
him he would gird up his loins for his journey and
proceed at once wherever it might be thought good
to send him. His father had sternly reminded him of
his promise; but, when so reminded, Tom had turned
himself in his bed and uttered groans instead of
replies. Now he had been brought up to London and
was no longer actually in bed; but even yet he had
not signified his intention of girding up his loins and
proceeding upon his journey. Nevertheless the
preparations were going on, and, under Sir Thomas's
directions, the portmanteaus were already being
packed. Gertrude also was a source of discomfort to
her father. She considered herself to have been deprived of her two lovers, one after the other, in a
spirit of cruel parsimony. And with this heavy
weight upon her breast she refused to take any part
in the family conversations. Everything had been
done for Augusta, and everything was to be done for
Tom. For her nothing had been done, and nothing
had been promised;—and she was therefore very
sulky. With these troubles all around him, Sir
Thomas was sitting oppressed and disheartened in
Lombard Street on Friday, the 11th of April.

Then there entered to him one of the junior clerks with a card announcing the name of Captain Batsby. He looked at it for some seconds before he gave any notification of his intention, and then desired the young man to tell the gentleman that he would not see him. The message had been delivered, and Captain Batsby with a frown of anger on his brow was about to shake the dust off from his feet on the uncourteous threshold when there came another message, saying that Captain Batsby could go in and see Sir Thomas if he wished it. Upon this he turned round and was shown into the little sitting-room. 'Well, Captain Batsby,' said Sir Thomas; 'what can I do for you now? I am glad to see that you have come back safely from foreign parts.'

'I have called,' said the Captain, 'to say something about your daughter.'

'What more can you have to say about her?'

At this the Captain was considerably puzzled. Of course Sir Thomas must know what he had to say. 'The way in which we were separated at Ostend was very distressing to my feelings.'

'I daresay.'

'And also I should think to Miss Tringle's.'

'Not improbably. I have always observed that when people are interrupted in the performance of some egregious stupidity their feelings are hurt. As I said before, what can I do for you now?'

'I am very anxious to complete the alliance which I have done myself the honour to propose to you.'

'I did not know that you had proposed anything. You came down to my house under a false pretence; and then you persuaded my daughter,—or else she persuaded you,—to go off together to Ostend. Is that what you call an alliance?'

'That, as far as it went, was,—was an elopement.'

'Am I to understand that you now want to arrange another elopement, and that you have come to ask my consent?'

'Oh dear no.'

'Then what do you mean by completing an alliance?'

'I want to make,' said the Captain, 'an offer for the young lady's hand in a proper form. I consider myself to be in a position which justifies me in doing so. I am possessed of the young lady's affections, and have means of my own equal to those which I presume you will be disposed to give her.'

'Very much better means I hope, Captain Batsby. Otherwise I do not see what you and your wife would have to live upon. I will tell you exactly what my feelings are in this matter. My daughter has gone off with you, forgetting all the duty that she owed to me and to her mother, and throwing aside all ideas of propriety. After that I will not say that you shall not marry her if both of you think fit. I do not doubt your means, and I have no reason for supposing that you would be cruel to her. You are two fools, but after all fools must live in the world. What I do say is, that I will not give a sixpence towards supporting you in your folly. Now, Captain Batsby, you can complete the alliance or not as you please.'

Captain Batsby had been called a fool also at Ostend, and there, amidst the distressing circumstances of his position, had been constrained to bear the opprobrious name, little customary as it is for one gentleman to allow himself to be called a fool by another; but now he had collected his thoughts, had reminded himself of his position in the world, and had told himself that it did not become him to be too humble before this City man of business. It might have been all very well at Ostend; but he was not going to be called a fool in London without resenting it. 'Sir Thomas,' said he, 'fool and folly are terms which I cannot allow you to use to me.'

'If you do not present yourself to me here, Captain Batsby, or at my own house,—or, perhaps I may say, at Ostend,—I will use no such terms to you.'

'I suppose you will acknowledge that I am entitled to ask for your daughter's hand.'

'I suppose you will acknowledge that when a man runs away with my daughter I am entitled to express my opinion of his conduct.'

'That is all over now, Sir Thomas. What I did I did for love. There is no good in crying over spilt milk. The question is as to the future happiness of the young lady.'

'That is the only wise word I have heard you say, Captain Batsby. There is no good in crying after spilt milk. Our journey to Ostend is done and gone. It was not very agreeable, but we have lived through it. I quite think that you show a good judgment in not intending to go there again in quest of a clergyman. If you want to be married there are plenty of them in London. I will not oppose your marriage, but I will not give you a shilling. No man ever had a better opportunity of showing the disinterestedness of his affection. Now, good morning.'

'But, Sir Thomas——'

'Captain Batsby, my time is precious. I have told you all that there is to tell.' Then he stood up, and the Captain with a stern demeanour and angry brow left the room and took himself in silence away from Lombard Street.

'Do you want to marry Captain Batsby?' Sir Thomas said to his daughter that evening, having invited her to come apart with him after dinner.

'Yes, I do.'

'You think that you prefer him on the whole to Mr. Houston?'

'Mr. Houston is a scoundrel. I wish that you would not talk about him, papa.'

'I like him so much the best of the two,' said Sir Thomas. 'But of course it is for you to judge. I could have brought myself to give something to Houston. Luckily, however, Captain Batsby has got an income of his own.'

'He has, papa.'

'And you are sure that you would like to take him as your husband?'

'Yes, papa.'

'Very well. He has been with me to-day.'

'Is he in London?'

'I tell you that he has been with me to-day in Lombard Street.'

'What did he say? Did he say anything about me?'

'Yes, my dear. He came to ask me for your hand.'

'Well, papa.'

'I told him that I should make no objection,— that I should leave it altogether to you. I only interfered with one small detail as to my own wishes. I assured him that I should never give him or you a single shilling. I don't suppose it will matter much to him, as he has, you know, means of his own.' It was thus that Sir Thomas punished his daughter for her misconduct.

Captain Batsby and the Trafficks were acquainted with each other. The Member of Parliament had, of course, heard of the journey to Ostend from his wife, and had been instigated by her to express an opinion that the young people ought to be married. 'It is such a very serious thing,' said Augusta to her husband, 'to be four hours on the sea together! And then you know——!' Mr. Traffick acknowledged that it was serious, and was reminded by his wife that he, in the capacity of brother, was bound to interfere on his sister's behalf. 'Papa, you know, understands nothing about these kind of things. You, with your family interest, and your seat in Parliament, ought to be able to arrange it.' Mr. Traffick probably knew how far his family interest and his seat in Parliament would avail. They had, at any rate, got him a wife with a large fortune. They were promising for him, still further, certain domiciliary advantages. He doubted whether he could do much for Batsby; but still he promised to try. If he could arrange these matters it might be that he would curry fresh favour with Sir Thomas by doing so. He therefore made it his business to encounter Captain Batsby on the Sunday afternoon at a club to which they both belonged. 'So you have come back from your little trip?' said the Member of Parliament.

The Captain was not unwilling to discuss the question of their family relations with Mr. Traffick. If anybody would have influence with Sir Thomas it might probably be Mr. Traffick. 'Yes; I have come back.'

'Without your bride.'

'Without my bride,—as yet. That is a kind of undertaking in which a man is apt to run many dangers before he can carry it through.'

'I dare say. I never did anything of the kind myself. Of course you know that I am the young lady's brother-in-law.'

'Oh yes.'

'And therefore you won't mind me speaking. Don't you think you ought to do something further?'

'Something further! By George, I should think so,' said the Captain, exultingly. 'I mean to do a great many things further. You don't suppose I am going to give it up?'

'You oughtn't, you know. When a man has taken a girl off with him in that way, he should go on with it. It's a deuced serious thing, you know.'

'It was his fault in coming after us.'

'That was a matter of course. If he hadn't done it, I must. I have made the family my own, and, of course, must look after its honour.' The noble scion of the house of Traffick, as he said this, showed by his countenance that he perfectly understood the duty which circumstances had imposed upon him.

'He made himself very rough, you know,' said the Captain.

'I dare say he would.'

'And said things,—well,—things which he ought not to have said.'

'In such a case as that a father may say pretty nearly what comes uppermost.'

'That was just it. He did say what came uppermost,—and very rough it was.'

'What does it matter?'

'Not much if he'd do as he ought to do now. As you are her brother-in-law, I'll tell you just how it stands. I have been to him and made a regular proposal.'

'Since you have been back?'

'Yes; the day before yesterday. And what do you think he says?'

'What does he say?'

'He gives his consent; only——'

'Only what?'

'He won't give her a shilling! Such an idea, you know! As though she were to be punished after marriage for running away with the man she did marry.'

'Take your chance, Batsby,' said the Member of Parliament.

'What chance?'

'Take your chance of the money. I'd have done it; only, of course, it was different with me. He was glad to catch me, and therefore the money was settled.'

'I've got a tidy income of my own, you know,' said the Captain, thinking that he was entitled to be made more welcome as a son-in-law than the younger son of a peer who had no income.

'Take your chance,' continued Traffick. 'What on earth can a man like Tringle do with his money except give it to his children? He is rough, as you say, but he is not hard-hearted, nor yet stubborn. I can do pretty nearly what I like with him.'

'Can you, though?'

'Yes; by smoothing him down the right way. You run your chance, and we'll get it all put right for you.' The Captain hesitated, rubbing his head carefully to encourage the thoughts which were springing up within his bosom. The Honourable Mr. Traffick might perhaps succeed in getting the affair put right, as he called it, in the interest rather of the elder than of the second daughter. 'I don't see how you can hesitate now, as you have been off with the girl,' said Mr. Traffick.

'I don't know about that. I should like to see the money settled.'

'There would have been nothing settled if you had married her at Ostend.'

'But I didn't,' said the Captain. 'I tell you what you might do. You might talk him over and make him a little more reasonable. I should be ready to-morrow if he'd come forward.'

'What's the sum you want?'

'The same as yours, I suppose.'

'That's out of the question,' said Mr. Traffick, shaking his head. 'Suppose we say sixty thousand pounds.' Then after some chaffering on the subject it was decided between them that Mr. Traffick should use his powerful influence with his father-in-law to give his daughter on her marriage,—say a hundred thousand pounds if it were possible, or sixty thousand pounds at the least.

## CHAPTER LVIII

### MR. TRAFFICK IN LOMBARD STREET

MR. TRAFFICK entertained some grand ideas as to the house of Travers and Treason. Why should not he become a member, and ultimately the leading member, of that firm? Sir Thomas was not a young man, though he was strong and hearty. Tom had hitherto succeeded only in making an ass of himself. As far as transacting the affairs of the firm, Tom,—so thought Mr. Traffick,—was altogether out of the question. He might perish in those extensive travels which he was about to take. Mr. Traffick did not desire any such catastrophe;—but the young man might perish. There was a great opening. Mr. Traffick, with his thorough knowledge of business, could not but see that there was a great opening. Besides Tom, there were but two daughters, one of

whom was his own wife. Augusta, his wife, was, he
thought, certainly the favourite at the present
moment. Sir Thomas could, indeed, say rough things
even to her; but then Sir Thomas was of his nature
rough. Now, at this time, the rough things said to
Gertrude were very much the rougher. In all these
circumstances the wisdom of interfering in Gertrude's
little affairs was very clear to Mr. Traffick. Gertrude
would, of course, get herself married sooner or later,
and almost any other husband would obtain a
larger portion than that which would satisfy Batsby.
Sir Thomas was now constantly saying good things
about Mr. Houston. Mr. Houston would be much
more objectionable than Captain Batsby,—much more
likely to interfere. He would require more money at
once, and might possibly come forward himself in the
guise of a partner. Mr. Traffick saw his way clearly.
It was incumbent upon him to see that Gertrude
should become Mrs. Batsby with as little delay as
possible.

But one thing he did not see. One thing he had
failed to see since his first introduction to the Tringle
family. He had not seen the peculiar nature of his
father-in-law's foibles. He did not understand either
the weakness or the strength of Sir Thomas,—either
the softness or the hardness. Mr. Traffick himself
was blessed with a very hard skin. In the carrying
out of a purpose there was nothing which his skin
was not sufficiently serviceable to endure. But Sir
Thomas, rough as he was, had but a thin skin;—
a thin skin and a soft heart. Had Houston and
Gertrude persevered he would certainly have given
way. For Tom, in his misfortune, he would have
made any sacrifice. Though he had given the
broadest hints which he had been able to devise he
had never as yet brought himself absolutely to turn
Traffick out of his house. When Ayala was sent away
he still kept her name in his will, and added also that
of Lucy as soon as Lucy had been entrusted to him.
Had things gone a little more smoothly between him

and Hamel when they met,—had he not unluckily
advised that all the sculptor's grand designs should
be sold by auction for what they would fetch,—he
would have put Hamel and Lucy upon their legs.
He was a soft-hearted man;—but there never was
one less willing to endure interference in his own
affairs.

At the present moment he was very sore as to the
presence of Traffick in Queen's Gate. The Easter
parliamentary holidays were just at hand, and there
was no sign of any going. Augusta had whispered to
her mother that the poky little house in Mayfair
would be very uncomfortable for the coming event,
—and Lady Tringle, though she had not dared to say
even as much as that in plain terms to her husband,
had endeavoured to introduce the subject by little
hints,—which Sir Thomas had clearly understood.
He was hardly the man to turn a daughter and an
expected grandchild into the streets; but he was, in
his present mood, a father-in-law who would not
unwillingly have learned that his son-in-law was without a shelter except that afforded by the House of
Commons. Why on earth should he have given up
one hundred and twenty thousand pounds,—£6,000
a-year as it was under his fostering care,—to a man
who could not even keep a house over his wife's
head? This was the humour of Sir Thomas when Mr.
Traffick undertook to prevail with him to give an
adequate fortune to his youngest daughter on her
marriage with Captain Batsby.

The conversation between Traffick and Batsby
took place on a Sunday. On the following day the
Captain went down to the House and saw the
Member. 'No; I have not spoken to him yet.'

'I was with him on Friday, you know,' said Batsby.
'I can't well go and call on the ladies in Queen's Gate
till I hear that he has changed his mind.'

'I should. I don't see what difference it would
make.'

Then Captain Batsby was again very thoughtful.

'It would make a difference, you know. If I were to
say a word to Gertrude now,—as to being married or
anything of that kind,—it would seem that I meant
to go on whether I got anything or not.'

'And you should seem to want to go on,' said
Traffick, with all that authority which the very
surroundings of the House of Commons always give
to the words and gait of a Member.

'But then I might find myself dropped in a hole at
last.'

'My dear Batsby, you made that hole for yourself
when you ran off with the young lady.'

'We settled all that before.'

'Not quite. What we did settle was that we'd do
our best to fill the hole up. Of course you ought to go
and see them. You went off with the young lady,—
and since that have been accepted as her suitor by
her father. You are bound to go and see her.'

'Do you think so?'

'Certainly! Certainly! It never does to talk to
Tringle about business at his own house. I'll make
an hour to see him in the City to-morrow. I'm so
pressed by business that I can hardly get away from
the House after twelve;—but I'll do it. But, while
I'm in Lombard Street, do you go to Queen's Gate.'
The Captain after further consideration said that he
would go to Queen's Gate.

At three o'clock on the next day he did go to
Queen's Gate. He had many misgivings, feeling that
by such a step he would be committing himself to
matrimony with or without the money. No doubt
he could so offer himself, even to Lady Tringle, as a
son-in-law, that it should be supposed that the offer
would depend upon the father-in-law's goodwill.
But then the father-in-law had told him that he
would be welcome to the young lady,—without a
farthing. Should he go on with his matrimonial
purpose, towards which this visit would be an important step, he did not see the moment in which he
could stop the proceedings by a demand for money.

Nevertheless he went, not being strong enough to oppose Mr. Traffick.

Yes;—the ladies were at home, and he found himself at once in Lady Tringle's presence. There was at the time no one with her, and the Captain acknowledged to himself that a trying moment had come to him. 'Dear me! Captain Batsby!' said her ladyship, who had not seen him since he and Gertrude had gone off together.

'Yes, Lady Tringle. As I have come back from abroad I thought that I might as well come and call. I did see Sir Thomas in the City.'

'Was not that a very foolish thing you did?'

'Perhaps it was, Lady Tringle. Perhaps it would have been better to ask permission to address your daughter in the regular course of things. There was, perhaps,—perhaps a little romance in going off in that way.'

'It gave Sir Thomas a deal of trouble.'

'Well, yes; he was so quick upon us, you know. May I be allowed to see Gertrude now?'

'Upon my word I hardly know,' said Lady Tringle, hesitating.

'I did see Sir Thomas in the City.'

'But did he say you were to come and call?'

'He gave his consent to the marriage.'

'But I am afraid there was to be no money,' whispered Lady Tringle. 'If money is no matter I suppose you may see her.' But before the Captain had resolved how he might best answer this difficult suggestion the door opened, and the young lady herself entered the room, together with her sister.

'Benjamin,' said Gertrude, 'is this really you?' And then she flew into his arms.

'My dear,' said Augusta, 'do control your emotions '

'Yes, indeed, Gertrude,' said the mother. 'As the things are at present you should control yourself. Nobody as yet knows what may come of it.'

'Oh, Benjamin!' again exclaimed Gertrude, tearing herself from his arms, throwing herself on the

sofa, and covering her face with both her hands.
'Oh, Benjamin,—so you have come at last.'

'I am afraid he has come too soon,' said Augusta,
who however had received her lesson from her husband, and had communicated some portion of her
husband's tidings to her sister.

'Why too soon?' exclaimed Gertrude. 'It can
never be too soon. Oh, mamma, tell him that you
make him welcome to your bosom as your second
son-in-law.'

'Upon my word, my dear, I do not know, without
consulting your father.'

'But papa has consented,' said Gertrude.

'But only if——'

'Oh, mamma,' said Mrs. Traffick, 'do not talk about
matters of business on such an occasion as this. All
that must be managed between the gentlemen. If he
is here as Gertrude's acknowledged lover, and if
papa has told him that he shall be accepted as such,
I don't think that we ought to say a word about
money. I do hate money. It does make things so
disagreeable.'

'Nobody can be more noble in everything of that
kind than Benjamin,' said Gertrude. 'It is only because he loves me with all his heart that he is here.
Why else was it that he took me off to Ostend?'

Captain Batsby as he listened to all this felt that
he ought to say something. And yet how dangerous
might a word be! It was apparent to him, even in
his perturbation, that the ladies were in fact asking
him to renew his offer, and to declare that he renewed it altogether independently of any money
consideration. He could not bring himself quite to
agree with that noble sentiment in expressing which
Mrs. Traffick had declared her hatred of money. In
becoming the son-in-law of a millionaire he would
receive the honest congratulations of all his friends,
—on condition that he received some comfortable
fraction out of the millions, but he knew well that he
would subject himself to their ridicule were he to

take the girl and lose the plunder. If he were to answer them now as they would have him answer he would commit himself to the girl without any bargain as to the plunder. And yet what else was there for him to do? He must be a brave man who can stand up before a girl and declare that he will love her for ever,—on condition that she shall have so many thousand pounds; but he must be more than brave, he will be heroic, who can do so in the presence not only of the girl but of the girl's mother and married sister as well. Captain Batsby was no such hero. 'Of course,' he said at last.

'Of course what?' asked Augusta.

'It was because I loved her.'

'I knew that he loved me,' sobbed Gertrude.

'And you are here, because you intend to make her your wife in presence of all men?' asked Augusta.

'Oh certainly.'

'Then I suppose that it will be all right,' said Lady Tringle.

'It will be all right,' said Augusta. 'And now, mamma, I think that we may leave them alone together.' But to this Lady Tringle would not give her assent. She had not had confided to her the depth of Mr. Traffick's wisdom, and declared herself opposed to any absolute overt love-making until Sir Thomas should have given his positive consent.

'It is all the same thing, Benjamin, is it not?' said Augusta, assuming already the familiarity of a sister-in-law.

'Oh quite,' said the Captain.

But Gertrude looked as though she did not think it to be exactly the same. Such deficiency as that, however, she had to endure; and she received from her sister after the Captain's departure full congratulations as to her lover's return. 'To tell you the truth,' said Augusta, 'I didn't think that you would ever see him again. After what papa said to him in the City he might have got off and nobody could have said a word to him. Now he's fixed.'

Captain Batsby effected his escape as quickly as
he could, and went home a melancholy man. He, too,
was aware that he was fixed; and, as he thought of
this, a dreadful idea fell upon him that the Honourable Mr. Traffick had perhaps played him false.

In the meantime Mr. Traffick was true to his word
and went into the City. In the early days of his
married life his journeys to Lombard Street were
frequent. The management and investing of his
wife's money had been to him a matter of much
interest, and he had felt a gratification in discussing
any money matter with the man who handled
millions. In this way he had become intimate with
the ways of the house, though latterly his presence
there had not been encouraged. 'I suppose I can go
in to Sir Thomas,' he said, laying his hand upon a
leaf in the counter, which he had been accustomed to
raise for the purpose of his own entrance. But here
he was stopped. His name should be taken in, and
Sir Thomas duly apprised. In the meantime he was
relegated to a dingy little waiting room, which was
odious to him, and there he was kept waiting for half-
an-hour. This made him angry, and he called to one
of the clerks. 'Will you tell Sir Thomas that I must
be down at the House almost immediately, and that I
am particularly anxious to see him on business of
importance?' For another ten minutes he was still
kept, and then he was shown into his father-in-law's
presence. 'I am very sorry, Traffick,' said Sir
Thomas, 'but I really can't turn two Directors of the
Bank of England out of my room, even for you.'

'I only thought I would just let you know that I
am in a hurry.'

'So am I, for the matter of that. Have you gone
to your father's house to-day, so that you would not
be able to see me in Queen's Gate?'

This was intended to be very severe, but Mr.
Traffick bore it. It was one of those rough things
which Sir Thomas was in the habit of saying, but
which really meant nothing. 'No. My father is still

at his house as yet, though they are thinking of going every day. It is about another matter, and I did not want to trouble you with it at home.'

'Let us hear what it is.'

'Captain Batsby has been with me.'

'Oh, he has, has he?'

'I've known him ever so long. He's a foolish fellow.'

'So he seems.'

'But a gentleman.'

'Perhaps I am not so good a judge of that. His folly I did perceive.'

'Oh, yes; he's a gentleman. You may take my word for that. And he has means.'

'That's an advantage.'

'While that fellow Houston is hardly more than a beggar. And Batsby is quite in earnest about Gertrude.'

'If the two of them wish it he can have her to-morrow. She has made herself a conspicuous ass by running away with him, and perhaps it's the best thing she can do.'

'That's just it. Augusta sees it quite in the same light.'

'Augusta was never tempted. You wouldn't have run away.'

'It wasn't necessary, Sir Thomas, was it? There he is,—ready to marry her to-morrow. But, of course, he is a little anxious about the money.'

'I dare say he is.'

'I've been talking to him,—and the upshot is, that I have promised to speak to you. He isn't at all a bad fellow.'

'He'd keep a house over his wife's head, you think?' Sir Thomas had been particularly irate that morning, and before the arrival of his son-in-law had sworn to himself that Traffick should go. Augusta might remain, if she pleased, for the occurrence; but the Honourable Septimus should no longer eat and drink as an inhabitant of his house.

'He'd do his duty by her as a man should do,' said Traffick, determined to ignore the disagreeable subject.

'Very well. There she is.'

'But of course he would like to hear something about money.'

'Would he?'

'That's only natural.'

'You found it so,—did you not? What's the good of giving a girl money when her husband won't spend it? Perhaps this Captain Batsby would expect to live at Queen's Gate or Merle Park.'

It was impossible to go on enduring this without notice. Mr. Traffick, however, only frowned and shook his head. It was clear at last that Sir Thomas intended to be more than rough, and it was almost imperative upon Mr. Traffick to be rough in return. 'I am endeavouring to do my duty by the family,' he said.

'Oh indeed.'

'Gertrude has eloped with this man, and the thing is talked about everywhere. Augusta feels it very much.'

'She does, does she?'

'And I have thought it right to ask his intentions.'

'He didn't knock you down, or anything of that sort?'

'Knock me down?'

'For interfering. But he hasn't pluck for that. Houston would have done it immediately. And I should have said he was right. But if you have got anything to say, you had better say it. When you have done, then I shall have something to say.'

'I've told him that he couldn't expect as much as you would have given her but for this running away.'

'You told him that?'

'Yes; I told him that. Then some sum had to be mentioned. He suggested a hundred thousand pounds.'

'How very modest! Why should he have put up

with less than you, seeing that he has got something of his own?'

'He hasn't my position, Sir. You know that well enough. Now to make a long and short of it, I suggested sixty.'

'Out of your own pocket?'

'Not exactly.'

'But out of mine?'

'You're her father, and I suppose you intend to provide for her.'

'And you have come here to dictate to me the provision which I am to make for my own child! That is an amount of impudence which I did not expect even from you. But suppose that I agree to the terms. Will he, do you think, consent to have a clause put into the settlement?'

'What clause?'

'Something that shall bind him to keep a house for his own wife's use, so that he should not take my money and then come and live upon me afterwards.'

'Sir Thomas,' said the Member of Parliament, 'that is a mode of expression so uncourteous that I cannot bear it even from you.'

'Is there any mode of expression that you cannot bear?'

'If you want me to leave your house, say it at once.'

'Why, I have been saying it for the last six months! I have been saying it almost daily since you were married.'

'If so you should have spoken more clearly, for I have not understood you.'

'Heavens and earth!' ejaculated Sir Thomas.

'Am I to understand that you wish your child to leave your roof during this inclement weather in her present delicate condition?'

'Are you in a delicate condition?' asked Sir Thomas. To this Mr. Traffick could condescend to make no reply. 'Because, if not, you, at any rate, had better go,—unless you find the weather too inclement.'

'Of course I shall go,' said Mr. Traffick. 'No consideration on earth shall induce me to eat another meal under your roof until you have thought good to have expressed regret for what you have said.'

'Then it is very long before I shall have to give you another meal.'

'And now what shall I say to Captain Batsby?'

'Tell him from me,' said Sir Thomas, 'that he cannot possibly set about his work more injudiciously than by making you his ambassador.' Then Mr. Traffick took his departure.

It may be as well to state here that Mr. Traffick kept his threat religiously,—at any rate, to the end of the Session. He did not eat another meal during that period under his father-in-law's roof. But he slept there for the next two or three days until he had suited himself with lodgings in the neighbourhood of the House. In doing this, however, he contrived to get in and out without encountering Sir Thomas. His wife in her delicate condition,—and because of the inclemency of the weather,—awaited the occurrence at Queen's Gate.

## CHAPTER LIX

### TREGOTHNAN

THE writer, in giving a correct chronicle of the doings of the Tringle family at this time, has to acknowledge that Gertrude, during the prolonged absence of Captain Batsby at Brussels,—an absence that was cruelly prolonged for more than a week,—did make another little effort in another direction. Her father, in his rough way, had expressed an opinion that she had changed very much for the worse in transferring her affections from Mr. Houston to Captain Batsby, and had almost gone so far as to declare that had she been persistent with her Houston the money difficulty might have been overcome. This was imprudent,—unless, indeed, he was desirous of bringing back Mr. Houston into the bosom of the Tringles. It instigated Gertrude to another attempt, —which, however, she did not make till Captain Batsby had been away from her for at least four days without writing a letter. Then it occurred to her that if she had a preference it certainly was for Frank Houston. No doubt the general desirability of marriage was her chief actuating motive. Will the world of British young ladies be much scandalised if I say that such is often an actuating motive? They would be justly scandalised if I pretended that many of its members were capable of the speedy transitions which Miss Tringle was strong enough to endure; but transitions do take place, and I claim, on behalf of my young lady, that she should be regarded as more strong-minded and more determined than the general crowd of young ladies. She had thought herself to be off with the old love before she was on with the new.* Then the 'new' had gone away to Brussels,—or heaven only knows where,—and there seemed to be an opportunity of renewing matters with the 'old.' Having perceived the desirability of matrimony, she simply carried out her purpose with a determined will. It was with a determined will, but perhaps with deficient judgment, that she had written as follows:

'Papa has altered his mind altogether. He speaks of you in the highest terms, and says that had you persevered he would have yielded about the money. Do try him again. When hearts have been united it is terrible that they should be dragged asunder.' Mr. Traffick had been quite right in telling his father-in-law that 'the thing had been talked about everywhere.' The thing talked about had been Gertrude's elopement. The daughter of a baronet and a millionaire cannot go off with the half-brother of another baronet and escape that penalty. The journey to Ostend was in everybody's mouth, and had surprised Frank Houston the more because of the recent termination of his own little affair with the lady. That he should already have re-accommodated himself

with Imogene was intelligible to him, and seemed to
admit of valid excuse before any jury of matrons. It
was an old affair, and the love,—real, true love,—
was already existing. He, at any rate, was going
back to the better course,—as the jury of matrons
would have admitted. But Gertrude's new affair
had had to be arranged from the beginning, and
shocked him by its celerity. 'Already!' he had
said to himself,—'gone off with another man already?' He felt himself to have been wounded in a
tender part, and was conscious of a feeling that he
should like to injure the successful lover,—blackball
him at a club, or do him some other mortal mischief.
When, therefore, he received from the young lady
the little billet above given, he was much surprised.
Could it be a hoax? It was certainly the young lady's
handwriting. Was he to be enticed once again into
Lombard Street, in order that the clerks might set
upon him in a body and maltreat him? Was he to be
decoyed into Queen's Gate, and made a sacrifice of
by the united force of the housemaids? Not understanding the celerity of the young lady, he could
hardly believe the billet.

When he received the note of which we have here
spoken two months had elapsed since he had seen
Imogene and had declared to her his intention of
facing the difficulties of matrimony in conjunction
with herself as soon as she would be ready to under-
go the ceremony with him. The reader will remember
that her brother, Mudbury Docimer, had written to
him with great severity, abusing both him and
Imogene for the folly of their intention. And Houston,
as he thought of their intention, thought to himself
that perhaps they were foolish. The poverty, and the
cradles, and the cabbages, were in themselves evils.
But still he encouraged himself to think that there
might be an evil worse even than folly. After that
scene with Imogene, in which she had offered to
sacrifice herself altogether, and to be bound to him,
even though they should never be married, on condi-

tion that he should take to himself no other wife, he
had quite resolved that it behoved him not to be
exceeded by her in generosity. He had stoutly
repudiated her offer, which he had called a damnable
compact. And then there had been a delightful
scene between them, in which it had been agreed that
they should face the cradles and the cabbages with
bold faces. Since that he had never allowed himself
to fluctuate in his purpose. Had Sir Thomas come to
him with Gertrude in one hand and the much-desired
£120,000 in the other, he would have repudiated the
lot of them. He declared to himself with stern resolution that he had altogether washed his hands from
dirt of that kind. Cabbages and cradles for ever
was the unpronounced cry of triumph with which he
buoyed up his courage. He set himself to work
earnestly, if not altogether steadfastly, to alter the
whole tenor of his life. The champagne and the
woodcocks,—or whatever might be the special deli-
cacies of the season,—he did avoid. For some few
days he absolutely dined upon a cut of mutton at an
eating-house, and as he came forth from the unsavoury doors of the establishment regarded himself
as a hero. Cabbages and cradles for ever! he would
say to himself, as he went away to drink a cup of tea
with an old maiden aunt, who was no less surprised
than gratified by his new virtue. Therefore, when it
had at last absolutely come home to him that the
last little note had in truth been written by Gertrude
with no object of revenge, but with the intention of
once more alluring him into the wealth of Lombard
Street, he simply put it into his breastcoat-pocket, and
left it there unanswered.

Mudbury Docimer did not satisfy himself with
writing the very uncourteous letter which the reader
has seen, but proceeded to do his utmost to prevent
the threatened marriage. 'She is old enough to look
after herself,' he had said, as though all her future
actions must be governed by her own will. But within ten days of the writing of that letter he had found

it expedient to go down into the country, and to take his sister with him. As the head of the Docimer family he possessed a small country-house almost in the extremity of Cornwall; and thither he went. It was a fraternal effort made altogether on his sister's behalf, and was so far successful that Imogene was obliged to accompany him. It was all very well for her to feel that as she was of age she could do as she pleased. But a young lady is constrained by the exigencies of society to live with somebody. She cannot take a lodging by herself, as her brother may do. Therefore, when Mudbury Docimer went down to Cornwall, Imogene was obliged to accompany him.

'Is this intended for banishment?' she said to him, when they had been about a week in the country.

'What do you call banishment? You used to like the country in the spring.' It was now the middle of April.

'So I do, and in summer also. But I like nothing under constraint.'

'I am sorry that circumstances should make it imperative upon me to remain here just at present.'

'Why cannot you tell the truth, Mudbury?'

'Have I told you any falsehood?'

'Why do you not say outright that I have been brought down here to be out of Frank Houston's way?'

'Because Frank Houston is a name which I do not wish to mention to you again,—at any rate for some time.'

'What would you do if he were to show himself here?' she asked.

'Tell him at once that he was not welcome. In other words, I would not have him here. It is very improbable I should think that he would come without a direct invitation from me. That invitation he will never have until I feel satisfied that you and he have changed your mind again, and that you mean to stick to it.'

'I do not think we shall do that.'

'Then he shall not come down here; nor, as far as I am able to arrange it, shall you go up to London.'

'Then I am a prisoner?'

'You may put it as you please,' said her brother. 'I have no power of detaining you. Whatever influence I have I think it right to use. I am altogether opposed to this marriage, believing it to be an absurd infatuation. I think that he is of the same opinion.'

'No!' said she, indignantly.

'That I believe to be his feeling,' he continued, taking no notice of her assertion. 'He is as perfectly aware as I am that you two are not adapted to live happily together on an income of a few hundreds a year. Some time ago it was agreed between you that it was so. You both were quite of one mind, and I was given to understand that the engagement was at an end. It was so much at an end that he made an arrangement for marrying another woman. But your feelings are stronger than his, and you allowed them to get the better of you. Then you enticed him back from the purpose on which you had both decided.'

'Enticed!' said she. 'I did nothing of the kind!'

'Would he have changed his mind if you had not enticed him?'

'I did nothing of the kind. I offered to remain just as we are.'

'That is all very well. Of course he could not accept such an offer. Thinking as I do, it is my duty to keep you apart as long as I can. If you contrive to marry him in opposition to my efforts, the misery of both of you must be on your head. I tell you fairly that I do not believe he wishes anything of the kind.'

'I am quite sure he does,' said Imogene.

'Very well. Do you leave him alone; stay down here, and see what will come of it. I quite agree that such a banishment, as you call it, is not a happy prospect for you;—but it is happier than that of a marriage with Frank Houston. Give that up, and then you can go back to London and begin the world again.'

Begin the world again! She knew what that meant. She was to throw herself into the market, and look for such other husband as Providence might send her. She had tried that before, and had convinced herself that Providence could never send her any that could be acceptable. The one man had taken possession of her, and there never could be a second. She had not known her own strength,—or her own weakness as the case might be,—when she had agreed to surrender the man she loved because there had been an alteration in their prospects of an income. She had struggled with herself, had attempted to amuse herself with the world, had told herself that somebody would come who would banish that image from her thoughts and heart. She had bade herself to submit to the separation for his welfare. Then she had endeavoured to quiet herself by declaring to herself that the man was no hero,— was unworthy of so much thinking. But it had all been of no avail. Gertrude Tringle had been a festering sore to her. Frank, whether a hero or only a commonplace man, was,—as she owned to herself,— hero enough for her. Then came the opening for a renewal of the engagement. Frank had been candid with her, and had told her everything. The Tringle money would not be forthcoming on his behalf. Then, —not resolving to entice him back again,—she had done so. The word was odious to her, and was rejected with disdain when used against her by her brother;—but, when alone, she acknowledged to herself that it was true. She had enticed her lover back again,—to his great detriment. Yes; she certainly had enticed him back. She certainly was about to sacrifice him because of her love. 'If I could only die, and there be an end of it!' she exclaimed to herself.

Though Tregothnan Hall, as the Docimers' house was called, was not open to Frank Houston, there was the post running always. He had written to her half-a-dozen times since she had been in Cornwall, and had always spoken of their engagement as an affair at last irrevocably fixed. She, too, had written little notes, tender and loving, but still tinged by that tone of despondency which had become common to her. 'As for naming a day,' she said once, 'suppose we fix the first of January, ten years hence. Mudbury's opposition will be worn out by old age, and you will have become thoroughly sick of the pleasures of London.' But joined to this there would be a few jokes, and then some little word of warmest, most enduring, most trusting love. 'Don't believe me if I say that I am not happy in knowing that I am altogether your own.' Then there would come a simple 'I' as a signature, and after that some further badinage respecting her 'Cerberus,' as she called her brother.

But after that word, that odious word, 'enticed,' there went another letter up to London of altogether another nature.

'I have changed my mind again,' she said, 'and have become aware that, though I should die in doing it,—though we should both die if it were possible,—there should be an end of everything between you and me. Yes, Frank; there! I send you back your troth, and demand my own in return. After all why should not one die;—hang oneself if it be necessary? To be self-denying is all that is necessary,—at any rate to a woman. Hanging or lying down and dying, or lingering on and saying one's prayers and knitting stockings, is altogether immaterial. I have sometimes thought Mudbury to be brutal to me, but I have never known him to be untrue,—or even, as I believe, mistaken. He sees clearly and knows what will happen. He tells me that I have enticed you back. I am not true as he is. So I threw him back the word in his teeth,—though its truth at the moment was going like a dagger through my heart. I know myself to have been selfish, unfeeling, unfeminine, when I induced you to surrender yourself to a mode of life which will make you miserable. I have sometimes been proud of myself because I have loved you so truly; but now I hate myself and despise myself because I have been incapable of the first effort which love should make. Love should at any rate be unselfish.

'He tells me that you will be miserable and that the misery will be on my head,—and I believe him. There shall be an end of it. I want no promise from you. There may, perhaps, be a time in which Imogene Docimer as a sturdy old maid shall be respected and serene of mind. As a wife who had enticed her husband to his misery she would be respected neither by him nor by herself,—and as for serenity it would be quite out of the question. I have been unfortunate. That is all;—but not half so unfortunate as others that I see around me.

'*Pray, pray,* PRAY, take this as final, and thus save me from renewed trouble and renewed agony.

'Now I am yours truly,
—'never again will I be affectionate to any one 'with true feminine love,

'IMOGENE DOCIMER.'

Houston when he received the above letter of course had no alternative but to declare that it could not possibly be regarded as having any avail. And indeed he had heart enough in his bosom to be warmed to something like true heat by such words as these. The cabbages and cradles ran up in his estimation. The small house at Pau, which in some of his more despondent moments had assumed an unqualified appearance of domestic discomfort, was now ornamented and accoutred till it seemed to be a little paradise. The very cabbages blossomed into roses, and the little babies in the cradles produced a throb of paternal triumph in his heart. If she were woman enough to propose to herself such an agony of devotion, could he not be man enough to demand from her a devotion of a different kind? As to Mudbury Docimer's truth, he believed in it not at all, but was quite convinced of the man's brutality.

Yes; she should hang herself—but it should be round his neck. The serenity should be displayed by her not as an aunt but as a wife and mother. As for enticing, did he not now,—just in this moment of his manly triumph,—acknowledge to himself that she had enticed him to his happiness, to his glory, to his welfare? In this frame of mind he wrote his answer as follows:—

'MY DEAREST,

'You have no power of changing your mind again. There must be some limit to vacillations, and that has been reached. Something must be fixed at last. Something has been fixed at last, and I most certainly shall not consent to any further unfixing. What right has Mudbury to pretend to know my feelings? or, for the matter of that, what right have you to accept his description of them? I tell you now that I place my entire happiness in the hope of making you my wife. I call upon you to ignore all the selfish declarations as to my own ideas which I have made in times past. The only right which you could now possibly have to separate yourself from me would come from your having ceased to love me. You do not pretend to say that such is the case; and therefore, with considerable indignation, but still very civilly, I desire that Mudbury with his hard-hearted counsels may go to the ——

'Enticed! Of course you have enticed me. I suppose that women do as a rule entice men, either to their advantage or disadvantage. I will leave it to you to say whether you believe that such enticement, if it be allowed its full scope, will lead to one or the other as far as I am concerned. I never was so happy as when I felt that you had enticed me back to the hopes of former days.

'Now I am yours, as always, and most affectionately,                    'FRANK HOUSTON.

'I shall expect the same word back from you by return of post scored under as eagerly as those futile "prays."'

Imogene when she received this was greatly disturbed,—not knowing how to carry herself in her great resolve,—or whether indeed that resolve must not be again abandoned. She had determined, should her lover's answer be as she had certainly intended it to be when she wrote her letter, to go at once to her brother and to declare to him that the danger was at an end, and that he might return to London without any fear of a relapse on her part. But she could not do so with such a reply as that she now held in her pocket. If that reply could, in very truth, be true, then there must be another revulsion, another change of purpose, another yielding to absolute joy. If it could be the case that Frank Houston no longer feared the dangers that he had feared before, if he had in truth reconciled himself to a state of things which he had once described as simple poverty, if he really placed his happiness on the continuation of his love, then,—then, why should she make the sacrifice? Why should she place such implicit confidence in her brother's infallibility against error, seeing that by doing so she would certainly shipwreck her own happiness,—and his too, if his words were to be trusted?

He called upon her to write to him again by return of post. She was to write to him and unsay those prayers, and comfort him with a repetition of that dear word which she had declared that she would never use again with all its true meaning. That was his express order to her. Should she obey it, or should she not obey it? Should she vacillate again, or should she leave his last letter unanswered with stern obduracy? She acknowledged to herself that it was a dear letter, deserving the best treatment at her hands, giving her lover credit, probably, for more true honesty than he deserved. What was the best treatment? Her brother had plainly shown his conviction that the best treatment would be to leave him without meddling with him any further. Her sister-in-law, though milder in her language, was, she feared, of the same opinion. Would it not be better for him not to be meddled with? Ought not that to be her judgment, looking at the matter all round?

She did not at any rate obey him at all points, for she left his letter in her pocket for three or four days, while she considered the matter backwards and forwards.

## CHAPTER LX

### AUNT ROSINA

DURING this period of heroism it had been necessary to Houston to have some confidential friend to whom from time to time he could speak of his purpose. He could not go on eating slices of boiled mutton at eating-houses, and drinking driblets of bad wine out of little decanters no bigger than the bottles in a cruet stand, without having some one to encourage him in his efforts. It was a hard apprenticeship, and, coming as it did rather late in life for such a beginning, and after much luxurious indulgence, required some sympathy and consolation. There were Tom Shuttlecock and Lord John Battledore at the club. Lord John was the man as to whose expulsion because of his contumacious language so much had been said, but who lived through that and various other dangers. These had been his special friends, and to them he had confided everything in regard to the Tringle marriage. Shuttlecock had ridiculed the very idea of love, and had told him that everything else was to be thrown to the dogs in pursuit of a good income. Battledore had reminded him that there was 'a deuced deal of cut-and-come-again in a hundred and twenty thousand pounds.' They had been friends, not always altogether after his own heart, but friends who had served his purpose when he was making his raid upon Lombard Street. But they were not men to whom

he could descant on the wholesomeness of cabbages
as an article of daily food, or who would sympathise
with the struggling joys of an embryo father. To
their thinking, women were occasionally very convenient as being the depositaries of some of the accru-
ing wealth of the world. Frank had been quite
worthy of their friendship as having 'spotted' and
nearly 'run down' for himself a well-laden city
heiress. But now Tom Shuttlecock and Lord John
Battledore were distasteful to him,—as would he be
to them. But he found the confidential friend in his
maiden aunt.

Miss Houston was an old lady,—older than her
time, as are some people,—who lived alone in a small
house in Green Street. She was particular in calling
it Green Street, Hyde Park. She was very anxious to
have it known that she never occupied it during the
months of August, September, and October,—though
it was often the case with her that she did not in
truth expatriate herself for more than six weeks. She
was careful to have a fashionable seat in a fashionable church. She dearly loved to see her name in the
papers when she was happy enough to be invited to a
house whose entertainments were chronicled. There
were a thousand little tricks,—I will not be harsh
enough to call them unworthy,—by which she served
Mammon.* But she did not limit her service to the
evil spirit. When in her place in church she sincerely
said her prayers. When in London, or out of it, she
gave a modicum of her slender income to the poor.
And, though she liked to see her name in the papers
as one of the fashionable world, she was a great
deal too proud of the blood of the Houstons to toady
any one or to ask for any favour. She was a neat,
clean, nice-looking old lady, who understood that if
economies were to be made in eating and drinking
they should be effected at her own table and not at
that of the servants who waited upon her. This was
the confidential friend whom Frank trusted in his
new career.

It must be explained that Aunt Rosina, as Miss Houston was called, had been well acquainted with her nephew's earlier engagement, and had approved of Imogene as his future wife. Then had come the unexpected collapse in the uncle's affairs, by which Aunt Rosina as well as others in the family had suffered,—and Frank, much to his aunt's displeasure, had allowed himself to be separated from the lady of his love on account of his comparative poverty. She had heard of Gertrude Tringle and all her money, but from a high standing of birth and social belongings had despised all the Tringles and all their money. To her, as a maiden lady, truth in love was everything. To her, as a well-born lady, good blood was everything. Therefore, though there had been no quarrel between her and Frank, there had been a cessation of sympathetic interest, and he had been thrown into the hands of the Battledores and Shuttlecocks. Now again the old sympathies were revived, and Frank found it convenient to drink tea with his aunt when other engagements allowed it.

'I call that an infernal interference,' he said to his aunt, showing her Imogene's letters.

'My dear Frank, you need not curse and swear,' said the old lady.

'Infernal is not cursing nor yet swearing.' Then Miss Houston, having liberated her mind by her remonstrance, proceeded to read the letter. 'I call that abominable,' said Frank, alluding of course to the allusions made in the letter to Mudbury Docimer.

'It is a beautiful letter;—just what I should have expected from Imogene. My dear, I will tell you what I propose. Remain as you are both of you for five years.'

'Five years. That's sheer nonsense.'

'Five years, my dear, will run by like a dream. Five years to look back upon is as nothing.'

'But these five years are five years to be looked forward to. It is out of the question.'

A.A.—28

'But you say that you could not live as a married man.'

'Live! I suppose we could live.' Then he thought of the cabbages and the cottage at Pau. 'There would be seven hundred a-year, I suppose.'

'Couldn't you do something, Frank?'

'What, to earn money? No; I don't think I could. If I attempted to break stones I shouldn't break enough to pay for the hammers.'

'Couldn't you write a book?'

'That would be worse than the stones. I sometimes thought I could paint a picture,—but, if I did, nobody would buy it. As to making money that is hopeless. I could save some, by leaving off gloves and allowing myself only three clean shirts a-week.'

'That would be dreadful, Frank.'

'It would be dreadful, but it is quite clear that I must do something. An effort has to be made.' This he said with a voice the tone of which was almost heroic. Then they discussed the matter at great length, in doing which Aunt Rosina thoroughly encouraged him in his heroism. That idea of remaining unmarried for another short period of five years was allowed to go by the board, and when they parted on that night it was understood that steps were to be taken to bring about a marriage as speedily as possible.

'Perhaps I can do a little to help,' said Aunt Rosina, in a faint whisper as Frank left the room.

Frank Houston, when he showed Imogene's letter to his aunt, had already answered it. Then he waited a day or two, not very patiently, for a further rejoinder from Imogene,—in which she of course was to unsay all that she had said before. But when, after four or five days, no rejoinder had come, and his fervour had been increased by his expectation, then he told his aunt that he should immediately take some serious step. The more ardent he was the better his aunt loved him. Could he have gone down and carried off his bride, and married her at once, in total disregard of the usual wedding-cake and St.-George's-Hanover-Square ceremonies*to which the Houston family had always been accustomed, she could have found it in her heart to forgive him. 'Do not be rash, Frank,' she said. He merely shook his head, and as he again left her declared that he was not going to be driven this way or that by such a fellow as Mudbury Docimer.

'As I live, there's Frank coming through the gate.' This was said by Imogene to her sister-in-law, as they were walking up and down the road which led from the lodge to the Tregothnan house. The two ladies were at that moment discussing Imogene's affairs. No rejoinder had as yet been made to Frank's last letter, which, to Imogene's feeling, was the most charming epistle which had ever come from the hands of a true lover. There had been passion and sincerity in every word of it;—even when he had been a little too strong in his language as he denounced the hard-hearted counsels of her brother. But yet she had not responded to all this sincerity, nor had she as yet withdrawn the resolution which she had herself declared. Mrs. Docimer was of opinion that that resolution should not be withdrawn, and had striven to explain that the circumstances were now the same as when, after full consideration, they had determined that the engagement should come to an end. At this very moment she was speaking words of wisdom to this effect, and as she did so Frank appeared, walking up from the gate.

'What will Mudbury say?' was Mrs. Docimer's first ejaculation. But Imogene, before she had considered how this danger might be encountered, rushed forward and gave herself up,—I fear we must confess,—into the arms of her lover. After that it was felt at once that she had withdrawn all her last resolution and had vacillated again. There was no ground left even for an argument now that she had submitted herself to be embraced. Frank's words of affection need not here be repeated, but they were of a nature to leave no doubt on the minds of either of the ladies.

Mudbury had declared that he would not receive Houston in his house as his sister's lover, and had expressed his opinion that even Houston would not have the face to show his face there. But Houston had come, and something must be done with him. It was soon ascertained that he had walked over from Penzance, which was but two miles off, and had left his portmanteau behind him. 'I wouldn't bring anything,' said he. 'Mudbury would find it easier to maltreat my things than myself. It would look so foolish to tell the man with a fly to carry them back at once. Is he in the house?'

'He is about the place,' said Mrs. Docimer, almost trembling.

'Is he very fierce against me?'

'He thinks it had better be all over.'

'I am of a different way of thinking, you see. I cannot acknowledge that he has any right to dictate to Imogene.'

'Nor can I,' said Imogene.

'Of course he can turn me out.'

'If he does I shall go with you,' said Imogene.

'We have made up our minds to it,' said Frank, 'and he had better let us do as we please. He can make himself disagreeable, of course; but he has got no power to prevent us.' Now they had reached the house, and Frank was of course allowed to enter. Had he not entered neither would Imogene, who was so much taken by this further instance of her lover's ardour that she was determined now to be led by him in everything. His explanation of that word 'enticed' had been so thoroughly satisfactory to her that she was no longer in the least angry with herself because she had enticed him. She had quite come to see that it is the duty of a young woman to entice a young man.

Frank and Imogene were soon left alone, not from any kindness of feeling on the part of Mrs. Docimer, but because the wife felt it necessary to find her husband. 'Oh, Mudbury, who do you think has come? He is here!'

'Houston?'

'Yes; Frank Houston!'

'In the house?'

'He is in the house. But he hasn't brought any- thing. He doesn't mean to stay.'

'What does that matter? He shall not be asked even to dine here.'

'If he is turned out she will go with him! If she says so she will do it. You cannot prevent her. That's what would come of it if she were to insist on going up to London with him.'

'He is a scoundrel!'

'No, Mudbury;—not a scoundrel. You cannot call him a scoundrel. There is something firm about him· isn't there?'

'To come to my house when I told him not?'

'But he does really love her.'

'Bother!'

'At any rate there they are in the breakfast-parlour, and something must be done. I couldn't tell him not to come in. And she wouldn't have come without him. There will be enough for them to live upon. Don't you think you'd better?' Docimer, as he re- turned to the house, declared that he 'did not think he'd better.' But he had to confess to himself that, whether it were better or whether it were worse, he could do very little to prevent it.

The greeting of the two men was anything but pleasant. 'What I have got to say I would rather say outside,' said Docimer.

'Certainly,' said Frank. 'I suppose I'm to be allowed to return?'

'If he does not,'—said Imogene, who at her brother's request had left the room, but still stood at the open door,—'if he does not I shall go to him in Penzance. You will hardly attempt to keep me a prisoner.'

'Who says that he is not to return? I think that you are two idiots, but I am quite aware that I cannot prevent you from being married if you are both determined.' Then he led the way out through the hall, and Frank followed him. 'I cannot understand that any man should be so fickle,' he said, when they were both out on the walk together.

'Constant, I should suppose you mean.'

'I said fickle, and I meant it. It was at your own suggestion that you and Imogene were to be separated.'

'No doubt; it was at my suggestion, and with her consent. But you see that we have changed our minds.'

'And will change them again.'

'We are steady enough in our purpose now, at any rate. You hear what she says. If I came down here to persuade her to alter her purpose,—to talk her into doing something of which you disapproved, and as to which she agreed with you,—then you might do something by quarrelling with me. But what's the use of it, when she and I are of one mind? You know that you cannot talk her over.'

'Where do you mean to live?'

'I'll tell you all about that if you'll allow me to send into Penzance for my things. I cannot discuss matters with you if you proclaim yourself to be my enemy. You say we are both idiots.'

'I do.'

'Very well. Then you had better put up with two idiots. You can't cure their idiocy. Nor have you any authority to prevent them from exhibiting it.' The argument was efficacious though the idiocy was acknowledged. The portmanteau was sent for, and before the evening was over Frank had again been received at Tregothnan as Imogene's accepted lover.

Then Frank had his story to tell and his new proposition to make. Aunt Rosina had offered to join her means with his. The house in Green Street, no doubt, was small, but room it was thought could be

made, at any rate till the necessity had come for
various cribs and various cradles. 'I cannnot
imagine that you will endure to live with Aunt
Rosina,' said the brother.

'Why on earth should I object to Aunt Rosina?'
said Imogene. 'She and I have always been friends.'
In her present mood she would hardly have objected
to live with any old woman, however objectionable.
'And we shall be able to have a small cottage somewhere,' said Frank. 'She will keep the house in
London, and we shall keep the cottage.'

'And what on earth will you do with yourself?'

'I have thought of that too,' said Frank. 'I shall
take to painting pictures in earnest;—portraits
probably. I don't see why I shouldn't do as well as
anybody else.'

'That head of yours of old Mrs. Jones,' said Imogene, 'was a great deal better than dozens of things
one sees every year in the Academy.'

'Bother!' exclaimed Docimer.

'I don't see why he should not succeed, if he really
will work hard,' said Mrs. Docimer.

'Bother!'

'Why should it be bother?' said Frank, put upon
his mettle. 'Ever so many fellows have begun and
have got on, older than I am. And, even if I don't
earn anything, I've got an employment.'

'And is the painting-room to be in Green Street
also?' asked Docimer.

'Just at present I shall begin by copying things at
the National Gallery,' explained Houston, who was
not as yet prepared with his answer to that difficulty
as to a studio in the little house in Green Street.

When the matter had been carried as far as this
it was manifest enough that anything like opposition to Imogene's marriage was to be withdrawn.
Houston remained at Tregothnan for a couple of
days and then returned to London. A week afterwards the Docimers followed him, and early in the
following June the two lovers, after all their troubles

and many vacillations, were made one at St. George's
church, to the great delight of Aunt Rosina. It cannot be said that the affair gave equal satisfaction to
all the bridegroom's friends, as may be learnt from
the following narration of two conversations which
took place in London very shortly after the wedding.

'Fancy after all that fellow Houston going and
marrying such a girl as Imogene Docimer, without
a single blessed shilling to keep themselves alive.'
This was said in the smoking-room of Houston's
club by Lord John Battledore to Tom Shuttlecock;
but it was said quite aloud, so that Houston's various
acquaintances might be enabled to offer their remarks on so interesting a subject; and to express
their pity for the poor object of their commiseration.

'It's the most infernal piece of folly I ever heard in
my life,' said Shuttlecock. 'There was that Tringle
girl with two hundred thousand pounds*to be had
just for the taking;—Traffick's wife's sister, you
know.'

'There was something wrong about that,' said
another. 'Benjamin Batsby, that stupid fellow who
used to be in the twentieth, ran off with her just
when everything had been settled between Houston
and old Tringle.'

'Not a bit of it,' said Battledore. 'Tringle had
quarrelled with Houston before that. Batsby did go
with her, but the governor wouldn't come down with
the money. Then the girl was brought back and
there was no marriage.' Upon that the condition of
poor Gertrude in reference to her lovers and her
fortune was discussed by those present with great
warmth; but they all agreed that Houston had
proved himself to be a bigger fool than any of them
had expected.

'By George, he's going to set up for painting
portraits,' said Lord John, with great disgust.

In Queen's Gate the matter was discussed by the
ladies there very much in the same spirit. At this
time Gertrude was engaged to Captain Batsby, if not

with the full approbation at any rate with the consent both of her father and mother, and therefore she could speak of Frank Houston and his bride, if with disdain, still without wounded feelings. 'Here it is in the papers, Francis Houston and Imogene Docimer,' said Mrs. Traffick.

'So she has really caught him at last!' said Gertrude.

'There was not much to catch,' rejoined Mrs. Traffick. 'I doubt whether they have got £500 a year between them.'

'It does seem so very sudden,' said Lady Tringle.

'Sudden!' said Gertrude. 'They have been about it for the last five years. Of course he has tried to wriggle out of it all through. I am glad that she has succeeded at last, if only because he deserves it.'

'I wonder where they'll find a place to live in,' said Augusta. This took place in the bedroom which Mrs. Traffick still occupied in Queen's Gate, when she had been just a month a mother.

Thus, with the kind assistance of Aunt Rosina, Frank Houston and Imogene Docimer were married at last, and the chronicler hereby expresses a hope that it may not be long before Frank may see a picture of his own hanging on the walls of the Academy, and that he may live to be afraid of the coming of no baby.

## CHAPTER LXI

### TOM TRINGLE GOES UPON HIS TRAVELS

WE must again go back and pick up our threads to April, having rushed forward to be present at the wedding of Frank Houston and Imogene Docimer, which did not take place till near Midsummer. This we must do at once in regard to Tom Tringle, who, if the matter be looked at aright, should be regarded as the hero of this little history. Ayala indeed, who is no doubt the real heroine among so many young ladies who have been more or less heroic, did not find in him the angel of whom she had dreamed, and whose personal appearance on earth was necessary to her happiness. But he had been able very clearly to pick out an angel for himself, and, though he had failed in his attempts to take the angel home with him, had been constant in his endeavours as long as there remained to him a chance of success. He had shown himself to be foolish, vulgar, and ignorant. He had given way to Bolivian champagne and Faddle intimacies. He had been silly enough to think that he could bribe his Ayala with diamonds for herself, and charm her with cheaper jewelry on his own person. He had thought to soar high by challenging his rival to a duel, and had then been tempted by pot courage to strike him in the streets. A very vulgar and foolish young man! But a young man capable of a persistent passion! Young men not foolish and not vulgar are, perhaps, common enough. But the young men of constant heart and capable of such persistency as Tom's are not to be found every day walking about the streets of the metropolis. Jonathan Stubbs was constant, too; but it may be doubted whether the Colonel ever really despaired. The merit is to despair and yet to be constant. When a man has reason to be assured that a young lady is very fond of him, he may always hope that love will follow,—unless indeed the love which he seeks has been already given away elsewhere. Moreover, Stubbs had many substantial supports at his back; the relationship of the Marchesa, the friendship of Lady Albury, the comforts of Stalham,—and not least, if last, the capabilities and prowess of Croppy. Then, too, he was neither vulgar nor foolish nor ignorant. Tom Tringle had everything against him,—everything that would weigh with Ayala; and yet he fought his battle out to the last gasp. Therefore, I desire my hearers to regard Tom Tringle as the hero of the transactions with which they have been concerned, and to throw their old shoes after him as he starts away upon his grand tour.

'Tom, my boy, you have to go, you know, in four days,' said his father to him. At this time Tom had as yet given no positive consent as to his departure. He had sunk into a low state of moaning and groaning, in which he refused even to accede to the doctrine of the expediency of a manly bearing. 'What's the good of telling a lie about it?' he would say to his mother. 'What's the good of manliness when a fellow would rather be drowned?' He had left his bed indeed, and had once or twice sauntered out of the house. He had been instigated by his sister to go down to his club, under the idea that by such an effort he would shake off the despondency which overwhelmed him. But he had failed in the attempts, and had walked by the doors of the Mountaineers, finding himself unable to face the hall-porter. But still the preparations for his departure were going on. It was presumed that he was to leave London for Liverpool on the Friday, and his father had now visited him in his own room on the Tuesday evening with the intention of extorting from him his final consent. Sir Thomas had on that morning expressed himself very freely to his son-in-law Mr. Traffick, and on returning home had been glad to find that his words had been of avail, at any rate as regarded the dinner-hour. He was tender-hearted towards his son, and disposed to tempt him rather than threaten him into obedience.

'I haven't ever said I would go,' replied Tom.

'But you must, you know. Everything has been packed up, and I want to make arrangements with you about money. I have got a cabin for you to yourself, and Captain Merry says that you will have a very pleasant passage. The equinoxes are over.'

'I don't care about the equinoxes,' said Tom. 'I should like bad weather if I am to go.'

'Perhaps you may have a touch of that, too.'

'If the ship could be dashed against a rock I should prefer it!' exclaimed Tom.

'That's nonsense. The Cunard ships never are

dashed against rocks.* By the time you've been three days at sea you'll be as hungry as a hunter. Now, Tom, how about money?'

'I don't care about money,' said Tom.

'Don't you? Then you're very unlike anybody else that I meet. I think I had better give you power to draw at New York, San Francisco, Yokohama, Pekin, and Calcutta.'

'Am I to go to Pekin?' asked Tom, with renewed melancholy.

'Well, yes;—I think so. You had better see what the various houses are doing in China. And then from Calcutta you can go up the country. By that time I dare say we shall have possession of Cabul. With such a government as we have now, thank God! the Russians will have been turned pretty nearly out of Asia by this time next year.'[1]*

'Am I to be away more than a year?'

'If I were you,' said the father, glad to catch the glimmer of assent which was hereby implied,—'if I were you I would do it thoroughly whilst I was about it. Had I seen so much when I was young I should have been a better man of business.'

'It's all the same to me,' said Tom. 'Say ten years, if you like it! Say twenty! I shan't ever want to come back again. Where am I to go after Cabul?'

'I didn't exactly fix it that you should go to Cabul. Of course you will write home and give me your own opinion as you travel on. You will stay two or three months probably in the States.'

'Am I to go to Niagara?' he asked.

'Of course you will, if you wish it. The Falls of Niagara, I am told, are very wonderful.'

'If a man is to drown himself,' said Tom, 'it's the sort of place to do it effectually.'

'Oh, Tom!' exclaimed his father. 'Do not speak to me in that way when I am doing everything in my power to help you in your trouble!'

'You cannot help me,' said Tom.

---

[1] It has to be stated that this story was written in 1878.

'Circumstances will. Time will do it. Employment will do it. A sense of your dignity as a man will do it, when you find yourself amongst others who know nothing of what you have suffered. You revel in your grief now because those around you know that you have failed. All that will be changed when you are with strangers. You should not talk to your father of drowning yourself!'

'That was wrong. I know it was wrong,' said Tom, humbly. 'I won't do it if I can help it,—but perhaps I had better not go there. And how long ought I to stay at Yokohama? Perhaps you had better put it all down on a bit of paper.' Then Sir Thomas endeavoured to explain to him that all that he said now was in the way of advice. That it would be in truth left to himself to go almost where he liked, and to stay at each place almost as long as he liked;— that he would be his own master, and that within some broad and undefined limits he would have as much money as he pleased to spend. Surely no preparations for a young man's tour were ever made with more alluring circumstances! But Tom could not be tempted into any expression of satisfaction.

This, however, Sir Thomas did gain,—that before he left his son's room it was definitely settled,—that Tom should take his departure on the Friday, going down to Liverpool by an afternoon train on that day. 'I tell you what,' said Sir Thomas; 'I'll go down with you, see you on board the ship, and introduce you to Captain Merry. I shall be glad of an opportunity of paying a visit to Liverpool.' And so the question of Tom's departure was settled.

On the Wednesday and Thursday he seemed to take some interest in his bags and portmanteaus, and began himself to look after those assuagements of the toils of travel which are generally dear to young men. He interested himself in a fur coat, in a well-arranged despatch box, and in a very neat leathern case which was intended to hold two brandy flasks. He consented to be told of the number of his shirts,

and absolutely expressed an opinion that he should
want another pair of dress-boots. When this occurred
every female bosom in the house, from Lady Tringle's
down to the kitchenmaid's, rejoiced at the signs of
recovery which evinced themselves. But neither
Lady Tringle nor the kitchenmaid, nor did any of the
intermediate female bosoms, know how he employed
himself when he left the house on that Thursday
afternoon. He walked across the Park, and, calling
at Kingsbury Crescent, left a note addressed to his
aunt. It was as follows:—'I start to-morrow afternoon,—I hardly know whither. It may be for years
or it may be for ever. I should wish to say a word to
Ayala before I go. Will she see me if I come at
twelve o'clock exactly to-morrow morning? I will
call for an answer in half-an-hour. T.T., junior. Of
course I am aware that Ayala is to become the bride
of Colonel Jonathan Stubbs.' In half-an-hour he
returned, and got his answer. 'Ayala will be glad
to have an opportunity of saying good-bye to you to-
morrow morning.'

From this it will be seen that Ayala had at that
time returned from Stalham to Kingsbury Crescent.
She had come back joyful in heart, thoroughly
triumphant as to her angel, with everything in the
world sweet and happy before her,—desirous if
possible to work her fingers off in mending the family
linen, if only she could do something for somebody
in return for all the joy that the world was giving
her. When she was told that Tom wished to see her
for the last time,—for the last time at any rate before
her marriage,—she assented at once. 'I think you
should see him as he asks it,' said her aunt.

'Poor Tom! Of course I will see him.' And so the
note was written which Tom received when he called
the second time at the door.

At half-past eleven he skulked out of the house in
Queen's Gate, anxious to avoid his mother and
sisters, who were on their side anxious to devote every
remaining minute of the time to his comfort and

welfare. I am afraid it must be acknowledged that he went with all his jewelry. It could do no good. At last he was aware of that. But still he thought that she would like him better with his jewelry than without it. Stubbs wore no gems, not even a ring, and Ayala when she saw her cousin enter the room could only assure herself that the male angels certainly were never be-jewelled. She was alone in the drawing-room, Mrs. Dosett having arranged that at the expiration of ten minutes, which were to be allowed to Tom for his private adieux, she would come down to say good-bye to her nephew. 'Ayala!' said Tom.

'So you are going away,—for a very long journey, Tom.'

'Yes, Ayala; for a very long journey; to Pekin and Cabul, if I live through to get to those sort of places.'

'I hope you will live through, Tom.'

'Thank you, Ayala. Thank you. I dare say I shall. They tell me I shall get over it. I don't feel like getting over it now.'

'You'll find some beautiful young lady at Pekin, perhaps.'

'Beauty will never have any effect upon me again, Ayala. Beauty indeed! Think what I have suffered from beauty! From the first moment in which you came down to Glenbogie I have been a victim to it. It has destroyed me,—destroyed me!'

'I am sure you will come back quite well,' said Ayala, hardly knowing how to answer the last appeal.

'Perhaps I may. If I can only get my heart to turn to stone, then I shall. I don't know why I should have been made to care so much about it. Other people don't.'

'And now we must say, Good-bye, I suppose.'

'Oh, yes;—good-bye! I did want to say one or two words if you ain't in a hurry. Of course you'll be his bride now.'

'I hope so,' said Ayala.

'I take that for granted. Of course I hate him.'

'Oh, Tom; you shan't say that.'

'It's human nature! I can tell a lie if you want it.
I'd do anything for you. But you may tell him this:
I'm very sorry I struck him.'

'He knows that, Tom. He has said so to me.'

'He behaved well to me,—very well,—as he always
does to everybody.'

'Now, Tom, that is good of you. I do like you so
much for saying that.'

'But I hate him!'

'No!'

'The evil spirits always hate the good ones. I am
conscious of an evil spirit within my bosom. It is
because my spirit is evil that you would not love me.
He is good, and you love him.'

'Yes; I do,' said Ayala.

'And now we will change the conversation. Ayala,
I have got a little present which you must take from
me.'

'Oh, no!' said Ayala, thinking of the diamond
necklace.

'It's only a little thing,—and I hope you will.'
Then he brought out from his pocket a small brooch
which he had selected from his own stock of jewelry
for the occasion. 'We are cousins, you know.'

'Yes, we are cousins,' said Ayala, accepting the
brooch, but still accepting it unwillingly.

'He must be very disdainful if he would object to
such a little thing as this,' said Tom, referring to the
Colonel.

'He is not at all disdainful. He will not object in
the least. I am sure of that, Tom. I will take it then,
and I will wear it sometimes as a memento that we
have parted like friends,—as cousins should do.'

'Yes, as friends,' said Tom, who thought that even
that word was softer to his ear than cousins. Then
he took her by the hand and looked into her face
wistfully, thinking what might be the effect if for the
last and for the first time he should snatch a kiss.
Had he done so I think she would have let it pass
without rebuke under the guise of cousinship. It

would have been very disagreeable;—but then he
was going away for so long a time, for so many miles!
But at the moment Mrs. Dosett came in, and Ayala
was saved. 'Good-bye,' he said; 'good-bye,' and
without waiting to take the hand which his aunt
offered him he hurried out of the room, out of the
house, and back across the Gardens to Queen's Gate.

At Queen's Gate there was an early dinner, at
three o'clock, at which Sir Thomas did not appear,
as he had arranged to come out of the city and meet
his son at the railway station. There were, therefore,
sitting at the board for the last time the mother and
the two sisters with the intending traveller. 'Oh,
Tom,' said Lady Tringle, as soon as the servant had
left them together, 'I do so hope you will recover.'

'Of course he will recover,' said Augusta.

'Why shouldn't he recover?' asked Gertrude. 'It's
all in a person's mind. If he'd only make up his
mind not to think about her the thing would be done,
and there would be nothing the matter with him.'

'There are twenty others, ever so much better
than Ayala, would have him to-morrow,' said his
mother.

'And be glad to catch him,' said Gertrude. 'He's
not like one of those who haven't got anything to
make a wife comfortable with.'

'As for Ayala,' said Augusta, 'she didn't deserve
such good luck. I am told that that Colonel Stubbs
can't afford to keep any kind of carriage for her.
But then, to be sure, she has never been used to a
carriage.'

'Oh, Tom, do look up,' said his mother, 'and say
that you will try to be happy.'

'He'll be all right in New York,' said Gertrude.
'There's no place in the world, they say, where the
girls put themselves forward so much, and make
things so pleasant for the young men.'*

'He will soon find some one there,' said Augusta,
'with a good deal more to say for herself than Ayala,
and a great deal better-looking.'

'I hope he will find some one who will really love him,' said his mother.

Tom sat silent while he listened to all this encouragement, turning his face from one speaker to the other. It was continued, with many other similar promises of coming happiness, and assurances that he had been a gainer in losing all that he had lost, when he suddenly turned sharply upon them, and strongly expressed his feelings to his sisters. 'I don't believe that either of you know anything about it,' he said.

'Don't know anything about what?' said Augusta, who, as a lady who had been married over twelve months and was soon about to become a mother, felt that she certainly did know all about it.

'Why don't we know as well as you?' asked Gertrude, who had also had her experiences.

'I don't believe you do know anything about it;— that's all,' said Tom. 'And now there's the cab. Good-bye, mother! Good-bye, Augusta. I hope you'll be all right.' This alluded to the baby. 'Good-bye, Gertrude. I hope you'll get all right too some day.' This alluded to Gertrude's two lovers. Then he left them, and as he got into his cab declared to himself that neither of them had ever, or would ever, know anything of that special trouble which had so nearly overwhelmed himself.

'Upon my word, Tom,' said his father, walking about the vessel with him, 'I wish I were going to New York myself with you;—it all looks so comfortable.'

'Yes,' said Tom, 'it's very nice.'

'You'll enjoy yourself amazingly. There is that Mrs. Thompson has two as pretty daughters with her as ever a man wished to see.' Tom shook his head. 'And you're fond of smoking. Did you see the smoking-room? They've got everything on board these ships now. Upon my word I envy you the voyage.'

'It's as good as anything else, I dare say,' said Tom. 'Perhaps it's better than London.'

Then his father, who had been speaking aloud to him, whispered a word in his ear. 'Shake yourself, Tom;—shake yourself, and get over it.'

'I am trying,' said Tom.

'Love is a very good thing, Tom, when a man can enjoy it, and make himself warm with it, and protect himself by it from selfishness and hardness of heart. But when it knocks a man's courage out of him, and makes him unfit for work, and leaves him to bemoan himself, there's nothing good in it. It's as bad as drink. Don't you know that I am doing the best I can for you, to make a man of you?'

'I suppose so.'

'Then shake yourself, as I call it. It is to be done, if you set about it in earnest. Now, God bless you, my boy.' Then Sir Thomas got into his boat, and left his son to go upon his travels and get himself cured by a change of scene.

I have no doubt that Tom was cured, if not before he reached New York, at any rate before he left that interesting city;—so that when he reached Niagara, which he did do in company with Mrs. Thompson and her charming daughters, he entertained no idea of throwing himself down the Falls. We cannot follow him on that prolonged tour to Japan and China, and thence to Calcutta and Bombay. I fancy that he did not go on to Cabul, as before that time the Ministry in England was unfortunately changed, and the Russians had not as yet been expelled from Asia;*—but I have little doubt that he obtained a great deal of very useful mercantile information, and that he will live to have a comfortable wife and a large family, and become in the course of years the senior partner in the great house of Travers and Treason. Let us, who have soft hearts, now throw our old shoes after him.

## CHAPTER LXII

### HOW VERY MUCH HE LOVED HER

WE have seen how Mr. Traffick was finally turned out of his father-in-law's house;—or, rather, not quite finally when we last saw him, as he continued to sleep at Queen's Gate for two or three nights after that, until he had found shelter for his head. This he did without encountering Sir Thomas, Sir Thomas pretending the while to believe that he was gone; and then in very truth his last pair of boots was removed. But his wife remained, awaiting the great occurrence with all the paternal comforts around her, Mr. Traffick having been quite right in surmising that the father would not expose his daughter in her delicate condition to the inclemencies of the weather.

But this no more than natural attention on the part of the father and grandfather to the needs of his own daughter and grandchild did not in the least mitigate in the bosom of the Member of Parliament the wrath which he felt at his own expulsion. It was not, as he said to himself, the fact that he was expelled, but the coarseness of the language used. 'The truth is,' he said to a friend in the House, 'that, though it was arranged that I should remain there till after my wife's confinement, I could not bear his language.' It will probably be acknowledged that the language was of a nature not to be borne.

When, therefore, Captain Batsby went down to the House on the day of Tom's departure to see his counsellor he found Mr. Traffick full rather of anger than of counsel. 'Oh, yes,' said the Member, walking with the Captain up and down some of the lobbies, 'I spoke to him, and told him my mind very freely. When I say I'll do a thing, I always do it. And as for Tringle, nobody knows him better than I. It does not do to be afraid of him. There is a little bit of the cur about him.'

'What did he say?'

'He didn't like it. The truth is——. You know I don't mind speaking to you openly.'

'Oh, no,' said Batsby.

'He thinks he ought to do as well with the second girl as he has done with the first.' Captain Batsby at this opened his eyes, but he said nothing. Having a good income of his own, he thought much of it. Not being the younger son of a lord, and not being a Member of Parliament, he thought less of the advantages of those high privileges. It did not suit him, however, to argue the question at the present moment. 'He is proud of his connection with our family, and looks perhaps even more than he ought to do to a seat in the House.'

'I could get in myself if I cared for it,' said Batsby.

'Very likely. It is more difficult than ever to find a seat just now. A family connection of course does help one. I had to trust to that a good deal before I was known myself.'

'But what did Sir Thomas say?'

'He made himself uncommonly disagreeable;—I can tell you that. He couldn't very well abuse me, but he wasn't very particular in what he said about you. Of course he was cut up about the elopement. We all felt it. Augusta was very much hurt. In her precarious state it was so likely to do a mischief.'

'It can't be undone now.'

'No;—it can't be undone. But it makes one feel that you can't make a demand for money as though you set about it in the other way. When I made up my mind to marry I stated what I thought I had a right to demand, and I got it. He knew very well that I shouldn't take a shilling less. It does make a difference when he knows very well that you've got to marry the girl whether with or without money.'

'I haven't got to marry the girl at all.'

'Haven't you? I rather think you have, old fellow. It is generally considered that when a gentleman has gone off with a girl he means to marry her.'

'Not if the father comes after her and brings her back.'

'And when he has gone afterwards to the family house and proposed himself again in the mother's presence.' In all this Mr. Traffick had received an unfair advantage from the communications which were made to him by his wife. 'Of course you must marry her. Sir Thomas knows that, and, knowing it, why should he be flush with his money? I never allowed myself to say a single word they could use against me till the ready-money-down had been all settled.'

'What was it he did say?' Batsby was thoroughly sick of hearing his counsellor tell so many things as to his own prudence and his own success, and asked the question in an angry tone.

'He said that he would not consider the question of money at all till the marriage had been solemnised. Of course he stands on his right. Why shouldn't he? But, rough as he is, he isn't stingy. Give him his due. He isn't stingy. The money's there all right; and the girl is his own child. You'll have to wait his time;—that's all.'

'And have nothing to begin with?'

'That'll be about it, I think. But what does it matter, Batsby? You are always talking about your income.'

'No, I ain't; not half so much as you do of your seat in Parliament,—which everybody says you are likely to lose at the next election.' Then, of course, there was a quarrel. Mr. Traffick took his offended dignity back to the House,—almost doubting whether it might not be his duty to bring Captain Batsby to the bar for contempt of privilege; and the Captain took himself off in thorough disgust.

Nevertheless there was the fact that he had engaged himself to the young lady a second time. He had run away with her with the object of marrying her, and had then, according to his own theory in such matters,—been relieved from his responsibility

by the appearance of the father and the re-abduction
of the young lady. As the young lady had been taken
away from him it was to be supposed that the intended marriage was negatived by a proper authority.
When starting for Brussels he was a free man; and
had he been wise he would have remained there, or at
some equally safe distance from the lady's charms.
Then, from a distance, he might have made his demand for money, and the elopement would have
operated in his favour rather than otherwise. But
he had come back, and had foolishly allowed himself
to be persuaded to show himself at Queen's Gate. He
had obeyed Traffick's advice, and now Traffick had
simply thrown him over and quarrelled with him.
He had too promised, in the presence both of the
mother and the married sister, that he would marry
the young lady without any regard to money. He
felt it all and was very angry with himself, consoling himself as best he might with the reflection
that Sir Thomas's money was certainly safe, and that
Sir Thomas himself was a liberal man. In his present
condition it would be well for him, he thought, to
remain inactive and see what circumstances would
do for him.

But circumstances very quickly became active.
On his return to his lodgings, after leaving Mr.
Traffick, he found a note from Queen's Gate.
'Dearest Ben,—Mamma wants you to come and
lunch to-morrow. Papa has taken poor Tom down to
Liverpool, and won't be back till dinner-time.—G.'
He did not do as he was bid, alleging some engagement of business. But the persecution was continued
in such a manner as to show him that all opposition
on his part would be hopeless unless he were to
proceed on some tour as prolonged as that of his
future brother-in-law. 'Come and walk at three
o'clock in Kensington Gardens to-morrow.' This was
written on the Saturday after his note had been
received. What use would there be in continuing a
vain fight? He was in their hands, and the more

gracefully he yielded the more probable it would be
that the father would evince his generosity at an
early date. He therefore met his lady-love on the
steps of the Albert Memorial,* whither she had managed to take herself all alone from the door of the
family mansion.

'Ben,' she said, as she greeted him, 'why did you
not come for me to the house?'

'I thought you would like it best.'

'Why should I like it best? Of course mamma
knows all about it. Augusta would have come with
me just to see me here, only that she cannot walk out
just at present.' Then he said something to her about
the Monument, expressed his admiration of the
Prince's back, abused the east wind, remarked that
the buds were coming on some of the trees, and
suggested that the broad road along by the Round
Pond would be drier than the little paths. It was not
interesting, as Gertrude felt; but she had not expected him to be interesting. The interest she knew
must be contributed by herself. 'Ben,' she said, 'I
was so happy to hear what you said to mamma the
other day.'

'What did I say?'

'Why, of course, that, as papa has given his consent, our engagement is to go on just as if——'

'Just as if what?'

'As if we had found the clergyman at Ostend.'

'If we had done that we should have been married
now,' suggested Batsby.

'Exactly. And it's almost as good as being married;—isn't it?

'I suppose it comes to the same thing.'

'Hadn't you better go to papa again and have it
all finished?'

'He makes himself so very unpleasant.'

'That's only because he wants to punish us for
running away. I suppose it was wrong. I shall never
be sorry, because it made me know how very, very
much you loved me. Didn't it make you feel how

very, very dearly I loved you,—to trust myself all alone with you in that way?'

'Oh, yes; of course.'

'And papa can't bite you, you know. You go to him, and tell him that you hope to be received in the house as my,—my future husband, you know.'

'Shall I say nothing else?'

'You mean about the day?'

'I was meaning about money.'

'I don't think I would. He is very generous, but he does not like to be asked. When Augusta was to be married he arranged all that himself after they were engaged.'

'But Traffick demanded a certain sum?' This question Captain Batsby asked with considerable surprise, remembering what Mr. Traffick had said to him in reference to Augusta's fortune.

'Not at all. Septimus knew nothing about it till after the engagement. He was only too glad to get papa's consent. You mustn't believe all that Septimus says, you know. You may be sure of this,—that you can trust papa's generosity.' Then, before he landed her at the door in Queen's Gate, he had promised that he would make another journey to Lombard Street, with the express purpose of obtaining Sir Thomas's sanction to the marriage,— either with or without money.

'How are you again?' said Sir Thomas, when the Captain was for the third time shown into the little back parlour. 'Have you had another trip to the continent since I saw you?' Sir Thomas was in a good humour. Tom had gone upon his travels; Mr. Traffick had absolutely taken himself out of the house; and the millions were accommodating themselves comfortably.

'No, Sir Thomas; I haven't been abroad since then. I don't keep on going abroad constantly in that way.'

'And what can I do for you now?'

'Of course it's about your daughter. I want to have your permission to consider ourselves engaged.'

'I explained to you before that if you and Gertrude choose to marry each other I shall not stand in your way.'

'Thank you, Sir.'

'I don't know that it is much to thank me for. Only that she made a fool of herself by running away with you I should have preferred to wait till some more sensible candidate had proposed himself for her hand. I don't suppose you'll ever set the Thames on fire.'

'I did very well in the army.'

'It's a pity you did not remain there, and then, perhaps, you would not have gone to Ostend with my daughter. As it is, there she is. I think she might have done better with herself; but that is her fault. She has made her bed and she must lie upon it.'

'If we are to be married I hope you won't go on abusing me always, Sir Thomas.'

'That's as you behave. You didn't suppose that I should allow such a piece of tomfoolery as that to be passed over without saying anything about it! If you marry her and behave well to her I will——' Then he paused.

'What will you do, Sir Thomas?'

'I'll say as little as possible about the Ostend journey.'

'And as to money, Sir Thomas?'

'I think I have promised quite enough for you. You are not in a position, Captain Batsby, to ask me as to money;—nor is she. You shall marry her without a shilling,—or you shall not marry her at all. Which is it to be? I must have an end put to all this. I won't have you hanging about my house unless I know the reason why. Are you two engaged to each other?'

'I suppose we are,' said Batsby, lugubriously.

'Suppose is not enough.'

'We are,' said Batsby, courageously.

'Very well. Then, from this moment, Ostend shall be as though there weren't such a seaport anywhere

in Europe. I will never allude to the place again,—
unless, perhaps, you should come and stay with me
too long when I am particularly anxious to get rid
of you. Now you had better go and settle about the
time and all that with Lady Tringle, and tell her that
you mean to come and dine to-morrow or next day,
or whenever it suits. Come and dine as often as you
please, only do not bring your wife to live with me
pertinaciously when you're not asked.' All this
Captain Batsby did not understand, but, as he left
Lombard Street, he made up his mind that of all the
men he had ever met, Sir Thomas Tringle, his future
father-in-law, was the most singular. 'He's a better
fellow than Traffick,' said Sir Thomas to himself
when he was alone, 'and as he has trusted me so far
I'll not throw him over.'

    The Captain now had no hesitation in taking him-
self to Queen's Gate. As he was to be married he
might as well make the best of such delights as were
to be found in the happy state of mutual affection.
'My dear, dearest Benjamin, I am so happy,' said
Lady Tringle, dissolved in tears as she embraced her
son-in-law that was to be. 'You will always be so
dear to me!' In this she was quite true. Traffick
was not dear to her. She had at first thought much
of Mr. Traffick's position and noble blood, but, of
late, she too had become very tired of Mr. Traffick.
Augusta took almost too much upon herself, and
Mr. Traffick's prolonged presence had been an eyesore.
Captain Batsby was softer, and would be much more
pleasant as a son-in-law. Even the journey to Ostend
had had a good effect in producing a certain humility.

    'My dear Benjamin,' said Augusta, 'we shall
always be so happy to entertain you as a brother.
Mr. Traffick has a great regard for you, and said
from the first that if you behaved as you ought to do
after that little journey he would arrange that
everything should go straight between you and papa.
I was quite sure that you would come forward at
once as a man.'

But Gertrude's delight was, of course, the strongest, and Gertrude's welcoming the warmest,—as was proper. 'When I think of it,' she said to him, 'I don't know how I should ever have looked anybody in the face again,—after our going away with our things mixed up in that way.'

'I am glad rather now that we didn't find the clergyman.'

'Oh, certainly,' said Gertrude. ' I don't suppose anybody would have given me anything. Now there'll be a regular wedding, and, of course, there will be the presents.'

'And, though nothing is to be settled, I suppose he will do something.'

'And it would have been very dreadful, not having a regular trousseau,' said Gertrude. 'Mamma will, of course, do now just as she did about Augusta. He allowed her £300! Only think;—if we had been married at Ostend you would have had to buy things for me before the first month was out. I hadn't more than half-a-dozen pair of stockings with me.'

'He can't but say now that we have done as he would have us,' added the Captain. 'I do suppose that he will not be so unnatural as not to give something when Augusta had £200,000.'

'Indeed, she had not. But you'll see that sooner or later papa will do for me quite as well as for Augusta.' In this way they were happy together, consoling each other for any little trouble which seemed for a while to cloud their joys, and basking in the full sunshine of their permitted engagement.

The day was soon fixed, but fixed not entirely in reference to the wants of Gertrude and her wedding. Lucy had also to be married from the same house, and the day for her marriage had already been arranged. Sir Thomas had ordered that everything should be done for Lucy as though she were a daughter of the house, and her wedding had been arranged for the last week in May. When he heard that Ayala and Colonel Stubbs were also engaged he

was anxious that the two sisters should be 'buckled,'
as he called it, on the same occasion,—and he
magnanimously offered to take upon himself the
entire expense of the double arrangement, intimating
that the people in Kingsbury Crescent had hardly
room enough for a wedding. But Ayala, acting
probably under Stalham influences, would not consent to this. Lady Albury, who was now in London,
was determined that Ayala's marriage should take
place from her own house; and, as Aunt Margaret
and Uncle Reginald had consented, that matter was
considered as settled. But Sir Thomas, having fixed
his mind upon a double wedding, resolved that
Gertrude and Lucy should be the joint brides.
Gertrude, who still suffered perhaps a little in public
estimation from the Ostend journey, was glad enough
to wipe out that stain as quickly as possible, and
did not therefore object to the arrangement. But to
the Captain there was something in it by which his
more delicate feelings were revolted. It was a matter
of course that Ayala should be present at her sister's
wedding, and would naturally appear there in the
guise of a bridesmaid. She would also, now, act as a
bridesmaid to Gertrude,—her future position as Mrs.
Colonel Stubbs giving her, as was supposed, sufficient
dignity for that honourable employment. But
Captain Batsby, not so very long ago, had appeared
among the suitors for Ayala's hand; and therefore,
as he said to Gertrude, he felt a little shamefaced
about it. 'What does that signify?' said Gertrude.
'If you say nothing to her about it, I'll be bound
she'll say nothing to you.' And so it was on the day
of the wedding. Ayala did not say a word to Captain
Batsby, nor did Captain Batsby say very much to
Ayala.

On the day before his marriage Captain Batsby
paid a fourth visit to Lombard Street in obedience
to directions from Sir Thomas. 'There, my boy,'
said he, 'though you and Gertrude did take a little
journey on the sly to a place which we will not

mention, you shan't take her altogether empty-
handed.' Then he explained certain arrangements
which he had made for endowing Gertrude with an
allowance, which under the circumstances the bridegroom could not but feel to be liberal. It must be
added, that, considering the shortness of time
allowed for getting them together, the amount of
wedding presents bestowed was considered by Gertrude to be satisfactory. As Lucy's were exhibited at
the same time the show was not altogether mean.
'No doubt I had twice as much as the two put together,' said Mrs. Traffick to Ayala up in her bed-
room, 'but then of course Lord Boardotrade's rank
would make people give.'

## CHAPTER LXIII

### AYALA AGAIN IN LONDON

AFTER that last walk in Gobblegoose Wood, after
Lady Tringle's unnecessary journey to Stalham
on the Friday, and the last day's hunting with Sir
Harry's hounds,—which took place on the Saturday,
—Ayala again became anxious to go home. Her
anxiety was in its nature very different from that
which had prompted her to leave Stalham on an
appointed day lest she should seem to be waiting
for the coming of Colonel Stubbs. 'No; I don't want
to run away from him any more,' she said to Lady
Albury. 'I want to be with him always, and I hope
he won't run away from me. But I've got to be
somewhere where I can think about it all for a little
time.'

'Can't you think about it here?'

'No;—one can never think about a thing where it
has all taken place. I must be up in my own little
room in Kingsbury Crescent, and must have Aunt
Margaret's work around me,—so that I may realise
what is going to come. Not but what I mean to do a
great deal of work always.'

'Mend his stockings?'

'Yes,—if he wears stockings. I know he doesn't. He always wears socks. He told me so. Whatever he has, I'll mend,—or make if he wants me.

> " I can bake and I can brew;
> And I can make an Irish stew;
> Wash a shirt and iron it too." '

Then, as she sang her little song, she clapped her hands together.

'Where did you get all your poetry?'

'He taught me that. We are not going to be fine people,—except sometimes when we may be invited to Stalham. But I must go on Thursday, Lady Albury. I came for a week, and I have been here ever since the middle of February. It seems years since the old woman told me I was perverse, and he said that she was right.'

'Think how much you have done since that time.'

'Yes, indeed. I very nearly destroyed myself;— didn't I?'

'Not very nearly.'

'I thought I had. It was only when you showed me his letter on that Sunday morning that I began to have any hopes. I wonder what Mr. Greene preached about that morning. I didn't hear a word. I kept on repeating what he said in the postscript.'

'Was there a postscript?'

'Of course there was. Don't you remember?'

'No, indeed; not I.'

'The letter would have been nothing without the postscript. He said that Croppy was to come back for me. I knew he wouldn't say that unless he meant to be good to me. And yet I wasn't quite sure of it. I know it now; don't I? But I must go, Lady Albury. I ought to let Aunt Margaret know all about it.' Then it was settled that she should go on the Thursday,— and on the Thursday she went. As it was now considered quite wrong that she should travel by the railway alone,—in dread, probably, lest the old lady

should tell her again how perverse she had been,—
Colonel Stubbs accompanied her. It had then been
decided that the wedding must take place at Stalham, and many messages were sent to Mr. and Mrs.
Dosett assuring them that they would be made very
welcome on the occasion. 'My own darling Lucy
will be away at that time with her own young man,'
said Ayala, in answer to further invitations from
Lady Albury.

'And so you've taken Colonel Stubbs at last,' said
her Aunt Margaret.

'He has taken me, aunt. I didn't take him.'

'But you refused him ever so often.'

'Well;—yes. I don't think I quite refused him.'

'I thought you did.'

'It was a dreadful muddle, Aunt Margaret;—but
it has come right at last, and we had better not talk
about that part of it.'

'I was so sure you didn't like him.'

'Not like him? I always liked him better than
anybody else in the world that I ever saw.'

'Dear me!'

'Of course I shouldn't say so if it hadn't come right
at last. I may say whatever I please about it now,
and I declare that I always loved him. A girl can be
such a fool! I was, I know. I hope you are glad,
aunt.'

'Of course I am. I am glad of anything that makes
you happy. It seemed such a pity that, when so
many gentlemen were falling in love with you all
round, you couldn't like anybody.'

'But I did like somebody, Aunt Margaret. And I
did like the best,—didn't I?' In answer to this Mrs.
Dosett made no reply, having always had an aunt's
partiality for poor Tom, in spite of all his chains.

Her uncle's congratulations were warmer even
than her aunt's.

'My dear girl,' he said, 'I am rejoiced indeed that
you should have before you such a prospect of
happiness. I always felt how sad for you was your

residence here, with two such homely persons as your
aunt and myself.'

'I have always been happy with you,' said Ayala,
—perhaps straining the truth a little in her anxiety to
be courteous. 'And I know,' she added, 'how much
Lucy and I have always owed you since poor papa's
death.'

'Nevertheless, it has been dull for a young girl like
you. Now you will have your own duties, and if you
endeavour to do them properly the world will never
be dull to you.' And then there were some few words
about the wedding. 'We have no feeling, my dear,'
said her uncle, 'except to do the best we can for you.
We should have been glad to see you married from
here if that had suited. But, as this lover of yours
has grand friends of his own, I dare say their place
may be the better.' Ayala could hardly explain to
her uncle that she had acceded to Lady Albury's
proposal because, by doing so, she would spare him
the necessary expense of the wedding.

But Ayala's great delight was in meeting her sister.
The two girls had not seen each other since the engagement of either of them had been ratified by their
friends. The winter and spring, as passed by Lucy at
Merle Park, had been very unhappy for her. Things
at Merle Park had not been pleasant to any of the
residents there, and Lucy had certainly had her share
of the unpleasantness. Her letters to Ayala had not
been triumphant when Aunt Emmeline had more than
once expressed her wish to be rid of her, and when
the news reached her that Uncle Tom and Hamel had
failed to be gracious to each other. Nor had Ayala
written in a spirit of joy before she had been able
to recognise the Angel of Light in Jonathan Stubbs.
But now they were to meet after all their miseries,
and each could be triumphant.

It was hard for them to know exactly how to begin. To Lucy, Isadore Hamel was, at the present
moment, the one hero walking the face of this sub-
lunary globe; and to Ayala, as we all know, Jonathan

Stubbs was an Angel of Light, and, therefore, more even than a hero. As each spoke, the 'He's' intended took a different personification; so that to any one less interested than the young ladies themselves there might be some confusion as to which 'He' might at that moment be under discussion. 'It was bad,' said Lucy, 'when Uncle Tom told him to sell those magnificent conceptions of his brain by auction!'

'I did feel for him certainly,' said Ayala.

'And then when he was constrained to say that he would take me at once without any preparation because Aunt Emmeline wanted me to go, I don't suppose any man ever behaved more beautifully than he did.'

'Yes indeed,' said Ayala. And then she felt herself constrained to change the subject by the introduction of an exaggerated superlative in her sister's narrative. Hamel, no doubt, had acted beautifully, but she was not disposed to agree that nothing could be more beautiful. 'Oh, Lucy,' she said, 'I was so miserable when he went away after that walk in the wood. I thought he never would come back again when I had behaved so badly. But he did. Was not that grand in him?'

'I suppose he was very fond of you.'

'I hope he was. I hope he is. But what should I have done if he had not come back? No other man would have come back after that. You never behaved unkindly to Isadore?'

'I think he would have come back a thousand times,' said Lucy; 'only I cannot imagine that I should ever have given him the necessity of coming back even a second. But then I had known him so much longer.'

'It wasn't that I hadn't known him long enough,' said Ayala. 'I seemed to know all about him almost all at once. I knew how good he was, and how grand he was, long before I had left the Marchesa up in London. But I think it astounded me that such a one as he should care for me.' And so it went on through an entire morning, each of the sisters feeling that she was bound to listen with rapt attention to the praises of the other's 'him' if she wished to have an opportunity of singing those of her own.

But Lucy's marriage was to come first by more than two months, and therefore in that matter she was allowed precedence. And at her marriage Ayala would be present, whereas with Ayala's Lucy would have no personal concern. Though she did think that Uncle Tom had been worse than any vandal in that matter of selling her lover's magnificent works, still she was ready to tell of his generosity. In a manner of his own he had sent the money which Hamel had so greatly needed, and had now come forward to provide, with a generous hand, for the immediate necessities, and more than the necessities, of the wedding. It was not only that she was to share the honours of the two wedding-cakes with Gertrude, and that she was to be taken as a bride from the gorgeous mansion in Queen's Gate, but that he had provided for her bridal needs almost as fully as for those of his own daughter. 'Never mind what she'll be able to do afterwards,' he said to his wife, who ventured on some slight remonstrance with him as to the unnecessary luxuries he was preparing for the wife of a poor man. 'She won't be the worse for having a dozen new petticoats in her trunk, and, if she don't want to blow her nose with as many handkerchiefs this year as Gertrude does, she'll be able to keep them for next year.' Then Aunt Emmeline obeyed without further hesitation the orders which were given her.

Nor was his generosity confined to the niece who for the last twelve months had been his property. Lucy was still living in Queen's Gate, though at this time she spent much of each day in Kingsbury Crescent, and on one occasion she brought with her a little note from Uncle Tom. 'Dear Ayala,' said the little note,

'As you are going to be married too, you, I suppose, will want some new finery. I therefore send a cheque. Write your name on the back of it, and give it to your uncle. He will let you have the money as you want it.

'Yours affectionately,

'T. TRINGLE.

'I hope your Colonel Stubbs will come and see me some day.'

'You must go and see him,' she said to her Colonel Stubbs, when he called one day in Kingsbury Crescent. "Only for him I shouldn't have any clothes to speak of at all, and I should have to be married in my old brown morning frock.'

'It would be just as good as any other for my purpose,' said the Colonel.

'But it wouldn't for mine, Sir. Fine feathers make fine birds, and I mean to be as fine as Lady Albury's big peacock. So if you please you'll go to Queen's Gate, and Lombard Street too, and show yourself. Oh, Jonathan, I shall be so proud that everybody who knows me should see what sort of a man has chosen to love me.'

Then there was a joint visit paid by the two sisters to Mr. Hamel's studio,—an expedition which was made somewhat on the sly. Aunt Margaret in Kingsbury Crescent knew all about it, but Aunt Emmeline was kept in the dark. Even now, though the marriage was sanctioned and was so nearly at hand, Aunt Emmeline would not have approved of such a visit. She still regarded the sculptor as improper,—at any rate not sufficiently proper to be treated with full familiarity,—partly on account of his father's manifest improprieties, and partly because of his own relative poverty and unauthorised position in the world. But Aunt Margaret was more tolerant, and thought that the sister-in-law was entitled to visit the workshop in which her sister's future bread was to be earned. And then, starting

from Kingsbury Crescent, they could go in a cab;
whereas any such proceeding emanating from
Queen's Gate would have required the carriage.
There was a wickedness in this starting off in a
hansom cab to call on an unmarried young man,
doing it in a manner successfully concealed from
Aunt Emmeline, on which Ayala expatiated with
delight when she next saw Colonel Stubbs.

'You don't come and call on me,' said the Colonel.

'What!—all the way down to Aldershot? I should
like, but I don't quite dare to do that.'

The visit was very successful. Though it was
expected, Hamel was found in his artist's costume,
with a blouse or loose linen tunic fitted close round
his throat, and fastened with a belt round his waist.
Lucy thought that in this apparel he was certainly
as handsome as could ever have been any Apollo,—
and, so thinking, had contrived her little plans in
such a way that he should certainly be seen at his
best. To her thinking Colonel Stubbs was not a
handsome man. Hamel's hair was nearly black, and
she preferred dark hair. Hamel's features were
regular, whereas the Colonel's hair was red, and he
was known for a large mouth and broad nose, which
were not obliterated though they were enlightened
by the brightness of his eyes. 'Yes,' said Ayala to
herself, as she looked at Hamel; 'he is very good
looking, but nobody would take him for an Angel of
Light.'

'Ayala has come to see you at your work,' said
Lucy, as they entered the studio.

'I am delighted to see her. Do you remember
where we last met, Miss Dormer?'

'Miss Dormer, indeed,' said Ayala. 'I am not
going to call you Mr. Hamel. Yes; it was high up
among the seats of the Coliseum. There has a great
deal happened to us all since then.'

'And I remember you at the bijou.'

'I should think so. I knew then so well what was
going to happen,' said Ayala.

'What did you know?'

'That you and Lucy were to fall in love with each other.'

'I had done my part of it already,' said he.

'Hardly that, Isadore,' said Lucy, 'or you would not have passed me in Kensington Gardens without speaking to me.'

'But I did speak to you. It was then I learned where to find you.'

'That was the second time. If I had remained away, as I ought to have done, I suppose you never would have found me.'

Ayala was then taken round to see all those magnificent groups and figures which Sir Thomas would have disposed of at so many shillings apiece under the auctioneer's hammer. 'It was cruel.—was it not?' said Lucy.

'He never saw them, you know,' said Ayala, putting in a goodnatured word for her uncle.

'If he had,' said the sculptor, 'he would have doubted the auctioneer's getting anything. I have turned it all in my mind very often since, and I think that Sir Thomas was right.'

'I am sure he was wrong,' said Lucy. 'He is very goodnatured, and nobody can be more grateful to another person than I am to him;—but I won't agree that he was right about that.'

'He never would have said it if he had seen them,' again pleaded Ayala.

'They will never fetch anything as they are,' continued the sculptor, 'and I don't suppose that when I made them I thought they would. They have served their purpose, and I sometimes feel inclined to break them up and have them carted away.'

'Isadore!' exclaimed Lucy.

'For what purpose?' asked Ayala.

'They were the lessons which I had to teach myself, and the play which I gave to my imagination. Who wants a great figure of Beelzebub like that in his house?'

' I call it magnificent,' said Ayala.

' His name is Lucifer,—not Beelzebub,'*said Lucy.
'You call him Beelzebub merely to make little of
him.'

' It is difficult to do that, because he is nearly ten
feet high. And who wants a figure of Bacchus?* The
thing is, whether, having done a figure of Bacchus, I
may not be better able to do a likeness of Mr. Jones,
when he comes to sit for his bust at the request of his
admiring friends. For any further purpose that it will
answer, Bacchus might just as well be broken up
and carted away in the dust-cart.' To this, however,
the two girls expressed their vehement opposition,
and were of opinion that the time would come when
Beelzebub and Bacchus, transferred to marble,
would occupy places of honour in some well-
proportioned hall built for the purpose of receiving
them. ' I shall be quite content,' said Hamel, 'if the
whole family of the Jones's will have their busts done
about the size of life, and stand them up over their
bookshelves. My period for Beelzebubs has gone by.'
The visit, on the whole, was delightful. Lucy was
contented with the almost more than divine beauty
of her lover, and the two sisters, as they made their
return journey to Kingsbury Crescent in another
hansom, discussed questions of art in a spirit that
would have been delightful to any aspiring artist
who might have heard them.

Then came the wedding, of which some details
were given at the close of the last chapter, at which
two brides who were very unlike to each other were
joined in matrimony to two bridegrooms as dis-
similar. But the Captain made himself gracious to
the sculptor who was now to be connected with him,
and declared that he would always look upon Lucy
as a second sister to his dear Gertrude. And Gertrude
was equally gracious, protesting, when she was
marshalled to walk up to the altar first, that she did
not like to go before her darling Lucy. But the
dimensions of the church admitted but of one couple

at a time, and Gertrude was compelled to go in
advance. Colonel Stubbs was there acting as best
man to Hamel, while Lord John Battledore performed the same service for Captain Batsby. Lord
John was nearly broken-hearted by the apostacy of
a second chum, having heard that the girl whom
Frank Houston had not succeeded in marrying was
now being taken by Batsby without a shilling.
'Somebody had to bottle-hold for him,' said Lord
John, defending himself at the club afterwards, 'and
I didn't like to throw the fellow over, though he is
such a fool! And there was Stubbs, too,' continued
his Lordship, 'going to take the other girl without a
shilling! There's Stubbs, and Houston, and Batsby,
all gone and drowned themselves. It's just the same
as though they'd drowned themselves!' Lord John
was horrified,—nay, disgusted,—by the folly of the
world. Nevertheless, before the end of the year, he
was engaged to marry a very pretty girl as devoid of
fortune as our Ayala.


## CHAPTER LXIV

### AYALA'S MARRIAGE

NOW we have come to our last chapter, and it may
be doubted whether any reader,—unless he be
some one specially gifted with a genius for statistics,
—will have perceived how very many people have
been made happy by matrimony. If marriage be the
proper ending for a novel,—the only ending, as this
writer takes it to be, which is not discordant,—
surely no tale was ever so properly ended, or with so
full a concord, as this one. Infinite trouble has been
taken not only in arranging these marriages but in
joining like to like,—so that, if not happiness, at any
rate sympathetic unhappiness, might be produced.
Our two sisters will, it is trusted, be happy. They
have chosen men from their hearts, and have been

chosen after the same fashion. Those two other sisters have been so wedded that the one will follow the idiosyncrasies of her husband, and the other bring her husband to follow her idiosyncrasies, without much danger of mutiny or revolt. As to Miss Docimer there must be room for fear. It may be questioned whether she was not worthy of a better lot than has been achieved for her by joining her fortunes to those of Frank Houston. But I, speaking for myself, have my hopes of Frank Houston. It is hard to rescue a man from the slough of luxury and idleness combined. If anything can do it, it is a cradle filled annually. It may be that he will yet learn that a broad back with a heavy weight upon it gives the best chance of happiness here below.* Of Lord John's married prospects I could not say much as he came so very lately on the scene; but even he may perhaps do something in the world when he finds that his nursery is filling.

For our special friend Tom Tringle, no wife has been found. In making his effort,—which he did manfully,—he certainly had not chosen the consort who would be fit for him. He had not seen clearly, as had done his sisters and cousins. He had fallen in love too young,—it being the nature of young men to be much younger than young ladies, and, not knowing himself, had been as might be a barn-door cock who had set his heart upon some azure-plumaged, high-soaring lady of the woods. The lady with the azure plumes had, too, her high-soaring tendencies, but she was enabled by true insight to find the male who would be fit for her. The barn-door cock, when we left him on board the steamer going to New York, had not yet learned the nature of his own requirements. The knowledge will come to him. There may be doubts as to Frank Houston, but we think that there need be none as to Tom Tringle. The proper wife will be forthcoming; and in future years, when he will probably have a Glenbogie and a Merle Park of his own, he will own that

Fortune did well for him in making his cousin Ayala
so stern to his prayers.

But Ayala herself,—Ayala our pet heroine,—had
not been yet married when the last chapter was
written, and now there remains a page or two in
which the reader must bid adieu to her as she stands
at the altar with her Angel of Light. She was at
Stalham for a fortnight before her marriage, in
order, as Lady Albury said, that the buxom ladys-
maid might see that everything had been done
rightly in reference to the trousseau. 'My dear,' said
Lady Albury, 'it is important, you know. I dare say
you can bake and brew, because you say so; but you
don't know anything about clothes.' Ayala, who by
this time was very intimate with her friend, pouted
her lips, and said that if 'Jonathan did not like her
things as she chose to have them he might do the
other thing.' But Lady Albury had her way, inducing Sir Harry to add something even to Uncle
Tom's liberality, and the buxom woman went about
her task in such a fashion that if Colonel Stubbs were
not satisfied he must have been a very unconscion-
able Colonel. He probably would know nothing about
it,—except that his bride in her bridal array had not
looked so well as in any other garments, which, I take
it, is invariably the case*—till at the end of the first
year a glimmer of the truth as to a lady's wardrobe
would come upon him. 'I told you there would be
a many new dresses before two years were over,
Miss,' said the buxom female, as she spread all the
frocks and all the worked petticoats and all the collars
and all the silk stockings and all the lace handkerchiefs about the bedroom to be inspected by Lady
Albury, Mrs. Gosling, and one or two other friends,
before they were finally packed up.

Then came the day on which the Colonel was to
reach Stalham, that day being a Monday, whereas
the wedding was to take place on Wednesday. It was
considered to be within the bounds of propriety that
the Colonel should sleep at Stalham on the Monday,

under the same roof with his bride; but on the Tuesday it was arranged that he should satisfy the decorous feeling of the neighbourhood by removing himself to the parsonage, which was distant about half-a-mile across the park, and was contiguous to the church. Here lived Mr. Greene, the bachelor curate, the rector of the parish being an invalid and absent in Italy.

'I don't see why he is to be sent away after dinner to walk across the park in the dark,' said Ayala, when the matter was discussed before the Colonel's coming.

'It is a law, my dear,' said Lady Albury, 'and has to be obeyed whether you understand it or not, like other laws. Mr. Greene will be with him, so that no one shall run away with him in the dark. Then he will be able to go into church without dirtying his dress boots.'

'But I thought there would be half-a-dozen carriages at least.'

'But there won't be room in one of them for him. He is to be nobody until he comes forth from the church as your husband. Then he is to be everybody. That is the very theory of marriage.'

\* \* \* \* \* \*

'I think we managed it all very well between us,' said Lady Albury afterwards, 'but you really cannot guess the trouble we took.'

'Why should there have been trouble?'

'Because you were such a perverse creature, as the old lady said. I am not sure that you were not right, because a girl does so often raise herself in her lover's estimation by refusing him half-a-dozen times. But you were not up to that.'

'Indeed I was not. I am sure I did not intend to give any trouble to anybody.'

'But you did. Only think of my going up to London to meet him, and of him coming from Aldershot to meet me, simply that we might put our heads

together how to overcome the perversity of such a
young woman as you!' There then came a look
almost of pain on Ayala's brow. 'But I do believe it
was for the best. In this way he came to understand
how absolutely necessary you were to him.'

'Am I necessary to him?'

'He thinks so.'

'Oh, if I can only be necessary to him always! But
there should have been no going up to London. I
should have rushed into his arms at once.'

'That would have been unusual.'

'But so is he unusual,' said Ayala.

It is probable that the Colonel did not enjoy his
days at Stalham before his marriage, except during
the hour or two in which he was allowed to take
Ayala out for a last walk. Such days can hardly be
agreeable to the man of whom it is known by all
around him that he is on the eve of committing
matrimony. There is always, on such occasions, a
feeling of weakness, as though the man had been
subdued, brought at length into a cage and tamed,
so as to be made fit for domestic purposes, and deprived of his ancient freedom amongst the woods;
whereas the girl feels herself to be the triumphant
conqueror, who has successfully performed this great
act of taming. Such being the case, the man had
perhaps better keep away till he is forced to appear
at the church-door.

Nevertheless our Colonel did enjoy his last walk.
'Oh, yes,' she said, 'of course we will go to the old
wood. Where else? I am so glad that poor fox went
through Gobblegoose;—otherwise we should never
have gone there, and then who knows whether you
and I would ever have been friends again any more?'

'If one wood hadn't been there, I think another
would have been found.'

'Ah, that's just it. You can know that you had
a purpose, and perhaps were determined to carry it
out.'

'Well, rather.'

'But I couldn't be sure of that. I couldn't carry out my purpose, even if I had one. I had to doubt, and to be unhappy, and to hate myself, because I had been perverse. I declare, I do think you men have so much the best of it. How glorious would it have been to be able to walk straight up and say, Jonathan Stubbs, I love you better than all the world. Will you be my husband?'

'But suppose the Jonathan Stubbs of the occasion were to decline the honour. Where would you be then?'

'That would be disagreeable,' said Ayala.

'It is disagreeable,—as you made me feel twice over.'

'Oh, Jonathan, I am so sorry.'

'Therefore it is possible that you may have the best of it.'

\* \* \* \* \* \*

'And so you never will take another walk with Ayala Dormer?' she said, as they were returning home.

'Never another,' he replied.

'You cannot think how I regret it. Of course I am glad to become your wife. I do not at all want to have it postponed. But there is something so sweet in having a lover;—and you know that though I shall have a husband I shall never have a lover again,—and I never had one before, Jonathan. There has been very little of it. When a thing has been so sweet it is sad to think that it must be gone for ever!' Then she leaned upon him with both her hands, and looked up at him and smiled, with her lips a little open,—as she knew that he liked her to lean upon him and to look,—for she had caught by her instinct the very nature of the man, and knew how to witch him with her little charms. 'Ah me! I wonder whether you'll like me to lean upon you when a dozen years have gone by.'

'That depends on how heavy you may be.'

'I shall be a fat old woman, perhaps. But I shall

lean upon you,—always, always. What else shall I ever have to lean upon now?'

'What else should you want?'

'Nothing,—nothing,—nothing! I want nothing else. I wonder whether there is anybody in all the world who has got so completely everything that she ever dreamed of wanting as I have. But if you could have been only my lover for a little longer——!' Then he assured her that he would be her lover just the same, even though they were husband and wife. Alas, no! There he had promised more than it is given to a man to perform. Faith, honesty, steadiness of purpose, joined to the warmest love and the truest heart, will not enable a husband to maintain the sweetness of that aroma which has filled with delight the senses of the girl who has leaned upon his arm as her permitted lover.

'What a happy fellow you are!' said Mr. Greene, as, in the intimacy of the moment, they walked across the park together.

'Why don't you get a wife for yourself?'

'Yes; with £120 a-year!'

'With a little money you might.'

'I don't want to have to look for the money; and if I did I shouldn't get it. I often think how very unfairly things are divided in this world.'

'That will all be made up in the next.'

'Not if one covets one's neighbour's wife,—or even his ass,' said Mr. Greene.

On the return of the two lovers to the house from their walk there were Mr. and Mrs. Dosett, who would much rather have stayed away had they not been unwilling not to show their mark of affection to their niece. I doubt whether they were very happy, but they were at any rate received with every distinction. Sir Thomas and Aunt Emmeline were asked, but they made some excuse. Sir Thomas knew very well that he had nothing in common with Sir Harry Albury; and, as for Aunt Emmeline, her one journey to Stalham had been enough for her.

But Sir Thomas was again very liberal, and sent down as his contribution to the wedding presents the very necklace which Ayala had refused from her cousin Tom. 'Upon my word, your uncle is magnificent,' said Lady Albury, upon which the whole story was told to her. Lucy and her husband were away on their tour, as were Gertrude and hers on theirs. This was rather a comfort, as Captain Batsby's presence at the house would have been a nuisance. But there was quite enough of guests to make the wedding, as being a country wedding, very brilliant. Among others, old Tony Tappett was there, mindful of the manner in which Cranbury Brook had been ridden, and of Croppy's presence when the hounds ran their fox into Dillsborough Wood. 'I hope she be to ride with us, off and on, Colonel,' said Tony, when the ceremony had been completed.

'Now and then, Tony, when we can get hold of Croppy.'

'Because, when they come out like that, Colonel, it's a pity to lose 'em, just because they's got their husbands to attend to.'

And Lord Rufford was there, with his wife, who on this occasion was very pressing with her invitations. She had heard that Colonel Stubbs was likely to rise high in his profession, and there were symptoms, of which she was an excellent judge, that Mrs. Colonel Stubbs would become known as a professional beauty. And Larry Twentyman was there, who, being in the neighbourhood, was, to his great delight, invited to the breakfast.

Thus, to her own intense satisfaction, Ayala was handed over to her

ANGEL OF LIGHT.

# EXPLANATORY NOTES

2 *Lombard Street*: originally occupied by Lombard
bankers and still containing many of the principal
London banks. Although comparatively small,
and overcrowded with buildings, in 1873 Walter
Bagehot described it as 'by far the greatest combination of economical power and economical
delicacy that the world has ever seen'.

3 *£900 a year from his office*: as a surveyor in the
Post Office, Trollope's basic salary never rose
above £700 per annum, even at his retirement.
By suburban standards, Reginald Dosett is not
badly off.

*genteel*: the word usually implies straitened
means in this novel.

*Notting Hill*: originally the hamlet of Kensington Gravel Pits, Notting Hill was reconstructed
as a Victorian suburb between 1825 and 1870, in
a pattern of terraces, gardens, crescents, and
squares. Although many contemporary accounts
stress the ugliness and uniformity of the building,
to modern eyes the concentric circles of the Lad-
broke Estate development (on which Kingsbury
Crescent is presumably based) have a character-
istic charm. See Florence M. Gladstone, *Notting
Hill in Bygone Days* (reprinted 1969).

*bijou of a little house*: *OED* Supplement lists
many examples of 'bijou' from 1860 onwards
applied to small, elegant, luxurious houses.

*South Kensington*: the 'bijou' probably lay in the
area that was once Brompton. In early Victorian
times this was almost exclusively the artist
quarter. By 1878, however, South Kensington was

more renowned for the various museums that had been constructed there to house the remains of the 1851 Great Exhibition than it was for artist life. The prestigious painters were mainly concentrated in Kensington proper, particularly in Melbury Road, where, at about this period, dwelt G. F. Watts, John Leech, Holman Hunt, Sir Luke Fildes, and Marcus Stone. Lord Leighton lived in Holland Park Road, and in 1878 Trollope's friend Millais moved to 2 Palace Gate, off the Kensington Road. Charles Dickens Junior's *Dictionary of London* for 1879 does, however, point out that 'votaries of the brush and chisel' still frequented the South Kensington area.

*blue china . . . painted cornice . . . satin hangings for his drawing-room*: blue china was an industry in suburban London in the 1870s and 80s, a cult carefully and tastefully fostered by Murray Marks, who began trading in Oxford Street in 1875. Oscar Wilde was denounced from the pulpit of the University Church for wishing that he might live up to the level of the blue china in his rooms at Magdalen, Oxford, in the 1870s (see Hesketh Pearson, *The Life of Oscar Wilde* (1946), p. 33). The rich fabrics and painted cornice in the 'bijou' are also typical of avant garde interior decoration at this time. A satirical description of an artist's suburban studio in *Punch* (7 September 1878) lists 'blue china, round mirrors, faded tapestry, carved oak-chests, high-backed chairs, brazen sconces, medieval arms and armour, an organ with beautifully painted pipes but no bellows, and other musical instruments'.

6 *Bond Street*: Bond Street was still fashionable and a centre for women's clothing of all kinds, but without its Regency prominence, and somewhat eclipsed, at this date, by Regent Street.

*Queen's Gate . . . Eaton Square*: the Queen's Gate area was developed in the 1850s; Eaton Square, part of the Grosvenor estate, dates from the 1820s, and vied in fashion and rents with Mayfair in the 1870s.

10 *Mudie's*: the largest and most influential of the mid-Victorian circulating libraries, Charles Edward Mudie's business opened in 1842. He purchased large quantities of newly-published books, which at retail price were beyond the pockets of all but the wealthiest readers, and loaned them to his subscribers. The straitened and practical Dosetts, however, find even Mudie's beyond their means.

12 *duty is to be hard*: 'The Lady of Launay', a short story Trollope wrote immediately before *Ayala's Angel*, and which was subsequently published in the magazine *Light*, makes extreme play of the tyranny of 'duty' in a middle-class home.

13 *Somerset House*: the work of Sir W. Chambers, built to house miscellaneous Government and semi-public offices. As a clerk in the Civil Department of the Admiralty Dosett's hours would have been from 10 to 4.

*Underground Railway to the Temple Station*: the 'inner circle' of the Metropolitan and District Railways was completed when the stretch from Westminster to the Temple opened in May 1870.

*the youth of nineteen enters an office*: such a clerk might expect to begin on a salary of £100 per annum. Trollope himself began his Post Office career on £90 in 1834, and his works are filled with references to the probability of £100 a year coming to grief 'on the rocks of Metropolitan life'. See particularly *An Autobiography*, World's Classics, pp. 51–2.

16 *reading the Idylls of the King*: which Trollope had read aloud to his family in November 1876; see N. John Hall, ed., *The Letters of Anthony Trollope*, II, p. 1033.

21 *Envy, hatred, and malice*: from the Litany or General Supplication in *The Book of Common Prayer*: 'Good Lord, deliver us: from all blindness of heart; from pride, vain-glory and hypocrisy; from envy, hatred and malice, and all uncharitableness.'

22 *gin and water*: generally a drink for the lower orders. In turning from port to gin and water Dosett has sunk even below those bastions of the Trollopian lower middle class, Moulder and Kantwise in *Orley Farm*, who ostentatiously order port at their commercial hotel (Ch. V).

29 *Nobody seemed to care for anything*: the Tringles' philistinism here should be compared with Trollope's description of the British abroad in his *Travelling Sketches* (1866).
*Campanile at Florence*: refers to the detached bell-tower (1334) of the cathedral in Florence. It is 275 feet high in black, white, and red marble, was begun by Giotto and completed by Taddio Gaddi.

31 *some old-fashioned idea ... purlieus of Kensington*: since William III established Kensington Palace in 1689 public access to Kensington Gardens had been more restricted than to Hyde Park, and the 'select' character of the Gardens persists to this day. In 1878 *Punch* still referred to Hyde Park as the resort of habitual criminals; in 1861–2 Mayhew described the 'Park Women' who were to be met in Hyde Park between the hours of 5 and 10 p.m. (when the gates were closed in winter). See *London Labour and the London Poor*, Frank Cass, 1967, IV, p. 213.

33 *all that art could do ... had better be an Englishman*: Trollope's other Italianate sculptor is the wastrel Bertie Stanhope, who 'opened an establishment, or rather took lodgings and a workshop, at Carrara, and there spoilt much marble, and

made some few pretty images' (*Barchester Towers*, Ch. IX). Such knowledge as Trollope possessed of Victorian sculptors in Italy was probably culled from those attached to his mother's Florentine Circle; and possibly from later visits to his brother Tom Trollope at Rome.

*a shoemaker*: Trollope notoriously draws parallels between the shoemaker and artists of all kinds, particularly the novelist. In *An Autobiography* he declares 'I was once told that the surest aid to the writing of a book was a piece of cobbler's wax on my chair. I certainly believe in the cobbler's wax much more than the inspiration.'

*San Sisto . . . Apollo*: San Sisto is presumably a reference to Michelangelo's ceiling for the Sistine Chapel in the Vatican Palace, Rome; Apollo is the Apollo Belvedere, a restored copy of a fourth century BC Greek statue, in the Vatican Museum, Rome.

40 *'64 Leoville' . . . my lips*: claret-wine from the St Julien Appellation, Haut-Médoc, and very popular with Victorian Englishmen. The year 1864 (vintage 17 September) is a *grande année* and, as Professor Saintsbury remarks in *Notes on a Cellar Book* (1920), 'was in perfection, but very dear likewise' when he laid down his cellar in the late 1870s. Such classified growths took ten years to mature. More evidence of Trollope's esteem for this wine is the 24 dozen Leoville '74 (another excellent year) he bought into his cellar at 72/- a dozen. See N. John Hall, ed., *The Letters of Anthony Trollope*, II, p. 938. Trollope's dealings with wine-merchants are humorously discussed in *London Tradesmen* (*Pall Mall Gazette*, 1880; reprinted 1927).

43 *a tricksy Ariel*: see *The Tempest*, V. i. 226.

44 *the Honourable Mr. Septimus Traffick . . . second son of Lord Boardotrade*: Trollope's sometimes

facile and facetious use of type-names persists in his later novels. Henry James takes exception to the practice in his *Partial Portraits* essay on Trollope (1888): 'It would be better to go back to Bunyan at once.' In addition to Lord Boardo-trade and his son, in *Ayala's Angel* see also Break-at-Last, the Huddersfield Manufacturer (p. 41), Lady Sophia Smallware (p. 41), the alco-holic Mr Montgomery Talbot de Montpellier (p. 148), Earl of Glentower (p. 180), and Lord John Battledore and Tom Shuttlecock (p. 584).

46 *all the Peerages*: a variation on one of Trollope's stock quotations regarding aristocratic pedigree:

What can ennoble sots, or slaves, or cowards?
Alas! not all the blood of all the HOWARDS.
(Pope, *Essay on Man*, IV, 215–6)

50 *'au première'*: of the first quality.

52 *the top of St. Peter's*: the ascent to the Loggia of the Lantern above the Dome of St Peter's is by no means easy. There are 537 steps from the pave-ment of the basilica, and it is perhaps not surpris-ing that Augusta objects!

55 *the Pincian*: a park laid out by Giuseppe Valadier in 1809–14 on the side of the Pincian Hill and on the site of the most magnificent of the monu-mental gardens of ancient Rome. Walking in the park became very fashionable in mid-Victorian times.

56 *the Forum . . . how many Romans could have congregated themselves . . . world's doings*: a dif-ficult question, as there are five separate imperial fora, and in the 1870s it was not recognized that they were interconnected in accordance with a definite plan.

*the Arch of Titus*: on the summit of the Clivus Sacer. Commemorates the Roman destruction of the temple of Solomon in Jerusalem in AD 70, and the removal of the spoils. Whether the reliefs depicting this process particularly gratified the acquisitive Mr Traffick is left for the reader to judge1.

59 *the weaver Bottom with the ass's head*: see *A Midsummer Night's Dream*, III. i. and IV. i.

*Bluebeard .. fond of his last wife*: *Blue Beard* is a popular tale in an oriental setting, translated from the French of Perrault by Robert Samber (1729). Blue Beard, who has murdered all his previous wives, is gentle and loving to his last wife Fatima, at least until she discovers that the bodies of her predecessors are hidden in his closet!

62 *the Coliseum*: the great amphitheatre at Rome, begun by Vespasian and completed by Titus in AD 80.

71 *a hobble-de-hoy*: Trollope, a late developer himself, always had sympathy for the hobbledehoy, of whom the two best-known examples in his fiction are Johnny Eames in *The Small House at Allington* (1864) and Charley Tudor in *The Three Clerks* (1857).

92 *castles in the air*: for Trollope's own youthful addiction to day-dreaming and 'castle-building' see *An Autobiography*, World's Classics, pp. 42–3.

103 '*in formâ pauperis*': appearing at law in the guise of a poor person, without liability for costs.

108 *cognate paterfamilias . . . the mantle of his noble blood*: Lord Boardotrade presents himself in the guise of a Roman patrician.

112 *seven houses of the Devil*: see Matthew 12: 43–5 (Luke 11: 24–6 is almost identical): 'When the unclean spirit is gone out of a man, he walketh through dry places, seeking rest, and findeth none. Then he saith, I will return into my house from whence I came out; and when he is come, he findeth it empty, swept, and garnished. Then goeth he, and taketh with himself seven other

spirits more wicked than himself, and they enter in and dwell there: and the last state of that man is worse than the first.' Ayala gains little of her knowledge from books, and when she does, the results, as here, are garbled.

117 *certain Irish Members having been very eloquent*: obstructionism by Irish MPs at Westminster had begun in 1875, but it was not until the influence of Charles Stewart Parnell on the Home Rule Party began to be felt in the sessions of 1877 and 1878 that the obstructionists came to real prominence. In July 1877 they twice kept the House of Commons up all night, the second time till 2 p.m., a 26-hour sitting. Trollope's last, incomplete novel, *The Landleaguers* (1883), deals in passing with Parliamentary obstructionism.

*Saturday, June 15*: Trollope's list of chapter divisions for serial publication (now in the Bodleian Library) suggests that from the Traffick marriage on Monday 15 April (see p. 108) he dated events carefully, and that he used a calendar for 1878–9 to do so. The novel ends in 'late May' of the year following the Traffick marriage.

119 *a month at Glenbogie from the 12th.*: that is, from 12 August, when grouse-shooting begins.

125 *Four-per-cent.*: a relatively high rate of interest, and would need careful investment. Government stock—gilt-edged securities—paid only three per cent.

*Onslow Gardens*: South Kensington, laid out in 1850 on the Smith's Charity Estates, after the designs of George Basevi (d. 1845), architect of the supremely fashionable Belgrave Square.

126 *jeunesse dorée*: a 'gilded youth', a term coined to apply to the fashionable counter-revolutionary group formed in France after the fall of Robespierre in 1794.

129 *"picters"*: Sir Thomas lapses into a (presumably) native cockney.

133 *Buncombe Hall*: another piece of coarse type-naming on Trollope's part. Buncombe is cynical oratory, after the member for that county in North Carolina who spoke in the 16th Congress merely to prolong the debate on the Missouri Question. Houston's 'love tale' to Gertrude Tringle is likely to be just as empty and just as self-interested.

134 *Allan-a-Dale*: Frank Houston parodies the song of Edmund of Winston in Sir Walter Scott's *Rokeby*. Allen-a-Dale, poacher and freebooter, is in search of a wife. The full passage runs:

> Allen-a-Dale to his wooing is come;
> The mother, she ask'd of his household and home:
> 'Though the castle of Richmond stand fair on the hill,
> My hall', quoth bold Allen, 'shows gallanter still;
> 'Tis the blue vault of heaven, with its crescent so pale,
> And with all its bright spangles !' said Allen-a-Dale.
>
> The father was steel, and the mother was stone;
> They lifted the latch and they bade him be gone;
> But loud, on the morrow, their wail and their cry:
> He had laugh'd on the lass with his bonny black eye,
> And she fled to the forest to hear a love tale,
> And the youth it was told by was Allen-a-Dale !
>       (*Rokeby*, Canto III, Oxford Standard Authors,
>         Sir Walter Scott's *Poems* (1964), p. 342.)

In *The Three Clerks* (1857) Charley Tudor face-tiously relates the adventures of one Sir Anthony Allan-a-dale, in a piece composed for the 'Daily Delight' newspaper.

136 *Brook Street*: Brook Street is the northern bound-ary of Mayfair, in the 1870s the *crème de la crème* of residential London. The addresses close to the Park were particularly desirable, as they were built on the highest ground. Charles Dickens Junior's *Dictionary of London* (1879) tells us that

'the smallest and most inconvenient house [in Mayfair] . . . lets readily at a rent which, in less sought-after neighbourhoods, would provide a handsome establishment'.

144 *when she did not consider herself to be quite out*: i.e. out in society, and eligible for a husband.

146 *marched across Africa*: this was the heydey of British military expectation in South Africa, after the annexation of the Transvaal (1877) and before the disaster at Isandhlwana (Jan. 1879). Trollope thought the annexation of the Transvaal high-handed but expedient. He was vehemently opposed to the Zulu Wars. See *South Africa*, 4th ed. (1879).

*defended the Turks,—or perhaps conquered them*: British foreign policy traditionally propped up Turkey, but in the period 1876–8 there was a hot debate as to whether it should continue to do so. Disraeli's government was strongly 'turcophil', and opposed Russian gains from the Turkish Empire through the Treaty of San Stefano. Gladstone, however, who had published a pamphlet (July 1876) condemning the atrocities Turkey had committed in suppressing a nationalist rising, believed the Turkish regime to be morally bankrupt. Trollope supported Gladstone, and read the 'Bulgarian Atrocities' pamphlet aloud to his family (see Hall, *The Letters of Anthony Trollope*, II, 1033); he also spoke publicly in support of Gladstone at a conference on the Eastern Question (see Eastern Question Association, *Report of Proceedings of the National Conference at St. James's Hall, London, December 8 1876*, pp. 19–21).

147 *There's a prejudice about Jonathan, as there is about Jacob and Jonah*: both the Biblical Jonathans died violently, David's great friend at the battle of Gilboa, fighting against the Philistines (2 Samuel 1), and the brother of Judas

Maccabeus was killed by the treachery of the Greeks (1 Macc. 12). Jacob, whose name means 'one who gets the better of another' is distrusted for his schemes to disinherit his brother Esau (Gen. 27); for Jonah's unpopularity with the sailors with whom he took ship rather than preach against the city of Nineveh, see Jonah 1 : 1–16.

150 *'Sallow, sublime, sort of Werther-faced man'*: I have not been able to identify the source of this quotation.

151 *realms of Lethe*: realms of forgetfulness. In Virgil one of the six rivers of the underworld. The souls gather on its shores to drink and forget so that they can be born again (*Aeneid* VI).

152 *the malt tax*: Disraeli, whose government was in power when the novel was written in 1878, had long been in favour of a repeal of the Malt Tax. He had stood for election on the point in 1834, had tinkered with the tax in his 1852 budget, and was tempted to remove it altogether during his 1874–80 administration. As Trollope was writing the novel, agricultural interests were lobbying strongly for the repeal of the tax, which would make the growing of barley more profitable and bring new land into production. Gladstone finally removed the tax in 1880.

*half-pay*: officers were retained on half-salary when not on active service, and pensioned on it when they retired. Usually suggests straitened means, as here.

153 *a stall next to yours*: at this time, under the influence of the Bancrofts, disreputable pit-benches were given over to respectable stalls at many of the West End theatres.

156 *the Fulham Road ... South Kensington*: development was extensive in the area between Fulham and Kensington Roads, west of Queen's Gate and Onslow Square, in the years following the Great Exhibition of 1851.

166 *Allan-a-Dale*: see note to p. 134.

167 *laughing on a lass*: see note to p. 134.

183 *chimes must be heard at midnight*: see 2 *Henry IV*, III. ii. 228.

184 *ortolans*: the garden-bunting, esteemed for its delicate flavour.

185 *like Adam, it is not good that I should be alone.*: Genesis 2: 18: 'And the Lord God said, It is not good that the man should be alone; I will make him an help meet for him.'

188 *lawn tennis:* the unenclosed court was first used for tennis in 1874, when the game was patented by Major Wingfield. It caught on at once: Isabel Boncassen, heroine of *The Duke's Children* (1880), is an adept, as is Lord Carstairs, the junior hero of *Dr Wortle's School* (1881). Its vogue in the 1870s is vouched for by numerous *Punch* cartoons: 'Not play lawn tennis in the dark? Stuff and nonsense! All you've got to do is just to mark out the courts with Phosphorus, and rub the balls with the same' (24 August 1878).

191 *Queen of Sheba . . . King Solomon*: 1 Kings 10: 1: 'And when the Queen of Sheba heard of the fame of Solomon concerning the name of the Lord, she came to prove him with hard questions.' Stubbs's exotic allusion well illustrates the Romantic side of his nature. Solomon, it will be remembered, found answers for all of the Queen of Sheba's questions.

193 *cockered up*: indulged with gourmet food, depending on the cook's skill to prepare it.

203 *glories of a hunt*: W. G. and J. T. Gerould in *A Guide to Trollope* (1948) list fifteen major hunting-scenes in Trollope's forty-seven novels. In addition, Trollope published widely on hunting. See the account of his own hunting history in *An Autobiography*, his *Hunting Sketches* (1865), his contribution on hunting to *British Sports and*

*Pastimes* (1868), which he also edited, and his controversy with E. A. Freeman over the morality of blood sports in the *Fortnightly Review*, October and December 1869. The hunting-scenes in *Ayala's Angel* are as fresh as any, and, as R. C. Terry has pointed out, are remarkably free from nostalgia, despite the fact that Trollope had himself hunted for the last time.

*Rufford and Ufford United Pack*: a development of the Rufford United Hunt Club of *The American Senator*.

204 *Adonis*: in Ovid a youth of great beauty killed by a boar.

*Lothario*: the 'heartless gallant gay' libertine in Nicholas Rowe's tragedy *The Fair Penitent* (1703).

213 *a mollified she-Cerberus*: Cerberus was the dog of Pluto stationed at the entrance of Hades to prevent the living from entering and the dead from escaping.

215 *he riding capacities of ladies . . . brothers*: Trollope seems to denigrate the riding capacities of women here, but the article 'The Lady Who Rides to Hounds' in *Hunting Sketches* redresses the balance: 'Women who ride, as a rule, ride better than men. [Men] do not acquire the art of riding with exactness, as women do, and rarely have such hands as a woman has on a horse's mouth.'

*old Tony*: also appears in *The American Senator*, Chs. IX–XI; his surname seems to be spelt variously Tappett and Tuppett.

218 *Sir Harry's drag*: a private vehicle of the type of a stage coach, usually drawn by four horses, with seats inside and on top (*OED*).

219 *Lord Rufford*: Lord Rufford's sporting 'youth' is described in *The American Senator*, where, after narrowly avoiding the clutches of the adventuress, Arabella Trefoil, he settled down to mar-

riage and domesticity with Caroline Penge, a wealthy young friend of Lady Penwether.

*that fence where poor Major Caneback got his fall six years ago*: for Caneback's accident, and the embarrassment his lingering death causes to the house-party at Rufford, see *The American Senator*, Chs. XXII–XXIII.

*I never wants 'em to jump . . .*: Tony Tappett belongs to the school of 'The Man Who Hunts and Never Jumps'. The type is discussed in *Hunting Sketches*.

221 *Mr Lawrence Twentyman*: a character in *The American Senator*. His hopeless love for Mary Masters is finally blocked when she marries her cousin, the squire of Bragton, Reginald Morton. After a suitable interval, he consoles himself with her younger sister Kate, and seems to have made a full recovery by the time of *Ayala's Angel*.

230 *Not to have a good place in a run . . . character as a sportsman*: Trollope took seriously his hunting and his whist, though he distrusted their addictiveness. He was especially wary of billiards: 'to play billiards well is a dangerous thing' (*Travelling Sketches*). Trollope's interest in whist is commemorated in his article 'Whist at Our Club', *Blackwood's Magazine*, May 1877.

231 *As was the heart of the Peri . . .*: Moore, 'Paradise and the Peri', *Lalla Rookh*. See A. D. Godley, ed., *The Poetical Works of Thomas Moore* (1910), p. 401.

238 *'From such . . . the sting'*: from Sir Henry Taylor's blank verse drama *Philip Van Artevelde* (1835), Part I, I. ii. Adriana Van Merestyn is wondering if it is possible to refuse her lover without hurting him.

242 *it was necessary to pass through the billiard-room*: as Trollope informs us on p. 342 'the real hall of the house was used as a billiard room.'

an arrangement which Mark Girouard in *Life in the English Country House* describes as common in large Victorian houses. Efficient bell systems had removed waiting-servants from the Great Hall, so the gentry had to find a new use for it.

248 *Carpe diem*: make the most of the present. Cf. Horace, *Odes*, I. xi. 8.

259 *CHAPTER XXVIII*: chapters beginning, like this one, *in medias res* are rare in Trollope; in *The Duke's Children* (Ch. IX) he discusses the pitfalls of the method. The setting of this chapter probably reflects Trollope's 1878 summer tour, on which much of *Ayala's Angel* was composed.

263 *Billingsgate*: foul language, after the London fish-market, proverbial for rough and abusive speech. Its manners seemed to have mended in this respect when Trollope, researching an article for *London Tradesmen*, visited it in 1880.

264 *a rivulet . . . a succession of little cataracts*: running water often accompanies Trollopian love-scenes where powerful feelings are engaged. Compare especially Emily Hotspur's walk with her cousin George in *Sir Harry Hotspur of Humblethwaite*, Ch. VIII.

267-8 *the world . . . carry a sword*: *The Merry Wives of Windsor*, II, ii. 2-3: 'Why, then the world's mine oyster, which I with sword will open.'

269-70 *he was one who thoroughly understood millions . . . would be lost*: in the 1870s London became a major centre for such deals, especially after the Bank of France suspended payments following the Franco-Prussian War. In *Lombard Street* (1873) Bagehot points out that 'English trade is carried on upon borrowed capital to an extent of which few foreigners have an idea.'

277 *he calmly tore the letter in little bits . . . waste-paper basket*: as R. W. Chapman points out, this is impossible; see note to p. 349 below. Chapman

notes other inconsistencies in the novel: Lady Albury's Christian name is given as Rosaline on pp. 252, 433 and 452, but as Rosilind on pp. 371 and 373; and the Marchesa Baldoni's Christian name as Beatrice on p. 190 and Julia on p. 505.

281 *tablets of his memory*: *Hamlet* I. v. 98.

*Confounded . . . means nothing*: Sir Thomas Tringle's distaste for fashionable slang is like that of the Duke of Omnium, who also corrects his sons. See *The Duke's Children*, Ch. LII, where the objection is to the word *awful*, and Ch. LVI, where it is to the word *beastly*: 'The Duke made another memorandum to instruct his son that no gentleman above the age of a schoolboy should allow himself to use such a word in such a sense.'

286 *Caelum non animum . . .*: 'they change their sky, not their mind, by hurrying across the sea', Horace, *Epistles*, I. xi. 27. This is one of the many occasions in the novel when literature adds little to a character's native wit; see Introduction, p. ix.

288 *the Campagna*: the gently undulating plain surrounding Rome, uncultivated and often marshy at this time, though schemes for reclamation were beginning.

299 *duels at present were not in fashion*: the duel in *Phineas Finn*, Ch. XXVIII (1869), is looked on as something most exceptional; the duel in Henry James's *The American*, which appeared in the year Trollope wrote *Ayala's Angel*, is looked on as an exotic anachronism. Even as early as the 1860s Englishmen who wished to fight duels had to go abroad to fight them.

301 *a new club . . . called the Mountaineers*: the Mountaineers has a very similar constitution to the Beargarden, that paradise of licensed dissipation in *The Way We Live Now* and *The Duke's Children*.

305 *old Faddle's name and yours on the same prospectus*: Sir Thomas Tringle probably lends his
name to speculative schemes like the South
Central Pacific and Mexican Railway in *The
Way We Live Now*; but he has no closer con-
nexions with what Trollope, in *An Autobiography* (p. 353), calls the 'commercial profligacy
of the age'. See Introduction, p. v.

306 *the old song . . .*: the first edition of the *Oxford
Dictionary of Quotations* (1941) lists this as an
inscription on a pillar erected on the Mount in
the Dane John Field, Canterbury, which was
quoted in *The Examiner*, 31 May 1829. The full
inscription is as follows:

Where is the man who has the power and skill
To stem the torrent of a woman's will?
For if she will, she will, you may depend on't.
And if she won't, she won't; so there's an end on't.

307 *to go off the Duke of York's Column together*:
a column in Tuscan granite 124 feet high erected
at the south end of Waterloo Place to the memory
of the Duke of York, Commander-in-Chief of the
British Army, 1795–1827. It provided excellent
views of London, and a panoramic perspective of
the city was made from the top in the 1840s.
Perhaps Tom would have had trouble throwing
himself down from it. If we can judge from
*Marion Fay* (written 1879) the authorities were
wise to such suicide attempts. 'They've caged up
the Monument,' a disappointed lover is told,
'and you're so looked after on the Duke of York's,
that there isn't a chance.'

313 *those things in the Marylebone Road*: Charles
Dickens Junior's *Dictionary of London* for 1879
refers to a 'little cluster of tombstone-makers' at
the Tottenham Court Road end of what was then
often termed the New Road.

*Italia United . . . Prostrate Roman Catholic
Church*: Italian unification was completed, and

the capital of Italy re-established at Rome, in 1870. This marked the end of the temporal power of the Pope.

320 *underground cavern at the Gloucester Road Station*: the station was opened by the Metropolitan Railway on 1 October 1868. The District Railway also ran tracks through the station, from South Kensington to Earl's Court, and this was responsible for its cavernous proportions.

324 *Faith, Hope and Charity*: 1 Corinthians 13: 13.

330 *in the hands of the Philistines*: Judges 10: 7.

333 *the institution had been stamped out . . . concerned*: see note to p. 299.

337 *Bolivia's . . . Leicester Square*: Leicester Square, seedy and disreputable in the sixties, was ceremoniously reopened after its refurbishment in July 1874. Tom Tringle's dissipations are probably less 'shady' than they would have been ten years earlier; however Baedecker in 1879 counselled visitors to London to avoid 'any unrecommended house near Leicester Square', and Signor Bolivia almost certainly would have lacked Baedecker's recommendation.

346 *Epernay*: one of the champagne-producing centres in France.

347 *long sea down to Aberdeen*: short for 'long sea passage'. Young Faddle is being taken out of harm's way.

*Kilkenny cats*: to engage in a mutually destructive struggle. The Kilkenny cats fought so long and violently that nothing was left of them but their tails.

349 *she found her own letter . . . opened, and thrust in among her father's papers*: see note above to p. 277.

350 *those hundred Argus eyes*: Argus was a monster with a hundred eyes sent by the jealous Hera to

watch her priestess and rival Io. Slain by Hermes, his eyes were transferred by Hera to the tail of the peacock.

359 *And now the Adriatic's free to wed another*: cf Byron, *Childe Harold*, IV. xi. 1–2.

363 *a certain line . . .*: *Video meliora proboque; deteriora sequor* (Ovid, *Metamorphoses*, vii. 20).

*Some god comes out of a theatrical cloud*: the *deus ex machina* of Greek drama, particularly Euripedean tragedy. A god was lowered on to the stage by a *mechane* so that he could get the hero out of difficulties or untangle the plot.

370 *Crichton*: James Crichton (1560–85?) was a formidably learned Scot who travelled Europe as a soldier and scholar. His title of Admirable originated in Sir Thomas Urquhart's narrative of his career (1652). Ainsworth's novel *Crichton* (1837) and James Barrie's play *The Admirable Crichton* (1902) are also based on his life.

405 *men have died from time to time . . .*: *As You Like It*, IV. i. 107.

410 *as many suitors as Penelope*: at the beginning of Homer's *Odyssey* it is generally believed in Ithaca that Odysseus has perished in the Trojan War. His wife, Penelope, is besieged by numerous lazy and luxurious suitors.

424 *the Haymarket Theatre*: at this time theatre-going was becoming socially more respectable. In the 1850s and 60s the Haymarket was celebrated for its 'Prima Donna' prostitutes, and for Kate Hamilton's 'Night House' (see Mayhew, *London Labour and the London Poor*, IV, 217). By 1880, however, Squire and Marie Bancroft had taken over the management of the Haymarket Theatre. They had already done much to restore the prestige of play-going in their work with T. W. Robertson at the Prince of Wales, and their lead had been followed by Irving and

by the Savoy Opera Series; and on a more modest scale, by Hare, the Kendals, and Wyndham. See George Rowell, *The Victorian Theatre 1792–1914* (1978).

436 *angels had come from heaven . . .*: Genesis 6: 4: 'When the sons of God came in unto the daughters of men, and they bare children to them, the same became mighty men which were of old, men of renown.'

438 *I believe he sits all day and has his toe kissed*: Ayala is probably recalling the custom of kissing the extended toe of the statue of St Peter in St Peter's Basilica, Rome. The foot has been worn away by the kisses of the faithful.

472 *Captain Glomax*: Master of the Ufford and Rufford United Hunt Club, in *The American Senator*; also appears in *The Duke's Children*.

477 *drawing-room*: an error on Trollope's part. Colonel Stubbs, Ayala and Lady Albury are in the drawing-room already. He probably means Ayala to walk towards the dining-room.

484 *evil things of violets and primroses*: the hunting season comes to an end in April.

521 *"Faint heart never won fair lady"*: according to *Oxford Dictionary of Proverbs,* proverbial from at least the close of the sixteenth century; see also Burns, 'To Dr Blacklock'.

522 *a minister's promise that the income-tax should be abolished*: first imposed as a war tax in 1799, Peel reintroduced the tax in 1842 and it has remained in force ever since. Gladstone, probably the minister Trollope is thinking of, thought income tax immoral, 'a tangled network of man-traps for conscience'. Whenever he had a chance, he liked to whittle away at the rate of taxation. Unfortunately the Crimean War interfered with his plans, and it was not until 1874 that Gladstone was able to promise abolition. But Glad-

stone lost the election of that year, and Disraeli, who was in power as Trollope was writing, retained the tax.

525 *turning out of a son . . .*: compare Lord Cashel's inability to evict his intelligent and cynical son Lord Kilcullen in *The Kellys and the O'Kellys* (Ch. XXXIII).

542 *A walk in a wood*: see Trollope's essay on the delights of woodland walks in *Good Words*, 1879. He found them conducive to hard thinking, to the construction of the plots and the conception of the characters in his novels.

547 *'a joy for ever'*: Keats, *Endymion*, I. 1.

573 *off with the old love . . . new*: one of Trollope's favourite quotations. The full stanza runs:

> It's gude to be merry and wise
> It's gude to be honest and true
> It's gude to be off with the old love
> Before you're on with the new.

N. John Hall identifies this as James Johnson's version of the 'old song' in *Scots Musical Museum*, Vol. V, 1796, no 412. He also lists and discusses uses of this stanza in Trollope's other novels. See Anthony Trollope, *The New-Zealander*, ed. N. John Hall (1972), p. xxxvii.

579 *'Cerberus'*: see note to p. 213.

584 *Mammon*: wealth. See Matthew 6: 24; Luke 16: 9–13.

587 *St.-George's-Hanover-Square ceremonies*: the church was built in 1713–24 by John James, a follower of Wren. It had been noted for its fashionable weddings since the late eighteenth century. Nelson's Emma Hamilton (née Hart) had been married there in 1791, and Disraeli in 1839. George Eliot was to marry her second husband, J. W. Cross, there in 1880.

592 *two hundred thousand pounds*: a clubroom exaggeration; Gertrude was never worth more

than £120,000. See p. 125. On p. 583 Lord John Battledore was better informed.

595–6 *the Cunard ships never are dashed against rocks:* Sir Thomas Tringle's trust in the Cunard line, here and on p. 461, may be due to the fact that Trollope travelled to Iceland in the yacht of John Burns, Chairman of the Cunard Steamship Company, in the summer of 1878, during the composition of *Ayala's Angel.*

*we shall have possession of Cabul . . . next year:* Chapter LXI was written in mid-September 1878, just three months after Disraeli had successfully concluded the Congress of Berlin, and prevented a possible Russian advance on Constantinople. The prestige of his government's foreign policy had never been higher. Disraeli's aspirations then turned to Afghanistan, and within months a British Minister was established at Kabul. It was only in September 1879 that news reached home that the Afghans had mutinied and massacred the British legation. As a result of this disaster, Disraeli ordered a withdrawal from northern Afghanistan, and Gladstone, who came to power in 1880, had no interest in recovering Kabul. Sir Thomas Tringle's 'jingoism' would seem outdated when the book came out in June 1881, hence Trollope's explanatory footnote.

601 *the girls put themselves forward so much . . . men:* Trollope's own experiences of the United States, as recorded in *North America* and the short story 'Miss Ophelia Gledd' in *Lotta Schmidt,* confirm this opinion; as does his mother's record of her experiences, *Domestic Manners of the Americans* (1832). Henry James's *Daisy Miller* (1878), almost exactly contemporary with *Ayala's Angel,* and *The Portrait of a Lady* (1880–1), which kept Trollope's novel out of *Macmillan's Magazine,* also deal with the phenomenon of 'outgoingness' among young American females.

603 *the Ministry in England was unfortunately changed . . . Asia*: see note to p. 596 above. Gladstone's Ministry, which had little desire to expand into Afghanistan, replaced Disraeli's in April 1880. It is probable that this sentence was added to the MS immediately before publication, but I have been unable to confirm this.

608 *on the steps of the Albert Memorial*: where she had arranged to meet Frank Houston. See p. 131. Here, as in her desire that each of her suitors should elope with her to Ostend, Gertrude's taste in romantic assignation is remarkably consistent. When *Ayala's Angel* was written the Albert Memorial in Kensington Gardens had something of the charm of novelty, as work on it had only been completed in 1876.

623 *Lucifer,—not Beelzebub*: interchangeable names for Satan, though in Milton, Beelzebub, like other Pagan gods, becomes one of Satan's henchmen. The name Beelzebub, means 'Lord of the Flies', and is derived from Beelzebul, a Canaanite god. Romantic Lucy prefers to think of Hamel's statue as Lucifer, who was himself originally an 'Angel of Light'.

*Bacchus*: the Latin name for the Greek god of wine, Dionysus.

625 *a broad back with a heavy weight upon it . . . below*: Trollope believed this to the bone. In *Orley Farm* he writes: 'There is no human bliss equal to twelve hours of work with only six hours in which to do it' (Vol. II, Ch. IX).

626 *except that his bride . . . invariably the case*: as the sentence stands, Trollope seems to suggest that Ayala looks less well in her bridal garments than in her ordinary clothes. R. W. Chapman suggests we delete 'as' here.